Also by Ha Jin

A FREE LIFE

Ha Jin

A FREE LIFE

PANTHEON BOOKS *New York*

COPYRIGHT © 2007 BY HA JIN

All rights reserved. Published in the United States by Pantheon Books, a division of Random House, Inc., New York, and in Canada by Random House of Canada Limited, Toronto.

Pantheon Books and colophon are registered trademarks of Random House, Inc.

Grateful acknowledgment is made to Henry Holt and Company, LLC and Jonathan Cape for permission to reprint an excerpt from "The Oven Bird" from The Poetry of Robert Frost, *edited by Edward Connery Lathem. Copyright © 1916, 1969 by Henry Holt and Company. Copyright © 1944 by Robert Frost. Reprinted by permission of Henry Holt and Company, LLC and Jonathan Cape, an imprint of The Random House Group Ltd., London.*

Library of Congress Cataloging-in-Publication Data
Jin, Ha, [date]
A free life / Ha Jin.
p. cm.
ISBN 978-0-375-42465-6
1. Chinese—United States—Fiction.   2. Immigrants—United States—Fiction.
3. Poetry—Authorship—Fiction.   4. Poets—Fiction.   I. Title.
PS3560.I6F74 2007
813'.54—dc22   2007006177

www.pantheonbooks.com
Book design by Iris Weinstein
Printed in the United States of America
FIRST EDITION
2 4 6 8 9 7 5 3 1

TO LISHA AND WEN, WHO LIVED THIS BOOK

PART ONE

1

FINALLY Taotao got his passport and visa. For weeks his parents had feared that China, even if not closing the door outright, would restrict the outflow of people. After the Tiananmen massacre on June 4, 1989, all the American airlines except United had canceled their flights to Beijing and Shanghai. At the good news, Pingping burst into tears. She quickly rinsed the colander in which she had drained the shredded turnip for her jellyfish salad, took off her apron, and set out with her husband, Nan Wu, for the town center of Woodland, where the office of Travel International was located.

The plane ticket cost seventy percent more than the regular fare because it had not been purchased three weeks in advance. The Wus didn't hesitate; as long as Taotao could get out of China in time and safely, it was worth any price. They also bought round-trip tickets from Boston to San Francisco for themselves.

Neither Pingping nor Nan could go back to China to fetch Taotao, who had been staying with Pingping's parents for the past three years. And since no one in Pingping's family had a passport—not to mention the difficulty in getting a visa from the U.S. embassy—the boy would have to fly by himself. Pingping's brother, a middle school physics teacher who had just returned to their parents' home for the summer vacation, had agreed to take his nephew from Jinan City to Shanghai. There Taotao would be left in the hands of the American flight attendants. Barely six, he wasn't allowed to change planes unaccompanied, so his parents would have to go and collect him in San Francisco. The travel agent, a bosomy brunette with olive skin and long hair, helped Nan make a reservation for the least expensive room at a hotel near Union Square, where the three of them would stay the first night before flying back to Boston. Altogether the trip would cost them close to $3,000. Never had they spent money so lavishly.

They arrived in San Francisco in the early morning of July 11. They hadn't expected it to be so chilly; nippy gusts were ruffling pedestrians' hair and forcing people to squint. A storm had descended the night before, leaving shop signs tattered and soggy; a few traffic lights were out of order, blinking endlessly. But the ebony facades of some buildings had been washed clean and glossy, and the vigorous wind smelled of the ocean. Pingping, without any warm clothes on, couldn't stop shivering and then began hiccuping violently on their way to the hotel. Nan tried massaging the nape of her neck to relieve her spasms, and once or twice he slapped her back in an attempt to shock her out of them. This trick had worked before, but it didn't help today.

Nan had called United Airlines twice to find out whether Taotao was actually on the plane, but nothing could be confirmed. He was told that the boy's name didn't come up in the computer. Things were still chaotic in China, and many passengers had been switched to this flight from other airlines that had canceled their services, so there wasn't a complete passenger list yet. "Don't worry, Mr. Wu," a pleasant female voice consoled Nan. "Your son should be all right."

"We were told zat he is on zer plane." Nan often mismanaged the interdental sound that the Chinese language doesn't have.

"Then he should be."

"Do you have anozzer way to check zat?"

"I'm afraid I don't, sir. Like I said, he should be okay."

But between "should be" and "is" stretched a gulf of anguish for the boy's parents. If only they knew where their son actually was!

Nan's brother-in-law had said on the phone that he left Taotao with a group of American air stewardesses, one of whom was an Asian and could speak a little Mandarin. Now the Wus just hoped he was on the plane.

Three hours after they had checked into the hotel, they returned to the airport by a shuttle bus. The plane wasn't supposed to arrive until 12:30. Since it was an international flight, the Wus were not allowed to enter the restricted terminal. All they could do was stand outside customs, staring at the chestnut-colored gate that seemed resolved to remain shut forever. Several times they asked the people at the information desk whether Taotao was on the plane, but nobody could tell them that for certain. A thin, broad-faced woman in a dark blue uniform appeared. She looked Chinese but spoke only English. Hoping there might be another way to find out their son's whereabouts, they asked her to help. Her stubby-chinned face stiffened. She shook her head and said, "If that lady at the desk can't do anything for you, I can't either."

Distraught, Pingping begged her in English, "Please check it for us. He is our only child, just six year old. Three years I didn't see him."

"Like I said, I really can't help you. I have work to do, okay?"

Nan wanted to plead with her too, but the woman looked annoyed, so he refrained. In her eyes, which had more white than black, Nan had caught a flicker of disdain, probably because she knew they were from mainland China and suspected they were still red inside, if not red to the bone.

He wrapped an arm around Pingping, whispering in Chinese, *"Let's wait a little longer. I'm sure he'll come out soon. Don't worry in advance."* Between themselves they spoke Mandarin.

The way his wife had begged that woman upset him. Pingping, though thirty-three, looked almost ten years younger than her age, with large vivid eyes, a straight nose, a delicate chin, and a lissome figure. Perhaps that woman was jealous of her pretty features and liked seeing her in agony.

At last the gate opened and spat out a string of passengers. Most of them looked exhausted, their eyes dull and inert, and several walked unsteadily, pulling wheeled suitcases or lugging bags. The Wus stepped closer and gazed at the new arrivals. One by one the passengers went by. A tall black man in a baggy blazer cried, "Hey, Toni, so great to see you!" He stretched out his right arm, a dark canvas ukulele case hanging from his left shoulder. Toni, a skinny girl wearing a nose stud and a full head of cornrows, buried her face in his one-armed hug. Except for that cheerful moment, though, most passengers seemed groggy and dejected. Some of the Asians seemed uncertain what to do, and looked around as if wondering who among those standing by were supposed to receive them.

Within five minutes all the new arrivals had cleared customs. Slowly the gate closed. A chill sank into Nan's heart; Pingping broke into sobs. *"They must have lost him! I'm sure they lost him!"* she groaned in Chinese, holding her sides with one arm. Tugging Nan's wrist, she went on, *"I told you not to let him take the risk, but you wouldn't listen."*

"He'll be all right, believe me." His voice caught, unconvincing even to himself.

The hall was hushed again, almost deserted. Nan didn't know what do. He said to Pingping, *"Let's wait a little more, all right?"*

"There was only one flight from China today. Don't lie to me! Obviously he was not on it. Oh, if only we had let him wait until somebody could bring him over. We shouldn't have rushed."

"I know."

Then the gate opened again. Two stewardesses walked out, the tall one, a blonde, holding a young boy's hand while the other one, slight and with smiling eyes, was carrying a small red suitcase. "Taotao!" Pingping cried, and rushed over. She swooped him up into her arms and kissed him madly. *"How worried we were! Are you all right?"* she said.

The boy in a sailor suit smiled, whimpering *"Mama, mama"* while pressing his face against her chest as if shy of being seen by others. He then turned to Nan, but his face registered no recognition.

"This is your daddy, Taotao," his mother said.

The boy looked at Nan again and gave a hesitant smile, as if his father were a bigger friend being introduced to him. Meanwhile, Pingping went on kissing him and patting his back and stroking his head.

The two stewardesses asked for Nan's ID, and he produced his driver's license. They compared his name with their paperwork, then congratulated him on the family's reunion.

"He was fine on the plane, very quiet, but a little scared," said the short woman, who looked Malaysian. She handed Nan the suitcase.

He held it with both hands. "Sank you for taking care of him on zer way."

"Our pleasure," said the blonde, who wore mascara and had

permed hair, her face crinkling a little as she smiled. "It's wonderful to see a family reunited."

Before Pingping could say anything, the women left as if this were their routine work. "Thank you!" she cried at last. They turned their heads and waved at her, then disappeared past the gate.

2

NAN had not seen his son for four years. Taotao seemed frailer than in the photos, though he was definitely more handsome, with a thin nose and dark brown eyes, like his mother's. Together the Wus headed for the bus stop, both parents holding the child's hands. Approaching an automatic door, the boy somehow stopped and wouldn't exit the building. He asked his mother, "*When are we going back?*" His Mandarin had a slight Shandong accent, since he had lived with Pingping's parents.

"*What? What are you talking about?*" said Pingping.

"*Uncle and Aunt are waiting for us in Shanghai.*"

"*Really?*"

"*Yes, they'll meet us there.*"

"*Who said that?*"

"*They told me to come and take both of you back. Let's go home now.*"

"*Can't we stay just another day?*" Nan stepped in, having realized that his in-laws must have tricked Taotao into traveling with the flight attendants.

"*No, I want to go home.*"

Nan forced a smile and choked back a wave of misery. "*Don't you want to see dolphins and whales?*" he asked.

"*Real ones?*"

"*Sure.*"

"*Where are they? Here?*"

"*No, we're going to make a stop in a city called Boston, where there're lots of whales and dolphins. Don't you want to see them?*"

"*Yes,*" Pingping chimed in. "*We'll visit a few places before heading for home.*"

"*All right?*" Nan added.

The boy looked uncertain. "*Then we'd better let Uncle and Aunt know our plan. They're still waiting for us at the Shanghai airport.*"

"*I'll call them. Don't worry,*" said his father.

So Taotao agreed to return to the hotel with them. Nan was carrying him piggyback on the way to the bus stop while Pingping went on talking with him, asking what food he had eaten on the plane and whether he had been airsick. The din of the traffic muffled the voices of mother and son, and Nan couldn't hear all their conversation. His mind was full, in turmoil; but he was happy. His child had come. He was sure that, eventually, the boy would become an American.

But what about himself? He was uncertain of his future and what to do about his life, not to mention his marriage. The truth was that he just didn't love his wife that much, and she knew it. Pingping knew he was still enamored of his ex-girlfriend, Beina, though that woman was far away in China. It seemed very likely to Nan that Pingping might walk out on him one of these days. Yet now he was all the more convinced that they must live in this country to let their son grow into an American. He must make sure that Taotao would stay out of the cycle of violence that had beset their native land for centuries. The boy must be spared the endless, gratuitous suffering to which the Chinese were as accustomed as if their whole existence depended on it. By any means, the boy must live a life different from his parents' and take this land to be his country! Nan felt sad and glad at the same time, touched by the self-sacrifice he believed he would be making for his child.

On the bus Taotao was sitting on his mother's lap. A moment after they pulled out of the airport, to his parents' astonishment, the boy said, "*Mama, there was a big fight in Beijing, do you know? Hundreds of uncles in the People's Liberation Army were killed.*"

"*It was the soldiers who shot a great many civilians,*" his father corrected him.

"*No, I saw on TV bad eggs attacking the army. They burned tanks and overturned trucks. Grandpa said those were thugs and must be suppressed.*"

"Taotao, Dad is right," his mother broke in. *"The People's Army has changed and killed a lot of common people, people like us."*

That silenced the boy, who looked cross, biting his lips, which puffed up a little. He stayed quiet the rest of the way.

It was two o'clock. They decided not to return to the hotel directly, and instead went to Chinatown for lunch. At a fruit stand Nan bought a pound of Rainier cherries for Taotao, who had never seen such yellow cherries, each as big as a pigeon's egg. Pingping rinsed a handful of them with the water from the bottle she carried. The boy ate a few and found them delicious; he saved the rest for his younger cousin Binbin, the daughter of Pingping's sister. He didn't want to throw away the stones and instead slotted them into the patch pocket on his jacket so that he could plant them in his grandparents' front yard, where there were already two apricot trees.

They didn't go deep into Chinatown but just entered a Cantonese restaurant close to the ceramic-tiled archway at the intersection of Bush and Grand. A stout middle-aged woman showed them to a table beside a window. As soon as they sat down, she returned with a pot of red tea and three cups and put everything before them. She glanced at them quizzically and seemed to be wondering why they were dining at such a place. She must have known they were FOJs—fresh off the jet—who would scrimp on food to save every penny.

After looking through the menu and consulting Pingping, Nan settled on two dishes and a soup and ordered all in the large size. He avoided the cheaper dishes on purpose, though he had no idea what "Moo Goo Gai Pan" and "Seafood and Tofu Casserole" tasted like. They sounded strange to him. The "Three Delicious Ingredient Soup" didn't make much sense either, but, unable to speak Cantonese and ashamed of asking what was in it, he just ordered it. He disliked these nebulous names. Why not call things what they were? The Chinese here just wanted everything to sound fancy and exotic.

The waitress smirked, collected the menus, and left.

"What's that?" Taotao asked his mother, pointing at half a side of roast pork hanging behind glass above a counter.

"Golden pig," she answered.

"And those?"

"Roast ducks? Want some?"

"*Not now.*"

"*It tastes no good, too fatty,*" Nan said. Then he chuckled as he remembered that when Taotao was a baby, barely able to use a spoon, the boy had liked meat and seafood so much that he'd hog them at a meal and even declare, "*I want to eat it all. I don't leave any for others.*"

Nan looked around and saw a few people eating noodles and wontons. The Cantonese ate lightly at lunch and wouldn't order so much food as he had. The air was rife with fried scallion and soy sauce. Nan usually liked those smells in a Chinese restaurant, but today the usual aromas somehow irritated his nose. Feeling that his hands were a little sticky, he got up and went to the restroom to wash them.

On his way back to the table, he caught sight of the community newspaper, *Asian Voice,* stacked on a steel rack near the restaurant's side entrance. He picked up a copy. Sitting down, he opened the paper and saw a full page of photographs of some recent scenes from Beijing. One of them showed a naked soldier hanging, by a piece of iron wire, on the window frame of a burned bus, his feet dangling and still in boots. Beside him stood a rectangle of cardboard bearing two vertical lines of words, which read: "He killed five civilians and was caught when he ran out of bullets. He got his comeuppance!"

The Wus' order came with plain rice. The steaming soup was made with slivers of chicken, shrimp, snow peas, and slices of bamboo shoot. Both dishes tasted good, though Taotao didn't like the squid in the casserole. He wanted more portabella mushroom, and his mother put several pieces on his plate. "*Why don't we have big bowls?*" he asked.

"*Here people use only small bowls for soup in a restaurant,*" Pingping answered.

Gingerly he took a bite of a sliver of chicken as if afraid it was underdone. But soon he became more confident, chewing without hesitation.

Halfway through lunch, Nan said to Taotao, showing him the photos in the newspaper, "*Look here, all these are civilians slaughtered by the People's Liberation Army.*"

"*Put that away! He's eating,*" Pingping protested.

"I just want him to see the truth. Well, Taotao, see how many people they butchered? Here are some bodies and bikes crushed by a tank."

His wife begged, *"Please let him finish lunch in peace."*

"Dad, isn't this an army uncle?" The boy pointed at the hanged soldier.

"Yes. But he killed some civilians and got his punishment. Don't you think he deserved it?"

Taotao was silent for a moment, staring at his plate, then mumbled, *"No."*

"Why not?" Nan felt frustrated and thought his son was stubborn and hopeless. His bushy mustache bristled.

"Even for that, people shouldn't kill each other," Taotao said in a small voice.

Stupefied, Nan didn't know how to respond for a good while. His wide-spaced eyes gazed at his son as something stirred in his chest, which was so full that he lost his appetite. He managed to finish the food on his plate, then refilled his teacup.

"Don't you want some more?" Pingping asked.

"I've had enough," he sighed. Then his voice turned husky. *"This boy is too good-natured and must never go back. He can't survive there. I don't know where I'll end up, but he must become an American."*

"I'm glad you said that," she agreed.

"I don't want to be American, Mama!" Taotao wailed. *"I want to go home."*

"All right," she said. *"Don't talk. Eat. You're a Chinese, of course."*

Nan's eyes glistened with tears, and his cheek twitched. He turned to look out the window. On the narrow street tourists were strolling in twos and threes, and a few Asian men wore cameras around their necks.

The waitress came again and placed in front of Nan a tiny tray that contained three fortune cookies, three toothpicks sheathed in cellophane, and a bill lying facedown. Although the lunch cost only twenty-six dollars, Nan left a five for tip. He meant to show the woman that some FOJs also had a fat wallet. Taotao had never seen a fortune cookie before; he pocketed them all.

In the hotel the TV was showing a Chaplin movie. Taotao was at once captivated by it, laughing so hard that he coughed and gasped continually. He kept brandishing his hands above his head and would jump on the bed whenever a funny scene came on. Pingping was worried and told him to sit down and not to laugh so loudly lest people in the adjacent rooms hear him. Yet when the starved shorty appeared on the screen, wearing a patch of mustache and walking with splayed feet and bowed legs, visualized his fellow worker as a plump chicken and set about chasing him with an ax, Taotao sprang to his feet again, skipping around and shrieking gleefully. Nan was amazed that, all at once, the boy had become so at home here. He couldn't help but grow thoughtful. Indeed, for a child, home is where his parents are and where he feels happy and safe. He doesn't need a country.

Nan was exhausted and soon fell fast asleep in spite of the racket Taotao was kicking up. After the silent film, the TV showed *Tom and Jerry*. Although Taotao didn't understand it all, the wild cartoon kept him rolling all the same. Pingping was afraid that he might get sick, he was so excited.

3

HEIDI MASEFIELD'S house sat at the center of two and a half acres of prime land in Woodland, a suburban town twenty miles west of Boston. Near the southern side of this antique colonial stood an immense maple, whose shade fell on several windows in the summertime and kept the rooms cool. From one of its thick boughs hung a swing, two pieces of rope attached to a small legless chair. Except for the terrace at the back of the house and the driveway that led to a country road, the land was covered entirely by the manicured lawn. A line of lilac bushes encircled the property, replaced by low fieldstone walls at the front entrance to the yard. During the summer the Masefields were staying on Cape Cod, in a beach bungalow near Falmouth, so the Wus could use the Woodland house for themselves. Heidi would be coming back every other week to pick up mail and pay bills. She and her two children wouldn't return until early September, when the elementary school started.

Two years ago Dr. Masefield, a plastic surgeon, had drowned in a sailing accident, so his wife had needed someone to help her with housework and to care for her son and daughter. Her sister-in-law, Jean, under whose supervision Nan had once worked as a custodian in a medical building, introduced the Wus to her. Heidi was so pleased when she saw the young couple, who looked steady and were so polite and cleanly dressed, that she hired them on the spot. She let the Wus use the two bedrooms in the attic in exchange for work—Pingping was to cook and do laundry while Nan would drive the children to school in the mornings, and, if their mother was too busy to fetch them, he'd pick them up in the afternoons as well. In addition to free lodging, Heidi paid Pingping two hundred dollars a week.

Although she was rich, Heidi was determined not to take her children to restaurants very often, to prevent them from falling into the habit of dining out. So Pingping cooked breakfast and dinner for them on weekdays. The housework wasn't heavy. Two black women, Pat and her daughter, Jessica, would come once a week to vacuum the floors and clean all the bathrooms except the one in the attic apartment—the mother did most of the work while the daughter, almost twenty, sat around reading. There was also Tom, a firefighter who worked the night shift at the Woodland Fire Station. He came regularly to mow the lawn and prune the flowers and bushes. He also plowed snow and sanded the driveway in the wintertime. Working for Heidi gave the Wus another great advantage they hadn't foreseen—their son now could go to the excellent public school here.

Amazingly, Taotao wasn't jet-lagged at all. For a whole day he skipped up or bounced down the stairs, his footsteps echoing in the house. But he didn't dare go out by himself yet. Now and then he looked out the windows of the kitchen and the study. He marveled at the detached garage that had recognized their car from a distance last night and opened automatically, as if welcoming them home. The lawn impressed him so much that he said, *"Mama, I'm going to tell Grandpa there's green carpet everywhere outside our house."*

"It's just grass." Pingping smiled. *"Why don't you go out and see it?"*

"Can you come with me?"

"Are you still scared?"

"Don't know."

Mother and son went out so he could touch the grass with his hands. She wore a lavender wraparound skirt, and Taotao had on white shorts and maroon leather sandals. The boy loved the feel of the grass under his feet and kept running about as if chasing a phantom ball. His legs were sturdy but slightly bandy, like his father's. After he had frolicked for a while, Pingping took him to the woods beyond the northern end of the Masefields' property to see if they could find a few mushrooms. Under her arm was a thick book; she had to depend on the pictures to tell the edible mushrooms from the poisonous ones here. Together mother and son left the yard, where parts of the grass were glimmering softly and the lawn was shaded in places by the long shadows of the house and the trees.

•

Nan saw his wife and son fade away into the woods. He was glad that for the rest of the summer they could use this house for themselves, but at the same time his mind was restless, teeming with worrisome thoughts. So many things had happened recently that he was still in a daze. Six weeks earlier, when the field armies were poised to attack the demonstrators in Beijing, some Chinese graduate students at Brandeis University, where Nan had been working toward a Ph.D. in political science, had discussed all the possible means of preventing the violence from being unleashed. They talked for hours on end, but were mainly blowing off steam. Then, without thinking twice, Nan tossed out the idea that they might seize some of the top officials' children studying in the Boston area, especially those at MIT, and demand that their fathers revoke martial law and withdraw the troops from the capital. He was prompted by anger, just having seen on TV soldiers beating civilians with belts, clubs, and steel helmets, many faces smashed, bathed in blood and tears. To his surprise, his fellow compatriots took his suggestion so seriously that they began planning a kidnap. But before they could seize any hostages, the massacre broke out in Beijing and it was too late to do anything. Instead they went to Washington to demonstrate in front of the Chinese embassy. Nan joined them and stood shouting slogans before that ugly brick building, in which the officials and staff hid themselves and wouldn't show their faces but would give the demonstrators either the finger or the victory sign through the window curtains.

Back from D.C., he was shocked by another incident. Hansong, a visiting scholar in East Asian Studies at Harvard, whom Nan had known quite well and who had been actively involved in the aborted kidnap plot, had kept a pistol that he was supposed to return to the gun dealer. Rumor had it that his girlfriend had disappeared in Tiananmen Square and that she must have been killed by the army and buried somewhere in a mass grave. Crazed, Hansong ran out one night and had a row with a homeless man in a park in Watertown. He pulled out his revolver and shot the old man in the head. Nan was so shaken by the killing and by his own involvement in the unexecuted kidnapping that he declared to Pingping that he would never participate in any political activities again. He also decided to give up his graduate work in political science, which he had never liked but which he had been assigned to study when he was admitted to college back in China. Later, he hadn't had any choice but to stay within the same field when he went on to earn a master's degree. Now he felt too sick of it to continue studying it.

He had decided to quit graduate school, but he had no idea what he was going to do. It was said that the U.S. government would take measures to protect the Chinese students and scholars who didn't return to their homeland, so he should be able to stay here legally, but what unnerved him was that from now on he couldn't rely on the university for financial aid anymore. Such an independent condition was new to him. Back in China he had always been a member of a work unit that provided a salary, shelter (usually a bed or at most a room), coupons for cloth and grain and cooking oil, medical care, and sometimes even free condoms. As long as he didn't cause trouble for the authorities, his livelihood was secure. Now he would have to earn a living by himself and also support his family. He was free, free to choose his own way and to make something of himself. But what were the choices available for him? Could he survive in this land? The feeling of uncertainty overwhelmed him.

A week ago, Hansong, the deranged man, had been committed to a mental hospital. Nan hadn't gone to see him, but his friend Danning, who had opposed the kidnap idea from the very beginning, had visited Hansong at the asylum and left him with a tin of jasmine tea, which made Nan wonder if an inmate in there could have free access to hot water. Danning had told Nan that Hansong grinned at him without any trace of remorse. *"He's a real psychopath now. His loony smile spooked me and made my scalp crawl,"* Danning said.

How fortunate it was that Hansong's mental state had prevented him from talking; otherwise he might have revealed their plan for the kidnap. Then every one of them would have been dragged to court.

Pingping and Taotao returned with just one fat yellow mushroom, the kind called Slippery Jack. There had been a drought, and most fungi in the woods had vanished. Nan noticed that since they'd flown back from San Francisco, his son hadn't even once mentioned returning to China. Taotao seemed to be adapting quickly. Although unable to read a word of English yet, the boy was fascinated by an old set of *Britannica,* which his parents had bought at a church bazaar. He looked at the pictures in some volumes and raised all kinds of questions. He was eager to test his father and even asked him which planet was bigger—Mercury or Saturn? Nan couldn't give a definite answer and just guessed, *"Mercury."*

"Wrong!" the boy announced, beaming. He seized every opportunity to make fun of his dad. One of his favorite tricks was to tie a long chain of rubber bands to Nan's toe so that the whole thing would hit his sole when released from the other end. Nan was pleased by his son's little pranks, which he felt indicated that the child had accepted him as his dad.

Even though the Wus had the entire house to themselves, they confined themselves to the attic except when they had to use the kitchen downstairs. In their spacious room upstairs stood a large bed, Nan's desk, a coffee table under the window facing the northern yard. Two of the walls were lined with books, most of which were the Masefields'. Nan had the habit of reading late at night, so he and his wife slept separately most of the time. Since their child shared the bed with Pingping now, Nan was left alone. He used the other room in the attic. It was smaller but fully furnished, with a pair of single beds and a redwood nightstand in between. This room had occasionally served as a guest room for the Masefields.

Before going to sleep, Nan opened a volume of Robert Frost's poems and began to read. He loved Frost, Auden, Whitman, Li Po, and Tu Fu, but sometimes he couldn't fully understand the poetry written in English. Tonight his eyes were heavy, and from time to time the words blurred into a solid block and then faded from the page. Before he could finish the long poem "The Death of the Hired Man," the book slid from his hand and plopped on the carpet. Without noticing it, he fell asleep, snoring lightly while the porcelain lamp still glowed on the nightstand.

•

The next day the Wus went to the mall in Watertown to buy toys for Taotao. The boy wasn't interested in cars, or guns, or bicycles, or stuffed animals. He wanted a large telescope so that he could watch the stars. His parents bought it for him for $105. The moment they came back, Taotao opened the long carton and began assembling the telescope. He couldn't read the instructions but wouldn't let his father help. Whenever Nan picked up a knob or screw, the boy would yell, "*Put that down!*" Somehow he managed to join the pieces together without a glitch, as if he had owned such a thing before. He wouldn't go down to eat dinner until he set the tube on the tripod.

Unfortunately it was an overcast night, so his parents wouldn't go out with him to stargaze. This upset him. After dinner, he was told to go upstairs and clear away the paper and the plastic bags, putting them in the trash can in the bathroom, and then come down again to look at a picture book together with his mother. Pingping had checked some childrens' books out of the town library to prepare herself for teaching him how to read English.

As she and Nan were talking about how to register him at the elementary school, suddenly something thudded on the stairs, followed by footsteps and a clack. "*Taotao,*" Pingping called out, "*are you all right?*"

There was no response. Then, to their amazement, the boy scurried into the kitchen, dragging his red suitcase, which now had a squashed corner. "*I'm packing, leaving for home,*" he announced, his face sullen.

"*What did you say?*" his mother asked.

"*I'm going back to Grandpa and Grandma.*"

That astounded his parents. After a brief pause, they burst out laughing. "*Well, you're welcome to leave,*" Nan told him with a straight face.

The boy was puzzled. "*I'm packing.*"

"*Sure. Do it, quickly,*" Pingping urged.

Taotao let go of the suitcase, dropped down onto the floor, and broke out crying. "*I miss Grandma and Grandpa!*"

That frightened his parents, who had thought he was merely bluffing because they wouldn't go out with him to stargaze. His mother picked him up, sat him on her lap, wiped away his tears with her fingers, and rocked him gently. Nan said, *"Come on, we'll watch stars when there are no clouds, all right?"*

"You're already a big boy," his mother added. *"You should know we can't go back anymore. We'll have to live here. China won't let us live in peace if we return. You know, Dad and Mom are going to work very hard so that we can have our own home someday."*

The boy blubbered some more, snuffling fitfully. He seemed to understand most of what she was saying, and kept nodding his head.

Somehow, after that, he didn't want to go out to gaze at stars anymore, and the telescope was just propped beside the window at the landing upstairs. Once in a while he'd observe the sky with it, but every time he watched for only a minute or two. Soon he stopped missing his grandparents as well. Whenever he was naughty or disobedient, his parents would say they were going to send him back to China by the express mail, but this threat scared him for only a few months.

4

THESE DAYS Pingping was so happy that even her limbs felt lighter. An internal glow expanded in her, and a pinkish sheen frequently came over her face. She often hummed Chinese folk songs when she was cooking or sewing. Whenever she went shopping or to the post office, she'd take Taotao along as if the boy might disappear the moment she left him alone. Even when Taotao played within the yard, she'd accompany him. Behind Heidi's house, beyond the blueberry bushes, lay a tennis court, green and springy as if coated with rubber, surrounded by a tall steel fence. But the Wus didn't go there. Instead, they often kicked a volleyball under a basketball hoop in the front yard. Taotao played only soccer.

Pingping understood that the joyful days were temporary, because the summer would end soon—the Masefields would come back and she'd resume doing the housework. Furthermore, Taotao would begin school in early September, which might be hard for him. She had been reading children's books in English together with him for five or six hours a day. Since he watched a lot of TV, he had begun to pick up words, able to say "Uh-oh," "Okey-dokey," and even "Get lost." Having him with her, Pingping felt more certain how she would live. In the past years she had prepared herself mentally for returning to China, because Nan had planned to go back and teach at his alma mater, a small college in Harbin City. Yet whenever she dreamed of home, she'd have nightmares, in which she rushed around looking for a clean toilet but couldn't find one. Nan told her that modern restrooms had been put up in many Chinese cities lately; in fact, there had been a campaign to modernize the public facilities, and to use some of them you'd have to pay, like buying a cup of tea. Nan would joke, "*Like no free lunch in America, there'll be no free bathrooms in China anymore. Too many people.*" Still, Pingping couldn't stop searching for a toilet in her dreams. But since Taotao came, her nightmares had mostly stopped and her head had grown clearer. Even if Nan changed his mind and returned to China someday, she'd live in America raising their child alone. She was sure of that.

Nan had come to the United States alone in the summer of 1985. A year and a half later Pingping had managed to leave China. But the officials wouldn't allow her to bring Taotao along for fear she might not return, so the boy stayed with her parents in Jinan City, a provincial capital more than two hundred miles south of Beijing. Soon after her arrival in Boston, Pingping told Nan that she wanted to save $20,000 before they went back home. That astonished Nan, to whom the figure was unreasonable, though he already had more than $3,600 in the bank. He had never cared about getting rich and would tease her, saying she was a born capitalist. Yet Pingping wanted financial independence, which meant a tidy sum in their bank account so that they wouldn't worry about getting a raise that had to be approved by officials at whose feet many people would grovel. So she resolved to make money and save as much as possible while they lived here. Among his compatriots at Brandeis, Nan was known as a rich man after his first year at the school, mainly because he had worked constantly to earn the money needed for his wife's visa—the U.S. embassy in Beijing required a bank statement that showed at least $3,000. Unlike the graduate students in the science departments, Nan didn't have a stipend and had to take care of his own living expenses. To save time for his study, he'd cook himself huge meals, each of which he'd eat for half a week. Sometimes he slept only three or four hours a day. He lived such an industrious life that he had lost more than twenty pounds by the time Pingping came to join him.

Two and a half years later, after Pingping had worked in a nursing home for a year and then for Heidi for a year and a half, and after Nan had done various odd jobs, the Wus had saved $30,000. Yet this sum didn't give them any sense of security, because now they were planning to live here permanently. If Nan quit his Ph.D. candidacy,

Pingping wasn't sure what he was going to do. Though she knew he didn't love her, she loved him deeply. Before she'd married him, her father had warned her that she might not live a secure life with Nan, who, though a decent young man, was by nature impractical, an incorrigible dreamer. Yet she had never regretted being his wife, though she did feel hurt from time to time and was even tempted to drink (though she disliked American wines and there was no way to find the kind of fragrant Luzhou liquor here, of which she had used to pilfer mouthfuls from her father's bottles when she was a child). She was certain Nan wouldn't just walk out on her. For better or worse, he was trustworthy and dependable. Now that Taotao was here, Nan was all the more willing to be the head of the household. In his own words, *"To be the draft horse pulling the cart of this family."*

"*I'll look for a full-time job soon,*" he told Pingping one afternoon. Their son was napping in the other room.

"*What kind of jobs do you have in mind?*"

"*Do I have a choice?*" Again a caustic edge sharpened his voice.

"*Don't be nasty. I always can work too.*"

That mollified him some. He sighed, "*I'll keep my eyes open for jobs.*"

Pingping remained silent, feeling guilty because Heidi didn't pay her during the summer. They had spent thousands of dollars recently and couldn't afford to stay home eating away their savings. Yet she wanted to teach Taotao some basics before his school started, so it was Nan who needed to look for a job.

It was reported that the U.S. government was going to issue green cards to the Chinese students who did not intend to return to China. Professor Nicholson in Nan's department, a specialist in American domestic policy, had assured him that the United States would definitely keep the Chinese students here. This baggy-eyed scholar said to Nan, "Believe me, any country will be willing to have the cream of China's young generation." That was probably true. Indeed, both Canada and Australia had just granted permanent residency to all the Chinese students and scholars living there. Pingping and Nan felt relieved to know they wouldn't have to spend thousands of dollars and wait years for green cards like most immigrants. Still, they were unsettled. Mentally they were not prepared for such a new life.

5

THE FALL SEMESTER would be starting in two weeks, and if he didn't register as a student Nan wouldn't be able to work in the university library anymore. For days he had been looking for a job but couldn't find one. He had liked his job as a custodian in the medical building very much; it was not demanding and gave him some time to read, though he was paid only $4.65 an hour, and though his fellow worker Nick, the maintenance man, often carried a dime bag on him and smoked a joint in their windowless office, mixed with tobacco to hide the scent. For years Nan had adhered to the principle that he would sell his brawn but not his brain. He wanted to save his mind for his study. Now graduate work was no longer his concern, so he wouldn't be too picky about jobs.

He responded to numerous ads, but no one was interested in a man without any employable skill. He went to several Chinese restaurants and they wouldn't use him either, because his accent betrayed that he was from northern China and because he couldn't speak any southern dialect. They didn't explain why, but he guessed the reason. At Nanking Village in Watertown, the owner of the place, an old woman with high cheekbones, told him, "*If only you had come last week. I just hired a waitress, that fat girl.*" Apparently she liked Nan and showed him some respect, as if he were a poor scholar in dire straits but might ascend to a consequential post someday. Nan even wrote to several Chinese-language programs in local colleges, one of which did respond, but in a form letter, saying they couldn't hire him although they might rue that they had let "a pearl" slip through their fingers.

A pearl only your mother can appreciate! Nan sneered to himself.

Without any hope he phoned a factory in Watertown that had advertised for a night watchman. A man named Don told him to come in and fill out a form. Nan was not enthusiastic about the job but went anyway.

Don was a middle-aged supervisor with a bald crown who spoke English with an Italian accent. Seeing that Nan was a foreign student and over thirty, he seemed more interested. They sat in the factory's office, which stank of tobacco and plastic. The room, with its grimy windows facing west, was dim despite several fluorescent tubes shining. "Have you done this kind of work before?" Don asked Nan.

"Yes. I worked for one and a half years at zer Waltham Medical Center, as a cahstodian. Here's recommendation by my former bawss."

Don looked through the letter, which Heidi's sister-in-law Jean had written for Nan when she got fired and had to let her staff of three go. Don tilted his beetle eyebrows and asked, "Tell me, why did you leave that place?"

"My bawss was sacked, so we got laid all together."

"You got what?" Don asked with a start. A young secretary at another desk tittered and turned her pallid face toward the two men.

Realizing he'd left out the adverb "off," Nan amended, "Sorry, sorry, they used anozzer company, so we all got laid off."

"I see." Don smiled. "We need you to take a physical before we can hire you."

"What's zat? Body examination?"

"Correct. Here's the clinic you should go to." Don penciled the address at the top of a form and pushed it to Nan. "After the doc fills this out, you bring it back to me."

"Okay. Do you awffer medical care?"

"You mean health insurance?"

"Yes."

"We do provide benefits."

"Cahver a whole family?"

"Yes, if you choose to buy it."

Nan was pleased to hear that. Having left school, he was no longer qualified for the student health insurance and would have to find a new one for his family. But the idea of taking a physical bothered him. He was healthy and sturdy, and the job paid only $4.50 an hour; there should be no need for them to be so meticulous. On second thought, he realized that the factory, which manufactured plastic products, would be liable to lawsuits filed by its employees.

•

Nan went to the clinic on Prospect Street in Waltham. It was a small office that had opened recently and had only one physician; there wasn't even a secretary around, probably because it was lunch hour. Nan handed the form to the bulky doctor, who showed him into a room that wasn't fully furnished yet. The dark leather couch was brand-new; so were the floor lamps. In spite of his pale face and brown stubble, the doctor reminded Nan of a Japanese chef he had once seen at a restaurant in Cambridge. The man had a pair of glasses hanging around his neck and against his chest. As he was checking Nan's hearing, Nan wondered whether the doctor was far-sighted or nearsighted.

After listening to his breathing, tapping his chest, and palpating his stomach, the doctor said, "All right, open your pants."

Nan started. "You need to check everysing?"

"Yep." The man grinned, putting on a pair of latex gloves.

Nan unfastened his belt and moved down his pants and briefs. On the right side of his belly stretched a scar like a short engorged leech. The doctor pressed it with his index and middle fingers, saying, "How did you get this?"

"Appendix."

"Appendicitis?"

"Yes."

"That shouldn't have left such a big scar. Does it still hurt?" He pressed harder.

"No."

"Fascinating. It's healed okay, I guess." He spoke as if to himself. Next, to Nan's astonishment, the doctor grabbed his testicles, rubbed them in his palm for three or four seconds, then squeezed them hard and yanked them twice. A numbing pain radiated through Nan's abdomen and made him almost cry out.

"Any prawblem?" he managed to ask, and noticed the man observing his member intently.

"No. Genitalia are normal," the doctor grunted, scribbling on the form without raising his puffy eyes.

Nan was too shocked to say another word. Having buckled up his pants, he was led into the outer room. Rapidly the doctor filled out the form and shoved it back to him. "You're all set," he said with a smirk.

Stepping out of the clinic, Nan wondered if the doctor was allowed to touch his genitals. He felt insulted but didn't know what to do. Should he go back and ask him to explain what the physical was supposed to include? That wouldn't do. "Never argue with a doctor"—that was a dictum followed by people back home. Even now, Nan couldn't understand some of the terms on the form. If only he had brought along his pocket dictionary. Perhaps the doctor had just meant to find out whether he had a normal penis. Still, the man shouldn't have pulled his testicles that hard. The more Nan thought about this, the more outraged he was. Yet he forced himself to let it go. What was important was the job. He'd better not make a fuss.

A boy on a skateboard rushed by on the sidewalk and almost ran into Nan. "Watch out, dork!" shouted the teenager with an orange mohawk. That stopped Nan from brooding, and he hurried to his car, parked behind the clinic.

6

NAN liked the job at the factory. He worked at night and on weekends when all the machines stopped and the workshops were closed. There was another watchman, Larry, a spindly student majoring in thanatology at Mount Ida College. He and Nan rotated. On Nan's first day Larry told him, "I can't hack it anymore, have to quit one of these days." Indeed the fellow looked sickly and shaggy, his face always covered in sweat, but he never missed his shift.

Once an hour, the watchman had to walk through the three workshops and the warehouse to make sure everything was all right. There were sixteen keys affixed to the walls and the wooden pillars inside the factory, and he had to carry a clock to those spots, insert the keys into it, and turn them, so that the next morning Don could read the record. As long as the clock showed enough of the hourly marks, Don would be satisfied.

Usually a round took Nan about fifteen minutes; after that he could stay in the lab upstairs, doing whatever he liked. A black-and-white TV sat on a long worktable strewn with pinking shears, large scissors, rulers, red and blue markers, and bolts of waterproof cloth of various colors. If he got tired of reading, he'd watch television. On weekends he could go up to the rooftop and stay in the open air. Behind the factory, close to the base of the two-story building, flowed a branch of the Charles. The green water looked stagnant; it was quite narrow, no more than a hundred feet wide, but it was deep. Sometimes one or two anglers would come fishing on the bank, and Nan, not allowed to leave the building, would sit on the rooftop and watch them. Most of the time they caught bass, bluegill, perch, pumpkinseed, and smelts, but the water was so polluted that they always threw their catches back, even a thirty-pound carp Nan once saw a man drag ashore, its rotund body motionless while its slimy tail kept slapping the grass.

Between his rounds, Nan read a good deal, mainly poetry and novels, and if he didn't read or watch TV, he let his thoughts roam. Recently many Chinese students in the humanities and social sciences, having realized they might have to live in the United States for good, had changed their fields in order to make themselves more marketable. Nan knew that some people who had been writing dissertations on Shakespeare or Dewey or Tocqueville had decided to go to business or law school. More amazing, in some cases their advisors encouraged them to switch fields and even wrote recommendations for them. Nan's professor, Mr. Peterson, was different and said it was unfortunate that Nan would be leaving the Ph.D. program, because he believed Nan could have become an excellent political scientist if he had studied the subject devotedly. Professor Peterson even tried to dissuade him, but Nan wouldn't change his mind.

Nan was determined to quit political science, but deep down he was disappointed about leaving academia. He had written to Professor Clifford Stevens at the University of Chicago to inquire about the possibility of doing graduate work in Chinese poetry or comparative poetics under his guidance, but he never heard a word from that distinguished scholar. Nowadays most American graduate schools were inundated with applications from China. Worse yet, after the Tiananmen massacre, the student enrollments in the Chinese language and studies had dropped so drastically that many American colleges had begun to scale down their Chinese programs. So, for the time being, there was no way Nan could study Chinese poetry.

Four years ago, a former professor of his in China had visited the United States as part of a Chinese delegation of American Studies, as an expert in U.S. political history because he had translated some essays by Thomas Jefferson. When his former teacher came to visit Harvard, Nan went to the Holiday Inn in Somerville to see him. The old man, beardless and browless like an albino, told Nan about his meeting with Professor Carolyn Barrow at Harvard. He said, "*The old lady was very nice and gave me six of her books. Do you know her writings?*"

"*I read some of her papers. She's well revered for her work in polit-ical theories.*"

"*I guessed that,*" the teacher went on. "*I gave her a stack of plates.*"

"*What do you mean?*"

"*I brought with me some fine porcelain, and I gave her eight pieces.*" He smiled, his lips puckered.

That account had scandalized Nan. His old teacher hadn't shown any trace of discomfort, as if the fact that his porcelain and Professor Barrow's books were at least equal in monetary value had canceled all the difference in the nature of the two sets of presents. Nan was sure that some other Chinese scholars had done similar things. Without telling anybody, he had made up his mind that he'd write many books after he finished his Ph.D. and returned to his home-land to teach. Someday when he came to revisit the United States, he'd bring only his own works as gifts for American scholars. Yes, he'd write a whole shelf of books and would never subject himself to his teacher's kind of disgrace.

Now that ambition, inflated with a sense of national pride, was gone. He might never go back to his native land, and it would be unimaginable for him to write scholarly books in English if he was no longer in academia. Worse, he had little passion left for any field of study except for poetry. But that was impossible for now.

7

AT WORK the night watchmen were not supposed to leave the factory. Nan noticed, however, that Larry often went out to buy things. Larry said that as long as you made your hourly rounds on the dot, Don wouldn't care. Sometimes Nan didn't bring food with him and would steal out to get a hamburger or fried rice.

One night, the moment he finished the ten o'clock round, he drove to Riche Brothers, a nearby supermarket open around the clock. He picked up a can of luncheon meat, a jar of gherkins, and a French bread. Hurriedly he checked out of the express lane and then headed for the front entrance. As he was striding out the automatic door, he almost bumped into a couple, both thirtyish, who had just come out of the adjacent liquor store. The man, his chestnut mane reaching his shoulders, was tall, with an athletic build, and carried three video tapes in one hand, while the woman, wearing a baseball cap, had a bony face and a slim body and held a half-filled paper bag in her arms. They were both in black leather jackets and jeans with frayed cuffs, but she wore blue high-tops whereas he had on heavy-duty boots. Nan stepped aside as she did the same to avoid a collision. "Sorry," he said with a smile. She rolled her large watery eyes, then peered at him.

Nan walked away toward his car. Strangely enough, the couple turned back and came toward him. The woman whispered to the man, who was nodding. When they caught up with Nan, the man said in a raspy voice, "Hey, buddy, wanna come with us?"

"For what?" Nan was startled. A gust of wind swept up a few scraps of paper tumbling past a corral holding two rows of shopping carts.

"For fun." The man blinked his eyes, the left of which was black as if bruised, and he opened his mouth to laugh, but only a dry cough came out. There was enough alcohol on his breath to cover a few yards around him.

The woman smiled suggestively, showing the gaps between her teeth. Nan shook his head and said, "I have work to do."

"Wanna have a drink?" the man asked.

The woman took out a can of Coors, snapped it open, and took a swig. "Mmm . . . it's nice and cold. Have this." She handed the beer to Nan.

"No, sanks. I reelly cannot."

"C'mon, don't you want some fun?" The man grinned, the corners of his mouth going up.

"What fun?"

"With purty girls."

Nan was too shocked to answer, while the woman crooked her forefinger, wiggling it at him. He hated that gesture, which to him suggested he was an obedient dog.

She coaxed, "Please come with us. We've never had an Oriental man there."

"No, I mahst go!"

"Whoa!" the man shouted after him. "Don't run, you gook. Don't you want some young pussies?"

They both laughed. Nan started his car and pulled out of the parking lot. To his horror, the couple hopped into their pickup, backed it out, and followed him. Nan's heart was throbbing, but he drove unhurriedly as if he hadn't noticed them. "Calm down, calm down," he repeated to himself while observing them in the rearview mirror. Their truck didn't accelerate and just followed behind at a distance of about two hundred feet. A white moth was trapped in Nan's car, fluttering at the windshield. He brushed it away with one swipe.

After four turns Nan swerved into the factory's front yard. He sprang out of his car while the pickup was rolling into the parking lot too. He dashed away to the side entrance of the building. His flashlight fell on the ground with a clash, but he didn't stop to retrieve it and kept running. He thrust the key into the lock and opened the door. Rushing in, he snagged his windbreaker's pocket on the handle with a rasp. Without looking at the rip, he locked the door, switched off the lights, and turned left into the dark storage room with windows facing the yard. He saw the couple out there. They seemed puzzled. Their truck was idling, but its front lights were off. They each carried a baseball bat under an arm and eyed the side entrance as if on the defensive. They whispered to each other for a while; then the man crushed his beer can on the side window of Nan's car. He picked up Nan's long flashlight and waved it at the building.

The woman cupped her mouth with both hands and shouted at the entrance, "Come out, you dumb prick!"

"We're gonna come in and bust ya!" the man cried, and he kicked the side door of Nan's car. He spat and blew his nose on the windshield.

Blood thudded in Nan's ears as he kept his eyes glued to the couple. He withdrew his face from the dusty windowpanes so that they couldn't see him. His mind was in a tumult of anger and fear, which made him queasy and out of breath. Stop kicking my car, you idiot! he shouted mentally. Heavens, what do they want of me? I'm not a sex maniac like they think. Go away! Go fuck yourselves!

But they wouldn't leave. They whispered to each other again and were evidently planning their next move. What should he do if they broke into the building? He wouldn't let them. He'd do anything to stop them. He'd hide in the darkness and knock them down with a steel bar. Yes, he'd lick them if they came in. Go, go, go! But they wouldn't move. Why were they so determined to hurt him? Just because they could? Just because his face was yellow, not as white as theirs? How come they thought he'd like to take part in their monkey business? Crazy! Stupid! They were barking up the wrong tree. Even if they paid him a thousand dollars, he wouldn't join them. Neither would he let them set foot in here. They'd better not mess with him.

They looked quite patient over there, waiting and gazing at the factory. How could he get rid of them? Were they planning to break in?

Finally, Nan pushed open the one-paned transom and cried, "Eef you don't leave, I shall call zer police."

"Oh yeah?" the man barked. "Bring all the cops over and line them up to suck my cock."

They both guffawed.

Nan shouted again, "I have a gahn here. I'm shooting if you don't leave right away." With a steel bar he knocked a metal bench, which sent out a dull clang.

That transfixed the couple for a few seconds. Then they scrambled back into the pickup and thunked the doors shut. The front lights came on; the man revved the engine, and after a long honk, the truck swerved onto the road and sped away. Its broad wheels squealed and crushed through dark puddles of rainwater.

Nan heaved a sigh of relief, wondering if they were high on drugs besides alcohol. How frightened he was! Had they grabbed hold of him, they might have dragged him to a secret place and hurt him. He suspected they must have intended to take him either to an orgy or a studio to make a pornographic film. He regretted having gone out at night and having smiled at that crazy woman.

The watchman's clock was still in his car, but for a long while he dared not go fetch it. Not until almost eleven p.m. did he retrieve it. Luckily, the side door of his car wasn't damaged much—just a few dings—but his flashlight was gone.

His fellow worker, Larry, had a pistol like a toy derringer, and now Nan couldn't help wondering if he should get a handgun or a knife. But he remembered his vow to Pingping that, besides shunning politics, he'd never resort to any kind of violence in his life, so he decided not to carry any weapon.

When he told his wife about the incident the next day, she was terrified, though she tried to loosen him up a little, teasing him, "*It serves you right. Don't ever eye up a woman again.*"

"*I didn't flirt with her, I just smiled. They must have been stoned.*"

"*They must have smelled something on you.*"

"*What?*"

"*You're a born lech.*"

"*That's not true.*"

"*Of course you are.*" She giggled and went on sewing up the tear in his windbreaker.

From that day on Nan wouldn't go out on the night shift anymore. He'd bring along an electric pot so that he could cook instant noodles or soup in the lab, but most times Pingping prepared food for him. She'd pack a banana or apple or orange. She made him promise he'd never sneak out of the factory again.

8

THE MASEFIELDS had been back from Cape Cod for three weeks. Heidi's children, Nathan and Livia, ages eleven and eight, had been pleased to see Taotao, especially Livia, who adopted a protective attitude toward the younger boy. The girl, who had a wide forehead and large deep-set eyes, was short and scrawny for her age. She had many friends in the neighborhood and often invited them over, but Taotao wouldn't join them. Neither would he play with Nathan. Most of the time he stayed upstairs in the attic. Whenever Livia found him in the kitchen with his mother, she'd teach him a few English words. "Say 'Thank you, please' when you want something," she told him; or "Say 'Can I have this, please?'" And Taotao would repeat after her. Sometimes she'd hold out her hands with the short fingers raised and ask him, "How many is this?" The boy always answered correctly in English. In every way she treated him like a friend. She seemed eager to please Taotao, who was still timid and quiet. She often said to Pingping and Heidi, "He's really smart. Why's he so shy?"

The Wus ate their own meals separately. They'd enter the large kitchen only after the Masefields were finished with dinner. This meant Pingping had to cook two meals in the afternoons. Unlike his parents, Taotao was fond of American food, which made his mother's cooking easier. Following him, his parents had begun to eat what they wouldn't touch before—pizza, cheese, spaghetti, macaroni, hot dogs. Cheese tasted like soap to Nan at first, but now he chewed it with relish and could tell if the flavor was sharp. Still, he found that milk would upset his stomach, so his wife gave him ice cream instead.

In the evenings Pingping spent most of the time reading aloud to

Taotao. She also taught him arithmetic, which was easier for him since she explained everything in Chinese. She had been a math teacher at a vocational school back in China, but she had hated teaching, a profession assigned to her by the state. Now she was happy to teach her son with the thick textbooks Nan had bought at a secondhand bookstore in Sudbury, a nearby town. She found that American math books were much better written than the Chinese textbooks, more detailed, more comprehensive, and more suitable for students to teach themselves math. Each book was chock-full of information, at least ten times more than a Chinese schoolbook contained.

With his mother's help at home, Taotao did decently at school, though he was still in the lowest reading group. Nan had gone to see his son at school a few times and noticed that a freckle-faced girl named Loreen often read to Taotao. He was moved by the sight in which the girl put her finger on a drawing, saying, "This is a jumbo jet heading for Miami," while his son listened attentively. Nan knew that the girl's father played basketball for the Celtics, and he had once seen him with Loreen sitting on his knee at a PTA meeting. The man was a giant, but somehow his daughter was weedy and frail. Taotao told his parents that Loreen was good to him and even gave him her milk at lunch. Yet not all the students were kind to him, and a few called him Conehead.

One afternoon in mid-October, Nan and Pingping went to have a conference with Mrs. Gardener, Taotao's homeroom teacher. The classroom was already empty of students, and the little chairs had all been pushed under the child-size tables. "Take a seat," the teacher said in a tired voice to Nan and Pingping, smiling kindly. She was in her early forties and had round eyes and a pudgy face.

They sat down in front of Mrs. Gardener, who began talking about Taotao's progress. Meanwhile, the boy was sitting on his heels in the corridor, waiting for his parents.

"I have just put him into another reading group, one level up," the teacher said about Taotao.

"Sank you for promoting him." Nan's eyes brightened.

"We are very happy about that," Pingping added.

"Mrs. Wu, does Taotao have a bladder problem?"

"Not really. He pee in bed a few times when he's baby, but that's okay."

"In class he goes to the bathroom every ten minutes. The other students are amused. He must feel embarrassed, I gather. I'm worried about that."

"He may be nervous," Nan put in.

"He could be. I've noticed that in the math class he doesn't go to the bathroom as often."

"I work hard with his reading at home," Pingping said.

"I can tell. He has made a lot of progress. Still, it's not easy for him to keep up with the rest of the class. That's why I want to ask you this—would you like to have him placed in a bilingual class? The school is going to start one soon."

"No!" Nan objected. "We don't want him to be in a class jahst for foreigners."

"Yes, he doesn't need that," Pingping chimed in.

Mrs. Gardener looked perplexed. "Why? That'll make him more comfortable."

"He comes here to stahdy, not to be comfortable," replied Nan.

"I don't understand, Mr. Wu, although I appreciate your taking his education so seriously."

"He can catch up wiz zer class, believe me. Please give him a chance," Nan said.

"Please don't get rid of him!" Pingping begged. "Taotao said a lotta good thing about you, Mrs. Gardener. He's unhappy if you take him out."

The teacher looked at her in astonishment, then was all smiles. "I don't mean to send him away. Don't get me wrong. If you insist, we won't put him in the bilingual class."

After that meeting, Pingping worked harder to help Taotao with his reading. Every week she borrowed a dozen or so children's books from the town library and read them together with him. Even when the boy was too tired to continue, she'd go on reading aloud so he could listen while working a jigsaw puzzle or playing with Legos or the toy robots Nathan had lent him. She didn't always understand what she read. Once, as mother and son were reading a story about

King William and his knights who conquered a fortress, the boy asked, *"Mama, what does* 'laid waste' *mean?"*

"Poop and pee everywhere." She then continued loudly, "The king was pleased with the raid and awarded his men . . ."

Another time they were reading an abridged biography of Queen Elizabeth. When they came to a scene in which Her Majesty was so furious with a courtier that she laid her hands on him, Taotao asked his mother, *"What is* 'boxed his ears'*?"*

"To cover up his earholes so he couldn't hear anything."

"It doesn't sound like that."

"All right, let's mark this and ask Daddy when he's back."

Among the titles Pingping had checked out of the library, she liked the simplified *Black Beauty* best. She'd sigh, saying, *"I'm like that horse, always moving from place to place and serving others. As long as the harness is on me, I can't take a run for joy or lie down for weariness. I have to work, work, work, until I die."* Her eyes would fill.

Taotao didn't fully understand what she meant, but her words upset Nan when he overheard her. He knew her life had been misspent. When Pingping was a child, her mother had prophesied her hard future, saying she had a princess's body but a maid's fate. Pingping resented that but never dared to talk back. She always dreamed of becoming a doctor like her parents and often went to her father's clinic to do voluntary work, giving injections, decocting medicinal herbs, performing acupuncture and cupping, boiling syringes and needles. Everybody praised her, many patients wanted her to treat them, and people believed she had life-nurturing hands and would make an excellent doctor someday. But when she had grown up, she couldn't even attend nursing school and was assigned to study applied mathematics in a technical school. How she envied those youths in her neighborhood who had gone to college or the army through their parents' clout. In her mind she had blamed her father for not pulling strings for her, even though she knew that the old man, born into a rich peasant's family and classified as a reactionary element, dared not, and could not, assert himself. Now she made Taotao study hard, hoping he could go to medical school someday. If that happened, she would spend her last penny helping him.

9

IN EARLY NOVEMBER, the Masefields left for Italy to visit Heidi's sister, Rosalind, who lived in Rome most of the time. Seizing the opportunity, Nan invited Danning and three other friends over for dinner. But except for Danning they all declined, saying they were too busy. True enough, two of them had to work the graveyard shift at the Chinese Information Center in Newton that had been established recently by a group of dissidents to help the underground democracy movement in China. But it was also true that since Nan had quit graduate school, most of his friends had distanced themselves from him. They probably viewed him as a loser. Pingping urged him to break with them completely. *"They're just a bunch of fair-weather snobs, not your friends,"* she told Nan. *"Who needs them?"*

Danning, however, was always eager to visit the Wus. He was almost thirty-five and had a seven-year-old daughter back in China. His wife had joined him in the United States two years before but had left him last winter. They had often quarreled, and she'd yell at him, calling him names and saying that one of these days she would quit being his "pretty slave." She liked bragging about her looks, which were by no means extraordinary; she merely sported a pair of sparkling eyes shaded by long lashes. Her nose was flat, her mouth wide, and one side of her face larger than the other. She told people that she had grown up always with a nanny for herself and had never cooked a single meal back home when she lived with her parents, but now she did all kinds of housework that made her feel humiliated. One night as she and Danning fought again, she grabbed a kitchen knife and swiped at him. "Ow!" he cried, feeling the pain in his back. At the sight of blood she dropped the knife and ran away. Their roommate, who shared the three-bedroom apartment with them, drove him to the hospital, where Danning received twelve stitches. His wife didn't come back after a few days, so he reported it to the police—not his wound, but her disappearance. She was nowhere to be found, though some people said they had seen her shopping at Ming's Supermarket in Chinatown. It was whispered that she was living with a wealthy businessman from Canton now. Although Pingping didn't like Danning's wife that much, she never blamed her. She'd say to Nan, *"Why couldn't Danning see that Anni meant to leave him? He always bragged about this and that but never saw the fire in his backyard."*

"Come on, have some sympathy," Nan would object. *"He's a smart man. How can we tell he wasn't aware of his marital trouble?"*

"I hope he can find her."

The truth was that Danning still didn't know her whereabouts. She hadn't written him a word and had never called. Oddly enough, he seemed to enjoy living as a bachelor, in no hurry to look for her. Their daughter was cared for by his parents back in Beijing.

Before dinner, Nan gave his guest a tour of the Masefields' place. He took Danning to the tennis court, its green surface studded with yellow balls; the frayed net was slack, betraying that nobody had played here recently. Next they went to the swimming pool beyond the tennis fence, the water wrinkling in the breeze and a pair of white plastic geese bobbing in a corner, their necks tethered to a steel pipe by ropes. Then Nan and Danning entered the workshop next to the garage, in which Heidi made pottery. The room had in it a hardwood floor, a ceiling fan, a tall electric heater, and a long workbench on which were stacked some terra-cotta pots. Near the window stood a potter's wheel and a side chair. A column of sunlight slanted in, specks of dust billowing in it. Danning was so impressed that he said, *"This makes me sad, very sad."*

"Why?" Nan was surprised.

"We all work so hard, but how could we ever get as rich as this family?"

"Heidi owns half a bank and an insurance company. Old New England money. We shouldn't measure ourselves against her."

Danning sighed. *"We'll never live like this. What's the good of working myself to a skeleton here?"*

"It took several generations for her family to build the wealth. She also inherited lots of money from her husband."

"I should give up. The American dream is not for me." Danning's nostrils flared as his face scrunched.

"I thought I was the only pessimist." Nan chuckled. He realized that for a long time he hadn't been interested in making money, perhaps because he had seen so much wealth at this place that he had gradually lost heart, no longer possessed by the hunger that drives new immigrants to wrestle with fortune.

Dinner was simple: eggplant stuffed with minced pork, a salad of assorted vegetables, preserved eggs, braised shrimp, and dumplings filled with beef and napa cabbage. Danning wanted beer despite Nan's warning that he'd have a long drive back to Belmont. Nan took a six-pack of Budweiser out of the refrigerator and opened a bottle for his friend. They were seated at the dining table in the kitchen, which had a bay window that looked onto the front yard. In the flower bed the yellow mums and marigolds had all withered, and some tattered blossoms drooped, touching the ground. The trees dropped leaves now and again, white pine seeds helicoptering listlessly and husks of oak leaves zigzagging down, sinking through the opalescent light. A couple of tufted titmice were busy pecking at the sunflower seeds contained in a glass feeder hanging from a bough of the bulky linden at the center of the yard. Danning ate with a good appetite and kept saying to Nan that it was great to have one's family together. He seemed to respect Pingping a lot and frequently patted Taotao on the head. He spooned some mashed garlic onto his plate and asked Nan, *"Have you decided what to do yet?"*

"No, but I've been thinking of doing something that moneyed people can't do. You see how rich the Masefields are. It doesn't make sense for me to dream of getting rich." Nan turned to Pingping, who looked alarmed, a shadow dimming her face.

"What do you plan to do?" Danning put half a dumpling into his mouth, chewing with his lips closed.

"Probably I'll write. I want to be a writer."

"Writing articles for newspapers?"

"No, poetry."

"Wow, you're such an idealist, a dreamer! I take off my cap."

"Don't be sarcastic. I'm just saying I might try to write some poems."

"Still, I admire you for that, for being faithful to your own heart and following your own passion. To be honest, I don't like physics, but I have to finish the dissertation to get the damn degree."

"What would you do if you were free to choose?"

"Well, I would write novels, one after another. I know I could be a prolific writer, telling stories about our experiences in America."

"You would publish them in China?"

"Of course, where else can you have your readers if you write in Chinese?"

"I can't think about writing novels. I don't have that kind of long wind."

"What will you do for money? Poetry won't fetch a salary."

"I always can work."

Nan was reluctant to talk more about his plan since he hadn't made up his mind yet. His wife put in about him, "He's always rich in the heart."

"That makes him remarkable, doesn't it?" said Danning.

"I hope we just live a life similar to others' here, making some money and having our own home, so that every day will be the same as the previous one," she replied thoughtfully.

"Come now," Nan said to her. "I'll work hard to bring in money, you know that."

That quieted her. She got up to take a bowl of fruit out of the refrigerator. As they started to eat the dessert, Danning said, "Nan, have you heard anything from the Chinese consulate yet?"

"No, about what?"

"They've been investigating your involvement in the planned kidnap."

"Really? How do you know?" Pingping broke in.

"Vice Consul Hu asked me last week about Nan's role in the case. I said I had no idea. It seemed they knew Nan had brought up the suggestion of seizing hostages, and he must be a target of their investigation."

Nan was so flabbergasted that he couldn't respond for a moment. Then he asked, *"What are they going to do to me, do you know?"*

"Don't be scared. They can't do anything to you here. But once you're back in China, that'll be different. So don't fall into their hands."

"How did they come to know about the plan?"

"I don't have the foggiest idea. Somebody must have given you away."

"Yuming Wang or Manyou Zhou?"

"It can be any one of those involved, but there's no way to identify the informer. Anybody could turn you in to save his own ass."

"You mean I've been singled out as a scapegoat?"

"Right."

Nan turned to Pingping, who looked panic-stricken, her eyes flickering. She placed her hand on Taotao's head, stroking his hair unconsciously.

"What should I do?" Nan asked his friend.

"Relax. Don't say anything against the government in front of others, not even in your letters or on the phone when you call home. If those top leaders' children confront you, just say you made a rash remark and never thought others would take it seriously. It won't hurt if you apologize to them."

"No, never."

"I know you won't."

When Danning was about to leave, Pingping thanked him for letting them know of the official investigation. Danning said, *"I planned to call and tell you about it even if I couldn't come today."* He grinned, his face a little lopsided. He had drunk three bottles of beer but wouldn't stay longer to let the alcohol dissolve some. He told Pingping he hadn't had a homemade dinner for two months. He was sorry about the troublesome information, but they shouldn't be scared. Nan should just be careful and avoid getting hotheaded again. Danning stepped into his rusty hatchback and drove away.

That night Pingping didn't go to bed until eleven-thirty, when Nan had to set off for the factory. They talked about their situation. Now it looked like Nan definitely couldn't return to China, and even in this country he'd have to keep a low profile. They'd be lucky if both of their families, especially their siblings, didn't suffer on Nan's account.

Recently Nan had mailed his passport to the Chinese consulate in New York for renewal, so he was now afraid that the officials might create difficulties for him and put his papers on hold. He felt powerless whenever dealing with them. It was as if invisible hands still manipulated his life even though he lived far away from China.

At work that night, Nan wrote to his parents, telling them to take good care and that everything was fine with his family here. He mentioned: "I have enclosed a hair of mine. If you don't find it in the envelope, that means someone has tampered with the letter. Let me know if you see it." He wanted to ascertain whether his mail was monitored. If it was, there'd be no doubt that he'd been blacklisted. How he regretted having blurted out the crazy kidnap idea in the presence of more than a dozen people. Now it had boomeranged on him. The more he thought about his situation, the more convinced he was that any one of those who had heard him could have informed against him. No wonder so many of his friends and acquaintances had grown estranged from him lately. They were probably all desperate to clear themselves.

10

"WELL, I'm sorry to tell you we're moving," Don said to Nan. They were in his tiny office in the middle of the main workshop, with a glass wall on every side. A few workers had just punched in, drinking coffee and making noises with tools, but all the machines were still quiet.

"Zer whole factory?" Nan asked Don.

"Yep."

"Where are you going?"

"We bought a place outside Fitchburg. If you want, you can come work for us there."

"Zat is hard. My son goes to school here." Nan turned silent and recalled Fitchburg, a town he had been to once. A year earlier he and Danning had gone to Keene, New Hampshire, to pick up two cheap computers assembled by a four-man company housed in a barn. On their way back they had stopped for lunch at Fitchburg, which had some lovely Victorian and colonial houses surrounded by woods. It was a long drive from Woodland, at least an hour.

"Anyway, think about it. We'll close this place by mid-January." Don screwed up his yellow eye.

"I will."

"Don't forget your bird."

"Sure, I won't." Nan had just finished his shift. Having hung the clock behind the door of the office for Don to check, he went over to a giant refrigerator, on the side of which was taped a large poster of a black sprinter drifting along with a star-spangled banner above her head. She looked as if she had just won a dash, her expression euphoric and beaming. But below her glistening legs stretched a line of words scribbled in blue ink by one of the workers: "If you can catch me, you can fuck me!" Nan opened the door of the fridge and picked out a turkey, a gift the factory offered to every employee.

It was snowing a little, the low clouds tumbling in the wind. Snowflakes swirled down and melted the moment they hit the black-top, which curved away toward the blurred townscape of Waltham in the west. Nan drove numbly ahead, still rattled by the news that the factory was moving.

Twenty minutes later he reached the Masefields'. He handed the package with the turkey to Pingping, who was making pancakes in the kitchen. Then he went upstairs to sleep without having had any breakfast.

•

At the sight of the large turkey, everybody got excited. Taotao, who had been chatting with Livia about a limping doe that had wandered into the front yard that morning, turned to ask his mother how to cook this huge bird. He had eaten deli turkey in school but wanted to know if this real turkey tasted the same. By now he had risen to the middle reading group in his class and could speak quite a bit of English, though he used only short sentences. Even when he talked with his parents, he'd mix English into Chinese.

Pingping drove all three children to school after they'd had break-fast. Before she set out with them, she had suggested to Heidi that they share the turkey for dinner that evening, though Thanksgiving was still two days away. "It's too big for us," she said. Indeed, it weighed more than twenty pounds. Heidi agreed happily. She'd be taking her children to her in-laws' for Thanksgiving dinner and wouldn't be buying a turkey this year.

For Nathan and Livia, it was extraordinary that Nan had brought back a turkey for free. They thought he was a security guard at the factory, somewhat like a policeman. "Wow, amazing!" Nathan said in the van, licking his chafed lips. He was a husky boy with russet hair and silken skin, but he wasn't bright. He had never once gotten an A for his homework and always remained below the average in his class. Good-humored and handsome, he'd flash a broad smile when-ever Pingping said he looked like the young Ronald Reagan when the president had been an actor in Hollywood.

Back from the school, Pingping cleaned the turkey, sprinkled salt and pepper on it, and put it into the refrigerator. She then went upstairs to prepare some arithmetic problems for Taotao. Nan was snoring loudly in the other room. He must have been utterly exhausted. Pingping wouldn't even use the bathroom upstairs for fear of disturbing him. Toward midmorning she went to Star Market and bought yams, potatoes, green beans, a pumpkin pie, and some vegetables. As soon as she came back, she began roasting the turkey, which she had never done before. Heidi helped, showing her how to baste the bird. This was easy for Pingping, who was so good at cooking that she dared to cook anything after she'd tasted it. She also mixed some flour with butter and raisins to make biscuits.

Soon the house was filled with a meaty aroma. Heidi was so happy that she walked around with a glass of Chablis, her hazel eyes shining and her cheeks pink as if rouged. Usually she uncorked a bottle of wine a day, though she never got drunk. In the cellar of her house there were hundreds of bottles of wine in crates or on racks, some of them more than twenty years old. The Wus didn't drink, so Heidi had never locked the cellar.

In the afternoon Nan told Pingping about the factory's move. Small wonder Don had hired him on the spot three months before. If Nan had been an American, Don would have been obligated to let him know the temporary nature of the job when he applied. Now what should Nan do? He wouldn't mind working as a night watchman for some years, but he'd need a more reliable car than his old Ford if he had to commute to Fitchburg every day. Without much consideration, Pingping and Nan agreed that he shouldn't go with them, because Taotao could have better schooling here. What's more, Nan's job paid less than two hundred dollars a week, and after taxes and gas there wouldn't be much left. For the time being they had best stay with the Masefields. In this way they could save at least what Pingping made.

Heidi had cleared the mail and bills from the table in the dining room, which was seldom used and where the wide floorboards creaked a little when stepped on. On the southern wall, between the windows, hung an oval mirror, below which was a pier table. In one corner was a mahogany shelf displaying antique English porcelain. Near the door stood a bronze elephant, two feet tall, brought back from India by the late Dr. Masefield and now serving as a doorstop. From the very beginning, this low-ceilinged dining room had reminded Nan of the one in Nathaniel Hawthorne's house in Salem, which he had once visited with a friend.

Pingping spread a salmon-colored cloth on the table, then began placing the food on it. Dinner started at half past four, earlier than usual. The two families sat down, Heidi at the head of the table, her half-filled glass standing beside the hand-painted plate she had made herself. The others all drank milk or orange juice. Nathan and Livia enjoyed the turkey, the biscuits, and the baked yams as if the meal were better than the food offered by any of the restaurants their mother had taken them to on weekends. Taotao liked the gravy and wanted more of it on his meat and mashed potatoes. Pingping helped him. The boy wouldn't touch the stewed eggplant, which was Heidi's favorite. Heidi had on her plate the first cut of turkey breast with the crispy skin, which she loved.

The three children soon finished dinner and left. Livia and Taotao went into the living room, where they drew pictures with crayons, their laughter ringing from there continually. That put Pingping at ease; that morning she had come across a tattered copy of *Playboy* in Nathan's bedroom, and she didn't want Taotao to join the older boy upstairs. She and Nan often wondered why Heidi hadn't dumped all the back issues of *Playboy, Penthouse, Hustler,* and other pornographic magazines left by her husband. Wouldn't they warp Nathan's mind, making him think of nothing but naked women and girls? How could he concentrate on his schoolwork if he filled his brain with smut every day? Pingping couldn't figure out why Heidi was so careless. Nan guessed that maybe Heidi wanted her son to know more about women. His wife disagreed. What sort of sex education was this? More like a perversion.

As the adults conversed at the dining table, Heidi asked Pingping, "What's the biggest difference between life in China and life here?"

Nan and Pingping exchanged smiles. He knew that despite her desperate search for a clean toilet in her dreams, she missed many things back home, especially the mountain outside the small town where she had grown up.

"Come, tell me what's so funny?" Heidi persisted, rolling her eyes. Two dimples deepened on her cheeks, and the skin above her cleavage had turned reddish. With her fork she lifted a length of sautéed broccoli onto her plate.

"You can take shower here every day, real convenience," Pingping said.

"How did you do that in China?"

"We go to public bathhouse. I carry Taotao on my back and a big basin in fronta me, got on bus to downtown. After we wash, I carry him and everything back. He's so tired he slept all way, but I almost can't stand on my leg anymore. The bus too crowded and I can't find seat."

"How often did you go to the bathhouse?"

"Usually once a week. There's too many people everywhere."

"Where did you live—I mean, in what kind of housing?"

"We have one room."

"Like a studio with a kitchenette and a bathroom in it?"

"No, just one room."

"Really? Do most Chinese live like that?"

"Some people."

"My goodness, I guess my house can accommodate a hundred Chinese." Heidi tittered, a hacking noise in her throat.

"Not true," Pingping said, coloring. "Nan's parents live in four-bedrooms apartment, and my younger brother have three huge rooms for his family."

"I was just kidding." Heidi smiled, rather embarrassed. She sloshed the wine around in her glass and took a mouthful.

Nan was amazed that Pingping, despite her preference for American life, would be so sensitive about Heidi's casual remark. She and he often complained about China in harsh language between themselves, but to Pingping, others mustn't say anything unjustifiably negative about their native land without giving offense. If only he and his wife could break off with China altogether and squeeze every bit of it out of themselves!

Heidi turned to Nan. "What's the major difference to you?" She narrowed her eyes as if sleepy.

"In China every day I wanted to jump up and fight wiz someone. On buses, in restaurants, and in movie theaters, anywhere I went, I wanted to fight. Zere you have to fight to survive, but here I don't want to fight wiz anyone, as eef I lost my spirit."

"It's true," Pingping put in. "He's real fighter in China."

"I don't understand." Heidi shook her fluffy, slightly grizzled head. "You mean you're more peaceful or more oppressed here?"

"I can't tell for sure," he said. "Back in China I knew how to deal wiz bad guys, so I eizer confront them or avoided zem, but here I can't fight anyone. I'm not sure how far I can go, where to stop."

"That's strange."

Pingping added, "What big temper he used to have. He's more like gentleman now. Some Chinese men are mean, think themselves superior than women. They treat their wife like house servant."

"A lot of American men abuse women too," Heidi said.

Nan didn't comment, lost in thought. What good would fighting and yelling do here? Who cares what noise I make? The louder I shout, the bigger a fool I'll make of myself. I feel like a crippled man here.

Pingping kept on, "I glad Nan stopped mix with his Chinese friends. When they're together, they talk nothing, only politics. How to save the country, how to run government, how to take Taiwan back, how to beat Japan, and how to deal with USA. Everybody like prime minister or something."

Heidi tittered while Nan grimaced, knowing his wife wasn't totally wrong. Heidi had by now emptied the whole bottle of wine. Before dinner she had heard from Pingping about the factory's imminent move, so she asked Nan, "Are you going to look for another job?"

"Of coss."

"You have a master's, don't you?"

"Yes, just got it."

"Do you want me to talk to the principal of West Oxford? I've known him for a number of years. They might need someone to teach Chinese."

Nan hesitated, unsure if he should express his interest. He didn't have a degree in Chinese, and that preparatory school might not consider him at all. He had looked for a teaching position in the language before and had been turned down again and again on the grounds that his specialty was political science. Pingping said, "Thank you, Heidi. I don't think Nan should teach little kids. He has best mind in our generation, a published poet in China. People know him like scholar."

Nan remained silent, moved but also abashed. He thought about his wife's words. She talked as if they were still in China. They were in America now and had to compromise.

He looked at Pingping and then at Heidi. His wife kept a straight face, blushing up to the ears, while Heidi, tipsy, simpered vaguely.

11

A LETTER from Nan's parents arrived two weeks after Thanksgiving. His father wrote that Nan shouldn't be too paranoid and that they had indeed found in the envelope a thick hair, which they could tell belonged to nobody but their oldest son. This verification enraged Nan, because in fact he had not enclosed a hair in his letter at all. The mail examiner must have put in a substitute. Now, Nan was convinced that he was blacklisted. Unsettled, he tried to recall his conversation with Danning from a few weeks earlier so as to grasp the implications he might have missed. He was afraid that his trouble with the authorities might affect the careers of his siblings back home, one of whom, his younger brother, was a reporter at an official newspaper.

In the postscript his father wrote:

My son, I hate to reiterate this, but I ought to say it again. At home you could depend on your parents, but in America you are on your own and should make as many friends as you can. Remember, one more friend is one more way of survival. Don't put on airs and insulate yourself. Try to befriend as many people as possible. You don't know who may hold out a helpful hand in your hour of need.

The old bugger is full of crap! Nan said to himself. Here we're alone and can't possibly depend on friends for our survival. Besides, all the Chinese here have changed and become self-centered and won't share time and resources with others. Everyone is struggling to keep himself from sinking. It's not like in China, where you can attach yourself to a high-ranking official and live in a network of friends snugly as long as you make no waves and don't get ahead of others.

Nan had never been close to his father, who had looked down on him because as a college instructor, Nan couldn't get decent housing for his own family and had to live in a room borrowed from his father's beverage research institute. The old man often said to Ping-ping that Nan at most had a second-rate mind, but Pingping would counter, *"He's better than you. He'll be a professor someday."* Her father-in-law would hoot, far from offended, though he still called Nan "a born loser." On his fifty-sixth birthday five years before, the old man had excluded Nan from the dinner party because he had invited some important guests and was afraid that Nan, gauche and absentminded, might make a gaffe. Nan's younger brother Ning, smooth-tongued and more outgoing, kept their father's friends company at the party. That hurt Nan. He didn't respect the old man, who lived in a network of officials and was nothing but an empleomaniac, foolishly perusing the histories of various dynasties, particularly the Ming and the Ching, to learn statecraft (or political trickery); this despite the fact that the old man was in charge of a department of only ninety people and was already close to retirement age. In private Nan called his father "a lifetime lackey."

•

The letter from home disturbed Pingping as well. She advised Nan to forgive his father and not to be annoyed. She even ventured, *"He might have a point. You shouldn't continue to live like this."*

"What can I do, eh?" asked Nan.

"Maybe go to school again?"

"To study what? Law or business or computer science?"

"I didn't say any of those. Why can't you specialize in something you like? You write in English better than most people. Why not put that to good use?"

"I need money for tuition. Nowadays there're so many Chinese students in America that schools don't give as many scholarships as before. After the Tiananmen massacre, who still wants to admit students from that ruthless country?"

"But it won't hurt to try."

They did have some savings, which both of them had agreed not to touch—they must keep some cash on hand in case of emergency, now that their child was with them. *"I want to be a writer, to write many books,"* Nan muttered.

"In Chinese?"

"Of course."

"You'll have no chance if you do that."

"Why do you say that?"

"Where can you have your writings published? Besides, you can't get along with those Chinese writers living in this area. Some of them are plain scoundrels. You're a different type and can never find acceptance among them."

"You worry too much. I don't need to befriend anyone to be a writer. If my work is good, of course someone will publish it. My problem is that I have to make a living as well, have to secure a regular income. That I don't know how to do." He grasped the chest of his olive green turtleneck and shook it. *"Never have I felt so useless. I don't know how to sell myself here, I don't know how to sell anything, I can never be a salesman! Oh well, as I'm already worthless, I'd better not dream of making a salary."*

Pingping fell silent. Nan's state of mind troubled her. How could they live decently if he indulged in writing poetry? She wasn't even sure whether he had talent for that, though he had published about a dozen short poems back in China, all in small magazines. She knew that if he studied any subject in the humanities or social sciences, he might become a scholar eventually. But somehow he had just lost interest in academia, though he was still a dreamer and read a lot every day. True, he had always worked since coming to America, but he seemed to be getting nowhere and had never held a real job. Among some of his compatriots at Brandeis, Nan had a nickname, Mr. Wagon Man, because he had once quoted Emerson at a party— "Hitch your wagon to a star"—in an attempt to dissuade a linguist from switching to the field of economics. A historian, an arch-browed man from Henan Province, admonished Nan not to *"parrot that so-called New England sage"* who was a racist and always despised the Chinese.

Nan let out a sigh and told Pingping, *"Don't worry. I'll figure out a way. I'll make certain Taotao will live a life better than ours."*

"Sure, that's why we are here."

She said no more, not wanting to pressure him. In a way, she was pleased to know he still wanted to write, which indicated that he hadn't lost his spirit, though at the same time she feared he might blunder into a blind alley. She had no idea what she could do here. Compared with her, Nan was far more capable and should be able to lead a full life if he found his way. In any case, he mustn't remain wobbly too long; this family depended on him.

12

"I'M YOUR FRIEND. *You can trust me,*" Nan said to Pingping two days later.

They were sitting on the sky blue carpet in Nan's bedroom while their son watched television in the other room, letting out peals of laughter from time to time. Pingping understood what Nan implied—no matter how he tried, he couldn't love her wholeheartedly. Accustomed to his confessions of this kind, she murmured while looking away and choking back her tears, "*Still, I love you.*"

He sighed. "*If only I could go somewhere nobody can find me. I'm so tired.*"

"*You always want to walk out on us!*"

"*No, I've never thought of doing anything like that.*"

"*Fine. I want a divorce so you'll have to support both Taotao and me.*"

"*You know I'll never have enough money for the alimony. Divorce will make matters worse, unless you marry a rich man.*" He forced a smile.

"*I hate you! You've turned me into your servant, your slave!*"

That silenced him. He dared not continue—more exchange on this subject would make her more distraught. She might even go to the lawyer's office next to the bank at the town center and file for divorce. He regretted having brought it up again.

It was true that he didn't love her, but it was also true that he had always cherished her as his wife, determined to be a decent husband and father. He felt for her, knowing she loved him devotedly. Many times she had said that death would be a great relief for her, and that only because Taotao was still so young did she have to live, to raise him. She'd accuse Nan of having a heart of stone—however hard she tried to please and comfort him, he'd be as impassive as before.

The truth was that, exhausted emotionally, he was incapable of loving any woman. Ever since his first love, Beina, had abandoned him eight years before, his heart had remained numb. Soon after that ill-fated relationship he had met Pingping, who had also been crossed in love, jilted by a naval officer. Nan married her soon afterward because they enjoyed spending time together and both were tired of dating, and because he assumed that the marriage would help him heal quickly, at least forcing him to forget the heartless Beina. He knew he didn't love Pingping passionately, but now that he was too tired to look for another woman, why not marry her to help her out? Also, love could always be developed and nurtured after they married. Afraid of hurting her feelings, he had told her he loved her and wanted to live with her for the rest of his life. She adored him, saying he was the most honest and intelligent man she had ever met, although he appeared a little absentminded and was so kind-hearted that some people would take advantage of him.

If only he could pluck Beina out of his heart! Now and then this scene would rise behind his eyes: He was standing in a cold drizzle and drenched through, in his arm a bouquet of carnations that had turned fresher and crisper in the rain. In the distance, horses' hooves were clattering on an asphalt road, the sound mixed with a muffled jingle of harness bells; a horn boomed from a ferryboat in the north as if to announce a solemn ceremony. He had been waiting more than three hours, but that wild-eyed woman never showed up. He guessed she must have gone to a beach resort to celebrate her twenty-sixth birthday with another man. How Nan was crushed! Why? Why? Why? His heart writhed with endless questions. He felt maimed, as though all of a sudden drained of lifeblood. When he met her two days later, she said with that impenetrable smile on her plump lips, "*I just didn't feel like coming out on that wet day. Didn't I tell you it was over between us?*"

"*Then why did you hint you were expecting a birthday present?*"

"*That's not what I meant.*" She laughed that ringing laugh and swung her waist-length hair. "*I just said, 'A real man should be fierce like an eagle and gentle like a dove. Give me a man like that. That*

would be a real gift.' I didn't mean I wanted something from you."
She kept her eyes up to the starlit sky as if speaking to someone up
there.

Too sick to listen to her anymore, Nan strode away and left her
alone waiting for the bus to go home. For a long time afterward he
lived in a daze, his heart often gripped by paroxysms of pain. Later he
learned that Beina's new lover, a translator of Japanese who worked
in the same information office as she, often went to Japan on behalf
of their sewing machine factory and brought back fancy merchandise.
The man had presented her with a red Yamaha scooter, which she
rode to work, catching envious eyes on the streets. By contrast, Nan
couldn't even buy her a new bicycle. Never had he thought she could
be bought that way. He felt as if she had stolen his heart, crushed it,
and dumped it somewhere he couldn't find it. If only he could shut
her out of his mind. If only he could get her out of his system!

Two years later, after his son was born, Nan ran into a former
classmate who talked at length about the wild Beina, who had recently gone to Beijing to take a test for an English interpreter position at the UN but hadn't even made the first cut. Nonetheless, that
impressed Nan, and coming home, he couldn't help but confess to
his wife that he still missed his ex-girlfriend terribly. Pressed by Pingping, he admitted he had married her not out of love but out of convenience and compassion. *"No,"* he confessed, *"I have no strong
feelings for any woman except for Beina. If only I had never met her."*

Wordlessly Pingping turned her face away. Tears, as if forced up
from her constricted chest, rolled down her cheeks. His confession
upset her so much that her breasts, swollen with milk, went dry the
next day.

After coming to America, Nan lived alone during the first one and
a half years. He assumed that the distance of an ocean and a continent might help develop his affection for his wife into love, since
sometimes he did miss her, but the numbness in his heart never
went away. He also thought he'd forget Beina; yet she wrote to ask
him to help her pay application fees at some American universities.
He did that, but afterward he never heard a word from her. Obviously
no graduate school admitted her. Somehow even her failure gave
him more pain.

Every once in a while he felt attracted to women, especially if they had red hair, but he knew he couldn't love anyone ardently. He had desire, yet little passion. So he didn't try to know any woman. As a matter of fact, as far as desire was concerned, he was normal and strong. Pingping often said he was good in bed, yet he knew that wasn't the reason she had stayed with him: it was because of their child. And he was grateful for that, since he too wanted an intact family for Taotao. In this place neither he nor she had another person to turn to. They were stuck together and had to depend on each other to survive.

If only he were able to love her passionately! If only he weren't so sick at heart! He was tired, and this emotional fatigue had been sinking deeper and deeper into his being. Yet strangely enough, these days the desire for writing often stirred him and demanded an instant release. At work in the factory he wrote several poems, none of which turned out promising, so he put them aside and spent his time poring over Frost's *Selected Poems*.

13

EVER SINCE Don had told him about the factory's move, Nan had been looking for a job. He had also been reading books on poetry writing. Sometimes at night he tried to write poems, but the words he put on paper ended up seeming flat and incoherent. Usually the beginning would be strong, but then the lines would sag as the poem proceeded, as if there were a leak that sank the speaking voice. Nan was afraid he no longer had the youthful energy for making poetry. A decade ago, when he had just fallen in love with Beina, he had written more than a hundred poems, all of which came with ease. At times he had poured out two or three pieces a day; every part of her became his subject—her lamplike eyes, her peachy face, her pearly teeth, her dainty hands, her swift mind, her quivering hips, above all her fearless spirit. But after she had jilted him, he burned the notebook containing all his love poems. If only he could be possessed by that kind of head-over-heels feelings again. In contrast, though the desire to write frequently spurred him on, every line now was a big struggle, marred by diffidence and sluggishness.

He wished he could hold on to his current job. Just a few years more would give him a period of apprenticeship, during which he could read many books and learn more about literature besides the craft of poetry writing. But that was just a fantasy. He had to find another job soon. He went to a steakhouse in Watertown and told the manager that he had waited tables at a Chinese restaurant. The balding man looked askance at him, twisting his swallow of a mustache with his long fingers. Apparently Nan couldn't lie without blushing. He was relieved two days later when the man told him they couldn't hire him. He had been daunted by their menu, which contained many Italian words. Just a glance at it gave him a headache, let alone the long wine list on which almost all the names were unfamiliar to him. Nan turned up at a drugstore near Harvard Square in Cambridge; its owner, a portly gentleman, was interested in hiring him as an evening-shift supervisor, but first the applicant would have to show him his green card. Nan produced his work permit, but the man wouldn't accept it, saying he'd be fined thousands of dollars if the INS caught him. He'd take nothing except a green card, which Nan had applied for but couldn't get until the next year. Then Nan entered a used bookstore with a HELP WANTED sign leaning against a stack of moldy, leather-bound tomes in the window. A fortyish woman wearing pince-nez said they needed someone to work at most twelve hours a week, not a full-timer.

At last, a week before Christmas, a security guard's position opened up at Hampden Park, a condominium complex in Newton, just off Route 9. Sandy, the manager, told Nan to come in and fill out some forms. He went there the next morning. The place consisted of three connected buildings, behind which were a swimming pool and a parking lot shaded by two long sheds. There were altogether about 120 condominiums, all sharing the same front entrance, and most of the residents were retirees.

Sandy was a stocky man of around forty, with salt-and-pepper hair, a squarish face, pale skin, and narrow eyes. Nan sat in the manager's office in the basement, a metal desk between him and Sandy. After describing the job and asking Nan a few questions, Sandy said, "You'll make good money here."

Nan grinned incredulously.

"You have a cynical smile, young man. You don't believe me?" asked the manager.

"Honestly, no. How can I make good mahney eef you pay me jahst five dollars an hour?"

"Well, I can't do better than that."

"I know I cannot make a lot of mahney here, but I need zer jawb and medical insurance."

"Believe me, for this kind of a job you won't get any benefits elsewhere."

"Zat's true."

"I like your honesty, though."

"The troos is that no matter how hard I work, I can never be more zan a Social Security nahmber." Nan blurted out the sentence that had echoed in his mind for days.

Sandy stared at him in amazement, then his face relaxed. He said, "I can't either. You're a smart guy and I know what you mean. Here's a uniform. Always put it on when you come to work."

•

Usually there were two security guards working on the same shift at Hampden Park. One serving as a concierge stayed in the office at the front entrance, which was so tiny that it could contain only one chair, while the other patrolled the parking lot behind the buildings. Nan was pleased to take charge of the backyard, because the guard at the front office had to pay attention to the people passing by, since every visitor must be announced. The guard in the parking lot was less busy. Nan could walk around, but was not permitted to sit down. If it snowed or rained, he could remain under either of the two long, wall-less sheds that covered the entire parking lot. But he couldn't read while standing below so many windows—the residents would have reported him to Sandy if they saw him do that. So he carried a pocket English-Chinese dictionary with him. Now and then he'd take it out and go over a few word entries he had marked in pencil.

The guard in the parking lot was also supposed to help the residents load and unload their cars. If they returned from shopping, he was supposed to give them a hand, carrying the grocery bags to their apartments. This was no problem for Nan; besides, most times people would tip him a dollar or two. If it was a good shift, he could make an extra ten dollars. Some middle-aged people avoided using him, reluctant to waste money on tips, especially those who drove cheap cars. A Hispanic woman named Maria, around thirty, always asked him to carry stuff for her. She was very close to Ivan, another guard who usually worked the night shift, and she tried to be friendly with Nan too, calling him "a great guy." But she'd never tip him. At most she'd offer him a drink, which he always declined. She had thick auburn hair and a fine figure, and would wave at Nan whenever she came to the parking lot.

Besides the day shift, Nan occasionally worked at the front office at night. He hated to be seen by everyone at the entrance and dared not look at his pocket dictionary before ten p.m. There were four other guards, but he was scheduled to work mainly with Ivan and Tim. Tim was a spare black man from Canada, around sixty, and wore a gray mustache and a lumpy ring though he was single, divorced long ago. He often talked to Nan about his retirement plan. He was working another job too, driving a shuttle bus between Logan Airport and downtown Boston. With a mysterious look and some pride he told Nan that he had to hold two jobs to make enough money for a mansion he had been building in a suburb of Toronto. That was his dream home, which he'd retire to and which would cost him more than half a million dollars.

"When are you going back to Canada to live in your big house?" Nan asked Tim one afternoon, standing at the glass door of the tiny office.

"As soon as I'm through with this job, in a year or two. I don't like it here."

"You mean Hampden Park or Boston?"

"I mean the United States."

"But zere's a lawt of snow in Canada, right?"

"I don't mind."

"Don't you have better jawbs here?"

"Give me a break!" Tim cackled. Then he rolled up the sleeve of his pale blue shirt. "Look here." He pointed at his forearm.

"What? You mean you have hair on your skin?" Actually, Nan found Tim's arm as smooth as his own.

"No. Pigmentation."

"Oh, you are cahlored," said Nan.

In fact Tim wasn't very dark, his skin at most mocha. "That's right. Blacks are treated like trash in this country."

"But you make more mahney here."

"Yes, plus I'm busting my ass."

"How much more do you make here zan in Canada?"

"It's not the number but the purchasing power of the U.S. dollars that counts. For example, for a pack of toilet paper you pay three bucks here, but you have to pay four in Canada."

"Is Canada a better place for blacks to live?"

"Yes, that's why I'm a Canadian citizen and proud of it."

"So minorities are tritted equally there?"

"No, of course not. Still, Canadians are more open-minded than Americans."

"How do they trit Chinese?"

"Similar to blacks, I would say."

Nan remembered something. "I have a question for you, Tim."

"What?"

"Is a Chinese also cahlored?" Nan had seen some job ads that encouraged "people of color" to apply, but he wasn't sure if he was considered colored. How odd that term was. Wasn't white also a color? Why were whites viewed as colorless? Logically speaking, everybody should be "colored."

"I'm not positive about that here," said Tim. "In Canada people don't call me 'colored' to my face."

"Come on, you have dark skin."

"Why should I lie to you? I'm black, but not colored. 'Colored' is a bad word in Canada."

"I wish I were cahlored, zough."

"Why's that?"

"If you are cahlored here, you can have better employment."

"That's baloney, Nan! Blacks only have the shitty jobs nobody wants." Tim's bleary eyes stared at him, their corners wrinkled in rays.

Nan didn't respond, wondering if that was true. Ads for government jobs and teaching positions almost always urged "people of color" to apply, and he wondered if he should try for one. He'd be happy if he could work as a fireman or postman. Any stable job would be great. It wasn't just for the pay, but for the benefits and the sense of security—some peace of mind. On the other hand, Tim might be right—Nan had never seen a black postman or fireman in Woodland.

Later Nan pondered his conversation with Tim. Although he admired the old man's hardiness, it made him uneasy. Despite his age, Tim held two full-time jobs, running like a machine without respite. People here worked too hard, obsessed with the illusion of getting rich. Americans often disparaged workaholism in Japan, but most of them worked as hard as the Japanese, if not harder. In this place if you didn't make money, you were a loser, a nobody. Your worth was measured by the property you owned and by the amount you had in the bank. On the radio, the host of *Money Matters* would ask callers blatantly, "What's your worth?" You couldn't answer "I hold two master's degrees" or "I'm a model worker" or "I'm an honest guy." You had to come up with a specific figure. On TV, jolly old men would declare, "I feel like a million bucks!" Nan once saw in a lonely hearts section of the *Boston Herald* that a man seeking women described his profession as "millionaire." Money, money, money—money was God in this place.

14

THE OTHER GUARD often paired with him was Ivan, a man in his mid-thirties, a recent immigrant from Russia. Ivan was a squat fellow, broad in the shoulders and thick in the stomach, and often wore a knowing grin on his face, whose rugged features showed a good deal of strength and cunning. He drove a white pickup that had a short body but four seats in the cab. Every night he brought along a laptop and typed away on it. Nan hadn't seen such a small computer before and was impressed by Ivan's dexterity in using the machine, for which Ivan said he had paid more than $4,000. One night when most of the residents had turned in, the two guards talked. Ivan claimed he was already wealthy, though he'd come to America only six years before.

"What are you doing wiz your computer here?" Nan asked him.

"Business."

"What kind?"

"Transport oil."

"To anozzer country?"

"To Europe."

"Have you been in zis trade for long?"

"Yes, very many years."

"So you're a rich man?"

"Yes, I am." Ivan smiled, and his fleshy cheeks broadened, reminding Nan of a giant owl.

"Zen why are you working at Hampden Park?"

"Look, I'm making money just sitting here while I can work with Russian companies for big deals. This way is better to use my time. Time's money."

"Zat's true." Nan remembered that back in China, where you had nothing but time, no one was paid by the hour but all by the month. But here you made money by selling your hours. He asked Ivan again, "You don't work during zer day?"

"Of course I do. I visit people for business. That's why I work here at night most the days."

"Do you already own a house here?"

"No. My wife and I lease an apartment in Dorchester."

"Why didn't you buy your own house?"

"What's a house? It's just shelter. Like a car, it's just a vehicle. There's no need for fancy products. Why should I let a house waste my capital? Tell you what, we own a very expensive apartment in Switzerland."

"Reelly?"

"On Lake Geneva, beautiful place. Did you ever visit Europe?"

"No. How mahch does it cawst? I mean zee apartment."

"That's classified information. We bought it to invest. Real 'state was skyrocking over there, you know."

"How come you got rich so quickly here?"

"I followed my ways."

"You don't share your expertise?"

"All right, let me offer you one advice, Nan," Ivan harrumphed, his large eyes gleaming in the dimly lighted room. "In America there're only two ways to acquire riches. First, use others' money; second, use others' labor. I'm doing both." He hee-hawed.

Although Nan knew what Ivan said was true, he felt discomfited. He had once spent a year and a half poring over Marx's *Das Capital,* and he understood how capitalists accumulated their wealth. In theory, all profits resulted from surplus labor, the blood and sweat of workers. Evidently Ivan had intuitively grasped the essence of capitalism. But how could he—Nan—act like a capitalist? Besides having no capital to invest, he simply couldn't imagine himself using others' money or labor. That would amount to exploitation, wouldn't it? Yet to succeed in this place, shouldn't he do something like what Ivan had been doing? Maybe he had to, but how?

In a way the situation at Hampden Park was quite unusual. If what Ivan said was true, then the boss, Sandy Tripp, was poorer than some of the guards he supervised. Sandy must have known that. That might be why he was polite to Tim and Ivan. He didn't interfere with Ivan's working on the computer at night even though some residents had complained about it. Nan liked his boss better than his fellow workers. Sandy wasn't strict with his staff and was often absent from the premises, leaving the place entirely to the care of the guards.

15

IN LATE FEBRUARY, a letter came from the Chinese consulate in New York, informing Nan that they couldn't renew his passport because he hadn't attached the approval from his former work unit, Harbin Teachers College. The official letter told Nan to write to the school's personnel office and obtain their permission to let him continue studying in America. Only then could the consulate renew his passport. Nan was outraged. None of his former leaders, all jealous of his being in America, would ever grant him such an approval. Worse, he had quit graduate school here, and if they knew his current non-student status, they'd demand he return with dispatch. Nan wasn't sure whether there was official contact between Harbin Teachers College and the Chinese consulate, which seemed determined to make things difficult for him. Probably so—officials were always in cahoots to bully and torment people. He called Danning, who had heard that recently several people couldn't get their passports renewed on account of their involvement with the student movement the summer before.

What should Nan do? He couldn't write to the head of the personnel office at his former college. That devious man had once asked Nan to buy him a refrigerator, but Nan, disgusted, hadn't answered his letter. Perhaps he should appeal for help from the chairwoman of his former department, pretending he was still registered at Brandeis. That could be a long shot, though, for he had never been close to her and hadn't written her a word since he was here. He wasn't even sure if she'd bother to respond. How miserable he felt as he walked around in the back lot of Hampden Park, brooding about his predicament. Why should he trouble so much about his passport if he'd get his green card soon? Why let himself remain in the clutches of those invisible hands? Why shouldn't he break loose and set out on his own? What a misfortune it was to be born Chinese, for whom a trifle like a passport renewal would be tantamount to an insuperable obstacle! If you were Chinese, any petty official could torment you and make your life unbearable. And wherever you went, the powers-that-be would demand your obedience. If only he were an American.

With those thoughts on his mind, Nan returned from work in the evening. He was hungry, but couldn't go into the kitchen to eat until the Masefields finished dinner.

•

Pingping cleared the table and took out of the oven the meal she had cooked for her family—a whole chicken, Tater Tots, and rice porridge. To this she added a salad of cucumber and lettuce. Taotao didn't like the roast chicken and wouldn't eat the drumstick his mother had cut off for him. He complained about the porridge too and left half a bowl unfinished.

Nan always hated to see food wasted, never having forgotten the hunger pangs he'd had during the three famine years in the early 1960s. "*We should send you back to China! Totally spoiled*," he said to his son.

"Bullshit!" the boy grunted in English.

"*What did you say?*" Nan sprang up and grabbed at him.

"*Please don't!*" Pingping wedged herself between them. "*We're not in our own home, please!*"

Nan sat down, glowering at Taotao. He demanded, "*Where did you learn that word?*"

The boy, stunned, looked tearful. Pingping ordered, "*Apologize to Daddy.*"

But Taotao wouldn't say anything. This incensed Nan more. He blasted, "*Such a heartless brat! I've lived in this country slaving away just for your sake. Instead of being grateful, you hold me in contempt and insult me at every turn. Let me tell you, if not for you, I'd go back to China tomorrow.*"

"*That's not true,*" Pingping said. "*We can't go back because of our own doings. You shouldn't have mixed our decision with his fault.*"

"*Of course it's true. I can always go back, but I want to waste my life here, for him!*" He pointed at their son.

"*Then why wouldn't the consulate renew your passport? Stop blaming others. We decided to live here, and we must cope with all the difficulties. Come, Taotao, apologize to Daddy.*"

The boy muttered, "*I'm sorry.*"

"*Sorry is not enough, too late,*" said Nan.

Pingping got up and held the boy's arm. "*Let's go. Leave him alone.*" She took him away.

"*If you use foul language again, I'll send you back to China by the express mail,*" Nan shouted after Taotao.

Without another word, mother and son went out of the kitchen, climbing the stairs to their quarters.

Nan resumed eating. He didn't feel hungry anymore, but was so angry that his appetite knew no bounds. He didn't care what he put into his mouth and just ate and ate and ate, chewing the food ferociously while not tasting it.

To his astonishment, he finished the whole chicken and most of the Tater Tots without noticing how much he had eaten. Strange to say, he didn't feel stuffed. He was sick at heart and regretted his eruption and began blaming himself. Taotao is right. You're full of it. You use self-sacrifice as a pretext for your own failure and uselessness, and you want others to pity you and share your bitterness. You're silly and pathetic!

In fact, his daily grouchiness was mostly due to his loathing for his job, which he kept mainly for its substandard health insurance. At work he had to walk around in the parking lot constantly, and at the close of the day his legs were heavy and stiff. He often returned home loaded with gas. His family kept out of his way most of the time and avoided eating with him. This aggravated him more. As a result, he ate without restraint and often finished whatever Pingping put on the table. His wife joked once that she was afraid he might eat the plates and bowls as well. Despite the voracious eating, he didn't gain weight and even looked more haggard than before.

16

THOUGH he didn't see his dad very often, Taotao would play pranks on him whenever he could. The boy loved his father and by now knew his parents couldn't possibly mail him back to his grandparents. On the last Saturday morning of March, Nan came back from a graveyard shift with a stiff neck and shoulders. The moment he pulled into the yard, Taotao ran to the front entrance of the house and locked the screen door from inside. His father saw him, but exhausted and moody, Nan shambled over without looking at his son and yanked the door open. The latch snapped. The boy stood stock-still as his father checked the broken catch.

Heidi had seen everything. She said to Nan, "Why did you bust the latch on purpose?"

"I'm sorry. It was already loose," he mumbled, though that was true.

"But didn't Taotao lock the screen door when he saw you coming in?"

"He did."

"Well, you should have it fixed."

"All right, I will do zat."

"I have Bob's phone number. You can call him."

"Sure, I will eef I need him."

Bob was the carpenter who had put the latch in the previous spring, and Heidi assumed Nan was going to call him in to install a new one. But after breakfast, Nan unscrewed the catch. Then he and Taotao set out for the hardware store at the town center, carrying the broken part in a brown paper bag. Nan wasn't sure if they could find a match. All the way he blamed his son for being so careless. This time the boy remained quiet.

Without difficulty the salesman at Motts Hardware, who eyed Nan enviously for his fatherhood, found the same kind of latch, which cost less than seven dollars. Although Nan needed only the catch, he had to buy the whole set. On his way back, his mood lifted and he began talking with his son casually. Taotao told him that he had several friends now, Mark, Ralph, Billy, and others. He had risen to the reading group of the second level and was doing superbly in the arithmetic tests.

"How about Loreen?" Nan asked in English, remembering the frail, freckled girl who had often read to his son.

"Her family moved."

"Where did zey go?"

"Her dad retired from the Celtics and they went back to Indiana."

"Do you miss her?"

"Not really."

"Wasn't she your friend?"

"She was okay."

"She helped you a lawt, didn't she? You shouldn't forget her."

The boy fell silent. Nan was amazed how easy it was for him to speak English with Taotao. Perhaps from now on he should talk with him more often to improve his own English.

Together father and son installed the catch. The whole job took just a few minutes. Heidi was impressed, saying, "Bob charged me eighty dollars for it last time. I didn't know it was so easy."

That was a major problem in this household, Pingping and Nan had noticed long before. People sometimes overcharged Heidi when they worked for her. Very often a mechanic or plumber or carpenter didn't finish a job and would soon have to come back again. Heidi didn't have the vaguest idea how much the cost should be. Over the winter a mechanic who spoke only Portuguese had come three times to fix the cooking range, just to make two burners work again, but he had billed Heidi more than $150 for each visit, plus the parts. Once a huckster had stopped by with a powerful vacuum cleaner that could pick up an iron ball four inches in diameter; Heidi was so taken with his demonstration that she paid $1,000 for the machine.

Heidi was impressed by Nan's ability to fix small things. He had always changed the oil in his car and replaced the battery by himself, and once even repaired the rear brake of Nathan's bicycle. The previous winter he had replaced the toilet flapper to stop a leak in the bathroom next to the kitchen. Pingping was pleased by his handymanship and praised him. Back in China he had been a clumsy man and couldn't even patch a flat bicycle tire, which most men could do. In their neighborhood he was known for being lazy. He wouldn't do any housework and instead raised four doves, which were snow-white and lovely, each wearing a brass whistle on its wing, so they'd emit a fluty sound when flying. Several times the wives in the neighborhood complained to Pingping that their husbands had begun to emulate Nan and had stopped doing household chores. They urged her at least to let him wash dishes and his underwear. She promised to make him work, but he seldom lifted a finger to help her. Even Nan's mother said that if a bottle of cooking oil fell over and spilled, he wouldn't bother to pick it up.

American life had changed him. Now he loved hand tools—oh, the infinite varieties of American tools, each designed for one purpose, just like the vast English vocabulary, each word denoting precisely one thing or one idea. What's more, Nan was always ready to run an errand for his wife, though he still grumbled on occasion. This was mainly due to the job he hated intensely but had to keep. Even he could feel the change in himself. He wasn't a feeble bookworm anymore; he was no longer ashamed of working hard to make a dollar.

17

NAN and Pingping sometimes quarreled when their son wasn't around. But they had agreed to stay together until Taotao grew up. Nan once asked Pingping, "*What will you do after that?*"

"*Either go to a nunnery or kill myself,*" she said. Ever since girlhood she had been infatuated with the image of a nun: the long gown, the flying headpiece, the white gloves, the glossy rosary.

"*I'll be a monk, then,*" said Nan.

"*Let's go to a temple together so we can often meet. Promise, you'll spend some time with me every week.*"

Nan always liked her peculiar kind of innocence, and replied, "*You're talking as if all the monks will leave you alone.*"

She punched his arm. "*I'm serious.*"

Nan said no more. How he wished he could work up more emotion to reciprocate her love. If only he weren't so exhausted and so sick at heart. If only he hadn't been wounded so deeply by that fox Beina.

Sometimes when Pingping couldn't stand his impassivity anymore, she'd pick up the phone and call someone. Nan would do the same when he was unhappy. He'd talk with Danning, and most times they'd chat for a long while. His friend would urge him to be more considerate to Pingping. For better or worse, she was willing to sacrifice everything for their family and was absolutely loyal to him. What else could he want from her? Where could he find a better woman? He ought to feel fortunate and grateful.

Unlike Nan, Pingping didn't have a friend of her own. Then who did she call when she was upset or angry? Nan often wondered and got unsettled. Sometimes the instant the line went through, she'd hang up. Once he asked who she was phoning. *"None of your business,"* she said. *"I can call anyone I want to."*

One evening in mid-April they quarreled again. She dropped his tea mug on the floor. About that he said nothing and just wiped the wet spot on the carpet with a rag. He was afraid she might go so far as to tear one of his books, which she'd done before. Yet today his silence incensed her more. She rushed out of the room, picked up the phone from the top of a wooden chest and began dialing. He followed her out and pressed down the plunger of the phone. She glared at him, her eyes flashing madly.

"Who do you want to speak to?" he asked.

"Leave me alone!"

"No. You must let me know."

"You never care anyway."

"Please! If you have someone you'd like to meet, I won't hold you back, I promise. Just let me know." He reached for the handset but couldn't wrench it off her hand.

"Let go of me!"

"Not until you tell me who you're calling."

"I dialed nobody but 911, all right?"

"What?" he gasped. *"You're insane!"*

The gravity of his voice stopped her. She released the phone, staring at him.

"They may come here with an ambulance," he told her, still in disbelief.

"No, I've never said a word to them. How could they get here?"

"Their machine must show the caller's number, so they can trace you to this place."

That stunned her and she started sobbing. Nan replaced the phone, enfolded her with one arm, and said, *"Come, stop crying. Nothing like that has happened yet."*

"I really didn't know they could find out I called. I just meant to make you jealous."

Her last sentence surprised him, but also somewhat pleased him. He smiled and told her, *"You acted like a small child. All right, no more crying. Don't dial 911 again."*

She nodded yes and muttered, *"I hate you as much as I love you. If only I could leave and never see you again."*

"Just give me some time, okay? I'll find a decent job and then my temper will improve. I'll be a better man."

"You really need to do something to save yourself and our family. We can't continue to live like this."

"I know we can't stay under Heidi's roof forever. I'll figure out a way."

"You're always a good talker."

"Only in Chinese." He grimaced.

"Remember what you said to me when we first met?"

"What did I say?"

"You said, 'Life is a tragedy, but its meaning lies in how we face the tragedy.'"

"That was just juvenile rubbish I had picked up from reading Hemingway."

"But I fell in love with you for that. You were a full man then, the first man who ever said something meaningful to me. I had always been angry whenever I was with another man. You were so different from others, but now you've been losing your spirit. You must brace up and save yourself."

"I know I'm just drifting along."

"We must find our way."

Nan nodded without another word. His heart was filled with pain and gratitude. If his wife had been of two hearts with him, this family would have fallen apart long ago. He must find a way to make a decent living and mustn't despair of himself.

18

PINGPING was mending Heidi's bathrobe in the kitchen while talking with Heidi. On the table were three stacks of laundered clothes she had just folded. Outside, the clouds had broken, electric wires and leafy branches still glistening with rainwater. The lilacs and young dogwood trees had lowered their white and pinkish blossoms in the glowing afternoon sun. Beyond the shrubs two rabbits scampered about, now nibbling grass and now chasing each other. Pingping and Nan were both allergic to pollen. Nan was extremely sensitive to oak and dogwood, whereas Pingping didn't know what she was allergic to. She was most miserable in late April, when her nose would dribble and swell and she'd keep a wad of tissue in her pocket all the time. Nan would repeat in English "April is the cruelest month," though his wife had no idea it was a line of poetry. The previous spring when pollen had set in, they had thought they were suffering from the flu and had taken Tylenol, Bayer, and other cold pills available over the counter, but none of the medicines helped much. Not until mid-May had Nan figured out what it was, but by then the miserable season was almost over for them.

Pingping was glad that a morning shower had washed away a lot of pollen so the air would be somewhat clean for a day or two. She and Heidi had been talking about yesterday evening's quarrel. Heidi told her that Eric, her late husband's younger brother, was a ladies' man, so she wondered if Nan was the same.

"Nan doesn't like woman," Pingping said.

Heidi looked surprised. "What did you say? You mean, he's more fond of men?"

"No, he's not gay."

"Then what's his problem? Most men like women."

"His mind."

"I don't get it." Heidi shook her newly permed hair, which made her head appear larger than usual, her cheeks shiny and pinkish, and her face three or four years younger than the past week.

"How can I say this?" Pingping said. "Back in China he like pretty womans—women, but now he always say he's tired." She was too ashamed to reveal he didn't love her.

"I know some men are like that, especially after they've had too many women."

"Nan doesn't have affair."

"How can you be so sure?"

"I just know. When he come to USA, I told him he can have another woman if he want, but just don't forget me and Taotao, and don't get disease."

"Wow, you said that?"

"Yes."

"What did he do then?"

"Nothing. He said he has no time to chase women, he's too tired. He want to study hard and then come back home."

"Something could be wrong with his mind. You know what? He should see a shrink."

"What is shrink?"

"A psychiatrist. Nathan has seen Dr. Blumenthal in Wellesley every Tuesday afternoon since his dad died."

"That help him?"

"Of course, a lot. He's steadier now. He used to be very moody."

"Maybe Nan should meet that shrink too. How much it cost?"

"It depends. I guess around seventy an hour."

"I see."

Heidi put on her reading glasses and began leafing through a mail-order catalog while Pingping spread the bathrobe on the table to see whether there was another spot that needed patching. She was impressed that Heidi wouldn't throw away the tattered robe. Both of them turned silent for the time being.

Later that afternoon Pingping asked Nathan what Dr. Blumenthal had done to him on Tuesday. The boy blinked his whitish eyes and said, "Nothing. He just listened to me talk."

"Really? He make money just by listen to you?"

"Sure. He also asked questions."

"What kind?"

"Like 'How do you feel today?' and 'Did Scott bug you again last week?'"

"I can do that." She was amazed.

That evening she told Nan about her conversation with Heidi and suggested he consider seeing a psychiatrist. He had just received his diploma for his M.A., which had come in a large envelope braced with a rectangle of cardboard, so he was in a pleasant frame of mind and was about to play checkers with Taotao. He said in response to Pingping's suggestion, "*I don't believe in psychiatry. Why should we throw away money like that?*"

"*Nathan said it made him feel much better.*"

"*But it doesn't really calm him down. Don't you see he still has an outburst every now and then?*"

"*I'm afraid you might lose your mind.*"

"*I've already lost most of it. I can't get worse.*" He gave a short laugh. "*Don't worry. I can talk to you. We can be each other's psychiatrists.*"

"*At least you should give it a try.*"

"*Even if it helps, I won't do that. You know how hard it is for us to make a dollar. We have to save as much as we can. In this country, without money you can't do anything. We should move out of this house soon and have to have more cash in hand.*"

In reality, Nan didn't often speak to Pingping about his feelings, which were disordered and unclear to himself. If he couldn't help it anymore, he just poured his misery out on her, and once in a while she did the same to him. In appearance he was peaceful and gentle, but at heart he felt as if he were running a temperature, about to collapse. But somehow he always managed to pull himself together and go through his daily drudgery without a hitch. He didn't have time to read books now, though at work he tried to dip into his dictionary whenever it was possible. How he missed his former job at the factory, where he had been able even to catnap if he was tired of reading. Nowadays, besides the dictionary, he also carried with him a small notebook in which he had copied out some poems, both English and Chinese. He wanted to memorize the lines he loved.

19

NEVER having contacted Harbin Teachers College, Nan couldn't send its approval letter to the Chinese consulate to have his passport renewed, but it was said that lately the policy for such a renewal had changed and that no permission from one's former work unit was required anymore. So when Nan received a letter from the Chinese consulate one day in mid-May, he was pleased, fingering the booklet enclosed in a manila envelope with the thought that it must contain his passport. It did indeed. But when he opened the gilt-worded cover, he was stunned by a scarlet seal that declared CANCELED.

Both he and Pingping were devastated, knowing this was the official revenge for his involvement in the plan for the kidnap. Though Nan, shocked and outraged, couldn't think coherently for hours, the significance of the cancellation gradually sank in. Now the door back to China was shut and he had become a countryless man. What was to be done? The more he thought, the more angry he felt. Why had he been so passive, letting the Chinese consulate deliver blows on him at will? Why should he remain an obedient subject of that ruthless country? Shouldn't people be entitled to abandon their country if all the authorities did was make them sacrifice and suffer? He'd get naturalized here as soon as possible. By any means, he'd better discard the baggage of China so as to travel light. He must become an independent man.

With a feeling of forced pride and a mind in turmoil, Nan went to Hampden Park in the afternoon. He didn't patrol the parking lot but instead leaned against a resident's SUV with two bullet holes in its door. He wasn't supposed to rest like this, but today he didn't care. As he was still musing about his revoked passport, Maria, the thirtyish

Latina living on the third floor of the north building, appeared and beckoned him over. Reluctantly Nan went up to her. "You need help?" he asked.

She beamed, batting her dark eyelashes. "One of my lightbulbs is dead—can you replace it for me?"

"Sure, my pleasure."

It was a warm day, and she wore jeans and a pink wrap-over top that revealed her belly button, under which bulged a small fold of flab. Nan had never seen such a navel, an innie almost two inches across. He followed her upstairs. Her wide behind swung provocatively as she was going up, and he observed her shapely waist, partly naked and well tanned. Her hip-hugging pants were held only by a button on the front. At the gooseneck of the handrail she told him, "My mother's coming to visit, so I need to tidy my place up a bit."

"Where's she coming from?"

"New Mexico."

The defective light was in the kitchen, where the north-facing window let in a flood of sunlight. The ceiling was so high that Nan had to place a stool on a tall chair, then climbed onto them.

"Be careful, dear. Don't fall," she crooned.

"I won't." Though he said that, his right leg was shaking a little.

The lightbulb was covered by a scalloped fixture, and he unscrewed the nut and handed the glass shade to Maria. The incandescent bulb was half black, burned out. "Can you turn zer switch off?" he asked.

She flicked it off and came over to hand him a new bulb. "Let me hold you, dear, so you won't fall," she said, smiling and showing her even teeth. She hugged his calves from behind and pressed her nose between them. "Hmm, you smell good. You have strong legs."

"And also strong arms." He was screwing on the shade. "Can you open zer light?" He caught himself using the wrong verb.

"What?" she asked.

"Turn on zer switch."

"Sure."

The light came on. Before she could sidle back to him, he jumped down with his right hand holding the top corner of the refrigerator.

As he landed on the ceramic tile, his dictionary fell out of his pocket and spread facedown at Maria's feet. She picked it up and flipped through some pages. "My goodness, you've marked the entire book!"

"Almost. I have to stahdy English whenever I can." His face was reddening.

She handed it back to him. "I used to read books, but I don't have the time anymore."

Without another word he put the stool and the chair back to their original places. She asked, "Can I give you a glass of wine?" She looked him in the face, her eyes intense and unblinking.

"No, sanks."

"Why are you always so polite, Nan?"

"I'm supposed to be."

"C'mon, just have some wine and loosen up a bit. It's not busy out there." She poured half a glass of zinfandel and handed it to him.

"No, sanks. It will make my face red and Sandy can see it."

"You're such a serious guy. I'm sure you don't talk to your girl-friend like this. Are you afraid of me or something?"

He smiled, rather embarrassed. "I'm not afraid of anyone."

"Not even a woman?"

"I have a wife and a son. When I don't work, of coss I can relax at home."

"So you're trying to be professional here." She tittered, then kept on, "I don't mind if you have a family. Can't we be friends, just friends?" She sipped her glass of wine, probably to cover her edginess, while her eyes held him as if pulling him toward her.

"Sure, but I must leave." He turned to the door. "Sorry, Tim needs me in zee office." In his confusion he forgot that Tim had just quit as a result of a lung problem, which Tim told others was pulmonary emphysema but Sandy suspected was cancer. Without enough hands, Sandy had to work in the front office these days.

"Thank you for the help, Nan," Maria said damply. "You're a sweet guy."

"It's my pleasure."

Though he didn't feel attracted to Maria, his heart was racing a little. But in her eagerness and affected manner he had seen a lonesome, flighty woman. She wasn't a bad person, but he wouldn't get entangled with her.

After that day, she continued to ask him to carry grocery bags for her and still wouldn't tip him. He was always polite, however cold she was to him.

•

Maria's calling him "a sweet guy" reminded Nan of his experience with another woman, Heather Burt, who had been a girlfriend of Maurice Fomé, Nan's fellow graduate student at Brandeis. Maurice, a slim black man often wearing a broad smile, was from Sudan and had attended the Sorbonne before coming to the United States. He was fluent in both French and English in addition to several African languages, and would call a car "means of conveyance" and water "dihydromonoxide." He had many girlfriends, both white and black, some of whom had come from England and France to visit him. Usually they stayed just a few days, then left and never came again. Heather Burt differed from the other women and would come to see him every other month, driving her old sky blue sedan all the way from Youngstown, Ohio. Since Nan and Maurice lived in the same building and had the same professor as their advisor, Nan got to know Heather quite well. She was in her late twenties, with fair skin and facial hair like peach down, and she had a sonorous voice almost like a man's, though she was delicate and short, just five foot one.

She came to see Maurice again in late July 1986, intending to stay two weeks and get engaged to him. But when she stepped into his apartment, Maurice was in a trance, sitting in a beanbag chair with foam at his mouth, murmuring something nobody could understand. He wouldn't talk to Heather or anyone and didn't even recognize her. His eyes were milky, the pupils almost invisible.

That evening, having nowhere to go, Heather stayed at Nan's apartment, her eyes red and her face crumpled. Sitting at the table in the living room, she told Nan that Maurice's father, a tribal shaman, was calling to him from a mountain in Sudan. "He's not himself anymore and didn't understand what I said," she sighed, dragging at a cigarette.

"You mean he can communicate wiz his father in Africa?" For all his fondness for Maurice, Nan suspected he was shamming.

"Yes, he can," she replied in earnest.

"Do you believe zat?"

"I do."

She took a swallow of the green tea Nan had poured for her, then told him that her father, an auto mechanic, after opposing the idea of her being engaged to a black man, had finally given her his approval and blessing. But some of her friends still disliked the idea. "They asked me," she said, "'You really don't mind having a black guy in your bed?' I told them, 'It makes no difference. He's good.' See now, I'm in the doghouse." Two whitish tears fell out of her eyes, and she blew her nose into a paper towel, then raised her hand to tuck a strip of ginger hair behind her ear.

"You mean you're cornered?" Nan had never heard that idiom.

"I mean I'm in serious trouble."

Several days in a row Maurice didn't recognize Heather, who continued to stay at Nan's apartment, in his roommate Gary's room. Gary had gone back to Israel for the summer. During the day Nan went to work in the library and in the evenings cooked dinner for both himself and Heather. Sometimes they'd converse for hours after dinner, sharing tea and ice cream. She seemed to have calmed down some.

One night, the moment he turned in, Heather knocked on his door, which he hadn't locked. "Come in," he said.

She stepped in and, with a misshapen face, asked him, "Can I spend the night with you?"

"You—you don't know me zat well."

"Please!"

In spite of the surprise, Nan did feel a stirring rush and waved her to come over. For a whole year he hadn't touched a woman, and sometimes he was afraid he might have lost his potency, so he was eager to have her. She dropped her nightgown and got into his bed.

After caressing him for a while, she asked, "Do you have a rubber?" Her silk panties fell on the floor.

"You mean candy?" he guessed, thinking of chewing gum. His fingers kept fondling her breast.

She laughed. "I love your sense of humor." She wrapped her arm around his neck and kissed his mouth hard as if to suck the breath out of him.

So they made love and even tried soixante-neuf in the way shown in Gary's copy of *Penthouse*. Nan didn't like it, though he made her come, crying ecstatically as if in pain. He was glad he still could have sex with a woman like a normal man. How relieved he was after he came. Soon he fell into postcoital slumber.

The next morning he went to work without disturbing her, and left her breakfast in the kitchen—a blueberry bagel and two fried eggs, sunny side up on a white plate. When he came back in the evening, she was gone without leaving a word, though she had finished the breakfast and washed the dish. For days he was worried, fearing she might have gotten pregnant since they hadn't used a condom. On the other hand, he felt she might have been on the pill. She would have herself ready for Maurice before coming to see him, wouldn't she?

Then the thought began to disturb him that he could have caught some venereal disease. A few years earlier he had read in a Chinese newspaper that more than a third of Americans and Canadians had gonorrhea, herpes, syphilis. The previous winter his mother had written to warn him not to have sexual contact with foreign women, saying that if he got syphilis, his nose would rot, he'd go bald and blind, and he would pass the virus on to his wife and children and grandchildren. She had told him that in the old China, every day people had to boil chopsticks and bowls used by syphilitics so that their families wouldn't be infected. The more Nan thought about the one-night stand, the more he regretted it. If only he had observed Heather's body carefully before having sex with her. She couldn't have fled without a reason, could she? When he ran into Maurice, Nan couldn't help but observe the whiteheads on his thin neck, wondering if they were herpes blisters.

For three weeks he felt agitated and miserable, and even thought of going to the infirmary for a checkup, but he decided not to. Then right before school started, a letter from Heather arrived. She wrote in a scraggy hand that leaned slightly to one side:

August 26, 1986

Dear Nan,

I hope this will reach you and find you well. I don't have your address, so I'm sending this letter to your department. Thank you so much for accommodating me when I was in Boston. Without your help, I couldn't have survived the crisis. I'm sorry to have dragged you into my personal trouble when I was there. You are a sweet man. That night you made me feel great, as if I became a woman again. But to tell the truth, afterward I felt guilty, so I left in the morning without saying good-bye.

Don't be angry with me, Nan. We both sinned, though I am the one who made you commit fornication. Last weekend I confessed everything at the church, and it lightened my mind considerably. God is large-hearted and has forgiven me. Perhaps you need to go to confession too. Try it. It really helps.

Please don't think ill of me. I know you're a kind, generous man. I will remember you fondly.

Yours,

Heather

Her letter bewildered him. Nobody had ever called him "a sweet man." Neither did he know what "a sweet man" was like. Weren't men supposed to be strong and fierce, full of spunk? How could he be sweet? He was baffled.

He had never considered that, similar to himself, eager to prove the adequacy of his manhood with the one-night stand, Heather had been desperate to restore her womanhood. How could a woman have the kind of crippled feeling like a man's fear of having lost his potency? Perhaps for Heather this was more psychological than physical, since she didn't have to depend on an erection to perform in bed. She must have wanted to convince herself of being desired by a man or of her ability to make love to a man.

Rather than feeling guilty, Nan was fearful and somewhat upset.

He had promised his wife that he wouldn't have another woman in America. But Heather was a different case. He wasn't really fond of her. The yearlong celibacy had tormented him and made him feel he might not be adequate between the sheets anymore. The idea of sin hadn't entered his mind until he read Heather's letter. He couldn't imagine kneeling in a box and exposing himself to a priest, though he had gone to a church in Waltham on two Sundays. He consulted his *Webster's Collegiate Dictionary* to see the difference between "fornication" and "copulation." Being a one-night fornicator didn't bother him that much. What worried him most was whether Heather had carried any disease. Her letter sounded calm, with no trace of anxiety. Did this mean she was a clean and healthy woman?

For the whole fall he was troubled by that question. He examined his genitals carefully whenever he took a shower, but noticed nothing abnormal. His body was still fine and vigorous; his vision and hearing were as clear as before. Everything was normal. Not until it snowed did he manage to put the worry out of his mind.

20

AT HAMPDEN PARK, Ivan often talked to Nan about women, complaining that it was too expensive to have a date here. In Russia, he said, women would take care of the expenses when they went out with him. Nan doubted whether that was true. Ivan claimed that he had been a junior officer in the Red Army in the late 1970s and that Russian women were always enamored of uniforms and epaulets. Nan wondered why the cost of dating a woman would nettle Ivan so much if he was a successful businessman. Didn't he own real estate on Lake Geneva? He must already be a millionaire. One night, when Ivan talked about American women again, Nan asked him, "Are you not afraid of catching AIDS?"

Ivan let out a bray of laughter. "I've known lots of girls and can take care of diseases."

"So you like American women?"

"Not particularly. I need female company sometimes."

"How about your wife?"

"She lives in Paris. I don't need to pay attention to her."

"You mean you two are separated?"

"No. She's bossing a business there. She's Frenchwoman by birth, you know."

"So she let you have anozzer woman when she is away?"

Ivan smiled without answering. The expression on his face seemed to indicate that he was good at handling women. It reminded Nan of the saying "A brazen face is a man's great leverage with ladies." He then noticed that Ivan's laptop wasn't there. "Where's your computer?" he asked.

"Its hard disk busted dead. I left it home."

"You do oil exports still?"

"Well, I changed my profession."

"Doing what now?"

"That's top secret." Ivan laughed again. "By the way, don't you like Maria? She talked very much about you."

"Maria is all right, but I'm too tired to sink about women."

"You're smart. Maria goes nutty sometimes. What an appetite she possesses. She ate two rib-eye steaks when we dined together last time."

"And she drinks a lawt too."

"Like a cow whale."

"So you're dating her?"

"Not really. We visited a restaurant last weekend. God, I won't do that again. It's just too much."

By now Nan saw that Ivan wasn't very different from himself, a mere nighttime drudge, though this man from Vladivostok appeared to be confident and thriving here. Unlike him, Ivan must still believe in the dream of becoming a man of means.

A few days later Sandy called Nan into his office and told him not to carry his dictionary to work again. He insisted that personally he wouldn't have minded as long as Nan did his job well. But someone at the recent residents' meeting voiced the complaint in front of others, so he had no choice but to stop Nan from reading anything at work. "No hard feelings, Nan," said Sandy. "As the manager here, I have to let you know."

"I understand." Nan promised he wouldn't bring any book with him again. He knew it must be Maria who had bitched about him. But why? Only because he wouldn't flirt with her, or take her out, or bed her? Or simply because she could hurt him? He felt outraged and disgusted. From now on, he'd turn his back on that woman whenever she came to the parking lot.

21

THE FIRST ANNIVERSARY of the Tiananmen massacre was approaching, and the Yenching Institute at Harvard University was holding a memorial meeting in its auditorium. Several Chinese dignitaries, ranging from celebrated historians to the student movement leaders who had recently fled China, were to speak at the conference, so on Saturday morning Nan and Danning went there to hear those famous people talk. Among them, Nan was particularly interested in a poet, Yong Chu, who had lived in the United States for more than two decades, teaching at a private college in Rhode Island. What was amazing about this man was that he had made his name in Taiwan, in mainland China, and in the Chinese diaspora as well, although he had lived in North America. Nan remembered being very touched by some of his poems, which were written in a slightly archaic style that reflected the influence of the lyrics of the Song dynasty. The poet was especially known for the famous lines: "The jenny donkey under me is unaware / She's trotting into a mistaken serenade."

The conference wasn't as interesting as Nan had expected. Two student leaders talked about their experiences in fleeing China through an underground channel. Because some of the audience couldn't understand Chinese, a young woman, a graduate student, sat on the stage interpreting. Her voice, however, was too soft, aggravated by her shyness, which kept her eyes downcast when she spoke. After the student leaders' speeches, a Yale professor, an expert in Chinese intellectual thought, began expounding on the necessity of the Confucian values for contemporary China, a country that, chaotic and ruined, was on the brink of a moral meltdown because there was no religion to guide its populace. Nan was bored and said to Danning, *"I shouldn't be here. What a drag!"* He definitely would skip the panel discussion in the afternoon.

After the professor's speech, a noted dissident named Manping Liu went up and began to speak. This man in his mid-fifties had once headed China's Central Institute of Social Reforms, but owing to his involvement with the student movement the previous spring, he had fled the country and was now living in New York City. He had a strong but lean face, and his voice sounded metallic and resonant. He talked about the necessity of developing democracy within the Communist Party, because there wasn't yet another political force in China that could rival the ruling party, and because the country couldn't afford to have a hiatus in governing power if the Communist rule was abolished. His argument and analyses were cogent and at moments subtle, able to hold the audience. He emphasized that China's hope lay in reforming the Communist Party. Nan had read some of Mr. Liu's articles and was familiar with his thoughts, but today he felt there was something unsavory in his speech that Nan couldn't put his finger on, though he hadn't lost his reverence for the scholar's sincerity. Everyone could tell that Mr. Liu was speaking from his heart. Somehow Nan kept observing the old man's hand, which was small and delicate like a young woman's and which was gesturing as he spoke. That hand, a true scholar's, was born to wield a pen.

Then Yong Chu, the poet, took the microphone. He had served as an aircraft pilot in the Chinese Nationalist Army for five years, dog-fighting the Communists' MiGs over Taiwan Strait. Though getting on toward sixty, he was the picture of health, with a dark, strong face like a peasant's. It was said that he could drink a whole bottle of vodka at one sitting without getting drunk. His poetry often showed a kind of masculinity that was rarely found in the works of contemporary Chinese poets. Mr. Chu announced in a booming voice:

"The Tiananmen Democracy Movement is the greatest event of mankind. It demonstrates the Chinese people's bravery and resolve. Weilin Wang, the young man who single-handedly stopped a column of tanks, is a national hero whose image has lodged in the minds of the whole world and whose name will be recorded in history forever.

In one fearless stroke he removed all the shame from my face. He showed the world that there are still courageous Chinese willing to lay down their lives for an ideal. He's our pride and China's pride, and so are all the heroes in Tiananmen Square who sacrificed themselves for democracy. Their immortal deeds have made our personal achievements look so trivial that I feel I have shrunk to nothing. Here I declare that the whole body of my poetry isn't even worth one drop of the blood shed by the martyrs in Tiananmen Square . . ."

The speech annoyed Nan, whose illusion of this master poet quickly vanished. He wondered why Mr. Chu had let national pride supersede the value of his poetry, as though patriotism and literary arts should be judged by the same criteria. As an accomplished poet, he should see that the function of his poetry was to transcend history and to outlast politics and that a poet should be responsible mainly for the language he used. Instead, he was haranguing like an official in charge of propaganda.

Before the meeting was over, Nan left the auditorium with Danning, who invited him to go to his place for dinner. Danning now had a girlfriend named Sirong, a visiting scholar from Beijing. But Nan would have to get home and have some sleep before going to work that evening, so instead they went to the Harvard Science Center for coffee.

In the cafeteria Nan took a decaf and Danning a mocha to a table. *"I'm going back to China next month,"* Danning told him the moment they sat down.

"Really? Are you going to teach somewhere?"

"At the People's University."

"Does it have a physics department?"

"They have a computer science program where I'll teach, but I'm not that interested in teaching. I've been writing fiction. Actually, I had a novella just accepted by Spring Breeze. *It will come out in the fall."*

"Congratulations!" Nan was amazed despite knowing the bimonthly was a provincial literary magazine.

"Thanks. I plan to devote myself to writing novels," said Danning.

"Then what will you do with your Ph.D. in physics?"

"I'll use it to earn a salary."

"*That's a good arrangement. I'm impressed, also jealous. You're on your way.*"

"*No matter where I go, I feel I'm a Chinese to the marrow. I'm terribly homesick recently, perhaps because I'm getting old and soft-headed.*"

"*You're only thirty-five.*"

"*But I feel I'm aging rapidly in this country.*"

"*To be honest, I don't worry about my nationality anymore. I wear my nationality like a coat.*" There was so much bitterness in Nan's voice that his friend was startled.

"*That can't be true. That's just your fantasy, Nan. For example, you speak Chinese like a news anchorman, but your English will never be as good.*"

"*Language and nationality are different issues. I just want to be a decent human being.*"

"*Can you be that without loving your country, your homeland?*"

"*China isn't my country anymore. I spit at China, because it treats its citizens like gullible children and always prevents them from growing up into real individuals. It demands nothing but obedience. To me, loyalty is a two-way street. China has betrayed me, so I refuse to remain its subject anymore.*"

"*Come now, you're not an American citizen yet.*"

"*I've wrenched China out of my heart.*" Nan grimaced, his eyes brimming with tears.

"*You're just angry. You know you can never do that, no matter how hard you try. I can see that China hurt you deeply. Your anger just shows you're still emotionally bound to our motherland and you cannot remain detached.*"

"*I wish I had more anger so that I could write genuine poetry. I feel crippled inside, numb here.*" Nan placed his hand on his chest.

"*That's because you've tried to cut yourself off from your roots.*"

"*Enough of that patriotic nonsense. Patriotism is the last stick in the authorities' hand. With it they strike whomever they don't like.*"

"*All right, I won't argue with you about that, Nan. We're going our separate ways from now on. But we'll remain friends, won't we?*"

"*Yes, forever buddies. I wish you all good luck and a great success.*"

"I wish you a happy family. You have a lovely wife and a fine son. I envy you. You ought to cherish what you have."

"I have trouble with Pingping."

"I sensed that, but that will pass. If you live in this land, a stable family means everything. It's like a sturdy boat in a rough sea, and you have to stay within the boat to cross the ocean."

"I'll remember that."

"Also, don't ever talk to any Chinese like you did just now. You'll get into more trouble. You don't know who will turn you in."

"I'll be more careful in front of others, of course."

On their way out, Nan said he was sick of his current job, which had turned him into a semi-coolie. Danning told him that a Chinese-language poetry magazine in New York City was looking for a managing editor, but he knew nothing about the pay and the workload. Nan was interested and got the phone number of the editor in chief from Danning. The two friends hugged and parted ways, walking in opposite directions along Massachusetts Avenue.

PART TWO

1

NAN decided to take the job in New York. The editor in chief, Bao Yuan, had said on the phone that he could pay Nan only $1,000 per issue of the quarterly, *New Lines,* but he could also offer him a small room, rent-free. And Bao might help him find work in Brooklyn or Manhattan. Pingping supported Nan's decision, fearing he might lose his mind if he didn't quit his job at Hampden Park soon. Also, New York must hold more opportunities for him. Though the managing editorship didn't pay much, Nan could use it as a foothold to get a start in something. The Wus had heard that a man from Shanghai, formerly a graduate student in anthropology at Tufts University, had gone to Wall Street and gotten so rich that he owned a huge apartment on Madison Avenue. Pingping's main concern, however, was health insurance, which Nan couldn't possibly get in New York for the family. But many immigrants without any coverage at all had managed to survive, so she let him take the job, which might be his only chance to get out of his plight.

"Daddy, I'll miss you," Taotao said to Nan as mother and son were seeing him off at the Greyhound station at Riverside.

"I'll miss you too. Listen to Mom when I'm not home, all right?"

"I will. When will you come back?"

"At the end of zis mons. Be a good boy. If you need anysing, let me know."

"Uh-huh."

Taotao, in knee-length shorts, looked sad, pressing his face against his mother's waist. He was two inches taller than the summer before, also a little thicker. Nan got on the bus, sat down in a window seat, and turned to his family. Taotao was waving his hand back and forth at him. Pingping smiled and blew him a kiss. Nan did the same, though his heart was sagging. Because he couldn't find a decent job in the Boston area, his family couldn't live in a place of their own, and Taotao from now on, without health insurance, would have to avoid taking part in sports at school in case he got hurt. If only he had been a better father. If only he hadn't been such a failure. He hoped he'd return soon, as a more capable man.

This was Nan's second trip to New York. Two years ago he had gone there to meet with a friend of his who was on a delegation of educators from China. The old guard at the entrance to the Chinese consulate wouldn't let him in even though Nan produced his passport and even though his friend stayed there. It was raining outside, and the guard insisted that no visitor was allowed to enter the interior of the building, so Nan and his friend could stand only in the doorway, which was already crowded with more than a dozen people. Outraged, Nan said to the gray-bearded guard, "*You've made me feel ashamed of being a Chinese.*" "*Be an American, then! As if you could,*" crowed the man, and his mouth jerked to the side. Later, Nan and his friend wandered along the Hudson in a steady drizzle without an umbrella. The memory of that miserable trip still rankled him.

This time he went to Brooklyn directly, taking the C train after alighting at Port Authority Bus Terminal. He got off at Utica Avenue and without difficulty found his destination, a house with a stone facade painted white, on Macdonough Street near an elementary school. Bao Yuan, the editor in chief of *New Lines*, welcomed him warmly. He was thirtyish and squarely built with a patchy beard and long hair that fell on his shoulders. He took Nan's suitcase and said, "*I have the room ready for you.*"

Together they went up the narrow stairs leading to the attic. Bao pushed the sloping-topped door, which opened with a rat-a-tat screech. On the floor of the slanting-pitched room spread a mattress. An oblong coffee table stood near the dormer window, beside which was a lamp with a tattered yellowish shade. A strong smell of mildew hung in here. "*I hope this is all right,*" Bao said, licking his compressed teeth.

"This is fine." Nan liked that the floor was carpeted so he could sit on it and wouldn't have to look for a chair.

"You can use the kitchen and bathroom downstairs."

"All right."

"People living in this house share the phone in the living room."

"Fine, I'll pay my share."

"We'll talk about the editorial work this evening."

"Great. I'm excited about it."

After unpacking, Nan went out to buy some groceries. He was struck by the garbage accumulated under the curbs—plastic bottles, Styrofoam cups, scraps of paper, blanched beer cans. The air was still rain-soaked, and a few sepia puddles interrupted the sidewalk, too long for him to jump across, so he skirted them. He walked along Malcolm X Boulevard toward the subway station, where he had seen some shops an hour ago. He entered a small supermarket and picked up a bar of cheese, a bunch of bananas, and a loaf of sourdough bread. On his way back, as he was passing a strip club bearing a flickering sign with an electric martini and triple neon X's, a paunchy black man accosted him, shouting, "Hey, do you have a quarter to spare?"

Nan shook his head no and hurried away with the paper bag in his arm. He hadn't expected to see so many blacks living in this area, but he felt lucky to have a room for himself, having heard that you'd pay three hundred a month to share a bedroom in New York.

That evening Nan and Bao had tea in the kitchen. The living room was noisy, occupied by two other tenants, who were watching a game between the Yankees and the White Sox. Bao's girlfriend, Wendy, sat with them at the kitchen table. She was a white woman with half-gray hair and a puffy face, almost twenty years older than Bao. She can easily be his mother, Nan thought. Why doesn't Bao have a younger girlfriend?

Bao didn't seem to mind the age difference, though he was reluctant to show his fondness for Wendy in Nan's presence. Wendy drank decaf coffee in place of the Tuo tea Bao had made. The original tea had been pressed into a lump like a small bowl, from which Bao had broken a piece and brewed the chunk of leaves in a pot. It tasted a little bitter, but Nan enjoyed it. The last time he'd drunk this kind of tea had been in Nanjing, where he attended a conference on reforming the power structure in the state-owned enterprises. That was seven years before.

Bao got excited as he was describing to Nan the journal, which, though a quarterly, sometimes came out with five issues a year. *"Have you seen the English part of* New Lines?*"* Bao asked Nan, scratching his short beard.

"Yes, it's interesting." As a matter of fact, Nan wasn't impressed by the translations, which formed almost a third of each issue, as the last section.

"Danning told me that your English is excellent. Do you think you can take charge of that part too?"

"I'll be glad to."

"Maybe occasionally you can translate some poems too."

"Sure. I'm writing poetry myself."

Bao looked at Nan in surprise, his heavy-lidded eyes doubtful. He went on slurping his tea and then put the cup into his left palm. He said, *"Our circulation has just reached three thousand. Let's hope we can make a profit soon."*

"Do we have to be on our own financially?"

"Not at the moment. I have begged around for money since I took over the journal five months ago. So far I've got some. Goodness knows what will happen if we don't get funding next year."

Wendy yawned and said in a weary voice, "Honey, I'm going to bed. Don't stay up too long."

"Yes," said Bao.

"Are you going to come to bed soon?"

"Yes."

Nan wasn't sure if Bao understood her. Wendy shuffled a little as she moved to the door of their bedroom. From the rear, she looked baggy, more aged. Bao said to Nan, *"Feel free to show me your poems."*

Nan's face brightened while his thick eyebrows lifted. *"I will definitely do that."* He had read some of Bao's poetry, which was experimental and sometimes made no sense to him, just an assembly of pretty, nebulous words. But Bao was well connected in the circle of the exiled artists and writers. If he was willing to help him, Nan might get a good start.

Bao got up and went into the living room to call his sister in Shanghai, and Nan climbed back to his sultry garret.

2

THE PAY Nan got from *New Lines* was barely enough for supporting himself, and he had to find additional work. On Saturday morning he took the A train to Manhattan for job interviews. He arrived an hour and a half early so that he could stroll around a little. What was amazing about Chinatown and Little Italy was that every street corner smelled different. There were many foods being cooked and sold on the streets, at quite reasonable prices. Nan enjoyed sniffing the air, especially the smells of popcorn, fried onion and pepper, and Italian sausage, though now and then a stench of rotten fruit would pinch his nose. He noticed that most girls here were pale, slim, and pretty, often wearing perfume, especially those working in clothing stores. Walking along Canal Street, he felt as if he were in a commercial district in Shanghai or Guangzhou. Signs in Chinese characters hung everywhere. The stands along the sidewalk displayed all kinds of merchandise for sale: embroidered slippers, tawdry jewelry, shirts, towels, hats, umbrellas, mechanic pencils, knockoffs of brand-name watches and Swiss army knives—all made in China. The seafood stalls were noisy and had many fishes on display. Salmon, red snapper, bighead carp, pomfret, sea bass, all lay on crushed ice and looked slimy and no longer fresh, with collapsed eyes and patches of lost scales. There were also crabs, oysters, lobster, quahogs, sea urchins, razor clams. Though all the fish were dead, some of the stalls flaunted signs claiming SEAFOOD, ALIVE AND FIERCE!

The first interview was at the Chinese cultural center, which had a massive front door, dark like an ironclad gate. Nan arrived fifteen minutes early, so he stayed in the entryway and opened a copy of the white pages at a pay phone. He looked through some names in hopes of finding someone he knew. Whenever he was in a new place, he'd thumb through parts of its local white pages, dreaming of stumbling on a friend or acquaintance. Of course, the first person he'd look for was Beina Su. Somehow wherever he went, he'd fantasize he might chance on her. How wild with joy she'd be on seeing him. How firmly she'd hug him. Yes, they could always start like new. Today, despite finding no familiar names, Nan was amazed by the large number of Chinese living in Manhattan. Just under "Wei Zhang," six people were listed.

It was time for the interview. A young woman told Nan to go to the second floor and see Lourie. To his surprise, Lourie, the manager of this place, was a tall man in his mid-twenties wearing a ponytail and a blue shirt that was so long, it made his legs appear short. He reminded Nan of a hippie, though he looked Mongolian, with bright eyes. Behind him spread a cork bulletin board on the wall, tacked with posters and flyers. He stretched out his hand, which felt meaty when Nan shook it. "I was very impressed by your Mandarin," Lourie said, smiling while licking his fleshy bottom lip. They had spoken on the phone two days earlier.

"Sank you for considering my application," Nan said.

"Thank *you* for applying. What are you doing at the moment?"

"I'm zer managing editor of a literary journal."

"Excellent. What's it called?"

"*New Lines.*"

Lourie lowered his head and tried to recall. Then he said, "It doesn't ring a bell."

"It's new."

"I see. Do you speak Cantonese?"

"No, I don't."

"Not at all?"

"To tell you zer truth, it's like a foreign language to me. But I can learn."

"That'll make it difficult for us. You see, many of our students speak Cantonese only. You'll have to explain everything in the language they can understand."

"So I'm disquawlified."

"I'm not saying that. We cannot make our decision until we've interviewed all the top applicants."

"Can you tell me how I'm ranked among zem?"

"That I can't. Tell you what, I can offer you a free ticket for our exhibition."

"Sure, sank you."

The other interview was at one o'clock, still an hour away, so Nan went into the Museum of Chinese Immigrant Culture, located on the top floor. The exhibition, however, disappointed him because it was very shabby. There were dozens of photographs on the walls, but just a few pieces of artwork were on display, one of which was an instrument called the Chum Kahm, a crossbreed of the guitar and the banjo. Some hardwood chests and colorful robes worn by early Chinese immigrants were also among the collection. Even newspapers, printer blocks, abacuses, writing brushes, and used ledgers were on show. The most impressive of all was a large bald eagle made of pinkish toilet tissue, standing atop a glass case and symbolizing the longing for freedom. Up close, Nan could see that it was composed of hundreds of miniature origami birds. It had been created by a group of incarcerated illegal aliens, who had been seized by the Coast Guard when the rickety boat smuggling them into America got stranded at Hawaii. As for written works, there were only a handful of books, by contemporary authors such as Maxine Hong Kingston, Amy Tan, and Gish Jen. Near a tall window stood a trash can collecting the water dripping from a leak in the ceiling. There wasn't another visitor in the poorly lighted room. The whole show was a letdown.

Nan came out of the building with a sinking heart. Questions, one after another, were arising in his mind. Why do they call that place a cultural museum? Why are there so few exhibits that can be called artwork? How come there's no Picasso or Faulkner or Mozart that emerged from the immigrants? Does this mean the first Chinese here were less creative and less artistic? Maybe so, because the early immigrants were impoverished and many were illiterate, and because they all had to slave away to feed themselves and their families, and had to concentrate their energy on settling down in this unfamiliar, discriminatory, fearsome land. Just uprooting themselves from their native soil must have crippled their lives and drained their vitality, not to mention their creativity. How could it be possible for an unfettered genius to rise from a tribe of coolies who were frightened, exhausted, mistreated, wretched, and possessed by the instinct for survival? Without leisure, how can art thrive?

The more Nan thought, the more upset he became.

3

WITH a sadness induced by those thoughts, with the conviction that the cultural center wouldn't hire him, Nan entered Ding's Dumplings on Pell Street. The owner of this place was Howard Ding, who looked weary, sitting behind the counter with his legs crossed and reading the *New York Times*. But when he raised his eyes to glance at Nan, his face turned alert and intelligent. He stood up and shook hands with the applicant. Though already in his fifties, he had a straight back and a full head of dark hair, which Nan thought might be dyed. Howard stood almost six feet, but every part of him was thin—thin eyes, thin nose, thin chest, thin limbs, and thin extremities. After talking with Nan for a few minutes, he handed him a book that had a gray cover and a red title: *Practical English for Restaurant Personnel.* He told Nan, "Your English is pretty fluent, but you may still need to familiarize yourself with some of the words and expressions in our business."

"Does zis mean you're going to hire me?"

"Yes. I like you." Howard was soft-spoken, but his voice was clear. "Let me ask you one more question, because I hate to change my staff too often. How long will you live in New York?"

"I don't know, probably a year or two."

"I won't hire temporary workers. We just lost two people who started only three months ago."

"You mean they're cawllege students."

"Right. They went back to Maryland."

"Zen I will stay longer. I don't go to school. No need to worry."

"Good, I'm glad to hear that. Have you waited tables before?"

"No."

"What kind of work experience do you have in a Chinese restaurant?"

"I don't have any."

"I like your candor. How about starting as a busboy?"

"Zat's fine." Nan frowned in spite of himself.

"Don't be discouraged. Everybody here starts from the bottom. I'm always fair with my employees. You can also help the chef in the kitchen. Your English is good, so you can wait tables, filling in for someone now and then. If you're really capable, you may end up a manager eventually. I have other restaurants in town and need all kinds of help." Howard peered at Nan.

"All right, I'll begin as a busboy."

"Keep in mind that you're also a helper in the kitchen."

"It seems you want me to know every part of zis business."

"That's exactly what I mean."

Nan had on his mind a newspaper job he had applied for, but he wouldn't let this opportunity slip away. He said, "When should I start?"

"Tomorrow morning at ten."

"All right, I'll be here on time."

Despite saying that, he wasn't certain whether he really wanted the job. He was going to call the newspaper today to find out his chances with them.

He crossed Canal Street and somehow wandered onto Mott Street, where crowds of people gathered at a fair. Many of them clustered around jugglers, palm readers, quoit throwers, toy gun shooters, psychics arranging tarot cards, even a fire-eater wearing a red cape. A lot of foods were for sale on the sidewalks: sausages as thick as a human leg, giant pretzels revolving in glass ovens, kebabs sizzling on skewers, ravioli bobbing in boiling pots. Three young men in black T-shirts with the ideogram for "tolerance" printed on the front were performing kung fu massage on the people straddling the chairs that all had a ring affixed to the top for the customers to rest their faces on. Toward the end of the fair, two Chinese painters sat on canvas stools, one in his early thirties and the other middle-aged, both wearing Chicago Bulls caps. The older man was crying, "Anyone want a portrait?"

Few people paid heed to them. A flock of fat pigeons landed nearby, strutting nonchalantly, pecking at bread crumbs and popcorn and sending out a *koo-koo-koo* sound. Nan looked at the large sample portrait standing between the two painters. Beneath it were listed the prices: BLACK AND WHITE—$20, COLORED—$40, FRAME—$8. So cheap. How could they make a living by doing this? The middle-aged painter tilted his lumpy chin and asked Nan, *"Want a portrait, brother?"*

"No." He shook his head.

The man smiled and whispered, *"Please sit down for us. We won't charge you."*

"I can't do that." Nan was amazed by his offer.

"Please help us. We have to work on somebody to attract customers. Sit down, please."

"I'll pay you ten dollars if you do a good portrait of me. How's that?"

"Fine, just sit on that."

The younger man handed him a folding stool. As soon as Nan sat down, people began gathering around to watch. The older painter wielded a charcoal pencil, and with a few strokes sketched out the contour of Nan's face. Then he proceeded to draw his bushy hair and broad forehead. From time to time he used a napkin to wipe his own pug nose, which somehow wouldn't stop dripping. He now lifted his head to observe Nan, and now bent forward, scratching the paper rapidly.

"Where are you from?" Nan asked the younger painter.

"Wuhan. We used to teach at Hubei Institute of Fine Arts."

"You were professors?"

"He was. I was a lecturer."

"Can you make a living by drawing portraits on the street?"

"It's not easy, but we've been doing this for several years."

The older painter raised his eyes, his brow furrowed. *"Don't talk too much. Keep still, or the portrait may not resemble you."*

Nan stopped. He looked away. In the distance two trees grew on a rooftop, beyond which a jumbo jet was sailing noiselessly through the fleecy clouds. He wondered whether the trees were planted in pots or in a flower bed on the roof. Three seagulls were wheeling in the air on sickle wings, squawking like babies in pain. Around Nan, people were palavering about the portrait in the making. "It's really like him," said a girl.

"A fabulous job," echoed another voice.

"For twenty dollars, not a bad deal."

"Maybe I should have a portrait done here."

"Yes, just twenty bucks."

"Look et de nose, exectly like de guy's."

"Hey, smile," a jug-eared man yelped at Nan.

"I'm not taking a photo." Nan purposely set his face straight while fiddling with the strap of his bag.

Twenty minutes later the portrait was done. Nan looked at it and was surprised by his own face, which was as forlorn as though he had just missed a train or boat, too muddled to know where to go or what to do. In the drawing his eyes gazed into the distance while his mouth was set as if he were suppressing some anguish or pain. This face belonged to a lost, exhausted man. Obviously the painter had captured the actual state of his mind. A miserable feeling surged in Nan's chest and his eyes misted over, but he managed a grimace— his cheeks twitched. The older painter bent down and inscribed the date and place at the right-hand bottom corner of the portrait. "Here you are," he said, rubbing his hands while the younger man took the sketch off the easel and rolled it up for Nan.

Nan paid the older man ten dollars and walked away with the drawing under his arm. On the train he wondered what to do with it. Who wanted to see such a woeful face? It would remind people of bad luck! On no account would he show it to his wife and son— Taotao might laugh about it, whereas Pingping would be disappointed. So when he got off at Utica Avenue, he dropped it into a trash can at the station.

In Wendy's house, a letter from the *North Star Times* was awaiting him, which informed him that the newspaper had picked someone else for the assistant editorship it had advertised. Nan was upset, suspecting that they might already have decided on the hire before they put out the ad. An applicant like himself must have been needed just to fill a quota. Now he had no alternative but to start at Ding's Dumplings the next day.

4

DING'S DUMPLINGS offered mainly Shanghai cuisine, which isn't spicy but a bit sweet. It also specialized in noodles and dumplings filled with several kinds of stuffing: lean pork, fish, shrimp, crabmeat, and beef, all mixed with various vegetables. The restaurant was small, with only twelve tables in it, but it enjoyed a fine reputation. Under the glass top of each table was a *New York Times* article praising the quality and the fair prices of the food offered here. Unlike in a regular Chinese restaurant, on each table here was a sugar shaker among the cruets of soy sauce, vinegar, and chili oil. The main wall in the dining area was glazed entirely with mirror, on which some sea creatures were blazoned: turtle, swordfish, lobster, crabs, skate. On the street-facing window was painted a fat boy carrying with a curved shoulder pole two huge baskets of money, one of gold coins and the other of silver ingots.

Nan's job was to wash dishes in the basement kitchen. Besides the chef and the busboy, there were three waitstaff, supervised by a hostess named Chinchin. Chinchin was from Taiwan, and was congenial but garrulous and giggly. She often wore a pink dress and beige pumps, her bright-colored outfit making her sallow complexion appear dark. Whenever possible, she'd chaff the waitstaff, who were all from mainland China. She'd say they were all Communist supporters, red to the bone, and hadn't yet shed their air of banditry, and still dreamed of communizing property and sharing others' spouses and children. Unlike Chinchin, the two waitresses and one waiter all had on the restaurant's uniform—a yellow T-shirt, black slacks, and a maroon apron. Nan wore the same clothes but stayed in the basement most of the time. When there were too many customers he'd go upstairs and help clear tables. Otherwise, the waitstaff would carry the used tableware downstairs for him to wash.

Howard, the owner, seldom showed up here and left Ding's Dumplings in the hands of Chinchin, a distant relative of his, who also managed the tiny bar. Usually customers just ordered ready-made wines and beers, so the bar was rarely used. Howard had other restaurants in the city, one in the World Trade Center and another on 55th Street, near the Museum of Modern Art. These days he was all tied up at a new place he'd just opened in Queens. He was such a wealthy man that he received a letter from George Bush each year, inviting him to the President's Dinner at the White House, though he had never attended such an event. "Too expensive," he once told his staff. "You think there are free meals in America? You'll have to pay fifteen thousand dollars for a fund-raising dinner like that. Besides, I'm not a Republican."

A week after Nan started at Ding's Dumplings, a stalwart black man appeared. As he was stepping into the doorway, Chinchin motioned to the waitresses and shouted, "*Be careful! Here comes a dark ghost.*" A month ago the restaurant had been robbed by two blacks, one of whom wore a mask of Ronald Reagan and the other that of Richard Nixon. The police were still investigating the case.

To their astonishment, the black man announced in standard Mandarin, "*Please rest assured, comrades. I'm not a hoodlum. I'm your friend.*"

Embarrassed, they looked at one another speechlessly. Then Nan broke into laughter and the others followed him. Maiyu, the slender waitress with slightly bulging eyes and hoop earrings dangling from below her bob haircut, led the customer to a round table close to the stairs. The man, more than six foot two, squared his shoulders and sat down, his hands clasped on the tabletop. He had grizzled hair and wore a tie with a pattern of antique coins on it and a dark blue suit, his yellowish shirt decked with cuff links. He smiled at Maiyu, showing his wide mouth and strong teeth. Plainly he was past forty, but the wrinkles on his face made him look masculine and quite handsome. "Hi, it's gorgeous out there, isn't it?" he said to the waitress.

"Yes. What would you like?" Maiyu's soft eyes wavered as she spoke.

"*Yangzhou Fried Rice and Three-Delight Soup.*" He spoke Mandarin as if he were an old customer.

"How come you speak Chinese?" put in Heng Chen, the waiter, standing by with arms akimbo. Heng was Maiyu's husband; they had married the previous year, right before he came to America.

"I studied it in Beijing Foreign Languages Institute for three years, in the seventies," the man said, watching the supple movement of Maiyu's shapely waist as she was heading away for the kitchen.

"What are you doing now? Teaching Chinese?" Nan asked him.

"No, I quit teaching long ago. That's an awful profession, I mean in this country, underpaid and tiresome. I'm a private investigator now."

"You're a detective?" the bespectacled Aimin cut in, fingering the tip of her thin braid.

"Yes. I help my clients find information on other people or companies."

Maiyu returned with a pot of tea. The black man gave her a sidelong look and said, "You're beautiful, a real knockout."

Though unfamiliar with his last word, she was blushing. She glanced at her husband, who was frowning.

"I'm David Kellman. What's your name?" the man asked her.

"Maiyu."

"Can you write it down for me?" He took out of his inside pocket a gilt pen and a dark blue address book and opened it for her to inscribe on.

He observed the characters she'd written for him. "This is a beautiful name, 'Mai-you.'"

"No, 'Mai-yu.'"

"Let me try again. 'Man-yu.' Did I get it right?"

"Almost."

"Thank you for writing it down. I'm going to look it up in my dictionary and work on it. Next time I come, I'll pronounce your name accurately. Here's my card. If you need any help, just give me a ring."

She looked astonished, staring at him, her face crimson. Heng Chen, her husband, jumped in, "She has no ring for you!"

"What?" Kellman looked puzzled, and then his face relaxed. He burst out laughing. "Oh my, this is so funny! You thought I was talking of an engagement ring or a wedding band? What a misunderstanding! I wish I could do that for this charming young lady, though."

Nan told his fellow workers, "He meant you should phone him eef you need his help."

"Exactly," Kellman said, still chuckling.

"Thank you," Maiyu mumbled. She turned and made for the kitchen to fetch his order. Still, Heng couldn't take his triangular eyes off Kellman. As his wife was passing him, he wagged his chin to indicate that she shouldn't talk too much with that self-styled Sherlock Holmes.

Nan went back into the kitchen and resumed chopping vegetables and slicing beef. Today the assistant to the chef was off work, so Nan took over the kitchen chores, which he liked doing, as he was eager to see how the chef cooked.

From that day on, Kellman would come to Ding's Dumplings at least three times a week. Whenever he was here, the room would echo with his laughter. Nan liked him, though he felt this man was reckless, flirting with Maiyu openly and never noticing her husband's furious eyes. Kellman would talk excitedly to the waitress, who at first seemed reluctant to speak, but her face would turn sunny whenever he was here. Heng hated to see him, yet he couldn't throw out a regular customer. He had neither the muscle and guts to confront this big man nor the English to spoil his conversation, which at times could be heard by the entire room. One day, after Kellman had left, Heng exploded, accusing his wife of having become Americanized and degenerated into a shameless broad.

Chinchin reproached him, saying he ought to have a large heart. She kept shaking her oval face, on which lingered the last trace of youth, and said to the waitstaff, "*You people have been brainwashed by the Commies and are too serious about what happens between a man and a woman. A husband should feel proud if his wife is attractive to other men. Heng, just because Maiyu spoke a few words with Kellman, you think she's carrying on with him? You're dead wrong. Truth be told, I'm pleased to see that Kellman has become a regular. If only we had more pretty girls here. Then you all could get more tips.*" She caught herself and glanced at the homely Aimin, whose eyes were fixed on Chinchin, glinting behind her thick glasses.

But Heng couldn't be appeased, and was visibly jittery and grumpy whenever Kellman was in the restaurant, so Chinchin scheduled Maiyu and Heng for different shifts. As a result, Nan often filled in, waiting tables in the daytime. He made four dollars an hour as a busboy and was glad about the tips he got. Unlike him, the waitstaff were each paid only $1.50 an hour because they kept the tips.

Nan would phone Pingping in the morning before he set out for work. Occasionally she called him, especially when she had run into difficulties. One recent day she was unable to use his credit card to order things on the phone because she couldn't recall his mother's maiden name. Neither she nor Nan actually knew what a maiden name was. Three years ago, when they were opening a joint bank account and a woman representative asked Nan for his mother's maiden name, he had been stumped, but on the spur of the moment had told her, "Fengkou," which was a rural town where his grandparents had lived. When Pingping was asked, she said to the woman, "My mother has same maiden name." The representative said, "How did that happen?" Nan explained, "It's common in China, where a billion people have only a hundred family names." From then on, both of their mothers had shared the same maiden name— "Fengkou," a word that might never have been applied to a human being before.

Once in a while Nan didn't have time to call Pingping before going to work; then she'd phone him at the restaurant around noon. His fellow workers often teased him, saying his wife was an insomniac without him in bed, and asking him if he and she had grown up together. He once answered with a poker face, "*Of course, we were engaged when we were tots. That's why I'm so henpecked.*"

They were amused but unsure if he had told the truth.

5

THREE WEEKS LATER Howard hired another busboy and promoted Nan to the chef's assistant, because the former kitchen aide had left for Miami to marry a Cuban Chinese woman. Nan got a one-dollar raise too. Chef Zhang needed a lot of help, and Nan's job was mainly to cut meats and vegetables, fry chicken cubes, and wrap dumplings. Nan watched carefully how the chef cooked. Zhang told him to memorize the entire menu and the ingredients of every dish, so that Nan could assemble all the things needed for each order in a bowl or a plate or a Styrofoam container before the chef cooked it. On occasion Zhang would let Nan make fried rice or noodle soup while he stood by to supervise. He also taught Nan how to concoct various sauces. When it wasn't busy, Nan would go upstairs to chat with the waitstaff. Chef Zhang, always cooped up in the basement, told Nan not to *"gab too much with those bitches up there."*

The waitstaff disliked the chef, partly because they made money in different ways. The chef was paid by the hour and so were Nan and Chinchin, but the waiter and waitresses depended mainly on tips. When business was good, both the boss and the waitstaff would get excited, whereas the chef would become grouchy, having to cook without respite. Old Zhang often struck his legs with his fists to help the blood circulate. He revealed to Nan that he suffered from piles because for many years he had stood for more than ten hours a day in the kitchen. Whenever the work turned hectic, his pain and itch would grow more intense, insufferable. He said to Nan, *"Lots of people in this business have this problem with their asses. Be careful—don't end up like me."*

At last Nan understood why there were advertisements for treating hemorrhoids everywhere in Chinatown. No matter how tired he was, he'd take a shower before going to bed. Also, at night he'd place his pillow under his feet instead of his head to prevent his legs from developing varicose veins, which were also a professional hazard as a consequence of standing for long hours. He wasn't interested in managing one of Howard's dumpling houses, but he was eager to learn how to cook. Neither did he feel he could be a good waiter, who would have to carry a loaded tray on his shoulder steadily while climbing up the narrow stairs. Worse yet, a waiter had to put on a smile in front of customers, some of whom were nasty and wouldn't leave tips on the grounds that the service wasn't good enough. So Nan felt that by nature he belonged in the kitchen, where he wouldn't have to face any customers. Chef Zhang seemed fond of Nan and taught him how to cook and how to make dumpling stuffings whenever it wasn't busy. He often said, "*You're lucky, Nan. When I started, I was not allowed to touch the rim of the wok during the first year.*"

Nan had heard a lot of stories about the difficulties in finding a job at a Chinese restaurant in New York. The waitresses told him that if you were unable to speak Cantonese, most places wouldn't hire you. Ding's Dumplings was one of the few restaurants in Chinatown where the owners didn't know Cantonese. Heng said he had once worked at a place where all the waiters had had to wear a short bow tie, which made him miserable, unable to breathe freely. Chinchin, the hostess, had worked in other restaurants before and also talked about how the Chinese waitstaff were exploited and humiliated by their bosses, and even mistreated by barkeeps, most of whom were Caucasians. In contrast, Howard was by far a better boss, who wouldn't dock your pay if you came to work an hour late because of an emergency. Nan felt lucky he had this job.

6

THE CIRCULATION of *New Lines* had dropped by nine percent in recent months. Bao was worried and held an editorial meeting, at which five people were present, counting himself and Nan. They were to decide whether they should expand the journal, namely to include articles on current events and social issues, and even a few advertisements. There were a good number of Chinese dissidents living in North America and willing to contribute political essays to the journal. However, except Bao, those at the meeting all opposed the idea, arguing that *New Lines* should remain strictly literary. Bao complained that there wasn't another way to revitalize the journal. As a compromise, they agreed to print two or three pieces of fiction in each issue, though at present they couldn't pay the authors.

Bao knew many Chinese dissidents living in New York. One Saturday morning he and Nan went to visit Mr. Manping Liu, the well-known scholar in political economy who lived near Nostrand Avenue in Brooklyn. They wanted to get the older man's endorsement for their journal. Nan had seen Mr. Liu at Harvard last June and was eager to meet him again. Mr. Liu opened the door, his eyes and mouth both sunken, and said to them, *"Welcome to my hovel."* His apartment had only two rooms and was on the ground floor, but in his tiny backyard were some wilting sunflowers and chrysanthemums, and also some tripods for supporting vegetables, made of whittled branches tied at the tops but all unloaded now. The living room cum study was lined with books, and a small desk stood next to the window, strewn with manuscripts. Liu was well respected in the Chinese community, not only for his incisive writings but mainly for his integrity. In June 1989, when the field armies began attacking civilians in Beijing, he had bought a large wreath and intended to take it to Tiananmen Square personally, but his friends had restrained him despite his wailing and struggling to break loose. Within a few days his name appeared on the Most Wanted list; fortunately he and his wife managed to flee to southern China and from there were smuggled to Hong Kong through an underground channel. Unlike the other dissidents in the United States, he had always refused to accept financial aid from any organization and to date had supported himself mainly by writing for Chinese-language newspapers and magazines. Also, his wife was very adaptable and worked in a gift store in downtown Manhattan.

After Bao and Nan sat down and made their case, Mr. Liu happily agreed to write a few words for their journal. But for a moment he looked rapt in thought, then moved to his small desk, uncapped his fountain pen, and wrote something on a card. He turned around and handed the endorsement to Bao. It read: "I greatly admire the young writers at *New Lines*. May their effort flourish and their work endure!"

Both Bao and Nan thanked him. Then his wife, a sturdy woman with a heart-shaped face, came in, holding a kettle of boiled water to make tea for them. She looked tired, saying she had worked late the night before. After serving tea, she went back into their bedroom.

Mr. Liu said he remembered an article Nan had published in the *Journal of Political Economics* a few years earlier. But on hearing that Nan had left the field, he said, "*I understand. Life is hard here, and you have to survive first.*"

"*Not only because of that,*" Nan told him. "*I made a vow not to be involved in politics again. I'm not cut out for it.*"

"*I see.*"

Bao put in, "*Nan has been writing poetry.*"

"*Good. Every road leads to Rome,*" said Mr. Liu. "*China needs all kinds of talents.*"

Nan turned reticent, not knowing what to make of the old man's remark. Mr. Liu talked as if he were still an official.

Soon their topic shifted to life here. "*I just bought a car,*" Liu told the visitors.

"*A new one?*" asked Bao.

"*No. How could I afford a new car?*"

"*How much did it cost?*"

"*Four hundred dollars. It's a pretty good Toyota. A friend of mine drove it and said it was better than his car that cost him over a thousand.*"

"*Can you drive?*"

"*I just got my license.*"

"*You're very brave,*" Nan put in. "*I wouldn't dare to drive in New York.*"

"*I have to be able to drive, or else I'd feel as if I'm missing a limb. Also, as long as I live here, I'll have to make a living on my own. A driver's license is a means of independence. Once I can drive really well, I'll deliver food for a restaurant.*"

"*You shouldn't do that. You have poor eyesight, don't you?*" said Bao.

The old man laughed heartily. "*Maybe I can deliver computer parts in the daytime. Anyway, driving a car on the highway gives me a feeling of freedom. What fun! What exhilaration! Do you want to see my car?*"

"*Sure, let's have a look,*" Bao agreed.

On their way out, Nan said, "*Mr. Liu, from now on we're going to publish two or three short stories in each issue of* New Lines. *If you come across any good fiction, please recommend it to us.*"

"*I'll keep that in mind. As a matter of fact, my wife used to write fiction under the pen name Purple Lilacs. She's working too hard now, but she may write again.*"

Bao said, "*When she finishes a piece, please show it to us first.*"

"*By all means. I'll tell her.*"

Her pen name reminded Nan that he had read a novella by Mrs. Liu back in China. It had felt to him like a piece of reportage, but she had indeed had a name.

The three of them walked out of the building. Along the curbs were parked many cars, some dented and rusted, one with both front lights smashed and another wearing a boot. Nan looked back and forth, unable to determine which one might belong to Mr. Liu. The old man was taking them farther down the street, chomping on a thick pipe, a puff of smoke wafting about his head.

"*This one,*" he said finally, pointing at a hatchback with a warped front fender.

Nan looked closely but couldn't decide what color the car was. It was battered and repainted. It appeared dark brown, but some bright orange patches were scattered all over it. "*This is a good car,*" Bao managed to say.

"*Impressive,*" echoed Nan.

"*Want a ride?*" Liu asked.

Bao and Nan exchanged glances. "*Actually, we should be leaving,*" Bao said. "*Nan's going to work in the afternoon.*"

"*Then I can take you to the train station.*"

"*Are you sure?*"

"*Of course. My driving skill isn't good enough yet, or I'd drive you all the way home.*"

They got into the car, Nan in back and Bao in front. The seats were broken, yellow foam stuck out in spots, and there were also cigarette burns on them. An acrid smell of sweat and tobacco emanated from the interior.

"*How old is this car?*" Bao asked Mr. Liu.

"*More than ten years old.*"

As soon as the engine started, the car began shaking, coughing and moaning as if it were an animal seized by a crippling pain. Nan was unnerved as he noticed a pedestrian turn to observe them. He craned to look at the odometer, which showed merely seven zeros in a row. "*How many miles are on this car?*" he asked Mr. Liu.

"*Hard to say. Probably two hundred thousand.*"

"*What?*" cried Bao.

"*Just a guess. A Japanese car like this can run forever.*"

The car jolted along as if running on cobblestones. Despite the bumpy ride, Nan soon turned thoughtful. Mr. Liu had formerly lived a privileged life, having his own chauffeur and secretary, but now he had to restart his life here, writing for newspapers and magazines like a hack and even ready to do menial work. Still, he seemed quite buoyant and didn't regret his exile at all. Nan was full of both sadness and respect.

At last they arrived at the Nostrand Avenue station. Even though he had stepped out of the car, Nan still couldn't shake off the jitters. "*It's a real experience,*" he told Mr. Liu.

"*Next time I can drive you all the way home,*" the old man said with a broad grin that revealed his tobacco-stained teeth.

"*Take good care, Mr. Liu,*" said Bao.

"*You too, young men.*"

They saw the jalopy roll away, dragging a tail of exhaust, and merge into the flow of the traffic. They turned and entered the station to catch the train. Nan asked his friend about Mr. Liu, "*Doesn't he often say he'll return to China?*"

"*Yes, but he must have realized that would be impossible in the near future. That's why he has been learning how to support himself.*"

"*He's a remarkable man.*"

"*And also an interesting character.*"

Nan was annoyed by Bao's flippancy but said no more. They parted company to take different trains, Nan going downtown while Bao headed back. All the way to work, Nan ruminated on their meeting with Mr. Liu, who, unlike himself, didn't show any bitterness about his truncated life, as if he were oblivious to all the evil he had suffered. How different the old man was from some Chinese dissidents who were well supported by universities and foundations. On the other hand, Nan was upset too, for he felt a man such as Mr. Liu couldn't possibly live decently in this land because he was too old to start anew. However hard he struggled to be independent, Mr. Liu would still belong to their native land, and his existence would still be shaped by the Chinese political center of which he had always been a part. The very fact that he thought of doing those odd jobs indicated that he didn't plan to stay in America for long. Perhaps at night he couldn't help but dream of his former life.

Unlike him, if Nan lived his type of life and drove that kind of car, he'd earn only contempt and ridicule. He had to find his own way here, living not as an expatriate or an exile but as an immigrant. He was still young and must put up a fight. If only he could figure out where his battlefield was.

7

UNLIKE NAN, Bao didn't work and had been writing his memoir, which he said might bring him fame and fortune once it was published. That was why he didn't edit the journal himself and had hired Nan to do it. He seemed determined to live an artist's life, concentrating on his writing and painting. In his studio, the room opposite Nan's in the attic, several unfinished gouaches leaned against the walls, and Bao told Nan that he had been experimenting with new techniques, including painting with fingers or with a palette knife. Whenever others asked him what he did for a living, he'd say, "I paint and write." In a sense Nan admired that, though at the same time he could see that Bao had been using Wendy.

What's worse, Bao was an alcoholic. He often came to Nan's room with a bottle of cheap wine and wanted to share it with Nan, but Nan usually declined. Bao seemed lonely, unable to speak with anyone during the day when Wendy would go out to meet friends or participate in community activities. After half a bottle of wine, he'd grow loquacious, but would slur his words so much that Nan couldn't always follow him. He'd talk about whatever came to mind. He described how at the age of nine he had pilfered money from his parents and bought candies and Popsicles for his pals, and how he and a bunch of urchins had stolen into an orchard, eating their fill of fruits and melons. Once when he was tipsy, he even bragged about how firm Wendy's breasts were because she had never suckled a baby, and how tight her vagina was since she hadn't given birth. Another time he confided that he'd had a crush on the young Chinese woman who had been the managing editor before Nan. One night he took offense at Nan's refusing to down the California Chardonnay he had poured for him. *"If you want to write poetry, you have to be fond of drinks, like Li Po, the Wine God,"* he told Nan. But Nan would have to read submissions the next morning before going to work and couldn't afford to get drunk. Besides, he didn't believe alcohol was a source of inspiration and could induce poetic spontaneity. To his mind, that was a mere excuse for would-be writers to indulge themselves.

One day Bao showed Nan a chapter of his memoir, nineteen handwritten pages, and asked him to read it. It was about how his father, a high school chemistry teacher, had been forced to collect night soil in their rural town and pull a trash cart on the streets at the beginning of the Cultural Revolution. Because of his father's disgrace, Bao, besides taking verbal insults every day, was often beaten by his schoolmates. The writing was rough, and the story too generic and too expository. As a result, the experiences remained opaque and dull, not substantiated by concrete details. After reading it, Nan told Bao, *"I don't think this is finished yet. You should make it fresher and more peculiar if not surprising."*

"Heaven knows how hard I worked on it."

Then, to Nan's surprise, Bao asked him to translate this chapter so that *New Lines* could print it. Grudgingly Nan agreed. The translation bored him and took him a whole week to finish. When working on it, he'd swear and slap his forehead as if he had been swindled. He'd rather dig ditches with a shovel than wrestle with this florid prose marred with clichés and clever but superficial jibes. How relieved he felt when he was finally done.

On seeing the pages in English, Bao turned ecstatic and even bowed to Nan, saying he owed him a dinner. He looked at the translation over and over, though hardly able to understand it. But Wendy read it and told Nan that she was impressed by his way of using English, which was fluid, elegant, and slightly old-fashioned, but suited the subject well.

These days Bao often said to Nan that he was terribly homesick. He even wondered if he should go back to visit his parents, though he didn't have the money for the airfare and for the gifts for his family and friends. Nan admonished him to forget about that, because Bao was known as a dissident, already blacklisted, and would be either refused entry or apprehended by the police at China's customs. *"It's not worth running the risk,"* said Nan.

"If only I were naturalized," Bao sighed.

"What difference would that make?"

"The Chinese police won't hurt you if you're an American citizen. Have you heard of Weifu Cai?"

"Yes, wasn't he arrested last time when he attempted to enter China?"

"Yes, but they released him a month later. He just got a huge grant from an American human rights foundation, thirty thousand dollars in total. See, he held a U.S. passport, so the Chinese government couldn't really harm him. Otherwise they could've sentenced him to five years at least."

"I didn't know he was back."

"I saw him a couple of weeks ago. He was a picture of health. If only I were an American citizen."

"Then you'd try to go back?"

"Definitely."

Nan remembered a saying popular in the Chinese diaspora: "Only by becoming a citizen of another country can you be treated decently by the Chinese."

8

AT DING'S DUMPLINGS, the waitstaff judged customers mainly by how much they tipped. Aimin and Maiyu often complained that some Americans were too demanding and too grouchy, and that if this restaurant had been Italian or French, they wouldn't have been so surly. *"They come here only because they're cheap,"* Aimin said, and bunched up her thin lips.

"Or we're cheap," Maiyu added.

A couple, an overweight white woman and a young black man wearing a Vandyke beard, came twice a week. They always bought wonton soup, Peking ravioli, and fish dumplings, but had never left more than one dollar for a tip, usually just some loose change scattered on the table. Whenever they showed up, the waitresses would avoid waiting on them, so Chinchin would assign Aimin and Maiyu to serve them by turns. Sometimes a whole family would dine here: tots crawled under the tables, and youngsters even snuck into the small banquet room upstairs when they used the toilets next to the landing. Two middle-aged gay men turned up every Wednesday evening and wouldn't hesitate to neck in front of others. One afternoon a Caucasian couple came with their four daughters, who looked similar in features, all pretty though a little pallid. Nan was told that this family ate here once a month, right after the father, a dapper man, received his pay. Obviously they weren't rich, but they had good table manners. Nan overheard the youngest girl, about six years old, ask for a walnut cookie for dessert, but her mother said no. The child didn't make another peep. Once they were done with the meal, the father left a ten for tip.

"They always give the same amount, very nice people," Aimin said to Nan, smiling with her nose wrinkled.

Compared with other customers, David Kellman was the most generous tipper. Usually he'd show up midafternoon, when diners were few, and would have Maiyu wait on him. He'd compliment Chinchin on her outfit, and then the two of them would tease each other in a friendly way. However, they'd stop their repartee when Maiyu brought over his order. He talked a lot to Maiyu, and once in front of everyone he invited her out, saying he'd take her to a Broadway show and then to a nice place where they could have a great time.

"I'm already married," she told him, simpering.

"Really? You look so young, like a teenager, but it doesn't matter. We'll have fun." He spoke so loudly that the other diners turned to look his way.

Nan kind of admired Kellman, who seemed good-humored and at ease with himself, and who appeared so well off that even the cuffs of his tailored jacket were monogrammed. In addition, Kellman seemed unafraid of anything and anybody and never minced his words. He said to Maiyu again, "Tell me who's your husband, the lucky guy."

"No, I won't."

"You'd better not, or I'll strangle him." He gave a belly laugh.

Apparently Maiyu was attracted to this man. Her fondness for him often exasperated her husband, especially when she and he worked the same shift. Heng would fume, his eyes smoldering. Through his rage Nan could see the kind of desperation that often marked a man unable to find his way in this place. Nan had met a good number of these men, who, frustrated and disoriented and desperate, would vent their spleen on their wives or girlfriends, though almost without exception they all appeared taciturn in front of others. Deep inside, every one of them was like a keg of gunpowder, ready to explode. Intuitively Nan felt Heng and Maiyu's marriage was floundering.

Soon Kellman stopped showing up, and then Maiyu quit. Rumor had it that she had moved out of her apartment and shacked up with that black man. Nobody dared verify this with Heng, fearing he might go into hysterics, but it was an open secret that his wife had walked out on him. Heng sighed a lot at work and was more reticent than before, though once in a while he'd yell at the other workers without provocation.

Howard, the boss, interviewed several people for the job left by Maiyu. He decided on Yafang Gao, a woman of twenty-four who had arrived in New York a week before. She had graduated from Fudan University and spoke English fluently. She smiled at everyone as if she had worked here for a long time. Her slightly chubby face showed some innate goodness, while her bulbous nose and tiny eye-teeth gave her a youthful look. Her geniality made Nan think she must have had a happy childhood. Howard hired her mainly because she could speak the Shanghai dialect, which none of the staff could understand but which matched the cuisine of the restaurant. Four decades before, Howard had lived in that metropolis too. So at the interview with Yafang he spoke the language, which sounded foreign and slick to Nan. At one point, he overheard Howard saying in English to the applicant, "I'm thrilled to speak our home dialect again!" The boss gave Yafang a copy of *Practical English for Restaurant Personnel* as well, and from then on called her "my hometown girl."

Because Yafang Gao had to settle in before she could start, Howard let Nan wait tables for a few days. When she began waitressing, Nan returned to the kitchen, where from then on he'd cook under Chef Zhang's supervision. He liked the work and enjoyed seeing raw materials change into toothsome dishes. He tried to learn as much as he could, believing Howard might put him in the chef's position someday.

Yafang turned out to know some of Nan's former schoolmates who had continued to do graduate work at her alma mater in Shanghai. She and Nan often chatted and got along well. Both were amazed that China, though a vast country, was actually a small world. Many people who had come out of their homeland knew of one another. Most of Nan's fellow graduate students had left China. As long as one could speak a foreign language, one would strive to go abroad. Some of them had even landed in Czechoslovakia, Poland, Hungary, Russia, South Africa. "*It took me three years to get the approval from my department for visiting America,*" Yafang told Nan. She had taught English at a technical college in Shanghai.

"*Why so long?*" he asked.

"*The chairman of my department said I was still young and should let the older comrades have a chance first.*"

"*So you feel lucky?*"

"*Certainly. You should have seen the long line of visa applicants outside the U.S. consulate in Shanghai. Some of them went there the night before their interviews, but the American officials turned most of them down.*"

"*I don't think people always know why they want to come to the United States.*"

"*Sure they know, for a better life.*"

"*But life here isn't easy at all.*"

"*Still, there's freedom.*"

"*Freedom is meaningless if you don't know how to use it. We've been oppressed and confined so long that it's hard for us to change our mind-set and achieve real freedom. We're used to the existence defined by evasions and negations. Most of our individual tastes and natural appetites have been bridled by caution and fear. It's more difficult to break the self-imposed tyranny than the external constraints. In short, we have lost the child in ourselves.*"

"*Wow, you speak like a philosopher, so eloquently.*"

Heng Chen broke his habitual silence, saying, "*Nan is also a poet.*"

"*Are you really?*" Yafang batted her glossy eyes, unconsciously licking her top lip.

"*I've been trying to write poetry,*" admitted Nan.

"*That means you still have a young heart.*"

Heng butted in again, "*Heh-heh-heh, Nan's a young-hearted man indeed, also very romantic. More impressive, he doesn't drink or smoke, absolutely a clean man, a model husband.*"

Nan wanted to call him "a loser" or "a new bachelor," but feeling reluctant to continue the conversation, he merely said, "*I've got to go down and cook some pot-stickers.*" He hurried away to the kitchen.

9

NAN went back to see his family at the end of September. Pingping and Taotao were overjoyed to have him home again, though Heidi greeted him lukewarmly. Pingping had explained to Heidi several times that Nan had gone to New York just to take a job; perhaps Heidi was afraid she might have to shelter Pingping and Taotao if Nan abandoned them. Nan had promised Heidi on the phone that he would come back as soon as he went through his training at the restaurant. Now, to convince her that he had been learning to be a chef, he cooked a dinner—wonton soup, lemon chicken, and shrimp dumplings—for the Masefields and his family. His cooking was a complete success. Livia loved the wontons so much that she wanted Nan to teach her how to make and boil them. Nan told Pingping what he had put into the stuffing, and she promised Livia that she'd get the wrappers from the Chinese grocery store in Burlington and show her how to wrap and cook wontons. Both Nan and Pingping knew that the girl would forget her interest in a matter of a day or two. Livia rarely persisted in doing anything.

Nan could stay only the weekend and would have to take Greyhound back on Monday morning. He didn't sleep in the same bed with Pingping, though they made love while Taotao was napping in the other room. She sighed afterward, saying she had missed him terribly and felt handicapped without him around, because there were many things she couldn't handle by herself. *"Why can't we stay together?"* she asked. *"When you're not home, I'm restless and can't sleep well at night."*

"I can't sleep well in New York either. Too noisy."

"Heidi asked me if we were separated."

"I'll come back soon. Honestly, I don't care about the editorial work, but the job at the restaurant is an opportunity for me to learn a trade. Just take my absence from home as a stint I'm doing, all right? I'll come back like a real chef in a few months."

"Taotao misses you too."

"I know."

"If you meet another woman you like in New York, you can spend time with her, as long as you don't catch disease and come back to us."

"Drop it! I'm too tired to have another woman. One's enough."

That stopped her. Nan remembered that before he left for America, she had said the same thing. Somehow she always thought he could make women weak in the knees. In reality he believed he wasn't attractive at all and was too quiet and too introverted to be a lady-killer. Worse, he had never been good at flirting or sweet-talking. Before coming to the States, he had heard that American colleges offered all kinds of bizarre courses. When he enrolled at Brandeis and got a copy of its curricula, he had thumbed through it to see whether there was a course in flirtation or seduction. If there had been such a class, he'd definitely have taken it.

Nan sighed, still fingering the tip of Pingping's hair while she was lying on her side, facing the back window. After the lovemaking, he still felt numb in the heart. This numbness made him gloomy. He knew she sensed his state of mind and must be feeling hurt.

What he didn't know was that she sometimes hated to go to bed with him, because sex made her feel miserable and degraded. "Cheaper than a whore," she'd chide herself afterward. Despite her undoubted love for him, despite her great effort to hold the family together, she simply couldn't always reconcile herself to the feeling that to have sex with a man who didn't love her was somewhat like self-violation. That was why she wouldn't mind that much if Nan slept with another woman, though she did fear losing him. If only he could understand how she actually felt.

She gazed at the sheets of rain rolling down the widowpanes as she listened to Nan snoring lightly.

•

The next morning Nan drove Taotao to the town library, where the boy checked out a stack of books. On their way back, father and son chatted about Taotao's pals at school while Nan was driving rather absentmindedly. The boy was on the math team now, but he disliked the practice for the future tournaments, which he said were more about the speed of your response than about your knowledge. There was a small traffic jam near the old town cemetery caused by an accident—a pickup had broadsided a white station wagon. Approaching the site, Nan swerved into the newly opened lane marked by orange pylons. As he was coming out of the stopgap way, somehow the right-hand side of his car touched the rubber-coated front shield of a coupe, but the contact was so light that Nan wasn't even aware of it. He continued driving away.

The bottle-nosed coupe honked, then sprang forward, following him. Nan ignored it as road rage and didn't stop. He drove faster. A moment later the car overtook him and beeped again. "Pull aside!" the driver yelled at Nan, who still didn't know what was going on.

He stopped before a speed bump and stepped out of his car, his son remaining inside. A stocky man in a trench coat leaped out of the coupe and rushed over. To Nan's astonishment, the man produced a police badge and flashed it at Nan's face, though his unbuttoned coat revealed that he wasn't wearing his uniform. His hawkish eyes blazing, he shouted, "I'm a police officer. Why did you hit my car and run?"

"When . . . when did I do zat?"

"Just now. Don't argue with me!"

"I reelly don't know what happened."

"Stop arguing. You committed a crime, d'you understand?" He slapped his flank. "I have a gun here." Indeed, he wore a pistol, though he was off duty. "Give me your driver's license!" he ordered.

"Why?"

"I said so. Give it here!"

Nan turned to look at Taotao, who was still in the car, unaware of the trouble outside. He handed his license to the policeman, who began to jot down the information while saying, "You're lucky today. If you don't stop next time, I'm gonna shoot you."

Seized by a sudden surge of heartsickness and self-pity, Nan begged, "Why don't you do it now? Keel me, please!"

"I can do that if I like." The officer kept writing without raising his eyes.

"Come on, awfficer, pull out your gahn and finish me off here. I'm sick of zis miserable life. Please shoot me!"

His earnestness surprised the man, who looked him in the face and muttered, "You're nuts!" Then he went on in an official tone of voice, "Stop bluffing! I've seen lots of wackos like you who don't give a damn about others' property."

At this point Taotao came over and stood by his father. The officer handed the driver's license back to Nan and said, "This is revoked. You can't drive anymore. You're in deep shit."

"Why not keel me instead? Come on, put me out of this suffering! I'm sick of zis uncertain life. Please fire your gahn!" Nan gulped back tears, his face twisted with pain.

"Get a grip here, man. We all have a cross to carry, and only death and taxes are certain in America. You gotta be more careful when you're driving, especially when you have your kid in your car." He glanced at Taotao, whose eyes were watering too. Without another word he turned and strode away.

On their drive back, Taotao said, "Dad, you shouldn't talk to the cop like that."

"Why?"

"You could get killed."

Nan wanted to tell his son that he'd prefer death to this life that seemed to lead nowhere and only to reduce him to nothing, but he throttled his impulse. A kind of shame washed over him. "I won't do zat again," he said.

The incident shook him deeply. He wasn't sure whether his license was really revoked. If it was, how could he get a new one? For the time being he could manage without it, but it would be indispensable when he came back to Boston eventually. He dared not ask Heidi for advice, for fear of arousing unnecessary suspicion. As a last resort, he phoned a local radio station that night, under the alias Jimmy, to ask the talk-show host.

The call went through. The gentleman told Nan on the air, "It doesn't work that way, Jimmy. An off-duty officer has no right to revoke anyone's driver's license. He isn't even entitled to issue a ticket for a traffic violation. That means your license is still valid. Don't worry about it."

"Should I do somesing to prevent zer trouble down the road?" His heart was pounding; this was the first time he was speaking on the radio.

"You may go to the police station and file a complaint. Do you know what station this officer is at?"

"I don't."

"Find that out and file a complaint. We mustn't let this sort of police brutality pass with impunity. It's outrageous to threaten people with a gun when he was off duty. All right, it looks like we're out of time. You're listening to *Legal Talk*. Our toll-free number is 1-800-723 . . ."

Nan didn't know the word "impunity," and neither would he bother to lodge a complaint, since it was impossible to find out what station the policeman belonged to. He was glad he still had his driver's license.

10

HENG CHEN hadn't shown up at Ding's Dumplings for several days, and Nan substituted for him. The staff upstairs often talked about Heng, and sometimes Nan joined their conversation. They felt that Heng must be too ashamed to continue to work here since everybody knew his wife had dumped him. Nowadays it was commonplace for young women from mainland China to leave their husbands for white men and Chinese Americans, but in his case, he had lost Maiyu to a black man who was at least fifteen years his senior. For that, Chinchin believed, he must have felt more humiliated. Nan didn't think so. He could see that Kellman was attractive to women, especially to those who needed a strong shoulder to rely on. Kellman was the kind of fellow who would buy flowers for his girlfriend a few times a week and would take her to the movies, the theater, museums, and concerts. In contrast, Heng had yet to find his bearings here. He just worked and worked, and he must have been boring to Maiyu, who couldn't tolerate it that her husband, formerly a promising young historian, had grown less and less competent than herself. More troublesome, some men from mainland China tended to have a devil of a temper because they had lost their sense of superiority, especially some college graduates who had been viewed as the best of their generation in their homeland; here as new arrivals they had to start from scratch like others, and mentally they weren't primed for such a drastic change. Worse still, their former privileged life had deprived them of the vitality and stamina needed for grappling with adversities in order to take root in the American soil; as a consequence, the emigration blighted many of them. Undoubtedly, Heng was one of those men.

Heng had once told Nan that his parents would call him collect from his home village every other week, even though they didn't have anything urgent to report. For them, this was a way to show off to the villagers, none of whose children had gone to college, to say nothing of making big money in New York. His parents would go to the village office and use the only telephone available for the two hundred households. Every call from home cost Heng at least fifty dollars, so he and Maiyu often fought over the phone bills. He admitted to Nan that in a way he himself was to blame, because he had once sent back a photograph in which his rear end leaned against a brand-new Jaguar parked in a driveway beside a grand Tudor house, as if he owned both of them.

Rolling her large eyes, Chinchin said to the waitstaff joshingly, *"You mainlanders, Communist supporters, must've been used to sharing husbands and wives, so it's no big deal to Heng. If Maiyu had a Taiwanese husband, she'd better be careful—he would kill her."*

"Heng is no man," Aimin said.

"You shouldn't blame him," Nan broke in. *"It's hard for him to survive here. How can he compete with Kellman, who has everything Maiyu wants?"*

"Kellman can't be as rich as he appears," Chinchin said.

"But he owns a business and has a lot of confidence." Nan tugged a piece of tissue out of a dispenser on the counter. *"Maiyu must feel vulnerable and want security."*

"Maybe Heng is no good in bed," Aimin said, gnawing her thumbnail.

"Come now, he's already down, no need to kick him anymore," Nan protested.

"I'm sure Heng hasn't had enough sex education and can't satisfy Maiyu."

"Aimin, you really have a mouth on you," said Chinchin.

Strangely enough, Yafang had been tongue-tied the whole time the conversation was going on. She looked pale today. Aimin asked, *"Yafang, what do you think of Heng? Does he look like a man to you?"*

"He's a hungry wolf."

"Wow, how come you're so angry?" Chinchin said.

"He's just a little crazy, horny man."

"How do you know he's horny?" Aimin asked.

"I just know it."

Nan was amazed by Yafang's remarks. She seemed to know more about Heng than the rest of them. Perhaps something had taken place between her and him when Nan was back in Boston over the weekend. What had happened? Why wouldn't Heng come to work? Why was Yafang so irascible?

Peeling scallions in the kitchen, Nan thought about his conversation with the female staff upstairs. Though Heng was physically small and weak, Nan felt that sex shouldn't be the reason Maiyu had run out on him. He remembered Gary Zimmerman, who had been his roommate during his first year and a half at Brandeis. Gary, skinny and poor, was crippled, with one leg shorter than the other and his left arm unable to stretch out freely, yet he never lacked girlfriends. Sometimes this Israeli would date two girls together and even frolic with both of them simultaneously in his queen-size bed, making such a racket that Nan, in the next room, couldn't sleep until they quieted down in the wee hours. Except for his sonorous voice, Gary had nothing extraordinary, but he spoke English fluently and was at home in America, so his demeanor and confidence attracted the females around him, especially those who were learning Hebrew from him and sympathized with his handicap. By contrast, Heng's problem was that he had been enervated and diminished here. Having little English, with neither hope nor confidence, how could he rival Kellman?

11

THAT NIGHT after they closed up, Nan and Yafang left together for the subway station. She was wearing a gabardine peacoat that gave her a cinched waist. It was sprinkling, and the murky puddles on Canal Street reflected the neon lights and would disappear whenever a car crushed through them. Nearby wisps of steam were rising from a manhole. There were still many people on the sidewalk, though most of the shops were locked up. Along the other side of the street a Chinese man was biking from the opposite direction against the slashing wind, the back of his white raincoat bellying out and making him anomalous, like a ghost. As if unable to see far, his eyes were fixed on the front wheel of his bicycle; on the handlebars hung a plastic bag still giving off steam. Nan turned to watch the back of the deliveryman, who vanished at the street corner a block away.

On the subway platform, Yafang told Nan that Heng might never come to work again. *"Why?"* he asked.

"He dare not."

With the slackening clank an A train came to a stop, disgorging passengers. Nan could have taken it, but it didn't stop at Kingston-Throop avenues, where Yafang would get off, so he waited with her for the C train.

After the platform quieted down some, he said to her again, *"I still don't understand why Heng won't come to work again. Who's he afraid of?"*

"Me."

"You? Why?"

"I'll knife him if he comes close to me again."

"What's going on?"

"He . . . he forced me to have sex with him."

"What? A man like him could do that?"

The C train appeared and screeched to a stop. Nan and Yafang stepped onto it. Only a few passengers were aboard, some of them nodding off. Nan and Yafang sat down near a corner. "*How did it happen?*" he asked her.

"*He tricked me.*"

"*How? I don't mean to be nosy. I never thought he could be so dangerous. He's such a wispy man.*"

"*Three days ago Howard's daughters worked at the restaurant, so Heng Chen and I were both off for a day. We live in the same area, and he said he'd like to take me to the movies in the evening. I asked him what pictures were good. He said, 'Have you seen adult movies?' 'No,' I said. I had no idea they were porno flicks. I thought they must be something too serious for kids to understand. So he took me to a place nearby. We saw how Americans were having sex. I'd never seen that kind of thing before and was astonished and, to be honest, also fascinated. In the dark Heng Chen began to caress me, and I didn't know how to resist him, too ashamed to make any noise. Afterward we went to his apartment.*" She sobbed and blew her nose. Her face suddenly aged, lines appearing under her cheeks. She went on, "*I was excited and never knew there were so many ways of doing it. Heng Chen said he was good at it and could teach me how to make love. I tried to reject his advances, but he begged me, saying, 'We're all drifters in this country and ought to help each other. It's just like you have food in your pantry while I'm starving. Sex can help you forget your misery and loneliness, can make you happy.' All of a sudden he became so talkative and so piteous that I was touched. I felt sorry for him and let him have his way. He was like a wild beast, even bit and pinched me, and he wouldn't let me go until after midnight. But it was too late for me to return to my place by myself, so I slept in his living room. He wanted me to share his bed, but I refused. I stole out of his apartment at daybreak.*"

Nan remained silent, not knowing what to say. She had gone to Heng's bedroom of her own accord, though no doubt he had planned to seduce her. Her story upset Nan, as he realized that those who were wounded would in turn wound others. It was hard for him to imagine that Heng, a timid man in appearance, could be so bold and so vile.

"*What should I do?*" Yafang asked him.

"*I don't know.*"

"*If this had taken place back home, I could've asked my brother and his friends to beat him up, but here I don't know anybody. In fact, I've told only you what happened. You're a good man I can trust. Tell me, do you think he raped me?*"

Amazed, Nan massaged the corners of his eyes with his fingertips, then put down his hand and said, "*In reality he did, but it will be hard to prove because you went to the movies with him and entered his bedroom. He can say you two had a date and the sex was consensual. It will be your story against his story.*"

She sobbed again, this time louder. Nan put his hand on her shoulder and whispered, "*Don't be so sad. In this place we have to be tough, and have to endure a lot of humiliation. Sometimes you even have to swallow a tooth knocked off your gum.*"

"*But I never thought my fellow countryman would . . . do . . . do this to me!*" she panted.

"*A man like him, not daring to hurt whites or blacks, can only turn on the Chinese.*" He removed his hand from her shoulder and sighed.

"*Can you come and stay with me tonight?*" she asked, and her eyes dimmed. "*I feel so lonely, also frightened. Nobody cares about me here. My roommates are not in tonight and the apartment feels deserted. Please come with me. I'll be nice to you.*"

"*Yafang, you're too emotional to think clearly. You're a good woman and will recover from this. I can't go to your place tonight. That will amount to taking advantage of you, and later you'll despise me.*"

She nodded, her head hanging low. "*You misunderstood me. I meant to invite you to stay in our living room. I'd just want to have someone in my apartment. I'm scared.*"

"*Forgive me for what I said then, but I can't come with you.*"

"*I understand.*"

"*Don't tell others about what happened to you unless you absolutely trust them. If you can't help it, call home and talk to your siblings.*"

"That I can't do. They'll tell my parents. So far I've always told them everything is excellent here."

"Then you can call me if you want to talk."

"Thanks. I might."

She got off at Kingston-Throop avenues, dragging her feet away as if her body were suddenly too heavy for her.

That night Nan reviewed Yafang's story in his mind. He felt low and somewhat regretted not having gone with her, but he feared he might get entangled with her too deeply. His life was already a quagmire. At this point he didn't want to be involved with another woman, and he had to concentrate on his own survival and that of his family. The more he thought, the more tormented he was by the notion Pingping had often expressed, namely that it was more dangerous to mix with your own people than with strangers. Yafang's trouble proved that. Many of their compatriots here were desperate and wouldn't hesitate to harm one another. In Heng Chen's case, there must have been more to it than just taking advantage of Yafang. His wife's betrayal might have turned him into a misogynist. No, not exactly. He obviously still lusted after women. Perhaps he was so desperate and so cornered that he couldn't help but move fast to seduce a young woman. But afraid of lawsuits and retaliation, he could only prey on a new arrival from their native land.

Yafang never phoned Nan. At work she was polite to him but remained aloof. Nan knew he must have hurt her pride, and she might have felt he had left her in the lurch. He noticed that she talked a lot with Aimin and Chinchin. Several times he caught her wistful eyes glancing at him, but whenever he joined their conversation, she'd turn taciturn. She seemed to avoid speaking to him, though she did tell him that she very much enjoyed the issues of *New Lines* he had given her.

12

MR. LIU called and said his wife, Shaoya, had completed a short story. He wondered whether *New Lines* could use it. If they could, he would send it along right away. Nan told him, "*By all means, we'd love to see it. What's it about?*"

"*About how hard a Chinese woman works in an underground sweatshop in New York.*"

"*That's good. We probably can run it.*"

"*Should I mail it to you?*"

"*No need. I'm going to the print center tomorrow morning, and I can stop by and pick it up. That will save you the postage.*"

"*Thank you for your thoughtfulness, Nan. I'll see you then.*" Mr. Liu sounded tired, as though he'd lost some of his voice.

Nan told Bao about Shaoya's story. They both believed they should publish it provided she was willing to resume her pen name, Purple Lilac; yet they couldn't make the final decision until they had read it. Bao kept saying this was a good sign: some fiction might bolster the circulation of the journal.

The next morning Nan went to the Lius'. It took him a good while to find their apartment, because he wandered into a neighboring tenement that looked identical. Finally, as he was approaching the correct entrance, he heard a woman screaming in Chinese, but he couldn't make out her words. A black man ran out of the stairwell and almost barreled into Nan, who stepped aside to let him pass. The front of the man's canary yellow pullover bore the large words SICK OF IT ALL! He nodded at Nan and sauntered away. Nan went to unit 127, and the female voice was intelligible now—it was Shaoya's.

"I've worked myself half to death to make the money while you just threw it away right and left," she shouted.

"I didn't mean to," came Mr. Liu's tamed voice.

"You must pay it back."

"You know I'm broke. If I had any money, you could have it all."

"Stop playing the stock market! Do you hear me?"

"Life is a risk. We—"

"Shut up! Just promise me never to do it again."

Should Nan go in? He decided to knock on the door. Mr. Liu answered and was surprised to see him. Then the old man grimaced, saying, *"Come in, please."* He spread out his arm as if ushering Nan to a meeting.

"Sorry, I understand this might not be a convenient time," Nan said.

"Don't worry. We're just having a small exchange of words. Right, dear?" he asked Shaoya, who still looked incensed, her face dark.

She said to Nan as if he were an old friend, *"He dabbled in stocks with the sweat money I made. Yesterday alone he lost more than two thousand dollars."*

"All right, all right," said her husband. *"The stock market is like a battlefield where it's normal to lose or win. It highly depends on luck. Right, Nan?"*

Nan was taken aback, totally ignorant of stocks. He forced himself to answer, *"That must be true. Losses and gains take place every day."*

"But he shouldn't have run the risk in the first place," she said. *"Heaven knows how hard I've worked at the gift store. Last week I put in fifty-eight hours, and my legs got swollen every night when I came back. But he stayed home playing ducks and drakes with the money I made."*

"All right, I won't do it again," said her husband.

Nan got the story and Shaoya's agreement to resume her pen name. On his way back he mulled over the scene at the Lius'. He was surprised that the old man would speculate in stocks. Everyone assumed that the Lius were poor, but Mr. Liu had just lost thousands of dollars. How could that be possible? Had he accepted some financial aid on the sly? Probably. Otherwise he wouldn't have squandered money that way.

On second thought, Nan was unsure of his reasoning. Mr. Liu had already established his image as an independent man; if he had taken money from someone, word would surely have come out, since the exile community was small and all eyes were focused on the funds available for the dissidents. No, the old man could hardly have accepted any financial aid without being noticed. Nan realized that Mr. Liu's apparent self-reliance was based mainly on his wife's hard work and sacrifice.

13

BAO knew a famous poet, Sam Fisher, who lived in the Village. He had invited Fisher to be on the honorary board of *New Lines* and the poet had agreed. The journal listed his name, together with several others, on the inside of its back cover. Bao also requested poems from Fisher, who was so generous that he said he'd give him three or four. One Sunday morning Bao and Nan set out for the poet's place to get the poems.

Fisher lived in a yellow-brick building on West Tenth Street. He greeted Bao and Nan with a little bow, his arm opened toward the inside of his apartment. He looked sleepy, but his droopy eyes were intense, as if they could bore into your mind when he peered at you. His crown was entirely bald, yet the hair at his temples curved upward like two tiny horns. His home was rather crowded, the walls lined with bookcases and many large photographs, some of which showed naked young men in different postures. One displayed a teenage boy sitting on his haunches and holding his erected member with his hand as if masturbating. Sam Fisher was also an accomplished photographer, selling his pictures to collectors regularly. In addition, he was a Zen Buddhist. On the wall of the corridor hung a long horn, the type used at Tibetan temples. He led the visitors into the living room, which smelled bosky and had a shiny floor, and then he called to his boyfriend to brew tea.

To Nan's surprise, a young Chinese man stepped in with a tray that held a clay teapot and four cups. "This is Min Niu, from Chang-sha," Fisher introduced him to the guests.

They greeted his boyfriend in Mandarin, and then Nan resumed speaking English with Sam. He observed the young man pouring tea.

Min was rather effeminate and had a smart face with a smooth, hairless chin. He must have been in his mid-twenties. How could he and Sam be lovers? Sam must have been at least thirty years older than he was.

On the glass coffee table lay two biographies of Sam Fisher, one almost twice as thick as the other. Sipping the piping hot jasmine tea, Bao pointed at the books and asked Sam, "Which is more true?"

"Neither," Sam said. "This one is from a Marxist point of view, and that one is Freudian. They're interesting, but the man they describe is not me." He laughed, a sparkle in his eyes. He got up and went into his study.

Nan turned to Min Niu. "*How long have you been in America?*"

"*Since last autumn.*"

"*What do you do?*"

"*I'm a graduate student at NYU.*"

"*Studying science?*"

"*No, Asian history.*"

"*Really? What period?*"

"*I'm not sure yet. Probably I'll write a thesis on homosexuality in ancient China.*"

Sam returned with a few sheets of paper and handed them to Bao, saying, "You can use these."

Bao glanced through them as if able to read English while his eyes brightened. He said, "Thank for your help."

"Your poems will make a huge difference to our journal," Nan added.

Sam nodded without speaking. Someone knocked on the door, and Min went to answer it. In came a tall young man with Beatles-cut hair and high cheekbones. "Hey, come and meet my friends," Sam shouted, waving at the new arrival.

"Dick Harrison," the man introduced himself, and shook hands with Bao and Nan. He sat down across from Sam, and Min put a cup in front of him. As Min was about to pour tea, Dick stopped him and asked Sam, "Aren't we going out?"

"Yes, we're going to have lunch at Lai Lai." He turned to Bao and Nan. "Let's go out together, okay?"

Min whispered in Chinese, "*He's in a sunny mood today.*"

"What did he say about me?" Sam asked.

"You're high-spirited," said Nan.

"Yes, I am happy. Let's go out for lunch."

"I have homework to do, Sam," Min said. "I can't join you."

"Stay home, then. We'll go without you."

After Nan called Ding's Dumplings and told Chinchin he'd be an hour late, the four of them went out of the building and headed east. As they passed a small bookstore called Smart Readers, a young woman with penciled eyebrows waved at Sam and cried, "Hey, Mr. Fisher, how are you doing?"

"I'm well."

She blew him a kiss and turned away, pulling a cart loaded with used books. Then a young man with a widow's peak stepped out of the bookstore, and at the sight of Sam, he said, "Wow, Mr. Fisher! Please wait a sec. Let me go in and buy a book of yours. Can you autograph it for me?"

"All right."

The man rushed back into the store while the four of them stood waiting. "Well, I'm often stopped on the street," Sam told Bao and Nan, apparently amused. His hands hung against his abdomen, his fingers interlaced.

In no time the man returned with a volume of Sam's poetry entitled *Oh—Oh—Oh—*, his thumb in between the cover and the title page. "Please sign this for me, will you? This will make my day."

"Sure." Sam took the felt-tip the man handed him and began inscribing. Nan craned to see him drawing a Buddha with a drumlike belly. Next Sam put several stars around the Buddha's head and wrote "Ha Ha Ha!" Then with a flourish he signed his name below the figure.

The man looked at the drawing and the signature. "This is awesome! Thank you." He held out his hand and Sam shook it.

They went on their way to Lai Lai on Sixth Avenue, which Dick told them was a noodle house Sam loved. Sam walked with his hands in his pants pockets and every once in a while kicked something on the sidewalk: a beer can, or a pebble, or a cigarette pack, or a paper cup. After another turn they arrived at the eatery, but before they could enter, an overweight man greeted Sam. "Mr. Fisher, I enjoy your new book. I'm a big fan."

"So," Sam looked annoyed, "you want me to fuck you in the ass?"

"No, no, please." The man backed away, but turned his head to smile at Sam.

Nan was flabbergasted by Sam's words. Dick explained, "That's Sam. People know him well and won't be offended."

"Damn it," Sam grunted. "I just don't want to be stopped every five minutes. If he'd bought my book, that would've been different."

They all laughed and went into Lai Lai.

14

THE NOODLE HOUSE was full of people. A young waitress, looking Vietnamese, piloted them into an inner room that had only two
tables in it. She asked Sam with a knowing smile, "What would you
like today?"

"Ask my friends first," Sam said.

"Sure." She turned to Bao. "What will you have?"

"Shogun Noodle."

Nan ordered the same; not having eaten the Japanese noodle
before, he wanted to try it. Dick and Sam chose Pad Thai.

While waiting for their food, they talked about religion. Sam said
he knew the Dalai Lama personally, and in fact his master was a distant cousin of His Holiness. "Do you practice Buddhism?" Nan
asked him.

"I meditate every day."

"We go to Ann Arbor every fall," Dick put in.

"Why?" Bao asked.

Sam smiled mysteriously. "My master's temple is there, so we go
there to pray every year."

"We also listen to our master preach," added Dick.

The noodle and the Pad Thai came, giving off a spicy scent. Nan
was fascinated by their involvement with the Buddhists. He spooned
a shrimp out of the soup and took a bite. It tasted fresh but a bit rubbery. He asked Sam, "Why do you study Buddhism?"

"It can calm me down. It also helps my constipation."

Nan burst out laughing, while Bao looked bewildered. Dick said,
"It can also enlighten the mind."

"Does your master impose any restriction on your life?" asked Nan.

"No, we're free," Sam said. "You can do anything in our branch of Buddhism. Drugs, sex, marriage, alcohol, you name it, anything but violence."

"We're a radical group," Dick said, "so lots of people are against us."

"I don't give a fuck about what they think of us." Sam thrust a bundle of rice noodles into his mouth. "Do you know when Tibet will be open to tourists?" he asked Nan.

"I have no idea."

"I hope I can go there next year. I've been trying to get permission from the Chinese consulate, but every time those bureaucrats turn me down."

"You must be on their list," Nan said.

"I'm a crazy Jew, on every government's list."

"Including zer U.S.?"

"You bet. My FBI file must be able to fill a whole cart. I'm an enemy of authorities."

Bao broke in, "If you go to China, you know what happen?"

"I know, some undercover agent will put a bullet into the back of my head and the government will claim I committed suicide."

They all cracked up. When lunch was over, Sam paid for everyone. "I make more than the three of you put together," he said, refusing to go Dutch.

It was getting cloudier and looked like rain. As they were saying good-bye at a street corner, Sam embraced Nan and gave him a loud smack on the cheek. Nan was surprised and a little embarrassed. Dick Harrison wrote down his phone number for Nan and said he might send along some poems too. They promised to see each other again.

Nan and Bao headed for the subway station. "*Sam is really fond of you,*" Bao said, and squinted at Nan.

"*Come now, I'm not gay. I'm drawn to women, can't stop thinking about them.*"

Despite that unsettling kiss, Nan was quite moved by their meeting with Sam Fisher, in whom he had seen the free spirit of a poet who wasn't afraid of anything or anybody, a complete individual. Nan hadn't read Sam's poetry, but he liked his personality. If he were gay, he wouldn't have minded seeing Sam more often.

Bao told him more about Min Niu. Min had been an English major at Hunan Normal University. He wrote to Sam to express his admiration for his poetry, and then a relationship developed between them through correspondence. As his sponsor in the United States, Sam helped him get his visa and even paid tuition for him at NYU. Min came and lived with Sam, working as the manager of his home. In fact, he also cooked for Sam and sometimes served as his secretary. Bao had once eaten dinner in Sam's apartment, and Min had made four dishes and a large bowl of soup within an hour. And everything he cooked that evening was delicious. Sam also paid Min a decent salary.

Nan was impressed, saying, "*What a lucky fellow Min Niu is.*"

"*I think you can replace him if you want.*" Bao winked at Nan.

"*No, I'm dying to work for a pretty woman poet as famous as Sam Fisher. Do you happen to know anyone?*"

"*What makes you think I'll provide the information gratis?*"

They both laughed. An old woman walking by turned to look at them. They stopped laughing and went on chatting about the poetry world in New York.

15

PINGPING phoned Nan at Ding's Dumplings and begged him to come back immediately. She had bickered with Heidi and was thinking of moving out. What had happened was that Nathan couldn't find his new calculator and suspected that Pingping had taken it upstairs for Taotao to use. Heidi went up and asked Pingping, "Do you have Nathan's calculator?" "No," Pingping said. She took Heidi to Nathan's room on the second floor and found the calculator lying on the windowsill behind his desk. Then she told Heidi to her face that however poor she was, she wouldn't steal.

Her words rendered Heidi speechless, for she knew that was true. Many times Pingping had come upon banknotes and coins when laundering their clothes, and without fail she had given the money back to Heidi, sometimes even thirty or forty dollars. Yet as Pingping's boss, Heidi wouldn't apologize and just went away without a word. That angered Pingping more, and she planned to quit, though she hadn't mentioned it to Heidi yet.

Nan told her on the phone not to think of moving out right now, because Taotao couldn't find a better school. They could not afford to leave Woodland until the school year was over. "*I'll come back soon, all right?*" he said to her.

"*How soon?*"

"*I've got to make arrangements before I go back. I can't just leave without notifying my boss.*"

"*All right, come back as quickly as you can.*"

For a whole afternoon Nan was absentminded at work and even nicked his fingertip while dicing a cucumber. He was angry with Heidi, who seemed to have mistreated Pingping because he wasn't around. Probably she feared that his wife and son might stay at her home forever, so she created some difficulties for them to chase them out.

Toward the end of the day, Nan told Chinchin that he wouldn't come for the rest of the week because there was an emergency at home and he had to go back. His fellow workers all thought he was just taking a few days off and would return the next week. He wanted them to think that way too, since he wouldn't burn his bridges.

But he decided to quit his job at *New Lines*. He didn't enjoy the editorial work and was afraid that sooner or later, Bao would ask him to translate his entire memoir if he continued editing the journal.

The next morning he went downstairs to explain his decision to Bao. As he was approaching the door of their bedroom, he heard Wendy berating her boyfriend. She sounded furious today. "You're just a sponge!" she cried.

"Don't cawl me that!" yelled Bao.

"You live like a parasite. I can't stand you anymore. Get out."

"It's just couple dollars."

"A couple of dollars? I only get seven hundred a month from Social Security, but you spent more than two hundred on alcohol, not to mention the phone bills you ran up. How dare you call that amount just a couple of dollars?"

"But you have rent money."

"That goes to the mortgage. Stop arguing with me. I've made up my mind and want you to move out."

"Okay, okay, I go out your house."

"Good. Bring your gay friend along."

"Damn you, Nan not gay!"

"Don't tell me that. I know what he is."

"You don't want to marry me no more?"

"I'm sick of you. You've just been using me to get a green card. I can't help you with that anymore. Get out."

"Okay, I don't carry old bag like you," he said calmly.

Nan knocked on their door. He was incensed by Wendy's remark and glared at her. She was taken aback by his fierce eyes and turned to the bay window. Outside, a few blackbirds were fluttering on the crown of a sycamore, and one of them was holding a strip of toilet tissue in its beak. Nan noticed a reddish patch rising on Wendy's cheek. She used to be friendly to him, and he had helped her repair the front door and put up the picket fence in the backyard, but all of a sudden she had begun bad-mouthing him. This hurt him to the quick.

"*I'm going home,*" he told Bao.

"*You mean for good?*"

"*Yes. My family has some trouble, and I have to go back without delay.*"

"*Well, I'm going to move out soon. Sick of this rotten cunt.*" He pointed at his girlfriend.

Nan glanced at Wendy, who didn't understand Bao's curse. Then the two of them talked briefly about the journal. Bao hadn't gotten the funding for the next issue, so this might be the time for Nan to leave after all. In his heart Nan couldn't help but despise Bao. If he was going to become an artist, he would be a different type. He'd be a self-sufficient man first. Now it was high time for him to start his life afresh. New York wasn't a place for a man like him; he had to return to his family and struggle together with them.

16

ON THE PHONE Pingping hadn't told Nan the whole story, which involved Taotao and Livia as well. A few days earlier the two children had been doing homework together in the kitchen while Pingping was outside the house, fixing the lid on the wooden trash bin. The girl and the boy were quite close by now, and Livia often claimed that Taotao was one of her best friends, though he still wouldn't join her pals when they were over. Several times Pingping told her son not to get too attached to Livia, yet the boy couldn't help but turn ebullient whenever the girl was around. Heidi didn't like Taotao that much, though she admitted he was bright and handsome. Bending over the trash bin, Pingping hammered two nails into the holes on the hinge affixed to the lid, then opened and shut it a few times to make sure it was no longer loose. The job done, she turned to go back into the kitchen. But then she overheard the two children and stopped to listen.

"I just don't think he'll come back," Livia said in a serious tone of voice.

"That's not true. My dad is just working in New York."

"Tell you what, grown-ups always lie."

"My dad isn't a liar."

"How do you know he isn't?"

"My mom told me so."

"He lies to your mom too. He walked out on both of you, that's what I heard."

"You're a big liar!"

"Don't be mad at me. I don't want you to lose your dad just because I don't have my dad."

"You're not my friend anymore."

"C'mon, I didn't mean to hurt your feelings. I just told you what my mom and her friends said."

Pingping stepped in and said to the girl, "They're just buncha miserable rich ladies, have nothing else to do. They just want everyone else have bad luck."

Livia gasped and winced. Pingping went on, "Don't believe that kinda crap. Nan is learning to be chef. Don't you eat the wonton he cooked?"

"I did. It was delicious, better than anything I ate in any Chinese restaurant." Livia seemed to relax a little.

"He's away just for short time."

"He told me so too," Taotao added. "He said we'd open our own business in the future."

Livia dropped her eyes, misting up. She said to Pingping, "My mom's friends all say you and Nan split up. My mom is afraid you'll stay with us forever. To be honest, I won't mind." That was true. Livia was fond of Pingping, who was the only one who had contradicted Dr. Hornburger's prognosis that the girl wouldn't grow taller than five feet. Even her mother believed that Kraut.

"They just gossip," Pingping said. "Nan won't walk out from Taotao and me. He's good man."

Despite saying that, Pingping got more agitated than ever. She could see the logic behind the rumor. What if Nan hit it off with some woman in New York who could win his heart? Wouldn't he start an affair and then abandon Taotao and her? If this happened back in China she might not be devastated, because she was a complete person there and could do anything by herself. But here she depended on him for many things, and Taotao needed him as his dad. Indeed, before they had decided to immigrate, she had even planned to divorce Nan after they returned to China, where she would raise their child by herself. That was why for years she had been determined to make money. But in this place she couldn't live separately from Nan, and at all costs she must hold the family together, to give Taotao a safe, loving home. What's more, recently she somehow could no longer bear the thought that Nan might go and live with another woman. She knew she'd get jealous like crazy if that happened. So now she must have him back. The longer he stayed in New York, the more trouble might start.

17

NAN came back and talked with Pingping, who agreed they shouldn't rush to move out. To their amazement, Heidi had made up her mind to dismiss them, although she would let them stay another half year. She said, "I'll need someone for house-sitting this summer anyway. But after August I won't be able to use your help anymore. Are we clear about that?" Her face was wooden. The Wus thanked her for offering them the extended period.

Nan wondered if he should return to New York, but decided not to, now that he could cook like a professional. He called Howard to apprise him of his decision. His boss said he understood and would send him his last week's pay. That moved Nan, who had never thought he could get the wages.

That night he and Pingping went to bed together, but he found all his condoms punctured or cut by scissors. *"That must be our son's doing,"* she said, tittering.

Nan didn't reproach Taotao, realizing that the boy must have resented his absence from home. He smiled and said to his wife, *"How could he understand sex? I knew nothing about it until I was thirteen."*

"Here children reach puberty earlier. He has read some small books on biology and knows a lot about how babies are made."

"Still, it's too early for him to be so interested."

"It doesn't matter, as long as we love him and raise him well."

He said no more and went on making love to Pingping, who soon began to come. But she dared not scream for fear of waking up their son. She murmured tearfully while licking Nan's chest, saying she couldn't live without him. If only she could keep him home forever!

The next day Nan began to look through job ads in the *Boston Globe* and *World Journal*. This time he wanted to be a cook. Two Chinese restaurants interviewed him, and the Jade Café in Natick hired him as a sous-chef. He was to start the following Monday.

PART THREE

1

ONE DAY in the early summer of 1991, Nan came across an advertisement in *World Journal* for the sale of a restaurant in Georgia. The asking price was $25,000; the owner claimed that its annual business surpassed $100,000, more than enough to make a decent profit. "Perfect for your family," the ad declared. Nan brought back the page of the newspaper and showed it to Pingping. They talked about it late into the night.

For months they had been thinking about where to go. Should they stay in the Boston area? Or should they migrate to another place where the cost of living was lower?

By now they had saved more money, having worked nonstop without spending a penny on rent for the past three years. They had two CDs in the bank, $50,000 altogether. Yet even with this much cash, they still couldn't possibly buy a home or business in Massachusetts, where everything was expensive. Nan earned ten dollars an hour at the Jade Café; wages like that wouldn't qualify him for a loan from the bank. He'd heard that some Chinese restaurants in Georgia, Florida, Mississippi, and Alabama were quite affordable. Nan had been following newspaper ads, which seemed to confirm that. After working at the Jade Café for four months, he was already an experienced cook.

But what about Taotao's schooling? They decided this wouldn't be an obstacle if they left the Boston area, because Pingping could teach him math while Nan could help him with his English. Despite the mistakes he made when he spoke the language, Nan knew English grammar like the back of his hand. The crux of the problem was whether they'd be willing to go to the Deep South, where they had heard that racial prejudice was still rampant, and where the Ku Klux Klan was active and even dared to march in the glare of daylight. On the other hand, they had also read articles, written by Chinese immigrants living in the South, that bragged about the quality of life there. One woman in Louisiana boasted that her family had sixty-four oaks and maples in their backyard, something they could never have dreamed of when they had lived in northern California. Others even praised the climate in the South, which was similar to that in their home provinces back in China, not dry in the summer and with no snow, to say nothing of blizzards, in the winter.

That night, the Wus decided to contact the owner of the Georgia restaurant. When Nan called the next morning, a feeble male voice answered the phone. On hearing of Nan's interest, the man turned animated and identified himself as Mr. Wang, the owner. "*I can guarantee you that you'll make good money here,*" he told Nan.

"*Then why are you selling the business?*"

"*My wife and I are getting old and can't run it anymore. Too much work. Sometimes we go back to Taiwan to visit friends and family, and it's hard to find someone to take care of this place when we're away.*"

"*How long have you owned it?*"

"*More than twenty years. Truth be told, it's an ideal family business, very stable. If we could manage it, we'd never sell it.*"

"*But the economy is in recession now, and lots of restaurants have folded in Massachusetts.*"

"*I know. Some people here have lost their businesses too. We have fewer customers these days, but we're doing okay. Believe me, the economy will come around. Like I said, this place is very stable.*"

Nan asked him about the living environment of the Atlanta suburbs, which Mr. Wang assured him was absolutely congenial and safe for raising children. He had only heard of the Klansmen but never seen them in the flesh. Besides, there were thousands upon thousands of Asian immigrants living in the Atlanta area, which, he claimed, was almost like virgin land just open for settlement. In fact, Gwinnett County, where Mr. Wang was living, was one of the fastest growing counties in the whole country, and every two years a new elementary or middle school had to be added. Still, all classrooms were bursting at the seams, and on every campus some students had to attend class in trailers. All these nuggets of information were encouraging. Nan wanted to go down to Georgia and take a look at the restaurant. He told Mr. Wang he would come as soon as he got permission from his boss at the Jade Café.

Pingping grew excited after Nan described to her his conversation with Mr. Wang. If this deal worked out, it would mean they'd have their own business and eventually their own home. She urged Nan to set out for Georgia that very week. He should pay a deposit if he believed that the restaurant was in good condition and the area adequate for living. He should also look around some to see how much an average house cost in the vicinity. As long as there were Asian immigrants living there, the place should be safe.

2

THREE DAYS LATER Nan set out for the South. He followed I-95 all the way to Virginia and switched to I-85 after Richmond. He drove for fourteen hours until he was too exhausted to continue and had to stop for the night. He slept in his car in the parking lot of a rest area near Ridgeway, North Carolina. Before sunrise, when tree leaves were drenched with heavy dew and a thin fog was lifting, he resumed his trip. Entering Durham, North Carolina, he caught sight of a burgundy motorcycle, which reminded him of the Yamaha scooter the wild Beina used to ride. He floored the gas pedal, but his car couldn't go fast enough. In no time the motorcyclist's white helmet, jiggling and dodging, disappeared in the traffic ahead. Nan sighed and shook his head vigorously to force the image of his ex-girlfriend out of his mind.

Because of the construction along the road, it took him almost a whole day to cross the Carolinas, and not until evening did he arrive at Chamblee, Georgia, a suburban town northeast of Atlanta. He checked in at Double Happiness Inn on Buford Highway, managed by a Korean man who spoke Mandarin fluently but with a harsh accent. Tired out, Nan showered and went to bed without dinner, although Pingping had packed a tote bag of food for him—instant noodles, a challah, two cans of wieners, fish jerky, macadamia cookies, dehydrated duck, pistachios, clementines, as if none of these things were available in Georgia. She had also wedged in a coffeepot, with which he could boil water for oatmeal and tea.

The next morning, Nan went to see Mr. Wang. The Gold Wok was in Lilburn, a town fifteen miles northeast of Atlanta. It was at the western end of a half-deserted shopping center called Beaver Hill

Plaza, where several businesses and a small supermarket clustered together. Among them were a fabric store, a Laundromat, a photo studio, a pawnshop, and a fitness center. A few suites were marked by FOR RENT signs, which gave Nan mixed feelings. The vacancies implied that it would be easy enough for the restaurant to renew its lease, but it might also mean there wasn't a lot of business.

Mr. Wang, tall with withered limbs and a scanty beard, turned out to be much older than Nan had expected. His back was so hunched that he seemed afflicted with kyphosis, and his neck and arms were dappled with liver spots. As he spoke to Nan, he kept massaging his right knee as if he suffered from painful arthritis. He made an effort to straighten up but remained bent. He grimaced, saying that his chronic back pain had grown more unbearable each year. Somehow Nan couldn't help but wonder whether he had a prolapsed anus as well, since both afflictions, he'd learned, were common among people in the restaurant business. The old man and his wife were glad to see Nan and eager to show him the place. Nan went into the kitchen and checked the cooking range, the ovens, the storage room, the freezers, the dishwasher, the toilets, the light fixtures. He was pleased that all the equipment was in working order, though the dining room looked rather shabby. In it there were six tables and eight booths covered in brown Naugahyde, and the walls were almost entirely occupied by murals of horses, some galloping, some grazing, some rearing, and some frolicking with their tails tossed up. From a corner in the back floated up a Mongolian melody, which was supposed to match the theme of the horses on the walls. The Wangs had hired only one waitress, a dark-complexioned young woman from Malaysia named Tammie, who spoke both Cantonese and English but no Mandarin. Nan opened the menu, which offered more than two dozen items, mostly for takeout, none of which cost more than five dollars. Although it was unlikely to generate $100,000 worth of business a year as the ad claimed, the restaurant was in good trim.

As Nan was coming out from the kitchen, a young man wearing aviator glasses and a gray jersey strolled in, clamping a toothpick between his lips. Nan stepped aside to let him pass. Without a word the man went straight in. Presently Nan heard the brisk ring of a spatula scraping a pan.

"*Like I told you, this place is perfect for a family like yours,*" Mr. Wang said to Nan.

"*Does your wife speak English?*" asked Mrs. Wang, a waistless and short-limbed woman wearing a seersucker shirt.

"*Yes, she can do anything. By the way, I haven't seen lots of customers. There aren't many, are there?*"

"*Tuesday is slow,*" she replied.

"*Can you cook?*" Mr. Wang asked Nan.

"*I'm a chef.*"

"*Excellent. That will make all the difference. I can guarantee you that you'll get rich soon.*"

"*Well, I'm not so sure.*"

"*Look, I pay the chef, the fellow in the kitchen, eight dollars an hour. I used to cook myself, but I'm too old to do that anymore. If you and your wife both work here, all the profits will go into your own pocket.*"

"*You use a chef?*" Nan was amazed, not having imagined this place could make enough to pay that kind of wages. He had taken the man wearing glasses for a family member or relative of the Wangs.

"*Yes. You can go ask him how much I pay him. That's why we can't keep this place any longer—most profits end up in his wallet. It's like I'm just his job provider.*"

This was encouraging. If they could afford to hire a cook, the restaurant must be doing quite well.

The old couple invited him to stay for lunch, saying this was the minimum they should do for a guest from far away. Nan accepted the offer and, together with Mr. Wang, sat down at a table. He poured hot tea for his host and then for himself, and they went on talking about life in this place. The old man assured him that Gwinnett County had excellent public schools. A girl in his neighborhood had gone to Berkmar High and was at Duke now, a premed. Nan was impressed. Mr. Wang also told him that compared with the other counties in the Atlanta area, Gwinnett had a much lower realty tax. That was why many recent immigrants from Asia and Latin America preferred to live here.

Ten minutes later, Mrs. Wang stepped over gingerly and put before them a lacquered tray containing a bowl of pot-stickers, a plate of sautéed scallops and shrimp mixed with snow peas and bamboo shoots, a jar of plain rice, two pairs of connected chopsticks, and two empty bowls. *"You can have a bite if you want,"* she told her husband.

"Sure, I'm sort of hungry." But the old man just picked up a pot-sticker, saying to Nan that he didn't eat lunch nowadays.

Nan broke his chopsticks and began eating. He wasn't impressed by the quality of the food. The pot-stickers had the stale taste of over-used frying oil.

Then he asked Mr. Wang about the lease, the various taxes, the cost of utilities, and the service of the local distributor that delivered vegetables, meats, seafood, condiments. Meanwhile, three customers showed up. One ordered a takeout, and the other two, a middle-aged couple, were led by Tammie to a corner booth. The wide-eyed waitress kept glancing at Nan as if she wanted to speak to him but withheld her words.

After lunch, Nan took leave of the Wangs, saying he would come again the next morning. He tootled through several residential areas in Lilburn and Norcross, mainly along Lawrenceville and Buford highways and Jimmy Carter Boulevard, and he saw numerous homes for sale. Most of them were new and had four bedrooms and a brick front, priced between $120,000 and $130,000, but outside those subdivisions developed recently or still under construction were older houses, some priced even below $80,000. He hadn't expected that a brick ranch would sell for under $100,000. In the Boston area, a three-bedroom house of this kind would cost at least three times as much.

Nan's car had no air-conditioning, and time and again he drank Pepsi from a bottle lying on the passenger seat. It was hot and humid, waves of heat lapping his face whenever he stepped out of the car. It was so muggy that his breathing became a little labored. For the first time in his life he physically understood the word *humid*. Back in Boston, when people said "It's so humid," he hadn't been able to feel it. Now at last his body could tell the difference between dry heat and damp heat. Yet the sultry weather shouldn't be a problem if his family lived here, because there was air-conditioning indoors everywhere. Back in China, he had once stayed in Jinan City for a month in midsummer; whenever he walked the streets, his shirt and pants would be soaked with sweat, and it had been hot indoors as well as outdoors. There you simply couldn't avoid sweltering in the dog days' scorching heat, but this Georgian humidity and heat shouldn't be a big deal. More heartening was that there were indeed many Asian immigrants living in the northeastern suburbs of Atlanta. Within four or five miles, Nan saw one Chinese and two Korean churches. Without question this was a good, safe place.

That night he called his wife and told her what he had seen and heard. Pingping was so impressed that she urged him to clinch the deal with Mr. Wang the next day, paying a deposit that should be less than twenty percent of the agreed price. Also, she warned him not to haggle too much. One or two thousand dollars wouldn't make much difference as long as the business was solid.

Before hanging up, she said in English, "I miss you, I love you, Nan!" Somehow her words sounded more natural from a thousand miles away. He hadn't heard her speak to him so passionately for a long time.

"I love you too." Despite saying that, he wasn't sure of his emotions. He still didn't have intense feelings for her, but he felt attached to her and understood that they had become more or less inseparable—neither of them could have survived without the other in this land, and more important, their child needed them. If they moved to Georgia, it would mean they'd have to live more like husband and wife from now on. In a sense he wasn't displeased with that prospect, since whenever he was with Pingping, he felt at peace. Still, these days his thoughts had often turned to Beina, who seemed to accompany him wherever he went, enticing him into reveries. When he closed his eyes at night, her vivacious face often emerged, as if she were teasing him or eager to talk with him. Then he'd again smell the grassy scent of her hair. If only he could love Pingping similarly so that she could replace that woman in his mind, who was, he knew, merely a flighty coquette.

Late the next morning, toward eleven, he went to the Gold Wok again, but he didn't immediately go in. He parked a short distance from the restaurant and stayed in the car, waiting to see how many customers would appear. It was drizzling, the powdery rain blurring the windshield. It wasn't hot, so he didn't mind staying in the parking lot for a while, listening to a preacher on the radio. The man was speaking about a verse from Matthew, expounding on the necessity of "fresh wineskins for new wine." Nan was fascinated by his eloquence and passion despite the man's oddly hoarse, croaking voice. Meanwhile, in less than half an hour, five people turned up at the Gold Wok, three of whom appeared to be Mexican workers from the construction site nearby. They looked like regulars, and when they came out, they each held a tall cup of soft drink besides the food in Styrofoam boxes.

When Nan told the Wangs that he wanted to buy the restaurant, they looked relieved. Then began the bargaining. Nan managed to beat down the price by $3,000 on the grounds that he didn't like the horse murals and the Formica tables in the booths. This was the first time in his life that he had ever haggled with someone, and he took great pride in the result, feeling like a real businessman. The amount he'd saved translated into 25,000 yuan, thirty times more than his annual salary back in China. Somehow, whenever Nan handled a large sum of money, he couldn't help but convert dollars into yuan in his mind, and the habit made him very frugal. At times, though, he wished he could grow out of this mind-set, because he believed that here people got rich not just by how much they saved, but more important, by how much they made, and that in America one should live like an American.

"*When will you come and take over?*" Mr. Wang asked Nan with a little chuckle.

"*Probably in a month or so.*"

"*Too long. How about two weeks?*"

"*I'll try. It shouldn't be a big problem. I'll let you know soon after I get home.*"

Nan wrote him a check for $2,200, a ten percent deposit. The Wangs asked that he keep Tammie, who had been working for them since her late teens, almost a decade by now. "*That's fine,*" Nan promised. He was going to need help anyway. Currently they paid her one dollar an hour because she kept all the tips.

That afternoon Nan hit the interstate, heading back north.

3

HE RETURNED to Woodland two days later. Pingping was over-joyed to hear about the restaurant and the Atlanta suburbs. They were both pleased to know Mr. Wang was from Taiwan, for generally speaking, the Taiwanese were more trustworthy than the main-landers, who often ignored rules and laws. The Wus knew some people who'd been swindled even by their fellow townsmen from the mainland.

One thing Nan and Pingping had forgotten to consider was where to live. Nan had noticed some apartment buildings in Norcross, a neighboring town north of Lilburn, but he hadn't brought back any information on housing. So the following day he called the Gold Wok and asked Mrs. Wang about affordable housing in the vicinity. The old woman said she was going to mail Nan an apartment book. *"There are some copies outside. They just arrived,"* she told him.

He remembered seeing a red wire rack beside the entrance to the restaurant that held several kinds of booklets and leaflets. *"Can you send it along right away?"* he asked.

"I'm going to do it today."

Everything seemed to have fallen in place, and the Wus began planning to move. Even Taotao had to decide what toys and books to take and what to donate to the thrift shop behind the town library, run by the Unitarian church.

The main difficulty was Nan's books, most of which were in the boxes stored in the small shed attached to Heidi's garage. Years ago when Nan still planned to return to China, he had collected more than forty boxes of used books, determined to establish his own library once he went back. But when they had come to stay with the

Masefields, Nan had had to leave the books behind in Watertown. He'd talked his landlord, Mr. Verdolino, into renting him a basement room for sixty-five dollars a month and had kept his three thousand volumes there for two years. Later he realized that the amount he paid for the rent would eventually buy him those books again. Ping-ping urged him to get rid of them, since he couldn't go back to China anymore. Nan took some boxes of the books to local libraries and bookstores, but no one wanted them, all telling him that the titles were too specialized. Indeed, who among general readers could use a book like Anna Akhmatova's *Complete Poems* in the Russian or Hans Morgenthau's *Politics Among Nations*? Heartbroken and having nowhere to send the books, Nan had just left the few boxes next to a bunch of trash cans on a sidewalk lined with dirty snowbanks. The following week he threw away another three boxes.

For a month afterward he felt miserable, almost ill. If only there were a way to keep those books. Try as he might, he couldn't steel himself to dump them all. Fortunately, a friend of his who was returning to China came and picked thirteen boxes from his collection. Nan helped her pack them up and even drove a van with her all the way to New Jersey to have them shipped to Tianjin City by sea. Then he persuaded Heidi to let him use a little space in her shed in which to store the remaining eleven boxes. Now, to save postage, he would have to get rid of some of them again. In America every town had a library; why should he keep hundreds of titles at home? After carefully going through them, he kept about two thirds of the books, seven boxes in all, and discarded the rest.

Everything else was easy to pack; the Wus didn't have many belongings. Pingping phoned Heidi, who was on Cape Cod with her children, to let her know of their imminent move. Heidi sounded excited and also relieved. Two days later she returned to Woodland. She gave Pingping $1,200 to buy mattresses—twelve one-hundred-dollar bills in an envelope—since the Wus couldn't take along the ones they had. She also told her to clean their attic apartment before they left. Livia had come back with her mother too, and on the way she'd bought Taotao a Rubik's Cube. Now, as the adults were talking, the girl and the boy were in the living room, Livia showing him how to work the puzzle. The girl had an appointment with her orthodontist at eleven a.m. to adjust her braces, so a few minutes later Heidi called her out, ready to go.

"Keep in touch, Taotao," said Livia as she followed her mother to the passenger van.

"Sure." The boy nodded.

"Remember, I'm your friend." She waved her thin, short-nailed hand. Her flip-flops seemed too big, pattering on the driveway.

"Sure, thanks for the cube."

The Wus waved as Heidi's van drew away. The boy returned to the living room, to the unsolved puzzle.

•

The Atlanta apartment book arrived, a thick volume containing hundreds of listings. Pingping and Nan were impressed by the rents, which were much more affordable than in the Boston area. They folded several pages that showed housing in the eastern suburbs. But to their dismay, there was only one listing in Lilburn, and that place was too pricey, so they had to look for an apartment in an adjacent town. They noticed that housing was much cheaper in some areas near Stone Mountain, a town six miles south of Lilburn in Dekalb County. Nan phoned two of those places. Without difficulty he rented a three-bedroom apartment at Peachtree Terrace, which was within Gwinnett County and, according to the map, just a fifteen-minute drive from the restaurant. Nan wanted a study for himself, hence the third bedroom. Ideally, Pingping had hoped they could walk to work, but Nan told her that unlike Boston, the city of Atlanta sprawled in every direction, one having to drive to get around, so they'd better stay at Peachtree Terrace. The rent was a reasonable $550 a month.

A UPS van came to pick up their boxes. Altogether there were thirty-five. The driver was a tall woman with a squarish jaw and a tanned face. She wore the brown uniform, the short-sleeved shirt showing her muscular arms and bulging chest. Nan helped her load the shipment and was impressed by the ease with which she lifted the heavy boxes and lodged them onto the shelves in the van. He liked to see the woman work with her sinewy hands and could feel energy radiating from her sturdy body.

When everything was loaded, she assured him that the whole

batch would arrive intact. With a ballpoint attached to a clipboard she scribbled an X at the bottom of a form for his signature, then handed the paperwork to him. He signed it and asked her to handle their boxes carefully, though he didn't reveal that the shipment contained a microwave, a roaster, a computer, even a TV set. He gave her a ten for tip, and she beamed, panting a little. She promised to stick FRAGILE labels to all their belongings when she got back to the local UPS headquarters.

What a woman, so hardy and so independent! Nan watched her hop into the brown van and pull it out of the yard.

4

ON THE MORNING of July 6, a Saturday, the Wus got up at four o'clock. Pingping had put blankets and pillows in the backseat of their car the night before. As Heidi had instructed, she checked all the doors and windows, then left the key on the kitchen table and locked the front door. It was still damp and chilly outside. She couldn't stop shivering as she walked toward their loaded Ford parked in front of the garage.

There was little traffic on I-95, and a faint mist veiled the land on both sides. The hazy air seemed stirred by the shafts of light projected by their car and was rolling by like strips of smoke. The woods on the roadside were dark and looked as solid as if they were a rocky bank. Pingping was happy and excited. Despite knowing that Nan didn't completely love her, despite getting carsick easily, she felt hopeful and safe with him. Their move to Georgia showed that he was willing to live and raise Taotao together with her. Don't mind going anywhere as long as we're together, she told herself. The more you move, the stronger you'll grow, not like a tree that can be killed if you uproot it. Sick of living under Heidi's roof. At last we can have a place for ourselves.

She looked at Nan, who seemed calm. In fact, he had been better tempered these days. He was driving steadily in spite of their old car that wobbled a little and couldn't overtake any vehicles on the road. Ahead of them, the blacktop looked endless and mysterious, yet Pingping was sure it was leading them to a new life. Deep down, she knew Nan would work hard and together they would make a decent living.

When they had passed New London, Connecticut, suddenly the

sun came out, a giant disk flaming a good part of the eastern sky. More cars appeared on the highway, and patches of ocean shimmered as they went. Pingping kept telling Taotao to look at the sun and the water, but the boy just grunted. He was too sleepy to open his eyes, dozing away all along.

Because their car was fully loaded, Nan wouldn't let Pingping behind the wheel at first. From time to time she kneaded the nape of his neck to relieve his tension. She could see that he was nervous, especially whenever a semi passed them, its powerful wake shaking their car a little. This happened more frequently as they were approaching Stamford. Yet somehow she felt peaceful. As long as the three of them were together, she wasn't afraid of restarting their life anywhere.

They didn't want to get stuck in New York City traffic, so Nan turned onto I-287 as soon as they cleared the Connecticut border. After he drove a dozen miles or so west, the Hudson River emerged, immense, serene, and as breathtaking as the ocean. A lighthouse stood on the eastern bank like a behemoth penguin gazing at the distance. Many white houses on the western shore were drenched in the sunlight and nestled in the woods on the hills along the water, against which herons and gulls were sailing and bobbing. Far away, a yacht was churning a whitish trail. Swarms of sailboats were moored in the southwest, their sails fluttering like wings. Other than those small vessels, there was no trace of disturbance on this wide and tremendous river. Near the lower end of the Tappan Zee Bridge, a red stubby boat was anchored and planted with fishing rods; two men were sitting on it, smoking and drinking beer. Nan veered into the outside lane and slowed down some so as to take in more of the view. If only he could live in a place like this, so clean and tranquil. The river, though mighty and vast, wouldn't be roughened by storms and hurricanes the way the sea was. The hills on the shore were as bright as if every treetop, though viewed from the distance, were distinguishable. What a sublime place! Who were the lucky people living in these hills? How fortunate they were to be able to enjoy the peace and quiet here. If Nan came back to this life again and could choose where to live, this would definitely be one of his choices.

"This sight beats the Yangtze," said Pingping.

"*Also the Yellow River,*" echoed Nan.

They both laughed, then Nan tooted the horn. "*Don't do that,*" Pingping said. "*You might confuse other cars.*"

Soon they entered New Jersey. It was getting hot, the wild grass on the roadside flickering in the withering breeze. Then hills appeared, most of them wooded heavily and some devoid of human traces. Pingping felt drowsy but forced herself to chat with Nan so he could remain alert. He told her to take a nap and not to worry about him, because enjoying the scenery would keep him awake.

After they turned onto I-78, the land was still rugged, and some places were crowded with houses and buildings. The Wus took a lunch break at the first rest area after the toll bridge over the Delaware River so as to avoid the gathering heat. Around two-thirty, they set off again. Taotao kept asking what crops were growing in the vast Pennsylvanian fields. His father told him they were corn and soybeans. Nan was struck by the undulating landscape, so sparsely populated that most farmhouses looked deserted. Few human beings were visible on the farms, while dappled cows with bulging udders grazed lazily in the meadows. There were also horses and colts walking or lying in the distance. The land was rich and well kept, though some pastures were enclosed by wire fences. The sight reminded Nan of his first impression when he had come to the United States six years ago—he had written to his friends in China that nature was extraordinarily generous to America; it was a place that made their native land seem overused and exhausted.

From I-78 they cruised onto I-81. Pingping and Nan began talking about what crops they'd like to grow if they had a farm of hundreds of acres. Nan thought he'd like to have an orchard of apple and pear trees, whereas Pingping thought she'd prefer a vegetable farm, which could be more profitable. "*That would be too much work,*" said Nan.

"*We're not old. We could manage it,*" she replied. "*A lot of work is done by machines here.*"

They both agreed that if they lived on a farm, they'd raise a big family and build a large house that had at least six bedrooms.

From the backseat came a little voice. "I don't want any siblings," Taotao whined in English, his hands busy working on the Rubik's Cube. His parents laughed.

"Don't worry," Nan told him. "We're just shooting zer breeze."

"Shoot what?" asked Pingping.

"Shoot zer breeze. Zat means just to chat away."

At twilight, they crossed the tip of Maryland and a little strip of West Virginia in less than forty minutes. As soon as they had passed the border between the Virginias, they stopped for the night at an Econo Lodge at Winchester. Once inside the room, Pingping started cooking noodles on her single burner while Nan, exhausted, dropped off to snooze in the bed near the window, breathing stertorously. The instant Taotao clicked on the TV, his mother told him to turn the volume down. He was watching *The Simpsons.* Whenever he cracked up in response, Pingping would say, *"Don't disturb Daddy."*

When dinner was ready, Pingping woke Nan up, saying he mustn't sleep like this for long and ought to take a shower after the meal. Groggily, he sat up and began eating the noodle soup and canned ham.

That night Nan snored thunderously, which frightened Pingping. She worried he might hurt his larynx and made him turn on his right side so as to reduce his snoring. She and Taotao slept in the other bed. Despite the noise Nan made, despite the air conditioner's whirring, mother and son did get a good night's sleep. The motel offered continental breakfast, and the Wus ate bagels with cream cheese and a plate of cantaloupe. Nan drank two cups of coffee. Then they started out to cross Virginia.

Nan loved seeing the farms and the mountains along the way. Even the animals seemed comfortable and docile in the grasslands. He asked Pingping time and again: How about settling down in Virginia? She said that would be great. What impressed him most was the openness of the land, whose immensity and abundance seemed to dwarf humans. Farmhouses with red or black roofs, barns, trucks, all looked like toys. There were few people in sight except that once in a while a stalled vehicle sat on the roadside, its driver and passengers sitting inside or nearby. Somehow Nan couldn't help but think that if he died, he'd like to be buried in such a place, so open, so unpolluted by human beings. This was indeed a pristine piece of land.

When Nan felt tired, he let Pingping take over the wheel so that he could nap. The most pleasant part of the trip was central Virginia. Toward noon a fine shower washed the temperature down, and the air became cleaner, shining softly. Everything seemed to have turned clear in the sunlight. The green hills rising ahead and moving on both sides looked impenetrable with foliage, though in the distance the massive mountains, still under the rain clouds, were indigo. Traffic was sparse on the highway, with only a few semis in view. What's more, all the automobiles seemed subdued—no horn blared and every car was gliding smoothly along the glistening asphalt like a boat.

The landscape changed when they got onto I-77, crossing the spine of the Appalachian Mountains down to North Carolina. As Nan drove along, heading south for Charlotte, the soil became a lighter color, more reddish. More and more cars appeared on the two-lane road. After Charlotte and along I-85, they began to see peanut and tobacco fields. Holsteins, with drooping dewlaps and bald patches, were grazing in pastures, their tails languidly thrashing their hindquarters. Then orchards emerged, peaches studded the luxuriant crowns of the bulky trees, with branches curving down under the weight of the fruit. Once in a while they came across a bunch of mobile homes sitting on the edge of an orchard. Those trailers looked vacant; apparently their occupants had gone deep into the groves to pick peaches. Whenever Nan and Pingping saw a cottage or a small house, they'd say they would have been content with a home just like that. They wouldn't mind living in one of those trailer homes. They asked Taotao what he was thinking, but the boy didn't respond; perhaps he preferred something better.

5

TOWARD EVENING they arrived in Gwinnett County, Georgia. Peachtree Terrace was easy to find, just off Stone Mountain Highway. Nan parked before a brick building and went away to look for the woman who had the key to the apartment. As Pingping and Taotao waited outside their car, a few black and Mexican boys, who had been roller-skating in the parking lot, came over to look at the new arrivals. They didn't speak to Pingping and Taotao and just stared at them curiously, some chewing bubblegum. They nudged and jostled one another. Pingping couldn't fully understand what they were saying.

"Dey ain't Japs," said a boy with a chipped tooth.

"How d'you know?" asked another.

"Dis ain't fancy car."

"Is Ame'can car. Yuh know what I'm sayin'?" a heavyset boy in short pants said and kicked the rear wheel of the car, its Ford logo missing.

"Yeah. Them Japs don' wanna live here."

"Must be Chinese den."

"Naaah!"

Taotao clung to his mother, who was also a little unnerved. It was getting dark, and the damp air felt solid and oppressive. Large moths zigzagged around the orange lights in the parking lot. Beyond the lampposts and the treetops, the sky was spangled with clumps of stars, partly obscured by the clouds and smog. From the highway in the west came the whirring of the traffic.

Nan returned with the key twenty minutes later, massaging his sore neck with his hand. The apartment was in the basement of the building, whose hallways stank of so much synthetic lilac that

Pingping held her breath as she walked through them. If only Nan had asked which floor the apartment was on before paying the deposit. No wonder the rent was so low. He couldn't help but blame himself for not having looked for a place two weeks earlier when he had been here. Pingping told him not to worry. They had arrived safe and sound, which was already something they should celebrate. As they went through the dingy rooms in the apartment, a fusty odor tickled their noses. The carpet in one bedroom and the living room was partly soaked with water. Dead cockroaches lay about, their claws stretched toward the ceiling. Nan picked up the telephone left by the former tenant—amazingly, it still had the dial tone. There was no time to think, and they had to unload the car without delay. Together Pingping and Nan carried in the bags and parcels and put them into the innermost bedroom, where the floor was dry, though also grubby.

Taotao was sitting on the only chair in the apartment, crying noiselessly. Pingping asked, "What's wrong?"

"I want a real home!" he wailed, chewing his lips.

"This is good home. Look how big it is." Indeed, the three bed-rooms were spacious.

"No, this isn't a home I want. It's wet and dirty like hell."

"Don't worry your head about that. We can make it clean and comfy. That's why we have hands, right? You will see how nice it look in coupla days."

"Where can we sleep tonight?"

That was indeed a problem, to which she hadn't figured out a solution yet. They didn't have a mattress, and the floor in every room was filthy. The walls were so inadequately insulated that they could hear people yammering next door. Worse, since they'd come in, the ceiling hadn't stopped echoing the clatter of someone's heels.

They were all hungry, so Pingping went about cooking dinner. This was easy, since they had a lot of canned food. As the tomato soup was bubbling on the stove, she brought out a head of lettuce and a bag of poppyseed rolls. Nan opened a can of fried anchovies and a jar of spiced bamboo shoots. Fifteen minutes later they sat down to dinner on a pink sheet spread on the dry floor of the innermost bedroom. While eating, they talked about where to sleep. Because the linoleum floor of the bathroom could be wiped clean, they decided to spend the night in there. Done with dinner, Pingping began wiping the bathroom with paper towels while Nan was doing the dishes.

She spread a blanket on the floor, and together they lay down in the narrow space between the toilet and the bathtub. With Taotao in between the parents, the family tried to sleep. In spite of the two thick blankets keeping them warm, both Pingping and Taotao remained awake, but Nan slept soundly, though he didn't snore as he would when sleeping alone. As long as he was fatigued, he could always fall asleep the moment his head hit the pillow. If he wasn't exhausted, he would read for a while, which would induce him to sleep within an hour. Tonight, dead tired, he slept deeply regardless of the damp and the confining space in the bathroom. The toilet bowl against his right shoulder would whistle and hiss whenever somebody flushed in a nearby unit, but nothing could wake him up. Meanwhile, Pingping and Taotao tossed and turned beside him. If only they could have adjusted the central air-conditioning, which, on full force, went on without letup as if to refrigerate the rooms. What's worse, the floor was hard and musty. Pingping was afraid a roach or a mouse might crawl on her. For the whole night she drifted off fitfully. Whenever she was awake, she'd pat Taotao to help him sleep.

Unsure whether the apartment was safe, they went to the bank first thing the next morning to open an account and deposit the certified check they had with them. Nan and Pingping sat patiently, with Taotao on his mother's lap, while a clerk, a young woman with a receding chin, was getting through the paperwork with them. It took a solid hour to set up the account. Back in Boston such a matter would have taken at most twenty minutes, but this was the South. The woman seemed surprised that they deposited such a large check—$50,000—and glanced at them from time to time. Pingping understood the meaning in her eyes and knew they didn't look like people who could have so much cash. There was no way this woman could imagine the sacrifice and labor this check embodied. Pingping had never once bought new clothes for anyone in the family. She had always chosen the cheapest foods at the supermarket for themselves.

From the bank they went to Mattress King at a shopping center.

Pingping insisted on buying three full-size mattresses, plus the box springs, though Nan suggested they get at least one larger one so that they could sleep two in the same bed more comfortably. But she didn't want a queen- or king-size mattress. In the matter of shopping she always had the final say; Nan wasn't good at comparing prices and often felt a bit disgusted with money, for which he had worked jobs he loathed. The sales representative, a man with a beer belly hanging over his belt, said to Pingping with a smile, "Ma'am, I'm going to have these mattresses treated for you, to prevent bugs, okay?"

"How much that cost?" she asked.

"Ninety-nine dollars apiece, ma'am. You should have them treated, or they won't last in this climate."

"Hmm . . . fine, fine." She was pleased that he was so polite. Back in the Northeast salespeople had often followed her in stores, suspecting she might shoplift, and nobody had ever treated her as courteously as this gentleman.

The final bill was $962.82, including the delivery fee. Pingping handed the salesman ten one-hundred-dollar bills. He looked amazed, hesitating as if reluctant to touch the cash; then he took the banknotes and went into the back room to make sure they were genuine. A moment later he stepped out and gave Pingping her change and a receipt. He promised to have the mattresses delivered that very day.

After that, the Wus stopped at a large thrift store on Memorial Drive, where they chose some used furniture—a sofa, three chairs, a desk, and an hexagonal dining table. They paid $170 for those pieces and another $25 for delivery. They also bought a vacuum cleaner at a department store, getting a good price on the already-assembled floor sample.

As soon as they came back, they opened all the windows to air out the rooms and dry out the wet carpet. Nan plugged in the vacuum and began cleaning the floors. The living room had a screen door facing the backyard, where grass grew on a narrow lawn closed in by holly shrubs, which were dense and tall enough to keep people out. But Pingping and Nan kept that door shut most of the time, afraid someone might sneak in.

Both the mattresses and the furniture were delivered that after-noon, dragged in through the screen door of the living room. After Pingping checked and smelled the mattresses, she said, *"I don't think these are treated."* Nan took a look, but couldn't determine whether the salesman had made good on his promise or not. There was no time to regret or complain, so they went on cleaning. In a wink the apartment was transformed into something resembling a home. Even Taotao couldn't stop jumping on the mattresses in the dry bedroom. He laughed loudly and poked fun at Nan, kicking his shins and pulling his belt from behind. His mother kept saying to him, *"Stop messing around! Do something to help."*

That night Nan phoned Mr. Wang. Then he set about writing down some notes of the landscape he had seen on their trip to Geor-gia, hoping he could make a poem or two out of them eventually. He was still moved by the splendid views, though he didn't know how to describe them dramatically to make them vibrant. Meanwhile, Ping-ping was teaching Taotao how to solve some math problems that combined multiplication and division.

6

IN THE SHANG LAW OFFICE at the Chinatown Plaza in Chamblee, the Wus and Mr. Wang were about to finalize the sale of the restaurant. To Nan's surprise, the paperwork didn't include Pingping's name. The attorney explained that Mr. Wang had never mentioned her as a cobuyer. Although Nan had left his wife's name with him, the old man had forgotten, probably because he had always been the sole proprietor of the Gold Wok. Now Nan wanted to have Pingping mentioned as a cobuyer in the papers. Mr. Shang, the lawyer, looked displeased and said it would take several days to reprepare the paperwork and to meet them again. Pingping intervened, saying this wasn't a big problem and there was no need to waste so much time. She urged her husband to complete the deal as quickly as possible. The truth was that she was worried about Taotao, who was staying with Mrs. Wang at the restaurant.

Nan signed the contract. Pingping wrote out a check for $19,800 and handed it to Mr. Wang. Then she made another check for $120 to the lawyer for his fee. "Congratulations!" said Mr. Shang, a spindly man wearing gold-rimmed glasses. "This is your first step toward becoming a millionaire," he said to Nan, scratching his fat ear. He leaned back on his large chair and laughed gratingly, his half-gray mustache waggling. He gave Mr. Wang and Nan each a copy of the contract, then shook hands with everyone.

Together with Mr. Wang, the Wus headed back to the Gold Wok. Pingping said she shouldn't have gone to the attorney's office and she hoped Taotao was all right.

Both Nan and Pingping were overwhelmed. Now they owned a business; they had become their own boss. Even though he knew the restaurant couldn't make them rich, Nan couldn't help imagining the prospect of managing a business of their own. A kind of euphoria possessed him. At the same time, he tried to remain levelheaded. All his life he had never been interested in making money, but now he'd flung himself into the thick of it and was bowled over by becoming a small restaurateur. He knew that without his wife's backing he wouldn't have dared to attempt such a thing.

The Wangs had worshipped the God of Wealth. In a tiny alcove in the restaurant's dining room, this deity was represented by a porcelain statuette, like a smiling Buddha, with a bulging belly and ruddy, smooth cheeks. At his bare feet sat bowls of tangerines, apples, peaches, cookies, two miniature cups of rice wine, and four smoking joss sticks stuck in a brass censer. Nan and Pingping had mixed feelings about this superstitious practice, but should they evict the god? What if there indeed existed such a supernatural power that could decide the vicissitudes of their fortunes? In any event, they mustn't offend this deity, so they decided to leave him undisturbed and make similar offerings to him.

For several days, even when Nan was working at the cutting board and the sizzling wok, Pope's lines would echo in his mind: "Happy the man whose wish and care / A few paternal acres bound, / Content to breathe his native air / In his own ground." He was aware that he wasn't completely at home here, but still he felt that his feet were finally standing on solid, independent ground.

Unlike the Wangs, the Wus kept the restaurant quiet and didn't play any music. They had grown up with loudspeakers everywhere, punctuating their daily life with roaring songs and jarring slogans, so they detested any kind of sound pollution that forced people to listen to it regardless of their states of mind. They had changed the menu; Nan added a few more dishes and decided not to use MSG in anything they offered. Also, he prepared some dishes differently. For example, formerly the cold cuts called Five-Spice Beef would be piled on a plate with sliced meat atop slivers of cucumber. This was misleading or deceptive, because there was actually more vegetable than meat. Now Nan put the beef and the cucumber in separate piles on the same plate, so the customer could see how much meat and vegetable were actually served. He wanted to be honest. He understood that, unlike in China, here honesty was one's best credit. His wife and son liked the various kinds of chicken he made, especially Strange-Flavored Chicken, a Szechuan dish. Another improvement was that he would change the frying oil every three days. Most Chinese restaurants did this once a week, which often contributed to the unfresh taste of their foods. Most American restaurants used new oil every day. For the Chinese, such waste amounted to a sin. For decades, cooking oil had been rationed in China, each urban resident entitled to only four ounces a month; as for the people in the countryside, a whole household had been allocated only a few pounds a year. These days Nan often thought that if his parents had seen him pour a trough of used vegetable oil into plastic jugs for disposal, they'd have chastised him, not to mention the piles of chicken skin and pork fat he dumped into the trash can every day.

Tammie, the waitress, was very fond of Taotao and talked to him whenever she wasn't busy. Since school hadn't started yet, the boy came to the restaurant with his parents every day. Pingping made him read books and do math problems in a booth when business was slow in the early mornings and afternoons. Nan noticed that Tammie often avoided speaking to Pingping, perhaps because his wife was much better-looking than she was. He realized that the waitress had probably lived a lonesome life. Very likely, she longed to have a family; she was at least twenty-seven or twenty-eight. With her broad cheeks and heavyset body, she couldn't easily fetch a bridegroom here unless she had a lot of money or a green card, neither of which she possessed. Nan knew he might get into trouble if the INS caught him employing her, but it was unlikely that the agents would swoop down on such a small restaurant. Tammie often said she missed her parents, who had emigrated to Malaysia from southern China in the 1940s. Nan paid her three dollars an hour besides letting her keep all the tips, because she also helped do dishes and kitchen chores, mainly stringing beans and wrapping wontons, dumplings, and egg rolls. This way he wouldn't have to hire another hand, and Tammie was pleased with the arrangement. What Nan liked most about her was that she spoke English all the time, which was good practice for him and Pingping. Tammie understood Mandarin but couldn't speak it fluently.

In the first week the restaurant made a profit of almost six hundred dollars. Nan and Pingping were amazed. This place was a little bonanza, and business would almost certainly go up in the fall. It looked like they might indeed build a small fortune if they ran the Gold Wok well.

The Wangs lived just on the other side of Beaver Hill Plaza. Their house, a two-story brick bungalow painted gray, was visible from the restaurant. Nan and Pingping envied the proximity of their house to the Gold Wok. If only they could own a home so close by. They asked Mr. Wang teasingly whether he'd sell his house to them as well. "*Give me one hundred and fifty thousand, it's yours,*" the old man told them in earnest. That was too high a price, at least $40,000 above its assessed value.

Because the Wangs lived nearby, whenever Nan needed help, he'd ask Mrs. Wang to come in and work a few hours. The old woman was more than happy to do that, to make a couple of dollars. Sometimes Mr. Wang would drop in and palaver with Nan and Pingping. He was often bored at home despite having on his roof the satellite dish called "the Little Ear," which enabled him to watch many TV shows in Mandarin and Cantonese. There were few Chinese living nearby—most of the Asian immigrants lived in Duluth, a town seven miles to the northeast—and the Wangs seemed to have no friends here. They had a daughter working for a Taiwanese airline in Seattle. She was there just temporarily, so the Wangs wouldn't go and join her. The old man would sigh and say to Pingping, "*America is a good place only for young people. Once you're old, you feel awful living here, just a nuisance.*"

"*Why won't you go back to China?*" Pingping asked, knowing he had been born in Fujian Province. "*I heard that lots of people bought retirement homes there.*"

"*I wish we could do that. It costs too much. Besides, I don't trust the mainland government.*"

"*How about Taiwan? Can't you live there?*"

"*The same thing. The legal system is a slum there, not a good place to retire to. Many people are desperate to leave the island. They don't want to get trapped there when the mainland launches an attack.*"

"*How about Singapore?*"

"That small country is just like another province of China. The Chinese government controls nearly everything there. Here's a copy of the United Morning Post, *published in Singapore. You should read it. Terrible. The paper not only uses the Communists' language but also reprints the news distorted by the mainland media."*

"Do you plan to stay here for many years?"

"Hard to say."

To a degree, Nan and Pingping felt uneasy about the Wangs' situation and often talked about the old couple. They couldn't help but imagine their own old age, though it was still far away. It must be frightening to lead such an isolated life. Would they end up like the Wangs, who wandered around like scarecrows, still out of place after living here for three decades?

Probably not. Unlike them, Nan and Pingping spoke English better and were never afraid of isolation. They wanted to take root here, having nowhere else to go. That was why Nan had seized every opportunity to learn English. He knew that in this land the language was like a body of water in which he had to learn how to swim and breathe, even though he'd feel out of his element whenever he used it. If he didn't try hard to adapt himself, developing new "lungs and gills" for this alien water, his life would be confined and atrophied, and eventually wither away.

Whenever Nan had a free moment at work, he would read his *Oxford Advanced Learner's Dictionary* because it was monolingual. He still used his bilingual dictionary, which was getting tattered, especially when he couldn't figure out what a noun referred to as described in English. He could see that on the whole the definitions of the word entries written in English were more accurate than those given in Chinese. In addition, using the monolingual dictionary was a way to make himself think in English. He highlighted the words and phrases unfamiliar to him so that he could review them after he went over the entire volume. He had also bought a softcover *New English-Chinese Dictionary* for Pingping, but she seldom bothered to open it. Even when she came across a new word in her reading, she wouldn't look it up, able to figure out its meaning from the context most times. She was so smart that she had little need for a dictionary.

7

ON SATURDAY MORNING a UPS van came to deliver their boxes, all of which bore the sticker FRAGILE, a few wrapped with duct tape and a broken one spewing foam peanuts. Nan found that a box, number 21, was missing. This upset him. He was sure it contained some of his poetry books, though he couldn't name the titles at the moment. The deliveryman promised to check on it and have it sent over within a day or two, which actually never happened. Nan used a hand truck to move the boxes into their apartment through the screen door of the living room, but the Wus had to leave for work and couldn't open them until they were back at night.

That night, after unpacking them, they found the microwave broken. Taotao helped his father set up the computer, which was out of order too. Only the Sanyo TV set still worked, but it had more noise now and could pick up merely two channels. Nothing had been insured, so there was no way to claim damages.

"*This is a minor loss that will preempt real disasters,*" Pingping said, just to console her son and husband. Yet Taotao was inconsolable and eager to have his computer fixed so that he could play chess with it again. For this machine assembled in a barn in Keene, New Hampshire, Nan had paid only seven hundred dollars, so it wasn't worth repairing. Taotao then wanted a new computer, but his parents refused to buy that, saying they'd have to save every penny for the home they'd purchase in the future.

"*Do you want to throw away five hundred and fifty dollars every month?*" Pingping asked him, referring to the rent they paid.

"*No.*"

"Then we mustn't continue to waste money this way. Once we have our own home, we'll get you a computer."

The boy knew it was futile to argue, yet he wouldn't drop the topic without another try. He said, *"I don't want to go to the restaurant anymore. Leave me at home."*

"That's illegal," put in his father.

"It's not safe here," his mom added anxiously. *"What if somebody breaks in and snatches you away? He'll sell you to a stranger and you won't be able to see us again. Would you like that?"*

"No. I just don't want to stay in the damned restaurant anymore. It makes me sick just to smell the air in there."

"You have to come with us."

The couple living upstairs started fighting again. That stopped the Wus' argument. Neither Nan nor Pingping had ever met the man and woman, having to go to work early in the morning and come back late at night. Yet they had heard enough of their exchanges to know them almost intimately.

Would that couple ever be quiet and peaceful? They always yelled at each other as if they couldn't live for a day without a fight. Sometimes they'd wake Pingping up in the middle of the night.

Taotao kicked a squashed box, sullen and tearful.

"You're a sex maniac," said the woman upstairs. "I've already let you have it twice this week—when will it ever be enough for you? I can't sleep afterward. I'm having an interview tomorrow morning. Just leave me alone tonight, okay?"

"Don't talk to me like that," the man snapped. "If you hate sex so much, why live with me?"

"Get real here. You begged me to shack up with you. I still hate myself for listening to you."

"I'll be damned if I can understand this."

"You can never understand a woman. Else your wife wouldn't have left you for the other guy."

"Shut the hell up!"

Then came a crash. Shoes started scraping the floor. They must have been grappling with each other.

Pingping noticed her son prick up his ears. She said, "Taotao, go to bathroom and brush your teeth." That also meant it was time for bed.

The next day they cleared out a space in the storage room in the back of the restaurant and put in a small desk, at which Taotao could do his work for the time being. Both Pingping and Nan felt for him. Every day the boy had to stay with them for more than twelve hours, and not until ten p.m. could they go back together. To make Taotao more comfortable, Nan got a thirteen-inch TV for him, but they made him promise not to watch it too often. They also put in a love seat bought at a Goodwill store, on which the boy could nap. When it wasn't busy, Pingping would go to the back room and check on him. If he was idle or watching TV, she'd urge him to do his "homework," assigned by her. Seldom would he come to the front to see his parents.

Pingping scolded her son one afternoon, saying, "Don't be so lazy and watch TV all time."

"Duh, I'm tired." He looked peeved.

"Tired? We're all living fast life here. You must do same."

"That's not proper grammar, Mom."

"What?"

"People say 'We're living a busy life,' not 'a fast life.'"

"I mean burn candle at two ends."

"How can you do that?"

"I mean make two hundred percent effort."

"Impossible!"

"All right, you live busy life. After this show, go back to homework."

"Okay, okay!"

Whenever she said something wrong in her unique ungrammatical English, the boy would correct her. Sometimes he even did that in the presence of others. She was annoyed but never discouraged him, because she was determined to learn the language. What she and Nan didn't know was that Taotao had been simmering, angry about their awkward English, which sometimes embarrassed him. He was especially discomfited by Pingping. She'd toss out malapropisms right and left, such as "gooses," "watermelon skin," "deers," and "childrenhood." One day the boy threw a tantrum, accusing his parents of having messed up his English, because that morning, his second day in school, he had blurted out the term "peach hair" instead of "peach fuzz," for which some of his classmates had ridiculed him. He knew he had picked it up from his mother. "You're ruining my career!" he screamed at Pingping that afternoon. She broke into peals of laughter after hearing him explain why, and she went into the kitchen to laugh more to herself.

Every day she assigned him some math problems in addition to his schoolwork. However much he complained, she'd make him finish the assignments before they closed up.

8

WHEN they moved to Atlanta, the Wus hadn't known that the children at Peachtree Terrace went to schools farther south, which belonged to another district. This meant Taotao wasn't supposed to attend an elementary school in Lilburn. If there had been a grown-up in their apartment to accompany him after school, his parents wouldn't have minded letting him go to Shiloh Elementary in Snellville, which had a fine reputation. As it was, the boy would have to join them when he got off the bus in the afternoons, so he needed to attend a school near the Gold Wok. Fortunately, the Wangs allowed the Wus to use their address so that Taotao could go to Rebecca Minor Elementary. When the secretary at the principal's office called the Wangs, Mrs. Wang said Taotao was their grandnephew, who had come to stay with them. Mr. Wang told the Wus that they ought to live closer to the restaurant, to save the time and hassle of traveling back and forth every day. Also, gasoline was expensive nowadays as a consequence of the Gulf War. The Wus realized they'd have to move to Lilburn soon, but this town had few apartments for rent, which were all expensive besides. Every weekday they dropped their son at Rebecca Minor Elementary before going to the Gold Wok, and in the afternoon Taotao would get off the school bus at the east side of Beaver Hill Plaza and join his parents at the restaurant.

At work, the Wus couldn't stop feeling antsy about what might happen to their apartment, because Peachtree Terrace wasn't a safe place. Sometimes at night they heard gunshots in their building. Police cruisers would come, strobe lights slashing the parking lot, and people would gather around to watch the police making arrests.

Whenever such an incident happened, Nan would say they must move out soon.

One night the Wus returned from work and found that a window in the bedroom used as Nan's study was open. At once Nan flicked on all the lights to see what was missing. The computer and the microwave were gone; so was a pair of Pingping's leather sandals. Other than those, they had lost nothing else. How fortunate it was that they'd kept all their papers in their safe-deposit box in the bank. On the carpet of the living room two pairs of muddy shoe prints stretched parallel to each other, one under eight inches long and the other about a foot. Apparently two people, a grown-up and an adolescent, had committed the burglary. At first, both Nan and Pingping were outraged and cursed the thieves. They wondered whether they should report the crime to the police, but eventually decided not to. The police might summon them to the station, and they didn't want to go through the tedious process. They couldn't afford to lose a whole morning, plus probably a good part of an afternoon. Actually, their loss was minimum, as both the computer and the microwave were already broken. Having calmed down, they couldn't help smiling, amused that the thieves had made fools of themselves and must be racking their brains trying to make those machines work.

"*I'm pleased they removed the junk. Good riddance,*" Nan said.

"*I want my computer back,*" wailed their son.

"*It was already broken down, not worth keeping anymore.*"

"*I want it back. It's mine.*"

His mother stepped in. "*Be reasonable, Taotao. This way we won't have to bother to dump them. We just paid those fools a pair of my old shoes.*"

"*It's my computer.*"

"*All right, once we have our own home, we'll buy you a new one,*" Nan said.

"*When can we have our house? I don't want to live here anymore.*"

His parents looked at each other. Nan realized Pingping was thinking the same thought. He managed to answer his son, "*I'll start looking for a new place soon.*"

"*Yes, Daddy will take care of that,*" Pingping said. "*You must stop hoarding things.*"

Neither Nan nor Pingping could say when Taotao had become a hoarder: he had never let go of anything that once belonged to him, not even a pencil stub or a paper clip. For some time his parents had wondered what was wrong with him. Then one day back north, on his way to work in Natick, Nan by chance listened to a psychiatrist on the radio discussing the psychology of hoarding with a caller whose son had the same problem—"a real dog in the manger," the boy wouldn't even let his newborn cousin wear the booties he had outgrown long ago. The man and his wife had been separated, and the psychiatrist said their shaky marriage might account for their son's obsession—unconsciously the boy wanted to hold things together. The thought came to Nan that Taotao must have been frightened all these years when Pingping and he were often absent from his life. Now the boy must still be afraid of losing his parents, and this fear was manifested in his clinging to all trifles. Look at his duffel bag, full of trinkets: assorted batteries, dead wristwatches, rulers, a shoehorn, key chains, dog tags, pencil sharpeners, baseball cards, seashells, coins from various countries that Livia had given him. He had even saved every section of comics from the *Boston Globe* back in Massachusetts; his parents had forced him to dump them before the move, but now he had begun collecting the funnies from the *Atlanta Journal-Constitution*. What puzzled Nan was that Taotao never looked at those pages again once he had thrown them into the pile in his closet, next to the carton containing issues of *National Geographic,* which his parents had subscribed to for him. The boy's hoarding saddened his parents. Nan and Pingping agreed not to talk about their marital trouble in front of their child again.

"*I wonder why the thieves didn't take Taotao's telescope,*" Pingping said to Nan when the boy was brushing his teeth in the bathroom.

"*The computer must have seemed worth a lot of money to them.*"

"*If they'd walked off with the telescope, that would have killed him.*"

"*Maybe we should store it in the restaurant.*"

So they took the thing along when they went to work the next morning. For the whole day Nan continually looked through apartment books and the "Home Finder" sections of the Sunday *Atlanta Journal-Constitution* for a safe nearby place, but he couldn't find one. There were a few houses listed for rent in Lilburn, all too expensive.

To Nan's delight, Mrs. Wang showed up the next afternoon and said that she and her husband were going to visit their relatives in Taiwan for at least three months. She would be happy to let the Wus "keep the house" for them. Nan and Pingping understood that also meant she'd want them to pay some rent. They offered her six hundred dollars a month, which Mrs. Wang happily accepted. *"Nan, we trust you like a son of ours,"* she said with feeling.

Her words made Nan's gums itch, knowing the Wangs had no son. But Pingping tittered and asked her, *"Then I'm your daughter-in-law, right? And Taotao is your grandson, right?"*

"Right."

"Then you should let us use your house for free, shouldn't you?"

Mrs. Wang looked baffled; her small eyes dimmed while a worm-like frown gathered at her forehead. Pingping said, *"Just joking. We'll take good care of your house."*

Nan was worried that the managerial office at Peachtree Terrace might not let him get out of the lease easily. He talked to Shona, the black woman in charge of the apartment complex, and she agreed to cancel his lease provided Nan was willing to lose the security deposit. He was unhappy but had no choice. However, a week after the Wus had moved out, Nan received a check of $275 from Shona. She didn't write a word and just refunded him half the deposit, which pleased the Wus.

Since moving into the Wangs', the Wus hadn't been able to figure out what the little red flag on the mailbox was supposed to do. Back in Massachusetts, the Masefields hadn't had such a thing on their box, and Heidi had always taken her mail to the post office. Now every morning before going to work, Nan would raise the tiny flag as a way to greet the postman, who drove on the right-hand side of his van. Then one day Pingping found a slip of paper in the mailbox, bearing these words: "Don't let your kids play with the flag! Keep it up only when you have mail to go."

Taotao loved the Wangs' house and often set up his telescope in the backyard at night to look at stars. He was happy that at last he could use the instrument freely. His parents joined him in observing the sky a few times, but unlike in the Northeast, the air in Atlanta was still a touch humid in the fall, so even such a large telescope, 225 power, couldn't penetrate the hazy atmosphere completely. Tao-tao once sulked and kept twisting the focus knob and the eyepiece. Nan told him, *"The sky will be clear in the wintertime. Why don't you wait until then? I bet you can see stars clearly when it's cold."*

The boy agreed and stowed away the telescope in a closet. However, when winter came, he didn't take it out. In fact, the frustration in the fall had squelched his craving for stargazing. He'd never touch the telescope again, as if it was just a toy he had outgrown but still wanted to keep.

9

BOTH Nan and his wife often dreamed of their native land. Yet neither of them missed their parents a lot, because they had grown up in kindergartens and boarding schools. Unlike Nan, Pingping sometimes remembered her father fondly. She didn't love her mother that much; she had been grouchy, especially when frustrated at work, and had often vented her frustration on her children. As the oldest child, Pingping had to do many of the household chores and look after her siblings. Her mother would scold her if she didn't rinse the laundry clean enough, and would even slap her if her siblings had fought with other kids whose mothers came to complain and make scenes. So Pingping had never missed her mother. Every so often, she still dreamed of China, but in the dream she was sometimes tormented by a full bladder; she'd toss in bed and shout, "*Where's the toilet?*" A few times she awakened Nan, who slept in the other bed in the same room.

Nan dreamed of different things and people. Once, in a nightmare, he appeared to be an escapee, hunted by men wielding truncheons and wearing helmets marked with a swastika, but the setting was his alma mater, the small college in Harbin, and all the Nazis had Chinese faces. As he was fleeing, from behind him rose ferocious barks made by the hounds sicced on those who lagged behind. Another time he dreamed that a friend of his was being arrested by the police and frog-marched to an execution ground below the dam of a reservoir. His friend wasn't shot but was booted half to death, and Nan woke up drenched in cold sweat. More often he dreamed of Beina, that capricious woman. She would come to him snickering or sobbing; once she even caressed his throat and kissed his cheeks with her moist lips. She was different from a decade before, her egg-shaped face smooth and pale as if she were ill. Never did she look cheerful, more often irritated and grimacing, her large eyes tearful; neither did she ever speak a word to him. He was upset about her silence because she had a lovely ringing voice, and because her reticence contradicted her reckless nature. Once Nan dreamed that he and she were jogging together on the sports ground behind the classroom building of their old college, she following him stubbornly despite her heavy boots and the piercingly cold wind. Several times she appeared when he was talking with someone else—she stayed in the background but within earshot, listening closely. Whenever he woke up from such a dream, he'd feel a numbing pain in his chest. If only he could forget her. If only he had just flirted with her instead of being deadly serious and getting himself wounded. He wondered whether she ever dreamed of him.

"*I know you miss her again,*" Pingping said to Nan one morning after putting Taotao on the school bus. Now that they lived near the restaurant, they didn't have to hustle to work.

"*Who are you talking about?*" He pretended to be puzzled.

"*Beina. You met her again in your dream last night.*"

"*I didn't mean to.*"

"*If you love her so much, why did you marry me? Liar! Why did you tell me you loved me?*" She turned away and broke into sobs.

He said no more as a cramping headache suddenly seized his scalp. He got up, slipped on his green raincoat, and made for the door.

"*Come back!*" cried his wife.

He went out without turning his head. It was chilly outside, a mizzle falling almost like a fog, but there wasn't a breath of wind. Most of the trees had already shed their leaves, which were scattered on the lawns along the street, a few plastered on tree trunks and some caught in evergreen shrubs. In Nan's mind was falling another drizzle, in which he and Beina were walking under his raincoat toward their classroom building. Their body heat mingled while he wrapped his arm around her shoulders firmly. She was so little in his one-armed embrace, like a child, and she couldn't stop laughing. Around the campus, frogs were croaking lustily. The path through the aspen grove was misty and seemed to lead to a place far away. If only they could walk like that for hours.

Nan was heading for the Gold Wok. The cars, parked diagonally in Beaver Hill Plaza, had been washed clean, brighter than usual, and the asphalt was spotted with oily sheen. He didn't go to the restaurant and instead continued toward Lawrenceville Highway, which was two hundred yards to the north. He thought about his dream of the night before, in which Beina again wept wordlessly. He wondered why she appeared so wretched. Did her husband abuse her? Was she in trouble? Did she need him to help her? To rescue her from that bastard? Why was she always sad in his dreams?

At the same time he tried reasoning himself out of his fantasies. How ridiculous you are. The dream was nothing but vagaries of your mind. She had no need for you then and has no need for you now. Have you forgotten her words—"I can't stand you anymore"? Like some women she too wanted a man of wealth or power. You're nobody, just a piece of garbage dumped by her. Drop all the illusions! Stop wallowing in despair. Pull yourself together and focus on what's going on here and now.

Still, the pain was real, constricting his throat. He crossed Lawrenceville Highway and strolled toward Kroger because the other shops weren't open yet. Once inside the supermarket, he poured himself a cup of coffee and picked up a half blueberry muffin, both free for sampling; he walked around, pushing a shopping cart, which he actually didn't need. At the end of an aisle he stumbled on a table that displayed wristwatches for sale, all at a big discount. His watch had died a few days before, so he decided to buy one. He disliked those with leather straps because in the summer he'd sweat so much in the kitchen that the leather would rot within a year. So he picked one made in Brazil with a steel strap and a calendar on its face. The original price had been $140, but now it was marked down to $19.99. He touched his pockets and realized he'd left his wallet home. Yet in his hip pocket he found a twenty and a ten. He was glad he had the money on him.

At the express lane a gawky, pink-faced boy checked him out and said, "Twenty-three forty-seven." The screen of the register showed the same amount.

Nan was puzzled but handed him the money anyway. As the cashier was making change, Nan said, "Zer marked price is nineteen ninety-nine. Why such a big difference?"

"Six percent sales tax, sir." The boy grinned while his pale blue eyes batted.

"Still, it shouldn't be so mahch."

The boy gave thought to that, then pointed at a counter, saying, "The computer must've made a mistake. Go to Customer Service. They'll help you. I'm sorry about this, sir." He handed Nan the change and the receipt.

At the counter a fortyish woman with amber hair looked at the receipt and the watch. Without a word she punched away at a keyboard. "I'm going to give the money back to you, all right?" she said to Nan.

"Fine."

She came over and handed him $23.47, together with the wristwatch. Perplexed, Nan said, "I want zer watch."

"You can have it."

"But you gave me all zer money back."

The woman, wearing a nametag with SARAH printed on it, beamed and narrowed her eyes. "The store has a new policy—if the computer overcharges you, we give you the purchase for free. We apologize for the mistake, sir."

"Wow, sank you!"

Nan put on the watch and stepped out of the supermarket, impressed by the store's effort to inspire the customers' trust. His mood was lifting, and he was amazed that he was actually so easy to please. Just a free little timepiece could cheer him up. As he was about to cross Lakeside Drive, he caught sight of a pack of Virginia Slims lying in the roadside grass, the cellophane wrap dotted with rainwater and a cigarette sticking out of the top of the case. He picked it up. He didn't smoke, but the pack was hardly used and its contents still dry, so he put it into his pocket. With a lightened heart he headed home.

10

SLUMPED at the kitchen table, Pingping was smoking while Nan was away. Usually she wouldn't touch cigarettes, but when distressed, she'd indulge in one. She always kept a pack around, secreted somewhere Nan couldn't find. If only she didn't love him so hopelessly. How often she was torn between love and bitterness; and she even tried to hate him, but never could she summon up any real hatred. Despite her misery and feeling of being misused, every night before going to sleep she'd repeat to herself, "I love my husband only," as though this thought were her only way out of the labyrinth of love in which both she and Nan were trapped. It was clear by now that she could never go back to China and live as a self-sufficient person again, yet she wouldn't regret having settled down in Georgia and was willing to accept the prospect that she and Nan would have to remain together for a long time, probably for the rest of their lives. Still, why couldn't Nan outgrow his feelings for his first love, for that heartless woman? Why would he continue letting her suck all the energy and lifeblood out of him? Stupid ass. He'll get feebler and feebler if he doesn't quit pining away for her. Why can't he see that her life belongs elsewhere and has nothing to do with his here? He's just a miserable man, just an automatic generator of suffering and pain.

Unlike him, Pingping had never missed her ex-boyfriend, compared with whom Nan was a better man; Nan hadn't hesitated to marry her and wouldn't shirk his responsibilities as a husband and father. If only he were more responsive to her love and devotion. If only there were a way to soften his hardened heart.

The kitchen door opened. At the sight of Nan, Pingping averted her eyes and took a short drag on her cigarette. He said harshly,

"*You're not supposed to smoke in this house.*" The instant he let out those words, he changed his tone. "*This isn't our home.*" He took out the Virginia Slims and inserted something into the case.

She blew out a puff of smoke. "*I don't care.*" Despite saying that, she stubbed out her cigarette in a saucer serving as an ashtray.

"*Then I have another pack for you.*" He smiled and handed her the opened Virginia Slims. "*It has two thousand lucky pennies in it too.*"

"*You bought this for me?*" She looked puzzled, her eyes wider. She shook the case. "*My, twenty dollars!*"

"*I told you, didn't I?*"

"*Where did you get this? You smoke too?*"

"*No. I found it on the street.*"

"*Who lost it, do you know?*"

"*No idea.*"

He also showed her the brand-new watch on his wrist. She was amazed he had gotten it free. Hurriedly she made oatmeal for both of them. After breakfast, together they walked to work as if their squabble had never happened. Nan was amazed that just a free wristwatch had actually averted the crisis between them. He felt rather trivial as he remembered he had never been like this before. He had despised money back in China and never cared to save any, and before he met Pingping, he had always spent every penny of his salary each month. On the other hand, he felt that a good life should be uneventful, having few dramatic moments; instead, it should be filled with small delights, each of which should be appreciated and enjoyed like a gift. Pingping and he had too few such delights in their life, so a tiny windfall, a free watch, could bowl them over and switch their emotions to another gear. He wondered whether this piece of luck had come his way at the critical moment purely by accident. Life was truly mysterious. If he were a Christian, he'd have believed this might be a gift from God, but he didn't belong to any church and so he didn't allow his thoughts to stretch heavenward.

11

AT BEAVER HILL PLAZA a jewelry store had opened recently. It was five doors down from the Gold Wok to the east. Its owner was Janet Mitchell, a woman in her late thirties, with rusty hair and sloping shoulders. She had come from New Jersey to Atlanta the previous year with her husband, who worked for GE. Despite her trim figure, Janet walked with a lurch, the result of a traffic accident three years before. The damages she had collected enabled her to start her own business, whose clientele consisted mostly of young women living in Gwinnett County. She hired a salesgirl to work at the counter of her store while she herself made earrings and necklaces in the back room, which had a glass cutaway. Two or three times a week she would come to the Gold Wok for lunch and was particularly fond of the noodles and Ma Po Tofu offered there. Janet had caught the Wus' attention from the very beginning, because she wouldn't use a fork and would pick up a sliver of meat or a piece of stir-fried vegetable with her fingers if her chopsticks couldn't do the job. She and Pingping liked each other, and whenever she was there, the two of them would chat and giggle. Janet was amazed that Pingping, having learned English mainly by osmosis, could read local newspapers.

Sometimes when it wasn't busy at the restaurant, Pingping would go to Janet's store to see how she made jewelry. Besides showing her the craft, Janet also told her where to buy the beads, shells, stones, pearls. She even let Pingping assemble a necklace, just for fun; the piece turned out as elegant as those for sale. Janet was greatly impressed. Whenever they were together they'd talk about all kinds of things. Janet asked Pingping many questions. Why did Chinese children do so well in school? How come there weren't many fat

Chinese? What did she think of the one-child policy in China? Why did some families abandon girl babies there? Did the Chinese really respect old people? Must Pingping take care of her parents even if she was far away from home?

To the last questions Pingping replied "Not really," though every year, before the Spring Festival, she'd send five hundred dollars to her parents, as well as to Nan's. Their parents had all retired with full pensions and free medical care, so the remittances were mainly meant to make their holiday more festive.

One afternoon at the Gold Wok, Janet asked Pingping why Chinese women looked better than Chinese men. The question stumped Pingping, who had never thought about it before, but she admitted that some Chinese men were skinny perhaps because they had starved when they were young. If a man didn't look physically strong, he might be viewed as a weakling, especially in America. "But there is many handsome men in China," she told her friend. "Nan is handsome, right?"

Janet smiled without speaking; apparently she didn't think so. She then came up with another question. "I saw on TV the other day that Chinese women prefer double-fold eyelids, like the Western type. Some girls in Shanghai went through cosmetic surgeries to reshape their eyes. They already looked pretty, why did they bother to do that?"

"They like double eyelid, but that isn't really Western. Look, I'm double, right?" Pingping's forefingers pointed at her dark brown eyes while she flapped her lids. "I'm natural, right?"

"That's true. People tend to assume Chinese have slit Mongol eyes."

"China is big country, have all kinds people."

Nan was slicing pork tenderloin in the kitchen and pricked up his ears to listen in on them through the window that opened onto the dining room. He liked Pingping best when she was happy and bubbly. Despite feeling uncomfortable about Janet's curiosity that bordered on nosiness, despite having warned his wife not to tell her friend too much about themselves, he wouldn't think ill of Janet, who was a regular and was so fond of Taotao that she often bragged about him to her husband, Dave Mitchell. Dave, a husky man with a boyish face and a barrel chest, would come to dine at the Gold Wok with his wife on weekends.

Nan craned his neck to glance through the window at Pingping and Janet, who were sitting in a nearby booth, a pot of tea between them. He returned to the cutting board, working slowly so that he could eavesdrop on them more. Janet said in her contralto voice, "Come on, don't tell me this place doesn't make money. Everybody can see it's a cash cow. You and Nan have transformed it totally."

"I tell you truth," said Pingping. "We need money for house. This business can't make enough for that."

"Well, it depends on what kind of home you're looking for."

"Just small house, enough for three of us."

"That shouldn't be expensive here. If you were living in New York or San Francisco, you could say you can't afford it, but here real estate is cheap."

"We really don't have enough money."

To Nan, the business of the Gold Wok wasn't bad, but it didn't fetch a large profit. By now he understood that a tiny restaurant like theirs could never make a lot of money, but it could save a good part of its earnings through tax breaks. His family's living expenses had been reduced considerably since they took over this business. They ate at the restaurant, and most of the stuff they bought was tax deductible, things like lightbulbs, coffee, tea, detergent, paper towels, even gasoline. Eventually they could save most of the profit the restaurant made. No wonder a lot of Americans kept a small business even though they held regular jobs in large companies. Everyone tried to outsmart the IRS.

12

EVER SINCE the Wus had revived the Gold Wok, Nan had been troubled by the fact that legally he was the sole proprietor of the restaurant. What if he died of illness or got killed in a traffic accident? He was afraid that the state would take away his business and deprive his family of their livelihood. He talked with Pingping about this and convinced her that they should have both of their names included in the deed for the restaurant. He called Mr. Shang one day in late October and made an appointment for the following week.

Together Nan and Pingping went to the law office in Chamblee early on Monday morning. Mr. Shang, in a tweed jacket with leather patches at the elbows, was sipping coffee when the Wus arrived. On his desktop lay a sticky doughnut half wrapped with a piece of glossy paper, a bite revealing the dark jelly stuffing. He beckoned to the couple to sit down in front of him. "I have your paperwork ready," he told them.

"Sanks," Nan said.

"Let me explain how we should do this—I'm going to file a straw for you."

"What's that?" Pingping asked.

Mr. Shang shot her a reproachful look. He pushed up his glasses with his thumb and resumed, "A straw is also called 'bail common,' which we borrowed from the English law. The procedure works like this: you sell the property to me for one dollar and then I'll sell it back to both of you at the same price."

Nan felt uneasy. "Is there anozzer way to do zis?"

"No, this is the only way, inasmuch as you're not allowed to transfer property within your family." Mr. Shang lifted his coffee mug and drank noisily. His secretary, a stout woman with large eyes and tawny hair, came in and placed a brown folder on his desk. "Don't go, Cathy," he told her. "We need you as a witness."

In an undertone Nan explained the procedure to his wife, who seemed uncomfortable about this straw thing. He said, *"Let's do it now, all right? It will be hard for us to come again."*

To their surprise, Mr. Shang said to Pingping in stiff Mandarin, *"Believe me, this is the only way to make you a proprietress."*

So in the presence of the secretary, Nan signed the sheet that specified him as the seller, and then Mr. Shang signed the other one that sold the restaurant back to both Nan and Pingping. The attorney assured them that he'd go to the deeds office and register the transaction soon. For the registration and the lawyer fees Nan wrote him a check for two hundred dollars, and Cathy gave the Wus a receipt.

Once they were back at the Gold Wok, Nan and Pingping talked about the straw and grew more agitated. What if the lawyer wouldn't file all the papers? In other words, Mr. Shang could register himself as the buyer of the property without carrying out the second part of the straw—not selling it back to them. The more they thought about this possibility, the more jittery they got. They regretted not having asked for a copy of the paperwork. Now all they had was a receipt for the fees they'd paid. Then again, Mr. Shang could shred the check so that they wouldn't have any evidence for the transaction.

The next morning Nan called the lawyer's office and asked for a copy of the papers, but Cathy said her boss wasn't in and had them with him. Stupefied, Nan couldn't help but imagine that they'd sold their business for only one dollar. At the same time, he kept reminding himself that he shouldn't be too paranoid or think ill of Mr. Shang. He could see that Pingping was a bundle of nerves, so he ought to appear composed and cheerful. According to the attorney, they'd receive a notice about the registration from the deeds office within two months. What could the Wus do in the meantime? It looked like they could do nothing but wait anxiously.

13

AFTER Thanksgiving Nan would call the lawyer's office once a week, but the secretary always answered ambiguously, saying Mr. Shang was not in and the Wus would receive the notice from the deeds registry soon, so they should set their minds at rest. But she couldn't confirm whether the papers had been filed. Sometimes Nan felt that Mr. Shang was actually in his office when he phoned but that the man avoided speaking to him.

The more Nan thought about the impasse, the more befuddled and outraged he was. Mr. Shang, as his business card indicated, had gone to law school in California and must have grown up in the United States. It was unlikely that he'd act like a corrupt official, yet Nan felt as helpless as if he were again under the thumb of a bureaucrat, like back in China. But what should he do? He was at a loss.

One day at noon, Janet came in to have Dandan Noodle. Pingping and she chatted again while Janet was eating. By chance Pingping mentioned their predicament. Janet was surprised. "You should sue this obnoxious lawyer!" she told Pingping, her violet-colored eyes flickering.

"But we're not sure about his crime."

"Press charges for your suffering, for the mental damage he has done to you. This is outrageous."

"That cost more money. He's lawyer and know how to guard himself."

"Maybe he does, so?"

"We just want our business back, no more trouble."

"Don't worry. He won't get away with this. Let me ask Dave. He may have a better idea what to do."

Nan wasn't positive about Pingping's revealing their trouble to Janet, who he felt gossiped too much. He was afraid she might spread their story, and that would make them appear stupid in others' eyes. Yet if she could help them figure out a solution, he'd be more than grateful. He simply couldn't bear this uncertainty any longer.

Janet came in the next afternoon and told the Wus, "Dave said it wasn't a big deal. You can always go to the deeds office and file the papers by yourself."

"Reelly?" Nan felt dumb for not having thought of this before. "Zer lawyer said he must do zat."

"He just wants extra business. People file their business deals by themselves all the time. That's what Dave told me."

"Where is zer deeds awffice, do you know?" asked Nan.

"It's inside the courthouse in Lawrenceville."

"Are you sure?"

"Positive."

The next morning Janet and Pingping went to the lawyer's office together. Mr. Shang was with a client when they arrived, so Cathy let them sit in the waiting room, saying her boss would be with them shortly. She offered them each a cup of coffee.

When Mr. Shang was done and came up to them, Pingping asked him whether he had filed the papers. He answered, "I've been too busy to go to the deeds office these days." He glanced at Janet, who was glaring at him.

"Can we file it by ourself?" asked Pingping.

"You sure can. Cathy, get her papers from my office and give her the refund. Mrs. Wu, I'm pleased you can do this by yourself." Somehow he sounded relieved. He went on, "Excuse me, ladies. I have to meet a client who's waiting." He motioned to a young woman sitting near the entrance of the waiting room and riffling through a fashion magazine. "Come in, Miss Han," he said.

Pingping noticed that the attorney's socks were not mates, one black and the other blue. For sure Mr. Shang wasn't an absent-minded man, so he might have been color-blind.

The secretary wrote Pingping a check for eighty dollars and handed her the papers. Pingping and her friend left the office and headed for Janet's passenger van. "He isn't that bad," Pingping said as they pulled out of the parking lot.

"Lawyers are all the same," Janet replied. "You should know your rights when you hire them."

"I didn't expect he refund the money."

"He had to. That's for the filing fee."

They stopped at Asian Square to pick up a *World Journal* for Nan. Nan always read the Sunday newspaper, especially the enclosed weekly magazine that carried a number of articles written by well-known journalists and experts. Mr. Liu, the dissident living in New York City, had a column in the weekly, and Nan enjoyed reading that old man's writings. On their way to the deeds office, Pingping wondered whether Mr. Shang had refunded the eighty dollars because Janet had accompanied her, ready to challenge him. He couldn't possibly have forgotten to file the papers, since he went to the courthouse frequently, representing his clients. Yet somehow she didn't feel that the attorney was as greedy and sneaky as she had imagined, though she knew he had intended to torment her and Nan. They should have registered the transaction by themselves long ago to save all the doubts and miserable feelings that could easily poison one's mind and spawn hideous thoughts. She wondered why Mr. Shang had looked relieved when she said she'd handle the papers by herself. Probably having tormented the Wus enough, he had felt it was high time to bring the whole thing to an end. Or perhaps her request foiled his attempt to rob his clients and thus checked the crime he had been hesitating to commit. If so, this meant he still had a heart and dared not act like an outright crook.

Pingping and Janet found the deeds registry in the courthouse and filed the papers. The whole procedure took just a few minutes, and Pingping was amazed.

14

NAN was anxious, because the Wangs, having stayed in Taiwan for three months, would be coming back in two weeks. The Wus would have to move again. For days Nan had been considering where to go. He and his wife were a little spoiled by living so close to their workplace that they now felt reluctant to move far away. If only they could afford the Wangs' bungalow. These days Nan often looked through ads in *Gwinnett Creative Loafing* in hopes of finding a safe, affordable apartment nearby.

By now the Wus had $32,000 in the bank. They noticed that there were some smaller houses for sale for less than $90,000, though all of them were far away from the Gold Wok. With their business worth so little, they couldn't possibly get a mortgage from the bank. It seemed impossible for them to think of buying a house now.

Then one morning in early February Janet stopped by and said, "Pingping, I saw a home for sale on Marsh Drive. It's not big, can't be too expensive."

That street was just a five-minute walk from Beaver Hill Plaza, so the Wus were all ears. Nan asked Janet, "Do you know zer price?"

"Uh-uh. I guess a hundred grand, tops."

"But we have no that kinda money," Pingping said.

"And we can't get a loan eizer," added Nan.

"If I were you, I'd talk to the owner and see if there might be a way."

Early the next morning, the moment Taotao left for school, Nan and Pingping went to Marsh Drive to see the house. It was a brick ranch sitting on the northern side of a small lake and in the middle of a lot bigger than a third of an acre. The backyard, covered by grass and gently sloping toward the green water, was flanked by two steel fences, and a flock of Canada geese perched on the edge of the lake, basking in the sunshine. A dozen pines and sweet gums cast shadows on two semicircles of monkey grass, which resembled two large flower beds but with only a few young cypresses and some dead leaves in them. A woodpecker began hammering away on the other shore, and except for the rapid knocking, all the other sounds subsided at once. Having looked at the outside of the house, the Wus went to its front and rang the doorbell.

An old man came out. Seeing that the Wus were potential buyers, he let them in. His name was John Wolfe, and he was a retiree living alone. He wore a hearing aid but looked in good shape, with thick shoulders, a flat belly, thin legs, and a bush of white hair. After giving them a brief tour through the house, which had a half-finished basement, two small bedrooms and one large master bedroom, and two bathrooms, he told the Wus that the asking price was $85,000. Somehow the house felt smaller than it looked from the outside. Seated on a sofa in the living room, Nan explained their interest and difficulty. "We can't get a mortgage from zer bank because our business is too small," he told Mr. Wolfe.

"I know the Gold Wok. Its soups are delicious. Has Mr. Wang retired?"

"Yes. We have zer place now."

"Do you own it or run it?"

"We two own it togezzer." Nan put his hand on his wife's shoulder.

"How much down payment can you plunk down if I let you buy this house?"

Nan looked at Pingping, then said, "Maybe sirty percent."

"Holy smokes! I didn't expect you'd pay that kind of cash. That will do—I mean, we can figure out a way. Now, how about the rest of the payment? Are you willing to pay some interest, say seven percent?" He tapped his right foot on the beige carpet.

"Zat's a little bit too high for us," Nan said. He turned to Pingping and asked, "*What do you think?*"

"*Seven percent is fine if he doesn't change it,*" she said.

"Seven percent fixed," he told the old man.

Pingping added, "We'll try to pay all your money in three and four years."

That was indeed possible, since the restaurant could fetch a profit of more than $30,000 a year. Mr. Wolfe seemed unconvinced and said, "I don't mean to be nosy. Tell me, how much can you two make a year?"

"Maybe sirty-five thousand," Nan answered.

The old man's face crinkled into a smile while his bell-shaped nose quivered. He confessed that he hated to let an agent take a five percent cut from the sale, so this would be a good arrangement. After some calculation, an agreement was reached: besides the thirty percent down payment, the Wus would give him at least $1,000 a month until the mortgage was paid off.

Nan was eager to buy this place mainly because he liked the lake on the south of the property; according to feng shui, that symbolized the abundance of life. What's more, a nameless creek flowed in the east, about two hundred yards away from Mr. Wolfe's property, meandering along the edge of the woods. That was also an auspicious sign, which might embody the spring of life. Nan had never taken feng shui seriously, but at the sight of this house, somehow he couldn't stop thinking of that occult system. As their conversation continued, the Wus realized why the old man actually couldn't wait to sell his home. His ex-wife had left him the year before and he had a girlfriend down in Florida, near Pompano Beach, and was anxious to join her there.

Pingping, however, was suspicious about the feng shui of this place, where at least one marriage had disintegrated. She couldn't share Nan's enthusiasm and superstitious thoughts, but she supported the deal and had paid a five-hundred-dollar deposit. The house was close to the shopping plaza and solid in every way despite its low ceiling. Mr. Wolfe had built it himself, so the brickwork and the woodwork were fine—the living room walls were oak-paneled and even the carport was constructed of cherry red bricks with zigzag furrows on their sides, the same as those used for the house.

Coming out of Mr. Wolfe's, Nan and Pingping headed back to the Gold Wok. They were excited, never having dreamed they might soon own a house on a piece of land they could call their own.

15

ON THURSDAY MORNING they took Mr. Wolfe to Mr. Shang's office to sign the contract. They used the attorney again because his fee was $120, half the price Mr. Wolfe's lawyer would charge. Pingping was surprised by the change of the law office in less than a month. Now the suite was divided into two parts, one of which had become a gift shop lined with shelves displaying merchandise for overseas Chinese to buy for their families and friends in Taiwan and on the mainland—Wisconsin ginseng, multiple vitamins, capsules of fish oil, dried sea cucumbers, Spanish fly, love lotions, growth hormone release formulas, cosmetics, electronic gadgets—whereas the other half of the suite was still used by Mr. Shang as his office. Apparently the attorney wasn't doing well. These days so many small businesses had gone under in this area that some suites and rooms in Chinatown were vacant, marked with FOR RENT signs. But Mr. Shang was effusive and congratulatory when he saw the Wus again. Beyond his desk sat a Chinese girl, plump and pimply, typing at a computer and wearing headphones. Beside the mouse pad was a tiny CD player. She was wagging her head rhythmically while punching the keyboard. Mr. Shang declared to Nan, "I told you that you were going to be a millionaire." Nan wondered why Cathy, the secretary, wasn't here. Probably she had been laid off.

"It's just small house," Pingping told him, smiling.

"This is a big step, though," said the lawyer.

Mr. Wolfe chimed in, "A home is where you start to build your fortune."

"That's right," Mr. Shang agreed. "This is a major step toward realizing your American dream."

Nan couldn't help but wonder why Mr. Wolfe suddenly sounded like an old Chinese. What fortune had he built at the house on Marsh Drive? Just a broken marriage.

The transaction was quite simple. Mr. Wolfe had already written out their agreement on the price and the format of payment, and the attorney was just supposed to go over the contract, serve as a witness, and ascertain the validity of the sale. Mr. Shang took the sheets of paper from the old man and read them carefully. Then he said to the three of them, "This is fine. Everything is clearly spelled out. Because there's no mortgage from the bank, the sale is very simple. It's just between you two parties."

"So we should go ahead and sign zis contract?" asked Nan.

"Yes."

Mr. Wolfe shook his head, but scrawled his signature without a word. The Wus followed suit, signing their names as cobuyers. Then Pingping took out an envelope that contained a certified check for $25,000 and handed it to Mr. Wolfe. At the sight of it, the old man was elated. He scrutinized the check and put it back into the envelope. Smiling faintly, he inserted the money into the inner pocket of his jacket.

In the parking lot of the office he praised Mr. Shang to the Wus. "He's a good guy and doesn't rip off his clients. I should've used him for my divorce."

16

MR. WOLFE departed for Florida a week later. The Wus went to clean the home every morning before they began their day at the restaurant. Along with the house, the old man had left them some furniture and all the household tools, which came in handy for their cleaning. One morning they happened upon a vase standing on the doormat and holding a bunch of mixed snow crocuses. Attached to it was a note saying, "Welcome to the neighborhood—Mrs. Lodge." They placed the bouquet on the round coffee table in the living room, which at once brightened as if the yellow and white flowers had become a vibrant center. They had no idea who Mrs. Lodge was and whether they should return the vase. Knowing that colored people weren't always welcome in a predominantly white neighborhood, the Wus hadn't expected such warm greetings. Mrs. Lodge's present made their day. On their way to work, they read the names on some mailboxes while walking along the left-hand side of the street so as to avoid the traffic coming from behind, since there was no sidewalk anywhere in this neighborhood. They found that the Lodges lived about a dozen houses away from theirs. On the front porch of that raised ranch hung a large wicker swing, and on the well-kept lawn stood a willow oak and a colossal magnolia, its broad leaves scintillating with dewdrops in the sun. A flock of grackles were walking on the grass, most of them with their bills ajar as if they were choking. Suddenly one of them took off, then the entire flock followed, whirring and swirling in the air like a twisting blanket. And a few were crying gratingly. Nan and Pingping thought of going in to thank Mrs. Lodge, but decided against it, unsure that this was an appropriate time. *"There's no hurry. We can always do something in return,"* Nan told his wife.

•

It was said that Lawrenceville, an adjacent town to the east, had once been a base of the Ku Klux Klan. The Wus had heard some white men sing the praises of the Klan and claim to feel proud of being rednecks, but they had never seen a Klansman in the flesh. And they were convinced that the area was safe and peaceful, though not without racial prejudice. For instance, at A&P, the supermarket at the plaza, where the Wus usually went shopping, two women cashiers, one twentyish and the other middle-aged, had often scowled at them. One day the younger one, with thin limbs and honey-colored hair in loose ringlets, even overturned every one of the Wus' purchases as she was ringing them up, while the older woman watched with a smirk. Thereafter, the Wus always gave those two women a wide berth. Nan noticed that their shunning them seemed to have embarrassed the older one. She once motioned for them to check out through her lane, but they pretended they hadn't seen her. A month later the supermarket went out of business. Despite their treatment by the two women, the Wus were upset and disturbed by its disappearance, because from now on they'd have to do their shopping at Kroger or Winn-Dixie, which were farther away. Also, if a big store had failed like that, the Gold Wok could easily go under if they didn't manage it well.

Pingping was always attached to old things. Once she got used to something, she'd automatically take it as a part of her life, so she missed the now defunct supermarket a lot. Two years earlier Heidi had gotten her worn-out washer and dryer replaced, and Pingping had been so disappointed that for months afterward she'd mention the old machines, saying they could still have run properly. Now, for weeks she talked about the vanished A&P and wondered what would become of its employees. Nan told her to stop worrying about that. This was America, where everything came and went quickly. Deep down, however, he too was shaken and was more determined to run their business well and never to miss the monthly payment to Mr. Wolfe.

The day before the Wangs returned, the Wus moved out of the bungalow and set up their residence at 568 Marsh Drive.

17

NAN remembered noticing a sly, gleeful look passing Mr. Wolfe's face when the contract was signed at the Shang Law Office two weeks before. He couldn't figure that out until his neighbor Alan Johnson talked with him. Alan, an engineer of fifty-three who worked for General Motors, was rearranging the worm fence on his lawn. At the sight of Nan he stopped to greet him. The two men chatted about the schools in this area. Recently the districts in the county had been redivided and the older teenagers on Marsh Drive had begun attending Parkview High, a top school in Gwinnett County, so their parents were all pleased. This also meant the houses on the street would appreciate more in value. As their conversation went on, Alan switched the topic and said, his chunky face grinning, "Have you spoken to Gerald?" Gerald's house was next to the Wus'.

"No, about what?" asked Nan.

"You should make him keep his property nice and clean. John, the former owner of your house, used to have an exchange of words with him every once in a while and even tried to take him to court once."

"For what?"

"Gerald is lazy. He's the shame of this neighborhood. People are mad at him. Look at the mess he's made of his property." Alan pointed at Gerald's house and yard. Indeed, the mailbox, flagless and partly squashed, sat on a stack of building blocks as unsteadily as if it could be swept down by a gust of wind. Numerous brown patches marred the lawn, on which stood a few spindly pines almost choked by wild vines. The front porch of the house was half shielded by plywood, and on it was piled all kinds of stuff Gerald had brought back from construction sites where he had worked as an electrician:

bundles of rubber-sheathed wire, cans of paint, scraps of rug, buckets of plaster, bricks, ceramic tiles, boxes of nails and screws, broken fans, even a used air conditioner. On the east side of the house was parked a truck, its windshield and a front wheel missing, and it was propped up with wood blocks. Although the Wus had noticed the sorry state of Gerald's house, they hadn't been concerned. The idea that the mess would affect the appearance and value of their property hadn't crossed their minds, because they had never owned any real estate before.

"What happened to him?" Nan asked Alan. "Out of work?"

"No, he makes good money. His wife divorced him two years ago and he has to pay child support."

"He has children? I haven't seen zem."

"He has a boy and a girl, nice kids. It's a shame the family fell apart."

Nan thought of asking him about John's wife, but held back. Why had there been so many broken marriages in this neighborhood? Wasn't this a bad omen? The other day he and Pingping had talked with Gerald, who said he made sixteen dollars an hour but had to pay so many bills that he couldn't have his roof replaced. Indeed, its brown shingles looked decayed, already bleached by the sun and partly damaged by hailstones. There was even a family of squirrels living in the roof, who had gnawed off the tip of the northwestern eaves and used a missing louver board on the west side of the roof as an entrance.

The Wus had noticed the junk cars, the oil drums, and the piles of firewood and plastic pipes in Gerald's backyard, in the middle of which sat a large trampoline. Toward the lakeside all the trees were entwined by vines, almost blocking the view of the water and giving a swampy impression. One pine had fallen into the lake; against its root leaned an overturned canoe, which Gerald had never rowed. Goby, the kinky-coated collie Gerald kept, was tethered to a fence post by a long chain all the time, and his doghouse looked like a chicken coop. Gerald never walked him, and the confinement seemed to have maddened the dog, who often gasped and coughed. Goby had angry eyes and yowled a lot, sometimes furiously in the dead of night, triggering the crescendo of baying as about a dozen dogs at the houses around the lake joined in. From the day the Wus moved here, Goby would growl and woof at them, even though Tao-tao tried to appease him with scraps of food over and over again. Once Pingping saw a white man enter Gerald's backyard to read the water meter, and the dog made no noise whatsoever. Indeed, Goby wouldn't bark at Caucasians, neither neighbors nor strangers. "That dog is racist," Pingping said. Both Nan and Taotao agreed.

The Wus weren't really bothered by the messy state of Gerald's home, and they didn't intend to talk with him as Alan had urged them to do. Instead, they felt sorry for him and decided not to pressure him like the other neighbors. Similar to Gerald, they viewed themselves as poor people.

Nan now understood why Mr. Wolfe had smiled secretively when Pingping handed him the check—the old man must have believed nobody would want to live with a neighbor like Gerald, whose wretched house would make the adjacent homes depreciate in value. The Wus didn't mind having such a neighbor, since they wouldn't be selling their house anytime soon. Their only regret was that, had they mentioned Gerald's house in the negotiation, they could have haggled down the price considerably with Mr. Wolfe.

18

IT SNOWED on Saturday night a month after they had settled into their new home. This was rare in Georgia. The three-inch snow on the ground excited the children in the neighborhood, some of whom came out the next morning, riding on makeshift sleds, frolicking on the white lawns, and throwing snowballs while shouting war cries. Owing to the weight of crusted ice, some branches, especially of pines, had snapped and fallen to the ground. Electrical wires were mangled here and there, and workers were busy repairing them. The din raised by chain saws came from everywhere. In the Wus' backyard icicles still hung on the sweet gums at the waterside, having expanded and thickened the shadows cast by the trees on the lake. The waterfowl were all out of view and nestled in the bushes on the other shore to keep warm. From time to time they let out lethargic cries.

Taotao, accustomed to being alone, didn't join the kids of the neighborhood and instead played with his mother on their own lawn. Through the sliding glass door Nan watched his wife and son in the backyard; both of them were in the winter gear they had worn in the Northeast—leather gloves and tall boots. Pingping donned a flesh-colored stocking hat and a quilted coat that came down to her calves. Taotao wore a blue parka. Together mother and son were pushing a snowball already two feet across, while their breath clouded before them. The boy wanted to save some snow, so they were rolling the snowball around. Observing them, Nan was moved by the tranquil sight. His wife and son looked so happy and intimate. Suddenly Pingping took a pratfall, having stepped on one of the terrazzo tiles set a yard apart to form a curved path toward the lakeside. Taotao broke out laughing and clapped his gloved hands while his mother picked herself up from the ice-crusted grass. Nan chuckled over his tea mug.

Although touched by the peaceful scene, he still felt a lingering pain in his heart. The previous night he had again dreamed of his first love, Beina. In his sleep the two of them walked outside the campus of their old college. Moonlight filtered through the aspen grove and was shimmering on the snow grayed by thawing. For some reason, they quarreled again, and angrily she hurried away to the entrance of her dorm building. He shouted, "Beina, Beina, wait a second, let me explain!" She wouldn't listen and faded into the darkness of the doorway. His friend Danning appeared from behind a thick birch and dragged him away, saying, "She's not worth your love. Forget her. My friend, you must save yourself!" Somehow later Beina embraced him at a train station and wept wretchedly. After he woke up, he mused about her tears but couldn't guess why. He hoped her husband hadn't treated her too badly. She had looked colorless and must have been ill. Why had Danning Meng, the man who had studied physics at Brandeis and returned to Beijing two years ago, appeared in his dream? Nan was positive that Danning and Beina hadn't known each other at all. What a bizarre dream.

Peals of laughter came from outside and brought Nan back to his wife and son. He went on observing them, happy to see them in such buoyant spirits. He had just finished reading *A House for Mr. Biswas* and still vividly remembered the struggle the protagonist waged for having his own shelter in his own corner of land. He felt fortunate that he might achieve such a goal in just a few years. Though their mortgage was unpaid, he was on his way to becoming an independent man. His heart was filled with joy and gratitude. At long last he was hungry for making money, a lot of money, so that his family could live in peace and security.

With the back of his hand he touched his face, which wasn't hot today. Ever since the outset of the winter, he had often run a low fever. He had lived in cold climates all his life, and now in the mild Georgia winter his body was ready to resist cold, of which there wasn't any. Small wonder, bugs abounded here in the summertime. Any insects could easily survive a mild winter like this. Nan had noticed that a lot of roaches hibernated in the firewood left by Mr. Wolfe, stacked along their western steel fence. Just now as he talked with Gerald, Gerald had told him, "This snow's killing all them bugs. There'll be a bumpa peach crop nex' summa." If only there were more cold days like this one.

On such a crisp morning Nan felt energetic and clearheaded. He was in the mood for writing a poem about the scene in the backyard, about the joy and serenity of life, but he couldn't decide how to begin. He thought a good while about such a poem, which should start with a line like this: "Snow has been falling in the Southeast," but he didn't know how to proceed from there. In an hour or so he'd have to go to the restaurant, where there were chickens to cut up, flounder to clean, and spring rolls to wrap. It was always busy on Sundays, and he had to get everything ready before noon, the opening time. So he returned to his room and lay down on his bed to rest some more before setting out for work.

19

NOWADAYS Taotao no longer stayed at the restaurant after school. Their house was so close by that he could walk back and forth. If he was at home alone, Pingping would call to check on him. Sometimes she'd go back to see if he was doing his homework. Nan had bought him a cheap computer because Taotao said he would build one by himself eventually. The boy knew two older kids who had just assembled their own computers, and his parents agreed to buy the parts for him. Both Nan and his wife felt fortunate about the way things had worked out. They were eager to get rid of their debt, though Pingping insisted on keeping a tidy sum in the bank as a backup fund. The economy was still in recession despite the start of a slow recovery. She wanted to make certain that they could have enough money for the monthly payment even in a lean time. On average they managed to pay Mr. Wolfe $1,500 a month.

Luckily the Gold Wok continued thriving. To increase its food variety, Nan added steamed dumplings and several kinds of noodles, such as noodles sautéed with beef and snow peas, or with shiitake mushrooms, or with dried shrimp and scallops. The new offerings helped fetch more customers. Their Yangzhou Rice had become a favorite choice for lunch, loved by the Mexican workers at the construction site of an apartment complex off Lawrenceville Highway. Nan had been wondering how to make the restaurant more profitable, but it was too small to expand further. Yet there was an obvious way, namely to install a bar. Alcoholic beverages were lucrative, but neither Nan nor Pingping knew how to mix drinks. The Gold Wok did have a license for alcohol, yet to date it had offered only a few bottled beers and wines. For weeks the Wus had been wondering whether they should set up a bar, which meant they'd have to hire a barkeep. That would cost a lot.

When working in New York, Nan had heard a good deal about bars in Chinese restaurants. Many of them were tended by Caucasians, because most Asians couldn't communicate with customers well enough in English. ABCs, American-born Chinese, didn't take bartending as a real profession, so they wouldn't man bars. In a Chinese restaurant, all too often there was unspoken contention between the barman and the waitstaff. At some places the bars even offered appetizers, directly taking business away from the dining tables. It was commonplace that a barman often acted like a lord in a Chinese restaurant and was feared by waiters and waitresses, because he could create trouble for them by slightly altering the drinks ordered by their customers. If a complaint came up and their boss intervened, the barman could simply say he couldn't understand the English used by the waiter or waitress who had placed the order. Worse yet, it was almost impossible for the boss to follow the sales at the bar, so the barkeep could give favors freely to barflies, especially to young women, and some barmen even pocketed the money that was supposed to go to the cash registers. In short, a bar could be a bonanza but also a major bugbear.

Pingping didn't know what a bar would entail, so Nan explained everything to her. He even thought of finding a Chinese fellow, sending him to a bartending school in Atlanta and then hiring him afterward. But Pingping was adamantly against setting up a bar, which she said would throw their business out of kilter. Since physically the restaurant couldn't be expanded any more, there shouldn't be a bar that might destroy their peace of mind. What they needed most was a stable clientele, which didn't even have to be large. Nan agreed.

For months Nan had been working at least fourteen hours a day, sometimes without seeing the sun for a whole week, as he had to go to the Gold Wok early in the morning to get things ready. He'd slice beef, cut chickens, boil the bones to make stock, heat up a samovar for tea, chop broccoli and scallions, steam rice, deep-fry pork and chicken cubes. In the afternoons his legs often felt heavy and bloated; he'd sit down whenever he could, even when working at the wok, so as to avoid developing varicose veins. The restaurant had fully occupied his body and mind. Even at night he often dreamed of greeting customers and cooking their orders, his head full of the din of the kitchen while his limbs remained hot and sore as a result of the long working hours. His hands, always marked by nicks or burns or blisters, would throb a little whenever he woke up in the morning. Despite the hard work, despite his fatigue, he felt content and was determined to succeed. At long last life had become simple and clear to him, as if all the confusion and uncertainties had never befogged his mind.

One afternoon Pingping handed Nan a letter. *"It's for you."*

"For me? From whom?"

"How can I know? Must be from a secret lover of yours." She tittered, seeing his eyes flash with annoyance.

He hadn't expected that Sam Fisher would write back. A month earlier Nan had sent the poet a letter to inform him of his move to Georgia. He told Sam about the Gold Wok and his intention to continue to write poetry, which he had almost stopped doing, actually. He just meant to keep in touch with Sam in case he might consult him on the craft of poetry writing. Besides telling Sam that he loved his book *Fire Sutra,* he also took the occasion to send his greetings to Dick Harrison, the tall young poet, who had been friendly to him when Nan was in New York. In his reply Sam Fisher encouraged Nan to write more poetry, saying that he had talent and should persevere to develop it, and that what was fundamental was "to sustain a great sentiment" in his heart. Sam also mentioned that he had lately fallen in love with some of Tu Fu's poems, which he hoped he could translate someday.

The letter touched and upset Nan at the same time. He had been so devoted to making money lately that his desire to be a poet was almost gone, though he still read poetry before going to sleep at night. He was very fond of a thick anthology called *Great Poems,* especially the short explanatory essays before each poem, and he pored over the book whenever he had time. He knew some of the poems, but some he had never read before. He wrote back to Sam Fisher and offered to help if Sam did embark on translating Tu Fu.

20

THE WUS knew very few Chinese living in this area. Neither had they gone to any Chinese church or visited the community center in Chinatown. They just wanted to lead an undisturbed life and didn't mind their isolation.

However, one afternoon in mid-March, two Chinese, a young man and a woman in her mid-thirties, came to the Gold Wok. They ignored Tammie's greetings and went straight to Pingping and Nan at the counter. The woman, who had a bony face, glossy skin, fierce eyes, and permed hair, introduced herself as the wife of a graduate student at Georgia Tech, whereas the man said he was a leader of the Chinese student association of that same school. They had come here to solicit a donation for the flood victims in mainland China. Nan wasn't interested and said he had no money.

The woman, named Mei Hong, persisted, *"Look, Mr. Wu, you're from China, aren't you? Even if you're a rich American businessman now, you shouldn't forget your ancestors and homeland. Think about what you can do for your country."*

"China is not my country anymore, and I'm not a rich man," Nan said. *"I've been working my ass off day in and day out to keep this place alive. Besides, you shouldn't parrot that JFK crap here. Every citizen has the right to ask what my country can do for me."*

Stumped, she stared at him for a moment, then kept on, *"Do you know how much damage the Yangtze flood did last autumn?"*

"I know, but it's over. It's spring now."

"No. Seventy million victims are still suffering from the aftermath of the calamity. Tens of thousands of them are homeless and waiting

232

for your help. Eighteen provinces are still struggling to recover from the losses—"

"*Give me a break! How can I be a savior of so many people? We've separated ourselves from China long ago, and for good. We don't owe it anything.*"

The young man tugged at Mei Hong's elbow, saying, "*Let's go. It's no use arguing with such a miser who has forgotten his roots.*" His eyebrows were tilting as he kept pushing his flat nose with his knuckle.

Pingping said to Nan, "*Why not give them a few dollars and send them away?*"

"*No, this is a matter of principle. I won't spend money this way.*"

Mei Hong went on, "*You act like the U.S. government. Don't you feel ashamed?*"

"*I'm not as rich as Uncle Sam.*" Nan raised his voice. "*I don't collect taxes from others.*"

"*All right, do you know China appealed to the United States for help last autumn? Guess how much the U.S. government offered our country.*"

"*How much?*"

"*Twenty thousand dollars.*"

"*Yes, that's just enough for one of those cars,*" the young man said, pointing at the parking lot. "*The United States, the richest country in the world, meant to humiliate China with that piddling amount of money.*"

"*What does this have to do with me?*" Nan asked. "*If my business went belly-up, China wouldn't come to my rescue, would it? Where could I get even one dollar?*"

"*But you're a Chinese and obligated to do something,*" Mei Hong said.

"*I've done enough for China. Don't want to be charitable anymore.*"

"*Don't you have your parents and family back home?*"

"*Yes, I do.*"

"*Then how can you be so cold and cut yourself off completely? How can you see your own people suffering and dying without lifting a finger to help?*"

"*Because even if I donated millions, the money would never reach the victims, and the officials would gobble it up. I don't want to fatten those parasites.*"

"*We know what you're saying might be true to some degree, but we have made sure that the money we give will be spent on the victims. That's why so many people have contributed. One fellow at Georgia State is so poor that he lives in a decrepit van, but even he gave twenty dollars.*"

"Yes," the young man added, "*a chemistry professor donated a thousand. He's from Nanjing originally.*"

Mei Hong went on, "*We ought to separate the Chinese government from the common people. In this case, we're helping the victims.*"

Their words mollified Nan some. Pingping put in, "*How about fifty dollars?*"

Mei Hong said, "*How about sixty? I gave seventy, but I'm not as rich as you. I came to America only last summer. Even my daughter gave twelve dollars—that was all she had for pocket money.*"

"*Give them sixty and let them go,*" Nan grunted to Pingping.

She opened their checkbook. "*Who do I make the check out to?*"

"*The Georgia Tech Chinese Student Association.*"

While his wife was writing the check, Nan said to the solicitors, "*We give this money not because the victims are mainlanders. If they were people in Hong Kong or Taiwan or elsewhere, we would do the same. We just don't want to have anything to do with the Chinese government.*"

"*We understand. Some old overseas Chinese said the same thing, because they were hurt by the revolution and the political movements,*" Mei Hong admitted.

That made Nan ponder. He knew that Pingping and he were actually making this donation to China, and that if they hadn't been from there, the solicitors wouldn't have come to them.

"*Here you are.*" Pingping handed them the check.

The solicitors accepted it with a bow, which made the Wus cringe. Before turning to the door, Mei Hong said with wholehearted sincerity, "*On behalf of all the suffering Chinese on the mainland, on behalf of our country, we thank you from the bottom of our hearts. You will receive a thank-you letter from the Chinese consulate.*" She bowed again, and so did the young man.

"No need to hear from them," Nan said. "*They wouldn't even renew my passport.*"

"*We know how you feel,*" said Mei Hong. "*For several days we've been begging around shamelessly for our motherland. We only hope our children won't repeat the same act in the future when our country becomes rich and strong.*"

Both Nan and Pingping were astonished and wordlessly saw them walking away. When they had gone out the door, Nan shook his squarish chin and said to his wife, "*Such hotheads! They acted like state delegates, so damned sincere as if the whole of China rested on their shoulders and they couldn't even feel the weight.*"

"*You shouldn't have said that.*"

"*Said what?*"

"*We have nothing to do with China.*"

"*I know,*" he sighed. "*I was just angry. If only we could squeeze the old country out of our blood.*"

Nan had once thought they could dissociate themselves completely from the Chinese community here and just live a reclusive, undisturbed life, but now it was clear that China would never leave them alone. Wherever they went, the old land seemed to follow them.

PART FOUR

1

SPRING in Georgia was miserable for Nan and Pingping, both allergic to pollen. The air turned yellowish in daylight, and even the surfaces of roads changed color in the mornings, dusted with the powder from trees. Every day before going to work, Pingping would sweep their deck clean of the yellow dust. Once she couldn't find their car in the parking lot of Winn-Dixie, pollen having coated all the vehicles parked there and dulled their colors. Here the pollen season was much longer than in New England, usually from late February to mid-May. Whenever Pingping went out, she'd wear a mask, a nose piece, regardless of the attention it drew, whereas Nan wouldn't do that, so his nose had swollen to twice its normal size. How eagerly they looked forward to the next rain, which might cleanse the air for a few days so that they could walk outside again. To fight the allergies, Pingping made Taotao and Nan take tablets of bee pollen every day, which helped some, though Nan would have gastric pain if he swallowed them on an empty stomach. The Wus also took plenty of vitamins to build up their resistance to the allergies. Not until mid-May when a drought set in did they begin to feel better. Miraculously Taotao's allergy had subsided considerably this year. Back in Massachusetts pollen had tortured him, but now he could play in the open air without a runny nose or itchy eyes. Nan joked about him, saying the boy had acculturated so well, he would become a redneck eventually.

"I ain't a redneck!" his son protested, imitating some of his classmates, with an upswinging lilt on the last syllable "neck."

"Don't use that kinda language," his mother warned him.

"Yes, ma'am."

They all laughed. Actually, like Taotao, Nan and Pingping had begun to adapt to life here as well. Sometimes Pingping made grits for breakfast, and they often ate kale and collard and mustard greens. Nan and Taotao also liked pork rinds, boiled peanuts, fried okra, hush puppies, barbecue sauce. But the boy disliked the cheese here, which indeed had a dull taste compared with that in the Northeast. Corn bread had become a favorite of theirs, like a kind of pastry, and they'd buy it whenever it was on sale. Back in China, Pingping and Nan had lived on corn buns for many years, but that was a different kind, with no sugar or milk mixed into the cornmeal. It was pure corn, one hundred percent. One day Pingping cooked a few corn buns—the Chinese type—for Taotao, who had asked her for them several times, but the boy, after taking a bite, wouldn't touch it again. "Tastes like crap!" he said.

Unlike him, his parents each ate a whole bun with relish. They also brought one to Tammie. At the sight of it, the waitress got excited, but after having a morsel, she frowned and said, "You mainlanders always insist on the reunification with Taiwan, but I bet no Taiwanese wants to eat this stuff. You should eliminate this sort of corn buns before you talk about the reunification. This is absolutely not for human consumption."

Despite saying that, despite eating only a quarter of the bun with a piece of smoked herring as Pingping suggested, Tammie was pleased by the Wus' sharing it with her. She wrapped the remainder of the bun and took it home to show her roommates.

2

FOR TWO YEARS Nan had often feared that his wife or son might fall ill, because they had no health insurance. Nan had once known a young man living in downtown Boston who was a Canadian citizen; the fellow had never bought any medical insurance, so if he had an illness, he'd go to Montreal to see his doctor. Nan wished his family could do that.

He talked with Jinsheng Yu, who had once served as a captain in the Chinese People's Liberation Army and was now a reputable insurance agent used by many Asians and Latinos in the Atlanta area. Jinsheng told him that it would cost $860 a month to get the standard health insurance for his family. There was no way the Wus could afford that. At the suggestion of Jinsheng, Nan bought only the emergency coverage for his family for about $90 a month. This was the best he could do. Such a minimum protection, however, did calm him down some. He knew that a lot of Asian immigrants had no medical insurance whatsoever. If they were ill, they'd first go to an herbal shop. With few exceptions, Chinese herbalists are also doctors and can treat ailments and prescribe herbs. Some of them in the Atlanta area had been professors in medical schools back in China, but they couldn't practice here because they specialized only in Chinese medicine and couldn't speak English, so were unable to pass the professional exams. Apprehensive of lawsuits, many of them avoided treating whites and blacks, to whom they sold only herbs and patent pills and boluses.

The Wus didn't believe in Chinese medicine despite its holistic approach, despite its emphasis on the balances between yin and yang and between hot and cold winds in the body, but their friend

Janet often asked Pingping about herbs. Janet had once been treated by an acupuncturist for her back injury, so she was fascinated by Chinese medicine. In addition, she also wanted to know if there was an herbal remedy for infertility, of which Pingping wasn't sure.

One afternoon, toward the end of May, Janet came to the Gold Wok, wearing pedal pushers and a thick ring on her second toe. Unlike other days, she overstayed her midafternoon break. She and Pingping were sitting in a corner booth, chitchatting and tittering while Tammie was wiping with a sponge the cruets and saltshakers on the dining tables, a basin of warm water on a stool beside her. On the wall beyond them pranced and frolicked the horses and foals in the mural painted a decade before. Putting her long-fingered hand on Pingping's forearm, Janet said, "I have something to ask you."

"What?"

"Would you like to have another baby?"

"I love babies, but I can't."

"Why?"

"I must make money and help Nan and Taotao. Nan like to have a lotta kids, but we can't afford."

"What if somebody gives you money, lots of money?"

"What you mean?"

"I mean, I'd love to pay you to have a baby for Dave and me."

"I don't understand."

"Dave and I cannot have a baby no matter how hard we try. It's my problem, my eggs are no good."

"How can I have baby for you?"

"There are two ways." Janet grew animated, her eyes fully open and glowing. "You and Nan have another baby for us, and we'll pay you ten thousand dollars. Or you and Dave have a baby, and we'll double that."

"That's disgusting. How can I have Dave's baby!" Pingping was blushing to the ears and felt insulted.

"Don't blow your top. You must've misunderstood me. Haven't you heard the term 'surrogate mother'?" Janet scratched her own freckled arm.

"I heard it on TV, but what it mean exactly?"

"The doctor can inseminate a woman's egg with a man's sperm, and then put it into her uterus. That'll make her pregnant."

"Then what?"

"After the baby is born, the father has the right to it."

"So the mother can't see her own child again?"

"In most cases she can't. She has to abide by the agreement she signed with the man and his wife before she went through the artificial insemination. But biologically she's still the mother." Janet's face tensed up, as though she were holding back a smile. "If I could get pregnant like you, I'd have a small army of kids and let them populate a whole town."

"This is hard, Janet." Pingping crimped her brows, then muttered, "Why can't you adopt baby? Lots American couples have Chinese girls."

"We've thought of that, but ideally we'd love to have a baby from you."

"Why you give me such big problem? This is very hard for me."

"Look, Pingping, you're so pretty and healthy that we'd love to have your baby. You're just a year or two younger than me, but look at you—your skin and figure are like a young girl's. You can easily pass for twenty-five."

"You don't understand, Janet. Chinese women don't get old very quick like white women before we are fifty. Chinese girls grow up slow. I have my first period when I was sixteen. But after we're fifty, we suddenly become old woman, very, very old."

"Anybody's old after fifty."

"But after fifty, white woman get old very slow, because better nutrition, I guess. Look at Mrs. Lodge. She's eighty-nine and still do yard work and grow her vegetable garden."

"Okay, I see your point. Dave and I will be blessed if you can give us a baby."

"I can't do that, sorry."

"You see, usually a surrogate mother is paid ten thousand dollars. We're willing to double that. Cash. You won't have to pay tax for it. Dave loves Taotao, you know, and I can see that he dreams we can have a son like yours someday."

"Why not girl? I like girls."

"A girl will be great too. We'll be thrilled to have her."

"I can't say yes, Janet. Maybe I should talk to my husband."

"Sure, I understand. This ought to be a family decision. Talk to Nan, okay?"

"All right."

Although reluctant to consider the offer, Pingping saw this as an opportunity to reduce their mortgage, which had agitated her all along. Never had she borrowed money before they bought the house. She had always dreaded debt and paid their bills promptly. What if their business took a downturn? Or Nan fell ill, unable to work for some time? Then they might lose everything. If they couldn't make their monthly payments, for sure Mr. Wolfe would come and take their home back just as banks would repossess houses and cars of insolvent mortgagors. The more she thought about this possibility, the more terrified she was. She felt they must pay off the mortgage as soon as possible.

That night, after Taotao went to bed, she talked to Nan about the Mitchells' offer. "*No way,*" said Nan, whose eyes suddenly blazed. "*You must be out of your mind. How can you think I'll let you be a surrogate mother, carrying another man's seed? I'm not that shameless. If you love babies so much, I can give you one. Do you really want one for ourselves?*"

"*That's not my point. We need money to reduce our debt, don't we?*"

"*But you mustn't use yourself that way. What will you say to Taotao if someday he asks you why you sold his brother or sister?*"

"*I don't mean to sell a baby. Only because Janet needs my help. She's a friend.*"

"*But the fact is that you'll have to disown the child if you accept her money. How can you face Taotao if he asks you what happened to his sibling?*"

This was more than Pingping could bear, and she burst into sobs, which startled Nan. He softened some and said, "*Come, don't cry. I won't let you take that kind of risk.*"

"*I know it will be hard and risky, but I can do it for you and Taotao. We must get rid of the mortgage as soon as possible. I'm so scared.*"

"*Scared of what?*"

"*We may lose everything we have if misfortune strikes.*"

"*Don't be a worrywart. Nothing will happen as long as we manage our business carefully. Look at Americans. Don't most of them have a mortgage? Do they fret like us? Many of them feel lucky if they can get a mortgage. We must shed our Chinese mind-set and learn to accept insecurity as a living condition.*" Despite saying that, he was touched by his wife's willingness to sacrifice, gratitude welling up in his chest.

She whimpered, "*From now on we mustn't have sex too often. We don't have any real health insurance and can't afford to get sick or have a baby.*"

"*All right, I'll try to control myself. Haven't I always slept in my own room?*"

She grimaced, her lips wet. "*Promise you'll never walk out on me and Taotao.*"

"*How can you think of that? I won't leave you, all right? You two are all I have. Where could I go?*"

Pingping told Janet about Nan's objection the next afternoon. To her surprise, her friend accepted the explanation without any resentment and even said, "I knew it would be difficult. Let's forget it."

Afterward, Janet still came to the Gold Wok for lunch regularly. Pingping continued to help her assemble necklaces for five dollars apiece; she could finish half a dozen a week. They remained friends. Both Pingping and Nan were amazed by Dave and Janet's lack of resentment. If they had turned down such a request from a Chinese couple, the friendship might have ended automatically. Nan began to treat the Mitchells better than before and always picked a bigger red snapper for them when they ordered Five-Willow Fish, a deep-fried fish topped with five shredded vegetables.

Once Pingping asked Janet why she had not resented her refusal. Janet said, "If you agreed to give us a baby, we'd have to run away after it's born, so that you couldn't see us again. See, now I still have you as my friend."

3

EVERY Monday morning Nan went to the Chinese bookstore in Asian Square to buy the Sunday *World Journal,* which, unlike English-language newspapers, wouldn't arrive until midafternoon every day. He couldn't get it on a daily basis, so once a week he'd drive ten miles to Doraville to buy the Sunday paper; this was his way to keep abreast of the news about China and the Chinese diaspora. Besides getting the newspaper, he'd also visit the stores and the supermarket there to check the prices of groceries. His Monday trip to the shopping center was a kind of diversion to him, a luxury, since he had never taken a day off except on major holidays when no customers would show up. One morning in late June he turned up at the Chinese bookstore again, which was owned by *World Journal,* whose regional editorial division occupied two rooms in the back of the store. Several editors and typists worked in there on the advertisements and the local news for the southeastern section of the newspaper. As usual, Nan picked up the Sunday paper, then looked through the new books on the two display tables and flipped through some of the journals and magazines on the shelves. Among all the publications he liked the *Mirror Monthly* best because it carried well-informed articles on cultural and current issues, mostly written by reputable authors and scholars living in Hong Kong, Taiwan, and North America.

He noticed a new book on American life entitled *Under the Star-Spangled Banner,* written by a recent visitor from mainland China to the United States. He disliked this sort of writing targeted to the readers who could never set foot in America, because the writers often told exotic tales that distorted the truth. He remembered that

one author had even bragged that American wives were so understanding toward their husbands that whenever their men were about
to travel, the women would pack condoms into their baggage, implying they wouldn't mind if their husbands had a brief fling away
from home, as long as they didn't leave behind their hearts with
other women. A novelist who was a political officer in the People's
Liberation Army boasted that he had walked alone at night through
Chinatown in New York without taking fright; in an interview, when
asked what the American democracy was like, he replied, "A lot of
paperwork and high taxes." A woman author claimed that she had
increased her worth from $300 to $5 million after living in the
United States for just six years, and that now she was a CEO of a tex-
tile company, her cargo containers always on the move, traveling all
over the Pacific and the Atlantic. An upstart in Florida even bragged
that his ambition was to own a few satellites in space.

Whenever Nan flipped through these books, his heart would
sink—almost every person described in them was a paragon of success. Who will speak for the failures? he wondered. What's worse,
these books were often crudely written, in a journalistic style, and
many of them were a mere mishmash of articles, each of which the
author could finish at one sitting. These writers rushed to report
sensational news of petty triumphs before they had lived here long
enough to develop genuine feelings for this lonesome, unfath-
omable, overwhelming land. Look at these titles on the shelf—*Here
Is a Real America, Conquering the United States, I Have Become a
Successful Lawyer in the Bay Area, Chinese Celebrities in North
America, Our Growth in the USA, A Boss on Wall Street, My Bite of
the Big Apple.*

As Nan opened the June issue of *Harvest*, a major literary
bimonthly published in Shanghai, an author's name caught his eye—
"Danning Meng" printed under a novella entitled *Winds and Clouds
at an Alaskan Seafood Cannery.* Nan was astounded to see his
friend's name in such a top-notch magazine. He turned to the first
page of the story and skimmed several paragraphs. Without doubt
the author was his friend Danning, since the story was set in America and even mentioned Boston. He bought that copy of *Harvest.*

On his drive back along Buford Highway, whenever he stopped at a red light, he'd pick up the magazine and look at the illustrations and the table of contents. Some of the authors' names were familiar to him, and some were not. At the intersection of Jimmy Carter Boulevard he almost bumped into a brand-new passenger van, which bore a silver Darwin fish and a large sticker with red letters: LICENSED TO BITCH! That frightened Nan, and he forced himself not to touch the magazine again until he reached the Gold Wok.

That day at work, whenever he had a free moment, he would read a page or two of Danning's novella. At home that night, he lay on his bed and resumed reading it. He didn't feel it was extraordinary; the writing was sloppy, though the story was interesting and enjoyable. It was told in the first person, in the form of a memoir, and it described how the owner of an Alaskan cannery exploited his workers, who were mostly recent immigrants from Vietnam, South Korea, China, Mexico, and Eastern Europe. The narrator, presented as Danning's doppelgänger, was a graduate student specializing in agronomy at the University of Wisconsin–Madison and went to work in Alaska during the summer to make money for the next year's tuition. The cannery was depicted like a Chinese factory, where industrious workers often got into trouble, bad-mouthed by others, while slackers were trusted and rewarded for their clever words and deeds. Many dawdlers would clock in early and clock out late, but would slack off at work; some would find every excuse for staying on so as to get paid overtime. Furthermore, racial prejudice was widespread, the supervisors acted like little bullies, and most of the workers ate seafood whenever their foremen turned away. Fights broke out among them every day, and some girls were at one another's throats over a hunk, though there were decent people among the working hands. One man had previously been a lieutenant colonel in the Vietnamese army, and another a philosophy professor in Romania who could hardly speak any English. It was a dark story in spite of the narrator's breezy voice.

Turning off the light, Nan thought about the novella, which had somehow disquieted him. The story was believable, full of authentic details that brought the setting to life. Apparently Danning had done a lot of research and thinking, and Nan knew his friend had once been to Alaska, though he didn't believe Danning had ever worked in a cannery. What troubled him more was the insouciant style, full of misfired digs and riffs, which tried too hard to be funny and tantalize the reader. As a result, the humor felt forced and glib, not arising from within the drama, as if the narrator laughed before the audience, as if the author had become the victim of his own wisecracks. More troublesome, Danning had overused four-letter intensifiers, which appeared on every page. Still, Nan was happy for his friend, who had made a breakthrough in just two years after his return to China. Beyond question, his friend had become a literary figure of sorts. The fiction editor at *Harvest* called the readers' attention to Danning's novella in her introduction to this special issue devoted to "literature by students studying abroad." Indeed, the other four featured writers had all lived or were still living in foreign countries. Among the stories Danning's novella seemed to be the center, since the other pieces were much shorter, one just two and a half pages long.

Nan gave the magazine to Pingping, who read the cannery story during the next few days. She shared his view about the writing. *"Danning didn't have to be that flippant and coarse,"* she told him. *"He forgot to mention that among all workers the Chinese were the worst, much worse than the Vietnamese and the Mexicans."* Pingping had once worked in a nursing home that hired many recent immigrants, among whom, she felt, the Korean women were the best workers.

"Danning must be doing quite well," Nan said.

"He's clever and knows how to sell. But don't take his novella too seriously."

"Look, this is Harvest."

"So? If you tried, you could write better. At least you won't use that many double exclamation marks."

"Are you jealous of him?"

"I never want to be a writer—why should I be jealous? Trust me, you can do a better job."

"Heavens, you're so arrogant."

"He tried too hard to please the reader. Also, this kind of writing might mislead the Chinese who have never been to America."

For some reason Pingping simply wouldn't praise Danning's

accomplishment. Why did she judge the novella that way? Nan pondered her remarks and concluded that he agreed with her. He couldn't accept Danning's fiction as literature either. It was at most a piece of creative reportage written by an experienced hack. Yet obviously his friend was making headway in a direction totally different from his own. Maybe someday Danning might grow into a literary figure in China, where the vicissitudes of celebrity defied logic. Nan decided to write to his friend.

4

NAN didn't write to Danning immediately. For several days he'd been experimenting with moo shu, a Mandarin dish he hadn't cooked before. But in his childhood he'd had spring pancakes once a year, which were prepared and eaten in the same way as moo shu except that his mother had used soy paste in place of hoisin sauce. In China the term "moo shu" referred to dishes whose main ingredient was wood ears, sautéed with eggs or pork or shrimp, and they had little resemblance to the Americanized moo shu. Nan realized that the beauty of this dish consisted in the flexible choice of its ingredients. You could sauté meat, seafood, eggs, and vegetables individually, so you were free to make the dish in your own way. This also meant moo shu could be various kinds, sumptuous, or simple and light, or even vegetarian. What's better, Nan could use high-quality tortillas instead of pancakes and serve them after warming them up in the microwave; this would save a lot of work. So he resolved to add moo shu to their menu, not as a regular offer but as a house specialty.

He put a plate of moo shu he had wrapped and cut on a table and asked his wife and Tammie to try it.

"Mmm, it's great!" said Pingping, chewing with relish.

Tammie loved it too. She strode to the storage room and shouted, "Hey, Taotao, come out and have some moo shu."

The boy had just gotten off the school bus and was paring carrots with a scraping knife. After washing his hands, he came out, rubbing his eyes, and yawned. He took a bite of a piece of the tortilla wrapped around bean sprouts and slivers of lean pork. "Is this a taco or something?" he asked.

"No, it's moo shu," Nan said.

"Oh, I remember it!" Taotao's eyes gleamed as he was chewing. "My grandpa cooked this too, but he put chives into it. It tasted much better than this."

"We cannot offer sautéed chives to our cahstomers, who won't like zat," said his father. "Also, zat's too expensive. Maybe we can use chives for ourselves once in a while."

In fact Nan seldom cooked moo shu for themselves. The Wus ate at the restaurant most of the time, just whatever was available. There were choices for Taotao anyway, so the boy wouldn't complain.

When Nan finally had spare time, he wrote a letter to Danning. It read:

August 3, 1992

Dear Danning,

I cannot say how amazed I was to find your novella in the last issue of *Harvest*. Congratulations! I am impressed and can see that you are on your way to an illustrious career. I wish you all the good luck and keep my fingers crossed for you.

I assume that you are married by now. If so, give your wife my regards. My family is well, and we moved to Georgia last summer. Now we live in a northeastern suburb of Atlanta, where I run a small restaurant. The work is hard and weary; most of the time Pingping and I have to put in more than twelve hours a day. But so far we have managed to survive. In truth, we have prospered to some extent. We bought a house nearby, which has a lake, about twenty acres large, in the backyard. You see, I am a laborer now, a professional cook, but I won't complain. Frankly, I feel rather content with our situation. At length we have settled down in a corner of land we can call home.

The other day when I was reading your story, I felt as if we had been separated for a lifetime. You must be a different man now, but I'm sure that with this publication your life must have changed, opened to great expectations.

Please keep me posted about your new publications. There is a decent Chinese bookstore here that carries some magazines

published in China, and I can follow your success from this side of the earth. Work hard and write with more heart and vision.
Your friend,
Nan Wu

He thought about expressing his view on the novella candidly in a postscript, but changed his mind, unwilling to let Danning suspect he was jealous. He didn't know Danning's current address, so he sent the letter in care of the editorial department of *Harvest,* trusting they'd forward it to him.

In front of the Dollar Store at Beaver Hill Plaza stood a mailbox. Nan went out to drop the letter. It was muggy and hot outside, a mass of heat rubbing his face, but two adolescent boys were biking around in the parking lot, crying at each other happily and from time to time letting go of the handlebars of their bicycles while their legs kept pumping away. The heat didn't seem to bother them at all. These days it was so humid that when Nan drove on the street, he often saw waves of water ahead of his car. He had thought he might be losing his mind, seeing things, but Pingping told him she had also seen such puddles on the asphalt. Overhearing them, Tammie giggled and said, "That's just a mirage. It always appears on roads in the summer, even in the North too." Tammie had once lived in upstate New York for a year and had dreaded the winter there.

"That's true," agreed Pingping, "but you see it here more often."

Nan had never seen such shadowy water on the roads in Massachusetts, but again, he could have been too absentminded to notice it. How he hated the Georgia summer, when the damp heat reduced people's appetite, causing his business to flag, its clientele dwindling. Mr. Wang assured him that this was normal and that business would pick up after mid-September.

5

JANET and Dave Mitchell came to dine at the Gold Wok one evening. Dave was six foot one and seemed to have gained weight recently, weighing at least 240 pounds. He was a little bald and wore glasses that barely shielded his large gentle eyes. Both Nan and Ping-ping liked this reticent man, who never raised his voice and always smiled like a young boy when Tammie brought him and his wife their order, to which Nan would add something extra, a plate of teriyaki beef or a bowl of Peking ravioli. Dave would wave at Nan and say in a thin voice, "Thanks!" When he lifted a teacup, it would almost disappear in his huge hand, whose skin was as fair and hairless as his face.

Dave had once told Nan that he was a Republican, though he had grown up in a housing project in Camden, New Jersey, raised by his mother alone. Nan wasn't a citizen yet and couldn't vote, or he'd have argued more often with Dave over politics and the upcoming presidential election. He couldn't understand why Dave, a beneficiary of the welfare system, was adamantly against it. Once he asked him about this, and Dave replied, "I don't want to pay too much income tax and I hate a big government. If the Democrats win the election, they'll jack up taxes again."

"But you don't have to be a Republican to oppose a big gahvern-ment," Nan said.

"No. I may join the Libertarian Party anytime."

"Why not be a Democrat?"

"The Democratic Party is anti–white males."

Nan didn't know what to make of that.

This evening the Mitchells had come later than usual. There were so many customers that Pingping couldn't chat with Janet and Nan had to stay in the kitchen, cooking constantly. But the Mitchells seemed purposely to outstay the other customers, and when the room had finally quieted down, Janet beckoned Pingping, wiggling her forefinger. Pingping went up to her and said, "Don't do that."

"Do what?"

"Move your fingers that way. It make me feel like slave or servant, like you can pull me around just by move your finger."

"All right." Janet smiled, her high cheeks coloring. "Golly, you're so sensitive. I won't do that again. Listen, I want to ask you something."

"Sure." Pingping sat down, hoping this was not about the surrogacy again.

"Have you been to Nanjing?" Janet asked.

"Where?"

"Nanjing, the big city on the Yangtze River."

"Ah, I see. No, I never be there, but my father's family is from somewhere near that city. You want to visit China?"

"I'm not sure. Dave and I have been thinking of adopting a baby girl."

"That's wonderful. But are you sure you want to raise Chinese kid?"

"Not one hundred percent sure yet. Tell me what you think."

"Everybody can see she's not your daughter."

"Dave and I thought about that too. We won't mind. As a matter of fact, we like Chinese babies."

"Why not adopt American baby?"

"That'll be very hard. You don't have a choice here. It's the biological mother who chooses the adoptive parents. Besides, you have to wait a long time, sometimes several years. And you have to hire a lawyer. It's outrageously complicated and expensive. That's why a lot of people go to other countries to adopt babies. Dave and I have met some couples who have Chinese baby girls. They're all happy."

"Why do the Chinese abandon girl babies?" Dave said.

"People in countryside need boys to work in fields, so they don't want girls," replied Pingping.

"Why won't some Chinese families adopt them?" asked Janet.

"I guess because each family can have one baby only."

By now Nan had joined them, standing by listening to their conversation. He put in, "Zer one-child policy has a lot to do wiz it. If you already have a baby, you cannot have anozzer. So some families throw away girl babies to save zer quota for a boy. Feudalistic mentality, you know."

"Are the babies healthy?" Janet went on.

"Don't worry about that," answered Pingping. "Very few Chinese in countryside eat drugs. Many people can't afford food, no money for drugs and alcohol. The parents are young, healthy, and clean, but some of them can't read and write."

"We're not worried about that," Janet said. "We can give a good education to the child we raise."

Pingping had meant to say that although the babies were healthy, you couldn't know anything about their parents' education and intelligence. She didn't explain and asked Janet instead, "You really think adoption?"

"We've contacted an orphanage in Nanjing. Once we hear from them, I'll let you know. We'll need your advice."

"Sure. Nanjing is famous for beautiful girls."

Nan added, "Women there usually have smoos skin and fine figures. It's a majar city, and I went there once for a conference."

"That's good to know. Dave and I may go to the orphanage if we decide to adopt."

As the conversation continued, Nan left quietly to tidy up the kitchen. He was glad that the Mitchells were thinking of adoption, which meant they might not bring up the subject of surrogacy again.

6

NAN didn't expect Danning would write back within a month. Usually a first-class letter traveled more than ten days from the United States to China. In this case, Nan's letter had reached his friend via the magazine; the detour must have taken an extra few days. Danning wrote in a loopy, cloudy hand:

August 29, 1992

Dear Nan Wu,

What a thrill it was to hear from you. How time has been speeding by! Yes, Sirong and I married last year, and we are living in Beijing now. I didn't go to the People's University to teach. Instead, I have stayed home, writing fiction and freelancing for magazines. But I cannot continue living like this and will soon look for a stable job. Probably I will work for the Writers' Association, which is interested in me because I can speak English.

To be honest, I am not satisfied with my Alaskan novella. The editor cut too much from the story, and as a result the prose feels choppy and crude. She also put in many sentences of her own, which are out of place. Some of them are plainly jarring. The magazine was eager to cater to the readers' interest in the exotic, so the editorial department demanded that all the stories be set in foreign countries, and we were supposed to make them as outlandish as possible. I had no choice but to concede, otherwise they would not have printed the piece. Well, you see this is China, where nothing has changed much. I often feel I'm living in a net, having to navigate through many invisible holes. Sometimes I miss my old days in Cambridge, MA, where I was left alone and could dream alone, lolling on a bench outside my apartment, basking in a sunny indolence, and watching the scudding clouds.

I have been working hard on two novels, both set in the United States. Stories about American life are hot nowadays. Have you seen the book *Manhattan's China Lady*? It's a runaway best seller here. My publisher is eager to have a blockbuster like that and has pressed me for the manuscripts several times. I have to finish my books soon, but I don't know how to write popular stuff and may disappoint my publisher.

Give my regards to Pingping and Taotao. Talk to you later.

Shake hands,

Danning Meng

Nan remembered the time when Danning had lived in Cambridge, but in reality his friend hadn't always had the kind of leisure described in the letter. Danning had once taken three days off from his lab, able to lounge around, but only because a tick had stuck to the top of his ear and given him a low fever and painful joints. After that letter, Nan and his friend kept up a correspondence, though they didn't write frequently, four or five exchanges of letters a year. Nan would follow the noise Danning went on making in China. Gradually Danning became a well-known author, though he never wrote anything better than his Alaskan cannery story.

Once Danning claimed that he was going to write his "great Chinese novel," which would exhaust the genre of the novel technically. Nan couldn't imagine such a monumental masterpiece and thought of asking him to define his vision, but he refrained, feeling that his friend had become a glib man, if not a blabbermouth. He mentioned Danning's ambition to Pingping, who smiled and said it might just be a boast. She simply couldn't enjoy that man's writings no matter how hard she tried.

7

WHEN it got cooler in late September, business began to come back at the Gold Wok, but Nan and Pingping couldn't feel relieved. Many people were still out of work, and about a third of the suites at Beaver Hill Plaza remained vacant, though the economy was reported to be improving. The large hall left by A&P had been filled by a Goodwill store, and the parking lot was again half full in the daytime.

One afternoon Nan sat slouching at the counter and reading his *Oxford Advanced Learner's Dictionary.* Beside his elbow, toward the wall, was a small aquarium in which a pair of angelfish was gliding. A string of bubbles kept spiraling up from the pebbles at the bottom of the water. As Nan was perusing the verbal idioms listed under the headword *point,* in came a tall man with dark hair; his ruddy face looked familiar, but Nan didn't recognize him. The man, wearing a black T-shirt, smiled and nodded at him, then stretched out his hand. "Hey, Nan Wu, don't you remember me? Dick Harrison," he said in a mellifluous voice.

Now Nan recognized him—the young poet, Sam Fisher's friend, whom he had met several times in New York. Delightedly Nan shook his hand. "What brought you here, Dick? I didn't recognize you because your hair is short now. You look so young zat I thought you were a student."

"Thanks. I took a job at Emory." Dick rested his elbows on the counter.

"What kind of jawb? Teaching?"

"Yes, poet in residence."

"You teach how to write poetry?"

"Yes, plus literature. Sam told me you had opened a restaurant in an eastern suburb of Atlanta, so whenever I saw a Chinese restaurant, I'd pop in to see if I could run into you."

"Sanks for looking for me."

"I'm so happy to find you."

After introducing Dick to Pingping, Nan led him to a booth and they both sat down. He asked his wife to make some appetizers and Tammie to bring over a pot of Dragon Well tea, a delicate green tea, not the red stuff offered to their customers. By now Pingping could cook as well as Nan, though she usually worked at the counter as the hostess and cashier. The two friends resumed conversing. Now and again they looked at each other and tipped their heads back laughing as if someone had cracked a joke nobody but they two had caught.

"How's Sam?" asked Nan.

"He's okay, but he drinks too much."

"I didn't know he was bibulous."

"Come again?"

"He's bibulous."

"Oh, yes, he's fond of alcohol."

"How about his boyfriend, Min Niu?"

"Min doesn't drink much. They had a big row the other day. Min moved out, then Sam apologized and Min went back."

"So they're still a cahple?"

"Of course, Sam depends on Min."

Nan was surprised that Min Niu had dared to quarrel with Sam Fisher, the famous poet.

"How about you?" Dick went on.

"I'm doing all right. We bought a house nearby and also zis business."

"This is impressive. I can see that you're becoming an American capitalist."

"Come on, I still have a mortgage to pay. How can you call me zat?"

"Okay, you're not rich yet, but you're on your way to realizing your American dream, aren't you?"

"I just want to be independent."

Tammie came and put the teapot and two cups on the table. Dick tilted his full head of hair and said to her in his one-toned Mandarin, *"How do you do?"*

She didn't reply and instead tittered. She stared at him, her round eyes intense and widened; her lips parted, then twitched a little. Still she didn't say a word. Dick lifted the cup of tea Nan had poured, and sipped. "Hmmm, excellent tea. Thank you!" he said to her.

She giggled and glanced at his pointy chin and hairy neck. "It's Dragon Well, this year's fresh leaves," she told him.

Pingping called to Tammie from the kitchen, so the waitress turned away. The two men went on talking about Emory, which Nan had heard was called "the Harvard of the South." Dick said the university had received a lot of funding from Coca-Cola and paid him well. He also mentioned that the previous year he'd had a book of poems published, his second, which had garnered numerous positive reviews. That was why another college had also made him a job offer. Nan was impressed, glad Dick had moved here.

Tammie came again with two plates, one loaded with spring and egg rolls and the other with fried fantail shrimp. The moment she placed them on the table, Dick picked up a spring roll and took a bite. "This is delicious, Nan. I've heard you're an excellent chef. I'll come and eat here every once in a while."

"You're always welcome. Bring your friends too."

Dick went on to tell him about his move to Atlanta. He had already settled down, having bought an apartment in the Buckhead area. Today he had gone to Lake Lanier, and on his way back got off the interstate and drove through the suburbs. He was lucky to come into the Gold Wok, though he didn't expect to find Nan so easily. He said, "What a miracle. I thought I'd be a total stranger in this redneck country."

"Now you have me here. In fact, Atlanta is not a bad place. Many people from southern China feel more at home here zan in New England."

"You're kidding me—why?"

"Zer climate is very similah to their home provinces, and houses are not expensive."

"I can see that. To be honest, this is the first time in my life that I can afford a condo. There are lots of restaurants and shops in Atlanta. Quite a convenient place to live."

"Have you been to a farmers' market yet? I never saw so many fruits and vegetables before."

"No, I haven't."

"Go to zer Dekalb Farmers' Market. It's absolutely fantastic."

"Oh, I love this shrimp. Thank you, Mrs. Wu." He waved at Pingping, who was clipping coupons at the counter.

She replied, "I'm glad you like it. Just call me Pingping. I didn't change last name after we marry."

"Sure. Thank you, Pingping," Dick said loudly.

They all laughed, Tammie included, and then the two friends resumed their conversation. They talked about Bao Yuan, the painter-poet and editor of the journal *New Lines,* which was defunct now. Dick said Bao was thinking of leaving New York, though his paintings had begun to sell. Actually, he had just held a one-man show in a gallery in Soho, which turned out quite successful and sold many pieces of his work. Still, Bao felt he couldn't continue living in New York and had been looking for a job elsewhere. Nan knew that would be difficult, since that fellow spoke little English and would make no effort to learn it. It was a shame that he had lived with Wendy for almost a year and still couldn't speak a correct sentence. As people believed, the best way to learn English was to do it in bed with a native speaker, but Bao had simply wasted the opportunity. If he refused to change, there would be no way he could survive in America. "He's too smart," Nan told Dick.

"How do you mean?"

"He had good opportunities, but his mind couldn't focus. He depends too mahch on cleverness and doesn't work hard."

Dick agreed. Then, as if remembering something, he said, "Sam told me you were still writing poetry. How's it going?"

"Oh, I haven't done mahch lately, but I've kept lawts of notes. I'm still trying to figure out how to use zem."

"Do you write in Chinese or English?"

"I haven't written a lawt since I came here, to be honest."

"I remember Sam once urged you to write in English. You should try. Your English is excellent."

"I don't think I can."

"Why can't you?"

"I don't know anybody who has written significant poetry in an adawpted language."

"That's not true. How about Charles Simic? He came to this country in his teens and became a marvelous poet."

"Who?"

"Charles Simic."

"I have never heard of him, but I'm going to look at his work."

"Nan, you should be bolder. Fuck the bunk that says you can't write poetry in your stepmother tongue. If nobody can, then you'd better try harder. That will put you in a unique position, to make yourself original. To tell the truth, I was quite amazed that your English has improved so much. You speak more fluently than before."

"Sanks for your advice. By zer way, what's 'bunk'?"

Dick gave a belly laugh. "You're so earnest. It means 'nonsense,' the abridged form of 'bunkum.'"

"I see," Nan said, not knowing that word either. His lips stirred as if he were tasting his own words and reluctant to let them out.

After three o'clock some customers came in, so Dick took his leave. He and Nan exchanged phone numbers, and he promised to come again.

8

DICK'S presence changed Nan's life somewhat. Every week the poet would come to eat at the Gold Wok at least once. Nan always did his best in cooking whatever he ordered, and together they'd talk about news, poetry, books, movies, and Buddhism. Nan didn't know much about the religion, while Dick had been studying a bilingual volume of the Lotus Sutra. He would bring along the book and ask Nan about the meanings of some Chinese phrases that he suspected might have been corrupted through the translation, though he respected the group of translators named Silent Tongues.

Nan was happy whenever Dick came. He admired his carefree manner, his devotion to poetry, and his seriousness about meditation. But Nan wouldn't try to write in English as Dick had advised, mainly because he was exhausted by his daily work, unable to gather his strength for such an endeavor. He was still unnerved by the lingering impact of the recession, which had lately forced another shop at the plaza out of business. The past summer his restaurant had made only $1,000 a month, and the Wus had had to withdraw money from their savings account to pay bills. Tammie had made much less than before too and complained a lot. Nan encouraged her to look for a more lucrative job elsewhere if she wanted, but she said things would come around, and she stayed. For that he was grateful. Although more people came to eat after the summer, the business wasn't as good as it should have been. Pingping had asked Janet to let her make more necklaces and earrings, but the jewelry store was faltering too and couldn't stock more inventory at the moment. What disconcerted the Wus most was that if someday they couldn't come up with $1,000 for Mr. Wolfe at the end of a month, they might lose their home. The fear made them more determined to pay off the mortgage as early as possible. After that, even if their restaurant didn't make enough, they could still have their home intact and manage to tide themselves over. Nan regretted having mailed Mr. Wolfe $1,500 a month for half a year. From now on he would send him exactly $1,000 each month and deposit more money in the bank. Once they saved enough cash, they would clear the mortgage with a lump sum. This way he could always have some savings for a rainy day.

•

Whenever Dick was around, Tammie was noticeably excited. She seemed very fond of him. Usually she was reticent, but with Dick she'd become voluble, explaining to him how the dishes were made and plying him with questions about his family, his students, and his writing. Dick would take the opportunity to learn some Chinese words from her. He'd laugh casually even though he was aware of her glad eyes. Seeing the change in Tammie, Pingping would shake her head, believing the waitress was too easily smitten with that man. But she didn't know how to broach the subject with Tammie, who sometimes still avoided speaking to her.

After Dick left, Tammie would ask Nan questions about that red-faced man. How did they meet? Where did his folks live? Had he had a lot of friends in New York? Had he always been so funny and upbeat? Wasn't it amazing that he had already become a big professor and published two books even though he couldn't be older than thirty-five?

Nan felt for Tammie, knowing what it was like when you fell for somebody, which often made you silly and act out of character. Love could be an addiction, if not a sickness. Nan and Pingping talked between themselves about Tammie's infatuation and knew the poor woman might get hurt. So one day Nan told her bluntly, "Actually Dick is gay."

"You mean, he doesn't like women?" She looked at him in disbelief, her large eyes glittering.

"Yes. I saw him wiz some men in New York. Most of his friends were gay."

"That's awful!"

"I'm afraid he may catch diseases if he isn't careful wiz too many boyfriends."

"He looks very healthy, though."

"Yes, I was just sinking aloud. He knows how to protect himself. Don't make too much of what I said."

For the rest of the day Tammie looked absentminded and remained quiet. Nan felt sorry for her, but it was better to stop her from daydreaming before she got hurt. Afterward, when Dick showed up, Tammie was no longer as vivacious as before.

9

"MOM, *can you drive me to school tomorrow morning?*" asked Taotao one afternoon the moment he stepped into the restaurant, carrying his heavy book bag on his back. Today he should have gotten off at Marsh Drive and stayed home, doing his homework.

"*Why can't you take the bus?*" his mother said.

"*I don't want to.*"

"*How come?*"

"*I don't like the bus anymore.*"

His parents knew there must be some reason he wouldn't say, so they demanded that he be forthcoming about it. Pressed time and again, Taotao confessed that he was afraid of two boys, Sean and Matt, who would twist his ears and pull his nose whenever they saw him on the school bus.

"*Why do they do that?*" asked his father.

"*They're just assholes and won't stop bugging others.*"

"*Then why not ignore them?*"

"No," his mother interrupted. "*He can't let others bully him like that.*"

"*Mom, they do it to everyone.*"

"*Then why aren't the others scared?*"

"*I'm new here.*"

"*That's not an excuse. You have taken that bus for more than a year. I won't drive you, and you must help yourself.*"

The boy looked crushed, his mouth compressed and his eyes brimming with tears. His father told him, "*You have to fight back by yourself.*"

His mother went on, "*Do you want me to go with you on the bus*

tomorrow? I'll question the squirts and find out why they keep pick-
ing on you."

"No, Mom! I don't want you to do that. You'll make me look like a crybaby."

"Then you'll have to confront them by yourself. From tomorrow
on, when they pull your ears, you do the same to them."

"But you mustn't fight with them," added his father. "Just show them that you're not afraid. Understood?"

The boy didn't reply and began sniveling. Tammie came over, pat-ted Pingping's upper arm, and pointed at two customers waiting at the counter. Pingping went up to them while Nan returned to the kitchen to cook the takeout they ordered.

Tammie stroked the boy's hair. "What's wrong, Taotao?" she asked.

"Everybody's so mean to me."

"Your parents just want to help you. Your mommy teaches you every day. Whose mommy does that? Come, be a big boy and stop crying."

Taotao made no reply. Tammie had overheard their exchange just now, so she went on, "You should listen to your parents. If you're afraid of those hoodlums, they'll bully you without a stop."

The next morning, on the school bus, Sean, whose father had just walked out on his mother, sat next to Taotao. Sean elbowed him whenever the bus turned, then flashed a grin fortified by a mouthful of braces, but Taotao ignored him and kept looking at his own new Velcro sneakers his mother had just bought for him at a rummage sale. Then Sean grabbed hold of Taotao's earlobe and twisted it. "Cute little thing," he said, pulling hard.

"Knock it off!" Taotao gave him a shove in the chest.

"Have a problem, munchkin?" Sean pushed him back and again cracked a metallic grin.

At that word Taotao was suddenly possessed by a fit of rage. "Don't call me that!" He punched Sean squarely in the cheek.

"Ow! You smashed my face, man! You made my gums bleed." Sean bent over and muffled his voice with his palm, and bloody saliva was oozing out between his fingers.

Matt, a red-haired fifth grader, jumped in, "Taotao, you crazy jerk! He was just having a bit of fun with you."

"I've had enough of his shit!"

In fact, Taotao hadn't hit Sean that hard, but the braces had stabbed his cheek from inside and made it bleed. At the sight of the bloody drool, Taotao shivered, his heart kicking.

Mrs. Dunton stopped the bus and came over. "You did this to him?" she asked Taotao in a severe voice, her lipless mouth displaying her tiny teeth.

"He twisted my ears every day. Just now he called me names."

"I just said 'munchkin,'" Sean wailed, sniffing back some snot.

"But you pulled my ear."

Indeed, Taotao's earlobe was still red. Knowing Sean was a troublemaker, Mrs. Dunton just fished out a piece of tissue and handed it to him. "Here, wipe your face. You two will have a lot of explaining to do in the principal's office."

Taotao was criticized by the vice principal, the bearded Mr. Haberman, who also wrote a letter to his parents, urging them to talk to their son and take steps to stop this kind of violence. Nan was disturbed and promptly wrote back to apologize and assure the school that Taotao wouldn't commit such an act again. He also agreed to let the boy meet with Mrs. Benson, a counselor at school, whom Sean must see as well. Nan blamed Pingping for encouraging their son to fight, but she wouldn't listen to him, saying, "*I'm already a frightened mouse in this country. We don't need another wimp in our family. I'd rather disown him than have him intimidated by those little bullies.*"

Nan didn't argue with her, knowing he couldn't make her change her mind, but he talked with their son, who promised not to fight with his hands again.

In reality there was no need for Taotao to keep his word—Sean and Matt left him alone thereafter. For several days smaller boys dared not sit close to Taotao, who was known as a tough kid. But soon they forgot about the fight and accepted him as one of them.

•

Despite her hard words, Pingping had been worried about the incident. She told Janet about Taotao's violent act. To her surprise, her friend assured her, "No big deal. As long as they don't bother him again, this is over. In a way, Taotao did the right thing. What else could he do to stop them? You should be proud of him. My brother once was bullied by a bigger boy in our neighborhood, and my mother wouldn't let him in unless he went to fight with the boy on the street."

"How is your brother now?"

"He's doing fine. He's a financial planner in North Carolina, making tons of money." Janet smiled, her upper lip shaded by blond fuzz.

Pingping didn't reveal Janet's opinion to her husband, unsure whether Janet was just partial to Taotao. She knew the Mitchells adored the boy.

10

AFTER mid-October business turned brisk at the Gold Wok. Because Pingping no longer had time to go home and check on Taotao in the evenings, she made him stay in the restaurant after dinner, doing homework and waiting for his parents to close up. At school, his classmates had been talking about Halloween. He was quiet about it, knowing he wouldn't be able to go trick-or-treating as he had done back in Massachusetts. His parents did ask him whether he wanted a costume, but he said he wasn't interested.

Pingping bought two large pumpkins and placed them at the front door of their house. Taotao hollowed them out and carved the jack-o'-lanterns, but didn't put a candle inside. Across the street, in Alan's yard, a pear tree was laden with dozens of tiny pumpkins, all made of plush and wearing a painted smile. Whenever a breeze blew, those orange-yellow fruit, resembling giant apples, would jerk and bob incessantly.

On Halloween Eve, just after dark, Pingping and Taotao returned home, carried out a folding table, and set it up in their driveway, near the carport. On it they put a lamp and three baskets of candies: peanut butter cups, toffees, and egg-shaped chocolates. Since they had to go back to the restaurant, they Scotch-taped to the tabletop a sign, an oblong of cardboard, which said PLEASE LEAVE SOME FOR OTHERS!

There were a lot of customers at the Gold Wok that evening, and Taotao looked unhappy and restless, even though his parents allowed him to watch TV in the storage room. Toward nine o'clock, Janet came and said to Pingping, "I waited for Taotao at home, but he

271

didn't show up. We prepared lots of goodies for kids. You should've let him join others to trick-or-treat in our neighborhood."

"Your house is too far away," said Pingping.

"Fiddlesticks, it's just a five-minute drive."

"Taotao has homework to do."

"Oh, Pingping, it's Halloween. Let him go out and have some fun."

"He can't go by himself. We are busy now."

"I can take him around to get some candies. Do you mind?"

"Of course not, but is not late?"

"Not really."

Pingping went to the storage room and called to Taotao. The boy was more than happy to leave with Janet, but he needed a getup. "I can't wear this," he said to his mother, pointing at his green V-neck.

"I ask whether you want special clothing, you said no. You can't blame me now."

"Don't worry," Janet stepped in. "We have a vampire mask at home. You can use that."

"I love that humongous thing!" The boy had seen that grotesque face hanging in the Mitchells' game room.

"Oh yeah?" Janet said. "You can wear that. I'll figure out what to put on myself."

Nan told his son to come home soon, which Taotao promised to do. After Janet and the boy left, Nan, Pingping, and Tammie went about wiping the tables and mopping the floor, though there were still six customers eating in the room.

When they had closed up, they set out for home without delay. It was a clear night, and the stars seemed less distant than usual. In the air lingered a smell of burned grass and wood. On the street across the lake, flashlights were flickering, and groups of children in ghostly garb were still walking back and forth, some accompanied by dogs and grown-ups. There was also a lantern bobbing in the distance like a will-o'-the-wisp. Merry cries and laughter surged up now and again.

In the Wus' driveway the lamp was still on. To Pingping and Nan's surprise, none of the baskets on the table was empty, all still half full. Into the original chocolates, toffees, and peanut butter cups were mixed some other kinds of goodies—3 Musketeers, gumballs, peppermint patties, jellybeans, M&M's. There was also a red apple half buried in the candies. Both Nan and Pingping burst into laughter, amazed that the children were so innocent that they'd thought the sign begged them to leave some of their own spoils for others. The Wus were touched. Nan said thoughtfully, *"If this were in China, the lamp, the extension cord, the baskets, the pumpkins, and even the table would be gone, much less the sweets."*

"That's true," agreed Pingping.

As they were speaking, a bunch of Ninja Turtles, each wearing a plastic carapace, appeared down the street, jabbering and capering. Nan cupped his hands around his mouth and cried at them, "Hey, do you want more candies?"

"Sure we do," a girl trilled back.

Immediately Pingping removed one of the baskets and placed it under their Ford parked in the carport. She wanted to save it for Tao-tao. The children raced over, brandishing their rubber swords, their capes fluttering.

A boy asked the Wus, "How many can we have?"

"As many you want," said Pingping.

In no time the children pocketed and bagged all the goodies from the two baskets, then headed away for the next lighted house.

Nan turned, enfolded Pingping with one arm, and kissed her on the cheek. Surprised, she asked with a smile, *"What's that about?"*

"I'm happy. If only we had once lived like those kids."

11

EVER SINCE they'd bought the restaurant, Nan and Pingping had been thinking of finding a legal guardian for Taotao. If they both died, they wanted their son to be safe and raised with care and love. They thought about a few Chinese couples they had known in the North, but none of them were suitable, mainly because those people already had children and might not treat Taotao like their own. If only they had a family member or relative in America. After long consideration, they decided to ask the Mitchells to be Taotao's guardians in case they both departed this life. Dave and Janet were good-hearted and financially secure. More important, they were fond of children and could give Taotao a loving home.

When Nan and Pingping mentioned this to Janet, Janet was amazed, her eyes aglow. She said, "We'll be more than happy to be his guardians."

"What we do and make this legal?" asked Pingping.

"We should see an attorney perhaps, if you want to spell it out on paper. Dave will be thrilled to hear this."

So on the first Monday morning of December the two couples arrived at the Shang Law Office in Chinatown. Mr. Shang had just undergone eye surgery and was wearing a green eyeshade, which somehow reminded Nan of a photograph of James Joyce. The Wus reiterated to him their intention—they wanted the Mitchells to keep their son and property if they both died. Mr. Shang said, "That's a good idea. You belong to the propertied class now." Three days earlier Nan had called and given him all the names and information needed for the agreement, so he assumed that the paperwork was already done.

Mr. Shang switched to Mandarin and asked Nan with a scratchy accent, *"You want them to have your restaurant and home too?"* His good eye glanced sideways at the Mitchells sitting on a sofa near his desk while his mouth went awry, revealing a gold-capped tooth. Dave was gazing at the attorney, his top lip twitching, as if he was irritated by being excluded.

"Yes. If they take care of our son, they should inherit everything we have," said Nan.

Mr. Shang reverted to English. "I understand. Just double-check."

"They're good couple," Pingping put in. "We know them long time. They're our friend."

"I'm not sure you've known them long enough." Mr. Shang wagged his head.

"We don't have any family or relative in America," Nan explained.

"You don't have a Chinese friend you can trust your boy to?"

"Not really."

"How sad! You're truly a marginal man. It seems to me that your white friends may not be suitable for your son. Everybody can tell he's adopted by them, not their own."

"We don't mind that."

"All right, all right, I'll do what you want. I just meant to make sure you were fully aware of all the consequences." Mr. Shang turned away to prepare the agreement on a computer below a small window. He had already written a draft and was typing it out. The gray screen of the monitor was flickering as he punched away at the keyboard. From time to time he combed his thin hair with his slim fingers. Beside the computer stood a can of Sprite, which he lifted to his mouth time and again. The Wus were seated on the sofa across from the Mitchells. Nan felt embarrassed that the lawyer had spoken Chinese with them just now, so he explained in a low voice to their friends what they had talked about. He said that Mr. Shang thought people would easily tell that Taotao was an adopted child if he ended up in Janet and Dave's care, but Nan and Pingping had told the lawyer they wouldn't mind that because the Mitchells were their friends and very fond of their son.

As the conversation went on, the four of them talked about where

Taotao should go to college when he grew up. "MIT is the best," Dave claimed firmly.

Nan didn't argue, but he'd prefer his son to have a liberal arts education.

From college they switched to the topic of life insurance, which Nan and Pingping didn't know how to buy. Neither did they see why they should get it. What was the point in having a lot of money if one of them died? Money, if you couldn't enjoy spending it, wouldn't buy you happiness. Unlike them, Janet had bought some insurance on Dave.

Mr. Shang returned to his desk, holding two printed sheets. He handed the couples each a copy, saying, "You should all read this."

Nan looked through the paper, which stated:

We, Nan Wu and Pingping Liu, of 568 Marsh Drive, Lilburn, Gwinnett County, Georgia, hereby agree to let Janet and David Mitchell, of 52 Breezewood Circle, Lilburn, Gwinnett County, Georgia, be our son Taotao Wu's legal guardians if we both shall die before Taotao Wu reaches the age of eighteen. We nominate Janet and David Mitchell to be our Executor and Executrix. We direct them to pay our legal debts, funeral expenses, and the expenses of administering our estate after our decease and to charge said expenses to the residue. We give Janet and David Mitchell all the rest and remainder of our estate, both real and personal, of whatever name, kind and nature, provided they remain a married couple. The Mitchells shall be obligated to raise Taotao Wu with love and care and to finance his college education.

This AGREEMENT is composed in the presence of both parties and cosigned by both willingly. It shall not take effect unless the decease of Nan Wu and Pingping Liu occurs before Taotao Wu is eighteen.

"It's pretty good," Nan said, then handed it to Pingping. Meanwhile, the Mitchells were reading their copy too. Both couples agreed about the wording, so they all signed on the agreement in the presence of two young women Mr. Shang had called in from the store as witnesses.

With some deliberation the attorney unscrewed the cap of his chunky fountain pen and with a flourish wrote out his name on all the three copies, then notarized them. He said to Nan, "Eighty dollars."

Nan gave him four twenties. Mr. Shang handed a page to the Mitchells and another to the Wus, and kept one for his records. "Well, I hope nobody will ever use this piece of paper," he said, and screwed up his good eye.

"We do too," Dave said, then laughed, tapping his balding crown with his fingertips. His wife and the Wus all smiled.

Once they stepped out of the office, Janet asked Pingping, "Why is the procedure so simple?"

"What you mean?"

"If you went to an American attorney, he'd spend hours going through many things with you and would charge you hundreds of dollars."

"That's why I said we go to Mr. Shang. He isn't good man, but he always make things simple for people and give what you want."

Nan put in, "Actually, he's an American lawyer and graduated from a law school in L.A. But he often does business in zer Chinese way. Besides, he doesn't charge a lot."

"Well," Janet said, "he certainly doesn't write like an attorney— I mean, his English isn't full of gobbledygook, like lots of 'thereofs' or 'theretos.'"

"He has to make zer language simple enough for his Chinese cahstomers to understand."

"Are lawyers in China like him?"

Pingping answered, "Before we come to America, we never use lawyer. I never knew lawyer in my life."

"True, me eizer," Nan chimed in.

"You mean, people don't sue each other?"

"Very rarely they went to court," Nan said. "Zer Party leaders, awfficials, and street committees controlled your life, so you didn't need a lawyer."

"How about now? Are things the same?" Dave piped up.

"I heard there are some lawyers, but they can't reelly be independent of politics. Zer law often changes."

Dave observed thoughtfully, "I'm amazed that Mr. Shang doesn't even use a secretary."

"He has one, but she works only part-time," Nan said.

After their visit to the attorney, Janet and Pingping grew closer, though Dave came to the Gold Wok less often, having to put in more hours at work. The Mitchells bought Taotao a joystick to go with his computer, which enabled him to play more games. Nan felt rather relieved, certain that Taotao would be happy and safe with Dave and Janet if Pingping and he both died.

12

NAN honestly thought Dick was a homosexual, but one evening in mid-January his friend came with a young blonde who looked like a graduate student. Dick introduced her to Nan and Pingping, saying, "This is Eleanor."

The woman, wearing jeans, was tall and quite masculine, with a long waist. In a southern drawl she said to Nan, "Dick talks a lot about you. He said you're a fabulous chef." She smiled, the beauty mark above the corner of her mouth moving sideways.

"Welcahm." Nan was glad that his friend had mentioned him that way.

After they sat down, Tammie came over and plunked a stainless-steel teapot on the table. "What do you want to order?" she asked in a disgruntled voice. Pingping took alarm and glanced at her from the counter.

"How are you doing today?" Dick grinned, then pointed at Eleanor while saying in his toneless Mandarin, "*She's my girlfriend.*"

"Do you want to order now?" Tammie asked without raising her eyes.

Though discomfited by the waitress's sudden temper, Dick turned to Eleanor. "What would you like?"

"How about moo shu?"

"It's great, but it'll take a long time to make."

"Shoot, I have to be at the Manleys' at eight."

"Then let's have something else."

"You said they served shark here. Why isn't it on the menu?"

"Nan cooks it only for friends."

"Can we have that? I've eaten shark only once in my entire life."

"Tammie, do you know if Nan can make that for us?"

"I'm not sure."

"Then I'll go ask him." Dick also ordered fried wontons for an appetizer, watercress soup, and Five-Spice Beef. In addition, they each wanted a beer, he a Tsingtao and Eleanor a Miller Lite.

Nan had learned how to stir-fry and steam shark from Mr. Wang, though he hadn't printed this dish on the menu for fear that some children, if they knew the restaurant offered shark, might dissuade their parents from dining there. In fact, Mr. Wang had once included this specialty on his menu, but several kids talked to him about all the virtues of the fish, and still the old man wouldn't give up serving the dish. As a consequence, the kids made some people boycott the shark-serving Gold Wok. Soon Mr. Wang stopped offering this dish and mailed his new sharkless menu to hundreds of households in the area.

Dick went into the kitchen and asked Nan, "Can you cook shark for us today?"

"Sure, we have some fresh steaks. Boy, you're quick—you got a girlfriend the moment you started teaching here."

"I should learn more about southern women, shouldn't I? Actually, Eleanor is a Ph.D. student in my department."

"Well, zat's not very professional. You're not supposed to date your student." Nan winked at him while tossing bok choy and shrimp in a wok.

"That's why I should make her happy. Cook a big shark for us, will you?"

"Stir-fry or steam?"

"Stir-fry."

"I'll get it ready in fifteen minutes."

As soon as Dick went out of the kitchen, Pingping came in and talked with Nan about the way Tammie was treating the couple. They guessed the waitress might be jealous; still, she shouldn't have been rude to the customers. To forestall trouble, Nan suggested that Pingping take over that table. If Dick had been here alone, he could have smoothed things over by chatting with him himself every now and again, but today Dick had a lady friend with him. Eleanor seemed at ease and even swigged beer directly from Dick's bottle. They must already have shared a lot together, so Nan wouldn't go over and interrupt them.

He felt relieved that Tammie was pleased with Pingping's help; she already had her hands full, waiting on the other tables and booths. Yet the waitress couldn't stop throwing glances in the direction of Dick and Eleanor. Her eyes were shining and her face flushed.

Done with dinner, Dick left a five for tip, which Pingping let Tammie take. When they were cleaning up before they closed, Nan said to the waitress, "Tammie, why do you look so unhappy today?" He spoke just as a way to start conversation, as he assumed he knew the reason for her sullenness.

"I dunno," she said.

"You should have tritted Dick and his girlfriend better."

She glared at him and asked, "Why did you say he was gay?"

Nan was taken aback as he remembered their conversation from long ago. He still believed Dick might be a homosexual, but was unsure how to explain, so he said, "I had no idea he had a girlfriend. I asked him just now, and he said he wanted to know more about souzzern women."

"Then how could he be gay?"

"Zis is beyond me too."

"I know you think I'm cheap and silly. You too, Pingping, always take me to be a fool."

"Not true, we never think that way," Pingping protested.

"Don't deny it! If not, why did Nan lie to me?"

"I didn't lie to you," said Nan.

"You told me Dick was gay."

"I saw him wiz some men in New York. I still sink he might be a homosexual."

"Then why was he with that snake-hipped woman?"

"Maybe he likes women too. How can I tell? I didn't know him zat well before he came to Atlanta."

"You lied to me, because you thought I lost my head about him. Let me tell you, I don't care a damn about what he is. I just have enough of your tricks."

"Please, Tammie, don't explode like zis. You reelly misunderstood my intention."

"Good night." She plopped the mop behind the kitchen door and picked up her shoulder bag. Without turning her fluffy head she tore out toward her car.

The next day Tammie didn't show up. Nan and Pingping were worried and called her, but nobody picked up the phone. She didn't have an answering machine. The Wus were at a loss. There wasn't a lot of business at the moment, and even without Tammie they could manage. But the understaffed situation mustn't continue, because Pingping couldn't possibly work as both the cashier and waitress for long. A few days in a row Nan called Tammie, to no avail. If he had known where she lived, he would have gone to her apartment and begged her to return, but there was simply no way to get hold of her. Once her roommate answered the phone and promised to pass Nan's message on to her, but Tammie never called back.

13

TAMMIE'S walkout upset Nan and Pingping. A week later they heard that she had started waitressing at Grand Buddha in Decatur; obviously she was making more money there. That Chinese restaurant was owned by a Korean family and had a full bar and more than forty tables. Now that Tammie was gone for good, Nan began looking for a new waitress. A few women showed interest, but he didn't hire any of them because they were all college students and might not stay long. He couldn't afford to have a disruption again and preferred to use someone who depended more on such a job.

Then the idea came to him that he could call Ding's Dumplings in New York and see whether somebody there might be willing to come to Atlanta and work for him. He knew that many Chinese had left the Northeast for the South because life here was comfortable and more affordable. Also, the staff at Ding's Dumplings viewed that restaurant as a transit place and would move elsewhere once they had enough work experience. Nan called New York one afternoon, and Yafang Gao happened to answer the phone. "*How have you been?*" he asked her. "*I thought you had left Ding's Dumplings.*"

"*I'm fine. I'm the hostess now.*"

"*Congratulations! You're in charge there?*"

"*Basically.*"

Nan went on to describe his need for a waitress and the kind of money that person could make at the Gold Wok, at least two hundred dollars a week, cash, if the business was good. He told her that rent here was very low compared with New York.

"*Maybe I should come,*" Yafang said in a joking voice, which surprised Nan.

"*No, I can't pay the kind of wages you're pulling in.*" He knew that as the hostess she was paid by the hour. Besides, her work at Ding's Dumplings was less demanding.

"*Here's the deal—I'll come if you divorce your wife.*" She giggled.

She sounded like a different person now, flirtatious and carefree, no longer the timid young woman tricked into an adult movie theater and then into bed by Heng Chen, that desperate man. She must be a capable hostess at Ding's Dumplings.

It happened that Yafang had a distant cousin studying somewhere in Georgia (she wasn't sure at which school), whose wife had just come to America from Jiangsu Province. Yafang wondered if his wife might be interested in the job, and gave Nan the phone number.

Then Nan inquired about his former fellow workers and acquaintances in New York. Yafang told him that David Kellman and Maiyu had married last spring, that Chinchin had gone to nursing school at the University of Connecticut, and that Aimin had started a snack shop with her cousin in Flushing.

"*How about Heng Chen?*" Nan paused. "*Sorry, I shouldn't have brought up his name.*"

"*That wretch has returned to China.*" She sounded flat and unemotional.

"*Really? What happened to him?*"

"*He couldn't make it here. Such a loser.*"

"*He got into trouble?*"

"*No, he had to go back. Maiyu said he was sick of America and he had come just to make money.*"

"*He must've taken back a fortune with him.*"

"*Not at all. He didn't even have enough money to buy gifts for his parents and relatives, so he sold a kidney.*"

"*What? Is that true?*"

"*Why should I lie to you?*" She sounded a little cheerful now.

"*How much did he get for his kidney?*"

"*Twenty-five thousand dollars.*"

"*I knew his parents often demanded he send them remittances, but I couldn't imagine he'd sell his own organ.*"

"*He's a typical 'small man' and couldn't survive in America. A born coward.*"

"Still, it must've taken a lot of guts to sell a kidney."

Yafang cackled. *"Nan, you haven't lost your sense of deadpan humor."*

Her remark puzzled Nan, who hadn't meant to be funny at all. In fact, the conversation saddened him. However, the relative she had mentioned turned out to be helpful. Yafang's cousin, Shubo Gao, happened to be a Ph.D. candidate at the University of Georgia and lived near Lawrenceville. He answered Nan's call and let his wife, Niyan, speak with Nan. She was very eager to take the job and said she was tired of living idly at home. The next day she came to the Gold Wok, accompanied by her husband. Pingping liked Niyan, who was in her late twenties and quite good-looking, with a button nose, long-lashed eyes, and an oval face. So the Wus hired her and she started to work two days later. Niyan knew English, though she sounded as if she were giving a spiel when she spoke to customers, making little distinction between the long and the short vowels. But the Wus were pleased to have her, and things were normal again at the Gold Wok.

For days Nan thought about the phrase Yafang had used on the phone—"small man"—which was a faddish term that appeared in the Chinese-language newspapers and magazines published in the diaspora. It had been coined a few months earlier by a woman in a scathing article entitled "Let Us Condemn Small Men." She criticized some male Chinese immigrants who, having encased themselves in the past, made no effort to blend into American society. According to her, these "spineless men," unable to adapt to the life here, would vent their spleen on their wives and girlfriends and blame America for their own failure. Under the pretext of patriotism and preserving Chinese culture, they'd refuse to learn anything from other cultures. To them, even American salt was not as salty as Chinese salt. All they knew about America was strip bars, casinos, prostitutes, MBAs, CEOs; they had no friends of other races and refused to learn English. They were like crabs trapped in a vat, striving against one another, but none could get out of it. Some of them, who had lived in this country for more than a decade, still couldn't understand movies like *Rain Man, Dances with Wolves,* and *Peter Pan.* They had never visited a museum, and neither would they travel to see Europe or Latin America. They didn't know how many innings a baseball game had. They had no idea who Elvis Presley was, not to mention an appreciation of his music; they couldn't tell jazz from rock, or country from gospel; whenever they got homesick, they'd sing revolutionary songs, and their number one choice was "The Internationale." Still, they believed they were geniuses hamstrung by misfortunes and stunted by the emigration, as if there were no other people in the world who suffered more than they. By nature most Chinese women in America didn't aspire to be strong women, but their small men forced them to be more responsible and play the role of both wife and husband. It was common sense that when yang was weak, yin would have to grow stronger and prevail. "These small men can be a scourge of your bodies and minds," the author concluded. "Sisters, let us shun them if we cannot change or get rid of them."

Since the publication of that vociferous article in the *Global Weekly,* there had been heated discussion of the topic. A lot of men were outraged, saying the author, as a compatriot of theirs, should at least have some sympathy for them. They had already been mentally dwarfed and socially handicapped by living in America and by the tremendous struggle they had to wage for survival, so they didn't need her sort of twaddle, which just gave them more stress. Several meetings were held in American and Australian cities to debate the author's views. Many men wrote articles condemning her as a traitor, "a mere banana"—yellow on the outside and white on the inside.

Nan had seen that some of the men had indeed grown feeble and trivial, yet they were all the more megalomaniac. As for himself, he felt he was a better man than before. On the other hand, he knew that most of the labeled men were lonely souls who suffered intensely here. It was said that if a foreigner or immigrant lived in America for five years without family or close friends, the person would develop emotional problems. If one lived here for ten years isolated like that, one would have a mental disorder.

Nowadays it was commonplace for a woman to insult a Chinese man by calling him a "small man." That meant the fellow was a hopeless loser all women should hold in contempt.

14

JANET came and told Pingping that Dave and she had decided to adopt a baby, but that they'd have to wait three or four months before they could get a definite answer from the orphanage in Nanjing. The waiting list was long because lately a lot of American couples had begun to adopt Chinese babies and thus overwhelmed the adoption system there. In the Mitchells' case, Janet and Dave weren't sure whether they should continue to work with their agent or find another way to get a baby sooner. Janet asked Pingping, "Do you have a friend or relative who lives in Nanjing or nearby?"

"I have a cousin in Nantong, in same province. But we are never close because he betray my father in Cultural Revolution to protect himself. He just want to join Communist Party. Why you ask?"

"Dave and I wonder if we can find someone in China who can help us adopt a baby quickly. The regular process will take forever."

"I can ask my cousin, but I don't trust him. Let Nan and I think about this, okay?"

"Sure. If you can help us find some inside connections, that'll make the whole thing easier."

Nan put in, "How much does an agent cawst?"

"Ten thousand at most. We paid three thousand up front."

"If I were you, I'd use zee agent instead of depending on personal pull, as long as your agent has a good reputation."

"Why? Don't most people use personal connections to get things done in China?"

"Yes, but you may end up paying more zan you pay zee agent, and there will be endless anxiety. Any petty awfficial can interfere and create trahble for you. Zee awfficial world in China is like a black hole, and few people can keep their bearings once they're sucked into it. Besides, your connections in China will have to bribe awfficials at every turn. You will pay for zer horrendous bribes, right?"

"I guess so. But we've been thinking of doing this both ways, using our agent and the inside connections at the same time."

"No, you should rely on your agent only."

"Nan has point," Pingping said. "There's a lotta trouble if you involve officials."

So the Mitchells continued working with a Chinese American woman based in San Francisco, who had successfully helped dozens of families adopt babies. Janet showed the agency's literature to Pingping and Nan, who both felt the woman was trustworthy. Pingping even talked to her on behalf of the Mitchells, saying they had been her friends for a long time and were a reliable, loving couple, who had just built their dream home, a big Victorian house in an affluent neighborhood. She also mentioned they would become Taotao's guardians should she and her husband die by accident. The agent, named Ruhua, was impressed and said in her Mandarin roughened by Cantonese, *"Thank you for the information. That's very helpful. I'm going to schedule a home study of the Mitchells."*

"You mean you'll come here?"

"Oh no, I'll contact a local person, a certified social worker, who will go interview Dave and Janet and make sure they're a responsible couple and financially capable of supporting a child. Also, they must have no history of child abuse and substance abuse. Both the INS and the Chinese side demand the information."

"I see."

Ruhua promised to try her best to help the Mitchells. At the request of Janet, Pingping wrote a reference letter for her and Dave, stating that they were virtuous, dependable, and compassionate. Nan put it into English because Ruhua wanted the translation attached to the original. Even though she could speak Mandarin fluently, the agent couldn't read the written characters. The Mitchells needed two more letters, and Janet asked another friend of hers and Susie, the salesgirl working at her jewelry store, to provide the other references.

15

THE SURFACE of the lake was glittering in the morning sunshine. In spite of the wintry weather, a flock of mallards was paddling in the water, which had grown drab due to the absence of green foliage. Nan had once liked observing the Canada geese, but he couldn't tolerate them anymore. To him they were robbers and gluttons. Whenever they came into the yard, they'd graze on the grass, each guarding an area for itself. If one of them wandered into another's territory, the other goose or gander would lunge at the trespasser with flapping wings, a stretched neck, and an open beak emitting ugly hisses. The lakeside was already naked, the grass eaten up by the waterfowl. Since the fall, the Wus' back lawn had been dwindling. The geese would browse closer and closer to the house. Sometimes they would even come below the deck, pulling and jabbing at the grass without pause. Pingping would chase them away whenever she saw them coming too close, but they'd soon return and resume grazing on the sward, always tearing the tender shoots first.

At the beginning of the previous spring, Pingping had planted some garlic and scallions in the semicircles formed by the monkey grass, but a few days after the sprouts pierced the loam, the geese had pulled them up and eaten them all. The backyard could have been cultivated into a vegetable garden, but the piggish waterfowl would have devoured all the seedlings.

To Nan's amazement, when the sweltering summer set in, the geese didn't leave for the North as they were supposed to do. Instead, they perched in the shady bushes on the other shore and came out only in the evenings and early mornings. The families living on the lake fed them, mostly bread and popcorn, so there was always plenty of food for them. Nan realized that these Canada geese had grown fat, lazy, and comfortable, no longer possessed of the instinct for migration.

That thought irked him, and a trace of disdain crept over his face. Just for easy food, the geese had chosen to live a riskless, stranded life. Nan noticed that seldom would they fly off to another body of water nearby. To the north, just ten miles away, there spread Lake Lanier, which abounded in fish and algae. It was reported that a catfish named Little Bobbie, weighing at least eight hundred pounds, lived in there, and every fall the radio would urge people to go catch him so that the captor could win a million dollars at the catfish derby. What's more, that lake's water was clean and vast, but these Canada geese wouldn't go there and confined themselves to this pond as long as food was offered to them. They had grown heavy and clumsy, yet their appetite remained gluttonous, as if they were no longer wild birds that were supposed to spend a part of their lives in the air.

"*What losers! These geese live like millionaires,*" Nan would say to his wife whenever he saw them paddling in the water.

Pingping would smile, saying he was just an angry man. Why couldn't he let the birds have an easy life? What was wrong with their inhabiting this lake?

"*Nobody should feed them from now on,*" Nan continued. "*Totally spoiled, they've lost their animal instinct. No wonder they're so fat.*"

"*By nature, who doesn't like comfort and ease?*" asked his wife.

"*But they've lost their wild spirit.*"

"*Why are you so serious about them?*"

"*They're not supposed to live like domestic fowls.*"

"*You act as if they're humans. Bear in mind that they're just geese.*"

"*We mustn't feed them anymore.*"

In spite of his complaints and disdain, he still brought back left-overs for the waterfowl. The geese and mallards liked the Wus' back-yard so much that a few ducks even nested in the thick monkey grass near the waterside.

Over the railing of the deck a bird feeder, caged in steel wire, hung on a goosenecked steel bar. The Wus had once used another feeder made of a white plastic tube, a gift Janet had given Taotao the spring before. The Mitchells also loved birds, and they had six feeders around their house. In the summer the Wus had often brought home leftover rice and noodles for the waterfowl and birds. All species of them would come: blackbirds, jays, cardinals, robins, golden finches, orioles, and even crows. Sometimes so many of them landed in the lawn that the grass changed color, and the Wus' deck was always scattered with bird droppings. Among the birds, cardinals seemed the most stupid, especially the females, who often merely searched the ground for seeds dropped by the males eating at the feeder. In the oak trees in the backyard lived two families of squirrels. Acorns were plentiful, so there was no need to feed them; yet the squirrels would come to steal the bird feed.

On this winter day, before Nan set out for work, he refilled the bird feeder with sunflower seeds. He liked songbirds, which would delight his heart whenever he saw them perch on the feeder, pecking at the seeds. At first he'd treated the birds like little visitors; feeding them had given him a kind of satisfaction, like playing the role of a friendly host. But he hadn't had that frame of mind for long and had stopped feeding them for several months when it was still warm. In the beginning, he had bought seeds mixed especially for mead-owlarks, finches, warblers, tufted titmice, but every day they'd eat up a whole tube of the feed. He was baffled by their voracious appetite and switched to sunflower seeds, which were cheaper—for six dollars he could buy twenty-five pounds at Wal-Mart. Still, every morning he found the feeder empty. One day he saw a squirrel stretch upside down on the white tube, eating the seeds from the holes. He shooed it away, but the squirrels would come to attack the feeder when nobody was around. Soon the holes on the tube were ripped wider, as if the rodents had intended to eat the plastic as well. Nan bought a new feeder caged in steel wire, which the ad claimed was "indestructible by squirrels."

To his bewilderment, even this feeder still couldn't keep the seeds from disappearing at night. True, the squirrels could use their tiny hands to scoop out seeds and drop them to the ground so that they could pick them up during the day, but how could they eat so much? Every night a good four pounds of sunflower seeds would be gone.

Nan talked with Dave about this, who was also perplexed, having run into the same problem. Dave called the squirrels on his property "a pain in the ass" and had trapped a number of them and released them in the woods three miles away near Snellville (one of the critters had even managed to return to the Mitchells', according to Dave); but for Nan that was too much because he could see no point in robbing the rodents of their current habitats. Besides, there were only four of them living in his backyard. Another family of three nested in Gerald's roof, and sometimes they also came to steal bird feed.

Then one night, as Nan was reading Tu Fu's poetry, suddenly a racket broke out on the deck as if some animals were tussling with one another. He went over to take a look, but it was too dark for him to see anything nearby. Only a car was flitting noiselessly behind the trees on the opposite shore. Nan flicked on the lamp under the back eaves and found a fat raccoon crouching on the top bar of the railing. Regardless of the light, the animal went on pulling and twisting the feeder, tossing the sunflower seeds helter-skelter. Nan knocked the glass back door with his knuckles, yet the rascal wouldn't scare, its bushy ringed tail flapping and swaying while its jaws clamped the cage and kept rocking it. Nan slapped the door pane; still it wouldn't pause. Not until he rushed out with a broom did the raccoon jump off the deck and vanish into the darkness.

From that day on, Nan would bring in the feeder every night and hang it out in the morning. A tube of seeds would last three or four days now, and a lot of birds gathered on the deck and around the feeder in the daytime. Even when it rained, some of them would stay around. Nan was not pleased that they had grown lazy and plump and taken the deck as a habitat of sorts, but he still fed them.

When he mowed the lawn in the backyard he noticed that there seemed to be more and more insects jumping out and darting away, and there were also more toads, frogs, and lizards in the grass. Then one day he was frightened to see a green snake, about three feet long, slithering away to the lakeside while the lawn mower was snarling and flinging bits of grass aside. He wasn't sure if it was poisonous, but he was positive it had come into the yard to hunt for toads and lizards. The thought came to him that lizards, frogs, and toads must have gathered here because insects were teeming in the yard. The insect proliferation must have been due to the fact that the birds he fed had quit searching for food in nature and let insects multiply in the grass. As a result, more frogs and lizards frequented here, and they in turn attracted snakes.

This realization made Nan stop feeding the birds. He didn't want snakes to lurk and crawl in the backyard, even if most of them were nonpoisonous. The birds would have to catch insects from now on. As the number of toads and lizards decreased in the grass, fewer snakes came around, although sometimes Nan saw them zigzagging in the lake, their tiny heads raised above the water. They probably lived among the rocks under the short bridge in the east.

In the winter the birds had to be starving, so Nan resumed feeding them. To his dismay, not many of them showed up now; still, he kept the feeder full every day and took it back in at night.

16

ONE MORNING Mrs. Wang called and begged Nan to come to her house immediately. Her husband had suffered a heart attack and had to be rushed to Gwinnett Hospital. She asked Nan to accompany her there because she wouldn't be able to understand some of the medical terms the doctors and nurses used. Nan set out after telling Pingping that if she and Niyan couldn't handle the business by themselves, they should close up for a few hours until he came back. As he was approaching the Wangs', an ambulance pulled into their driveway and two paramedics hopped out. Nan hastened his pace and caught up with the men. Mrs. Wang let the three of them in. Her husband was lying in bed, his eyes closed and his papery hand resting on his abdomen. But he was aware of the people around him and nodded as his wife told him that they were taking him to the hospital. Somehow Mr. Wang had lost his English and murmured Chinese in response to the paramedic who spoke to him while carrying him out.

In the ambulance Nan sat next to Mr. Wang, whose face was colorless and shriveled. The old man kept saying to his wife, *"I'm bone tired."* His lips were bluish and his white hair wet and mussed up.

Finally his wife gave way to her emotion, begging him not to leave her so suddenly. He opened his puffy eyes and murmured, *"I want to go back."*

"Where do you want to go?"

"Home."

"We'll go home soon."

His mouth stirred as he tried to smile, obviously tormented by angina. He began gasping for breath again, a gurgling sound in his throat. One of the paramedics, a stocky fellow, put an oxygen mask on his face, which eased the patient's breathing within a minute. Nan wasn't sure whether by "home" the old man was referring to their house here or to Taiwan or Fujian, his native province on the mainland.

Mr. Wang was rushed into a trauma room in the ER. His wife and Nan waited outside, sitting on orange chairs. Nan told Mrs. Wang to take a nap, since she might have to stay here a whole day and should rest some now. Soon she dozed off in spite of all the activity in the lounge. Meanwhile, Nan paced the floor and regretted not having brought along a book. He inserted two nickels into a pay phone and called the Gold Wok to check on Pingping and tell her about Mr. Wang's condition, which seemed critical. His wife couldn't talk with him for long because she and Niyan were overwhelmed with work there.

About half an hour later, a young doctor with tired eyes and curly sideburns stepped out of the trauma room and said to Mrs. Wang, "He isn't doing too well."

"Please save him!" she begged.

"We're doing our best." The doctor handed his half-drained coffee cup to a nurse and returned to the patient.

"Is he on Medicare?" the nurse asked Mrs. Wang.

"Yes, here's his card." The old woman took the card out of her purse and handed it to her. The nurse gave her two forms clasped to a clipboard. Mrs. Wang didn't know how to complete them, so Nan filled them out for her.

Again she closed her eyes and tried to drop off while Nan sat there watching people milling around. His head was numb and couldn't focus on any thought, partly because he had drunk two mugs of coffee that morning to gear himself up to the work in the kitchen. An hour later, a tall nurse wearing a laminated ID badge around her neck came out and said that Mrs. Wang could now go in and see her husband. The old woman and Nan followed her into the trauma room. At the sight of them, the young doctor smiled, his eyes sparkling and his bulky nose filmed with perspiration. "Well, he's stable now," he told them. "We're going to move him into another room for observation. He can check out tomorrow if he's still stable by then. The nurse will let you know how to take care of him at home."

"Thank you, doctor," said Mrs. Wang.

"Sure. I'm going to put him on medication before we decide if he needs an angioplasty. That's a minor operation using a little balloon to clear the narrowed artery." The doctor also said he wanted Mrs. Wang to bring her husband back regularly so that he could see him on an outpatient basis.

Nan translated the doctor's words to Mrs. Wang while she nodded agreement. He was surprised that they wouldn't keep the old man in the hospital for a few days. He remembered that Uncle Zhao, his father's painter friend in China, had once suffered a minor heart attack and had been hospitalized for a good month.

Mr. Wang was lying on the bed and lifted his withered hand to wave at his wife and Nan. Color had returned to his face, and his eyes were animated again. A thin hose was still attached to his arm, and a yellow defibrillator perched beside the bed. He said almost naughtily to his tearful wife, "*I thought I couldn't make it this time. Thank heaven, they brought me back.*"

A nurse pulled over a gurney. They moved Mr. Wang onto it and pushed him away. Nan didn't follow them to the ward, and instead told Mrs. Wang that he must go back to help Pingping and that she should call him when the old man was discharged so that he could come and drive them home. She looked a touch dismayed but didn't ask him to stay. Nan hailed a taxi and headed back to the Gold Wok.

•

Hearing that Mr. Wang had survived the heart attack, Pingping felt relieved. She was pleased that Nan had come back before midafternoon; otherwise she'd have had to put Taotao, who was just ten, to work at the counter as the cashier.

Although Mr. Wang could walk around afterward, the Wangs had been shaken by his heart attack and decided to move back to Taiwan, where free medical care was available to everyone. They had thought of joining their daughter in Seattle, but her airline job there was temporary and she might be transferred elsewhere. Soon they put their house on the market, selling it for $145,000. The price had been drastically reduced, so a lot of people stopped by to look at the brick bungalow. Niyan and Shubo went there to see the property too. They loved it, especially its convenient location, but the price was still too steep for them. What's more, Shubo Gao hadn't defended his dissertation yet and might go elsewhere to take a job. Nonetheless, his wife said to Mrs. Wang, "*We'll buy your house if you lop twenty thousand off the price.*"

"*No way.*" The old woman shook her full head of gray hair. "*We've already underpriced it for a quick sale. Ask Nan and Pingping whether we offered them the home for a hundred and fifty. That was two years ago.*"

Niyan and Shubo did ask Pingping, who proved that was true, so they gave up coveting the bungalow. A week later a retired couple from Illinois bought the house, and within a few days the Wangs left for good.

Their departure was a quiet affair that few people in the neighborhood noticed, but it saddened Nan and Pingping. The Wangs didn't like Taiwan that much; still, they could return to it. By contrast, the Wus, having no recourse to a place they could call home, had to put down roots here. They liked Georgia, yet they could see that life might be lonely and miserable here when they were old. They often talked to Niyan about the isolation the Wangs had experienced, but Niyan thought the old couple had asked for that kind of life, saying they could always have joined a community. Niyan said in a crisp voice, "*They should have gone to a church. That could've made them feel more or less at home here. If they didn't think Taiwan was a safe place, they should never have gone back to it. Your homeland is where you live and die.*"

Niyan's words made Nan and Pingping think a good deal. Husband and wife talked between themselves about joining a church, but decided not to rush. By any means they mustn't make light of the matter of religion, and neither should they go to God's house just for human companionship. Nevertheless, isolation and loneliness often made Nan ill at ease. Unlike him, Pingping was unusually calm, saying they wouldn't need others as long as their family stayed together. "*Who has many friends?*" she said to him. "*Most people only have associates. We have no need for lots of friends.*"

Nan was abashed as he realized she was much more enduring and solitary than he was. She didn't even miss her parents and siblings that much, although she'd write them regularly. He wasn't attached to his parents either, but he was unaccustomed to an isolated life and couldn't yet differentiate loneliness from solitude. By nature he was gregarious and had liked noisy, bustling crowds, but life had placed him at a spot where he had to exist as an individual completely on his own. How lucky he felt to have Pingping with him.

17

NAN also felt fortunate to have Dick Harrison as his friend, whose presence in his life had intensified his interest in poetry. One day Dick invited Nan to a reading given by a famous poet. At first Nan was reluctant to go, because whenever he was away, he'd have to ask Shubo to help at the restaurant. Shubo had been writing his dissertation in sociology at home, so he was available most times when the Gold Wok needed him. Still, Pingping would be unhappy about Nan's absence, which would cost them six dollars an hour to Shubo, who would work at the counter. This also meant Pingping would have to cook in the kitchen. Yet fascinated by Dick's praise of the poet, Edward Neary, Nan begged his wife to let him attend the reading at Emory University. Pingping didn't want him to go at first, but she later yielded.

The reading was held in White Hall on campus, where many buildings had marble exteriors and roofs of red ceramic tiles. At the entrance to the auditorium stood two folding tables, on one of which were stacked Edward Neary's books for sale, the table manned by a strapping man from the university's bookstore. Nan, in a double-breasted blazer, went into the auditorium, which had already filled up with students, faculty, and people from the city. The crowd overflowed onto the steps alongside the walls. There were more women than men among the audience. Unable to find a seat, Nan stayed in the back and leaned against the steel banister of the stairs that led up to the projection booth.

Around eight o'clock the poet arrived, accompanied by Dick and several other faculty members. Mr. Neary was a lanky man with a short neck and a web of wrinkles on his face, but he must have been quite handsome when he was young, as his Roman nose and pale green eyes suggested. They all sat down in the front row, which had been reserved for them. A moment later Dick went over to the podium. He introduced Mr. Neary briefly, enumerating the awards and grants the poet had garnered and calling him "a major poetic voice of our time."

Then Edward Neary took the microphone and began reading a long poem, "An Interpretation of Happiness," which he said he was still working on. His tone was languid and casual, as if he were talking to a few friends in a small room, but the audience was attentive. Now and then somebody would "huh" or "hah" in response to a playful line or a clever turn of phrase. Neary kept reading without lifting his head and seemed to have some difficulty concentrating, shifting his weight from leg to leg. His right hand rubbed his chin time and again. Whenever he did this, he'd muffle his voice a little.

Nan couldn't understand everything Neary was uttering. Soon he grew absentminded, looking around at the audience and noticing that some others were bored too. It took the poet at least twenty-five minutes to finish the poem. As he was flipping through a book, searching for another piece to read, a female student cried out, "Let us hear 'Tonight It's the Same Moon.'"

"Yes, read that, please," chimed in another young woman.

"All right," the poet said. "It's a love poem I wrote many years ago, for a girlfriend of mine whose name I've forgotten." The audience laughed while Mr. Neary grinned, running his fingers through his grizzled flaxen hair. "I guess I'm too old to write this kind of poetry anymore, but I'm going to read it anyway. Here it is." He lifted the book with one hand and began reading the poem with some emotion. Nan liked it very much. It was an elegy spoken by a young widow in memory of her late husband, lost in a recent plane crash. The cadence was supple and tender, in keeping with the pathos.

After that, Neary read seven or eight poems from different volumes. Then unhurriedly, he stacked his books together, indicating he was done. Dick stood up, clapping his hands. After a burst of applause, he announced, "Let's adjourn to the reception in the lobby, and Mr. Neary will be happy to autograph his books. Please join us for a glass of wine. Also, don't forget the colloquium Mr. Neary will give tomorrow afternoon, at three, in this room."

In the lobby Nan drank a cup of punch and ate a piece of cauliflower and a few squares of honeydew. Though Dick had announced there was wine, only some soft drinks were on the tables. Nan felt out of place here because he didn't know anybody except Dick, who was busy taking care of the poet's needs while talking with some people standing in line to get their books signed. Nan went up to him and said, "I'd better go."

"Don't you want to join us after this?" asked Dick.

"For what?"

"We'll have a drink somewhere. Come with me—we'll spend some time with Ed."

Nan agreed. He was curious about the poet, who seemed passionless, carefree, and a bit cynical, remarkably different from the ardent Sam Fisher. He went over to a table and picked up a small bunch of red grapes and stepped aside, waiting in a corner.

When the reception was over, Dick and a group of young women took Edward Neary to a bar just outside the campus. Nan tagged along and accompanied the poet all the way while Dick was talking and laughing with the five women walking ahead of them. Mr. Neary walked with a shuffling gait. He had been to China a few years before and talked to Nan about how hot it was in Beijing in August. He remembered fondly a young woman assigned by China's Ministry of Culture to serve as his interpreter.

Then he asked Nan, "Do you happen to know Bao Yuan, an exiled Chinese poet living in New York?"

"Of coss I know him! We were a kind of friends and once worked togezzer at a journal."

"He's an interesting guy. He's been translating some of my poems."

"Reelly?"

"He also interviewed me."

"Does he speak English now?"

"He had a young lady interpreting for us. He can read English but cannot speak it well."

Nan couldn't believe that Bao, despite his deplorable English, would attempt to translate Neary's poetry. He must have relied on someone to produce the notes first, from which he might be able to do the translation. "Where is he going to send zer poems? I mean, to which Chinese magazine?" Nan asked.

"He had six of them published in a journal called *Foreign Letters*."

"That's a prestigious monsly, very literary."

"So I've heard."

"I'm glad Bao is still writing poetry. He's also a painter."

"Yes, he showed me some of his work, very impressive. He has fine sensibility and a lot of talent. But the exile must have stunted his development considerably. He said he never had time to write the work he planned to do."

As they passed the side entrance of the university, Mr. Neary asked Nan about the average price of the houses in the Emory neighborhood, which he had seen on his way to the campus that afternoon. Many of them looked grand, built entirely of bricks. Though uncertain of the price, Nan ventured a figure, guessing upward of $400,000, but that didn't impress the poet. Mr. Neary said he owned a larger house than these in Newport, Rhode Island. Nan was surprised, because to his mind most poets were struggling artists without that kind of money.

In the bar Mr. Neary ordered beer, wine, chicken nuggets, and nachos sprinkled with cheddar cheese and bits of jalapeno. The young women were effervescent; apparently they all admired Neary's poetry. Laura, the tallest of them, with cloisonné bracelets on both wrists, smiled at the poet all the while, her eyes flashing. Emily, the only Asian woman among them, seemed shy, though she giggled happily and nudged her friends now and again. Her sweet face resembled a teenager's. Mr. Neary liked her and asked about her life in Atlanta and her family. Her parents had immigrated from Korea, but she was born and raised in Missouri. She had moved to Georgia three years earlier and liked it here. Mr. Neary thought she was Chinese, but she said her last name was Choi and considered herself Korean American.

The shortest of them, Anita, was a budding poet and middle school teacher. She could even quote Mr. Neary's lines with ease, which pleased the author greatly. The other two women, also fans of the poet, worked at Barnes & Noble. The five of them belonged to a poetry group and met regularly to read and discuss one another's poems. Nan said little and just listened to them.

As they were chatting and drinking, Mr. Neary grew louder and more talkative. He said he had been editing an anthology of poetry by young poets for a New York publisher, whose name he wouldn't disclose. He squinted at Dick, who smiled knowingly. Then he told the women, "My babysitter has been helping me sort out the poems. Without her I don't know how I could do it. I don't have time to read all the books and journals people send in. You should all show me your work. Nan, you should send me your poems too."

"I will do zat when I have somesing finished," Nan replied in earnest. But none of the women responded to the invitation enthusiastically. He wondered why they wouldn't jump at such an opportunity, since they were all writing poetry and must have been struggling to get published.

Laura asked the poet casually, "Does your babysitter write poems too?"

"No, not now. She might have in her teens."

The women glanced at one another. The short Anita smirked, then covered her mouth with a napkin. Mr. Neary said to them again, "Feel free to send me your work. I'm a maker and breaker of poets. I'm a powerful man, you know."

Nan could see that the poet was tipsy. He caught a dubious expression flitting across Dick's face. Mr. Neary smiled to himself as if to recall something, his hand holding a barbecued chicken nugget. Then he lifted his head and asked the women, "So you don't believe me? You think I'm just an old loony?"

Emily Choi said, "You're not old. Your poems are wonderful and powerful."

"I'm also a rich man, you know," Mr. Neary went on. "Imagine, a poet paid sixty thousand dollars for federal tax last year. This is indeed a great country where even a poet can become a millionaire."

"Amazing," Emily mumbled, lowering her eyes.

Anita put in, "So Canada is no longer your homeland?"

"No. I'm an American."

Dick winked at Nan, who was bemused, knowing Neary had been born in Ontario and had come to the United States in his early thirties. He wondered why the poet would talk so much about power and money. How did those bear on his poetry? Why was he acting more like a business magnate?

A waitress came and placed the bill on the table, which Mr. Neary picked up. Nan noticed that it was more than eighty dollars. The young women looked at one another. Anita said, "Mr. Neary, let us take care of it. We're taking you out."

"No, no." The poet waved, licking his upper teeth. "This is on me. But I'm open to another drink with you at another place, individually or collectively." He laughed and screwed up his eye as he folded the receipt and placed five twenties in the bill sleeve.

The women said no more. They all got up, ready to leave. The bar was closing, and together they made for the door.

Outside, the night was clear, the street shimmering in the whitish moonlight. A breeze came, shaking the sprouting aspens a little. The traffic was still droning in the distance. The women said good-bye to Mr. Neary and presently faded into the darkness beyond North Decatur Road. Dick was going to walk his guest all the way back to the Emory Inn, which was about half a mile to the north. Nan kept them company for about two hundred yards, then parted from them and veered toward the garage behind the university's main library, where he had parked. He turned his head to look at them while walking away.

He overheard Mr. Neary say, "Let me give you the receipt for tonight."

"Sure." Dick took the slip from the poet.

18

DURING the next few days Nan thought a lot about his meeting with Edward Neary, about what the poet had said at the bar. When Dick came to the restaurant on Friday afternoon, Nan asked him what Mr. Neary had meant by being "a maker and breaker of poets." Dick explained that generally speaking, the inclusion of a young poet's work in a significant anthology could help establish the poet. As the editor, Edward Neary decided whom to include, so he was a maker of poets. Conversely, he'd have to exclude some people from the book—those poets, once left out, would suffer a setback in their careers. Therefore he was also a breaker of poets.

"Do you sink he'll leave someone out on purpose?"

"Sure, everyone does that to his enemies and people he doesn't like."

Nan was surprised that poets could be so vindictive and malevolent. "Is he reelly so well endowed as he bragged?" he asked again.

"Ha ha ha!" Dick laughed. "You're so funny. I don't know if Ed has a big penis, but he's a MacArthur fellow."

"What's that? He's related to General MacArthur's family?"

"No, no, it's a foundation that gives huge fellowships to talented individuals, at least three hundred thousand dollars. For Ed's age, it must be worth more than that, because the older a fellow is, the more money he gets."

"I never imagined a poet could be zat rich."

"Some poets live like a prince or princess."

"How about Sam?"

"He makes a lot too."

Nan thought it rather absurd that Mr. Neary was so powerful that he could decide the fates of some young poets. "Will he include your poems in his anthology?" he asked Dick.

"You bet, or I wouldn't have had him invited over and paid three thousand dollars."

"Reelly! He made mahney so easily? He just worked two or three hours and made more zan Pingping and I can make in a month."

"Life's unfair, isn't it? But that's the price for poets of his stature."

"How about you?"

"I'll be lucky if a school invites me just to read. Occasionally I get five hundred dollars for a visit."

"Zat's not bad."

"No, I can't complain. I can't think of money and power at this point in my career."

"You're right," Nan said sincerely. "If you reelly like power, you should run for zer governor."

Dick chortled. "I'll remember that." He turned his fork to twist some noodles into a bundle, then added, "Because what's at stake is so piddling in the poetry world, the competition is all the more fierce. In fact, it's a rough-and-tumble territory. Also, most poets live in cliques, otherwise it would be hard for us to survive. The network is essential."

"So you belong to Sam's group?"

"You can say that."

To some extent Nan was disillusioned by what Dick said. To him the poetry world should be relatively pure, and genuine poets free spirits, passionate but disinterested. Yet according to Dick, many of them were territorial and xenophobic. Could someone like himself ever belong to a coterie? Unlikely. He couldn't imagine being accepted by any clique. Besides, above all, he wanted to become a self-sufficient individual.

Dick lifted the teacup and took a swallow. He grinned at Nan while dipping his pointed chin. He looked secretive and leaned forward, whispering, "I want to show you something, Nan." He fished out of his hip pocket two small tubers like shriveled ginger roots, dried thoroughly. They looked familiar to Nan, but he couldn't remember what they were called. Dick asked, "Do you use this herb too?"

"What are these?"

"Dong quai, a kind of aphrodisiac. I thought you Chinese all used it."

Nan broke into laughter, which baffled his friend. "What's so funny?" Dick said.

Instead of answering, Nan asked, "You have used Tiger Balm for sex too?"

"Sure, but that's not as good as Indian God Lotion and burns your skin like hell."

Nan cracked up again, his eyes squeezed shut. "To tell zer truth, in China women use dong quai to regulate menstruation. It nurtures zer yin in your body, not zer yang. I've never heard zat any man eats zis herb to strengthen a dick."

Dick was amazed, then grinned. "Nan, you're a poet."

"How so?"

"You just made a pun with my name."

"Oh yes." Nan was surprised by his unintended feat.

"To be fair, this is powerful stuff," Dick went on. "I've used it for a while and it has really improved my performance and made me feel strong. It helps my writing too. As for Tiger Balm, I've removed it from my medicine cabinet."

"People in China mainly rub zer balm on zeir foreheads to prevent sunstroke, or on their temples to sooze headaches. Even kids use it too. We call it 'fresh and cool ointment.' Nobody trits it as somesing zat can increase sexual pleasure."

"Ah, this is a case of significant misunderstanding in cultural exchange, don't you think?"

"Of coss it's meaningful. It reflects zer core of American culture zat's obsessed with two s's."

"Two s's? What are they?"

"Self and sex."

"Very true." Dick's eyes lit up as he gave a hearty laugh. "Where did you get this idea? Is there an article or book on this?"

"No, just my personal impression."

"That's excellent."

After that conversation, Dick came to the restaurant more often, though Eleanor rarely accompanied him. He seemed fascinated by Nan, by the kind of off-kilter humor Nan had. Also, Nan always offered him something free along with his order—a couple of steamed dumplings, or a pair of egg rolls, or a scallion pancake. Ping-ping once asked Dick why Eleanor hadn't come with him. He shook his head and said, "She wants to play the field."

Pingping didn't understand that idiom. When she asked Nan, he said, *"Eleanor wants to see as many men as possible."*

"No wonder Dick has such a sad face these days," she said thoughtfully.

"He's lonely, I guess. He said I was his only friend here." Nan was surprised by his own words, because he had never believed Dick felt isolated in Atlanta.

"I don't think that's true. He has a lot of colleagues at Emory."

"But that doesn't mean they're his friends."

"He's just a big boy, inside weak."

"Anyway he's my friend." Nan looked at Pingping, who smiled at him quizzically. *"What?"* he asked.

She said nothing. Nan took hold of her ear, tweaking it, and ordered, *"Confess."*

"Let go!" she shrieked.

The instant he released her, she grabbed a flyswatter from the counter and set out to chase him. Nan was running around the table in the middle of the room, clockwise or counterclockwise, opposite the direction she moved in. Both of them seemed to have forgotten what had caused the pursuit, and despite their panting and red faces, they looked happy. Niyan laughed and watched them while shaking her head.

19

PINGPING felt uneasy about Nan's going out with Dick, though he generally did so at most once a month. Together they had gone to a Shakespearean play, a puppet show, and a reading given by John Updike. She understood that Nan needed some diversion once in a while, but the work at the Gold Wok would get hectic without him around. Shubo could cook a few things now, but Pingping would have to bustle about in the kitchen most of the time when Nan wasn't there. What's worse, Nan's absence would make her fidgety and make the place feel as strange as if it belonged to someone else. Why does he have to spend so much time with that frivolous Dick? she often wondered. Will they go elsewhere after the reading? Will they be alone, just the two of them? I really don't mind that they're friends, but I want Nan to stay here. He shouldn't act like a bachelor and ought to pay more attention to our family. He should spend more time with Taotao.

Whenever Pingping complained about Nan, Niyan sympathized with her. One day Niyan said to her, *"Why don't Nan and you go to church on Sundays? You can meet lots of interesting people there and have fun too. You won't feel isolated or insecure once you belong to a church."*

"In fact," Pingping said, *"a number of people have shown up on our doorstep to invite us to join their churches, but we're not Christians, so we don't go."*

"Aiya, why have only a one-track mind? You don't have to be a Christian to attend Sunday services." Niyan fingered her drop earring while biting her bottom lip. Her eyes, slightly bulging, were fixed on Pingping.

"We don't believe in Jesus Christ yet," Pingping said.

"Why so serious about that? How many of us are real believers? The church is a place where you can meet people and make friends. It has night schools and dance parties for singles. It can make you feel better with so many Chinese around."

"We're not singles."

"All I'm saying is that once you join a church, people will help you and your life will be safer and easier."

"Do you really feel that way?"

"Of course, why should I lie to you?"

"All right, I'll talk to Nan about this."

"Tell him that Shubo and I have had a great time in our church. You can attend the sermons on Sunday mornings. That will make you feel good, calm inside."

Pingping agreed to persuade Nan, mainly because she had something else on her mind. Dick Harrison had just broken up with his girlfriend, and Pingping was afraid he might be a bisexual and start an affair with Nan. She couldn't understand why Nan was so attached to that flighty man. There must have been some mutual attraction between them. To prevent her husband from turning gay, she even gave him several vitamins every day, since she had read in an outdated book that many cases of homosexuality were due to vitamin deficiency. She dared not express her concerns explicitly to Nan, who just swallowed whatever pills she gave him, never raising any question about them.

On their way to the Gold Wok the next morning Pingping brought up to Nan the subject of attending church. It was mizzling, and all trees and houses blurred. She and Nan shared a large candy-striped umbrella. She was shivering a little from the damp wind. Nan wrapped an arm around her shoulders to give her some body warmth. He said, *"We mustn't be lighthearted about this matter. If we go to church, we ought to believe in God. A church is a place for worship."*

"If you don't ever attend the service, how can you understand Christianity?"

"At this point of my life, I don't feel like joining any religious

group. I want to be independent. Also, I can take poetry as my reli-gion if I need one. If you want to go to church, feel free to do that."

"Why can't we be more flexible? As a matter of fact, we may get some business from Niyan's parish." Lately Pingping had noticed some customers greeting the waitress like a friend. Niyan told her that they belonged to her congregation in Lawrenceville.

"No, the church is a sacred place, a house of God," Nan said. *"If I'm not a Christian, I won't feel comfortable there."*

A few days ago he had said similar words to a craggy-faced black seminarian who had come to their home to read a few passages from the New Testament.

Pingping said no more, knowing she couldn't bring him around. Besides, she agreed with him in a way. It was better to be yourself. Here nobody could really help you, and only you could save yourself. In addition, she didn't want to be a fake, as she had tried to be back in China, where people had to lie to get things done and to keep themselves from danger. When she had come to the States six and a half years before, she hadn't been able to speak comfortably for months because she didn't know how to talk without lying. As a result, she would remain taciturn most of the time. It took more than half a year for her to get used to speaking her mind. Now she wanted to live and act honestly, just as Nan insisted.

20

PINGPING told Nan that the adoption agent had mailed Janet and Dave the photographs of two girl babies and asked them to choose one. Obviously Ruhua, the agent, had meant to do the Mitchells a favor, but this threw them into a terrible dilemma. How could they keep one child while abandoning the other? Janet called Ruhua and implored her to let them have both children, who would make perfect sisters, but the agent disallowed her appeal, saying all the paperwork had been filed for only one baby and it would be too difficult to restart the whole thing, and besides, there were many people desperate to adopt. The Mitchells were distressed and wanted to discuss the matter with the Wus that very day. Since the restaurant wasn't a suitable place for such a conversation, Pingping told Janet to come to their house around ten-thirty p.m.

Both Nan and Pingping were exhausted when they arrived home. Taotao was at his computer, playing the game Mortal Kombat. *"Turn it off,"* his mother told him. *"Time for bed."*

"Let me finish this round, all right?"

"Remember to brush your teeth."

As soon as Nan had taken a shower, the Mitchells came. They showed the Wus the photos and wanted them to suggest which one of the babies they should keep. Dave lounged on the sofa and looked upset, now and then letting out a feeble sigh. He asked for coffee since he and his wife would have to stay up late to make the decision. Nan put a kettle on the stove.

"What kinda daughter you have in your mind, Janet?" asked Pingping.

"I don't know."

"How about you, Dave?"

"Both of them look good to me. God, I've never felt it so heart-wrenching to decide on something." He was obviously in pain, and his deep-set eyes dimmed.

"It's my fault," Pingping said. "I shouldn't ask Ruhua to do you special favor."

"No," Janet put in. "We appreciate your help, Pingping. But now we're stuck with this two-baby problem. What should we do? Help us decide."

Nan dropped a bit of hazelnut extract into each cup of the instant coffee he made for the Mitchells, and then joined Pingping in observing the photos. The babies looked quite similar, with little cute noses and almond eyes, though one's face was broader than the other's. Nan sighed, "Zis is beyond me. I don't know what to say. How could I tell which of zem will turn out to be a better daughter for you?"

"That's not really our concern," Dave said, putting down his cup on a straw coaster on the coffee table. "Our main problem is that it will be hard for us to handle the guilt. The two girls are in different orphanages. If the one we leave behind is adopted by a good family, that will be okay with me. But what if she ends up in a bad family or remains an orphan?"

"Yes, that's the hardest part," Janet agreed.

Nan was amazed. Then to the Wus' astonishment, Dave broke into sobs, wiping his lumpy face with a tissue. "I'm sorry. It's too painful to choose."

Both Nan and Pingping were touched. Nan knew the Mitchells often went to church on Sunday mornings. Probably it was their Christian faith that had instilled in them the sense of guilt and enabled them to commiserate with the babies more than they—the Wus—could. Nan had never thought about the fate of the child the Mitchells would have to give up. He surmised that the Mitchells' minds must have another dimension that was absent from his.

Pingping said, "Think this way, Janet. When you saw the photos, which one of them you suddenly feel grab your heart?"

"This one." Janet lifted the one with a wider face from the coffee table. "I felt a jolt at the sight of her."

"How about you, Dave?" Pingping asked.

"To me, it was the other one."

"Heavens, no way we can help you!" Pingping raised her hand in defeat.

Nan stepped in, "I feel you two have to do some soul-searching and figure out a solution by yourselves. When will you let zee agent know your decision?"

"Tomorrow afternoon," replied Janet.

"Sorry," Nan said. "We reelly can't help you, not because we don't want to share zer guilt. If only there were more information. On zee other hand, even if we had enough information, you would still feel guilty if you adawpt just one of zem, right?"

"I guess so," said Dave.

Despite the impasse, the Mitchells stayed late into the night, talking about their plan to travel to China and bring back their daughter. Not until twelve-thirty did they take their leave.

21

TWO DAYS LATER, Janet told the Wus that Dave had gone with her choice of the baby with the wider face, since it was she who had first thought of adoption. They had gotten more information on the child and were going to contact the INS to apply for a green card for her. From now on they must wait patiently for the time they could go to Nanjing and pick up their baby. They were sort of surprised that the process wasn't as intimidating and tedious as they had thought.

For days, Nan, moved by Dave's sobbing of the other night, had been pondering the Mitchells' sense of guilt, which made him change his mind about going to church. He began to think that any religion might improve humanity, at least be able to make people more compassionate and more humble. So he decided to visit the Chinese Christian Church in Duluth, a nearby town to the north, just to see if he liked it. Pingping planned to go with him, but on Sunday morning she felt under the weather, having sore shoulders, and stayed home. Before Nan set out, he gave her a back massage, which eased her pain considerably.

The church was in a modern stuccoed building sitting atop a gentle rise planted with cypress saplings. It was a hot day, and the heat was rising from the newly paved parking lot, flickering like purple smoke. As Nan entered the church, some people were standing around exchanging pleasantries in the foyer, which resembled the lobby of a hotel or theater. He saw a few familiar faces, but didn't know anyone except the woman who had once come to the Gold Wok to solicit donations for flood victims. He remembered her name, Mei Hong, and was sure she recognized him; yet for some reason she turned away after giving him a once-over. Nan went into the nave, sat down in a back pew, and picked up a hymnal. Hundreds of people were already sitting in there, and on the wide chancel platform were seated two men wearing dark blue suits and crimson neckties, both bespectacled. A potbellied vase holding a large mixed bouquet stood on the floor, in front of the lectern.

The service started, and the younger clergyman on the chancel went to the microphone and called for the people to rise. Together they started singing a hymn, "A Mighty Fortress Is Our God," accompanied by a huge piano played by a mousy woman in a corner. Next, they bowed and meditated for a moment. The hall turned quiet while Nan glanced right and left and noticed an old woman in front of him thumbing through a Bible rested atop the back of the pew before her. A baby let out a cry but was stopped immediately by its parent. Then a choir, eight women and six men in scarlet-collared gowns, went onto the chancel steps and sang "Sweet Hours of Prayer." Their singing was passionate but serene, swelling and ebbing as if they were leading the piano. After that, the pastor wearing tinted glasses, surnamed Bian, took the lectern and began preaching the sermon, entitled "New Hope." His voice was soft most of the time, but now and then it grew strong, fervent and exultant. He spoke about Paul, the apostle, as a model follower of the Lord and an ideal man. He quoted from the New Testament to illustrate that Paul was originally a sinner and a persecutor of Christians, but then changed into a man with a big heart. Paul never lost hope and always remained modest, not taking pride in his own accomplishments and praising only the Lord. He loved his siblings despite their tricks against him, despite their transgressions and sins, because he could forget the past and look ahead only. *"Think about the sprinters at the Olympic Games,"* the preacher announced in Mandarin softened by his Fujian accent. *"How can they run that fast? Do they look back when they're dashing toward the finish line? Of course not. Brothers and sisters, we have to lay aside our old disputes and animosity and look forward and think about the future, where our hopes are. Otherwise, how could we see any light? . . ."*

Nan's eyes were glued to the pastor's long, heavy-chinned face. He believed he had seen him before. But where? He couldn't remember. He was positive this man had come from mainland China.

Pastor Bian now was speaking about how to get rid of one's sins. He said, "*If you have a glass of water mixed with soy sauce, how can you get the water clean again? Very simple. You keep pouring pure water into the glass until the soy sauce is washed away. Brothers and sisters, our Lord is the most abundant fountain of pure water. Tap into that divine source and you will be cleansed, clean like a newborn baby and bountiful with love.*"

Then he went on to talk about the necessity of accumulating one's rewards in heaven by doing good deeds on earth. He even claimed that he couldn't wait to meet God and collect the rewards he had deposited in God's bank up there.

Nan was fascinated by the analogies the pastor hurled, though he wasn't fully convinced by his eloquence. He remembered that his friend Danning Meng had told him that he couldn't stop weeping once at a Sunday service. In Massachusetts, Danning had gone to a Catholic church in Watertown at least once a month. In contrast, Nan now felt calm and detached. When the sermon was over, the choir again went to the front and belted out "Take My Life and Let It Be." After the singing, the pastor announced the birth of a baby to a couple in the congregation; it weighed seven pounds and five ounces, and mother and child were both safe and well. He also spoke about the amount of donations the church had received lately and urged people to give more so that they could reach the annual goal of collecting $50,000. After the announcements, the younger clergyman called everybody to rise again, and together they sang the final hymn, "I Praise My Lord Only," following the lines projected on the wall beside the chancel.

The moment they finished singing, the young clergyman said, "*Please receive Brother Shiming Bian's benediction.*" People sat down and bowed their heads while the pastor raised both hands to deliver his final words: "*Precious God, we thank you for making this church flourish and prosper. We ask for your blessing on every member of our community. Please make us strong and humble, brave and meek, righteous and compassionate. Please grant us the eyes that can see far and deep. Please grant us the ears that can hear your voice and the unpronounced truth. May your light and love guide our everyday existence so that we can forever remain yours—*"

"Amen!" the hall cried.

Nan hadn't lowered his head during the benediction, because at the mention of the pastor's name, he had realized that the man was an exiled dissident who had once been a preeminent journalist in China, famous for his reportage that exposed official corruption and power abuse. Each year photographs of this man would appear a few times in Chinese-language newspapers and magazines, and there was a famous saying attributed to him: "We have gained the freedom of the sky but lost the gravity of the earth," which described the existential condition of the Chinese exiles living in North America. No wonder his face looked so familiar. After the benediction, instead of filing out with others, Nan went up to the pastor and introduced himself as a local businessman. He told Mr. Bian that he admired his articles and was happy to meet him in person. He handed him his card and said, "*Please stop by at my restaurant whenever you like. Your friends are welcome too.*"

Mr. Bian glanced at the card. "*Nan Wu, I know of you,*" he said in surprise. "*I liked the poems you published in* New Lines, *especially the one called 'This Is Just Another Day.' Are you still editing the magazine?*"

"*No, I'm a chef now.*"

"*That's good. I too have put my feet on the ground finally, working to earn my keep. By the way, you know Mr. Manping Liu, don't you?*"

"*Of course, I visited him in New York.*"

"*He's going to speak here next Tuesday evening.*"

"*Really? On what?*"

"*On the relationship between Taiwan and mainland China. I hope you can join us. He'll be delighted to see you.*"

Then Mr. Bian went on to tell Nan that the talk would be given at the public library in Alpharetta, an affluent town full of brick mansions, about ten miles northwest of Lilburn. Nan promised to attend the meeting.

22

NAN was excited, not having seen Mr. Liu for almost three years. At work that day he even called him in New York and invited him to stay at his home. The old man was pleased, but said his friends in Atlanta had already made arrangements for his lodging and board. He sounded glad to hear from Nan, saying he looked forward to seeing him on Tuesday evening. Nan promised to attend his talk, though he hadn't mentioned it to Pingping yet.

When he brought it up, Pingping was reluctant to let him go, but later Nan persuaded her. On Tuesday evening, after eight-thirty, when the busiest time had passed at the Gold Wok, he arrived at the library, where the talk was already under way. He took a seat in the back corner. Mr. Liu had aged considerably, his mouth more sunken, but his voice was still metallic and ardent. He was speaking about the necessity for Taiwan to be reunified with mainland China, because if it went independent, China would lose its gateway to the Pacific Ocean, and Japan, in addition to the United States, would control the China Sea entirely. Nan was amazed that Mr. Liu's view dovetailed with the Chinese government's. It was as if all the years' exile hadn't changed the old man's mind-set one bit.

After the talk, the audience raised questions for the speaker, and some of them also stood up to add their opinions to Mr. Liu's answers. A young man who must have come from Taiwan asked, "*Mr. Liu, you're one of the foremost figures in the Chinese democracy movement and may hold an important office in the Chinese government someday. If you become China's president, what will you do if Taiwan declares independence?*"

Mr. Liu remained silent for a moment, then replied, "*First of all, I* can never become a national leader. But if I were the president, I might have to order the People's Liberation Army to attack Taiwan. There isn't another way out of this. China must protect its territorial integrity. Whoever loses Taiwan will be recorded by history as a criminal of the Chinese nation."

Some people applauded. Liu's words surprised Nan, who raised his hand and was allowed to speak. With his legs shaking, Nan said in a calm voice, "Mr. Liu, I can see the political logic of your argument. But if we look at this issue in a different light, that is, from the viewpoint of humanity, we may reach another conclusion. For the individual human being, what is a country? It's just an idea that binds people together emotionally. But if the country cannot offer the individual a better life, if the country is detrimental to the individual's existence, doesn't the individual have the right to give up the country, to say no to it? By the same token, all the regions in China are like members of the Chinese family—if one of the brothers wants to live separately, isn't it barbaric to go smash his home and beat him up?"

The audience was thrown into a tumult, with many eyes glowering at Nan, who forced himself not to wince. Mr. Liu smiled and said, "Nan Wu, my friend, I see your point. I can sympathize with your concern for humanity, but your argument is infeasible and too naive. If China doesn't get Taiwan back, another country will take it and set up military bases there to threaten China. Sometimes a nation must sacrifice to survive."

Mei Hong, the short, bony-faced woman, stood up and spoke in a shrill voice. "I totally agree with Mr. Liu. John F. Kennedy said, 'Ask not what your country can do for you; ask what you can do for your country.' Even Americans put their national interests before the individual's interests. Without Taiwan, our shoreline will be cut in half. Also, if Taiwan goes independent, then how about Tibet, Inner Mongolia, and Sinkiang Uighur? If we let this happen, China would break into numerous small warring states. Then chaos will rule our homeland, millions and millions of people will be homeless and die of famine, and the world will be swarmed with refugees."

Nan challenged, "You're a Christian. Does your religion teach you to kill? Are there not enough crimes committed on the pretext of patriotism in this century?"

Shiming Bian, the pastor, broke in, "*Christianity doesn't tolerate evil. Anyone who wants to destroy China deserves his own destruction. Nan Wu, you're too emotional to think coherently. Even a democratic country like the United States fought the Civil War to keep the country from going separate.*"

Nan cried, "*Isn't the current Chinese government an evil power that banished you? Why do you see eye to eye with it?*"

Mr. Liu put in, "*We must differentiate the government from our country and people. The government can be evil, but both our people and our country are good. I'm optimistic because I cannot afford to lose hope for our nation. The world already has too many pessimists, a dollar a dozen, so we ought to take heart.*"

That shut Nan up, but he wasn't persuaded. He thought of retorting with the aphorism Mr. Liu had often quoted from Hegel, "the nature of a people determines the nature of their government," but he sat down and remained silent. The question-and-answer period continued.

Nan left the meeting before it was over. The next morning he phoned Pastor Bian's residence, where Mr. Liu was staying, and left a message on the machine: he invited both of them to dinner at the Gold Wok. But they didn't return his call. Nan was disappointed by both Mr. Liu and the pastor, so for a long time he didn't set foot in that church again.

23

THERE WERE hundreds of Tibetans living in the Atlanta area, some of whom were graduate students. They gathered in a lecture room at Emory University on weekends to meditate and listen to a monk preach on Buddhist scriptures. Dick was involved with this group and often urged Nan and Pingping to join them, but the Wus couldn't, having to work on weekends. They had noticed that whenever they slackened their efforts at the Gold Wok, problems would crop up and customers would complain. They had to do their utmost to maintain the quality of their offerings, keep the restaurant clean and orderly, and see to it that every part of the business went without a hitch.

A few days after Mr. Liu's talk at the public library, Dick told Nan excitedly that the Dalai Lama was going to speak at Emory that week. Both Nan and Pingping were interested in hearing the holy man's speech and asked Dick to get tickets for them. Dick promised to help.

The next morning he called and said all three thousand tickets were already gone. Nan and Pingping were not overly disappointed, since it would have been difficult for both of them to leave the restaurant at the same time. They had seen the Dalai Lama on TV recently and respected him. He had a natural demeanor that belied his role of a dignitary. At a conference broadcast on TV, a reporter asked him what the major events of the next year would be, and he laughed and said, "What a question you gave me, Ted! I don't even know what I'm going to eat for dinner. How can I predict anything about next year?" The audience exploded in laughter.

Later that night Dick phoned to inform Nan that the Dalai Lama would meet with a group of Chinese students at the Ritz-Carlton hotel at two p.m. the next day. "If I were you, I would go," he told Nan. "This is a rare opportunity."

Then Dick described to him the public speech the Dalai Lama had delivered in the university's stadium two hours before. It had gone well at first, and His Holiness had spoken about forgiveness, benevolence, love, happiness. People were captivated by his humor and candor. But as soon as the Dalai Lama finished speaking, a stout politician took the podium and began condemning China for occupying Tibet, for starting the Korean War and the Vietnam War, for the genocide committed by the Khmer Rouge sponsored by the Chinese Communists, for oppressing the minorities and dissidents, for supporting the dictatorial regimes like Cuba and North Korea. He went so far as to claim that the Chinese national leaders should be grateful to the United States for the very fact that every morning they woke up to find Taiwan still a part of China. As the result of his diatribe, the spiritual gathering suddenly turned into a political battle. Some Chinese students shouted at the speaker from the back of the stadium, "Stop insulting China!" "Get off the stage!" "Stop China-bashing!" The meeting was chaotic until the politician was done.

The next day Nan and Pingping drove to Lenox Square in Buckhead. The timing was good, since Niyan and Shubo could manage without them in the early afternoon. When Nan and Pingping stepped into the hotel, the lobby was swarmed with people trooping out of a large auditorium. In the hall the Dalai Lama was standing on the stage and shaking hands with a few officials; he had just given a talk to four hundred local community leaders, two pieces of white silk still draped around his neck. There were so many people pouring out of the entrance that the Wus couldn't get closer to look at the holy man. Seeing some Chinese students heading down the hallway, Nan and Pingping followed them, pretending they were graduate students too. One man wearing thick glasses said in English, "I'm going to ask His Holiness how often he jerks off."

Pingping didn't understand the expression, but Nan was shocked. Then a pallid young woman said, "Yes, we must grill him."

Following them, the Wus entered a room in which a dozen rows of folding chairs occupied almost half of its space. About seventy Chinese students and scholars were already seated in there. At the front stood a small table and two wing chairs. A few moments after Nan and Pingping had sat down, the Dalai Lama stepped in, accompanied by a thickset man who had a broad, weather-beaten face. His Holiness bowed a little with his palms pressed together before his chest. The audience stood up. The Dalai Lama shook hands with some people at the front. "*Sit down, please sit down,*" he said in standard Mandarin.

He and his interpreter sat down on the chairs. He looked rather tired, without the beaming smile he had worn a moment before. "I'm very glad to meet all of you here," he said in halting English. "It's important for us to communicate with each other. I always tell Tibetans, let us talk with Chinese people. Try to make friends with them. Now here we are."

A short, squinty fellow with a crew cut stood up and asked, "*Since you left China in 1959, you have attempted to create an independent Tibet, but in vain. Where do you see your movement leading you?*"

The interpreter translated the question. The Dalai Lama said solemnly, "There's some misunderstanding here. I have never asked for an independent Tibet. Check my record. You will see I never seek independence from China."

"What do you want, then?" the fellow pressed on in English.

"More autonomy and more freedom for my people so we can protect Tibetan life and culture. We need the Chinese government to help us achieve this goal. The Tibetans are entitled to a better livelihood."

Nan was surprised by the modest but dignified answer. Prior to this occasion he too had assumed that His Holiness demanded nothing but the complete independence of Tibet.

A female graduate student got up and asked, "As a political leader, you can represent the Tibetans in India and elsewhere, but who gave you the right to represent the Tibetans in China?"

A dark shadow crossed His Holiness's face. He replied, "I'm not a political leader, not interested in politics at all. But as a Tibetan, I am obligated to help my people, spiritually and materially. I have to speak for those who are not listened to."

Then a tall man raised his hand. He asked in a thin, funny voice, "What do you think of the slave system in Tibet before 1959?"

His Holiness answered without showing any emotion, "We always had our problems and backwardness. To be honest, I planned to abolish the slave system myself. Like any society, ours was never perfect."

Someone in the back stood up and spoke huskily. *"For centuries Tibet has been part of China, and your predecessors used to be the spiritual fathers of the Chinese people. You're wise not to pursue an independent Tibet, which China will never allow, because China has to maintain its territorial integrity. Truth be told, Tibet can never be a vacuum of external power. If it weren't part of China, other countries would occupy it and pose an immediate threat to China . . ."* The voice sounded familiar to Nan. He turned around and to his astonishment found Mr. Liu standing there and speaking. He'd thought the old man had left Atlanta.

The Dalai Lama didn't respond to Mr. Liu directly and said only, "I've heard the same argument before, but it is not based on justice. It's not difficult to rationalize injustice."

Some of the Chinese here were so belligerent, so devoid of empathy, that Nan and Pingping felt embarrassed. Nan could see that the Dalai Lama was miserable and at moments cornered by the questions. His Holiness was obviously a suffering man, totally different from his public image. Nan had come to see his beatific face, but ever since the conversation started, not even once had His Holiness smiled.

A stocky male student asked sharply, "Can you tell us what kind of life you lived before you fled to India?"

Some eyes turned to glare at him and a few voices tried to shush him, but the short fellow seemed impervious to the resentment from the audience, some of whom felt the question was frivolous. The holy man answered calmly, "I lived like my predecessors, well clothed and well fed, but I also worked hard to manage things and earn my food and shelter. Sometimes it can be exhausting to be the Dalai Lama."

Some people laughed; so did His Holiness. The intense atmosphere lightened some.

Then an older man, who looked dyspeptic and professorial, rose and said, "I've always sympathized with you Tibetans, although I'm from China originally. Can you tell us how much Tibetan culture has been lost under the Communist rule?" Many eyes stared at the man, who obviously hated the current Chinese government.

The Dalai Lama sighed. "Some Tibetans just came out and told me, a lot of people don't eat barley and buttered tea anymore. They eat steamed bread—*mantou*—and rice porridge. Even children curse each other in Mandarin now, and many young people can write only the Chinese characters, not the Tibetan script."

From this point on, the meeting turned lively, and His Holiness laughed time and again. So did the audience. His humble manner and witty words were infectious. Most of the audience could feel the generosity and kindness emanating from him. When the last question was answered, His Holiness said, "Please forgive my old, slow English because the Dalai Lama is old too."

The audience broke into laughter again. Then they all went to the front to take photos with His Holiness. Nan and Pingping stepped forward and stretched out their hands; to Nan's surprise, His Holiness, after shaking their hands, put his left palm on Nan's shoulder while signing a book a girl held open before him. A crushing force suddenly possessed Nan, as though he were going to collapse under that powerful hand. He was trembling speechlessly. When the hand released him, he still stood there, spellbound. The holy man kept nodding as numerous people surrounded him for a photo opportunity. The crowd pushed the Wus aside.

Mr. Liu came up to Nan and said he appreciated his invitation, but couldn't come to the Gold Wok because he was leaving that very evening. Then he said about the Dalai Lama, "*He's quite shrewd.*"

"But he's a great man, isn't he?" Nan said.

"*You're always naive, Nan Wu. With an M.A. in political science, how come you still don't understand politics?*"

"*That's why I quit my Ph.D. candidacy.*"

Mr. Liu slapped Nan on the shoulder and laughed, saying, "*You *should be a poet indeed.*" They shook hands again, for the last time, and said good-bye.

"*Let's go.*" Pingping tugged Nan's sleeve.

Arm in arm they headed for the garage. "*I'm disgusted with some of them,*" Nan said, referring to the audience at the meeting.

"*Yes, they're malicious.*"

"*We'd better avoid them.*" Nan jutted his thumb backward.

"*They take pleasure in torturing others.*"

"*They seem to know everything but humility and compassion.*"

Touched by his meeting with the holy man, for several days Nan felt almost ill, as if running a temperature. What moved him most was that the Dalai Lama had never shown any anger while talking with those bellicose Chinese. He was sweet and strong, probably because he was beyond destructive emotions, though Nan believed that deep inside, His Holiness also suffered like a regular man, and was perhaps even more miserable than most.

24

THE WEEK AFTER the meeting with the Dalai Lama, Nan went to Borders in Snellville to buy a book by His Holiness. There were several volumes on the shelf, and he picked the most recent one, *Ocean of Wisdom: Guidelines for Living*. It gave him pure pleasure to visit the bookstore, where he'd stay an hour or two whenever he was there. Today he went through books on some shelves, especially the poetry section, to see what books had come out recently. He found Sam Fisher had published a new volume, *All the Sandwiches and Other Poems*. He bought that book too.

On his drive back, he couldn't help touching his purchases in the passenger seat from time to time. The minute he stepped into the Gold Wok, Pingping handed him a letter and said, *"From your dad."* Eyes rolling, she stepped away.

On the envelope was a stamp of a red rooster stuck askew. Nan took out the two sheets, pressed them on the counter, and began to read. The old man had written with a brush and in India ink:

August 22, 1993

Nan:

Not having heard from you, your mother is deeply worried. Write us more often from now on. Let Taotao write a few words too.

Recently I read several articles on the Chinese dissidents in the United States. Beyond question those are devious people, whom you must shun. Nobody can be a good human being without loving his country and people, and nobody can thrive for long by selling his motherland. Some of the dissidents are just traitors and beggars, shamelessly depending on the money proffered to them by the American capitalists and the reactionary overseas Chinese. Do not get embroiled with them. Do not do anything that may sully the image of our country. Always keep in mind that you are a Chinese. Even if you were smashed to smithereens, every piece of you would remain Chinese. Do you understand?

I'm also writing on behalf of Uncle Zhao. He has finished a large series of paintings lately. He wants you to help him hold a show in America. Nan, Uncle Zhao has been my bosom friend for more than three decades. He had a tough childhood and is an autodidact. For that people think highly of him. When you were leaving for America eight years ago, he presented you with four pieces of his best work. You must not forget his generosity and kindness. Now it's time to do something in return. Please find a gallery or university willing to sponsor his visit to the United States. It goes without saying that the sponsor of the show should cover his travel expenses. Also, try to explore the possibility of having him invited as an artist in residence so that he can stay there a year. He is already sixty and this may be his only chance to have an international exhibition. He told me that his visit to America would automatically eclipse all his rivals and enemies here. So do your utmost to help him.

Blessings from far away,

Words of your father
No need for my signature

Nan sighed, then said to Pingping, "*What is this? He thinks I'm a curator of a museum or a college president? I told him on the phone that I couldn't help Uncle Zhao hold a show here. I'm nobody.*"

"*Your dad still treats you like a teenager. You're already thirty-seven.*"

"*This is sick. I won't write back.*"

"*We have to respond to his letter one way or another.*"

"*You write him.*"

"*What should I say?*"

"*Tell him I regret having accepted Uncle Zhao's paintings. Tell*

*him we're working like coolies every day and have nothing to do
with the art world. Tell him he and my mother should know we're
merely menial laborers at the bottom of America—we're useless to
them."*

"He'll be mad at you."

"Let him. The old fogey is full of crap, as if he owns me forever.
He's too idle and has too much time on his hands. He just wants to
use me. If our business goes under, we'll lose our home and everything. Can my parents help us? They'll continue to ask for money
every year. They'll never understand what life is like here. They still
believe I'm heading for a professorship, even though they know I'm
working my ass off in a restaurant. They're just selfish. Damn them,
let them disown me! I couldn't care less."

"They'll never do that," Pingping said cheerfully.

"Sure, they think we're making tons of money here, eating nutritious food, drinking quality wine, and living like gods."

The more Nan spoke, the more vehement he became, so Pingping
left him alone and went to the storage room with a bundle of towels
to wash.

Indeed, Uncle Zhao had presented Nan with four paintings, but
two of them had fallen apart on account of the shoddy mounting.
The other two had gone to Professor Peterson and Heidi Masefield
respectively many years before. Nan had wondered why Uncle Zhao
had mounted those paintings with such cheap materials that just a
little damp air could warp them. The two broken pieces, still in the
closet of Pingping's bedroom, were absolutely unpresentable, and he
didn't know what to do with them, unwilling to spends hundreds of
dollars to have them framed.

After the letter from his father, Nan never wrote to his parents
again. He felt they couldn't possibly understand or believe what he
told them. Taotao didn't write to his grandparents either, because he
had lost most of his characters, which he had been able to inscribe
when he came to America four years before. These days, despite his
protests, Pingping and Nan made him copy some ideograms every
day, but he had been forgetting more of them than he learned. Evidently he'd never be really bilingual, as most Chinese parents here

hoped their children would become. He could speak Mandarin but might never be able to read and write the characters.

Every time a letter from Nan's parents arrived, Pingping would reply. She didn't complain about this, since Nan devoted himself entirely to their business. In a way she relished handling the correspondence, because after they married, Nan's mother had often bragged to Pingping, "A monkey is smart enough to ride a sheep and supervise her." Nan was born in the year of monkey, whereas Pingping was a sheep, so according to his mother, he was supposed to keep her under control. Now, her writing letters to his parents would show that the relationship between Nan and her was reversed. That surely wouldn't please her mother-in-law, that control freak, and Pingping secretly gloated over the old woman's irritation.

Recently Nan had reorganized the service at the Gold Wok, which now offered a lunch buffet on weekdays and the regular menu at dinner. This change improved the business considerably. A lot of people working in the area would come in for lunch, which consisted of two soups, four appetizers, and ten dishes, all for $4.75. Nan and Pingping would arrive at work before eight a.m. and cook the food and get everything ready by eleven-thirty. After they closed up at night, he'd stay a little longer preparing the meats and vegetables for the following day. This made him busier, but the restaurant fetched ten percent more profit than before, and even Niyan got extra tips. The Wus were determined to pay off their mortgage in the near future.

PART FIVE

1

IN THE SPRING of 1994, the Mitchells were preparing to leave for Nanjing to bring back their daughter, Hailee. "Hailee" was a name they had given her, though they'd kept her original first name, Fan, as her middle name. Her family name was Zhang, which had actually been assigned to her by the orphanage. Dave arranged to take a ten-day leave from work; Janet's jewelry store would remain open when she was away. She told Susie, the salesgirl, to contact the Wus if anything turned up that she couldn't handle by herself.

The Mitchells had originally thought of stopping in Hong Kong for a day or two as a transition, because Dave had been to that city before and liked it very much. But they decided to go directly to mainland China together with two other couples living in Atlanta who were also adopting Chinese babies. Janet called them "our group," and indeed they often met to compare notes and share their anxiety, frustrations, and happiness. All of them would have to go to the U.S. embassy in Beijing to get visas for their babies, so the Mitchells decided to use the capital instead of Hong Kong as their base in China. Janet had bought a Mandarin phrase book, and both she and Dave had been learning to speak some words and simple sentences. She often went to ask Pingping how to say pleasantries and order things in Chinese. Despite her good memory, she had trouble with the four tones, speaking some words as if she had a blocked nose.

The Mitchells had recently decorated Hailee's nursery on the second floor of their home with a band of wallpaper, two feet wide and just high enough for a toddler to reach. The paper had frolicsome animals on it—dancing bulls, bears playing the violin, wobbling penguins, elephants rearing up, dogs blowing the saxophone. On the ceiling of the room were numerous phosphorescent stars that would shine in the darkness but were almost invisible when it was light. A new crib sat by the window that overlooked the back garden, fenced in by white palings. On the floor were stacks of baby clothing, some of which the Mitchells would take to Nanjing and donate to the orphanage. They'd also bring formula and diapers for their daughter to use. Pingping had seen the stuff they planned to take along. There were so many things that she wondered if the Mitchells could possibly carry them all. They were going to pack in two lap robes, a bunch of baseballs, a stack of hats with the Braves logo on them, granola bars, water crackers, fruit candies, laundry soap, clotheslines and clothespins, fanny packs, billfolds, batteries, painkillers, tubes of sunscreen and insect repellent, a shortwave radio, not to mention a luggage trolley and a dozen boxes of Polaroid film. They'd shoot a lot of photos as mementos of Hailee's native place. Pingping told them to take pictures of the people they wanted to thank and give them the photos on the spot, which would be a small present, appreciated by most Chinese.

The Wus talked between themselves about the Mitchells' preparations. In the past they had noticed that Dave was very frugal, almost stingy, and would always ask for a doggie bag after he dined at the Gold Wok, even if the leftovers were just a morsel. In the early days of their friendship, whenever Nan had offered him a beer or soft drink, Dave would beam but wouldn't indicate that he planned on paying for it. Nan and Pingping never minded that, amused to see Dave was easy to please. But now he and Janet must have spent thousands for the trip and would donate an extra $5,000 to the orphanage that had kept Hailee.

Four days before the Mitchells' scheduled departure, out of the blue the Chinese side informed them that they had to postpone their trip for two months. Why such a delay all of a sudden? The Mitchells called around and couldn't find a definitive answer. Their agent told them that the Chinese side wanted to ascertain that the girl was really an orphan. This threw the Mitchells into turmoil. What upset them more was that the other two adopting couples would leave for China as planned. Confused, Janet and Dave went to the Gold Wok and talked with the Wus, who couldn't figure out a reason either. Janet kept saying, "We've already bonded with Hailee. Now we feel like someone has snatched our child away from us. This is more than we can bear."

"It's awful!" Dave shook his head and blew his large nose into a tissue, his eyes moist and glistening.

Pingping said, "Officials in China don't care about your feeling, so you should make yourself happy. Maybe you can use this time to study Chinese or learn how to be parent."

"That's an interesting thought," said Janet. "Maybe I can attend a parenting class in the evenings. But we're afraid that if Hailee is not an orphan, we might lose her."

"Don't worry too much," Pingping said. "The delay is just excuse for officials. If she's not orphan, how can she stay in orphanage? Officials never care who is the girl. They just want to create trouble for you. Don't let them torture you. Remember, in China, officials' job is to make people suffer."

"Our agent didn't think this had anything to do with our baby's identity either. She said it was just bureaucracy."

"Zere will be a lawt of heartaches once you become parents," Nan put in, "so don't get distressed too easily."

"Well," Dave said, "I guess this is just the beginning."

They all smiled. Dave lifted the teapot in front of him and refilled his cup. A black woman holding a toddler stepped in and ordered two panfried noodles, so Nan went back into the kitchen after giving a lollipop to the baby girl, who clutched a nub of carrot.

A few days later, Janet enrolled in a parenting class and went to Atlanta to take the lessons two evenings a week. Whenever there was news about Hailee, she'd share it with Pingping.

2

"TURN *your heel toward me*," Pingping told Nan, holding a pair of large scissors in her hand, which was sheathed in a latex glove. She was scraping his feet for him. Both of them were sitting on low stools, a stainless-steel bowl between them. His left foot was steeped in the warm water while his right one rested on her lap covered with a khaki apron. It was early morning and their son had just left for school. A cuckoo cried from the depths of the woods across the lake and set the air throbbing. Between the pulsing calls surged a scatter of birdsong. A flock of mallards was quacking in the backyard, waddling around, and some flapped their wings so vigorously that they sent out a faint whistle. Two ducks had been hatching eggs in the monkey grass along the lakeside, so these days the Wus didn't go there for fear of disturbing them. On the dogwood tree near their deck two squirrels were chasing each other, shaking dewdrops off the branches in full flower.

"Your athlete's foot looks better than last time," Pingping said. *"Be careful. It can easily get worse in the spring."*

Nan nodded, still immersed in a volume of selected poems by Auden, whose photo appeared on both the front cover and the spine of the book. He loved Auden and had learned some of his lines by heart when he was in China. Yesterday morning he had chanced on this copy of poetry at the Goodwill store on his way to work and had bought it for a quarter. To his delight, he found the poem "September 1, 1939" within, a poem Auden himself had excluded from most of his collections. Nan was still happy about the bargain. In Gwinnett County, the public libraries would discard all the books that hadn't been checked out for more than a year and would sell them dirt cheap, so Nan, now that he had his own house, had started collecting books again. He'd rummage through the book sections in thrift stores and go to libraries' book sales whenever he could. Sometimes Pingping complained that the house would soon be cluttered up with books, but he simply couldn't stop.

Since they had married, Pingping had scraped Nan's feet five or six times a year, because he couldn't do it thoroughly by himself. In the beginning she had been frightened by his feet, the heels and the skin between the toes gnawed by fungi, and she had wanted to have them cured so that she and their baby wouldn't catch the ringworm. She'd soaked his feet in warm water, then cut the calluses with scissors, rubbed away the dead skin with a chunk of emery wheel, and applied antifungal cream to them. This gradually developed into a habit, and Nan enjoyed being treated by her. Although his athlete's foot was never cured, she had managed to keep it under control. Still, Nan wore socks all the time, even in bed. He liked taking a hot bath, which she urged him not to do, afraid the fungi might be spread to the other parts of his body. But a bath was so relaxing that he couldn't help running one every few days. To date, his body had never been affected by fungi. Ever since moving to Georgia, the Wus had noticed that many people here suffered from skin diseases, probably on account of the humid climate. Sometimes at supermarkets they came upon cashiers whose hands and forearms were scaly with scabs and running sores.

"*Ouch!*" Nan cried.

"*Did I hurt you?*" Pingping stopped the scissors.

"*Don't scrape too hard.*"

"*All right, but I won't be able to scrub your feet again this spring. We'll be weak until summer.*"

Indeed, pollen had already set in and had begun to torment them. From now on they had to conserve their energy and keep all the doors and windows shut. These days they each carried a bottle of nasal spray in a pocket to prevent their allergies from becoming fullblown. The miserable season enervated and even pacified them—they became more gentle to each other, as if too tired to raise their voices.

On top of that, Pingping was no longer worried about Nan's obsession with his first love. Seldom did she see the woeful clouds that used to darken his face. She was right: Nan had indeed mellowed a lot. He hadn't often thought of Beina in the past two years, although she'd appear in his dreams now and then. The numb pain still lingered in his chest, but it was no longer as acute as before. Every day he was too occupied to indulge in fantasies. When he got home at night, he'd go to sleep within an hour after taking a shower and reading a few poems. He felt that physically he was strong now, but his mind was empty. He simply didn't have the energy to think of ideas, much less write anything.

To some extent he was pleased by this state of affairs. In his mind would rise the lines by the ancient poet Tao Chien: "Human life runs the same course, / Whose end is to secure shelter and food." Nan was peaceful, determined to stand on his own ground and willing to be a devoted family man.

3

SHUBO GAO had received his Ph.D. from the University of Georgia the previous fall. He was still looking for a teaching position in sociology, but so far without success. He often talked with Nan about job hunting and would joke that he was ready to "turn a new leaf," meaning to abandon his sociology specialty. The past winter he had gone to six interviews at a convention held in San Francisco, but the interviewers had all found that he spoke English with a grating accent, so despite his impressive résumé that boasted a book published in Chinese, none of the schools invited him over for a campus visit. Afterward, Shubo mailed out more than a hundred applications. He would receive a batch of refusal letters every week, which didn't bother him much, though Niyan couldn't stand it anymore. During the day she would not check the mail for fear of spoiling her appetite.

Despite his bad English, Shubo was fond of clichés. He'd use all kinds of sayings, some of which were Chinese expressions he translated into English, such as "one hill cannot be inhabited by two tigers," "search for a needle in the ocean," "pour oil on fire," "kill two eagles with one arrow." He had a little notebook in which he'd collected more than a thousand English idiomatic expressions. Nan would tease him, calling him a social linguist. He also told Shubo, "*If you really want to master English idioms, get a good dictionary, a* Longman *or* Collins, *and learn the real thing.*" He explained that unlike the Chinese, who respected a person knowing a great many sayings and proverbs, a good English speaker wouldn't repeat clichés, but Shubo continued filling his notebook with hackneyed expressions and tossing them out right and left.

Though a Ph.D., Shubo respected Nan and often bantered with him, saying that Nan was a sad case and shouldn't waste his talent by running a small restaurant. He once read Nan's palms and said with a straight face, "*You were born to be an official, deciding the fates of thousands. You know, you should've risen to prominence long ago. But now you're a phoenix grounded and stripped of its wings, inferior to a chicken.*"

Nan rejoined, "*Why don't you go back to Szechuan? With your Ph.D. from UGA, I'm sure you can get a professorship at a Party school or a police academy.*"

"*I'd prefer to be my own boss.*" Shubo's face fell.

In fact, Shubo often said he'd never return to China, because when he was applying for his passport so that he could go to the University of Georgia to do graduate work, all the officials had treated him like a semicriminal and wouldn't issue the papers to him until a whole year had passed, after the school had withdrawn its financial aid. He told Nan that not a single Chinese had ever said a good word to him when he went to their offices, and that only a young American woman of Indian descent at the U.S. embassy in Beijing, noted for her record of turning down most visa applications, had beamed at him, saying, "Congratulations!" when she handed him his visa.

Although Shubo could joke about his situation, his wife had lost her peace of mind. Now that it was unlikely that he would find a teaching position, what should he do? Niyan often spoke to Pingping and Nan about him. Recently his cousin, Yafang Gao, had promised that if he went to New York, she could help him find a job at Ding's Dumplings; but he'd have to work there at least a whole year because her former boss, Howard, wouldn't hire a temporary hand. Niyan told the Wus that Yafang herself had left Ding's Dumplings a few months earlier to attend business school at NYU.

Shubo talked with Nan about the restaurant work in New York; he wasn't sure if he should go, reluctant to be away from his wife. Nan was uncertain whether Shubo still meant to remain in academia, but his friend assured him that he wouldn't think twice about leaving his field if he could find a full-time job. Shubo hated teaching and had once taught an introduction to sociology course to more than thirty students, some of whom wouldn't turn in their homework on time and would frown at his accent, a few even pretending they couldn't understand him. During the first few weeks of teaching, he felt sick and often knelt on the floor of the bathroom at home and vomited into the toilet, his guts twinging while his wife slapped his back to ease his pain. Later, he attempted to make a joke or tell an amusing story from time to time in class. Once he even compared Americans to turkeys (fat) and the Chinese to cranes (thin), but only one big black woman laughed besides himself. The whole course was sheer torture to him, yet he had to get the teaching experience so that he could find employment in the future. In the course evaluations one student wrote "Bathetic & pathetic!" Now, still haunted by that class, Shubo wouldn't hesitate to leave academia. On hearing that he really wouldn't mind abandoning his field, Nan suggested he go to a bartending school. Once Shubo knew how to mix drinks, he could always find work at a Chinese restaurant. Niyan and Shubo thought this was a good idea, so Shubo paid $3,000 and enrolled in a bartending class in downtown Atlanta.

Different from the Wus, Niyan and Shubo were still like newlyweds, seeking each other's company whenever they could. They loved Georgia for its low cost of living and warm climate, which resembled that of their home province, and they didn't think about moving elsewhere. Yet they had been so busy struggling to survive ever since they landed here that they wouldn't dare to have children. Some of their friends had given birth to babies and then sent them back to China, to farm them out to the grandparents. But both Niyan's and Shubo's parents were in poor health and couldn't look after a child, and neither could they come here to help them if Niyan had a baby. As a result, she was still wearing an intrauterine ring. "Look, I'm already thirty," she said to Pingping one afternoon. "How many years do you think I can wait?"

"I know how you feel. Back in China I was never worried about bringing a child into the world."

"Maybe Shubo and I will end up adopting a baby like the Mitchells," quipped Niyan with a grimace.

"You're too young to think like that."

Since it was impossible to have their own child now, Shubo and Niyan had grown very fond of Taotao. They'd tell Pingping and Nan that they envied them their fine son. Whenever Taotao's report card arrived, they'd look at it and sing his praises. Many times Shubo said Nan was a lucky man who had everything—a devoted wife, a smart son, a lakeside house, and a business of his own. His words would put Nan in a reflective mood and make him wonder why he himself didn't feel as content as he should.

4

IN LATE SPRING Taotao, with the help of his friend Zach, who was an eighth grader, assembled a large computer. The machine was so powerful, he told his parents, it worked like a small station. With the new computer, he spent a lot of time surfing the Internet and chatting with his friends—they mainly let off steam by bad-mouthing their teachers. He also played games with some children in Europe and Asia. Because his parents were always busy working at the restaurant, they couldn't supervise him. Once he was online, he'd enter cyberspace unknown to his parents, who would accept whatever he told them about it.

Both Pingping and Nan tried to curb him from surfing the Internet, warning him over and over again not to waste too much time. The boy promised not to use the computer very often when his parents weren't home. At work, every evening Pingping would call back at least twice to check on him, but most times the line was busy. Evidently Taotao was using the Internet. Whenever this happened, Nan and Pingping would get angry and take their son to task when they came back at night.

Taotao had never been really close to Nan, perhaps because Nan hadn't spent enough time with him and had left for America when the boy was merely two. In recent years Nan had worked constantly and tended to confine himself to his business and books. As a result, father and son didn't talk much. If Nan spoke to him harshly, Taotao would ignore him or mutter "Shut up," at which Nan would lose his temper, calling his son a heartless ingrate. Yet the boy always listened to his mother, who knew how to make him behave. Sometimes she called him "Little Donkey," meaning that as long as she coaxed him, he'd be obedient.

One evening in late May, Nan phoned home. At the busy signal he got enraged, telling his wife he was going back to catch Taotao red-handed. She was angry too and couldn't stop fulminating against their son under her breath. Nan set out for home along the dimly lighted street. The air was very humid, and his hurried pace made him pant a little while the cries of insects cascaded from the trees. He wondered whether they were chirring to attract mates or were maddened by the heat. As he passed Mrs. Lodge's, the old woman, lounging in a cane rocker on her porch, waved at him. "Closed early today?" she asked cheerfully, flapping the palm fan Pingping had bought for her from a Korean grocery store.

"No," Nan shouted. "I'm going back to get somesing."

"Tell Pingping I have some geraniums for her."

"Sure, sanks."

He continued homeward, wondering how come mosquitoes didn't bother Mrs. Lodge at all. The old woman was so hale and hearty that, already past ninety, she still took care of her yard and garden. Over the crown of a giant oak in Alan's backyard, the North Star, slightly obscured by the smog, glowed with orange light, while traffic whirred from a distant main road. Fireflies pulsed here and there, drawing short arcs. As Nan entered his own front yard, a young maple suddenly rustled as if startled by his approaching. Then the air conditioner kicked on, humming at the side of the house. Taotao's room was dark, but Nan saw the light of his computer through the half-closed slats of the venetian blind. He unlocked the door stealthily and tiptoed in.

At the creaking of the floorboards in the corridor, Taotao lurched up from his swivel chair. He gulped as if to say something, but no word escaped from him. Nan flicked on the light, which made his son's eyes smart. The boy's mouth dropped open. A spasm of rage seized Nan, who rushed up to Taotao, grabbed his shoulders, and threw him down on the bed. *"Why are you playing with the computer again?"* he demanded. *"Damn you! You promised Mom and me to do your homework and read when we were not home. Why did you break your word?"*

"*I just turned it on. I did my homework already.*"

"*Liar! The phone line has been busy for two hours. I'm going to smash this damned machine now.*" Nan picked up a large magnet from a corner shelf, about to throw it at the monitor.

"*Please, Daddy, don't! I won't do it again!*" Taotao was holding Nan's arm with both hands and begging him tearfully, but his father wouldn't let go of the magnet. Nan raised it above his head, struggling to pitch. As father and son were tussling, Nan caught sight of some words on the monitor's screen. He dropped the magnet on the chair and leaned forward to read the message, which said:

Hi, Taotao,

I miss you. You're my best boyfriend. I often tell my friends here what a great guy you are. They don't believe we are sweethearts and say I just brag. Write me some sweet, sweet words, so I can show them.

A thousand kisses,

Livia

Again anger overtook Nan, who grabbed his son's chest and began slapping him across the face. "*You little beast! No wonder you always turn on the computer. You've been carrying on with Livia.*"

As Nan went on striking him, Taotao stopped resisting. He wailed, "*I didn't write the message. Ow, don't hit me! You're hurting me, Dad!*"

But his father's merciless slaps kept landing on his face and head. In a flash his cheeks turned puffy, streaked with handprints. When Nan's temper had subsided some, he saw his son's face, which horrified him. He released Taotao, who was still gasping for air. For a moment Nan stood there motionless as if dazed. Suddenly he remembered his promise to Pingping long ago that he'd never resort to violence in his life. How shocked he was by his own use of brute force on the boy, who couldn't defend himself. He averted his head, too ashamed to face his son.

Then he rushed off into the kitchen, picked up the cordless phone, and came back. "*All right, stop crying,*" he said, panting, and gave Taotao the phone. "*Call the police and tell them I beat you up.*"

"No, I won't call." The boy put both hands behind him, his mouth twisting.

"Call them!" Nan thrust the phone to him. *"Let them come arrest me. Tell them I'm a violent man and should be sentenced to life."*

"No, I won't."

"Damn it, call them! Help me—I have had enough of this miserable life. Let them come and take me away. That will spare me all the worries and hopelessness. Let the police slam me into jail so that you can play with your computer day and night and have as many girlfriends as you want. Here, dial the number." He pointed at one of the emergency numbers on the sticker stuck to the handset.

"I won't call."

"Why? I just beat you up. Why not have me arrested? I'm an abusive parent and should be sentenced to prison. Now call!"

"No, I won't."

Nan began punching the police's number madly. Taotao lunged forward and snatched the phone from his father's hands. Nan wrapped one arm around the boy as his other hand tried to loosen Taotao's grip on the phone. Father and son scuffled, and then both fell on the bed, but the boy still held the phone with both hands. Hard as Nan tried, he couldn't pry it free.

"Let go!" Nan huffed.

"No!"

Gradually Nan eased off some, then stopped to sit up. He peered at his son, who got up and moved away. The boy, still snuffling and panting, thrust both hands behind him so that his father couldn't see the phone. He stood in the corner with his back firmly against the walls. Seeing Taotao's tears and terror-stricken face, Nan froze, at a loss. In a flash he realized that his son desperately wanted to keep him home. Look at his face, so scared. Wouldn't surrender the phone even if you smashed his hands. Awash in contrition, Nan stood up and went out of the house without another word. He headed back to the Gold Wok, continually wiping his eyes with the back of his hand, weeping all the way.

5

WHEN Nan told Pingping of what he had discovered at home and what he'd done, her first response was a punch on his shoulder. Then she warned him, *"Don't ever whale Taotao again, or I'll give you endless trouble."*

Nan promised he would never hit the boy again.

Though Pingping smacked their son once or twice a year, she wouldn't allow anyone else to touch him. Yet in her heart of hearts she believed Taotao deserved his beating, so she couldn't help but grumble about him and even said she too would whack him. Niyan overheard her and protested, *"Please go easy on him. He should have some fun."*

"Fun?" Pingping retorted. *"He was flirting with a girl while we work ourselves half to death here."*

"He's almost eleven and should be interested in girls."

"I don't want him to have a girlfriend until he graduates from college. It's a waste of time."

"Heavens, you're such a fuddy-duddy. We're not living in China anymore. Here kids reach puberty earlier. By any standard Taotao is a fine boy. You should feel lucky to have a son like him. I have a friend whose teenage boy often visited porn sites on the Internet. He even called some women. At the end of a month his father received a phone bill for more than nine hundred dollars."

"My goodness, when did this happen?"

"Two years ago when that boy had just turned thirteen."

"What did his parents do about him?"

"His father strapped him, but the boy kept visiting porn sites,

*addicted to cybersex. He even threatened to sue his parents for child
abuse."*

"There's no way to straighten him out?"

*"His parents sent him back to Beijing the summer before last, but
last year they took him back because he couldn't survive middle
school there. He didn't know enough Chinese to understand his lessons. If you had a son like that, how would you feel?"*

Pingping said no more, though deep down she was still fuming at
Taotao for carrying on with Livia. The greatest regret in her life was
that before she met Nan she'd had a boyfriend who had wasted five
years of her life. She had gone to the young man's home on weekends, hand-laundering and cooking for his family. Because of serving them, she couldn't concentrate on her schoolwork, though she
always got good grades. Without the boyfriend she could have gone
to graduate school and achieved much more in her life. Those years
spent with the man who later jilted her were the most miserable and
empty period of her life. At any cost she wouldn't let her son repeat
the same mistake.

After returning home from work that night, she said to Taotao,
"You must stop writing to Livia."

Nan added, *"She must have a dozen boyfriends, and you're just
one of them, like a toy."*

"How do you know?" asked Taotao.

His mother put in, *"I took care of her for several years, and I know
what she's like. She's not a serious girl. She's boy crazy and just
playing games with you."*

"She's my friend."

"You must never take a girlfriend like her."

"Why?"

*"Why? Our family is not their kind and we're poor. We don't have
eight fireplaces in our house, do we?"*

"No. But that doesn't mean she's bad."

*"Stop arguing. I served the Masefields long enough. Do you want
me to be a servant of my daughter-in-law?"*

"What are you talking about, Mom?"

Nan also felt that Pingping had stretched this too far, but he didn't say another word. He didn't want Taotao and Livia to be close friends either. He'd feel uncomfortable to see the Masefields again and was afraid they might not treat Taotao well.

"Do you want to be a servant boy all your life?" Pingping asked their son.

"No."

"Then drop Livia. You're a poor boy, and a rich girl like her will treat you like a piece of trash. Do you remember Phil?" Phil was Heidi's brother-in-law, a Spaniard without a penny of his own, and the Masefields would frown at him even in the presence of Heidi's sister, Rosalind, the one Phil had married.

"Yes, he's a good guy," Taotao said.

"Do the Masefields respect him?" asked his mother.

"Not really."

"Do you want to be like him?"

"Damn it, Mom! I'm not going to marry Livia, okay? You're crazy and imagined the whole thing."

"Then why do you carry on with her?"

"We just have a good time."

"Stop this American 'fun' crap! I don't want you to learn how to toy with girls. You must be a serious and responsible man."

Taotao turned pensive, but looked unconvinced. His mother went on, *"It just wastes your life to have a girlfriend so early. I want you to concentrate on your schoolwork. As for a girlfriend, you can wait until you graduate from college."*

The boy made no reply and turned to his father, gazing at him beseechingly. Nan sympathized with his son, yet he felt the boy shouldn't be so close to that girl or he might get hurt. On the other hand, it would be better for Taotao to know some girls before he grew up and entered into any serious relationship. If Nan could have restarted his life, he'd have dated many girls casually before losing his heart to a woman. *"All right,"* he said to both his wife and son, *"time for bed."*

"I want him to promise us to break with Livia," insisted Pingping.

"I'll take her just as a regular friend, okay?"

Pingping said no more, knowing Taotao was too stubborn to make a full promise right now. She went into her room and picked up a towel for a shower, still grumbling about what a weakling her son had become.

·

The next day Mrs. Spiller, the geography teacher, asked Taotao in class, "What happened to your face? Somebody hit you?"

"No, I bumped into a wall when I was going to the bathroom last night." Though a little flustered, the boy forced a smile.

"You look awful."

"It hurt like hell, but I'm all right now."

"Uh-uh, language."

"Sorry." He lowered his head and resumed working on his map. The teacher had assigned the class to create a country of one's own, and each student was to draw a map of an imagined territory containing different time zones, several cities, forests, plains, highways, harbors, sea routes. Taotao loved the project.

6

THE MITCHELLS left for Nanjing in early June. The two-month delay had been prolonged for another month, and as a result, they'd had to rebuy some clothes for Hailee, who wore larger sizes now. Even so, the Mitchells were elated by the final approval of the Chinese side. At long last they could bring their daughter home, they kept telling others. When Janet and Dave were away in China, Pingping would stop by at the jewelry store from time to time, chatting with the tall Susie, who kept everything in good order, as if she owned the business. Since the previous spring Susie had been working full-time for Janet. She told Pingping that her boss was a cheapskate and wouldn't give her a paid vacation. Pingping defended her friend, saying, "Look, you have health insurance, right?"

"Yes, but it's not that good. Every time I go see the doctor, I have to spend twenty bucks for the co-pay." Susie made a pout, then licked her upper lip.

"We have a child, but we don't have any real insurance. You're lucky. It cost Janet a lotta money to cover you."

Susie looked annoyed and kept flexing her henna-nailed fingers. She was wearing so much rouge that she looked sunburned. "I know you two are close," she muttered. "Don't tell Janet I bad-mouthed her."

"Of course I don't do that."

Susie often went to the Gold Wok for lunch, mainly because it was convenient. She didn't have a car, and her boyfriend, a young carpenter who had a centipede tattooed on each bicep, would drive her to work and pick her up when she closed up in the evenings.

Today there were few customers at the restaurant after two o'clock, so everybody could take a breather. Pingping and Niyan settled at a table drinking tea and paring apples to eat. Nan was reading *Time* magazine, to which he had subscribed for business use. Usually they didn't have lunch; whoever was hungry could take a bite from the kitchen. But they'd eat a meal together late in the evening before they called it a day. Nan often cooked light, homely food for their dinner, such as fish-head soup, sautéed watercress, and tofu with peas and pickled mustard greens.

As Nan lifted his coffee mug absentmindedly to his lips, the phone rang. Pingping picked it up. "Where are you calling from, Janet?" she asked excitedly.

"Where can it be? I'm in Nanjing!" Janet said.

"Do you have Hailee already?"

"Not yet. We have to wait another day."

"It's very hot there, right?"

"Yes, it makes me miss Atlanta. I've never been in such weather. It's scorching outside during the day, but that doesn't seem to bother the locals."

"That's why Nanjing is called 'Furnace.'"

"We went to see the other baby yesterday."

"What baby?"

"The one whose photo came together with Hailee's, remember?"

"Yes, how she's like?"

"She's a lovely girl too, a bit taller than Hailee. My heart went out to her. The good news is that a single woman in Philadelphia is going to adopt her. That makes Dave and me feel better."

"So no more guilty, okay? Did you go to other place? I mean, look around and buy things?"

"We went to the Yangtze River and a park. Nanjing is a fascinating city. There's a lot of good food here."

"Did you walk on Yangtze Bridge?"

"Yes, it was kind of scary."

"How come?"

"It trembled whenever a train passed beneath us. Dave and I were afraid it might collapse. You know he can't swim."

Pingping laughed. "You're so funny, Janet. Everything is all right so far?"

"Yes. I'm calling to see how things are at home."

"Everything is fine. Your house and yard is safe and clean. I went there yesterday morning. Your grass is cut, and everything look nice. Don't worry. Susie keep your store good too. She's very careful about everything."

"Thanks a lot, Pingping. After we get our daughter, we'll have to go to Beijing to get her papers. Then we'll go see the Great Wall before we fly back."

"Why you do that? Isn't hard to go there with baby?"

"We figure we won't be able to travel for a long time once we have Hailee. Also, we want to take some photos, to show them to her in the future."

"I see. Travel safely then. Don't worry about anything here."

Having hung up, Pingping said to Nan, *"They're going to see the Great Wall with the baby. Isn't that crazy?"*

"Hailee is really a lucky girl," Nan said poker-faced. *"If some American family had adopted me when I was an infant, I could have become a movie star, or at least a CEO."*

That cracked everybody up.

Late that afternoon Nan read an article in a week-old *Overseas Daily,* reporting that Mr. Manping Liu had gone back to Beijing to get cancer treatment. The old exile had suddenly collapsed one day as he was patching the muffler of his jalopy with duct tape, and had been rushed to a local clinic for poor people. The diagnosis was liver cancer, and the doctor said his days would be numbered if the treatment wasn't effective. It was rumored that the old dissident had written to a member of the Political Bureau, begging for permission to go back to China. "Please let me die in our motherland," he wrote. Out of pity or political expediency, they let him return and even assigned him a hospital bed in Beijing, provided he'd remain silent about sensitive issues and would inform the police beforehand if he was to meet with any foreigner. He could resume receiving the same salary as before he had fled China. Mr. Liu accepted the provisos and went back quietly, together with his wife.

His case evoked mixed feelings in Nan, and for days he'd been thinking about the implications of Mr. Liu's return. Why did the old man stoop to the authorities so easily? True, he was nostalgic and might get better medical treatment and live longer in Beijing. But wouldn't his return compromise his principles and impair his integrity? Nan couldn't answer definitively. His mind couldn't help but turn to Mr. Liu even when he was busy cooking.

Gradually he figured out the essential difference between himself and the old scholar. Mr. Liu was an exile, whose life had been shaped by the past and who could exist only with reference to the central power that had banished him from China. Here lay Mr. Liu's tragedy—he couldn't possibly separate himself from the state's apparatus that could always control and torment him. Without the frame of reference already formed in his homeland, his life would have lost its meaning and bearings. That must be why so many exiles, wrecked with nostalgia, would eulogize suffering and patriotism. Physically they were here, but because of the yoke of their significant past, they couldn't adapt to the life in the new land. In contrast, Nan was an immigrant without a noteworthy and burdensome past. To the authorities, he was nobody, nonexistent. He didn't even have a Chinese official to beg. Who would listen to a man like him, a mere immigrant or refugee? People of his kind, "the weed people," survived or perished like insects and grass and wouldn't matter at all to those living in their native land. To the people in China, they were already counted as a loss. Small wonder that a senior official had recently declared to a group of overseas Chinese, "You must be qualified to become a real patriot," implying that China needed only those who could make substantial contributions to its economic and technological development. The more Nan thought about these issues, the more upset he became. On the other hand, he was willing to accept the immigrant life as the condition of his existence so as to become a self-sufficient man. He felt grateful to the American land that had taken in his family and given them an opportunity for a new beginning.

7

A THUNDERSTORM warning was broadcast the following day, and many people went to supermarkets to buy nonperishable foods, bottled water, and other supplies. No customers showed up at the Gold Wok after four o'clock, so the Wus closed early and went home to prepare for the severe storm due to hit the area in the evening. They were worried about the massive oak near the east end of their house. If it fell, it might crush the roofs of their carport and living room. The tree belonged to both the Wus and Gerald, the property line going right through its trunk. Several times Nan and Pingping had talked to Gerald about bringing the oak down, since it could fall on his roof as well, but he wouldn't share the cost of six hundred dollars, saying he had no money. However, Alan had told Nan that oaks had deep roots and wouldn't fall easily. It was pines that were more likely to cause damage; that was why Alan had taken down nineteen of his pine trees two years ago and had kept the oaks in his yard. Now all the Wus could do was cross their fingers and watch the television showing destroyed houses and overturned vehicles in the wake of the storm. A newsman said, "Besides the thunderstorm, it's reported that some places in the northern suburbs got hammered by a tornado. We'll bring you more on that once we have the details."

The Wus moved a couch into the dining room, where they could stay to avoid being crushed by the oak if it fell. Around nine o'clock, after a series of thunderclaps, the night suddenly turned whitish— all the trees and lights beyond the lake vanished at once. Then came the ghostly rustle that sounded like a harvester cutting crops, though at a much faster speed. Taotao wanted to look out the window, whose panes kept up a steady rattling, but Nan stopped him for fear that the storm might crash into the room. In no time the power went out. The Wus realized this was a tornado, and wordlessly they cowered on the couch, set in a corner. Try as he might, Nan couldn't hear the earth-shaking booms made by trees hitting the ground, and somehow all the noises were muffled, though their roof creaked and echoed with objects pelting it. He wondered if it was hailing as well.

Three minutes later the tornado passed, but the night was darker than before as all the lights were gone. The Wus looked out the broad window of the dining room and saw some boughs and branches on the grass. To their relief, all the trees were still standing in the backyard. In the north a fire engine or ambulance was howling. Because electricity might not come back on soon, they went to bed early.

After Taotao left for school the next morning, Nan took a walk in the neighborhood to see the havoc. Several houses had been damaged by fallen pines, and on the streets electric wires were mangled here and there. Fortunately the tornado hadn't touched Beaver Hill Plaza, and there was still electricity at the Gold Wok. Nan was pleased to find his freezer and refrigerators all droning as before. He realized there might be a lot of business today since many households in the area had no power. Hurriedly he went back and told Pingping to stop cleaning the front yard. Together they set out for work.

Indeed, for a whole day people came in nonstop. The Wus and Niyan had a hectic time, though all were happy about the business. Owing to the power outage, Taotao stayed at the restaurant after school, doing his homework. Toward dark, electricity finally came back to the neighborhood, where the smell of barbecued meat and fried chicken from cookouts still hovered.

Shortly after the Wus returned home that night, Gerald knocked on their door. Nan answered it. Gerald had been ill lately and out of work. He looked gaunt and aged, in jean overalls smudged with grease; the stubble on his chin was grizzled, and his eyes shone with a stiff light like a crazed man's. He had lost his dog, Goby, a week earlier. It was Taotao who had found the dog dead the other morning— a pair of crows were standing on Goby's belly, shrieking like mad, so the boy called to his parents, who went out but couldn't rouse the animal. Goby had died of heartworm. According to Gerald, the collie had carried the disease since it was a puppy. In a way, the Wus were pleased by Goby's disappearance, because now no dog would bark in the dead of night and wake them up.

"Kin—kin I borra some juice from ya?" Gerald asked Nan, apparently embarrassed.

"Orange juice?"

"No. I mean 'lectricity."

"Oh, what happened to your house? Your power isn't back yet?"

"No. I called 'em. They said they gonna come work on it tomorra."

"How can you borrow electricity?" Nan was puzzled, though he knew Georgia Power must have cut off Gerald's supply because of unpaid bills.

"I kin connec' a cord to your carpo't."

"I see." Indeed, there was a wall outlet near the side door of the house. "Two days. You don't have to borrow it from us. I can let you use zer line for two days."

"Two days're plenty. I'll git my powa back by then."

Gerald looked hungry and probably had not cooked that day. As a matter of fact the Wus hadn't seen him for a long time. He wouldn't come out of his house nowadays, as if in hibernation, though their neighbor Alan would bang on Gerald's door to remind him that his lawn needed mowing or that he should trim his trees. Gerald would rejoin, "I'll take care of that when I feel like. I won't be push' around by nobody." But he never did anything to put his property in order, except that once in a while he cut his grass with a tractor mower. When he drove that thing in his front yard, he'd kick up a thundering din and clouds of dust. To show his gratitude to the Wus, he once mowed their lawn with his machine as well, but its blades had been set so low that after the mowing, the grass turned yellow and shriveled for many days. So Pingping begged him to leave their lawn alone.

By nature Gerald was a kind fellow and a sort of craftsman, always ready to give a hand to someone. He'd get on Mrs. Lodge's roof and blow down leaves for her. He had laid drainage pipes for the Utleys, a retired couple living a few houses down the street, so that rainwater could flow directly into the lake instead of sluicing and furrowing the roadside and their yard. Also, he had helped two families set their hardwood floors. People in the neighborhood went to those houses to look at the superb work, and everyone agreed that Gerald had done "a beautiful job." Yet he simply wouldn't bother about his own property, perhaps because no one would pay him for working on it.

"*The other day I saw his ex-wife and daughter in his front yard,*" Pingping told Nan after Gerald left.

"*What's she like?*"

"*She looks very young, with permed hair. She waits tables at the Waffle House near Berkmar High School.*"

"*But I remember Gerald once said his ex was older than he was.*"

"*I guess she is, but she really looks young and pretty. She said she couldn't stand Gerald because he always collected too much junk. She called him a 'pack rat.'*"

"*That can't be the reason for the divorce.*"

"*She also said he used to drink a lot.*"

"*But he isn't an alcoholic anymore.*"

"*She seemed happy without him. Maybe she has another man now, I don't know. His daughter looked happy too.*"

Nan turned the tap and let warm water fall into a plastic bucket, in which he was going to bathe his feet. Tonight he was too tired to take a shower, which he'd do tomorrow morning. He thought about Gerald's situation and realized that if his life were like that fellow's, he might have killed himself by now. In a way, Gerald was tough. Nan felt fortunate that he could hold his family together.

8

THE MITCHELLS came back with their daughter, and the Wus went to see them the next morning. Dave and Janet lived in a mansion secluded away in a cul-de-sac. A private driveway crossed a wooden bridge and led to their front yard, where a thin pine tree was lying beside a marble birdbath, felled by the storm a few days before. A beige portico supported a balustered balcony at the main entrance to their Victorian house, which boasted a sloping turret and arched windows. Their home was one of the most expensive in Breezewood Park, a subdivision off Five Forks Road.

With delight the Mitchells received Pingping and Nan. Despite exhaustion, Janet and Dave were in high spirits and both seemed to have shrunk a little, probably withered by the heat in Nanjing. The floor of the nursery was strewn with stuffed animals, among which was a puppy, lying on its stomach, its long ears touching the rug. There was also a miniature toy elephant sitting on its ass with its trunk raised above its head, and beside it was a bassinet, maybe already too small for the baby. Hailee was lying in the crib, half wrapped in a red blanket. Now and again she prattled and put out a hand, which reminded Pingping of a tiny fresh bun. The baby was happy and comfortable, as if eager to talk to the grown-ups bending over her. In every way she was an ordinary Chinese infant, with slightly chafed cheeks and almond-shaped eyes, at the corners of which gathered a bit of crust. Despite her strong bone structure and energetic voice, Hailee didn't look healthy. Janet said that the child had suffered from pneumonia in the past spring, which was the actual reason their trip had been postponed, and that she was going to take her to the doctor early the next week.

Dave's face was flushed with happiness, his large forehead shinier than before. When he held the baby, Pingping thought his big hands might squash her, but he was careful and let Janet hold Hailee most of the time. He often followed his wife around when the baby was in her arms. The two couples returned to coffee in the living room. The Mitchells said their trip to China had been an eye-opener. The country wasn't as backward as they'd thought and most people seemed to live comfortably there, and everywhere there was construction under way. Among the American visitors there was a joke that said China's national bird was the building crane. Obviously the country was developing rapidly. Janet asked Pingping and Nan why the Chinese in Nanjing looked different from those in American Chinatowns. In Nanjing and Shanghai they had seen a lot of handsome men and women. Girls were slim and had smooth skin, often dressed to the nines, and many young men were well built, some athletic. The Mitchells couldn't figure out why the Chinese here seemed like a different race. Pingping told them that if they'd gone to the countryside, they'd have met many people who bore more resemblance to the residents in Chinatowns. The truth was that nowadays young people in the big cities had better nutrition, so they grew taller than their parents.

"Don't Chinese kids eat nutritious food here?" asked Dave. "Still they look so different from the people in China."

"Maybe zeir genes have been Americanized," said Nan with a straight face.

"Then they should be bigger and taller," Dave went on.

They all laughed. Pingping explained that most people in Chinatown originally came from the southern coastal provinces, where people ate rice and didn't grow as tall as a result of the hot climate and the diet. Generally speaking, northerners are taller than southerners, but weren't Shanghai and Nanjing in the south, where people should be shorter? Hard as they tried, neither Nan nor Pingping could come up with a convincing explanation, though they believed the Mitchells' observation must be right. They too had noticed some physical differences between the Chinatown Chinese and those in mainland China.

The Mitchells showed them a lot of photos they'd taken on the trip, of temples, parks, English corners, the staff at the orphanage, banquets, and also of the girl baby they'd had to give up. Janet brought out another album, with plastic sleeves containing memorabilia for Hailee, among which, in addition to small artwork like colorful feather bookmarks and cut-paper creatures wrapped in onionskin, there were even the stubs of their plane tickets, taxi receipts, and a small map of Nanjing City. Pingping was so touched that she couldn't stop thinking what a lucky girl Hailee was, and her eyes filmed over with tears for a good minute.

Then she unwrapped the onionskin and scrutinized the set of paper cuttings, composed of six creatures—a hog, a buffalo, a chow chow, a deer, a magpie, and a rooster. Janet told the Wus, "We bought these from a peddler. Aren't they exquisite?"

"Not very good," said Pingping. "Look at this pig. His nose is too long, like elephant nose slashed half."

"Pingping can do better," Nan put in. "Her mozzer won prizes for paper cuttings."

"This is *art*." Janet sounded incredulous.

"Sure, that's why I married zer girl with zer deftest hands." Nan laughed, scratching his crown.

"Don't believe him," said Pingping.

Janet looked her in the eye. "Can you really make artwork like these?"

"Yes, I can cut these things."

"Then you should make some for me."

"It take a lotta time." Pingping smiled blithely.

As the conversation went on, the Mitchells brought up the topic of Hailee's biological parents, but husband and wife couldn't see eye to eye on this subject. Janet had asked the leaders of the orphanage to send her information on Hailee's biological parents, ideally some pictures as well; although they didn't promise to provide anything more, the head of the orphanage, a good-looking young man with a chipped tooth, had assured her that he'd try to gather the information for her.

"I don't think you will hear from zem," Nan said to Janet, and put down his coffee cup on the glass end table.

"What use to know her ex-parents?" asked Pingping. "You and Dave are her parents."

"That's right," Dave chimed in.

But Janet couldn't be persuaded. "I want to see what her biological parents look like and also to know the medical history of the family."

"They don't have medical history," said Pingping.

"What do you mean?" Janet looked puzzled, her eyes blinking.

"People in Chinese countryside don't write down their disease," Pingping explained.

"They don't have a medical record," added Nan.

"But certainly they know who died of what disease in the family," said Janet.

Nan answered, "You shouldn't bozzer to look for her biological parents. Even if you find zem, they might give you a lawt of trouble down zer road."

"That's what I think too," said Dave. "Hailee is our daughter, period. No matter what happens, she's ours and we'll take care of her. I don't have to know the medical history of her biological family."

"I don't mean we might give her up if anything bad happens," Janet said. "You'll have to kill me before you can take her away from me."

They kept talking about parenthood. To the Wus' surprise, the Mitchells asked them to be their daughter's godparents. Pingping said, "I don't go to church, how can I be godmother? I can be her stepmother."

The Mitchells were astonished, while Nan laughed. He told them, "Pingping means she can be a nominal mozzer. That's zer Chinese way and has nothing to do wiz religion. A child can have nominal parents in China."

Janet said, "I heard of nominal parents in Nanjing."

So Pingping agreed to be Hailee's nominal mother, but Nan was reluctant, saying he couldn't be a good father. Both Janet and Dave looked dismayed. Indeed, they had promised to be Taotao's legal guardians if his parents died. Why wouldn't Nan reciprocate the favor? Pingping explained, "Nan can never be good father. You see, Taotao and he is not close."

"That's because I didn't spend a lawt of time wiz him when he was little," said Nan.

Ignoring his words, Pingping went on, "After Taotao was born, he doesn't sleep with us for three month. He sleep in his father's office every night."

Nan kept silent, awash in shame. Pingping had often dredged that up and he'd defend himself by insisting that he'd have to attend seminars in the mornings and must sleep well at night. Now, in front of their friends, he felt it futile to argue with her. He told the Mitchells about the nominal fatherhood, "Let me think about zat, okay?"

"Sure, no rush," said Janet. "We thought it would be wonderful if Hailee has Chinese godparents or nominal parents."

"I'm not sure eef I can bring her up like my own child," admitted Nan, as if mumbling to himself.

"You wouldn't have to do anything for Hailee if Dave and I were both gone."

"All right, I will let you know my answer soon."

After the Wus left, Janet carried Hailee upstairs to the nursery, Dave following her. Dave liked Nan but sometimes found it hard to communicate with him. Undoubtedly Nan was a decent man, but he was too introverted and often as aloof as if he were in a kind of trance. It was impossible to talk with him about fishing, sports, dogs, cars—not to speak of women and girls. He'd call an SUV "a big jeep" and wouldn't listen carefully when Dave explained to him the rules of football, though he bragged that he used to play soccer in college, a halfback. By nature Nan was a bookish man who could have thrived in an academic environment, yet somehow the restaurant business suited him as well—he was an excellent cook and knew how to please customers. What Dave didn't like about him was that at times Nan acted like a spoilsport. Dave had once heard him telling Janet, Pingping, and Niyan that all soap operas were trash. That was really embarrassing.

"Nan's such a flake," Dave said to Janet, who placed their baby in the crib.

"I was surprised too that he didn't want to have anything to do with Hailee."

"He doesn't like kids, I guess."

"Then why did he get married and start a family in the first place? Wasn't that unfair to Pingping and Taotao?"

"A guy like him thinks too much." Dave tucked in an edge of the baby's red blanket.

"I hope he'll change his mind about Hailee."

"It doesn't matter. We have lots of others willing to be her godfather."

"I'm glad Pingping agreed, though."

"Me too. She's always been more helpful than Nan."

9

NAN truly felt he couldn't be a good nominal father. He wasn't sure if he'd be capable of assuming all the parental responsibilities if Dave and Janet really died. If that happened, by the Chinese custom, he'd be obligated to raise Hailee as his own. Different from Dave, he wasn't very fond of children and felt that in his heart he was unwilling to make the sacrifices needed for raising another child. His friend Dick Harrison often went to New York to see his godson, attending the boy's birthday parties, cello performances, soccer tournaments, bar mitzvah. Nan wouldn't want to be like Dick. He already had his hands full with Taotao.

Another problem bothering him was that if Pingping and he were supposed to raise Hailee in the event that her parents died, the Mitchells had never mentioned whether Nan and Pingping would inherit their property, whereas the Wus had entrusted them with everything they owned. Dave had a lot of family and relatives in the South, and perhaps he and Janet didn't intend to leave Hailee in the Wus' care, not wanting their property transferred to them. That must have been why Janet said, "You wouldn't have to do anything for Hailee if Dave and I were gone." Nan, making little distinction between a nominal parent and a legal guardian, gathered that Dave and Janet would want them to be only a lesser kind of nominal parents, probably because the Mitchells were rich, unwilling to share their property with them. Pingping hadn't considered the matter in this light and now could see Nan's point. She wouldn't reproach him for refusing to be Hailee's nominal father right away. It was unfair for the Mitchells not to reciprocate the kind of absolute trust the Wus had placed in them. *"Is it because we're yellow and they're white?"* Pingping asked Nan.

"Their daughter is Asian too. I think it's more likely because they're rich and have more family, not loners like us."

Then husband and wife wondered if they should cancel the agreement on Taotao's guardianship they'd signed with the Mitchells. They decided not to, because they were uncertain who, beside Janet and Dave, could treat Taotao better if both of them died. They had best let the matter stay as it was. This wasn't equal, they both agreed, a little mortified, but they had no choice. To make the whole thing worse, Mr. Shang, the attorney who had prepared the papers for them, had left Chinatown and nobody knew his whereabouts. The Wus had thought of informing the Mitchells of Mr. Shang's disappearance, but now they changed their minds and preferred to put the matter on the back burner for the time being. They only hoped that nothing fatal would happen to them before their son reached eighteen.

At the restaurant two weeks later, when Nan told Janet that he couldn't be Hailee's nominal father, she said, "Don't worry. Hailee has three godfathers already." Janet had been so happy these days that her eyes couldn't stop smiling, making them less round than before.

The mention of the triple godfatherhood surprised the Wus. Pingping asked her friend, "How many godmothers she has?"

"Four, yourself included."

"My goodness, why so many?"

"We want to share Hailee with friends."

A lull ensued. Both Pingping and Nan were perplexed, as the idea of sharing one's child with other people was utterly alien to them. This multiple godparenthood also indicated that the Mitchells hadn't been serious about the nominal parents they wanted the Wus to be, because, by definition, a nominal father or mother was almost like a child's other parents and at least should be treated as a family member. That's why a child mustn't have more than one nominal mother or father. Pingping was glad Nan had declined the Mitchells' request.

A young mestizo, a temporary roofer, came up to the counter, and Nan turned to take his order.

"I want to show you something," Pingping said to Janet.

"What?"

Pingping went behind the counter, pulled open a drawer, and took out a thin notebook. She came back to Janet and opened the first page, proudly displaying a red cut-paper duck. "I made this for you. It's my mother's type."

"My, this is gorgeous! Is it really for me?"

"Yes."

Janet touched the duck gently with her forefinger as if afraid to break it. Indeed, the duck was not only delicate and lifelike but also in motion, with its feathers ruffled by a breeze and with waves of water beneath it. More striking, it carried a pair of tiny ducklings under its wing. Anyone could see that the scissor-work in this piece was clean and elegant, much superior to that in the paper cuttings the Mitchells had. Janet enthused, "Look at the duck's eye! Even with exquisite lids. You're a true artist, Pingping."

"I wish I can make more. My sister can do better than me because my mother like to teach her more often. I'm oldest daughter, so I always work."

"Here's an idea, you should open a studio."

"For what?"

"Teaching people how to create art with paper and scissors."

"I don't like to teach, you know that. Before I leave China, I swear I will never be teacher again."

When Nan returned, he put a carton of roast pork rice into a plastic bag, placed it on the counter, and threw in a few napkins and a spork for the customer. Instead of rejoining his wife, he sat down and resumed looking through *Consumer Reports* while listening in on the ladies. After they talked awhile about the art of paper cuttings, Janet told Pingping, "I've enrolled in the Chinese class at Emory. God, the language is so hard to learn. No wonder you Chinese are so patient and industrious."

"Why you want to study it?"

"I want to teach my daughter. She should know her mother tongue."

"Why? She will grow up speak English like American."

"But Chinese is her heritage. We ought to help her keep it."

"I have idea. Why don't you hire Chinese babysitter? Hailee can learn the language with her easily?"

"No. According to the experience of some adoptive parents, that's the last thing you should do."

"Why? It's good way to learn Chinese, I'm sure."

"You know, the adoption of a child is actually mutual. Hailee has also adopted us, so Dave and I must also try to adjust. Dave wants to learn some Chinese too. From now on we'll celebrate the Moon Day and the Spring Festival."

Pingping didn't know how to respond to that. Later the Wus talked between themselves about the idea of "mutual adoption," and Nan believed that the Mitchells were right, though he doubted if they could ever speak Chinese, not to mention read and write the ideograms, which were almost impossible for non-native speakers to master.

10

ON THE NIGHT of July Fourth the Gold Wok was closed. Some people in the neighborhood went downtown to watch fireworks in spite of the overcast sky. The Wus stayed home, glad to have a break. Nan was lying in bed reading Frost's poetry. He was moved by the wise ending of the poem "Provide, Provide" and was contemplating how truthful the phrase "boughten friendship" was. Suddenly Pingping burst in and threw a sheet of brittle paper on his face. He sat up with a start and asked, *"What's this about?"*

"About you and your sweetheart. Disgusting!" Her mouth twisted as she was speaking. Then she spun around, marched out, and slammed the door shut.

Nan glanced at the paper and recognized it was a letter from Beina. He had kept it in the unabridged *Webster's* and had almost forgotten it. What must have maddened Pingping was that the letter was dated on November 12 without a year, as if it had been written recently. In it Beina asked him to help her with the application fees at three American graduate schools. He had paid $140 for her but hadn't heard a word from her afterward.

He went into the living room, where his wife, lying on a sofa, had been singing in English repeatedly, "I love you. You love me. We're a happy family!" Though she covered her face with a towel that had just come out of the dryer, her voice was sharp and crazed. Nan stepped over and touched her upper arm, shaded by downy hair that he always liked to caress. He said, *"Come now, don't be so paranoid. That's an old letter. I haven't heard from her for almost eight years."*

She paused to stare at him. He kept on, *"I really have no contact with her."*

"*But you tried to bring her to America!*" Pingping raged, dropping the towel to the floor. "*Who knows? You're a big liar. Maybe you're still thick with her like before. You always do things behind my back.*"

"*Honestly, I'm not in touch with her and have no idea where she is.*"

"*Leave me alone! You spent our sweat money on that heartless woman. If she were good to you, I wouldn't complain. You're just bewitched by that fox spirit.*"

"*Like I said, this was before you came to America.*"

"*I see, you really meant to bring her here. If I hadn't come and joined you, you would've lived with her instead.*"

"*This is crazy. She just used me.*"

"*But you like being used by her and always miss her. You're so cheap that the worse she treats you, the nicer you'll be to her.*"

Their son stepped into the living room and listened to them. Nan told Taotao to go away, but the boy wouldn't leave. Nan begged Pingping, "*Don't be so nasty. I'm sorry. I shouldn't have kept the letter.*"

"*Why not? That's your receipt for the favor she owes you. She'll do something in return one of these days. But why didn't you hide it in a secret place? I don't care what you do on the sly as long as you don't let me know.*"

"*Honestly, I'm not carrying on with her.*"

"*Go away! I don't want to see your face.*"

Wordlessly Nan flounced toward the door while Pingping resumed singing behind him, "I love you. You love me. We're a happy family! . . ."

Nan wandered away from their house, alone with his numb heart. On occasion when he and Pingping quarreled, he'd get away awhile. His absence from home often enraged her more, but today she had chased him out. If only there were a place where he could stay a few days when his house got too raucous and too maddening. If only there were a friend to whom he could unburden himself. Dick Harrison lived fifteen miles away in Buckhead, but Nan felt Dick might be bored and look down on him if he went to him for consolation, which was the last thing he'd do. Every time after he and Pingping fought, he'd go either to the town library or to a bookstore for an hour, or just work off his anger in the kitchen of the Gold Wok. But this evening he had nowhere to go, so he walked along the lakeside alone. In the air hovered the effluvium of skunks, which had grown more intense as the summer deepened. Insects were shrieking explosively as if a large battle were in full swing, and time and again some waterfowl let out a sleepy cry from the dark woods of the other shore. Fortunately, the air was damp and few mosquitoes were flying about. In the southern sky a helicopter was ticking faintly, now buried in the clouds and now flickering like a drifting lantern.

Nan's mind was teeming with thoughts. Deep inside he knew he was at fault. Pingping had lashed out at him not so much because of the money he had spent on Beina as because he had kept her letter as a kind of memento. Before they married, she had let him read all the love letters the naval officer, her former boyfriend, had written her, and then she burned them all in his presence. Oddly enough, he didn't have any letter from Beina at that time and couldn't convince his bride-to-be that there had been no correspondence between him and his former girlfriend since they had lived in the same city. To make her believe him, he showed her a photo of that woman, then dropped it into a stove. Now his wife must have thought he had been in touch with Beina all these years and that from the very beginning he hadn't leveled with her. To her, he was a double-faced man.

It took him almost an hour to walk around the lake, which should have taken at most half the time. Approaching his house, he wondered if he should enter it now. All the lights were off in there, and the windowpanes kept reflecting the slashes of the lightning in the north, where the sky was beginning to jump a little. It threatened rain, the oak leaves fluttering in the gathering wind, so he decided to go in.

As he stepped into the living room, a pair of arms wrapped around him and Pingping's hot face came against his cheek. She whispered, *"Nan, forgive me. I can see the letter is old, the edges of the paper already yellowed. I was nasty just now. Can you . . . ?"* Her words were muffled as he pressed his lips on her mouth. In response, she began kissing him as hard as if she wanted to breathe with his lungs. He could feel her heart knocking against his half-numbed chest. He touched her breasts, which were warm and heaving. A knot of feeling was quickly unfolding in him, and his hand slipped behind her to unbutton her dress.

"*Don't. Taotao can hear us,*" she said.

He stopped and went into their son's room. The boy was dozing on his bed, his feet rested on the floor and his face toward the ceiling. Nan covered Taotao's stomach with a shirt, closed the door, and returned to Pingping. "*He's sleeping. I'll be careful,*" he said, and his hands resumed caressing her.

She slid down to the floor, pulling him down with her. Then they started peeling off each other's clothes.

Soon she began panting and trembling a little. A few tears welled out of her eyes. Instead of being rough with her, he licked her wet cheeks, and her tears tasted a bit tangy, reminding him of the bitter-melon soup they'd eaten two days before. He adjusted her body to make her lie comfortably so that he could stay in her for a long time.

"*Don't cry,*" he murmured. "*Just relax and imagine we're on our honeymoon.*"

At those words she broke into smothered sobs, which startled him. He regretted having said that because never had they honeymooned anywhere and his words must have caused her to feel sad about their life. He said, "*Forgive me for saying that.*"

"*Make me happy.*"

He nuzzled her neck and nibbled her ear.

11

DESPITE their reconciliation, Pingping's furious response to that letter brought the memories of Beina back to Nan. For two days he couldn't stop thinking about his ex-girlfriend. He tried to sidetrack his mind, yet somehow it couldn't help but stray to that woman, the fountainhead of his misery. Every remembered detail—a peculiar frown of hers or an indolent gesture or a petulant pout—seemed pregnant with meanings he hadn't thought of before, and whenever he was unoccupied he'd attempt to decipher those hidden messages as if they had really been there all along but he had overlooked them. One incident still stung his heart whenever he thought of it. Three months after Beina declared she'd washed her hands of him, Nan had run into her one morning in a park, where she and her new boyfriend were walking, her hand on his arm. It was windy and the ground was frozen, cobblestones glazed with ice on the path leading to a white building beyond a grove of trees. Nan turned away, pretending he hadn't seen them. But suddenly he slipped and his legs buckled; he stretched out his hand and grabbed a birch sapling to break his fall. Yet his copy of Friedrich Engels's *The Origin of the Family, Private Property and the State* dropped on the ground, and the author's bushy beard on the front page kept fluttering, ruffled by the wind. From behind came that woman's ringing laughter, silvery and icy, which pierced his heart. He picked up the book and dashed away, sending flocks of crows and pigeons into explosive flight. He ran, ran, and ran until he could hardly breathe, until his heart was about to burst.

He was unsure whether she had laughed out loud to make him

mad so as to bring him back to her or just to wound him. He'd prefer to believe it was just another wile of hers.

A few weeks before, he had burned the notebook containing the poetry he had written for her. He declared to her face that he had gotten rid of all the silly poems. Yet there still remained one piece that he had never shown her, known only to himself. He wrapped it into the jacket of his copy of *Book of Songs,* an ancient poetry anthology compiled by Confucius. He brought the book to America and had kept the poem in it all these years.

One night after his wife and son had gone to bed, he took out the poem and read it again. It went:

The Last Lesson

Again the ferryboat was canceled,
you told me on the phone.
This time the captain didn't grab a passenger
and get his own face smashed.
The boat was really falling apart,
docked for an emergency overhaul.

On the beach my shadow has doubled in length.
The life ring I just bought lies nearby,
half withered in the afternoon sun.
Alone, I'm sitting on an apple crate
and watching youngsters diving
in the shallows to compete for
the championship of holding breath.

What an idiot! Why volunteer
to teach you how to swim
while I myself can hardly keep my head
above the whirlpools you randomly spin?

He smiled after reading the poem, which he couldn't say he still liked and which was probably sappy and unfinished. But it was something that had once been close to his heart, and he wanted to keep it. He wrapped it back into the jacket of the book and put it on the shelf beside his desk.

Lying on his bed, again he wondered whether he had been too impatient with Beina. For example, after she hadn't shown up at the beach, he had simply stopped offering her swimming lessons. Then came another breakup of theirs. Although tough in appearance, he couldn't really disentangle himself from her. One day he even went to the cafeteria near her dorm, just to look at her. She caught sight of him but pretended not to have seen him and kept talking loudly with the man in front of her in the mess line. Now and again she tossed a glance at Nan. When she had bought her lunch, she turned around and headed in his direction, but her eyes looked away. As she was drawing near, he spun around and rushed out of the dining hall.

If he had spoken to her, probably he could have resumed teaching her how to swim the next summer. That would have given him an opportunity for more physical contact with her. Sure, she wouldn't change much, but he could take her willfulness and caprice with aplomb to show he had a large heart. Eventually he might have gained the upper hand with her. Yet he was bitter and too proud of himself. It was his silly self-pride that gradually cemented the barrier between them. If only he'd had thicker skin; if only he had played fast and loose with her; if only he could have made her suffer.

"What sickness, sickness . . ." With those words on his lips, he drifted off to sleep. The fluorescent tube remained on until daybreak.

12

HEIDI MASEFIELD called the Gold Wok and asked Pingping whether she had heard from Livia recently. The girl had run away from home, and for days her mother had been looking for her. Shocked, Pingping wondered if Taotao was still in touch with the girl despite his agreeing to stop e-mailing her. She told Heidi that she'd talk to her son and find out whether Taotao knew Livia's whereabouts. "I will call you tonight, Heidi," she said.

"Please do. I don't know why she did this to me."

"I hope she is not with someone."

"How do you mean?"

"Did you tell police?"

"Not yet. She disappeared three days ago. I thought she might have gone to her grandparents' or a friend's home."

"Maybe you should let police know."

"If I still haven't heard from her by this evening, I'll do that."

Pingping didn't ask her why Livia had run away. Neither would she express her fear that Livia might have fallen into a molester's hands. From the brief conversation she guessed that the girl and her mother had quarreled over a boy who could be a bad influence. Livia was just thirteen and seemed already entangled with a number of boys. On the phone Heidi had revealed that recently Livia had often "played hooky." Pingping had almost gasped at that, not knowing the exact meaning of the idiom, and assumed it had something to do with "hookers." She went into the kitchen to tell Nan about the phone call. The radio was on in there, sitting on a shelf, and Nan was listening to *Car Talk*. He enjoyed the show, especially the hacking laugh of Tom, the older of the Magliozzi brothers. Tom's wild laughter was contagious and often made Nan chuckle or giggle when he was cooking. It was boring in the kitchen, so every Saturday he'd listen to *Car Talk* from beginning to end. He liked the seemingly casual way Tom and Ray treated their callers—teasing them a little so that everyone could have a good laugh. He often wished he could crack up like Tom, who would ha-ha-ha with total abandon and from the depths of his gut. Pingping, who liked Tom's laughter too but felt he cackled way too much, came in and turned down the radio, saying, *"Heidi just called. Livia ran away from home."*

Nan's face stiffened. *"I hope it hasn't implicated our son."*

"She's a bad girl and 'played hooky.' "

"I 'played hooky' *when I was in elementary school."*

"What did you say?" She widened her eyes at him.

"We just fooled around in the mountains, doing kids' stuff."

"That's not what you would do with 'hookers.' "

Nan broke into laughter.

Discomfited, she went on, *"This is not funny!"*

" 'Play hooky' *means to skip school. It doesn't pertain to prostitution."*

"Oh, I see." She laughed, then went on, *"Still, Livia is a bad girl."* She removed the lid from a pot, as the broth in it was about to bubble over.

That afternoon they talked to their son about Livia. The boy had no idea about her disappearance but knew she didn't get along with Heidi. Recently Livia had often complained to him about her mother, who had a boyfriend named Joe. She disliked that man and thought he was just "a smarty-pants." Both she and Nathan tried to dissuade their mother from seeing Joe, but Heidi was obsessed, because, unlike the other men she had dated, Joe would always pick up the tab when they went out. Together they had traveled to Paris and London. Joe was a banker, but in her e-mail to Taotao, Livia had called him "a little jerk." She also wrote: "I never thought my mom was such a cock-tease."

"What that mean?" Pingping asked her son.

Nan explained, "A woman who is too fond of men."

"Something like that," agreed the boy. "That's a gentle expression."

"I don't believe you," Pingping said. "Livia is never gentle to her mother."

"I mean Dad's explanation."

"Anyway, she can't talk about her mother like that. She's bad girl and crazy."

That night Pingping phoned Heidi and told her that Livia was angry about her taking a boyfriend. Heidi said someone had seen Livia at the train station three days before. She was worried sick and had reported her disappearance to the police. She didn't mind whatever Livia called her, as long as the girl could return home safe and sane.

13

TO THE Wus' astonishment, Livia showed up at the Gold Wok two days later. The girl was a foot taller than three years before, almost as tall as Pingping now. She wore a jeans skirt and high heels, her lips thickly rouged, nearly purple. Despite a few flecks of acne on her cheeks, she was handsome, as well as curvaceous. Her frizzy auburn hair was pulled back into a ponytail, giving her the look of a young woman. Both Pingping and Nan couldn't help but marvel at the girl they had never imagined Livia would grow into. Though unsettled by her sudden appearance, Pingping hugged her and said, "I told you you will grow tall."

Livia beamed. "You were the only person who knew me."

At those words Pingping's unease melted, and she called Taotao to the front to meet his friend. The boy came over, and the two of them hugged awkwardly, smiling without a word as if shy in the grown-ups' presence, as if he had known all along that she was coming.

Livia had no extra clothes with her and reeked of tobacco, which she said she'd caught from a man sitting close to her at the Greyhound station. "Anyways, don't think I smoke," she told Pingping. Then she caught sight of the God of Wealth sitting in the alcove and asked Taotao, "Who's this cross-eyed guy? Why offer him so many goodies?"

"He's the money god. We inherited him from the former owner of this place, and my parents don't want to disturb him."

"Can he make your family rich?"

"I've no frigging clue."

She patted the deity's porcelain belly and caressed his smiling face. "He's so pudgy, a model of obesity. Can I have an orange from this plate?" She lifted one of the fruits Pingping had placed at the deity's feet that morning.

"I'm not sure if you can now. They were was just offered to him."

Pingping said, "We have orange at home. Let's go." She wanted the girl to take a shower and change her clothes. Livia put the fruit back on the plate, and together she and Pingping went out, heading for Marsh Drive.

It was early August, and despite the clear sky, the air was so muggy that Pingping and Livia both opened their mouths to breathe as they walked. The roadside near an intersection was littered with napkins, a squat whiskey bottle, a few chicken nuggets and fried shrimp; the grass had been grooved by a truck's wheels, red mud exposed like festering wounds. Several photos were scattered around, all torn in half. "Whew, it's so humid!" Livia said to Pingping.

"This is Georgia, not Boston. It's not hottest time in summer yet."

"Hotter than this?"

"Of course, it can reach ninety-eight degree."

"God help me! How can human beings live here!"

Pingping didn't respond, but she was glad that her son didn't seem involved with the girl's running away, though she wasn't sure whether Livia had come to stay with them or mainly to see Taotao. In some sense she was pleased that the girl had shown up here, which meant that Livia must have felt somewhat attached to them, and now her mother could stop looking for her.

A snapping turtle appeared ahead of them, crossing the street. At the sight of the creature, Livia let out a cry and bounded over. "Wow, he's so cute!" She patted its dark shell and scared it to a halt, its head withdrawn from view. With her toes she overturned the turtle, whose underside was brownish and rubbery, semitranslucent. Pingping bent down, held one side of its shell, and put it back on its stomach. Still it wouldn't move, playing dead. Around them a pair of blue dragonflies hovered, their wings zinging and flickering with sunlight.

"There's lake nearby," Pingping told Livia, "so you can find a lotta bird and animal around here."

Livia tried to lift the turtle, but Pingping stopped her, saying it might snap at her hand if she wasn't careful. Yet the girl feared that a passing car might crush it if it stayed in the middle of the road. Pingping stretched out her foot and gently pushed the creature all the way across the street into the roadside grass. The turtle began crawling away, its beak stretched out again and its eyes clear like a bird's.

As soon as Pingping and Livia got into the house, the girl went to the bathroom for a shower. Pingping put a change of clothes on the lid of the toilet beside the bathtub while the girl stood in the cone of spraying water, shielded by the screen of ground glass. "You can wear my clothing, okay?" Pingping said.

"Thanks a million," said Livia. "Oh, it's so nice to take a warm shower again! I must stink like a skunk."

"How many days you didn't wash?"

"Four."

"Take your time and wash yourself thoroughly. There are orange in refrigerator. You can eat as many you want."

"Sure, I'll have one."

Pingping looked at Livia behind the semitransparent screen, but she could see only the contour of that pubertal body. Apparently Livia had grown into a fine, healthy girl, though she still seemed flighty and fragile. Pingping went out to call Nan to discuss what to do about Livia.

•

At the Gold Wok, Taotao was sitting in a booth and eating a pork bun. His father asked him, "Is Livia your girlfriend?"

"Nah, she's just a friend. Why? Why are you grinning like that?" the boy growled.

"I jahst asked. What's the difference between a girlfriend and a friend?"

"You date a girl, then she's your girlfriend. I don't date Livia, so she's just my friend."

"That's good. She's not suitable for you."

"None of your business! How can you tell if she suits me or not?"

"She's too big, almost like a woman. Look at yourself. You have no hair on your tawp lip yet."

The phone rang and Nan picked it up. Pingping asked him how they should handle Livia. They were both worried that something might happen between their son and the girl, so they had to figure out a way to prevent the two youngsters from being alone together.

Having talked briefly, they decided to let both Taotao and Livia work in the restaurant and would pay them each five dollars an hour. Although business was slow at present, this was the only way to keep the girl in line.

The moment Pingping hung up, Nan called Heidi. Heidi dissolved into sobs at the news. She implored Nan and Pingping not to disturb her daughter, saying she would come and pick her up without delay. "Don't wahrry yourself sick, Heidi," said Nan. "We'll take good care of her. In fact, we're going to hire her to work for us."

"Do you think she'll do that?" came Heidi's concerned voice, broken up by a burst of static.

"Here is not like in Boston, where you have a lawt of places to visit. Livia cannot go anywhere. Taotao will work wiz her too. We hire them as a team so zat we can keep watch on them."

"That's a great idea, Nan. I can't thank you and Pingping enough."

Nan wondered if he should invite Heidi to stay with them, but unsure if their home was too shabby for her, he said nothing, knowing she'd surely make arrangements for her lodging anyway. In the back of his mind lingered a touch of discomfort from having the two juvenile workers at the Gold Wok, because their wages might consume a good part of the profit the business could fetch in a slow season like now. Besides, he'd have to pay Niyan as well and might even lose money this week. He hoped Heidi would arrive within two or three days.

14

LIVIA and Taotao didn't mind being kept at the Gold Wok. Never paid five dollars an hour before, they followed Pingping's instructions with alacrity and worked zestfully, busing tables, taking plates and bowls out of the washer, peeling fruits, shelling nuts, picking vegetables. Livia did ask Nan what places in Atlanta were worth seeing; he told her that there was the Martin Luther King Center and also the World of Coca-Cola, where you could have a "Soda Safari" and partake of all kinds of soft drinks for free. The girl wasn't interested in either place, and said, "Coke just makes you fat. I quit drinking it long ago." To Nan's disquiet, Taotao mentioned Stone Mountain Park, saying a boat ride on the lake there could be fun, but Livia thought it was too hot to stay in the open air. Nan felt relieved that she didn't want to go sightseeing.

Compared with Livia, Taotao seemed much younger, like a little brother, so his parents weren't really worried about his being with the girl. Yet Nan noticed that with Livia around, Taotao had become more animated and talkative. The boy even tried to ingratiate himself with Livia, who he assumed had come all the way to see him. Nan was certain that if Taotao were a few years older and able to drive, he would have taken Livia to the movies, or Stone Mountain Park, or Lake Lanier, and wouldn't have been willing to work at the restaurant. Maybe it would do him good to have a girlfriend. At least that might teach him how to get along with girls and eventually make him relax when dating a woman. Nan always regretted that he had taken girls too seriously when he was young.

Livia reveled in the free food at the restaurant. She told the Wus that both her brother, Nathan, and she had missed Pingping's cooking. Now there were more choices here and everything was better made, no longer the homey fare Pingping used to cook. Livia kept asking Nan and Pingping, "Can I work here for the rest of the summer? I hate the fishy smell of the Cape."

"In fact, we can't hire you for long," said Nan. "You're underage, and I may get into trahble for exploiting children."

"Nobody will know, please!"

Pingping said, "We have to ask your mother."

As if she were a full-time employee here, Livia would mimic Niyan's manner and even asked the waitress how much she made. Niyan wouldn't tell her and just smiled, amused by the carefree girl. The truth was that there wasn't enough work for the youngsters to do. When idle, the two of them would settle in a booth, cracking spiced pumpkin seeds and roasted peanuts and talking about their schools and the kids they both knew. Now and again they would laugh, which drew attention to them.

Livia leaned forward in her seat and whispered to Taotao, "Do your parents get along?"

"Sure. They've worked very hard. My dad is a real chef now. You see, people like what he cooks."

"I mean, your parents don't fight anymore?"

"Very rarely."

"So Nan won't walk out on Pingping?"

"What makes you still think of that?" The boy stared at her and puckered his brows.

"Never mind."

"C'mon, tell me why you said that."

"Are you sure your dad isn't seeing another woman?"

"You have a sick mind. He'll never abandon us."

"Then how come your dad and mom sleep in different rooms?"

"They always do."

"I don't get it."

"My dad reads and writes late at night. He doesn't want to disturb my mom."

"That's odd. So they don't go to bed together anymore?"

"That's just your stupid way of thinking. Husband and wife must sleep in the same bed or the marriage is in trouble."

"My aunt stopped sharing her bed with Phil before they were divorced."

"But that doesn't apply to my parents!" the boy flared at her, his eyes sparking.

"There, there, don't be an asshole."

Indeed, Nan and Pingping hadn't slept in the same room since they moved to Marsh Drive. But contrary to Livia's assumption, they did make love from time to time, mostly when Nan sneaked into Pingping's bed early in the mornings, and the marital crisis Livia had intuited long ago had been eased considerably. The couple lived a stable life now, totally preoccupied with their business and their child. When Livia arrived, they had moved Taotao out of his room and let the girl use his bed. The boy stayed with his dad, sleeping on a futon next to the south-facing window. He didn't complain and had surrendered his room willingly, whereas Livia felt it bizarre that Nan would sleep in the same room with his son instead of staying with his wife. In fact, Pingping had asked Taotao to sleep in her master bedroom, but the boy wouldn't do that. Thanks to the girl's presence in the house, he adamantly insisted on staying with his father. Nan was pleased to have him in his room.

But at night Taotao and Livia would watch TV together in the living room and wouldn't go to bed until after midnight, whereas Nan and Pingping would turn in as soon as they got home. One night Nan saw the two children lounging on the sofa and watching a John Wayne movie. Livia kept yawning, while Taotao looked dreamy, his eyes glassy, somewhat clouded over. He didn't respond to his father's sudden appearance, as if he were dozing. His delicate fingers were holding something like a tiny cigarette. Nan looked closely—it wasn't a cigarette but a joint. He shouted, "Damn it, you're smoking marijuana!"

"Just a little bit."

"It's drugs!"

"Not that much different from tobacco."

The boy gave him a silly smile, his nose quivered a little, and he seemed too dazed to speak more. Nan snatched the joint from him and snuffed it out with his thumb and forefinger. He turned to Livia. "You gave him this, right? Damn you!"

"He—he asked for it. I told him he shouldn't smoke in the house, but he wouldn't listen."

"Still, you're a drug dealer. I'm going to call zer police."

"Please don't, Nan! I just happened to have a little bit of the weed on me."

"Give it to me." He stretched out his hand.

She pulled out of her pocket a white envelope, six inches by four in size and about a third full, and handed it to him. At this moment Pingping stepped in, wrapped in a nightgown, and said loudly to nobody in particular, "You can't smoke in here." She peered at Taotao, who looked dumb. "What's wrong with him?"

Nan explained and showed her the stump of the joint. She burst out at Livia, "How dare you teach him to eat drug! I'm going to call your mother now."

"Please, Pingping, don't be mad! My mom knows."

"What, she know you are drugger?"

"I'm not a druggie! I just got a bit of the weed from Neil, who's my boyfriend. My mom chased him out of our house when she discovered it."

Nan broke in, "Are you telling us zer truth?"

"Swear to God, I am."

Pingping switched off the TV. "Taotao, how many times do you smoke that stuff?"

"Only once."

"This is his first time," put in Livia.

"Clearly you're a bad influence," Nan said.

The girl hung her head without another word. After making her and Taotao promise never to do drugs again and sending them to bed, the parents sat down and talked between themselves. Nan wondered if they should inform Heidi of Livia's drug problem, but Pingping believed Heidi already knew. For better or worse, the girl wouldn't lie. Probably she had fled home because she and her mother had fought over this matter. Nan and Pingping decided to keep a closer eye on the two children until Heidi arrived.

15

HEIDI arrived two days later. She looked much older than she had three years before, with more wrinkles on her neck, and her grizzled bangs were almost white now. She had lost weight, though she was still broad in the beam. She hugged and kissed both Pingping and Nan and thanked them for accommodating Livia, who seemed happy to see her mother.

Nan had to cook in the kitchen while Heidi and Pingping were sitting at a table and conversing. Taotao was at the counter, working as the cashier, and Livia helped Niyan as the busgirl.

Heidi had checked in at the Hilton Hotel in downtown Atlanta, where she also had a bed for Livia, but she hadn't mentioned this to the girl, unsure if she'd be willing to stay with her. Heidi, having eaten brunch, took only a beef ravioli from the appetizer platter Nan had placed on the table. Now and then she'd steal a glance at her daughter, who paid no heed to her and was ogling a young man in a maroon silk shirt seated near the window with an Indian woman, whose face was so heavily made up that Pingping couldn't tell her age—probably under thirty.

"Livia's hopeless," Heidi whispered to Pingping. "She started to have trouble with boys last winter and didn't do well in school."

"She is good girl in heart," consoled Pingping.

"If only I could talk some sense into her."

Afraid their conversation might annoy Livia, who seemed to be eavesdropping, Pingping offered to give Heidi a tour of their house. Together they went out to the Wus' passenger van. Usually Nan kept the car's backseats down, using it as a freight vehicle as well, but after Livia arrived, Pingping vacuumed it and put all the seats up.

Heidi was amazed by the Wus' home, not only by the brick ranch but especially by the lake and the immense trees in the backyard. She turned to Pingping. "Now, tell me again, how many years have you been in the United States?"

"Nan is here nine year, me seven and half years."

"Wow, in less than a decade you already have your own business, a house, and two cars. I'm so happy for you, to see you doing so well."

"We just try to manage. Still have mortgage to pay."

"Is it a big one?"

"Not really, about forty thousand dollars left."

"Amazing. This can happen only in America. I'm very moved by the fact that you and Nan have actualized your American dream so quickly. I'm proud of this country."

Pingping smiled, a bit embarrassed by her effusion. Heidi waved at the old Romanian man sitting on the opposite shore and holding a fishing rod. That florid-faced man spoke no English and often went angling there alone, a small metal bucket sitting next to him. Once Pingping saw that he had caught six large fish, two bass and four bullheads. That had made her feel as if she'd been robbed, as if the lake weren't public property but her family's. The feeling probably arose because every morning when she looked out the window, she'd see fish skip out of the surface of the shimmering water.

When they turned to observe a gray egret that stood on one leg in the shallows, Pingping said to Heidi, "Livia said you have a boyfriend now."

Heidi nodded. "His name is Joe, a good guy, but Livia and Nathan are not pleased."

"They will grow up and leave home. You can't be old lady live in that big house by yourself."

"You're right. I have my life too."

They also talked about the public schools in Gwinnett County. Pingping said that in general, the language instruction here was quite good, with students reading and writing a great deal, but the science part was rather weak. She had heard several neighbors complain that the high school didn't offer science projects and had invested too much in sports because its football team had won the state championship several times. Last winter Taotao's English teacher had assigned each student to write a novel as homework, and Taotao had started the project but wouldn't show his parents what he had been writing. At first Pingping was amused by the assignment, but soon she suspected that the teacher might have cut corners in her job, knowing few of her students would finish the homework and hand it in for grading.

Their conversation turned to Nan. Pingping told Heidi that he was more like a family man now and worked hard to keep the Gold Wok afloat. "Are you happy here?" Heidi asked, and her clear hazel eyes looked straight at Pingping's smooth face.

"Yes, I'm happy as long as our family are together," she answered, scratching the welt of a mosquito bite on her forearm.

The egret took off from the lakeside, sailing away like a kite. Heidi had stepped on some geese droppings and kept scuffing her pumps on the grass. While shuffling, she gazed at Gerald's yard, in which things were more disordered than before. The trampoline was standing on its side like a makeshift wall, and the doghouse had collapsed, hardly recognizable. Against one of the junk cars was a pile of split firewood, having waited to be stacked since the past winter. Worst of all, the porch behind the house was half installed with gleaming glass, while a part of it remained a gaping hole, as if the house had been disemboweled. Gerald had been working at the thing on and off for more than a year, and it seemed he could never finish it.

"Who's living next door?" Heidi asked Pingping, pointing at the decaying house.

"Gerald Brown. He's electrician, a good guy. His wife left him."

"What a shame he doesn't take care of his property. The neighborhood should do something about it. If he doesn't put his home in order, he should be thrown out of the community. What an eyesore this mess is in the middle of such a nice area."

Pingping said nothing. A bad taste was seeping into her mouth, and she sighed, shaking her head to indicate that it was impossible to make Gerald mend his ways.

16

WITHOUT much persuasion Livia left with her mother, and Pingping and Nan felt relieved. For days the Wus had been talking about
their neighbor Gerald, who lately wouldn't come out of his house. He
had been ill and unemployed since June, and his front yard was
messier than before. Sometimes at night pickups would even park on
his lawn for trysts and leave behind beer bottles, paper bags, Styrofoam boxes, and even used condoms on the grass, which hadn't been
cut for three months. Whenever Nan or Pingping mowed their lawn,
they would cut the part of Gerald's front yard adjacent to theirs, but
that had made Gerald's lawn appear even more neglected.

Then one morning as the Wus were about to leave for work, three
police cruisers pulled into Gerald's driveway and lawn. In his front
yard gathered dozens of people from the neighborhood, to watch him
being evicted. Mrs. Lodge, shaped like a potato, was among them and
kept shaking her white head and saying, "Poor guy. What a shame."

Alan was also standing nearby. He sidled up to Nan and Pingping.
With a grin that made his eyes crinkle, he said, "It's high time for
him to go. Finally they're doing something."

Still bewildered, Nan asked, "Where's Gerald?"

"I've no idea. They couldn't find him."

"Why they're doing this?" Pingping said.

"Gerald hasn't paid his bills for a long time, so the bank was sick of
him. Now they've come to repossess his property."

Dumbstruck, the Wus stared at the commotion, never having
seen somebody being thrown out of his own home. From inside the
house and its basement, a team of Mexican workers was dragging
out Gerald's possessions and dropping them on the grass. There was

all kinds of stuff, most of which he had taken from construction sites: scraps and rolls of rugs, broken chairs and tables, battered floor lamps, utensils coated with grease, stacks of plastic pails, two wheelless barrows, hundreds of old magazines, boxes of electric wires, assorted pieces of lumber, several rusty jigsaws, a brand-new toilet with an oak lid, two used air conditioners. A beefy policeman with a pair of handcuffs on his hip kicked a floppy baby carriage and told the spectators, "Gerald Brown has twenty-four hours to remove his stuff. After that, you can pick up whatever you want."

From the backyard came the moaning of a tow truck. One of Gerald's junk cars emerged from the corner of the house and was hauled away. Nan noticed many eyes eagerly searching through Gerald's belongings scattered on the grass, and he was sure that before dark some people would come and scavenge through this mess. He was afraid they might damage his lawn, since some of Gerald's possessions had already overflowed onto the Wus' front yard. Unable to delay any longer, Nan and Pingping set off for work, talking about the eviction all the way.

Both of them were shaken by the scene, which reminded them that they hadn't paid off their mortgage yet. They still owed Mr. Wolf $38,000. If their business folded or if they fell ill, their home might be repossessed as well. By all means they must get rid of the mortgage as soon as possible.

Shubo stopped by at noon to get from Niyan the key to their safe-deposit box in the bank. Nowadays he worked at Grand Buddha as its barkeep and made decent wages. He and Nan got along well, so he often came in to chat or to give Nan a magazine or newspaper that carried something interesting. Nan was amazed by Shubo's manner, which bore no trace of his academic background. Who could imagine this fellow had earned a Ph.D. in sociology? In every way he looked like a menial worker, with a weather-beaten face and shadowy eyes. When the Wus told him about their neighbor's eviction, Shubo said, "*Americans are tough. They live more naturally, close to animals.*"

Nan laughed and asked, "*What do you mean by 'close to animals'? Animals don't have to work to make money and pay mortgages and car loans.*"

"*I mean, if you're strong you survive here, if you're weak you die.*"

"It's the same everywhere."

"But lots of Americans won't grumble if bad luck strikes. They take it just as something that happens."

Nan wasn't certain if Shubo's observation was accurate, though he had noticed that in general Americans didn't complain much and seemed more able to endure frustrations and misfortunes.

Early that afternoon, when the busy hours were over, Nan went back to see the eviction again and also to check on his own property. He feared that the movers might have damaged the steel fence dividing his backyard from Gerald's. As he was approaching his home, suddenly hundreds of blackbirds took off from Gerald's front lawn, veering away, their wings whirring, and casting a drifting shadow on the ground. Nobody was at Gerald's, and his possessions were strewn around the house, which was sealed, a lockbox hanging on the door handle. Other than the two wheelless barrows, everything was still there. Nan walked around a little and saw that his backyard fence was intact. He entered Gerald's front porch. On a windowsill was propped open a magazine displaying a young couple copulating in doggie fashion. Nan swiped it to the ground; it was an old copy of *Hustler.* Most of its pages had been crinkled by rainwater. Gerald must have picked it up somewhere, maybe from a trash can. Nan thought about keeping it for a day or two, then changed his mind and kicked it to a pile of newspapers and posters.

As he stepped from the porch, to his surprise, he saw Gerald standing at the edge of his yard, holding a blue bicycle and gazing at the piles of his belongings with large, dazed eyes. The man looked as if he were afraid to step on the lawn, his feet on the pavement, his right hand holding the handlebar of the bike. He raised his head and caught sight of Nan. Nan had never seen Gerald so small and so frail, his eyes lackluster and his chin covered with grizzling bristles. Nan waved and walked toward him, wondering what consoling words he should say. But Gerald spun around, leaped on the bicycle, and trundled away, the chain clinking its guard and the rear-wheel fender. A gust of wind lifted his hair into a tuft and swelled the back of his gray shirt, making him resemble a large bird. Nan exhaled a long sigh.

17

HAILEE was going to be one year old on September 16, and Janet had been busy preparing the birthday party, to which the Wus were invited. As the nominal mother Pingping had agreed to go, but Nan was reluctant. Six weeks ago he and his wife had attended a party at the Mitchells', and he had felt out of place among the crowd there. This time, afraid he might again feel left out, he decided to stay at the Gold Wok that evening. Besides, there was so much to do at the restaurant that either he or Pingping had to be around during the busy hours. So Pingping went to the Mitchells' alone with a picture book in Chinese as a present for the baby. When she arrived, most of the people hadn't shown up yet. Janet told Pingping that several of Hailee's godparents were coming too.

Dave was watching a baseball game with their daughter on his lap while Janet was busy in the kitchen, unwrapping cheese and pouring a jar of salsa into a soup bowl. A large woman holding a glass of seltzer came up to Pingping, introducing herself as Christine, and they entered into conversation. To Pingping's surprise, Christine had taught nursing at a medical school in Taiwan for a year and was reminiscing about her experiences there fondly. She said she missed the night snacks sold at the streetside eateries in Taipei. Pingping noticed that her left eye was bloodshot and a little puffy, so she asked her, "What happen to your eye?"

"Oh, I just had laser surgery." She touched the root of her plump nose with her fingertips as if she were still wearing glasses. There was a sprinkling of freckles across her cheeks.

"So you can see better now."

"Absolutely. For the first time in my life I can see individual leaves on treetops with my naked eyes. I began to wear glasses at seven, and before that, my poor eyesight had always made me think a tree crown was just one block of green, not made of individual leaves. This is wonderful. I can drive without glasses on now."

The door chime rang and two couples stepped in. Christine knew the new arrivals and hurried to greet them. Janet, holding a plate of lox, stopped on her way to the dining room and asked Pingping to help her remove the spinach turnovers from the oven, because she had to go and welcome the guests. Gladly Pingping entered the kitchen, put on a mitt, and began taking out the hors d'oeuvres. After that, she resumed the work left by Janet, mashing avocado to make a dip for corn chips. Janet had cooked the buffet dinner already, and several platters were filled with meats and there were also two large bowls of salads, mixed organic greens. Presently Janet came back and together the two of them started carrying dinner to the oval table in the dining room.

The house was noisy now, ringing with chuckles and chitchat. After everything was ready, Pingping went to join the guests. A rotund man with a domed forehead was sitting alone on a love seat. He looked sleepy on account of his doughy face and thin eyes. Despite his fleshy lips and fair skin, he somehow reminded Pingping of Vladimir Lenin. She went up to him and said pleasantly, "Hi, how are you?"

The man raised his eyes, and his face suddenly tightened, his pupils shifting. He seemed flustered and didn't know how to respond. As Pingping wondered about what to say, a raccoon-faced woman came over with two glasses of red wine. She glared at the man, then asked Pingping sharply, "Can I help you?" The plunging neckline of her dress revealed her tanned cleavage.

Confused, Pingping stammered, "I—I'm Pingping. Janet and Dave are substitute parents for my son." In panic she forgot how to say "legal guardians" in English.

"You mean godparents?" the woman asked, handing a glass to the man.

"Something like that."

"Oh . . . I'm sorry. I'm Kim and he's my boyfriend, Charlie. So you adopted a baby too."

"No. My son already in middle school."

"I see. Charlie is Hailee's godfather and I'm her godmother."

Pingping thought of mentioning herself as a kind of godmother to the baby too, but refrained. She was amazed that the Mitchells had an unmarried couple as their daughter's godparents. Somehow she felt uncomfortable talking with Kim and Charlie, though she couldn't say why. She was sure Kim had been rude to her just now, so she said a few more words, then went away to play with Hailee.

She didn't enjoy Janet's cooking and ate just a piece of chicken breast and some cherry tomatoes, which she always liked. Yet she had a good time with the baby, who was chewing on a tiny rubber fish. She removed the teether from Hailee's mouth and tried to teach her how to say "Mommy" and "Daddy" in Mandarin, but the girl could speak only one syllable at a time. Hailee laughed a lot, her mouth drooling, and she held Pingping's thumb and dragged her along when she crawled around on the Persian rug. No guests stopped to talk with Pingping, probably assuming she was a nanny. Indeed, she looked as young as if she were in her late twenties.

When the large birthday cake was brought out, the house turned noisy again. As people began singing "Happy Birthday," Pingping carried Hailee to the living room while a few ladies, Susie among them, walked backward in front of the cake, chorusing and clapping their hands. Hailee was puzzled and wouldn't blow at the single candle, so Janet did that for her.

After nine o'clock, Nan arrived to pick up his wife, having left the restaurant for Niyan to close up. This time he mixed well with the Mitchells' guests, especially with a wiry man sporting a goatee, who was a librarian in Decatur and liked Chuang Tzu, the ancient Chinese philosopher. The man also knew Dick Harrison and had invited him to read in his library. Nan and he conversed over wine for a good while. Then Nan turned to talk with Christine about which Chinese cities she should visit, because she had applied for a teaching fellowship. If that came through, she'd love to go to China to teach.

Dave came, beaming, and placed his hand on Nan's shoulder. "Did you try the Parmesan chicken I made?" he asked.

Nan hadn't but prevaricated, "I didn't know you can cook."

"I've just begun to learn to make a few things."

Christine chimed in, "He's a father now and should be a well-rounded family man." She laughed; so did Nan and Dave. In fact, the chicken was undercooked, half of it left in the two platters.

On their way back, Pingping was unhappy and wouldn't speak to Nan. She had often complained that Nan would leave her unaccompanied whenever they went to a party. This time he had done that again, not staying with her for a single minute. She shouldn't have gone to the Mitchells' today. She simply didn't like some of Hailee's godparents. Nan knew why his wife was fuming, so he remained quiet.

The next morning, Pingping dropped in on Janet at the jewelry store on her way to work. When Janet asked her if she had enjoyed the party the night before, Pingping said, "Not really. I like Christine, but to be honest, I don't like Kim and Charlie. They're rude to me, like afraida me or something."

Janet smiled quizzically. Pingping pressed on, "What? I'm never nasty to them."

"You know, Kim is vulnerable. Charlie has been her boyfriend for almost two years, and she cannot afford to lose him."

"Crazy. How can she think I want her boyfriend, that chubby Charlie? I have Nan, he's already more than I can handle. One more man will kill me."

Janet stowed away a box of assorted beads on the shelf, turned back, and said, "A few years ago Kim lost her boyfriend to a Japanese girl, so she must've feared you might do the same to her."

"She's sick."

"Come on, Pingping, you don't know how pretty you are. You can easily bewitch a lot of men. In fact, after you left yesterday, both Kim and Charlie said you and Nan were a lovely couple. Kim was really relieved to know you were married." Janet tittered, rubbing her nose with the back of her hand. "Have you heard the expression 'yellow fever'?"

"Yes. A kinda disease?"

"Yeah, you're right. It also means that a lot of men are crazy about Asian women. Believe me, if you weren't married, you could have lots of dates."

"I don't want to date man, I want marriage. Nobody, only Nan want to marry me."

•

After Pingping left, Janet thought about their conversation, amused by her friend's innocence. She often talked with Dave about Pingping and Nan, knowing they'd had marital trouble all along. Dave would say Nan was a lucky man who didn't seem to know how to appreciate his luck. What amazed the Mitchells was that Nan and Pingping, in spite of their rocky marriage, seldom quarreled and wouldn't have extramarital affairs, as if both were content with the situation and would make no effort to improve it. Janet once urged Pingping to take Nan to a marriage counselor, but her friend refused, saying, "We don't need shrink." Probably thanks to the hard work at the restaurant, neither Pingping nor Nan had the time and energy to look for another lover. Also, their son kept their hands full and held them together.

More amazing was that the Wus always shared everything—they had the same bank accounts and paid all the bills together. Whatever they owned was under both names. In fact, Nan let Pingping handle all the money that went through the Gold Wok. By contrast, Janet and Dave each had personal bank accounts and each would contribute $3,000 a month to their joint account, from which all their household expenses, including the mortgage and dining out, were drawn. On holidays and birthdays, they'd buy each other presents paid out of the givers' own pockets. Janet noticed that when Pingping bought clothes or shoes for her family, she'd get the same kind for both Nan and Taotao, as if Nan were just another child of hers. In addition, the Wus never got presents from each other. Once, on Pingping's birthday, Janet asked her why, and her friend said, "I don't need gift from Nan. He spend my money if he buy anything. If I buy something for him, I spend his money."

Janet could see the logic of those words and was even more fascinated by their marital state, which seemed quite stable despite Pingping's denying that Nan loved her. Aren't passion and sex essential parts of the married life? Can a marriage last without those basic ingredients? Sometimes Janet raised those questions to herself and couldn't answer them, unable to imagine living with Dave without the desire to possess him and without deep love for him. She was sure that if Dave hadn't loved her, he could definitely have started an affair with another woman, and then their marriage would disintegrate. But in the Wus' case, Pingping and Nan seemed in harmony, and neither was really bothered by the absence of passion in their marriage. On the other hand, Pingping had admitted to Janet that she and Nan did make love from time to time, and that the longer they lived together, the more comfortable she felt with Nan in bed. Strange. Maybe they did love each other, but in their own peculiar way.

18

NAN was peeling ginger while watching CNN. The TV, hung up in a corner behind the counter, had tiny refulgent spots on its screen. As the camera shifted to a street crowded with Asian faces, the anchorwoman with kohl-rimmed eyes said, "A Chinese dissident was arrested yesterday afternoon in Beijing. Mr. Bao Yuan, an exiled artist living in New York City, returned to China last week with the intention of publishing a literary magazine in his homeland. The charge is still unclear, but our CNN source reports that he's accused of the crime of sabotage . . ."

Nan was flabbergasted and stopped the peeler in his hand, his eyes fixed on the screen. He was eager to see Bao's face, but it never appeared. Instead, a scene that didn't directly bear on his apprehension emerged: a group of policemen frog-marched four handcuffed criminals toward a six-wheeled truck, whose back was canvased, as if they were heading for an execution ground.

At once Bao became the topic at the restaurant, though neither Pingping nor Niyan had ever met him. Nan told them how he had lived off Wendy and how she had called in her brother, who threw Bao out of her house. They all felt that Bao might have planned to get arrested for the sake of publicity; otherwise only a fool would have run the risk of sneaking back into China, where the police were awaiting him. Shubo stopped by on his way to work and left a copy of *World Journal* for Nan, saying Bao Yuan must have been out of his mind. He had to hurry to Grand Buddha and couldn't stay to join them in their conversation. Before Nan could tease him, saying Shubo's unshaven face brought to mind a koala today, his friend was already outside, striding away toward his car. Shubo's bald patch was more eye-catching when viewed from behind.

Nan opened the newspaper. The front page listed Bao's arrest as a major piece of news. On the third page was a long article about the incident, entitled "China's New Human Rights Violation." Together with the writing was Bao's photo, in which he wore a sardonic grin as if trying hard to fight down a wild laugh. The article reported that he had taken with him a hundred copies of New Lines and intended to distribute them in China. He also wanted to explore the possibility of publishing the journal on the mainland, but before he could find a business partner, the police seized him and confiscated all the copies of the journal. Rumor had it that the authorities were going to put him on trial, which Nan doubted would ever take place, because it might raise more international uproar. He was sure Bao already had a green card, so it would be difficult for the government to imprison him like a regular Chinese citizen. More troublesome for the authorities, the dissident communities in major U.S. cities were already on the move, launching protests and staging condemnations. The article stated that a group of freedom activists in New York and Washington, D.C., had started collecting signatures and appealed to some U.S. congressmen to intervene on Bao's behalf.

Nan talked with Dick on the phone about Bao's trouble. Dick chuckled and said, "I've heard about it. He's famous now, and even my colleagues in Asian Studies have been talking about his bravery."

"What? Zey believe he's brave?" asked Nan.

"Sure, how could they think otherwise?"

"He might have meant to attract attention."

"Probably. Still, it takes a lot of guts to smuggle the journal into China personally, don't you think?"

"I guess all zer copies must have been back issues. Zer journal was dead long ago, you know zat."

"Maybe he meant to resurrect it in China."

"Well, I'm not sure."

"Jeez, Nan, you're too cynical. Come to think of it, the guy might do many years behind bars just because he believes in free speech and free press."

"It's not zat simple. I don't feel he'll become a prisoner of conscience."

"What makes you think that way?"

Nan couldn't explain it in detail on the phone, so he suggested they meet and talk about it. Dick was busy going through his copy-edited poetry manuscript, which he had to send back to his editor that weekend, so he couldn't come until the following Wednesday.

19

WHEN Dick came to the Gold Wok on Wednesday afternoon, Bao had just been released and expelled from China. It was reported that some in the U.S. Congress had pressured the Chinese government for his release. Nan felt vindicated and said to his friend, "See, I told you he wouldn't be in jail for long."

"I don't get it. Why wouldn't they sentence him to a prison term?" Dick shook his chin, on which sweat was beading.

"Zat would make him more famous," said Nan.

"I guess now he has quite a bit of material for a book."

"He was writing a memoir when I worked for him in New York."

"I know. I saw some chapters of it in translation. Utterly atrocious. I told him to scrap the whole thing and start over."

"Maybe he has finished it." Nan wanted to say that perhaps Bao could easily find a publisher now, but he checked himself.

Out of his back pocket Dick pulled a mock cover of his new book. It was a piece of glossy paper, fourteen by ten inches and divided down the middle, the right half red and the left half white. Two large handwritten words stood in the center of the right-hand side, *Unexpected Gifts,* above which was the author's name, "Dick Harrison," and below which was a basket of fruit: apples, pears, tomatoes, grapes. The opposite half of the paper bore some words of praise for Dick's other books and a blurb on this volume by Sam Fisher, commending Dick for "his unerring ear." Nan disliked the cover on the whole, but was impressed by the fruits embodying the gifts.

"How do you like this cover?" Dick asked.

"To tell zer truth, I don't like zer crimson, too loud, like a cover of a revolutionary book."

"The color's fine. Red is eye-catching and will help it sell better."

Dick's reply surprised Nan, who had never thought that a poet would be so concerned about the sales of his book. In spite of his own hard effort to make money, when it came to poetry Nan couldn't imagine it as a commodity. He didn't know how to say this to his friend, so he pointed at the wicker basket on the cover, saying, "Zese fruits look nice."

"I hate it!" said Dick.

"How come?"

"It's so banal. Why can't they have a basket of more peculiar things, like squash, or pinecones, or trout, or pheasants? I quarreled with the publisher this morning before I went to class. Gosh, he's impossible."

"Are they going to change zis?"

"I don't know. The guy said it was too late. I told him it wasn't too late because they just started working on this book. We yelled at each other on the phone. He's a schmuck, but he's my publisher. Maybe I shouldn't have had the altercation with him."

"A mediocre cahver shouldn't be a big deal. People will judge zer book by its content."

"I want everything to be perfect."

Nan said no more. He felt Dick had overreacted to the cover, trite though it might be. Dick told Nan that the first run of this volume would be one thousand and that if all the copies were sold, the book would be a success. Nan was surprised by the small number and couldn't figure out why Dick was so eager to sell the book if he could hardly make any money from the sale—the publisher had agreed to pay him merely five percent of the list price for royalties. Dick mentioned that some journals might write about *Unexpected Gifts*. If the reviews were positive, they'd bolster the sale of the book.

"Yes, a favorable reception is more important," Nan said.

"That's true," agreed Dick. "Actually, I care more about the reviews than about the sale."

"Zat's a right attitude. Poetry isn't profitable anyhow." Despite saying that, Nan didn't fully understand Dick's reasons. Neither did he know that Dick could make money indirectly if the book was well received, because his school would give him a bigger raise and he'd get invited more often to read and conduct writing seminars at colleges and writers' conferences.

While the two friends chatted away, Pingping and Niyan were wrapping wontons in a corner. Dick was the only customer in the room, so Nan could sit with him for a while before business picked up.

20

DICK had continued his weekend meditation with the Buddhist group at a temple north of Emory. He tried to persuade Nan to join him, saying it would alleviate stress and make him peaceful. Nan wondered why Dick needed peace of mind if he wanted to write poetry. Didn't the poet need strong creative impulses? Wasn't it true that the more explosive his emotions were, the more powerful his poems would be? Yet out of curiosity Nan went to see the Buddhist group one Sunday morning.

Their temple was just two long ranch houses in a large wooded yard. It had been built recently, and each house was surrounded by a veranda and had more than a dozen doors. The place reminded Nan of a motel, with a large paved parking lot in the front and a few flower beds grown with clematis, jasmine, and chrysanthemums. Except for some tiny paper lanterns hanging under the eaves, nothing seemed to differentiate this temple from a family-run motel. Dick took Nan to the second house, but on the way there, they came upon the group they meant to join. The disciples were all sitting cross-legged in the lotus position on the expanse of grass in between the two houses. About half of them were locals, but there were four Tibetan men among them, all with leathery but energetic faces. It was a splendid fall day, warm and dry without a single fly or midge in the air. The stalwart Nepalese master, wrapped in a mud-colored robe, waved at Dick and Nan and nodded smilingly. He had a wattled chin and prominent eyes, which broadened some when he smiled. He was sitting on a round cornhusk cushion, and beside him on the grass was a cassette player. In front of him sat a small brass pot containing sand, wherein were planted sticks of incense, sending up coils of smoke.

Dick and Nan sat down beside a young woman in a sweater vest and white slacks. Another few people arrived. When everyone was seated on a hempen hassock provided by the temple, the master began to speak about the day's exercise. His English was nasal and undulating, which made it hard for Nan to make out every word, but he could follow the drift of what the man was saying. He was talking about meditation as a way to cleanse one's mind. "In fact," the master said, "our minds are in a state of chaos before we make effort to improve them. An unimproved mind contains a mixture of many things, benign and destructive, base and noble, good and evil. We all know that a person has biological genes, but the truth is that one also has cultural genes and spiritual genes. All these inherited elements affect one's inner life . . ."

Nan marveled at the master's expanded notion of the genes. The man must be quite learned, he decided. Nan glanced at the white woman sitting beside him, her face smiling with innocence and joy. "In our exercise today," the master went on, "we shall try to empty our minds and hearts. Forget everything and try not to feel any emotion, neither happiness nor sadness. Above all, forget yourself and who you are. In this way we can sink deep into our origins, experience total emptiness, and achieve genuine tranquillity."

A pair of cymbals started tinkling, and then from the cassette player came the slow, gentle, aerial music played on the bamboo flute. The sound often subsided as if about to disappear, but it always swelled back. The master's voice turned inaudible, though his lips were still stirring. All the disciples, eyes shut, were breathing relaxedly with their hands on their laps, their palms upward. Nan followed suit. But he closed his eyes only halfway and felt as if the master were levitating.

Unlike the others, Nan couldn't concentrate on his breathing. He opened his eyes and looked around. Every face seemed carefree and serene, and many of them wore a knowing, inward smile that looked a bit mysterious. Nan shut his eyes and tried to let himself be transported by the music; still he couldn't get close to the nirvana that seemed to be admitting the others. His thoughts couldn't help but wander. He wondered if he should continue to write in Chinese. He had mailed out three poems to a literary journal in Taiwan two months earlier, but so far he hadn't heard from it. As for the magazines in mainland China, he wouldn't send them his work anymore after an editor had once written back and asked him to delete several lines that were too sensitive politically. Nan hadn't responded to that, so the poem had never seen print. Maybe he should translate some of his poems into English and try his luck with small magazines in America. Probably the miserable feelings that often surged in him originated from the fact that he couldn't see any possibility of publishing in Chinese, let alone establishing himself as a poet here. It was as if in front of him stood a stone wall inviting him to bump his head against it. If only he had come to America ten years earlier! Then he could definitely have given up his mother tongue and blazed his trail in English . . .

Somehow two ancient lines cropped up in his mind: "No prairie fire can burn the grass up / When the spring breeze blows, it will again sprout." Yes, he must have the spirit of the wild grass. However thick and impenetrable the wall before him, he must grow beneath it and even on it, like the invincible grass with blades that eventually would dislodge the rocks. This was the American spirit Whitman eulogized, wasn't it? Yes, definitely. He must figure out his own way of making poetry, and—

"All right, you can wake up now," said the master in an even voice.

All the people opened their eyes, their faces softened and their voices smaller. The master told them, "May you hold the peace in you. See you next Sunday."

When all in the group were on their feet, Dick asked Nan, "Well, what do you think?"

"I can see it works on everyone except me."

Dick laughed and slapped his back. "Come, let me introduce you to a few friends."

Nan looked at his wristwatch and said, "I have to go now. It's already past eleven." The Gold Wok opened at twelve noon on Sundays, so he had to rush back.

Dick didn't insist but asked Nan to join him here the next Sunday. Nan said he'd try his best. Actually, he wasn't interested in meditation. He wouldn't join the group again.

21

FINALLY Gerald's house was put up for auction, TO BE SOLD ON PREMISES as the sign on the lawn announced. For weeks people would stop by to look at the property, and when they saw the Wus in the front yard, they'd ask them about the neighborhood and the former owner of the home. Although empty of all the junk at last, the house looked more dilapidated than before. A pipe had burst in the basement and flooded a good part of the floor; the unfinished glassed-in porch looked like a boat cut in half, displaying a dark, gaping cabin. Worse yet, two of the windows had smashed panes now—someone had thrown rocks into the house. The neighbors all looked forward to the auction, which had been postponed once already.

One Saturday morning Alan said to Nan about the house, "I won't buy it unless it's under ten grand."

"Eef you can fix it and sell it to someone, you can make a lawt of money," said Nan.

"But the renovation will cost a fortune. Too many things have to be replaced." Alan slapped his thigh as if an insect had gotten into his pant leg, and his other hand was holding a tiny spade with which he dug dandelions out of his lawn.

Nan went on, "My friend Shubo may be interested in buying it, but he doesn't know how to repair a house."

"Who's your friend?"

"You know zer waitress at my restaurant?"

"Yes, she's a pretty gal." Alan swatted a mosquito that had landed on his sinewy neck.

"Shubo is her hahsband. Zey live outside Lawrenceville and want to move closer."

"I think I met the guy. Well, tell him he's not welcome." Alan's tone was rather casual, but he seemed to speak accidentally on purpose.

Nan was taken aback. "Why?"

"I like you and Pingping, to be frank, and you're good neighbors. But there're too many Chinese in this neighborhood already. We need diversity, don't we?"

"But we are probably zee only Chinese here."

"How about the big family across the lake?"

"Oh, they're Vietnamese." Nan remembered seeing seven or eight cars parked in the yard of that brick raised ranch the other day. He had also noticed two young Asian couples in this area, but he was sure they weren't Chinese.

Alan continued, "Mrs. Lodge, Fred, Terry, and Nate, we all talked about this. We don't want this subdivision to become a Chinatown."

Nan was scandalized but didn't know how to argue with him. He managed to say, "All right, I will tell Shubo what you said. You want to keep Chinese as minority here, but don't you sink our neighborhood should be a melting pot?"

"But some people are not meltable."

"Maybe the pot is not big enough. Make it a cauldron, zen everybody can melt in it, yourself included."

They both laughed. Alan said, "To be honest, the worst-case scenario is that a slumlord will buy this house, fix it up, and rent it out. That'll cause a lot of trouble to our neighborhood."

"See, my friend will be a mahch better choice."

"Sure, compared with a slumlord."

The thought flashed through Nan's mind that some people in the neighborhood had taken his family to be interlopers all along and probably would continue to do so whether they were naturalized or not. When he passed Alan's words on to Shubo, his friend was so outraged that his eyes turned rhomboidal and his face nearly purple. The opposition from the neighborhood made Shubo all the more determined to bid for the house, even though he was uncertain how to renovate it and even though originally he and Niyan had worried that the property might depreciate in value because it was right next to the Wus'. He didn't know anyone in the house-repairing business and would have to use a contractor, who might rip him off. Worse still, it would be impossible for him to keep a close watch on the renovation because he'd have to bartend at Grand Buddha six days a week. All the same, his anger didn't abate, and the more he thought about Alan's words, the more resolved he was—he and his wife must enter into the neighborhood like a thorn stuck in those racists' flesh.

By now Niyan had befriended Janet, so Janet volunteered to accompany her and Shubo to the sale on November 6, which they all expected would be something like a Dutch auction. Shubo had drawn a certified check for $15,000 from the bank, as the flyer had indicated would be needed in order to seal the bargain on the spot. Nan urged the couple to be cool-headed about this matter, advising that they should treat it just as a regular business deal. After exchanging views, everybody agreed that Shubo and Niyan should pay no more than $40,000 for the house. If it went higher than that, they should forget it.

To everybody's amazement, the auction was such a quiet affair that few people in the neighborhood even noticed it. Seven real estate brokers showed up and Shubo was the only nonprofessional bidder among them. There was no chair for anyone to sit on, and the auctioneer, a tall man from Southtrust Bank, didn't shout out any offer from the bidders; neither did anyone hold a paddle with a number printed on it. Besides owing a mortgage of $65,000, Gerald hadn't paid real estate tax and several other bills for years. By any means the bank, the town, the utility companies, and even a used-car dealer had to recover the arrears, so the starting price for the property was $81,000. Shubo, Niyan, and Janet were dumbfounded, just standing there and watching others outbid one another. There were no raised voices, as if they all were at a coffee break from a meeting, making small talk. A man with a marzipan face was sucking a large Havana cigar the whole time and just flashed his fingers at the auctioneer without speaking. Two of the brokers quit at $90,000, but they showed no emotion, as if tired of the whole thing.

The final bid was $93,000, and the house went to a young Hispanic real estate broker. Shubo and Niyan returned to the Gold Wok, still in disbelief. Niyan told the Wus the purchasing price. Everybody was surprised and couldn't imagine that after paying that amount someone could still make a profit from the house. Shubo kept shaking his round chin and said, "*Without money you can't fight racism in America.*"

"*Just as you have to be rich enough to love your country,*" added Nan.

Like their neighbors, the Wus also feared that the buyer of the house might be a slumlord; otherwise, who would pay that kind of price for the property? Maybe the broker meant to convert it into a two-family house and rent it out so that he could make a larger profit. The more people talked about this, the more agitated they became.

To the Wus' bewilderment, for a whole winter the buyer left the house untouched. Though the season was less convenient for construction work, people in Georgia don't stop building or repairing homes in the wintertime. The new owner, who was said to intend to fix up the house and then sell it, seemed to have forgotten the property and didn't even come and look at it again until the next spring.

In mid-March the renovation finally started. A group of Mexican workers washed the walls and the roof, painted the doors and windows, and spread grass seeds into the loosened dirt of the lawn. They dismantled the glass porch and built a new deck. A real mailbox was erected at the end of the front yard. Despite the bright appearance of the renovated house, Nan knew that all the inner damages were covered up. The roof should have been replaced, as well as some of the pipes inside. Within two weeks, a sign was planted in the yard with a sheaf of flyers sheathed in a plastic pocket attached to the board. The asking price was $123,000, which pleased Nan and Pingping in a way, because it indicated that their own home must have appreciated considerably in value. Still, they couldn't help wondering who would pay that kind of money for such a house.

Their anxiety proved unjustified. A month later, Judith Goodman, a middle-aged single woman, bought it. She was an optician at the Gwinnett Mall and liked the quiet neighborhood and the lake. Then her mother, previously living down in St. Petersburg, Florida, moved in with her. Many people in the subdivision were relieved to see the Goodmans here. Again, Mrs. Lodge placed a vase of flowers, tulips this time, on their welcome mat the day after they moved in.

PART SIX

1

FOR ANOTHER YEAR Nan devoted himself to making money. The quality of his cooking was so good and the prices so affordable that the *Gwinnett Gazette* wrote about the Gold Wok, praising it as "the best bargain." Sometimes customers arrived groups and Niyan couldn't wait on so many of them, so Shubo, if available, would come in to help. The Wus had thought of hiring another waitress but decided not to, fearing business might flag again.

In the meantime, Pingping had cut as many household expenses as possible so as to pay off the mortgage. In the winter, during the day she wouldn't turn on the heat to warm the whole house and instead put a column radiator in the dining room, where Taotao did his homework. In the summer she shut off the wall registers in the living room and her own bedroom so that the air-conditioning would start up less frequently. She cooked as rarely as possible at home. If Taotao didn't go to the restaurant for dinner, she'd bring back something for him. He was allowed to stay home in the evenings, but he mustn't use his computer for more than one hour a day. Pingping also saved on taxes. She even filed their son as a part-time employee (the boy did do some kitchen chores) and claimed he had earned two thousand dollars the past year. Nan often joked with his wife, saying, *"I'm a fork that rakes in money while you're a box that holds money. It doesn't matter much if the fork loses a tine, but it will be a disaster if the box has a hole."*

She would say, *"I scrimp and save for you, not for myself. Don't make fun of me."* That was true; she had never bought a single item of new clothing for herself.

In December 1995, they sent Mr. Wolfe the final big check and asked for the title to their house, which the old man mailed them two weeks later. At last they had put their feet on the ground they could call their own. Confidence surged in Nan, who had finally earned the security for his family, and a kind of elation possessed him for a month or so. Now, even if the restaurant went under, his family would be safely sheltered. As long as he did some work, he could easily bring food home. This is freedom, he reasoned: not owing anybody a penny and having no fear of being fired.

But his joy was short-lived. Somehow he was puzzled by the home ownership, which he hadn't expected to come true in less than five years. He remembered *A House for Mr. Biswas* and still could feel for the protagonist, a small man whose lifetime struggle was to have his own roof. But here in Georgia, where land was cheap and realty in a buyer's market, he hadn't had a prolonged struggle for owning a home at all. In a way he wished this miracle had taken place in Boston or San Francisco or New York City, where one could claim success by owning a house. But here most people who worked hard could eventually become a home owner. Then his former neighbor Gerald came to mind, reminding him that there were a lot of losers even in Georgia and that he ought to be grateful.

Nevertheless, as time went by, a kind of disappointment sank into his heart. The struggle had ended so soon that he felt as though the whole notion of the American dream was shoddy, a hoax. In his mind he wrestled with the bewilderment that had begun to enervate him and made him work less hard than before. He tried to convince himself that the house was really theirs, and so were the van and the restaurant, that the realized dream wasn't merely an empty promise. If his family hadn't come to America, he couldn't have imagined owning these things, not in his wildest expectations. He was baffled, wondering what was wrong with him. Why couldn't he be as happy as his wife? Why couldn't he enjoy the fruits of their hard labor? He should feel successful. But somehow the success didn't mean as much to him as it should.

Gradually he figured out what had happened—in just a few years he'd gone through the journey that often took most immigrants a whole lifetime. Usually the first generation drudged to feed and shelter themselves and their families, and toward the end of their lives they might own a house or an apartment, and if they were more fortunate, a business. Their children, having grown on the bases the parents had built, would have different kinds of dreams and ambitions, going to college and becoming professionals and "real Americans." Most of them wouldn't repeat their parents' lives. In other words, the first generation was meant to be wasted, or sacrificed, for its children, like manure used to enrich the soil so that new seeds could sprout and grow.

But Nan was merely forty, and still had many years of life ahead. What should he do next? Work hard to acquire another business? Absolutely not. Of that he was certain. He didn't want to die a successful businessman.

Nan remembered the credo he had repeated to Danning six years before: Do something moneyed people cannot do. The memory occasioned a sudden pang in his heart. It seemed that he had forgotten his goal and gotten lost in making money. Why hadn't he devoted himself to writing poetry? Instead, all these years he had been working like a brainless machine. He tried to convince himself that this "detour" might be a necessary procedure, a step toward some achievement of higher order, since logically speaking, only after you were fed and sheltered could you mull over ideas and enjoy the leisure needed for creating arts. Yet his disappointment wouldn't abate, its heaviness weighing down his mind.

He couldn't help fulminating against himself mentally. "You've been living like a worm and exist only in the flesh. You're just a channel of food, a walking corpse." He was so irascible these days that his wife and son again avoided eating with him at the same table.

2

SHUBO often came in to give Nan *World Journal* after he himself had read it. If the restaurant wasn't busy, the two of them would chat at length. One afternoon, Nan told his friend that he should have spent more time writing poetry, Shubo shook his balding head and said, *"You're too impractical."*

"Why should I be practical?" countered Nan. *"The world has been created by impractical people."*

"I mean, you shouldn't bite off more than you can chew."

"If you speak Chinese, you don't need to mix in English idioms. When did you learn that expression, yesterday?" Nan felt his temper rising.

"See, that's exactly your problem," Shubo said, and took a swallow of oolong tea.

"What are you getting at?"

"You're impatient and always talk and act as if your bottom were on fire."

Nan hated that expression and asked, *"What do you mean by 'impatient'?"*

"We're new here and cannot go a million miles in one life. Writing poetry can be a profession only for your grandchildren. For example, I don't think Taotao will write poetry. You want him to study science to earn a meal ticket, don't you?"

"Maybe, but that has nothing to do with my life."

"Forget about your life. You're supposed to sacrifice yourself for your children, who are an extension of your life and who will do the same for their children. That's how we Chinese survive and multiply—each generation lives for the next."

"That's why children must be filial to their parents, isn't it?"

"Yes."

"Guess what, I don't buy into that crap. Why should I sacrifice myself? I'm done sacrificing—I've had enough. Besides, 'sacrifice' is just an excuse for our cowardice and laziness. My son has his life and I must have mine." Nan wanted to remind Shubo that he didn't even have a child and was unqualified to talk about parental sacrifice, but he held back.

"Nan, you're too impatient. In your life span you want go through the course of three generations. You'll be better off if you scale down your ambition. If you really want to write, do it in Chinese. That will be more reasonable."

"I don't want to be reasonable," sneered Nan. "We're too often emasculated by reason and pragmatism."

"We shouldn't continue talking like this, going in circles. All I'm saying is that one must be financially secure first and then think about making arts or writing books. In other words, it takes generations for the immigrants to outgrow the material stage."

"That's a philistine mentality," said Nan.

"No, it's the American way. Remember, Ben Franklin's father forbade his son to be a poet, saying most verse makers were just beggars?"

"Then Franklin's dad was a major American philistine," Nan said crossly, his long eyes glinting. "I don't believe artists starve in America. I've met many of them. They can be poor and wretched, but they don't starve. Take Dick Harrison for example, he's living a good life by being a poet."

"Nan, you're too stubborn. Dick's great-grandparents came to the States last century. Like I said, your grandchildren will be able to live Dick's kind of life, but that's not for us."

"So we have to compromise?"

"Do we have another choice?"

Niyan came over and put their checkbook in front of her husband, who was off work today. Their air conditioner had been struck by lightning the night before, and a technician was scheduled to come and look at it at three o'clock. Shubo rose and stretched up his arms, then rubbed the small of his back with both hands.

He'd suffered a backache recently, having to do a ten-hour shift six days a week at Grand Buddha. *"We'll talk more about this next time,"* he told Nan, and thrust the checkbook into his pocket, ready to leave.

Nan grimaced without speaking.

3

NAN decided to write poetry again. It seemed he couldn't get anywhere if he continued writing in Chinese. Obscure and unpublished, he was completely isolated from the Chinese writers' community, which was centered in New York. In Toronto there was also a group of novelists who, though having emigrated, were still writing in their mother tongue and sending their works back to China for publication, but their manuscripts were often censored there or rejected on the grounds that the subject matter wasn't right. In Nan's case, it was clear that writing in Chinese would lead him to a dead end. Could he do it in English? The same old question again tormented him these days. He knew that to him Chinese meant the past and English the future, the identification with his son. He also understood that by adopting another language he might wander farther away from his Chinese heritage and have to endure more loneliness and run more risk; eventually he might have to estrange himself from his mother tongue, in which a writer of his situation, in fact all writers in the Chinese diaspora, would be marginalized. But to write poetry in English was like climbing a mountain with a summit he couldn't see or envision. It was very likely that he might mess up his life without getting anywhere. Still, was there another way if he was determined to write?

The following Thursday when Dick came for lunch, Nan asked his friend to give him a list of books of contemporary poetry in English that he should know. Without hesitation Dick wrote eleven titles on the notepad Nan had placed before him. They included:

Darker, Mark Strand
Scream! Sam Fisher
The Fortunate Traveller, Derek Walcott
Descending Figure, Louise Glück
The Book of the Body, Frank Bidart
An Explanation of America, Robert Pinsky
North, Seamus Heaney
Elsewhere, Linda Dewit
The Ether Dome and Other Poems, Allen Grossman
Dien Cai Dau, Yusef Komunyakaa
An Appointment in the Afternoon, Richard Harrison

"Thanks, thanks," Nan said. He tore off the sheet and folded it carefully. "I've made up my mind to write in English."

"Good. You've been dillydallying too long," Dick said.

"Do you sink I can make it eventually?"

"Depends on what you mean by 'make it.'"

"I mean whezzer I can become a decent poet in English eef I persevere."

"No doubt about that, Nan. You'll be a fine poet."

"I may also mess up my life."

"That's common. I've already ruined a good part of mine." Dick laughed and blinked.

"Why did you say zat?"

"My parents wanted me to be a lawyer. I even went to law school at Columbia for a year, then I quit. My dad was mad at me for wasting so much money. In my parents' eyes I was a loser."

"But you're a success now. You have an excellent jawb."

"I may lose it anytime. If Emory doesn't give me tenure, I don't know where I'll go. Look, you have your wife and kid and you have a home. That's already a success. I have nothing but myself. Most poets in America are worse off than I am. I knew a middle-aged poet who died of pneumonia because he had no health insurance and couldn't go to the doctor when he was ill. To tell the truth, in a way you're lucky, Nan. Whatever happens to you, your family will be with you and love you. To top it all, you have your own home and business, a solid base."

Dick's words surprised Nan. Never had he thought his family could play such a vital role in the writer's life he tried to imagine for himself. Indeed, even if he ruined himself totally, his wife and son would remain with him. Without question, to Dick he was a kind of success, at least domestically. This realization gave him some confidence, now that he knew he had little to lose. All he could do was try.

He drove to three local libraries and found seven of the eleven poetry books Dick had listed for him. To get the other four titles, he went to Borders at Gwinnett Mall and bought two of them. He also ordered Linda Dewit's *Elsewhere* at the bookstore. But they couldn't find Richard Harrison's *An Appointment in the Afternoon*. The young saleswoman searched in the computer, but to no avail. "Are you sure this is the right title?" she asked Nan, biting the corner of her mouth, beside which a pair of thin lines emerged. Nan wondered whether they were wrinkles or scars.

"Yes. Do you carry ozzer books by zis author?"

"No, I don't see any here." She kept her eyes on the monitor.

"Have you ever stocked zis title?"

"No, we haven't."

Nan didn't try further, since the nine poetry books already in his hands would occupy him for two or three months. Besides, he was sure that Dick had a copy he could borrow.

When Dick came to the Gold Wok the next time, Nan mentioned his inability to get hold of Richard Harrison's book. Dick reddened, lowering his eyes while slurping seaweed soup. "What's zer matter?" Nan asked. "Don't you have a volume of his poetry?"

"Of course I do. I wrote it."

"What? But your name is Dick, not Richard. Your new book has 'Dick Harrison' as zee author."

Dick laughed nervously, his face puckering a little. "You don't know Dick is a nickname for Richard."

"Oh, I really don't know. You mean it's like Bob for Robert or Bill for William?"

"Exactly. From now on I go by Dick for my author's name."

"My, I never thought you would be on zer list."

"Why? You think I'm unqualified?"

"No, I don't mean zat. We Chinese would never do that!"

"Do what?"

"To put down your own name on such a list. I didn't imagine it was you. Hey, I don't mean to hurt your feelings. I'm just telling zer truth."

"I'm not that fragile. But I have to assert myself, even to pat myself on the back. A lot of poets just write dreck, but still they have every-thing—fame, money, and women."

"So you write for those?" asked Nan, half joshingly.

"Why not? Poets are not saints. We have to make our way in the world too."

"But poetry seems useless to me."

"You have to take it as a matter of life or death if you want to write well," Dick said in earnest, and unconsciously put down his spoon.

Nan thought about his friend's words afterward, but he was uncon-vinced. He couldn't see how poetry could be used as a means of get-ting fortune and fame, much less women. In the Chinese tradition, poets often celebrated poverty, believing their art could improve and mature with hardship and impoverishment. On the other hand, Nan remembered that Wallace Stevens once said money could become poetry. Yet that statement was mainly about the time and energy the poet needed for writing; it didn't bear on the fortune and fame Dick had in mind. Nan didn't agree with his friend, and neither would he believe in the principle upheld by traditional Chinese poets who had ritualized poverty. He felt that too much hardship could dull a poet's sensibility and smother his talent, just as in his own case the hard work over the years had stunted his growth as a poet. Now he had to keep his mind alert and clear and find his way.

4

IN MARCH, Mrs. Lodge bought eight ducklings, each already more than half a foot long, and kept them in the lake. They grew rapidly and in two months looked like adult ducks, waddling about with heavy asses. When swimming in the green water, they looked blazingly white. Though they didn't fly away to other bodies of water, they took off occasionally, darting from one end of the lake to the other end and quacking gutturally. Because of their ability to fly, Nan often wondered whether they were a hybrid of some domestic and wild ducks. The eight of them always stayed together. When they paddled around, the largest drake would lead the flock, and together they resembled a miniature cruising fleet. Taotao called the head drake the bully, because the rascal would chase female ducks and even geese. If a goose was too large and too tall for it to tread, it would just sit on her back as she sailed around in the water, both of them shrieking like crazy.

One morning in May, Nan and Taotao returned from the supermarket with the Sunday *Atlanta Journal-Constitution*. The moment they got out of the car, the boy caught sight of the bully duck perching near the gate to the backyard and shuddering in silence. Taotao went up to it, but the drake wouldn't move or make any noise. He pushed it with his foot; still it wouldn't budge, trembling without pause. Nan came over too. They saw blood on its head and feathers. "He must have been injured," Nan thought aloud in English.

The boy ran into the house, flapping his hands above his waist like a pair of penguin flippers. He shouted, "Mom, we have the bully duck in our yard. He won't go away."

Mother and son came out together while Nan held up the drake and saw that it had been mangled by fishing lines and hooks, its tongue hanging out, slashed by a large fishhook that had gone through it from underneath. Several pieces of fishing line were twined around its neck, choking it. One of its wings had collapsed, unable to move. Stroking its feathers, Nan found another hook stuck in its good wing. He managed to dislodge this one and some other hooks, but he couldn't take off the one on its tongue, which, when he tried to remove it, hurt the duck more and made its mouth bleed again. The poor creature was so damaged that it couldn't make any noise.

Pingping cut the fishing lines with scissors, but they couldn't get rid of the fishhook without further injuring the drake's tongue. She went back into the house and returned with a pair of pliers, her apron pocket stuffed with a bottle and cotton balls. With both hands Nan severed the hook so that the barb wouldn't cut the tongue again when he pulled the shank out. The steel of the fishhook was so hard that it had even dented the edges of the pliers. "Open his mouth," Pingping said to Nan while taking an aspirin tablet out of her apron pocket.

Father and son pried the duck's bill apart. Pingping, who had worked on a poultry farm for two years back in China and knew how to treat sick chickens, broke the aspirin in half and inserted one piece into the drake's mouth. It swallowed the medicine, and she rubbed its throat to ensure that the aspirin sank into its craw. Next, with a pair of sticks she picked off the maggots from its wounds. Then she gingerly rubbed the gashes with a cotton ball soaked with hydrogen peroxide; the wounds kept foaming while the drake's legs twitched fitfully. After the treatment, Taotao and Nan carried the creature to the lakeside and released it. It paddled away listlessly, hardly able to keep its head above the water.

For the rest of the day, Nan and Pingping talked about the bully duck, which must have stayed in their yard for a whole night. The drake had been the strongest of the brood, but when it was injured, it had been left to die alone and none of the flock had accompanied it. All the other ducks perched in the shady bushes on the other shore, sleeping, feeding, and mating as usual. Once in a while they'd get into the water, frolicking or catching fish or insects. Their life wasn't in the least disrupted by their ex-leader's absence. Pingping sighed, *"It's just like human beings—when you're weak, you're left to die alone."*

To their amazement, two days later, the bully drake led the flock swimming in the lake again, its head raised high, and it quacked as lustily as before. Again it would chase female waterfowl. These ducks and the mallards were very fond of the Wus' backyard. They'd bask in the sun on the shore and lay eggs in the clumps of monkey grass. The lake couldn't sustain too many of them, so Pingping left only ten of the duck eggs in the grass to be hatched. She took the rest home and salted them in a jar of brine.

5

TAOTAO had been on a Scholars Bowl team, but his parents made him quit because he'd miss classes, having to travel frequently for the tournaments, and because when they stayed at a motel, two boys would share one bed, which Taotao disliked. Furthermore, he didn't learn much from the answers to the questions—to win, all you needed was a strong memory and quick response. Still, he was unhappy about leaving the team and often threw a fit at home, yelling at his father.

He wrote an essay about the injured drake for his English class and got an A for it. Mrs. Ashby, his teacher, put "Super!" on his homework, which pleased him and his parents. Nan also wrote about the incident, but he couldn't complete the poem, whose ending simply didn't work no matter how hard he tried. By chance Taotao saw a draft of the poem Nan had thrown away. Outraged, he told his father, "That's my story. You shouldn't steal from me."

His parents were stumped. Nan said, "W-what do you mean?"

"I wrote about the duck already. If you did the same, you committed plagiarism."

"What's that?" asked his mother.

"Stealing ozzers' ideas," Nan explained, then turned to his son. "It's our story. We all took part in rescuing zer duck. And I didn't use any of your ideas or sentences and my speaker is zer duck. How can you accuse me of plagiarism?"

"But I've already written about it. You can't use it again."

"Who says I can't?" Nan was losing his temper, his eyeballs throbbing.

"The law says."

"Give me a break! You're not a lawyer."

"Fuck you!" The boy dropped his cereal bowl on the dining table and stood up.

"Say that again!" Nan jumped to his feet and grabbed at his son. Then he stopped and withdrew his hand, just glaring at him.

Pingping intervened, "Taotao, you apologize to Daddy. You curse him first, you must apologize."

Ignoring her order, the boy hoisted his book bag over his shoulder and tore out the door for the bus stop. These days he was often annoyed by Nan, who would in secret search his drawers and book bag every two or three days to make sure he was drug-free, and who would read his e-mail messages whenever he forgot to shut off his account. How many times had he told him not to invade his privacy? But his father just wouldn't mend his ways, treating him as if he were a culprit on parole. What a stupid asshole.

As Taotao was striding away, his mother caught up with him. She grasped his upper arm and stopped him, saying, "You must apologize to Daddy."

"He started it. Ow! Don't break my humerus!"

"I don't care who start. You curse him, you apologize." She was still clutching his arm.

"No, I won't!"

"He's your father. In whole world, if you can find another man who is better to you than Daddy, you don't need apologize. If you cannot find such man, you must apologize to him."

Taotao looked at her with a knotted brow, then ambled back to the house. Yanking open the screen door, he shouted, "I'm sorry, Daddy, okay?"

"That's fine," said Nan.

•

Although the exchange with his son spoiled Nan's desire to work on his poem about the injured duck, he was amazed that during the whole altercation none of them had spoken a single Chinese word. He went out to the deck and swept away the pollen and dust, pleased he had contained his temper this time.

On occasion Taotao still showed animosity toward Nan. One sentence he often hurled at him was "You were never there." Nan knew what he meant—the boy still resented Nan's absence from his early childhood. Yet Nan would reply, "Who said I wasn't there? I was the first person who saw you coming out of your mahther. Your head appeared first, with sleek hair." That would exasperate his son more.

Without doubt, Taotao viewed Nan as a kind of rival in the household. Whenever possible, he'd strive to monopolize his mother's attention and love, interrupting Nan's conversations with Pingping or sitting between his parents, or pinning blame on Nan whenever something went awry. Nan told him to act his age. The boy was almost thirteen, five feet tall, but he wouldn't change. "You have Oedipus complex and may end up a mama's boy," Nan often told him. That would make matters worse. Enraged, Taotao would call him "douche bag." Nan didn't know this word, nor could he find it in his dictionaries. He assumed that it must be a slang neologism, too recent for lexicographers to pick up. He once asked his son how to spell it, but the boy wouldn't tell him.

Sometimes Nan wondered what it would have been like if he'd had a daughter instead of a son. Deep down, he'd have preferred a girl, who might have treated him with more affection and attachment, and who might have helped him more with the work at the restaurant—not like Taotao, who would feel ashamed of clearing tables in the presence of the kids he knew and would complain to his parents, "Haven't I been a servant boy long enough?" Nan wouldn't respond to that, though he felt Pingping had spoiled their son. If only they'd had a daughter.

6

IN THE SPRING of 1996 Pingping found herself pregnant. The expectation of a new arrival in the family agitated everyone. Taotao was furious and said his parents were outrageous. "I'm almost thirteen. Am I going to be an uncle of the baby?" he blustered.

Nan countered, "Once you go to college, we need anozzer child at home."

"I don't want any siblings."

Pingping remained silent. The boy seemed afraid that the new arrival would become the center of the family.

"Selfish brat," said his father.

"Shut the hell up!"

Nan throttled his impulse to yell back at his son. In fact, he was the only one in the family who was happy about Pingping's pregnancy, because he imagined that the baby might provide a new focus for his life. He wouldn't mind spending the rest of his years raising the child if it was a girl.

Unlike him, Pingping was frightened, for she was already forty and might not be able to give birth easily. Also, this wasn't like in China, where her parents, both doctors, could help her. Here she was alone and couldn't rely on Nan, who wasn't good at taking care of others. More worrisome, the medical expenses would be enormous since their health insurance covered only emergencies. What if she died in childbirth? Then Taotao would be motherless and Nan would be wretched too. There were so many risks to consider that she had gotten restless. She told Nan about her fear, but he replied, "*Don't worry. Everything will work out fine. We have some extra money now and can afford to raise another child.*"

An ultrasound at the Norcross Medical Center showed it was a healthy baby, though it was too early to find out its sex. Somehow both Nan and Pingping had no doubt that it was a girl. From a tiny black box like a camera a nurse let the Wus hear the baby's heartbeat, which raced rapidly like a bird flapping its wings. "Very strong," Nan said, beaming as thin creases grooved the skin under his eyes.

Stacy, the nurse, told them, "Actually, the pulse is rather shallow, but it will get stronger as the baby grows." Her chubby fingers kept pressing Pingping's belly, which hadn't bulged out yet. The baby was just two months old.

Despite paying $236 for the checkup, Nan was elated. During the following days he and Pingping began thinking what name they should give the baby. Whatever they came up with, Taotao would say it sounded silly. Ignoring the boy's grouchiness, Pingping and Nan settled on "May," which is phonetically identical with the Chinese characters *beauty* and *plum blossoms*. Indeed, such a name was commonplace, but the plainness might make the child easy to raise. Back in China, especially in the countryside, parents often purposely gave babies nondescript names, even calling them Doggy or Donkey or Dolly, or just Kiddo or Lassie, so that ghosts might not notice and snatch them away.

Gradually Taotao cooled down, willing to accept a sister as a new member of their family, though his mother was still anxious. Sometimes Pingping was an insomniac at night, tossing in bed and thinking about all the unpredictable things. What if the baby turns out to be retarded or has a congenital illness? I'm already forty—anything like that can happen. What if I die in childbirth? That'll destroy Taotao and devastate Nan—our family will collapse. I won't worry about Nan, who can get along without me. If I'm dead, he might find another woman soon and might even go back to China to look for Beina. Although he says he's too tired to love anyone, I know him better than he knows himself—he could forget me and marry another woman soon after I'm gone. But I wouldn't begrudge him that. He deserves to go on with his life, to form a new family. What I cannot set my mind at ease about is that Taotao will be motherless. Nan loves him, I'm sure, but he doesn't know how to take care of a child. Not to mention the baby, who will need nursing and looking after. Nan can be a good provider but can't be a true family man. He was born to be a writer and scholar, though he can be neither here. That's what makes him angry all the time. If only my parents were here! They could help me figure things out and make arrangements. With them around I wouldn't mind having two more babies. I love children; so does Nan. We should've had a large family. That would make him happy, and with a girl baby he'll definitely try to be a good, indulgent father. Well, I'm not so sure. It seems like he can't live without making himself and others suffer. Still, I love him. He's a good man for all his shortcomings, and he can't wait to see the new baby. Never is he worried about the difficulties I might get into. Always absentminded like that. You may be able to remove a mountain, but you can't change a man's nature. Stop thinking so many negative thoughts. Get some sleep. Tomorrow is Monday, and there'll be a lot of work for the buffet.

In the morning Pingping's face would be sickly and bloated. She also retched a lot, convulsing with the dry heaves. There were many things her stomach wouldn't digest, such as cheese, tofu, spinach, fish, chicken. Yet she got hungry so frequently that she ate seven or eight meals a day. "This baby is a monster," she kept saying.

Nan tried to calm her down. He wouldn't let her do any heavy work in the restaurant. All of a sudden his life seemed to have a purpose, a center, and he felt invigorated. He was grateful for a second opportunity, because he hadn't helped his wife much in raising Taotao. This time he was determined to be a better father.

7

NAN wrote four short poems in English. He was pleased with them and wondered if he should show them to Dick. He decided not to for the time being; instead, he mailed them to Sam Fisher and Edward Neary, since both poets had told him to send them his work. He hoped they would comment on his poems and ideally help him publish one or two.

A few months earlier Dick had suggested that Nan write a memoir. Nan was bemused by the idea and shook his head, saying he had no such intention and couldn't imagine being a memoirist. To him, such a book should be written by someone who had experienced something extraordinary. But Dick said, "Your life can be a very interesting subject according to what I've heard." Still, Nan didn't want to attempt that. Besides, a book of prose would demand a lot of the author—a long-lasting concentration and total immersion in the writing. It meant he'd have to live as a full-time writer for a year or two, a luxury he couldn't afford. He'd better focus on poetry, which mainly needed short bursts of energy.

Now that the poems had been mailed out, he expected to hear from the two poets any day. But three weeks passed without a word from them. He was puzzled, wondering if he should write to them again, but his good sense got the better of him, so he waited patiently.

One afternoon Dick arrived at the Gold Wok with a sullen face and puffy eyes. He looked a few years older than the cheerful Dick that Nan had last seen. Nan drew up a chair upholstered with red vinyl and sat down at the table across from his friend. "What's eating you?" he asked, using the expression he had just learned from Shubo.

Dick uttered a long sigh. "My publisher is eating me. Oh, help!" His face contorted as he suddenly began sobbing. He stretched out his hand and held Nan's forearm as though intending to stand up but unable to. Surprised, Nan handed him a paper napkin, which Dick took and used to blow his nose.

"They want you to sell more books?" asked Nan a moment later.

"No. They refused to publish *Unexpected Gifts*."

"Why? I wondered what happened to zer book. It should have come out long ago."

"First they postponed its publication, then they decided not to do it at all."

"How come?"

"They said my last book hadn't reached the sales standard. That's just an excuse. I know some books they published have done much worse than mine. They just wanted to get rid of me, probably because I quarreled with them about that cover."

"Don't you have a contract?"

"I signed the contract, but they've never sent me the cosigned copy. So the contract isn't valid."

"Zat's awful!" Despite saying that, Nan didn't fully understand why his friend was so heartbroken. He asked again, "Didn't they already cawpyedit it?"

"Yes, but the publisher changed his mind. I'm through, Nan. I'll never recover from this blow."

"Don't be so pessimistic. You can always look for anozzer publisher, can't you?"

"You don't get it, Nan. Once you've lost your publisher, you're ruined."

"How so?"

"You belong to a different category of poets now and few publishers will take your work seriously. It's like you've become homeless."

"There's no room for negotiation?"

"With whom?"

"Zer publisher."

"No. The series editor was a sorry poet whose book I once reviewed negatively, because he'd lifted lines from others' poems. This made the whole thing worse. I knew that snot might stab me in the back, but I didn't expect he and the publisher would connive to destroy me. This got me right here." He pointed at his heart. By now he had stopped sobbing, though his eyes were still misty.

Still baffled, Nan said, "Zis shouldn't be zee end of the world. As long as you keep trying, there will be a way to get your book pahblished."

"You've no idea how the poetry world works. It will take me at least half a year to find another press willing to consider the manuscript, if I'm lucky. This winter I'll be up for the pretenure review. If I don't have a book accepted soon, Emory might fire me. If that happens, I'll be half dead as a poet and will have to start my career all over again."

At last Nan realized the enormity of his friend's setback. He asked, "Did zer series editor know zis would damage your career so much?"

"Of course he knew. He must be gloating over my suffering. Poets can be more vicious than politicians."

"It's disgusting."

"I may have to file for Chapter Eleven soon."

"You mean zer bookstore in Decatur? How can Chapter Eleven help you?"

Dick broke out laughing, his eyes suddenly filled with sparkling tears. His laughter perplexed Nan. Dick explained, "To file for Chapter Eleven means to declare bankruptcy. You're such a funny guy, Nan."

"I see. But you reelly haven't lawst any capital. No need for Chapter Eleven. Just try and wait."

"Yes, I'm not dead yet." Dick thumped the table. "I have to pull myself together and put up a fight. I'll start looking for a new publisher right away."

Since it wasn't the busy hour yet, Nan asked Pingping to cook some noodles for Dick and himself. Together the two friends had a late lunch, with a plate of roast duck and Kung Pao Chicken between them. Dick cheered up a little as he was eating. He said he was going to ask Sam Fisher to help him. He had to get his manuscript accepted by the end of the year so that he could become ready for the pretenure review. Nan assured him that he'd definitely find a new publisher.

Dick's setback upset Nan. It offered him a glimpse of the strife in the poetry world. If Dick was this vulnerable, what about a budding poet like Nan himself, unconnected and unpublished? Still, uncertainty and lack of luck shouldn't be the excuse for him not to try. He must try and try harder.

Despite his tough-mindedness, he actually avoided using any spare moment to write, because his wife was pregnant and needed care. For several weeks he fussed over Pingping so much, even patting her belly or hooking his arm around her in the presence of others, that at times she'd shoo him away, though whenever he wanted to kiss her she'd tilt her face for him to peck.

8

PINGPING was happy with Nan's sudden transformation into a devoted husband. She reveled in his attention and small loving gestures. He loved their baby girl so much that he often smiled for no apparent reason, as if relishing something secret. She was still unsure if he loved her, but with this new baby she'd be able to keep him occupied for many years. She knew he might still miss Beina even though he wouldn't let on about it. A few days ago she had looked through some drafts of his poems, some of which were evidently addressed to his first love. She was still hurt by his feelings for that coldhearted woman, who had probably forgotten him long ago. Sometimes Pingping couldn't help but believe that Nan just imagined a lover in order to fill his soul with sorrow so that he could suffer more.

These days she felt out of sorts, her body lacking strength and her mind agitated. She'd be thirsty no matter how much water she drank. A checkup indicated that she suffered from type 2 diabetes. The diagnosis frightened Nan and Taotao. Having heard that some people died of the disease, the boy was afraid he might lose his mother. He cried and blamed his father for making her pregnant. "I hate you! I hate you!" he yelled at Nan.

Though also worried, Nan believed that Pingping's diabetes would probably be temporary. The nutritionist had said that many pregnant women were afflicted with this disease, especially Asians, whose diet contained too much starch, but most of them would recover soon after they gave birth.

Following the menu provided by the nutritionist, Pingping ate five meals a day, all of low carbohydrates and high protein. She didn't like the prescribed food but dared not eat what Nan cooked at the restaurant, fearful of messing up her blood sugar. Despite being careful about her diet, she was still ill, always exhausted and sleepy during the day. Her face was swollen and her eyes watery. Every night she got up many times to vomit into the toilet. She suffered so much that she claimed the baby meant to torture her and wear her down.

Nan often begged her to stay home in the afternoons. Shubo had lost his job at Grand Buddha, which had just folded, and could fill in for her. In fact, Shubo disliked bartending and preferred to be a chef, so he often came to the Gold Wok to learn how to cook from Nan. He was picking up the skill quickly and was delighted whenever Nan asked him to cook an order. *"You're a born chef,"* Nan bantered one day.

"I shouldn't have acted on your advice, playing ducks and drakes with my money on the bartending school," said Shubo.

Whenever Nan asked him to come and help, he'd show up readily. Pingping often noticed Shubo caress his wife's arm or peck her on the cheek when they were alone. It would be more appropriate to say that he came to help Niyan rather than relieve Pingping. He'd seek every opportunity to be with his wife, as if the two were newlyweds. Pingping and Nan were amused, saying they were like a pair of mandarin ducks that always accompanied each other.

Shubo suggested that Nan get a karaoke machine, which might attract more customers and make the Gold Wok a lively spot where a lot of people would gather in the evenings, especially those professionals who, after speaking English all day long at work, needed to unwind some in a Chinese-language environment. *"To make this place popular, you need to put an accent on atmosphere,"* he said to Nan.

"I don't want to turn this place into bedlam. I'm afraid of crowds, you know." Nan smiled and refilled Shubo's teacup.

"Then how can you attract more business?"

"We have enough customers."

"If more people come, you'll make more money."

"God, you're such a party animal," Nan said in English. Seeing his friend flummoxed, he added, *"Never heard that expression, huh? Write it down in your notebook*—a party animal."

"You're an awful man."

Shubo knew many people in the Chinese community here, most of whom were lonely souls and would have come in and sung the old-time songs and opera snatches with which they had grown up. But Nan wouldn't buy a karaoke machine, because most of his clientele were Americans who might dislike a noisy Gold Wok. Besides, he hated noise. Once he had dined in a Taiwanese restaurant where some well-dressed college students sang so loudly that his ears kept buzzing the next morning and he never set foot in that place again. In addition, he was reluctant to rub shoulders with the Chinese professionals here, some of whom might look down on him. In Nan's eyes they were just clever snobs, full of themselves. Once they began singing at this restaurant, they might want to drag on into the small hours. He couldn't possibly keep this place open that late for them. He joked with Shubo that if he promised to come every night, he, Nan, would install a karaoke machine. That was impossible, since two nights a week Shubo had to go to a part-time job in Atlanta. Later, Nan explained to his friend that he ought not to create more work at the moment so that Pingping wouldn't be stressed. Shubo smiled, saying to Nan, *"You're a model husband."*

Niyan said, *"Yes, you must learn from Nan."*

•

Knowing about Pingping's pregnancy, Janet often came to the Gold Wok to see her. She also talked a good deal about Hailee, who could walk now. But Janet was worried: the child was pale and flaccid, as if shrinking. Sometimes Hailee cried wheezily as if in pain. Although Dave didn't come to the Gold Wok as often, the Wus had seen him holding Hailee in the jewelry store or walking with her in the plaza, always leading her by the hand and taking short and slow steps. Besides asking Pingping questions about parenting, Janet seemed afraid Hailee would grow up lonely. She said to Pingping, "When your daughter's old enough, can you let her play with Hailee?"

"Don't be silly," said Pingping. "We're friends. So they will be friends too. But I'm afraid my baby not healthy."

"What makes you say that?"

"I don't know, I feel terrible these days."

"You'll be fine. Try to think positive. We all hear the patter of tiny feet."

Janet was puzzled when Pingping told her that Nan was eager to have a daughter, because she and Dave had thought Nan disliked babies, especially girls, which was why, they believed, he had refused to be Hailee's nominal father. Pingping couldn't explain Nan's change either, but she felt it was probably because he was getting older and their life was relatively stable now.

9

DICK phoned one evening in May and said to Nan in a cracked voice, "The old man died." He sounded drunk and hoarse.

"Who's dead?" asked Nan.

"Sam."

"Reelly! When did it happen?"

"Yesterday afternoon he had a heart attack and died soon after they rushed him to the hospital. I'm going to New York tomorrow to attend his funeral."

"Yes, you should go. Tell Min Niu I'm sorry about Sam."

"I may not see Min. Oh, didn't I tell you he was no longer Sam's boyfriend?"

"No, you didn't tell me. What happened?"

"He left Sam a few months ago to marry a woman, but nobody knows his whereabouts exactly. I heard he was teaching at a college in Hong Kong."

"I can't believe zis."

Though surprised that Min Niu was a bisexual, Nan made no further comment. He told Dick to have a safe trip and not to grieve too much since Sam had passed away without much suffering. After he hung up, he couldn't help but wonder if Min Niu had used Sam without genuine love for the poet. Without Sam's sponsorship and paying his tuition, Min couldn't possibly have come to America. Then after Min had earned his M.A. from NYU, he left Sam to start the kind of life he had probably desired all along. Nan suspected that Min could be that kind of schemer.

Sam's death grieved Nan in a peculiar way. He hadn't known the poet well enough to feel very attached to him, but the loss saddened him nevertheless. Sam, who could have helped him in his writing, had left a small hole in Nan's life. His passing made Nan feel more isolated. He couldn't stop wondering whether Sam had read his poems before he died. Perhaps not.

Dick returned on Monday, having to teach the next morning. He came to the Gold Wok for a late lunch on Wednesday afternoon. He didn't look grief-stricken. His gray eyes radiated a soft light, and he kept smiling mysteriously. Nan went on gazing at his animated face as Dick talked about how Sam, prior to his death, had planned to buy an apartment in Brooklyn for his stepson and how he had still dreamed of visiting Tibet. When Niyan brought over his order, Bang Bang Chicken, Dick said to Nan, "My book was taken by a New York press, thanks to Sam."

"Congratulations!" Nan was happy for him. "How did this happen?"

"Sam called the president of Four Continents and sent him my manuscript personally. After reading it, the publisher told Sam he would print it. Now that Sam is dead, he's all the more eager to honor his word."

"A good deed. Sam gave you a big hand."

"It's a miracle. Four Continents runs a better poetry series than my former press."

"See, I said you would find a publisher soon. Now you won't have any problem wiz your pretenure review."

"Right."

Chewing a piece of chicken, Dick changed the subject and began talking about Bao Yuan, who had also attended Sam's funeral. Nan was excited to know that Bao was quite a success in the art world, having sold many of his paintings. Dick said with a grin, "He told me that he has a fiancée in China."

"He's engaged?"

"Yes, he went back for the engagement two months ago. He was very happy and invited you and me to visit his studio."

"Did zer Chinese gahvernment let him go back?"

"Obviously they did. I don't know how he worked that out."

"So he remembered me?"

"Yes, very fondly. He said you were brilliant."

"You're jahst pulling my leg." Nan laughed with some bitterness that misshaped his face into a sad expression, as if he had a sudden pain in his chest. He added, "A brilliant cook, maybe. Jahst now you said he has a studio—where's zat?"

"On a mountain in Tennessee."

"So he's a professional now?"

"Yes, and quite rich. His paintings are selling well."

Dick relayed that Bao had moved to Tennessee half a year before and begun teaching a small group of local amateur painters. One of them was a wealthy lawyer who owned a piece of land on the mountain, so the man had a studio built there for his teacher. Also, this way his fellow students could have a place to stay when they gathered to take lessons from Bao. Dick's explanation piqued Nan's curiosity. Never had he thought Bao, formerly a mere sponger, would make it in America. Perhaps that fellow had changed; perhaps he had become a diligent artist.

Nan and Dick decided to visit Bao together. The Gold Wok didn't open until noon on Sundays, and there wouldn't be many customers until late in the afternoon. So Nan asked Shubo to stand in for him so that he could go to Tennessee with Dick the next weekend.

10

DICK and Nan set out early on Sunday morning. It was a gorgeous day, cool and clear after a mist had lifted. Sunlight fell on the dew-drenched tree leaves, which flickered in the breeze. They drove along Route 575 for an hour and a half, took a break at Blue Ridge, then continued north. Half an hour later they crossed the Georgia border, and then after a few miles of hilly gravel road filled with doglegs, they found Bao's place on the mountain. To Nan's amazement, Bao was cut off from the outside world, living like a recluse. No house was visible from his studio, which was a large, high-pitched wooden shack with broad windows. The fresh wood, not painted yet, was whitish and rough-hewn, giving off an intense pine scent. Behind the studio was parked a brown travel trailer in which Bao cooked his meals and slept at night. Beside the trailer sat a burgundy passenger van. Sometimes he'd drive to a Chinese restaurant in Postelle, a tiny town about five miles to the north, to have lunch or dinner. On weekdays he devoted himself to painting and would meet his students only on weekends.

Bao hugged both guests warmly. He was more like a middle-aged man now, wearing a crew cut and having gained about twenty pounds, but he was the picture of health. His bronzed face reminded Nan of a peasant who worked in the elements. Bao told them that he swam in a nearby man-made lake every day.

In the studio were lounging three students of his. One of them was Frank, a fortyish man wearing glasses. He was the lawyer who owned the land and the studio. The other two were in their mid-twenties, Brian and Tim. Tim was tall and thin, but muscular like a basketball player, with a reddish mustache; Brian was a Vietnamese

American, born in Vietnam, with a handsome face that was rather Mongolian. Brian told Nan that his last name was Ho. His father had fled to the United States in the 1970s after Saigon fell, and a year later his mother, carrying him on her back, had come to America and joined his dad. Unlike these two hardy young fellows, Frank looked studious, skinny, and heavily myopic. The students' demeanor showed a good deal of respect for their teacher, though Bao was casual and often patted them on the shoulder and back. He was louder and happier than before. He spoke English as if yelling at someone and often added a high-pitched laugh after a sentence. Nan wondered when Bao had started to speak English like this, without hesitation.

Nan scanned the studio. Against the walls leaned about twenty paintings, mostly still lifes of fruits, flowers, trees, bowls of food, rocks, clumps of stars in the indigo sky. There were a few idyllic pieces of animals and young women, which were reminiscent of French impressionism.

"I work very hard these days," Bao said to the guests. "One day, one painting."

"So you must've made a lot of money," Dick said.

"I'm impressed," Nan admitted.

He noticed that these paintings differed palpably from Bao's former works. Most of them were bright and buoyant, full of life, sunlight, and exuberance, without any trace of the violent colors and tragic tones that used to suffuse his paintings. Evidently Bao's life in America had affected his art. These pieces had shed the depressive agitation, the jaundiced view of the world, and the dark despair; instead, they gave the feeling of warmth and contentment—there was light everywhere. Yet on second thought, Nan wasn't sure whether the change had stemmed from within the artist or from his effort to meet the needs of the American market. He could find little originality in these paintings.

"Each piece here is worth at least a thousand dollars," Tim told the visitors.

"So that's your price?" Dick asked Bao.

"Actually his Washington, D.C., series sold for more than forty thousand," Frank broke in, pushing up his glasses with his thumb.

"Here, I show you." Bao led the visitors to a long trestle table on which sat three bulky albums. He opened one of them and said, "Here's the series."

Nan and Dick looked at the photos of the paintings, which were indeed impressive, presenting the U.S. capital in a fresh, bright way, as if the city were a large park where woods gleamed in the morning sun and where shimmering cathedrals, half shaded, were massive like hills. "I just did one series," explained Bao. "My agent want me to do more, but I refuse."

"Why?" asked Dick.

"I don't want to repeat my work."

That answer puzzled Nan. By nature Bao was shrewd and pragmatic. Perhaps he meant to keep something unique in his repertoire so as to maintain and increase the value of his work. Nan didn't ask more and went on thumbing through the albums. They contained hundreds of photographs of Bao's paintings in different styles: landscapes that revealed the influence of traditional Chinese painting, avant-gardish pieces like advertisements, impressionistic gouaches and aquarelles, still lifes, portraits of girls and various kinds of artists. Among them Bao took great pride in the few he had painted with a palette knife. Indeed, these pieces of cityscape and waterside looked vigorous, striking, and primitively spontaneous. He said he himself had invented the technique, called "knife painting." Though impressed by the scope of Bao's works, Nan asked him, "*Do you still write poetry?*"

"*Not anymore. I've found painting suits me better.*"

"*How about your memoir?*"

"*I'm still working on it.*"

Nan realized Bao would never complete that book, which he must have scrapped.

A moment later Bao cut open a huge watermelon, and together they sat on the deck, conversing, drinking beer, and eating watermelon and grapes. Tim and Brian edited an art magazine called *Blue Stars,* which had just published a lengthy article on Bao and his works, praising him as "a master on the mountain." Tim was its author and prided himself on the writing.

Because of his poor English, Bao couldn't fully make out the elaborate sentences in the article, so he asked Nan to tell him what they meant. He insisted that Nan translate every word for him orally on the spot. Although aware of Brian's slightly ironic grin, Nan went ahead and explained the article sentence by sentence while Bao kept nodding and listening intently, his eyes blinking constantly. Nan felt his host was like a small boy, vain but in an innocent way. Somehow Bao differed remarkably from his former self, carefree and natural, though there was still a little edginess in his bearing and his face still betrayed a small bit of uncertainty. He laughed loudly whenever Nan rendered a flattering phrase into Chinese.

It took twenty-five minutes for Nan to finish translating the article. Then they resumed talking about the people they knew living in New York. Bao confessed he had fallen in love with a Chinese woman two years before, but her parents despised him and wouldn't let her marry him. In their eyes he was a ne'er-do-well, not a match for their daughter, who was now working on a Ph.D. in biology at Vanderbilt. He followed her to Nashville, though her mother had said to his face that he was merely a toad dreaming of nabbing a swan. "I give them ten my best paintings," he told the guests.

"They must be rich now," Dick said.

"I don't think so."

Brian put in, "They used his paintings as tablecloths, and one by one they ruined them. Then, last fall, they went to Bao's show in D.C. and were flabbergasted at the sight of the prices. They couldn't take their eyes off the price tags, man: six or seven thousand bucks apiece. The fact is that those paintings they destroyed were worth much more."

"That's old story," Bao said calmly. "It's over between she and I. We have no luck, no chance, no together. After she go away for another guy, I move to the mountain and work harder here. I'm stupid man, no luck with ladies."

Nan laughed, then checked himself. He remembered that Bao had once been a goatish fellow. How come this libertine had changed so much? Probably his success had given him more confidence and made him want to be a responsible man.

Bao let out a feeble sigh and said to Nan, "*That relationship hurt me deeply. It changed me. All of a sudden I felt old, eager to settle down and start a family.*"

Nan thought about that and decided Bao might be a better man now.

Dick and Tim got up and went out to the trailer to use the toilet. Nan was curious about Bao's success, wondering why he would paint at such a pace, one piece a day, which must have made him work like a manufacturer. No artist should force himself to do such a thing. He ventured, "*Why do you paint so fast?*"

"*There will be a show in Raleigh next month. I must give them ten pieces.*"

"*Do you really need to rush?*"

"*I ought to keep the momentum. My paintings have been selling very well in Hong Kong and Taiwan. People often ask, 'Who is this fellow, Bao Yuan?' They saw my work hang in the same halls as those done by some master painters.*" His tone of voice betrayed some complacence, which made Nan uneasy.

"*To be honest, Bao,*" Nan said, "*you shouldn't work at such a reckless pace. Slow down a little. Now it's time to consolidate your success. Don't rush.*"

Bao looked amazed, then said, "*Tell me honestly what I should do, Nan. If truth be told, success can be nerve-racking. It frightens me sometimes. I just dabble a piece for an hour or two and it can sell for hundreds of dollars, sometimes even more than a thousand. This gives me the willies.*"

"*Forget about making money. Remember your true ambition. Your rivals are not your contemporaries but some dead masters.*"

Bao's eyes sparkled. "*That's a brilliant thing to say, Nan. I told Dick you're one of the most intelligent men I knew. Now I must say you're also wise. Very true, I should think of immortal work now. All wealth and fame are transitory and extrinsic, not an inherent part of myself.*" He stretched up his arms as if lifting a weight.

"*Yes, we're already middle-aged and should plan our ambitions carefully.*" Nan sighed, remembering his own situation. He had written little in the last five years, always offering himself the excuse that his English wasn't sufficient.

"*Yes, I must keep that in mind,*" agreed the host.

Then Bao told him that he was going to China to do some paintings, because his agent loved his Venice series so much that he wanted him to paint a Shanghai series to accompany it. Bao would leave for China after the Raleigh show. Also, he wanted to marry his fiancée in the fall if everything worked out in his favor. Nan asked, "*So the Chinese government will let you go back? Didn't they arrest you two years ago?*"

"*I'm no longer a democracy activist, they know. I can return as a working artist anytime. Things have changed. Don't you want to go back and see your parents?*"

"*I do, but my situation is different—I'm not afraid of the government but the children of some top officials. There's some bad blood between them and me. Once I'm naturalized, I may go back for a visit.*" As they were conversing, Nan realized that his friend might have written a statement, as required by the Chinese government, declaring that he had quit political activities once and for all.

Brian came back from Postelle, the nearest town, with some cartons of Chinese food for lunch. While they were eating, Bao again talked to Nan about his bride-to-be.

"*Where is she now?*" asked Nan.

"*She's in Guangzhou with her family.*"

"*Why don't you bring her here?*"

"*I've been trying. That's why we'll get married as soon as possible. I've also applied for naturalization. Once I'm a citizen, she can immigrate.*"

"*So before you're naturalized she can't come?*"

"*She can, but she's quite comfortable with her folks there. Her family owns a factory, is prosperous. I have to make a lot of money to let her live well here. I'm thinking of building a home in this area.*"

"*You mean near your studio?*"

"*Correct. I can buy a piece of land from Frank.*"

"*That's crazy. What makes you think your bride can stand this kind of isolation? You have your work, but what will she do here? Raise chickens and ducks? You can't treat her like that.*"

"*Good, I need your advice.*"

"*Maybe you should build a home in a city, Knoxville or Atlanta or*

D.C., *with a studio in the backyard. You can't let your bride live your kind of life. Besides, you'll have children. You have to take their schooling into consideration too."*

Shaking his stubbly chin, Bao said, *"You're such a wise man. Why don't you learn how to paint so that we can work as a team?"*

"I have my own difficulties. I've been trying to write poetry."

"In English?" Bao asked matter-of-factly.

Nan realized he must have heard about this from Dick. *"Yes, a big struggle,"* he admitted.

"But you're a brave man, determined to blaze your own path."

"Honestly I don't know what to do exactly. My wife is pregnant and we're going to have a baby girl. That's what I really care about now. I want to be a good, responsible father, a real family man."

"That's very meaningful too," Bao said thoughtfully. *"Not many Chinese men of our generation are good fathers and considerate husbands. Some of us don't even know how to fend for ourselves. We're often possessed with ideals and ambitions, too high-minded, but in all candor many of us are just ignoramuses."*

Nan was moved by Bao's words, but on second thought wondered whether his friend had spoken from his heart or merely rehashed someone else's remarks. Bao loosened his belt a notch, then bent forward a little. Although none of the others could understand Chinese, he said to Nan in a voice just above a whisper, *"May I ask you a favor?"*

"Sure."

"Can you translate Tim's article for me? You don't have to do a thorough job, just make the meaning clear."

Tim heard his name mentioned and squinted at his teacher. Hesitantly Nan answered, *"I can do that. I'll mail the translation to you."* In spite of his agreement, he felt as uneasy as if he had been taken in. Bao jotted down his address on the back of his former business card. He used a post office box in Postelle.

After lunch, Frank left for Chattanooga to meet a client, and the rest of them went to a reservoir on the mountain to swim. On the low dam stood a small power plant, no longer in operation. They parked the van at the waterside and shed their T-shirts and pants. Brian, Tim, and Bao wore swimming trunks while the guests had on their briefs. As Nan put his wristwatch into his sneaker, he noticed Dick stealing glances at Brian's slender, muscular body, which was remarkably well proportioned and much more youthful than his face. With a loud, exhilarated whoop, Bao jumped into the cool water, and the others followed him. Their shouting and splashing echoed off the mountain while a few waterfowl glided slowly against the woods on the distant shore, crying softly.

Nan floated on his back in the shallows as the others rushed toward the middle of the reservoir. Dick swam freestyle while Tim and Brian did the breaststroke, puffing and gurgling like giant frogs. The water was clear, almost transparent, reminding Nan of his childhood when he had gone swimming with his pals in a pond surrounded by jagged rocks. The children had divided themselves into two teams and fought each other in the water, pulling and pressing their opponents down. Whenever a boy accidentally swallowed water, he'd curse his attacker without stopping. Laughter would surge in the afternoon air. What fun they had had! That was almost thirty years ago. Now, in this land, the water felt similar but people were different; so were the birds and the woods. This changed life was full of mysteries. Who could have predicted Nan would land here?

As he was swimming breaststroke toward the middle of the reservoir, lost in thought, suddenly a tiny triangular head rose above the water; then the creature, brownish and sinuous, swung aside, now tightening, now slithering on the surface of the water. "Snake!" he yelled, and turned around, crawl-stroking to the shore.

The others stopped to look in his direction, laughing and hollering from the center of the reservoir. Nan reached the beach and dropped on his knees, gasping for breath. His right calf had a cramp, so he held his big toe and stretched the leg as straight as possible, which did ease the muscle pain somewhat. He cried at the others, who were still treading and looking at him, "Hey, there's a snake in zer water, zis long." He stretched his hands over four feet apart.

"No big deal," shouted Tim. "Just a water snake. It won't bite."

Beyond him, Brian was doing the butterfly, splashing the water rhythmically.

Nan dreaded snakes, both poisonous and harmless ones, so he didn't enter the water again. Finally Bao came ashore. He said to Nan, "*Boy, I didn't know you were so scared of snakes. As long as you leave them alone, they won't come close to you.*"

"*It dashed right to my face.*"

"*Come on, it wouldn't attack you. Snakes are afraid of people, who are much more poisonous.*"

Nan sighed, "*This is my problem in the South. I can't blend myself into the landscape. Always at odds with the flora and fauna here.*"

"*I thought you were quite at home in Atlanta, much more adaptable than me.*"

"*I'm weak in my own way.*"

"*I guess we all are.*"

•

An hour later, on their way back to Atlanta, Dick couldn't stop talking about Brian and Tim. He hoped to see them again and make fun of each other some more. He was attracted to Brian, Nan knew. The moment they entered Georgia, a fine shower trickled down, washing everything clean. But the rain stopped abruptly fifteen minutes after they had come out of Blue Ridge. The sun had dispersed the clouds and shone softly on the blacktop, which had turned darker. Their wheels were rolling on the wet asphalt with a crisp sound. Ahead of them was a blue Volvo cruising with a small mist in its wake. As they were catching up with it, they saw a sticker on the car's rear, announcing PUBLISHED AUTHOR ABOARD!

"What a braggart!" said Nan.

"Let's see what the driver looks like." Dick floored the gas pedal. With a jolt his Mustang charged forward, passing the Volvo. He slowed down a little so that they could get a better look at the authorial driver. A stout woman with heavy makeup and a big bouffant hairdo was steering absentmindedly. Her head was bobbing and jerking, perhaps to music.

"Did you recognize her?" asked Nan when they had passed the car.

"No. She looks like a freak."

"Maybe the car is not hers."

"If she's an author, she must write romance novels."

They tipped their heads back and laughed. Dick said he should have a bumper sticker designed for his car, proclaiming PUBLISHED POET ABOARD! That might attract a lot of women.

Also men, Nan thought, but he didn't let that out.

11

FINALLY Edward Neary wrote back to Nan, saying he liked his poems, particularly the one entitled "Pomegranates." But the poems were unfinished yet and needed "some tightening." He didn't return the poems and instead said he'd like to discuss them with Nan in person. In September he was going to conduct a workshop at Key West, so he hoped Nan could attend his class there. He had enclosed a brochure that described the Key West seminars taught regularly by distinguished writers.

At first Nan was excited by the personal attention the poet had paid to him. Then, reading the letter again, he found something strange between the lines. At one point Mr. Neary wrote: "I vividly remember the night we spent at the bar outside Emory. Your sweet smile impressed me greatly. In fact, it comes to mind from time to time. Please go to Key West, where we can meet and talk about your work. Clearly you have a good deal of talent, but you need tutoring. You're still a diamond in the rough. So do make the best use of this opportunity. I wish to know you better."

Nan wondered if Edward Neary was making a pass. In the Gold Wok's bathroom he observed himself in the mirror and found his face quite masculine, with a squarish chin, a broad nose, and wide-spaced, shining eyes. He couldn't see how he could be attractive to men. Yet several times in the bank and bookstores he had caught men's furtive glances shot at him. This had never happened in China and was troublesome to him. If only those stealthy eyes had belonged to women. That would have boosted his confidence considerably. Now Mr. Neary's suggestion perplexed Nan, who was uncertain whether he should go to Key West. Probably he shouldn't even think about it, because Pingping would enter the third trimester of her pregnancy in September and he must be around. Also, he couldn't afford to be away from his business for more than two days, let alone an entire week. Still, it was extraordinary to have such an offer from a famous poet, and Nan couldn't stop musing on the invitation.

When Dick came the next time, Nan showed him Neary's letter. After reading it, Dick put it on the table and grinned mischievously.

"What?" Nan asked. "What do you make of it?"

"I think he's an old lech."

"You mean he's gay?"

"No, everybody knows Neary is an inveterate womanizer."

"Zen why did you smile like zat?"

"He remembered you wrong and took you for another person."

"I don't get it."

"Remember Emily Choi, the Korean girl at the bar? He must've gotten you and her mixed up."

Blushing, Nan muttered, "Zat's ridiculous." He recalled the young woman, who had indeed had a sweet face and also bright, smiling eyes.

"Look, your name Nan must have suggested to him a female, like Nancy and Nanny and Nanette. As a matter of fact, Nan is a diminutive of Anne and Anna."

"Actually, Nan means 'male.' My name means 'martial man.'"

"But Neary doesn't know Chinese."

"I see. He just wants to sleep wiz me, right?" Nan burst out laughing hysterically.

Dick looked startled, staring at his friend, whose face was distorted by the laugh. When Nan had stopped, Dick said, "Forget about this letter, okay? You can always show me your poems, and I'll tell you what I think honestly."

"I will do zat, sanks." Nan felt better, though his cheeks were still twitching. He remembered that when he was at Brandeis, he had once received a small package containing a pair of tampons mailed to him as a target consumer. Over the years he had run into many Chinese who had transformed themselves into Barry, or Harry, or

Mary, or Larry, or Carrie, and he had wondered whether he should have changed his name too, but he had always chosen not to.

•

Having translated the *Blue Stars* article on Bao, Nan mailed it to his friend. To his surprise, *Cathay Herald,* a Chinese-language newspaper circulating in Tennessee, Georgia, and Florida, published the article two weeks later. The translator's name wasn't given; that bothered Nan a little. He was also annoyed by the author's new tone, which had been altered quite a bit from the English, more formal and more authoritative now. Evidently, either Bao or the editor had tampered with his translation. In the space of a month the same piece was reprinted in a magazine called *Art World.* Obviously Bao had been busy promoting himself. Why did he take his student's article so seriously? The original publication was only in a new, obscure journal. Why should Bao be so obsessed with such an amateur piece of writing? He was too vain. No wonder he couldn't concentrate on real work.

Then Nan realized that in this case his friend had indulged his fraudulence more than his vanity. Bao tried to utilize the gap between the two languages—since few Chinese were familiar with the journal *Blue Stars* and Tim's writings, they could be misled into believing that it was a magazine as reputable as any major Chinese-language publication and that Tim Dullington must be an established art critic. *Art World* is a top-quality magazine printed outside China, so the transferring of the original article into such a major publication would present Bao in a different light, as if he were already a celebrity in America. In short, the whole misleading process helped to raise Bao's image to a higher level to the Chinese audience.

It was clever chicanery. Bao would have been better off, Nan thought, if he had spent the time working on his art.

A few days later Nan received a painting from Bao, a bizarre piece in which Sakyamuni, the founder of Buddhism, was riding a white horse and leading a batch of his disciples. It was signed as a gift for Nan. Nan didn't like it because it looked dark and muddy, lacking in life. Without his friend's explanation in the note, he could hardly have figured out what it was about. Still, the piece was an accomplished painter's work, so he was glad to have it. Then the thought came to him that Bao must have meant to pay him for his translation with this painting and wanted him to keep mum about the original article. This realization further dimmed his interest in the gift, and he didn't even bother to write back to thank Bao.

12

PINGPING'S diabetes was under control through her low-carb diet. By late June she had been pregnant for five months. Dr. Walker, her obstetrician at the Norcross Medical Center, suggested that Pingping go to the headquarters of their medical group in Dunwoody to be examined regularly, since that clinic had more advanced equipment and eventually the baby would be delivered there. It would be better for the Wus to acquaint themselves with the people at that place. Nan phoned the clinic and made an appointment with Dr. Smith.

On Friday morning Nan and Pingping arrived at Dunwoody Circle at nine. The clinic was almost like a small hospital and occupied an entire four-story building. Before meeting with the doctor, Pingping was to go through a comprehensive checkup, including an ultrasound, a urine test, and a blood test. Accompanied by Nan, she was ushered into a dim room with a single window covered by teal curtains. She lay down on a sloping bed, as she was told.

A tall nurse with blond hair stepped in and said to Pingping, "I'm going to do an ultrasound for you, okay?"

"Sure."

"Happy about having a baby again?"

"Yes." Pingping smiled faintly.

Nan was sitting on a low-backed chair in a corner and watched the nurse putting on a pair of latex gloves. She then rubbed a bit of gel on Pingping's abdomen and began massaging the lubricated area with the black transducer, turning the thing slowly clockwise. As she proceeded, her mouth fell ajar. Nan gazed at the sonogram and saw the shape of the tiny baby but not the twinkling star they had last seen at the Norcross Medical Center.

"I can't find the baby's heartbeat," said the nurse. A mournful expression widened her face as her eyes dropped. Silence filled the room.

Nan was staggered, choking and motionless, his eyes still fastened on the dark screen. A few seconds later the woman asked Pingping, "D'you understand what I mean?"

Pingping nodded without a word. Nan's heart contracted as if a hand were tugging and twisting it. He finally stood up but still didn't know what to say.

"I'm so sorry," said the nurse. "You should go see Dr. Smith right away."

So they skipped the urine and blood tests and went to the doctor's office. Dr. Smith, a portly black man with an amiable face and a graying mustache, said to Pingping in a soft voice, "I'm sorry about the loss. This often happens with women your age. It's hard to explain why nature does this."

Nan felt sobs rising in his throat but he choked them down. He glanced at his wife, who somehow looked emotionless, though more pallid than a moment before. She seemed too benumbed to say anything and just nodded at Dr. Smith as he was telling her to go home and wait for her obstetrician to call. "Dr. Walker will let you know what to do next," he said.

The Wus thanked him and left for the garage.

On the way back they were silent, their car zooming down the bypass. In the blue and cloudless sky, a blimp was sailing, dragging along a Coca-Cola ad. Nan was stunned by the sudden descent of death in the family. Now and again he felt a wave of nausea surging in his chest, but he was driving carefully, his hands in the ten and two positions on the steering wheel. His mind couldn't focus on any thought, yet he tried to remain calm and avoid saying anything that might trigger an outburst from his grieving wife. Meanwhile, Pingping looked distant, her face stony, as though she were oblivious to things around her. Before they reached the junction of I-85, she said finally, "*Let's go to the Korean supermarket.*"

"*Why?*" He was amazed she felt up to doing some shopping.

"*I promised Taotao to get garlic stems for him.*"

Nan got off I-85 and pulled onto Buford Highway. In the half-filled parking lot before the store, a pigeon dropped a load on the door of their van, and Nan didn't bother to wipe off the two white stains. As he and his wife headed for the entrance, he wanted to hold her arm to support her, but he couldn't do that, hardly able to lift his own hands. His legs were so weary that he was afraid they might give way at any moment. He had to exert himself to follow her.

13

ONCE HOME, Pingping broke down, sobbing wretchedly and blaming herself for the loss of the child. She went on saying, "*Our baby sacrificed herself for me, because she was afraid I couldn't survive the childbirth. She didn't want to put my life in danger.*" The more she raved, the harder she cried.

Nan could no longer control himself either and wept too. He felt a numbing pain sinking deeper and deeper in him and squeezing every ounce of his strength out of him. If only he had thought of the possibility of such a loss. If only he hadn't raised his hopes. Now his world was upside down.

Pingping lit two squat white candles and placed them on the bar table in the living room, on either side of a large yellow chrysanthemum stuck in a cylindrical vase. Not absolutely sure of the result of the sonogram, Nan phoned Dr. Walker at the medical center. The bad news had already reached there, and the obstetrician wanted Pingping to come that very afternoon for another checkup, but he told Nan that the accuracy rate of the ultrasound was more than ninety-nine percent. Nan called the Gold Wok and asked Niyan and Shubo to tend the restaurant for the rest of the day. In the afternoon he took his wife to see Dr. Walker. The result of the reexamination was the same. Now that it was beyond any doubt that the baby was lost, the dead fetus would have to be aborted soon, for which Nan agreed to take his wife to Northlake Hospital three days later, on Monday morning.

Although she sautéed the garlic stems with slivers of pork for Taotao, Pingping couldn't help lashing out at the boy at dinner. She declared that only Nan had been good to the baby and that both

Taotao and she herself had been heartless and selfish. She said to her son, "You never want baby sister. Now we lost her, you're happy."

"Mom, I'm sad too," Taotao wailed.

Nan intervened, "We shouldn't blame each ahther. We have to live on, zat's what our baby wants us to do."

That evening Janet came. She had heard the bad news from Niyan. She embraced Pingping and wiped away tears from her own cheeks. "This is too cruel," she said, shaking her roundish chin. Pingping took her friend into her bedroom and showed her the clothes she had made for the baby: a miniature jacket, two bibs, a pair of woolen socks, a silk quilt, and a cotton mattress that was yet unfinished. Janet stayed until ten o'clock.

Nan wanted to inter their child in their backyard; so did Pingping. He planned to lay her down beside the large Russian swan that had died two years ago in the lake, buried under the tallest sweet gum. He had marked the spot with a brown boulder. Now they must bring their baby home after the abortion. But how? They were unsure whether there was a coffin made for such a tiny body. It was already the weekend, and the funeral home on Lawrenceville Highway was closed. Nan went to the Korean supermarket again and bought a large jewelry box. He dismantled its tiny drawers and made it empty, like a casket. He planned to take their daughter home in it, and when the funeral home was open the next week, he'd go buy a real coffin for her, which should be large enough to contain this makeshift pall. Meantime, Pingping finished sewing the little cotton mattress. She made the bed for the baby inside the box with the clothing she had prepared. In a way, the interior of the container resembled a tiny, comfortable cradle.

14

ON MONDAY MORNING Pingping didn't eat breakfast, as the doctor had instructed. The Wus arrived at Northlake Hospital before nine o'clock. Dr. Walker wasn't there yet, but a Filipino nurse in scrubs led Pingping into a curtained area in a large room. Pingping undressed and lay down on a gurney; then the nurse covered her with a sheet, checked her vital signs, and gave her an IV. An anesthesiologist came and began administering an anesthetic to her. He said to Nan, "My wife lost a baby last year too. It was hard. I know how you feel." As he spoke, his large Adam's apple was joggling.

Nan said, "Doctor, we would like to take our baby home."

The stumpy man looked surprised, but told him, "You should talk to her obstetrician. To my knowledge, this hasn't been done before."

Pingping said in a frightened voice, "We want her stay with us forever."

"I understand."

The man's eyes dimmed, and he turned and hurried out. Nan kissed Pingping and said, *"Don't be scared. Everything will be all right."*

She nodded, smiling a little. Then the nurse unlocked the wheels of the gurney with her toe, pulled it into the hallway, turned it around, and pushed it away. As they were moving toward the operating room, Pingping still fastened her eyes on Nan as if eager to pull him along. His stomach lurched, though he forced a smile, waving to assure her that she'd be fine.

Nan was pacing up and down along a wall in the lobby with a canvas bag containing the casket slung over his shoulder. He was worried about his wife and prayed that she would come out of the operation safely. At last the warty-faced Dr. Walker appeared and hurried up to Nan. He said in an adenoidal voice, "We have everything in place. Pingping will be all right." But when Nan said he wanted to take the baby's body home, the obstetrician looked away. His blue eyes were downcast, but then they turned back to look at Nan. Dr. Walker told him, "I can feel your pain, but the baby would look very messy, an awful sight."

"Can you let us have her?"

"I have no objection to that, only because people usually don't do this. In any case, don't worry about the baby. We have to focus on the mother now."

That was true, so Nan didn't press further. Dr. Walker headed away and disappeared past the red-brown door to the operating section.

Nan resumed pacing the floor while thinking about the obstetrician's words. The thought grew clear to him that the baby would be shapeless, maybe torn to pieces in the operation. That might be why people didn't take the fetus home after an abortion. All the same, he hoped Dr. Walker could let him keep his daughter's body, broken or intact. If only Nan had given him the casket. Yet he didn't blame himself for not having handed it to Dr. Walker, who might have refused to take it even if Nan had insisted. The doctor was right— what was at stake now was Pingping's safety. Her life might indeed be in danger. That thought frightened Nan. He tried to imagine how she was suffering on the operating table. Were the doctors using all the blunt metal instruments to open her and tear out the dead fetus? Could the anesthetic they'd given her suppress all the pain? That was unlikely. However effective the drug was, she must have felt she was being butchered.

A full hour passed, and still there was no word about Pingping. Nan asked the old woman at the information desk how his wife was doing, but she had heard nothing from the operating room yet. He got so tensed up that he couldn't stop walking back and forth at the end of the waiting lounge. People sitting in the scooped plastic seats glanced at him from time to time. Something stirred in his gorge and set him hiccupping. He pressed his fist against his solar plexus, but the visceral spasms wouldn't stop. If only his parents-in-law were here. That would have made Pingping feel protected. When she had given birth to Taotao, her parents, both retired then, had taken care of her during her two months' maternity leave because Nan had to stay at school attending seminars. Her father, a skinny chain-smoker despite his hacking cough, cooked special meals for her every day so that she could have enough milk for Taotao. Her parents nursed her so well that most of her small illnesses, such as a weak bladder and occasional light-headedness, were cured when her leave was over. In addition, her hair had grown thick and abundant. Never had she felt so healthy as when she rejoined her husband in Harbin. Recently Pingping and Nan had talked about asking her parents to come and stay a few months, but they dared not invite them, afraid Nan's parents would be jealous and make trouble, at least wanting to come as well. It would be impossible for Pingping to get along with Nan's mother, who was too manipulative and would boss her around.

As Nan was pacing up and down the floor, the old woman at the information desk came up to him and said, "Hey, your wife's coming out of the operation momentarily. Go to the front door of the medical building and pick her up there."

"How is she?" he asked.

"She's doing all right. Bring your car there quickly."

Before Nan could leave, Dr. Walker appeared, his eyes shifty: he looked rather shaken. He told Nan that Pingping was safe, but the operation had taken longer than anticipated. He didn't mention the baby's body and Nan was so worried about his wife that he forgot to ask about the aborted fetus. Handing him his card, the obstetrician said, "Feel free to call anytime you need me. I'll call this afternoon to check on Pingping."

The instant Nan took the card, Dr. Walker turned around and strode away.

Nan rushed out of the lobby through the side door. He gave the numbered brass tag to a gangly black valet, who hurried away to fetch his car. Several people were waiting for their vehicles at the side entrance too. A bony middle-aged man told everybody excitedly that his wife had just given birth to a healthy boy. He turned to Nan and beamed. Nan managed to say, "Congratulations."

"How about you? Gonna be a father?" the man asked.

"We just lawst a baby girl."

"I'm sorry, really sorry." The man looked a bit abashed. He turned away and gave a tip to a short black fellow who handed over his key.

"Thank you, sir," the valet said cheerfully.

A moment later Nan got his car key from the other valet and tipped him a dollar. He drove to the front entrance of the medical building, where Pingping was sitting in a wheelchair, a young nurse standing behind her with both hands on the back of the chair. Seeing his wife empty-handed, Nan knew Dr. Walker hadn't let her have their baby's body, but he didn't ask her about it. He opened his car door and helped her get in. "She's very weak. Be careful," said the nurse, still wearing a pale blue cap.

Pingping seemed half paralyzed and could hardly move her head and limbs. Nan buckled her up. Without delay he pulled out of the driveway, as there were many cars waiting behind to pick up other patients. He drove out of the hospital and got onto I-285. On the way home he observed his wife now and again. Her eyes were closed, the lids twitching. Apparently she hadn't fully come out of the anesthesia yet. Her cheeks were swollen with a ghastly pallor and her mouth seemed flabby, reminding him of rising dough. Yet the expression of pain and suffering on her face touched him and made him want to weep. He kept taking his eyes off the road and peering at her. He felt a sudden onrush of emotion, his heart aching. Never had he found her face so ugly yet so moving; he was sure her sorrowful features would be embedded in his mind as one of those images that could always unloose a flood of tenderness and compassion in his heart. He remained silent for a long while lest he might let out the sobs gathering in his throat.

Having turned onto I-85, he finally asked her, *"How do you feel, dear?"*

"I almost died. I've never felt so awful, so like death."

"Did they let you have our baby's body?"

"I don't remember anything. The drug knocked me out."

"I asked Dr. Walker before the operation. He said he'd see to it."

"They just tried to keep me alive, I guess."

Now Nan understood why the obstetrician had looked so nervous when he handed Nan his card.

That afternoon Dr. Walker called and asked if Pingping was still bleeding. Nan told him she was not. "Thank God, she's strong. She lost a lot of blood," said the doctor. He ordered her to eat a lot of chicken soup and rest in bed for at least two days.

15

THE WUS kept candles burning on the bar table in the living room for a whole month. A bunch of flowers, mums or roses or daisies, constantly stood in the vase between the two tiny halos of candle flames. Physically, Pingping was recovering rapidly, but she often looked absentminded. Sometimes she heard their baby calling her in a cry, "Mommy, Mommy, take me home." When she stood at the glass door of the living room, she often caught sight of a red-cheeked girl toddling on the deck, as if her daughter, May, were frolicking there. Even the flickering of the surface of the lake in the sunlight would remind her of the blinking star, the baby's heartbeat in the sonogram. Every night she'd sleep with the empty casket beside her pillow, and at times she woke up hearing the baby prattle to her mysteriously. It would take more than two years for her to outgrow most of the grief and to stop talking to her husband about the child.

Nan grieved in his own way. He didn't hear any voices or see any images, but he was depressed. For months after the loss of the baby, he couldn't pull himself together to do anything other than run the restaurant. A numbing pain was sinking deeper and deeper in him. He felt deceived by fate. Originally he had thought that the arrival of his daughter would bring him a lot of joy and solace and would open a new page of his life. Even though his life had been truncated and enervated by the immigration, even though he had accomplished nothing here, even though he was a total failure in others' eyes, he'd still have a lovely daughter to raise, to love, and to be proud of. How often he had pictured the girl as good-looking as her mother. He imagined teaching her how to read and write, how to ride a bike, and how to drive, then seeing her dress up for her high school prom, taking her to college, and eventually walking her down the aisle and handing her to a fine young man. Having her would have made his life more bearable and lessened his misery and loneliness in this place. She could have become his American dream.

Now all the figments of his imagination were gone and he was thrown back to the hard reality again. He realized that he had been selfish in a way, eager to make his daughter's life a part of his own; that's to say he wanted her to come into this world for his sake, so that he wouldn't have to live his life fully or wage the fight against adversity. In other words, subconsciously he wished to use her as a pretext for wasting his life. The truth was that he had been frightened by the overwhelming odds against writing in English artistically, against claiming his existence in this new land, and against becoming a truly independent man who followed nothing but his own heart. To date he had tried every way to wriggle out of the struggle. For several years he had devoted all his energy and passion to the restaurant business and gotten the mortgage paid, but the disappearance of the debt had also ended his excuse for not writing, for not doing something his heart desired. Then he was obsessed with his unborn daughter so as to have his energy and life consumed in another way. Not until now did he understand his mind-set. What a shirker he had been! How disgusted he was with himself!

His self-hatred paralyzed his will to do anything other than his routine business. For months he was in despair and acted like a robot moving between the Gold Wok and his house. At times he felt the urge to write something, but whenever he took up his pen, his mind remained numb and vacant, a coldness still permeating his being. He knew he had to get out of this lethargic state before long. No matter what kind of destiny awaited him, he'd have to put up a fight. He must resume working on his poetry. By now it was clear that he should write exclusively in English, which was the only way to go. He had been shilly-shallying for too long; it was the radical beginning that had intimidated him. This realization made him loathe himself more, but it still couldn't motivate him enough for a wholehearted start. These days he thought a lot about writing as if it were a new subject to him.

"Have you read the novella Good-bye, My American Boss?*"* Niyan

asked Nan one afternoon. The waitress liked reading popular magazines, and her husband would write short articles for some Chinese-language newspapers every now and then.

"*No, who wrote it?*" asked Nan.

"*Danning Meng. It's a very interesting story that shows how badly some Americans treated the Chinese in Philadelphia. You should read it. It's in the last issue of* October Quarterly."

"*I know the author. We're friends.*"

"*Really? He's famous.*"

"*I got a letter from him two weeks ago.*"

Nan had noticed several new titles by Danning in the World Bookstore. He had read two of them, but was underwhelmed. Danning, despite his fame as the leading figure in the overseas student literature, pandered too much to the Chinese readers' taste and depended too heavily on exotic details and on nationalistic sentiment to make his stories work. That in effect made his fiction simplistic, glib, and even clunky in places. Nan didn't mention to Niyan that he disliked his friend's work. If he went on to write, he'd emphasize similarity instead of difference. He imagined a kind of poetry that could speak directly to the readers' hearts regardless of their cultural and ethnic backgrounds. Above all, his work should possess more strength than beauty, which he believed often belied truth. He wanted to produce literature, or else he ought never to bother about writing at all.

16

THE WUS didn't go to the Olympic games because of the traffic in downtown Atlanta, but they watched TV and followed the news. It was so hot that some athletes fainted during competitions. The local Chinese-language newspapers carried articles on how the American staff at the Olympic Village based at Georgia Tech had inconvenienced the Chinese athletes to ensure they couldn't perform at their best. One night the fire alarm in the dorm building housing the Chinese women swimmers went off, and the police came and ordered everybody out. The athletes stayed in the damp night air a whole hour, and few of them could sleep well afterward. As a result, they did poorly in the events the following day. What's worse, the schedules and maps provided by the Olympic Headquarters were often inaccurate, and some people missed their events or arrived so late that they had to forfeit their games. The Chinese officials lodged a complaint; so did some other countries.

The Wus half believed those reports, but Shubo and Niyan were convinced of them all. There was also a long protest letter in the local newspapers, condemning the NBC commentator's remarks on China at the opening ceremony. The protesters were soliciting more signatures. True, the commentator had criticized China's human rights record, its military threat to Taiwan, its athletes' doping, and its tolerance of counterfeiting intellectual property. Many Chinese here resented his comments, believing this was another case of China-bashing. These days torrents of angry words had poured in to the Olympic Headquarters, demanding an apology from NBC and from Robert Coleman, the commentator. Some Chinese students urged people to fax more letters to the media company so as to "jam their machines." Funds were being raised for a full-page protest in the *New York Times*.

Nan said to Shubo, "*If China is so sensitive to criticism and public opinion, why doesn't it apologize to its people for the Tiananmen massacre? Compared with the Chinese government, this NBC man is completely innocent. I don't see why people are so furious and even want to have him fired.*"

"*This isn't just politics. It's about national pride,*" said Shubo. He had come in to watch the games on the TV hung in the corner, which had a larger screen than the one in his home.

"*National pride, my butt,*" Nan said. "*What can the Chinese be proud of nowadays? The largest population and cheap labor?*"

"*Still, that anchorman had no right to condemn China at the opening ceremony.*"

"*How come? Only because he's an American, not entitled to criti-cize China? I don't understand why the Chinese here also believe that domestic shame mustn't be made public.*"

"*Our athletes were guests of the United States. You can't invite them over and then humiliate them publicly. It's the host's responsi-bility to make the guests feel welcome.'*"

"*The reason every country is here is to win medals. Who cares about friendship or politeness or hospitality? That's just Chinese idiosyncrasy and hypocrisy.*"

"*You have a heck of a mouth, Nan. So hard to please.*"

Shubo held a full-time job in a marble quarry now, so he could no longer always fill in for Nan when his help was needed. Nan found an old chef, Mr. Mu, who was good at Hunan cuisine but didn't have a work permit, so Nan couldn't use this sleepy-eyed man regularly. If the INS caught Mr. Mu working they could fine Nan $5,000. These days Shubo would come in the evenings, mainly to watch TV. Also, he wanted to keep his wife company whenever he could. Pingping often said to Niyan, "*I wish Nan were as sticky as Shubo.*" By "sticky" she meant "attached." Niyan would smile with-out speaking.

Then one day the same woman who had solicited a donation for the flood victims in China from the Wus four years earlier turned up at the Gold Wok again. Nan remembered her name, Mei Hong. This time she said pleasantly to him while patting his forearm, *"Nan Wu, we need you to help feed the Chinese athletes."*

"We don't donate anything," he said as his wife stepped closer.

"I'm not asking for donations. We'll pay you for the food. Only because you're a Chinese, we can trust you."

"That's why you came here?" He was nonplussed.

"Yes, the other Chinese restaurants have offered their help too. We dare not get food from foreigners."

"Why can't the athletes eat inside the Olympic Village? There are cafeterias in there. I saw them on TV."

"They can't stand American food—cheese, hamburgers, French fries, sandwiches, hot dogs. Yuck, the stuff makes you heavy and sick."

"How about Tyson *chicken? That's as good as any Chinese-style chicken, braised or roasted."*

She made no reply, apparently unfamiliar with that brand. What she wanted from the Gold Wok was five helpings of plain rice and shrimp sautéed with vegetables every day for two weeks. She would come toward midday to pick up the food and pay thirty dollars for it. The lunch was only for the athletes who were going to have events in the afternoon, a kind of treat. Nan prepared the rice and the dish as well as he could and was generous with the portions. Mei Hong would come to collect it and then drive all the way to a gas station outside Georgia Tech, since she didn't have a pass for the Olympic Village. A Chinese official would meet her there to receive the food. The Olympics had suddenly activated many local Chinese and united their minds and energies.

Although Nan said they were all being ridiculous, he couldn't help feeling delighted whenever he saw the Chinese national flag rising in the stadium. When he opened a newspaper, he'd check to see how many medals China had won. Sometimes even a Chinese face on TV would attract his attention in a peculiar way, as if he knew that person. He realized that emotionally he couldn't separate himself from those people completely. This realization troubled him, and for days he was cranky. His mind remained confused until he saw a performance on the pommel horse by a stolid-faced man named

Donghua Li, a former Chinese gymnast but a Swiss citizen now. That performance moved Nan and threw him deep into thought. Li had quit China's national team in order to marry a Swiss woman. He left his native country in 1988, but couldn't compete in international events because he had to wait five years to be naturalized. Now, at age twenty-nine, he was here in Atlanta representing Switzerland alone in gymnastics. While the other athletes loosened up for the pommel horse competition, he was napping in a corner with an opened magazine over his face and with his shoes stacked together as a pillow under his head. Few people took notice of him. Not until it was his turn to perform did he get up from the floor. The commentator joked, "He's woken up finally."

Li performed on the horse with aplomb, keeping his feet pointed while his legs swung high, nimbly executing the scissors movement, as if they had no weight. Then with ease he circled above the horse, keeping his feet together and his legs straight at a right angle to his upper body. He obviously was superior to all the other competitors. Throughout his program, never did his pants touch the horse. Nan watched closely. Despite the lightness of his movement, Li's facial muscles were all knotted, and sweat was glistening on his forehead. Swinging up his legs, he made a flank vault and landed stock-still. Applause burst out all around. He earned 9.875, high enough for the gold. After the event, he blew a kiss to his wife sitting among the audience, but he refused to be interviewed by the Chinese reporters following him. Instead, he turned to shake hands with the leading Russian gymnast, Aleksei Nemov, and gave him a thumbs-up. Nan was eager to see this fellow again in other events and to root for him, but Li never reappeared on the screen.

Another scene, however, troubled Nan. It took place in the women's soccer game between China and the United States. The TV showed several signs bearing Chinese characters being flaunted in the audience. A long horizontal one, held by two men, declared MARCH FORWARD, MARCH FORWARD! BRAVE SISTERS, YOU MUST WIN FOR YOUR BROTHERS WHO ARE FULL OF HATRED. An American woman reporter asked the men what the sign said, but they shook their heads, grinning and pretending they didn't understand her.

Those words were a parody of the beginning of the theme song in the revolutionary ballet *The Red Women Detachment*. The reporter had some inkling of the message, but she couldn't get the men to level with her. The sign bothered Nan and Pingping; they surmised that the two men had probably failed to find a decent job here or get a green card.

17

ONE MORNING Mei Hong came and said to Nan, "*We need some mung-bean soup. This Atlanta heat is too much for our athletes. Some of them have had sunstroke. We must help them relieve the heat.*"

"*We don't offer mung-bean soup,*" Nan told her.

"*No place does. That's why I came to you.*"

"*What do you want me to do?*"

"*Boil a large pot of the soup and I'll personally take it to them.*"

Nan wanted to ask her how much she'd pay him, but seeing her earnest face filmed with perspiration, he didn't mention money. Mung beans weren't expensive—two pounds, enough for a pot of the soup, cost just over a dollar.

The next morning he boiled the soup in a cauldron and ladled it into a tall stainless-steel pot. Mei Hong came and sealed the lid of the pot with duct tape. Nan helped her load it into the back of her SUV. Having promised to return the pot that very day, she drove away.

Pingping disliked Mei Hong, saying that she was like a village leader or a Party secretary of a small work unit. "*She acts as if she runs our life,*" Pingping complained.

The pot didn't come back that evening. Two days passed without any trace of it. When Mei Hong arrived to get the shrimp and rice, Nan asked her where it was. At first she dodged the question and just promised to bring it back, but then admitted she didn't know its whereabouts either. She explained, "*I told them it was mung-bean soup, but they wouldn't let the athletes drink it. They were afraid the soup might affect their urine tests.*"

"*What?*" Nan couldn't believe his ears. "*It had nothing in it but a few beans. I didn't even dare to put in sugar.*"

"*I know. They wouldn't listen to me, because their higher-ups had ordered them not to accept any drinks from outside. So they wanted ice instead of mung-bean soup. We used the pot to carry ice into the Olympic Village.*"

"*What happened to the pot? Why didn't you bring it back?*"

"*I tried to personally take the pot filled with ice into the compound, but the guards blocked me. One of them shouted, 'No taggy, no entry, Mama-san.' Damn that camel! Do I look like an old Korean woman?*"

Nan quenched his impulse to laugh. "*So you dumped the soup, didn't you?*"

"*Yes, I'm sorry. I couldn't follow the pot.*"

"*I want it back. I spent nineteen dollars for it.*"

"*I'll see what I can do.*"

After that conversation, Mei Hong stopped coming to fetch food, so Nan gave up cooking lunch for the athletes. The Wus were glad that finally the woman seemed to have disappeared from their lives.

18

DICK'S book, *Unexpected Gifts,* came out in August and was well received. These days he was busy reading at colleges and libraries and seldom came to the Gold Wok. Nan saw a brief but positive review of the book in the Sunday *New York Times,* which he often bought at Kroger. He could tell that Dick was now taken more seriously by critics. He phoned his friend, who was not in, so he left a congratulatory message. Dick didn't return his call. He was traveling a lot lately.

Nan wondered whether his friend had abandoned him. Then one afternoon Dick showed up, the same disheveled man in an unbuttoned denim jacket. He didn't look happy and told Nan, "My book is doing well, but the press won't reprint it."

"Why? Don't zey want to sell more books?"

"I don't know. They've never planned to make money from poetry. Once a book has sold out, it's dead."

"Dead in just two mons?"

"Well, not yet. They still have three hundred copies in stock, but once those are gone the book will be out of print." He let out a sigh.

"Zat's terrible."

"See, whenever I finish a book, I'll go through a big crisis, not knowing who will publish it. Whenever my book is doing well, it will create another crisis, because it means the book will be gone soon. It's very hard to keep a book of poetry in print for up to three years."

"Man, you have depressed me," Nan said gravely.

"Don't get upset. We write poetry because we love it. To tell the truth, if I didn't write, I don't know if I could have lived so long. I don't regret doing it."

That baffled Nan, who felt Dick could easily live without making poems. Dick might just have wanted to sound theatrical. Look at Nan himself—he hadn't written anything for a long time, and still he was breathing normally, in the pink, as it were. So he had his doubts about Dick's confession. Not until several years later did he fully understand the truth of his friend's words.

19

THE BERNSTEIN GALLERY in Atlanta was going to hold its fall show, at which some painters in the Southeast would be featured. Bao mailed Nan a card that bore a painting from his Shanghai series and the information on the exhibition. He wrote that he hoped to see Nan there and that he had invited Dick as well. Nan knew Dick wouldn't be there, for these days his friend was always out of town giving readings, except when he had to come back and teach.

Nan managed to go to the show on the opening day. He arrived ahead of the crowd in the afternoon, as he'd have to leave early before the busy hours started at the restaurant. Bao wasn't there yet, so Nan was able to walk around and look carefully at the works by all twenty-three artists. He found only a few of them remarkable. He noticed the prices for the paintings were not as high as he had expected; the most expensive piece was marked for $6,000. Among these paintings, Bao's didn't stand out at all. Most of his works were priced around $3,000; evidently Tim and Brian had overstated the case when Nan had met them. He wasn't impressed by Bao's new works either. The whole Shanghai series looked like an imitation of van Gogh, dull and even clotty in places, without the master's brightness and vibrations. The Hunagpu Bund was presented like a streetscape; without the title, few people could have related it to the Shanghai waterside. The view of a thoroughfare in one painting lacked specifics, as if it were a scene of nineteenth-century Paris. Below Bao's central piece sat a large bin containing numerous smaller objets d'art made by him: a still life of chrysanthemums, a pencil drawing of a Himalayan cat, a gouache of a dancing girl, a miniature seascape. These were priced between $150 and $300.

They reminded Nan of a Chinese buffet that offered numerous choices, none of which was refined or sumptuous. Obviously Bao, cashing in on his success, had diffused his energy and lost his creative center. This troubled Nan.

Ian Bernstein, a thickset, swarthy man and the owner of the gallery, greeted the early arrivals with a tumbler of mimosa in his large, veined hand. Nan talked with him while they stood in front of his friend's works. "What do you sink of Bao's new paintings?" he asked Mr. Bernstein, who was also Bao's agent.

"I'm not bowled over by them." The host screwed up his left eye.

"Not as good as his Venice series, right?"

"Who would buy these? They don't have enough life in them. Even the colors are too dull for me."

"I agree."

Bao appeared in the entryway. Mr. Bernstein went up to him and they hugged warmly. Then Bao came over and shook hands with Nan. He was fatter than five months before and looked stiff and rustic in his dark green three-piece suit and canary yellow necktie. Nan was determined not to praise his new works, so he asked about his health and his family. Bao was not only married but also an expectant father; his wife was due the next spring. After the birth of their baby, mother and child would come to join him here. *"I'm going to buy a piece of land in a suburb of Atlanta and build my home on it,"* Bao told Nan proudly.

"That's great. Have you decided in what area yet?"

"Probably somewhere in Cobb County."

"It has a good school system."

"So I have heard."

Frank, Bao's lawyer student, emerged from behind. He had brought along his family, his wife and two sons. Bao turned away to greet them.

Seizing this opportunity, Nan disengaged himself. He was afraid his friend would ask him to comment on the Shanghai series. Part of him wanted to tell Bao the truth, which would have been embarrassing to both of them. He moved around to look some more and came upon a set of landscapes by a Floridian painter named Kent Philips. Unlike the other artists, who each had at least half a dozen paintings on show, this man had only three pieces here, none of which was fancy. But Nan liked them very much, fascinated by their dark, luminous quality. In these landscapes, every stream, every tree, every animal, every rock possessed a shimmering spirit that seemed transcendental and mysterious. The paintings had depth and a kind of darkness that reminded Nan of the forests in New England. Nan greeted the short, pudgy artist who stood beside his works as if unable to mingle with others, though his three pieces were all priced above $5,000.

"I love your work," Nan said sincerely.

"Thanks. That means a lot."

"Is zis someplace in Florida?" He pointed at the middle piece.

"No, I painted them in Montana."

"No wonder zer vegetation wasn't lush. So no everglades and gators, huh?"

"No." Kent Philips chuckled, rather shy. "I wanted to make the landscape sparse but infused with light."

"Zat's clear. These pieces don't blaze but shimmer. Zat's what I like most about zem. Zey're full of a quiet dignity."

"Thanks! Do you paint?" Obviously he regarded Nan as a fellow artist.

"I write," Nan said reluctantly.

"What kind of work do you write?"

"Poetry."

"Wow, I can't imagine doing that, although I like poetry too. You must give me the titles of your books so I can get a copy at the bookstore in my town."

"I haven't pahblished a book yet." Nan was slightly embarrassed.

"I know poetry is hard, but don't give up. When you reach a certain point, good things will happen, as long as you persevere."

"I'll remember zat."

A young waiter came over holding a tray of green olives stuffed with pimento, which they both passed up. Kent gave Nan his card and invited him to come visit if he was ever in Florida. Nan was pleased and felt a kind of warmth rising in him, though he knew it was unlikely he'd see this man again. It was odd that he felt so uncomfortable to be with Bao despite having known him for years, whereas with Kent Philips, a stranger, he was at ease, not having to weigh his words or resort to social rhetoric.

Before leaving the show, Nan looked around for Bao to say goodbye. In the section of handcrafted works, he saw his friend conversing with a delicate black woman dressed in red silk and holding a flute of champagne. She was the artist who had made the gorgeous, menacing masks hanging on the wall behind her. As Nan approached them, he overheard Bao praise the lady's work, "Beautiful hand-job, very special."

"Handiwork!" she corrected.

"Yes, I mean everything done by hand."

Nan edged away while fighting down the laugh rising in his throat. He slipped into an anteroom and went out of the gallery. A chilly wind swept up a few dead leaves, which were rattling and scuttling before a Dumpster on which perched half a dozen crows. The moon looked bloody, like a giant rotten orange. Nan sank into thought on his drive back, and wondered if Bao would be displeased by his French leave. For the rest of the evening in the kitchen he couldn't stop imagining a kind of dark poetry that possessed a luminosity similar to that in Kent Philips's paintings.

20

THESE DAYS Nan and Pingping were priming Taotao for the SATs. The boy was just an eighth grader, but he had been selected to join in a talent survey, whose participants were to take the regular SATs in November. Nan gave his son a clothbound *Oxford American Dictionary* and asked him to highlight all the word entries he didn't know and then review them later on. Once Taotao finished the whole book, Nan would pay him a hundred dollars. The boy was reluctant, but his father convinced him that this would increase his verbal score considerably. More important, he would learn many new words. Even if he couldn't finish reading the dictionary before sitting for the SATs, he could continue to work on it afterward and earn the promised money. Taotao was eager to use the cash for a sound card for his computer, so he agreed to do the work. As for math, Pingping took care of that. In fact, she hardly needed to do anything, already having taught him a great deal.

"I know I'm going to blow it," Taotao complained to his parents. "I'm going to make a fool of myself. Nobody in my grade will take the SATs this year. This is silly and outrageous. And if I come out all right, people will think of me as a whiz kid. I don't want to be a whiz kid who's just a parrot. I want to be like everybody else."

"It's an honor to be a part of zer talent search," Nan said.

"I have no talent and don't want the honor. Let them experiment with other rare birds, not me. I won't take the tests."

"You just scared," Pingping put in. "If you don't do it, I won't teach you anymore. You can decide yourself."

"Mom, you're so cruel!"

Despite his protests, Taotao did sit for the SATs on the last Saturday in November. He wasn't sure if he had done well. His parents told him not to worry since there'd still be three years before he took the real tests for college. Four weeks later the scores came: math 710 and verbal 580. His parents were very pleased. For years Nan had worried about how to pay his son's college tuition; now it was clear that the boy would be able to get a scholarship from a decent school provided Taotao became an American citizen. Nan felt relieved and urged his son to continue to read the dictionary, of which Taotao had covered merely 350 pages, less than half the book. The SAT results got Taotao qualified for the summer programs for gifted kids at both Duke and Johns Hopkins, but he wouldn't be able to attend either of them because his parents didn't believe in them and couldn't afford the tuition. There was a chance that he could get a scholarship for the programs, but he preferred to stay home in the summertime.

21

NAN had applied for U.S. citizenship three months earlier. The naturalization would take at least half a year to complete. Only after he became an American citizen could Taotao and Pingping begin their naturalization. Nan hadn't applied for the citizenship with a light heart, but this was the only sensible thing to do. Besides the need for Taotao to become an American, Nan felt he had been disowned by China long ago. There wasn't another place where he and his family could and wanted to live. His home and livelihood were here. The previous spring he had read an article by Yong Chu, the old poet teaching Chinese at a college in Rhode Island, whom Nan had seen six years earlier at the memorial meeting for those killed in the Tiananmen massacre. In his article, "Why I Don't Want to Be an American Citizen," Mr. Chu wrote candidly that he was unsure which side he would take if the United States went to war with China. The citizenship would require him to be willing to bear arms to defend the U.S. Constitution and fight any foreign enemy, at least participating in noncombatant service in wartime. Chu stated that his heart wouldn't allow him to side against his motherland and that he wanted to live honestly, so he wouldn't get naturalized. Now Nan wasn't certain which side he'd take if a war broke out between China and the United States. This uncertainty tormented him, but he also knew that once he swore his allegiance at the oath ceremony, he'd have to abide by his word. To him, a promise should weigh more than a country.

He thought of a pair of metaphors, comparing China to his mother and the United States to the woman he loved. He was sure that someone else had used this trite analogy before; nonetheless, it helped him sort out his emotions. As a grown man he couldn't live with his mother forever and must choose to join the woman of his heart. Certainly he wouldn't taunt or beat his mother if there was a fight between the old lady and his beloved. All he could do was help them understand each other even though they might never see eye to eye. It was with this intention that he went to a meeting held in the community center in Chinatown.

Recently two young journalists in mainland China had published a book entitled *China Can Say No,* which vehemently condemned the United States as China's archenemy. The book was poorly written and full of errors and distortions, but it had gone through many reprints. The authors went so far as to claim that China would "incinerate Hollywood" and "let the United States suffer the ax of war." Clearly some top officials had endorsed the publication of this book, using hatred and fear to unify the populace. The book caused quite a stir in the Chinese diaspora as well, so the Chinese community in Atlanta had invited scholars, writers, students, and people of various walks to discuss it on a Saturday afternoon in early January.

The conference room at the community center was packed, some people standing along the walls. Nan was sitting on a folding chair close to the front, having arrived ten minutes early. Two men and one woman were seated at the table facing the audience. Since many of the attendees didn't know English, the discussion was to be conducted only in Chinese. After the moderator introduced the speakers, the older man, a historian wearing horn-rimmed glasses, harrumphed, then began to speak in a squeaky voice. He criticized the book, saying it merely echoed "the Boxers' sentiment and cheap jingoism." Also, its main points, mostly supported by wrong information and inaccurate statistics, were shaped to serve current politics in China and had nothing to do with real scholarship. While speaking, he grew more animated, his glasses flashing. He stressed that the United States had never robbed China like other foreign powers had, and that it was Japan and Russia that China should condemn and worry about. Anyone with some knowledge of modern history could see this plainly. In short, the book was superficial, unprofessional, irresponsible, and shouldn't be taken seriously. He went on to recommend several titles that could inform people better about the relationship between China and the United States. As he spoke, grumbles were rising from the audience.

Nan agreed with the speaker's views, but he didn't like the old man's jarring voice and supercilious manner, especially his use of his thick index finger to point at the listeners as if they were his students.

The second speaker was a younger man with large weary eyes, a political scientist at Georgia Tech. He believed the book was too emotional, but he could see two causes for the desperate emotions the authors manifested. First, the Chinese government had ruined its image with the Tiananmen tragedy, and people in the West had begun to view China as a totalitarian state; for this the Communist leaders had to be responsible. Second, the U.S. policy toward China had lacked consistency in recent years. That hurt the self-respect of the Chinese people. For example, in May 1995 the American government had allowed Denghui Li, the former president of Taiwan, to visit the United States and thus deviated from its one-China policy and accelerated the crisis over Taiwan Strait.

"*Shut up!*" a spindly man yelled, and he stood up in the back. "*You're talking dog crap and trying to please the Nationalists from Taiwan who control this community. Why do you want to shoot down the authors of this book just because they're young and emotional? We Chinese must have our pride and must stand up to Americans. I've been here for two years. How much bitterness have I swallowed? I was a doctor back in Tianjin City, but here I'm a custodian wiping windows and toilets. Who can relate to me? Who will speak for me? Who can know how a Chinese actually feels here? Why do you defend Americans instead of your own compatriots?*" The man broke out sobbing and couldn't speak anymore. He sat down and covered his face with both hands. Someone in the front howled with laughter.

For a moment silence fell on the room. Then people began jabbering, either condemning the U.S. government or denouncing the authors of the book. Nan turned around to look at that vociferous man in the back, who was still weeping. The moon-faced moderator waved to quiet the audience down and then let the woman on the panel, a Taiwanese essayist, speak.

The middle-aged writer moved the microphone closer and leaned forward a little. She said, "*I want to cry. Such a vulgar, mindless book has become a best seller. This shows the deteriorating mental state the people on the mainland have sunk into. How could the authors use such obscene language to describe Taiwan? I didn't understand the word 'sichu,' so I looked it up in a dictionary. How dare they say Taiwan is China's 'private parts' that no foreign power can touch! The authors were crass and foolish if not demented. They don't think of the Taiwanese as human beings. All they care about is the so-called Chinese nation, the great China. They made me want to puke! They went so far as to claim Taiwan was China's testicles, grabbed by the United States now. How ignorant and shameless they are! In the postscript they even say New York's highways are inferior to China's highways, and that New York has no new architecture. You have all seen America and can form your own opinion. If you're not blind, you can judge for yourselves.*"

She became too emotional to continue. Then a lynx-eyed man, perhaps a visiting scholar, seized the microphone in the audience and shouted: "*Compatriots and friends, to the vacillation of the U.S. foreign policy toward Taiwan we must say no!*"

People applauded.

He boomed again, "*To the Japanese anti-China activities we must say no!*"

Again applause broke out.

"*To the U.S. Congress's China-bashing we must say no!*"

More people clapped their hands.

"*To American imperialism and hegemony we must say no!*"

Applause thundered again.

"*To all those who are hostile to our Chinese nation we must say no!*"

Some of the audience stood up applauding. Then the man spoke calmly as if clarifying his points. He told the audience, "*Even as we say no, we must be rational and base our ideas and judgments on accurate information and facts. Otherwise we might make disastrous mistakes. While we blame others for being prejudiced and for double-dealing, we ought to prevent ourselves from getting too hot-*

headed." He was certain that the twenty-first century would belong to China, meaning that the country would grow into the number one world power, so the Chinese, he said, should be confident and mustn't follow American ways.

Nan was bewildered by this man's performance, wondering which side he was actually on. The man spoke like a seasoned official, manipulating the emotions of the audience, some of whom kept nodding approval.

Then a skinny woman in a coffee-colored woolen sweater took the microphone. She was wearing at her waist a small thermos made of stainless steel. Despite her new hairdo, Nan recognized her—Mei Hong. "*I have to take issue with you notables on the panel,*" she said emphatically. "*You say the authors are young, emotional, and ignorant. Do you know that being young is not necessarily being wrong? Napoleon started conquering Europe when he was a young man. You say they're too emotional. What can be accomplished without deep, sincere emotion? A few years ago I went to visit the Yuan Ming Park outside Beijing that was burned by the Eight-Power Allied Forces last century. Seeing those felled stone pillars and charred beams, I couldn't hold back my tears. My heart was aching and bleeding. How could I not be emotional? You say the authors are ignorant, but they plucked up courage to confront the American imperialists. Even if you have a great deal of knowledge and professional training, why haven't you done anything to expose the conspiracy against China? Why do you talk like running dogs employed by the U.S. government? Shame on you!*"

A smattering of applause rippled across the audience. The three panelists looked astonished. The woman writer sighed, now shaking her head, now pinching the bridge of her nose.

Mei Hong continued, "*The other day my daughter told me that a Korean boy in her class broke into tears because some students called him 'Chinese.' That made me remember that once a homeless bum had yelled 'Chinese' at me simply because I didn't respond to his panhandling. He didn't know my ethnicity for sure, but why did he call me that? And why did the Korean boy feel so humiliated by the word 'Chinese'? I did some research on this, and here, let me share my discovery with you.*" She pulled out a square of paper from her pants pocket, unfolded it, and went on to explain, "*In English the suffix '-ese' suggests 'inferior, insignificant, weak, weird, and diminutive.' You all know what 'China' means. It means 'hardened clay or dirt.' So combining the two parts together, 'Chinese' means 'tiny, petty, and odd stuff made of dirt or clay.' After looking up the verbal roots in* The Oxford English Dictionary, *I finally understood that 'Chinese' was a racial slur, originally used by the British imperialists to put down our people and break our spirit. Not only us, but also other races, such as* Japanese *and* Vietnamese, *as if we were all peewee peoples, lightweights. By comparison, the suffix '-an' designates people of 'superior' races, for example,* Roman, American, *and* German. *This discrepancy in naming different peoples means that racial prejudice is already coded in the English language. Germany produces sausages—why not call its people* Sausagese? *Italy is known for pizzas—why not call Italians* Pizzese? *England used to export woolen textiles—why not call the British* Woolese? *America yields a lot of corn—why not call the people here* Cornese? *Or the Swiss,* Cheesese?" Many people hooted with laughter while Mei Hong looked around, her face taut and her chest heaving, as if she were a stern teacher in front of a noisy class.

As the audience quieted down some, she went on, "*Obviously the English language is meant to discriminate against us and other colored races. Now I can see why so many people from our homeland call themselves 'Asians,' because they've intuitively sensed that words like 'Chinese,' 'Vietnamese,' and 'Japanese' were coined to diminish them. Therefore we, people from the 'Central Kingdom,' must refuse to be called* Chinese, *just like the blacks refuse to be called 'niggers.'*"

Her tirade made her short of breath. She sat down, her cheeks red and puffy. The audience was puzzled, so most of them remained silent. A few were snickering.

Nan rose and took the microphone. He said, "*I don't want to dispute the accuracy of Mei Hong's linguistic research, since I haven't touched the OED for ages. Let me just appeal to your common sense. We're all human beings and should be reasonable. The great poet*

Czeslaw Milosz said, 'Human reason is beautiful and invincible,' so let us rely on nothing but our own intelligence. America didn't force us to come here, did it? China is our native land, while America is the land of our children—that's to say, a place of our future. If a war breaks out between China and the United States, how can any one of us here benefit from it?"

"What's your point? Out with it!" a female voice burst out from the back.

"My point is that we must stop stoking animosity and must remember that the authors of this mean book don't speak on our behalf. They're just hate-mongers. We have different interests from them because we don't live in China anymore. We mustn't follow them in railing against the United States blindly."

Mei Hong cried sharply, "That's outside the parameters of my subject."

Her overbearing tone of voice enraged Nan. He exploded, "You haven't returned my soup pot yet! You promised to do that five months ago—why haven't you kept your promise? I can never trust you again. You talk so much about national pride and honor, but why wouldn't you honor your own word? Why can't you be more decent as a human being?" To his surprise, his questions shut her up. Mei Hong dropped her eyes, her face dark. Several people cackled.

Then a young woman stood up and challenged Nan, "Are you a Chinese or not?"

"I was born in China and—"

"Give us a simple yes or no answer!"

"I'm going to be a U.S. citizen. I believe most of you will—"

"Get out of here, you shameless American!" shouted a male voice.

"Let him speak," a man interrupted. "I'm going to be a citizen too."

"Americans out! Americans out!" a few voices cried in unison.

"This is a free country and I have the right of free speech," Nan said.

"We don't want to listen to you."

"Yes, get out of here!"

"Let him finish."

"Achoo!"

"*Listen,*" Nan went on. "*You people always talk about your nation, your China, as if every one of you were a kingpin of that country. Has it ever occurred to you that this obsession is dangerous? I mean to let a country dominate an individual's life and outweigh everything else. What's the definition of fascism? Do you know?*"

A hush fell over them.

Then someone brought out, "*Don't give us another lie.*"

Nan replied calmly, "*The first principle of fascism is to exalt country and race above the individual. If you don't believe me, look it up in* Merriam-Webster's Collegiate Dictionary, *the tenth edition. If we don't stop this nonsense of China's pride, we may end up ruining our own lives here.*"

"*You never cease to amaze me.*" Mei Hong stood up. "*A madman is what you are. Let me tell you, you're also a banana!*" She jabbed her finger at Nan. "*You always despise China and our language. That's why you've been writing in English and dreaming of becoming another Conrad or Nabokov. Let me tell you, you're just making a buffoon of yourself! Get real—stop fancying yourself a great poet!*"

Flustered, Nan felt his throat congesting. But he scrambled to answer, "*To write in English is my personal choice. Unlike you, I prefer to be a real individual.*"

"*Yeah, to be a lone wolf,*" scoffed Mei Hong.

"*Exactly!*"

That somehow gagged her, and some people giggled. Nan said to the audience, "*All I'm saying is that we ought to be decent human beings first, to be fair and upright to others and to ourselves.*"

The moderator rapped the table with her pen, but nobody took heed of her. "*Stop bickering!*" she begged, yet more people were jabbering now. The room was in a tumult. Many of the audience stood up, watching or whooping. The three panelists rose too, gathering their materials and about to leave. The scraping of chairs and shuffling of feet filled the room.

A few pairs of eyes were glowering at Nan, who pretended not to notice them. If only he had listened to Pingping and stayed at the restaurant. He shouldn't have come to this pandemonium to seek unhappiness. There was no way to reason with some people in this crowd, to which he felt he no longer belonged. Their ilk had the herd mentality that assumed the fulfillment of one's selfhood depended on the rise and growth of a tribe. Nan wondered whether he should go up to the old historian on the panel and talk with him for a while, but he decided not to. He preferred to stand alone.

22

WHILE Nan was at the meeting, Pingping and Niyan were diligently preparing for the evening. It was Saturday, so they'd be busy after three o'clock. Nan had promised to come back before three-thirty. Pingping took out of the freezer the beef and chicken Nan had cut the previous night and let them thaw. She planned to wrap some egg rolls after putting a new ribbon of paper into the cash register. She hadn't fully recovered from the abortion yet, and though most of her diabetic symptoms were gone, a numbing pain still tightened her lower back from time to time. In the dining room Niyan was chasing a fly with a long plastic swatter. She had been placing silverware and paper napkins on the tables.

As they were working, a shaggy man in a maroon windbreaker came in with a half-empty bottle under his arm. He lurched directly to the counter, plunked beside the cash register the stout amber bottle printed with "Wild Turkey," pulled out a snub-nosed revolver, and hissed at Pingping, "Give me all the dough you have here."

For a moment she was too transfixed to respond. The man said again, "Empty your drawer and give me all the cash!" His reddish beard, so thick that his mouth was invisible, quivered as he spoke, blowing hot, alcoholic fumes on Pingping's face.

Silently she unlocked the register and took out the tray that contained about a dozen singles, four fives, two tens, and some coins. Inside the machine, under the tray, was a sheaf of twenties, more than two hundred dollars, which she always kept in there for emergency use, but she didn't touch it. With trembling hands she placed the tray before the man and said, "We haven't star' yet." Through the corner of her vision she saw Niyan scurrying out the front door. The thought that she was left alone to face the robber petrified her, and she broke into sniffling sobs.

Her crying seemed to startle the man, who grabbed the money and thrust all banknotes into the pocket of his windbreaker but left the coins untouched. "What lousy luck!" he grumbled, his boozy eyes flickering.

"Please go away!" begged Pingping.

"Nope. I'm hungry and want some food."

"We not open yet."

"Don't tell me that!"

"I don't know how to cook."

"Sure you do. I've been here before and saw you cookin' in there."

"What do you want?"

"Let's see." He flipped open a menu on the counter. "Mongolian Beef, this one, spicy."

"My husband is chef. Me can't make Mongolian Beef." She was really unsure how to cook his order, because the dish wasn't sup-posed to be spicy.

"Don't lie to me. I'm not a fool. Let me have some spicy Mongolian Beef."

"I don't know how to cook that."

"D'you want me to come in and help you?" He slitted his eyes, leering at her.

"Okay, okay, I will see what I can do." She retreated into the kitchen.

As she was about to make for the back door, a piercing siren shrilled, rising louder and louder. The man was frightened. He spun around and rushed away to the front door. Before he could get out, three policemen came in and pointed their pistols at him. "Hold it there!" one of them ordered.

With a groan the man slumped to the floor. He wailed hoarsely, "I'm sorry! I'm really down and out. I need money to buy a birthday gift for my kid."

The police fell on him, pressed him on the floor, and handcuffed him. Then they pulled him up. Niyan came in and spat at the man's face, saying, "Shame on you! The bank is right across the street. Why don't you go there? We're poor too." She raised her hand and pulled off his marled hat, woven of black and orange wool and still bearing a Wal-Mart tag marked with the price—$3.75.

"Hey, hey, don't touch him!" said the short policeman with a beer belly, flipping the cylinder of the small revolver to remove the bullets. His colleagues were inspecting the crime scene, one in the kitchen.

"Can't make it anymore," the man mumbled to Niyan.

"Stop lying!" she snapped. "You still have money for a new hat."

"It's a gift from my girlfriend," he grunted.

Niyan turned to Pingping. "*Good heavens, hear this? He keeps a woman while he's totally broke.*" She thrust the hat into his left pocket.

Pingping said to him, "You should feel shame yourself."

"I'm sorry, ma'am," the man muttered, and hung his head, showing a whitish spot on his crown.

Pingping inserted his half bottle of whiskey under his arm. "Take your stuff." She then pulled all the cash out of his right pocket while explaining to the officers, "He grab all money from our machine."

"All right, let's go." The short policeman slapped the criminal on the back, then steered him toward the door.

An older officer began asking Pingping and Niyan questions. The waitress boasted that she could have grabbed the gun left by the man on the counter and shot him, but she phoned the police instead. "He's stupid, you know," she said, one palm on her hip.

"Never take the law into your own hands. You did the right thing," said the stalwart officer in a nasal voice, writing on a clipboard.

Pingping thanked him again and again for coming to their rescue.

●

When Nan came back, his wife, still beside herself, shouted at him, "*I thought you had forgotten this place. Why are you here?*"

He was taken aback by her tear-stained face and didn't respond. She was trembling a little as she spoke. After hearing about what had happened, he apologized and promised he wouldn't go to any of those meetings again.

Pingping went on, "*If Niyan hadn't called the police, that robber would have rushed into the kitchen and killed me in there. I was so scared! My legs still can't stop shaking.*"

Niyan tittered. Nan threw an arm around his wife and told her,

"We're poor too. I never thought someone would rob us. Don't cry, Pingping. I won't leave this place to you alone again. That man must have been really destitute."

"Maybe so. He wasn't like a professional robber. Probably he was scared too. I'm sure he was drunk."

Niyan put in, "Maybe we should keep a gun here."

"No, no, absolutely not!" Nan said. "If a robber shows up again, just give him what he wants. The most important thing is not to get yourself hurt. Understood?"

"Yes, sir," replied the waitress with a grin.

23

THOUGH Taotao read *The Oxford American Dictionary* from time to time, he refused to learn Chinese anymore. Whenever his parents urged him to write some characters, he'd claim his hand hurt so much that he was suffering from carpal tunnel syndrome. What was that? His parents had no clue. They believed the problem lay in his mind and it was his laziness that had caused the constant slippage with his Chinese writing. He could speak and understand Mandarin but could no longer read or write the words. Even when he spoke the language, he used it only in a rudimentary way. He was tired of his parents' litany of the advantages in being fully bilingual. One afternoon his father yelled at him in the storage room, demanding that the boy promise to work hard on the written characters, but Taotao wouldn't give him his word and instead complained about the uselessness of Chinese in his life. Shubo happened to be present and tried to convince the boy of the necessity of keeping his mother tongue.

"It's too hard," Taotao said. "I've already spent so many years on it and can't even keep the words I had learned before I was six." Recently he had begun to resent the more difficult characters. Among those he could recognize, he hated the killer ideogram *cang* (hide) most, never able to remember the order and number of its strokes.

"You've never poot your heart into it. Of coss you have regressed so much," Nan said.

Shubo coaxed, "Taotao, don't give up. Stroke by stroke you can fell an oak."

"I don't want to cut down any tree!"

502

"I mean, no pains, no gains—if you keep to try, you will master Chinese."

"Fat chance," grunted the boy.

"Yes, you still have a big chance."

"I don't mean that."

His father broke in, "I know what you mean—'a very slim chance.' No matter what, you must continue to learn Chinese."

Unlike Nan, Pingping sympathized with their son and in private pointed out to Nan that Taotao would never learn enough of the language for taking the SAT II Chinese test. Her argument sank in, and for several days Nan left him alone.

Now it was time for the boy to decide what foreign language to study in middle and high schools. There were Sunday Chinese classes at Emory University, which many children attended, but on weekends Nan and Pingping had to work and couldn't drive their son into Atlanta. Moreover, Pingping didn't believe Taotao would benefit much from knowing Chinese. She felt English was much more expressive and more useful. Back in China she could hardly write anything, but here once she learned a little English, she had found herself able to write a lot, as if whatever she put on paper became interesting. Nan agreed with her. Compared with written Chinese, English was indeed a language of common people, despite being hard to master, its grammatical rules too loose and its idioms defying logic. Without question, their son should devote himself more to this alphabet.

So they stopped badgering him to inscribe the characters. If the boy didn't like Chinese, he would never master it by copying the words. Maybe someday they could send him to Pingping's parents during the summer; that way he could regain his fluency and literacy in his mother tongue. In his school Latin was very popular, and he applied for it but couldn't get into the class. It was said that some students had learned Latin so well that they kept diaries in the dead tongue so that their parents couldn't tell what they wrote. Nan knew that the knowledge of Latin would strengthen his son's English, so he was displeased that Taotao couldn't enroll in the class.

Later Pingping found out that besides English, most papers in science were published in three other languages: French, German, and

Japanese. So it would be better if Taotao took up either German or French, both offered at his school. At the beginning of the next semester he chose to learn French, which turned out to be so easy for him that he soon excelled in the class.

Once he asked his parents, "Can I major in French in college?"

"You should study to be doctor," Pingping said. "What profession is better than save people's life?"

"I don't like medical science. How about art history or English? Can I major in art history?"

"Zen you will be a poor scholar for zer rest of your life," Nan said.

"I don't care."

"You don't care because we work night and day to make money for you," retorted his mother. "You act like rich kid who don't need profession."

Taotao turned to his father. "Didn't you tell me to follow my heart? You said, 'As long as you do something well, you won't starve.'"

"Sure, I said zat. But you should take your mozzer's opinion into account too."

"If I get a scholarship, can I study anything I want?"

His parents didn't answer, knowing there was no way to dissuade him. Nan knew Pingping would be happy if Taotao became a premed, but he believed they shouldn't force their son to do anything against his will. Yes, he wanted the boy to follow his own heart.

24

"SOMETHING good happened," Dick said to Nan when he stepped into the Gold Wok. There was a note of delight in his voice. He pulled his maroon scarf off his neck, his hair damp with rainwater and his cheeks steaming a little. It was still drizzling outside, and it had been a slow afternoon at the restaurant.

"What happened?" asked Nan.

"My book won the National Book Critics Circle Award." Dick's eyes were sparkling and his face was so radiant that he seemed many years younger.

"How big is zis prize?"

"Almost like a Pulitzer."

"My goodness, congratulations!" Nan gave him a bear hug, patting his shoulder several times. "So now you're as famous as Edward Neary?"

"I'm getting close."

"You inspire me," Nan said in all sincerity. Indeed, just yesterday he hadn't thought of Dick as a significant poet; now overnight his friend had become a literary figure.

"Now my task is how to manage success," said Dick.

"How do you mean?" Nan was puzzled, unable to see how success was something to be managed.

"I must capitalize on the opportunity to promote myself and my work, also to raise my fee."

"What fee?"

"The fee for my readings and talks."

"Oh, you'll rake in zer kind of mahney like Edward Neary?"

"You bet."

That surprised Nan, because Dick was talking like a businessman. Yet Nan said, "We must celebrate."

"Yes, let's do that. Thank you."

Nan went into the kitchen to make Crabmeat Fu Rong and Scallops with Black Bean Sauce. Both dishes were easy to to cook, and the latter was one of Dick's favorites. Nan told Niyan to take two bottles of Tsingtao beer to Dick. He said to Pingping, "*Dick just won a top prize for his poetry book. He's a star now.*"

"*No fooling? What prize?*"

"*I forgot what it's called, similar to the Pulitzer.*"

"*My, I should go and congratulate him.*"

"*Tell him I'll be done in a few minutes.*"

Both Pingping and Niyan gave their congratulations to Dick, who was so wild with joy that he wouldn't use the glass on the table and drank the beer directly from the bottle and in long swigs. His eyes turned watery. He now smiled and now sighed, shaking his head as if bemused by such good fortune.

•

A few weeks later Dick told Nan that he had received a job offer from the Iowa Writers' Workshop and decided to accept it. Nan had heard of that place and knew this was a major development in his friend's career. At least Dick wouldn't have to worry about his tenure at Emory anymore. Nan felt upset that from now on he'd be entirely alone as a struggling poet. He had been writing poetry in English these days, though somewhat halfheartedly, and had been planning to show Dick a few of his poems about animals once he polished them. Now his friend was about to leave; it was almost like a blow to him.

Nan managed to be congratulatory, though deep down he wished Dick could stay in Atlanta a few more years. Dick seemed to have sensed Nan's disappointment, so he promised to keep in touch with him and even said, "You must come see me in Iowa."

"I shall try." Nan grimaced.

"I'll miss the Gold Wok, you know."

They both laughed. "You are always welcahm to eat here. Do come back and visit us," Nan told him.

Seeing that Dick didn't respond and knowing he must be elated to leave Atlanta, Nan added, "Winter is mild here."

"Yes, of course. I'm sure we'll meet again, one way or another."

So in May 1997, Dick sold his condominium and left for New York. After spending the summer there, he started teaching at the University of Iowa. As promised, he kept up a correspondence with Nan.

PART SEVEN

1

JANET and Dave were worried about their daughter's health these days. Hailee, already three years old, caught cold continually and often lost her appetite. She ate so little that she seemed to have stopped growing. Even when she cried, which she often did, she no longer screamed gustily as she used to, and neither would she kick her legs or flail her arms, where the skin was so pale that the blood vessels were visible. One night her nose bled; the blood stained the front of her wrap-over vest and frightened her parents.

The next morning Janet took her to the hospital. Dr. Williams, a tall, haggard-looking woman, listened to Hailee's chest, palpated her abdomen, and discovered that her liver and spleen were tender, probably swollen. Immediately she sent her to the lab to have her blood tested. A nurse drew three tubes of blood from Hailee's arm and said the result would be available in two days. On her way back to the jewelry store, Janet stopped at the Gold Wok and chatted with Pingping. Pingping held Hailee in her arms, cradling her and cooing at her, but the girl was subdued, her eyes dim, and a line of drool flowed out of the corner of her mouth, which seemed partly collapsed. With tears in her eyes Janet told Pingping, "I've prayed and prayed and prayed, hoping she'll be okay."

"Don't worry before it's time. I'm sure Hailee will be all right. Babies always have problem. If they don't get sick often, they won't be smart."

"What kind of logic is that?"

"I tell truth. My younger sister is always sick when she's little, so she's smartest in our family."

"I would rather have Hailee healthy than smart."

"She will be fine."

Hailee looked sleepy, so Janet left a few minutes later. Nan had been busy working in the kitchen and had overheard their conversation; he said to Pingping about the Mitchells, *"Now they know what it's like to be parents."* Over the years Nan had grown to be very fond of Hailee. For some reason, whenever the girl saw him, she'd raise her little arms and cry, *"Baobao* [Hold me]," as if to claim a special tie with him. And without fail Nan would take her into his arms. If the Mitchells asked him to be Hailee's nominal father now, he would agree happily, but they never asked him again.

•

Dr. Williams called Janet two days later and in a soothing voice told her the result of the blood count. An abnormal number of white blood cells had been found, which might indicate leukemia, but she'd have to give Hailee a bone marrow biopsy to get enough information for an accurate diagnosis. She advised the Mitchells not to panic.

The next morning Janet took Hailee to the hospital again. A browless male nurse gave the child a local anesthetic on her hip and said she wouldn't feel any pain, so Janet, who covered her daughter's eyes with her palm, was not to worry. Then he inserted a long needle into Hailee's hip bone. Slowly the crimson marrow appeared, filling the syringe. Janet averted her head in terror, feeling as though a hand were yanking and twisting her insides. The girl let out a feeble groan but didn't kick her legs.

The result of the biopsy was the same. Dr. Williams told the Mitchells that Hailee had acute leukemia. From now on, the girl would be treated by a group of doctors in the hospital, though Dr. Williams would remain her primary pediatrician. She insisted that the child be hospitalized without delay. She also said that Janet and Dave shouldn't feel hopeless, because almost seven out of ten leukemia patients had been cured in the United States and the cure rate was even higher among children.

Still in disbelief and confusion, the Mitchells wanted to consult another doctor for a second opinion. Dr. Williams encouraged them to do that and had the results of Hailee's blood test and bone marrow biopsy faxed to an expert, Dr. Caruth at Emory Hospital. The following day Dr. Caruth sent back his diagnosis, which was also leukemia.

After crying in each other's arms, Janet and Dave took their daughter to Gwinnett Hospital, where the child went into chemotherapy. A transparent tube was put into a vein in Hailee's chest, through which anticancer drugs were pumped into her bloodstream. Her initial response to the treatment frightened her parents. Her face turned greenish and she often vomited, unable to stop groaning. She seemed too tired to cry loudly. No matter how Janet and Dave coaxed her, she'd hardly eat any solids, though she still drank fruit juices and milk. Then the girl's hair began falling out, but Dr. Williams said this was normal. She assured the Mitchells that these side effects would go away and that her hair would grow back once the chemotherapy was stopped.

Pingping and Nan went to see Hailee one morning in mid-March, bringing along a jar of fresh fruits for Janet, who often forgot to eat these days. Hailee smiled at Pingping and called her "Aunt"; then she called Nan "Uncle," but was too ill to raise her arms to let him hold her.

"Do you still feel pain here?" Pingping asked, and patted her forearm, pricked by needles.

"No," she mouthed.

Nan was about to stroke her cheek, but Janet stopped him—the girl's immune system had been so weakened by the medication that nobody was supposed to touch her face without wearing a glove.

Despite Hailee's good spirits, she looked withered and had lost weight, her skin tight over her strong bones. "Eat more food," Pingping told her. "You will recover soon, like new."

The girl smiled again, as if she had grown a few years older in just two weeks. Her mother told the Wus that Dave would come in the evening to attend to Hailee. They had a foldaway cot in the closet, so Dave could sleep beside their daughter at night. Before coming to the hospital he had to change and shower at home, as the doctor had instructed.

An old nurse came in to put some medicine into the intravenous line. The Wus took their leave, having to get to the Gold Wok before ten a.m.

Afterward they called the Mitchells now and then to see how Hailee was faring. Three weeks after the chemotherapy had started, another blood test showed a remarkable reduction of white blood cells. Apparently her leukemia was in remission. The girl was regaining her strength and began to eat solids; her pulse was stronger and even her voice sounded lively again. Both Janet and Dave were grateful and hopeful, though they were told that it would take a long time for their daughter to recuperate fully.

Once in a while Janet would come to the restaurant to talk with the Wus about Hailee, asking them how to locate the child's biological parents so that she could know something about her family's medical history. Pingping even called Seattle and talked to Ruhua, the fruity-voiced agent, and begged her to help the Mitchells. Ruhua promised to inquire into this matter, but she phoned back a week later, saying there was no way she could find any trace of Hailee's biological parents—the Chinese side had just hemmed and hawed without answering her questions. On behalf of the Mitchells, Nan wrote directly to Mr. Peng, the head of the orphanage in Nanjing. The man replied in less than a month and apologized for his inability to assist the adoptive parents, because the baby girl had been found near a local pig farm and there was no way they could identify her biological mother, who could have lived in any one of the two hundred villages in the county. He expressed the solicitude of the orphanage's leaders and staff, saying Hailee was still their daughter.

2

NAN had read and reread all the poetry books recommended by Dick. He liked them but felt Robert Frost and W. H. Auden were more to his taste, so these days he resumed reading Frost. In addition, he had been writing poetry in English whenever he could. Lately he had focused on a longish poem entitled "Heaven," which he planned to dedicate to Dick, as a surprise. Hard as he tried, he couldn't produce anything he liked. His lines were devoid of gravity and verve, and he could tell he was getting nowhere if he continued this way. He had to find a different angle from which he could reconceive his project, which had the ultimate goal of making his poems dark, luminous, and starkly elegant, a quality he vividly remembered from the paintings by Kent Philips. He knew that, living in Georgia, he couldn't possibly present that kind of landscape in his poetry, but he didn't have to avail himself of the physical world. What he should have was a restless soul from which vibrant lines might originate.

For months he couldn't feel excited about what he wrote, as if his mind hadn't wakened from a dormant state yet. He rented some movies and watched them late at night, but they didn't help create any poetic impulse either, and he got tired of them soon. He went to downtown Atlanta on a Saturday afternoon in April to attend a celebration of the imminent reversion of Hong Kong to China, but he felt more lonesome among the large crowd, though a soprano, singing at the proscenium with the curtain behind her, moved him to tears with two songs that brought back the memory of his childhood. He wondered whether this inert state of his mind might be connected to the fact that for many years he hadn't met a woman he loved wholeheartedly and with the passion from the depths of his soul. Of course there was Beina, who still bewitched him. But he had no idea where she was now, perhaps still in Harbin. If only he knew how to get in touch with her.

By now he honestly loved his wife, but in a steady and mundane way. With Pingping he felt peaceful. He took care of the restaurant and the yard work while she spent more time with Taotao, cooking breakfast for the boy and supervising him in his study. What's more, she kept their books, wrote checks, went to the bank to deposit or transfer money every day, and paid taxes by the end of each season. Their solitary life had strengthened their mutual dependence and emotional attachment, which had ripened into love and trust. Still, the marriage didn't offer the kind of excitement that Nan hoped could spur him into song. He imagined that what he needed was an overpowering emotion that could become an inspiration.

His desire for poetic stimulation often made him think of those women in literature who inspired poets and even became the subject of poetry, such as Petrarch's Laura, Dante's Beatrice, and Yuri Zhivago's Lara. If only there had been such a woman in his life! A woman just the thought of whom would set his soul on fire. He believed that if he had met such a woman, he might have written like a possessed devil and his mind could have turned into a fountain-head from which lyrical lines would overflow. Sometimes he realized this was silly, but he couldn't help himself and kept indulging in the illusion.

Out of this secret sentiment he rented the film *Doctor Zhivago*. He and Pingping watched the movie until two a.m. The picture touched them so deeply that they both felt sick for several days. They recommended it to Niyan and Shubo, who also enjoyed it. It reminded all of them of the life they had led in China, where, similar to the turbulent Russia, human lives had been worthless, where hatred and blind rage had run amok, and where the gun ruled the law. For days Pingping had a stuffy nose, and whenever they talked about the scenes in the movie the Wus would mist up a little.

Yet they were also moved by the beauty and strength of the film. Nan wished it had shown how Dr. Zhivago managed to write poetry when forced to serve the Bolsheviks. The poet in the story wasn't shown trying hard to develop his art. Once, in a deserted ice-clad mansion, he did take up his pen and write while Lara was sleeping and wolves were howling. Still, that couldn't explain how he became an accomplished poet.

Nan borrowed the novel from the town library. Fifteen years ago he had read it in the Chinese translation and had been underwhelmed, mainly because he couldn't grasp it structurally. This time he worked through it carefully and found it magnificent. Pasternak wrote as if no novels had existed before. The loose structure of the book seemed improvident, yet after finishing the last page, Nan felt everything hung together, uncannily unified. What an amazing book! Still, he wished it had shown how the protagonist struggled to write poetry, the development of which was hardly mentioned in the novel. He pondered over the poems at the back of the book and couldn't see how they were related to the content of the prose. He recommended the novel to Pingping. She read a few pages, then gave up. She didn't like the way the story was told, and preferred Steinbeck, whose books she would read whenever she had spare time. Sometimes even if she didn't understand a paragraph fully, she still loved to be lulled by that great author's natural, colloquial voice, just like listening to a wise friend talking.

Over the years Janet, a big fan of Stephen King and Anne Rice, had tried to persuade Pingping to join her book club, but Pingping wouldn't participate. She had very little time, and besides, she liked reading older books.

3

BOTH Nan and Pingping had gingivitis, a problem common among Asian immigrants because there was little dental care in their native countries. Without dental insurance, the Wus couldn't go to the dentist regularly. Ever since Taotao came to America, they'd had at most one dental cleaning a year. Recently two molars bothered Nan a lot, and the gums in the back of his mouth were inflamed, giving him a sore throat, though he'd had his tonsils out sixteen years before. He went to see Dr. Morell at Sunrise Square near the Lilburn public library, and the dentist suggested Nan have his four wisdom teeth extracted, or he might lose them and some other molars in the near future. The doctor told him, "They won't last, to be sure. All have deep pockets, seven or eight. We should take steps to save your other teeth."

"I don't have dental insurance."

"I'll charge you only two hundred dollars for it."

"Let me talk wiz my wife."

"Sure. Give me a call if you want to do it."

Nan didn't agree on the spot because Pingping disliked Dr. Morell, a pudgy man in his mid-thirties. In the beginning the dentist hadn't been good to the Wus. Once, right before he performed a minor surgery on Pingping's gum, he had said, "So, thirty-seven, eh?" He smirked, his face rippling with flesh. Apparently he'd gotten the information from the form she had just filled out. She angled her head in disgust but said nothing. Throughout the procedure she shut her eyes so she wouldn't have to see his ugly face. Despite that bad experience, she admitted that Morell was skilled, so she would let her family see him once a year.

This time Pingping urged Nan to have his wisdom teeth drawn without postponement. She feared he might fall ill, since the bad teeth often gave him a low fever. He went to the dentist a week later. The extraction wasn't very painful and took less than an hour. Dr. Morell told Nan that his teeth had unusually deep roots. That was why the last tooth alone had taken him almost twenty minutes to pull. Gingerly the tip of Nan's tongue probed the holes left in the back of his mouth, each of which reminded him of a smoldering bomb crater or volcano. Before leaving the dentist's, he asked for his teeth, which a nurse wrapped for him in a wad of gauze.

Coming out of the office and still in a haze, he looked at his four molars, each of which was ringed with tartar and stained with blood. One still had a tiny piece of flesh attached to it, and another had split in two along the middle, thanks to the force used to extract it. As Nan's tongue searched the cliffs and valleys in the back of his mouth, a warm pain filled his mind with a strange sensation, which reminded him of a passage in Nabokov's *Pnin*. Pnin did the same after his dental surgery. The author described his tongue as a fat, sleek seal "plunging from cave to cove" under icy water. In an endnote to the novel provided by the Chinese translator, Nan had read that this passage reflected Nabokov's own experience of having his teeth pulled. Somehow the memory of that passage distressed Nan and made him feel more wretched.

Having parked his car behind the Gold Wok, he unwrapped the gauze and observed the teeth again. Should he keep them? What for? To show them to his wife and son and later to his grandchildren?

Strangely enough, his mind went off on a tangent. He remembered the hearsay that Sakyamuni, the founder of Buddhism, had left two of his teeth on earth. In fact, their whereabouts were still discussed and disputed today. Every few years someone in Asia would proclaim a new discovery of the relic. In China some pagodas were erected to store the sacred teeth said to be Sakyamuni's.

Then Nan's anesthetic-inspired reverie ran wilder. He envisaged that teeth left by Nabokov, Joyce, Yeats, Frost had all become relics displayed in libraries together with their manuscripts and letters. How precious would their teeth be? How many visitors would pay homage to those tiny things? Some might even touch them in hope that the divine inspiration might rub off on them. This bizarre vision brought tears to Nan's eyes. He remembered that Keats died at twenty-five, but his gorgeous poetry was still read today. By comparison, he himself had lived only in the flesh. Why should he live like this? What was the meaning of an existence that was altogether bodily?

The more he thought, the giddier he got, something hammering his temples without letup. He looked pale and ill, and he leaned his shoulder against a bit of graffiti on the back wall of the restaurant, a circle of red hearts with a huge lip print in the middle. How valueless his rotten teeth were, because he had accomplished nothing in his life! How ludicrous and megalomaniacal he was to think of the value of his teeth!

Beside him a black lizard with a blue tail zigzagged down the wall and got into a hole beneath the back door of the Gold Wok. A moment later, Nan curbed his teeming mind and warned himself, "This is crazy. Stop this self-pity! These teeth are no different from a dog's." He walked across to the Dumpster and tossed them into it, then went into the restaurant.

At the sight of him Pingping asked, "*How do you feel, Nan?*"

"*All right, a little woozy.*"

"*Your face is narrower now. My God, let me look at you. You're more handsome now!*"

Niyan put in, "*Nan, you really look better.*"

He observed himself in the mirror in the men's room. Indeed, with the four big molars gone, his jawline was less squarish than before, and the new smooth contour gave a touch of maturity to his face. Even his chin had a clear angle now. How extraordinary this was! As if he had just received cosmetic surgery—a chin job. He scrunched up his face, then gave himself a mocking grin.

4

HAILEE suffered a relapse and was hospitalized again. This time the doctor said chemotherapy might not be effective, because after three months' treatment, the cancer cells would have developed resistance to the medicines. Indeed, despite the use of combined drugs, the sign of remission had diminished and then stopped. Instead, a large number of leukemic blasts, young and immature white blood cells, were found in Hailee's blood. The group of doctors in charge of her case recommended a bone marrow transplant, which would have to be done at a larger hospital.

For weeks the Mitchells looked in vain for a donor, who would have to have the same white blood cell proteins as their daughter did. Dr. Caruth at Emory Hospital faxed the description of Hailee's tissue details to the National Bone Marrow Donor Registry in St. Paul, Minnesota, which kept a list of more than a million potential donors, but the center couldn't find a match, partly because only a very small percentage of the registered donors were Asians. According to the literature Dr. Caruth had given the Mitchells, the match rate was much higher among people of the same ethnicity, so Janet asked the Wus if China might also have a program that listed potential bone marrow donors. Pingping called around and even talked with an official at the Chinese consulate in Houston, but nobody had ever heard of such a registry in China. If only the Mitchells could find Hailee's biological parents. They were certain that one of her siblings or cousins might have the tissue type that matched hers.

Both Nan and Pingping volunteered to have their blood drawn to see if they could be a donor, and later Taotao did the same, but none of them was a match. The Mitchells were quite touched nonetheless. Dave said to Nan, "We appreciate you trying to help her. You're a good man."

"Sure. Eef you or Janet had leukemia, we'd do the same. Don't sink I volunteered only because Hailee's a Chinese girl."

"I understand."

Then Nan hit on an idea. Why not contact the local Chinese community and see if they could help? Both Janet and Dave liked the suggestion, but they didn't know many people except the few whose children attended the Sunday Chinese classes at Emory. Nan didn't have a lot of contacts either, yet he nerved himself to call Mei Hong and ask her to help, though he believed she must still hate his guts. To his surprise, she eagerly agreed to spread the word among the Chinese students and the people in Chinatown. Also, she was going to contact all the Chinese churches in the Atlanta area and plead with them for help. She even said she'd go to Emory Hospital and have her own blood drawn.

As it turned out, she didn't need to go there, because after the local Chinese-language newspapers wrote about Hailee's case and published the Mitchells' plea for help, so many people offered to have their blood tested that a temporary clinic was set up at the Chinatown Plaza in Chamblee. A week later, to everyone's amazement, a thirteen-year-old girl in Duluth, named Moli, was found to be a match. At first, Moli's parents were unsure if they should let their daughter donate her bone marrow, but Mei Hong convinced them, saying that if they didn't help to save Hailee, they'd be despised by all the Chinese here. She also told them that a bone marrow transplant was similar to a blood transfusion, with no harm done to the donor's health. So the girl's parents, both recent immigrants working at Peace Supermarket, yielded and even let Mei Hong take their daughter to an interview with a reporter.

When the good news came, the Mitchells were overjoyed and broke into tears. Dave hugged Nan and wept like a little boy. With trepidation he and Janet spoke with Mei Hong on the phone and were reassured that the girl's parents wouldn't go back on their promise. In fact, Mei Hong had become the spokeswoman for the girl's family, since her parents couldn't speak a word of English. To

Nan, that woman had simply taken the whole thing into her own hands as if she were Moli's aunt.

Nan was puzzled. To him Mei Hong was just a jingoistic firebrand who couldn't think straight. He wondered whether she'd have let her own daughter be a donor if her child had been a match. When he talked with her about Moli, she said with her eyes fixed on him, *"You think I'm a hypocrite, huh? Let me tell you, if Moli were my daughter, I would let her do the same. Every member of my family had our blood tested. Hailee is a Chinese girl, so we must do whatever we can to save her. Wouldn't you donate your bone marrow if you were a match? No?"*

"Of course I would. I had my blood drawn too," Nan said.

After a thorough exam, which ascertained that Moli was healthy, Dr. Caruth explained to the girl's parents the process of marrow donation through Mei Hong's interpretation. The couple was fully convinced that it wouldn't impair their daughter's health, and they signed the paperwork. Nan and Pingping wondered why the girl herself hadn't said a word about the decision made for her by others. Did she want to donate her bone marrow or not? Wasn't she scared? Pingping asked Moli once, but the pumpkin-faced girl just replied, "Aunt Hong says I should help save Hailee, and if I were sick, others would do the same for me." Asked further, she'd say no more. Pingping felt for her so much that she packed a box of assorted appetizers for her, but Moli wouldn't accept it, not until Mei Hong told her to take it home and let her parents know it came from the Gold Wok.

A few days later Moli's bone marrow was injected into Hailee. The child's initial reaction was disheartening. She ran a high fever, and fluid was building up in her lungs, which made her wheeze. An X-ray showed her heart was enlarged considerably. She had to be kept in intensive care. The doctors at Emory Hospital, where Hailee stayed, said these problems were normal after a bone marrow transplant and it was too early to conclude that the treatment had failed. The Mitchells kept their fingers crossed.

Then, a week later, Hailee's fever subsided some and a soft sheen returned to her cheeks. When she smiled, a sparkle appeared in her eyes again. Her lungs began to clear and the size of her heart was shrinking. All the tests indicated that the transplanted bone marrow had been producing new blood cells. Now, positively, her leukemia was in remission.

Hailee's leukemia was cured eventually, and Mei Hong became another of her godmothers, though the Wus still avoided her.

5

IN EARLY JUNE, Nan had won a prize in a raffle at Grand Panda Supermarket. He was offered the plane fare for a round trip from Atlanta to Beijing. By now he had become a U.S. citizen and would have no difficulty getting a tourist visa from the Chinese consulate in Houston. Should he go back to visit? He asked his wife, who disliked the idea. Then should they let the tickets, worth $650, be wasted?

Nan begged Pingping to allow him to go back for a short visit. It was so hot these days that the restaurant didn't have much business. With the help of Chef Mu, everything would be all right at the Gold Wok. But Pingping wouldn't let him leave. He continued pleading with her for a few weeks, to no avail. Finally he said he wanted to see his parents before they died. Those words made his wife relent.

Nan decided to depart within a week. He wondered if he should visit his parents-in-law in Jinan City as well, but Pingping, after giving thought to that, told him not to—she wanted him to come back as soon as possible. She planned to return and see her parents once she was naturalized. Nan promised he'd make a quiet trip and come back in just a week or so. She also warned him not to speak against the Chinese government publicly. In the past the police had often questioned his siblings about his activities abroad. Not until two years ago had they stopped harrying them, because his father had assured the authorities that Nan had "cleaned up his act" and was no longer a dissident.

What Pingping didn't know was that Nan wanted to return to China for another purpose also—to see Beina. He didn't intend to resume a relationship with her; he just needed that woman's face and voice to rekindle his passion so that he could write poetry. He needed the vision of an ideal female figure for his art, just like a painter who uses a model. Yes, he wanted to use her just as she had once used him.

Nan boarded a Boeing 737 bound for Beijing one morning in late July. As the plane taxied toward the runway, somehow he didn't feel excited. He looked around and saw that almost half the passengers were Chinese, and nobody paid heed to the imminent takeoff. He remembered the intense excitement he and the other passengers had experienced twelve years ago when he flew for the first time in his life, from Beijing to San Francisco. As the plane was taking off, many of them had applauded and some had leaned aside toward the portholes to catch through the ragged clouds a bird's-eye view of the cityscape of the capital, which tilted while the plane banked a little. He also remembered how he and his fellow travelers, most of whom were students, had been nauseated by a certain smell in the plane— so much so that it had made some of them unable to swallow the in-flight meal of Parmesan chicken served in a plastic dish. It was a typical American odor that sickened some new arrivals. Everywhere in the United States there was this sweetish smell, like a kind of chemical, especially in the supermarket, where even vegetables and fruits had it. Then one day in the following week Nan suddenly found that his nose could no longer detect it. Another memory of his first flight brought a smile to his face. Like some of the passengers crossing the Pacific Ocean for the first time, after eating the lunch he had wiped the plastic fork and knife clean and noticed people looking at one another and wondering what to do with these things. Some of them put the knives and forks into their pockets or handbags, carrying them all the way to their destinations in America, because they couldn't imagine that all the plastic containers and tools were disposable. They had no idea what kind of plentitude and waste they were going to encounter in this new land.

This trip, however, excited Nan in a different way. He planned to visit his friend Danning in Beijing, then his parents in Harbin, where Beina must be living as well. He hadn't told any of them about his return and meant to give them a surprise.

He brought along a poetry anthology, *The Voice That Is Great*

Within Us, which he read from time to time during the flight. But he dozed off frequently since he hadn't slept well the night before. He was glad he was seated in an exit row and had more leg room. On his left lounged a lumpy-faced man, who was on his way back to his job in Shanghai but would stop in Beijing for a day or two on business. The man introduced himself as Yujing Fang and complained he couldn't smoke the whole way. Because he was in a window seat, unable to talk to others, now and then he tried to converse with Nan. He said he had earned an M.B.A. from the University of Chicago and worked for GE in China. But his wife and two children lived in New Jersey, and he could visit them a few times a year, plane fares paid by the company.

"*That's hard,*" Nan said. "*I mean, to be separated from your family.*"

"*Yes, in the beginning just the phone bills would cost five hundred dollars a month, but now I use phone cards and we're accustomed to the separation.*"

"*Why don't you find a job in the States?*"

"*My position in Shanghai is important and lucrative. I manage a branch of our company there.*"

"*Do they pay you an American salary?*"

"*Of course.*"

"*Then you must be a millionaire.*"

"*Truth be told, I don't count pennies when I go shopping.*"

"*Tell me, what are the fashionable gifts in China at the moment?*"

"*Color TV sets are still presentable. Air conditioners, digital cameras, computers—ah, yes, vitamins.*"

"*Do people take vitamin pills?*"

"*Sure. Twenty bottles of multiple vitamins can grease a large palm. Wisconsin ginseng is always popular too.*"

"*Life must be better for many people in China now. Few of them could afford those supplements ten years ago.*"

"*Another very expensive present is just coming into fashion in Shanghai.*"

"*Which is?*"

"*Enemas.*"

"*What did you say?*"

"Enemas, having your intestines rinsed once in a while."

"Why?"

"To prevent cancer and other diseases."

"But how can they be a gift?"

"That's easy. You buy a book of tickets for enemas at a hospital and give it to another person who can go there for the treatment."

"I see." Nan chuckled, still thinking this was odd. Maybe only people in Shanghai would use such a present.

"It's expensive, though," said Yujing. *"Only rich people, like entrepreneurs, athletes, and actors, can afford to have an enema regularly."*

"Still, how could I give my dad a gift like that?"

"Oh, I thought you meant to bribe an official or some big shot. Actually, this enema thing might just be a passing fad. Last year electric shavers were all the rage, but they're already passé. By the way, for youngsters, brand-name clothes and shoes are always welcome."

"Like what kind?"

"Like Polo shirts and Nike sneakers."

Nan felt lucky that he hadn't bought any presents for his parents and siblings. If he had, he'd have picked two or three foolproof cameras, a few calculators, a pair of electronic keyboards for his nephew and niece, and a dozen wristwatches. According to his fellow traveler, most of those were no longer appropriate. Nan had $3,000 cash on him, planning to give each member of his family a few banknotes, real American dollars. That was a bad idea, according to Pingping, who feared that her parents-in-law would keep the money quietly and then tell people that Nan hadn't brought back anything for them. At most the old man and woman, both tightfisted, might spend some of the cash on food, for which no one could know they had taken money from Nan. It would have been far better if he had bought them some high-quality clothes so that everyone could see it plainly when his parents donned an American coat or jacket or hat. But Nan had left in too much of a hurry to visit any clothing stores. Besides, he knew nothing about brand names and wanted to travel light.

For the rest of the trip he was reluctant to talk more with Yujing, fearing the fellow might ask him about his profession. He wouldn't mind saying he was a restaurateur, but it would be embarrassing to admit he had only one employee. So whenever Yujing tried to chat again, Nan would appear tired and give a yawn. He kept his eyes shut and nodded off most of the time like the old woman with knotted hands seated on his right, who slept nearly all the way.

6

BEIJING was now hardly recognizable to Nan. He got out of a taxi at the train station and found out the schedule of the train bound for Harbin. He planned to stay one day in the capital and depart for home the next morning. Outside the station, so many automobiles were running on the streets that he was a bit unnerved and stopped to observe the rushing traffic for a while. In the distance several cranes stood motionless, like dark skeletons, over buildings encaged by scaffolding. Around him people were hustling and bustling. To his surprise, there were yellow cabs here too, like in New York City. The plaza before the temple-like station was more crowded and more chaotic than it had been twelve years before when he had come to apply for a visa for the United States. Here and there gathered knots of young men in gray- or blue-collared T-shirts, some sitting on bedrolls and smoking pensively, and some lying on newspaper spread on the concrete slabs and dozing off. Apparently these country people had come here to seek work. Their leathery faces showed the kind of numbness that reminded Nan of the homeless in Atlanta. He wondered if there were soup kitchens in Beijing. Maybe not.

Nan called Danning Meng from a pay phone. On hearing of his arrival, Danning turned ecstatic and gave him directions to his home, insisting Nan stay with him. Nan agreed. He hailed a taxi and headed for Danning's place in the Hsidan area. There was so much traffic that bicycles seemed to move faster than automobiles. Now and then the cabdriver beeped his horn at the pedestrians who didn't step aside fast enough to make way for the car. At a red light a few vendors stepped over to hawk grapes, ice lollies, peaches, tomatoes.

To Nan's amazement, Danning lived in a small traditional compound with a scarlet gate, which, topped with black ceramic tiles, was in the middle of a high brick wall. A leaf of the gate was ajar, so Nan went in unannounced. Inside was a small stone-flagged quadrangle, formed by four houses. He hadn't expected Danning to live in such a spacious home, which was old-fashioned, a rare find nowadays. Two crab apple trees stood beside the entrance to the main house, and several wooden pots planted with kumquats and bamboos sat alongside the wing houses. *"Anybody home?"* shouted Nan.

Danning Meng stepped out of his living room and hugged Nan so tightly that the guest almost let out a moan. *"At last we're together again!"* the host said with emotion. Though thicker and a bit gray now, he hadn't aged much.

"You live like the nouveau riche, such a nice place," Nan said, beaming.

"I paid thirty thousand dollars for this piece of property, but we may have to move soon." Danning couldn't stop looking at Nan, and his smiling eyes curved a little, their outside corners drooping. He took Nan into the living room furnished with antique carved furniture.

"Why give up this place? It's a luxurious home, better than any apartment," Nan said the moment he sat down on a sofa.

"A company wants to build a hotel in this area, so the entire neighborhood will be gone in a year or two."

"What a shame. This quadrangle is the real old Beijing."

Danning's daughter, Weiwei, stepped in, called Nan "Uncle Wu," and then told her father that she had dragged Nan's suitcase into the guest room, which was in the east wing house and adjacent to Danning's study and their family room. The girl wore glasses and looked studious and undernourished. Though already fifteen, she was so thin that she seemed well under the age of puberty. Her father told her to prepare a basin of warm water so that Uncle Wu could freshen up.

As the two friends were talking, Nan felt an itch in his throat. Unconsciously he massaged the area below his Adam's apple with his thumb and forefinger. He didn't give more thought to this discomfort and just kept drinking the jasmine tea Danning poured him.

When Weiwei got the water ready, Nan went out to wash. On a stone bench under a crab apple tree sat a brass basin, beside which were a folded towel and a plastic case containing a bar of green soap. Nan soaked the towel in the water and rubbed his face and neck with it.

Quickly he went back into the house, eager to resume conversing with his friend. Although he felt refreshed after the washing, his throat still itched. His breathing went rough, but he tried to ignore it.

Over tea the two of them caught up with each other. Danning now worked at the Beijing Writers' Association and had been writing a script for a TV series. He disliked the show because the story was set in the Ming dynasty, six hundred years ago, but it paid well, much more than fiction. *"Why write an ancient story?"* Nan asked.

"It's safe to do that. Many, many writers are working on ancient stuff nowadays."

"Isn't it hard to make such work literary?" Nan said in earnest.

Danning slapped the top of his thigh and laughed. *"If you lived here, Nan, you'd have to forget about literature. The higher-ups want us to write about dead people and ancient events because this is a way to make us less subversive and more inconsequential. It's their means of containing China's creative energy and talents. The saddest part is that in this way we can produce only transient work."*

"I see, it's a trap."

Danning sighed and said he had been misusing his time for too long and must return to the real work soon. Nan didn't ask him what kind of writing he had in mind as "the real work" and instead expressed his admiration for the number of books (half a dozen) his friend had written. *"None of them is any good,"* Danning insisted. *"I've just been frittering away my life. Unlike in America, here I have no real struggle for livelihood. You see, I live comfortably. I just take up a project, finish it, and get paid."* He looked languid, as if already an old man in spite of his relatively young looks. Nan noticed that his hairline had retreated quite a bit, giving him a larger forehead than before. Also, Danning had a double chin, but that was almost covered by his chin-strap beard. Despite his easy life, despite his spacious home, despite his success, Danning was definitely unhappy.

Nan drank more tea to soothe his throat; still he couldn't breathe easily, his windpipe tight. Danning called his wife at work to see if she'd like to join them for lunch at a café. She was delighted and said she would. Before they set out, Nan finally told his friend, *"My throat feels dry and funny. Something is wrong."*

"So you have trouble breathing, don't you?" Danning smiled quizzically.

"Yes, like having asthma."

"You know what? You must have an allergy."

"Really? An allergy to what?"

"To the air, the smog. When my wife came back from America she had the same problem. It took her a month to get used to the air here, to become a Chinese again." He tossed his head back and laughed. *"Let me see if we still have some Benadryl."* He went into a bedroom and came out with a brown bottle. *"Here, take this."* He shook out two caplets into Nan's cupped palm.

Knowing the pills might make him drowsy, Nan swallowed them anyway. Then together they headed out. Weiwei, watching a movie on TV, didn't come with them. She asked her father to bring back a meat pie for her.

7

FOREVER LOVE CAFÉ was a very small place. Its side windows looked onto a man-made lake, which, ringed with white sand, was more like a pond, without any trace of fish or waterfowl in it. Two teenage boys were swimming near the opposite shore, their red and white caps bobbing on the green water. Danning knew the owner of the restaurant, a handsome, lean-faced man, and introduced Nan to him as his friend from overseas. "*Welcome back,*" the man said warmly, waving the cigarette held between his fingers.

They sat at a table beside a window. The room had a faintly vinegary smell, emanating from the cold dishes contained in the enamel basins in the glass display case. A waitress with squarish shoulders came and put a porcelain teapot and two cups between them. "*Their specialities are braised pork tripe and beef tendons,*" Danning told Nan. "*They also serve panfried noodles and rice for lunch. But their offerings may be far below the standard of your restaurant, so please bear with them.*"

"*Come on, you think I'm rich and finicky about food?*"

"*You're a businessman now.*"

"*I'm still struggling to survive there.*"

"*Yet you're rich.*"

"*Only by Chinese standards.*"

"*That's what I mean.*"

Sirong, Danning's wife, appeared, a petite woman smiling with a broad mouth and bulging eyes. She reminded Nan of a giant goldfish, though she looked good-natured and carefree. She held out her hand to him and said, "*It's so nice to meet you finally. Danning often mentioned you. When did you arrive?*"

"*Three hours ago.*" He shook her hand, which was small and soft.

"*Well, what do you think of Beijing now?*"

"*There are more cars, more buildings, and more people.*"

The couple cracked up. "*That's a very accurate observation,*" Danning said, turning to his wife. "*I told you he's a sharp fellow. He's having the same kind of allergic reaction as you did.*"

"*You are?*" she asked Nan. "*No wonder you look so pale. But don't worry. You'll be all right soon. It's just the process of getting readjusted. You'll feel normal within a month.*"

Nan thought of telling her that he'd be going back to the States the next week, but he refrained. He didn't feel like talking much and just enjoyed listening to them. The waitress came again and put a teacup before Sirong. Sirong ordered a wonton soup.

When the panfried noodles, the wontons, and the shredded beef tendons arrived, Sirong said to Nan, "*I must confess I miss America, a lot.*"

"*What do you miss most?*"

"*Things like big apples, big salmon, and big lobster,*" she said in all sincerity. "*Also, I'm a chocoholic and miss all kinds of chocolates they have there.*"

Nan laughed and told her, "*We serve salmon in our restaurant every day. You should come and visit us.*"

"*I'd love to. Mmmm, I still remember the lobster and shrimp we had at a crab shack in Plymouth, near the* Mayflower. *You see, here fish are skimpy and fruit puny. We Chinese eat too much and have used up our land.*"

Danning added, turning to Nan, "*Overeating is a big problem among children now.*"

Nan nodded. "*I saw some big fat kids this morning, like in the States.*"

"*Not just children who overeat, grown-ups too,*" said Sirong. "*Danning goes to dinner parties at least four times a week. Look how fat he is now. Besides, he has high cholesterol and hypertension.*"

Indeed, Danning had gained at least thirty pounds. Nan said to him, "*You've got to be careful about your health. You're no longer a young man.*"

"*In fact,*" said Danning, "*I'm doing better than most of my colleagues. Many of them have to battle diabetes and high blood fat levels, having eaten too much meat and sugar. My boss's triglycerides are over seven hundred. He often says he might have a stroke or drop dead anytime. Speaking of dinner parties, I'm supposed to attend one with a group of writers tonight. Nan, would you like to come with me? It'll be fun. You'll meet some important people.*"

"*All right, I'll come.*"

Sirong had to return to work before one-thirty and left the moment she was done with her wontons. The two friends strolled back, Danning holding a thick pie stuffed with pork and chives for his daughter. At a clothing stand Nan bought a tartan skirt as a present for the girl despite her father's protesting, "She already has too much stuff."

While they walked, they chatted about people they both knew. Danning mentioned that Mr. Manping Liu had died a month before and that only one small newspaper had printed a brief obituary, because the old scholar had refused to retract his statement about the necessity of democratizing the Communist regime and write the self-criticism the Party committee of his research institute had admonished him to do. Danning had gone to his funeral service, attended by only thirty people. The two friends also talked about Bao Yuan, whose paintings had been exhibited in a gallery in Beijing last fall, together with two other artists' works; Danning wasn't sure how well his work had been received here, but some of his colleagues had liked the show. A high-circulation weekly, *Art News*, even published a long article on Bao, written by an American art critic named Tim Dullington. Without commenting on that, Nan realized that as before, his own name as the translator must have been suppressed.

Exhausted and groggy, Nan slept for the rest of the afternoon in the guest room. He snored loudly, which fascinated the girl in the next room, who had never met anyone who made such thunderous noise in his sleep. On her dad's instructions, she lowered the volume of the TV, yet when Nan's snores penetrated the wall, interfering with the voice of the math teacher on the screen, she turned it up again. But whenever she did this, her father would come out of his study and order her to keep it down. Besides not wanting to wake Nan, he couldn't think clearly with the TV blasting.

8

TOWARD EVENING, a midnight blue Audi with tinted windows came to pick Danning up. He and Nan got into the air-conditioned car, which rolled away noiselessly and headed for Haidian District. The chauffeur, wearing aviator glasses and a peaked cap, seemed savvy and apparently knew Danning well, but he was reticent while the two passengers in back were talking about Beijing's real estate market, which had kept booming in recent years. The average home price had increased by twenty percent annually, and some people had unexpectedly become millionaires, having bought a couple of apartments for a song a few years before. Danning urged Nan to buy a pied-à-terre here, for which there'd be no realty tax, but Nan chuckled, saying he didn't have $30,000 to spare.

The chauffeur tooted the horn, urging a cyclist to make way for their car, which bucked again and again as if about to crush the bicycle, but its rider simply didn't respond. Not until the man rounded a corner could their car resume a normal speed. Dangling from the rearview mirror was a tiny oval portrait of Chairman Mao with a golden tassel. Nan wondered if that was some sort of amulet.

As they were approaching a crossroads, the light turned red, but their car didn't stop. The chauffeur signaled and drove left, ignoring the honking of other vehicles. A green motorcycle puttered up behind them, and a policeman in the side car shouted through a bull-horn, "*Pull over to the side!*"

"*Fucking cops!*" cursed the driver without moving his head. He clicked on the blinker, slowing down, and brought the car to a stop.

"*Are they going to give you a ticket?*" Nan asked him.

"*Oh well, I've never paid a fine.*"

Nan turned around and saw the two policemen hop off the motorcycle and stride up to their car. But as they were approaching, one of them pointed at the rear of the Audi, then they both veered off to a newsstand as if to deal with a more urgent incident over there first. Nan was bewildered.

The chauffeur said in an undertone, "*Bastards, they're not that stupid.*" He pulled away smoothly.

"*Why did they change their minds?*" Nan asked.

"*This is an army vehicle,*" explained Danning. "*They just saw the plate on the back.*" He pointed his thumb over his shoulder at the rear window.

"*So army vehicles don't have to follow the traffic rules?*" asked Nan.

The chauffeur said, "*They can give me as many tickets as they like, but there's no way they can collect the fines.*"

Danning winked at Nan, then spoke in English so that the driver couldn't understand. "You see, power comes out of the barrel of a gun."

Nan said, "Zis is crazy, still like two decades ago."

"Yes, things are basically the same."

They pulled into the yard of a medium-size hotel, and the chauffeur told them that he would come around nine-thirty to pick them up. Through a moon gate Danning and Nan entered the yard behind the building, where a two-story manor was half shaded by tall, dusty cypresses. In front of that house was a tiny pond, with a few mossy rocks erected in its middle and inhabited by orange carp and goldfish, whose tails and fins spread in the water like floating tulle. Danning and Nan went into the house and then turned in to the restaurant on the first floor, in which sat only a few people. The dimly lighted room felt damp, four long-fluked ceiling fans revolving with a rasping sound.

"*Welcome!*" a roly-poly man cried at them. Obviously the host, he was wearing a herringbone suit and shiny oxfords. He showed them to a table in a corner where five men were already seated. At the sight of Danning, they all got up and stretched out their hands, which Danning shook one by one.

With pride he introduced Nan to them as his American friend.

They were all pleased to see Nan. On the table were two saucers containing condensed milk and a bamboo basket holding tiny steamed buns, both serving as an appetizer. They went on gossiping about some recent events in Beijing's literary circles: the nominations for this year's major prizes and what offices were involved; which one of the pretty young women writers had outsold the others; the two poets who had just been offered a trip to Paris the next spring; an editor who had been fired last week for publishing a book offensive to the authorities, which had changed the policy, punishing editors in place of authors; how there was going to be a conference on a first novel by a young man whose father was a high-ranking official in the State Council. Nan knew nothing about their world and just listened.

Mengfei, the loudest among them, was a lieutenant colonel in the air force and a well-known fiction writer. It was this fleshy-faced man with a bull's neck and shoulders who had sent the Audi to fetch Danning. Sometimes he taught literary theory and modern fiction at the Arts Institute of the People's Liberation Army. He had just published a novella in *Flower City*, a top-notch magazine, so he had gathered his writer friends here to celebrate. Among them there was another officer, a captain who was a poet, and the rest were all civilians. Nan vaguely remembered seeing in a newspaper the photograph of the bald man sitting across from him. The man had introduced himself as Fanlong, an editor in the Writers' Publishing House. Seated next to the colonel was a spare man who was a journalist specializing in reportage literature, but he didn't speak much because he'd stutter whenever he opened his mouth. Unlike them, Nan didn't touch the Luzhou whiskey, which was too strong for him; instead, he sipped Five Star beer from a tall glass.

A waitress came and handed them the menu. Nan was puzzled by the names of the dishes. There were so many unfamiliar items that he wasn't sure what to order. He asked Danning, "*What is this—* '*Parents and Children'?*"

His friend grinned. "*It's just pickled soybeans and soy sprouts.*"

"*Then I won't eat the whole family.*" Nan chuckled but didn't ask about the other fancy names. The rest of the men didn't bother to open the menu and instead let Fanlong order for them. The man, well known for his ability to plan parties and dinners, mentioned a dozen dishes to the waitress and also asked for more liquor and beer for everyone.

"*Nan, what are the hot novels published in the United States recently?*" asked Mengfei, who seemed quite knowledgeable about contemporary American fiction. As a matter of fact, he had been to the States as a visiting scholar at Stanford, and in their conversation he often trotted out the phrase "when I was in America," which Danning told him not to use just for this occasion, at which there was no need for him to impress others.

"*A novel called* Cold Mountain *is very popular at the moment,*" Nan told Mengfei.

"*Who wrote it?*"

"*A new writer named Charles Frazier, but I haven't read the book yet.*" Nan paused, then added, "*I brought back a copy of* American Pastoral *for Danning.*"

The spare man with slanting eyebrows seated next to Mengfei spoke in a shrill voice. "*Th-that's Philip Roth's ne-new novel!*"

"*Yes,*" Nan said.

Fanlong butted in, "*I like Roth a lot, especially his* Ghost Writer."

"*I think Saul Bellow is better,*" mumbled the bespectacled man sitting next to Danning.

"*Ah, Bellow is smart and funny,*" Mengfei said, and smacked his lips as if tasting his own words.

In addition to parading their knowledge of American literature, they also talked about Calvino, Kundera, and Duras, none of whom was familiar to Nan, though at present they were popular here. So when Mengfei asked his opinion, Nan said, "*I don't read fiction very often. I read more poetry.*"

"*Wonderful,*" the bright-eyed captain put in.

Fanlong added, "*We just bought Derek Walcott's new book.*"

Nan was startled and realized that these men might be bureaucrats in the Chinese literary world. Now he should be more careful about what he was going to say. Probably they did indeed know a lot about American authors through translations.

The dishes came, loaded on a serving cart. Two young waitresses in pea green aprons began placing the courses on the table. "*This is*

'Trotting on a Country Path,'" declared one of them. Nan batted his eyes to look at the dish closely. Heavens, it was just braised pig trotters garnished with a few sprigs of parsley! Despite his bewilderment, he said nothing. Then together the waitresses lifted a large platter containing a fried flounder. There were also several cold cuts and sautéed vegetables. Finally the taller woman put the last plate on the table with both hands and said, "Here's your 'Whispers.'" Nan tried hard to stifle his laughter on looking at the dish, which was nothing but smoked beef tongues lying in aspic.

The waitresses had scarcely pulled the cart away when Nan burst out laughing, a bubbling sound in his nose. He said to the others, "Let's whisper, let's whisper." They got the joke and all cracked up.

"Lucky we still have our tongues," said Mengfei with a straight face.

They laughed more. As they were eating and chatting, more people appeared in the restaurant and most of the seats were taken. There were several gatherings in the room, but each group of diners paid little attention to the other tables. Nan liked the fish and ate several pieces of it. Everything else, though, tasted mediocre, but he tried to show his appreciation. By now he realized this place must be a kind of club for officials, businesspeople, and the cultural elite.

A moment later Nan mentioned to Fanlong, the senior editor, Dick Harrison's new book, Unexpected Gifts. The man looked blank, blinking his baggy eyes and saying, "I don't know enough about contemporary American poetry. Tell me more about this poet."

Without mentioning his friendship with Dick, Nan described him as a rising star in American poetry. He even recited the final stanza of Dick's poem "A Son's Reason," and they all laughed at the last lines—"Mother, I love you / only from far away."

"Dick Harrison just started teaching at the Iowa Writers' Workshop," Nan told Fanlong.

That soaked in. They all knew that workshop and the Iowa International Writing Program. The latter would admit two or three Chinese writers a year. The competition for such an opportunity was especially fierce among poets, because it was also a way to get a bit of money. After spending a semester at the University of Iowa, one could save $2,000 or $3,000 besides having the honor of attending such a prestigious program.

Danning declared to them, *"In fact, Dick Harrison is a close friend of Nan's."*

The faces at the table changed visibly. Fanlong, who was also a published poet, began to listen to Nan more closely and went on asking questions about American poetry. He even said to Nan in an orotund voice, *"I hope I can visit you in Georgia one of these days. Atlanta must be a big international city."*

"Sure, you're always welcome." Nan felt like a fake, uncertain whether Pingping would like that. But he had to appear friendly.

Some people at the tables near a low platform started singing a song, following the karaoke machine that had just come on. Mengfei stood up and said, *"Let's go have some fun."* They all went over to watch the crowd.

Several young women who must have been on the waitstaff were among the singers. A moment before, everyone had been quiet and subdued, but all of a sudden the men and women were so clamorous that Nan wondered whether they were all depressed and desperate to vent their frustrations through singing. They belted out song after song—sometimes only one man and one woman sang together, and sometimes a number of people chorused at the top of their lungs. Fanlong went to the front and began to sing an old folk song with a woman with a bleached blond pageboy who wore a red cheongsam. They were singing:

> *In a distant mountain lives a beautiful girl.*
> *Whoever passes her cottage will turn,*
> *Hoping to catch a glimpse of her.*
>
> *Her small pink face shines like the sun.*
> *Her lovely eyes move*
> *Like the moon in a cloudless night.*
>
> *O I'm willing to give up all I have*
> *And just follow her flock of goats,*

So every day I can see her small pink face
And her pretty dress frilled with gold.

O I'm dying to be her little goat
And always stay at her side,
So she can flick her tiny whip
To stroke my behind.

Having finished the song, Fanlong wagged his big ass and bleated twice, which set off whoops of laughter. He then held the woman's hands and did a little jig under the miniature chandelier, swinging his legs briskly while his cheeks glistened with sweat. The woman followed his steps, swaying her hips while holding her face up and straight. Despite the noisy audience, the two looked quite natural.

Nan was a little tired, but he thought he ought to keep his friend company. Danning was playing cards with Mengfei, the captain, and the journalist at their own table now. They had asked Nan to join them, but he had forgotten how to play One Hundred Points and just stayed around watching them.

Two girls, heavily made up, came over and sat beside the men. One of them said to Mengfei, "*Colonel, don't you want some fun and comfort today?*"

"*Wait until I lose another five pounds.*" Mengfei rolled his bovine eyes. Except Nan, all the others cackled. Nan was puzzled by the colonel's answer, but said nothing.

The other girl turned to Danning. "*Hey, big writer, you've forgotten me already? Where's the perfume you promised me?*"

"*Next time, Dailian, all right? I'm with my friend here.*" His chin jutted at Nan.

"*Doesn't your friend feel lonely? He's so quiet.*"

"*Ask him then.*"

The girl was all smiles. She scooted closer to Nan and asked coquettishly, "*Don't you want to know me?*"

"*Sure,*" Nan replied out of politeness.

"*Would you like to spend some time with me?*"

"*For what?*"

Mengfei gave a belly laugh and said, "*Nan's so innocent. Different from us. He's still uncorrupted.*"

"*Just follow her,*" Danning told Nan. "*She'll let you know for what.*"

"*Who will pay for it?*" Nan asked.

"*You will, of course.*" Mengfei pointed at him. "*Now I see that you're not so innocent as I thought. I pay for food and drinks but not for fellatio or sex.*"

The girl sitting near him pouted. "*He's always so shameless and barbaric.*"

Jokingly Nan said to the girl beside him, "*I don't have money, unless you're willing to spend time with me for free . . .*"

"*You don't have to pay now.*"

Danning intervened, "*Nan, don't tease her. She knows you're from abroad. If you're not interested, just say you don't want it. She'll hold me responsible if you get anything free from her.*"

"*All right.*" Nan turned to the girl. "*I'm too tired today. I just flew all the way back from America, almost twenty hours, and I'm still jet-lagged.*"

"*America? That's beautiful. Don't you want my phone number just in case?*"

"*I'm a married man.*"

That set the whole table roaring with laughter. "*We're all married men,*" Mengfei said, and slapped his broad forehead three times with the heel of his hand. "*Nan, please don't remind us of our depravity.*" He stared at the girls, who turned quiet at last. A moment later they both moved to a nearby table.

On their way back, lounging in the Audi, Nan asked Danning, "*Why did Mengfei tell the girl to wait until he lost another five pounds?*"

"*Ah, he has a theory—the intensity of sexual pleasure is in proportion to the weight you have lost.*"

"*Strange. Do you believe him?*"

"*Too much body fat dulls the physical sensation, doesn't it?*"

"*I see, you fellows are experts. By the way, why did the restaurant give those common dishes all the fancy names?*"

"*To get more business. Everybody wants to sell and sell and sell, to make money by hook or by crook. People don't call things by their names anymore.*"

Then Nan asked him what kind of place was that restaurant. "*It's like a brothel,*" he said.

His friend laughed and told him that there were many bars, salons, and hotels like that in Beijing. Using women to attract business was common practice nowadays. Nan thought of asking him whether he had often spent time with the girls, but he checked himself. Without question Danning was a regular customer; so were his friends. Nan wondered whether he himself would have become one if he lived here.

9

AFTER a whole night's train ride, he arrived at Harbin in the early morning. The train station had been renovated, and, with a new veranda and a massive gateway, it looked more welcoming than it had twelve years before. People here were dressed more colorfully than Beijingers, though they had much less money. The city appeared dormant and aged; the old Russian buildings in the southeast looked gray and shabby in spite of their copper cupolas. In the square before the station a few boys and girls in sweat suits were practicing martial arts, jumping around, or kicking and punching air, or directing their energy to different parts of their bodies while standing still with their knees bent at a right angle. On the west side of the square stretched a line of food stands that sold fried dough sticks, soy milk, sugar pies, jellied tofu soup, roasted beans and peanuts. Several customers sat on canvas stools there, eating breakfast while palavering or reading newspapers; a woman had a beagle on a long leash that kept wagging its docked tail. Nan flagged down a cab and set out for Nangang District, where his parents' home was located.

The city hadn't changed much. Indeed, there were more cars on the streets, but unlike in Beijing, not many of them here seemed privately owned. Nan liked the new tall buses, which looked roomy, like tourist coaches. Five minutes later he asked the taxi to stop at Friendship Boulevard, about three hundred yards away from Wind Chime Street, on which his parents lived, because he wanted to walk a little. He gave the cabbie, a young man with a missing front tooth, twenty yuan and let him keep the change. Then he headed toward his parents' home, lugging his wheeled suitcase without looking at the street signs as if his feet knew where to take him.

When he entered the residential compound, he heard a man chanting, *"Breathe in, breathe out, breathe in, breathe out . . ."* Accompanying those amplified singsong words was slow, dangling music that sounded ancient and listless. Rounding the corner of the first building, Nan caught sight of a group of old people, about thirty of them, doing morning exercises in the open space between two concrete tenements. They stepped around rhythmically, putting down heel first and swinging their arms left and right, all with their eyes half shut. They looked funny to Nan, as if sleepwalking or wrestling with shadows. Among them he saw his parents, who were swaying their shoulders indolently, his father wearing a flat brown cap while his mother was in purple slacks and a white short-sleeved shirt. To his amazement, neither of them had changed much; only their midriffs seemed thicker than before and their limbs looked a little stiff. All the people were expressionless, and their bodies moved in time with the male voice and the music as if they were in a hypnotized dance. Unconsciously Nan stopped in his tracks, his chest so full of feeling that he could hardly breathe. His eyes filmed over. Then he came around and decided not to address his parents, not to wake up the whole crowd. He went along and passed them with his face toward the wall of the building.

He climbed the stairs and reached his parents' apartment. The door was locked, so he leaned against the steel banister at the landing, waiting. His father and mother had retired several years ago with pensions equal to their full salaries, and they lived comfortably. Nan could see why, whenever he complained about the Chinese government in his letters, his father would write back upbraiding him and saying he was too naive and too rash. The old man, a staunch Communist, had never doubted the superiority of socialism to capitalism. He had once even condemned his son, saying that even though Nan lived in an American house, drove an American car, spoke American words, ate American food, and cut American farts, still all those privileges couldn't justify Nan's "vituperation" against the Chinese government. Now Nan understood that his parents' livelihood depended on the support of the state.

"*Who's there?*" his mother shouted as she was climbing up the stairs.

"*Mom, it's me.*"

"*Nan! Are you really Nan?*" She ran up, stumbled at a step and put out her hand to break the fall.

"*Don't run.*" He hurried down to meet her.

She threw her arms around him and broke into happy tears. "*Oh, my son, how I miss you! Are you back alone?*"

In his arms, she was like a meatball with love handles. He said, "*Yes, Pingping and Taotao couldn't come with me.*"

"*Let me take a good look at you.*" She pushed him away a bit and observed him with creased eyes. "*Nan, you're a middle-aged man now. You've changed so much. Life must be hard in America.*"

"*It's not easy, but we've managed. You look great, Mom. I saw you and my dad outside just now, but I didn't interrupt you.*" They turned toward the door. Viewing her from the side, he found her more bent than before, but her hair was jet-black, apparently dyed.

"*Oh, you should've stopped us,*" she went on. "*We were doing this new breathing exercise. It's like magic and everybody feels better after doing it for a week. Hey, my old man, our son is home.*"

Nan's father appeared in the stairwell. He saw Nan and hastened his steps. The moment he came in, he asked, "*When did you arrive?*"

"*A few minutes ago.*"

"*Why didn't you tell us beforehand?*" He smiled, crinkling his weather-burned face and unable to contain his happiness.

Nan explained the raffle prize that had enabled him to fly back. His mother had already started making breakfast in the kitchen, from which the clatter of pots and bowls could be heard. Nan saw steaming water falling out of the faucet in there—that was something new.

The old man and Nan sat down on the sofas in the living room. He said to his son, "*You were right not to come up to us when your mother and I were at the exercise. Uncle Zhao was right behind me. He's still unhappy with you.*"

"*Because I didn't help him get his paintings exhibited in the United States?*"

"*Right.*"

"*That was several years ago. He still bears a grudge?*"

"*Sometimes he complains that you're ungrateful, and I have to pretend to agree with him.*"

"But I'm nobody in America. How could I help him hold an art show?"

"*I'm not blaming you, Nan. He's just pigheaded, but he's an old friend I don't want to lose. So don't go out during the day in case people in the neighborhood see you, because then Uncle Zhao will know you're back.*"

"All right, I'll remain indoors." Nan was tired and sleepy, preferring to stay home anyway.

"*If you want to go out, use the back alley and wear sunglasses. Don't go by the front gate.*"

"You mean the alley is still there?"

"*Yes, nothing really changed except for people getting older.*"

At breakfast Nan asked about his brother and sister. His parents said their family was lucky that neither of Nan's siblings was out of work. There were so many unemployed people nowadays that pickpockets were everywhere in town. Nan had better be careful with his wallet on buses and in shops, especially in movie theaters, where the darkness could facilitate theft. His mother also told him that his younger brother, Ning, was addicted to gambling. Sometimes Ning would go out for a whole night. His wife griped about his bad habit all the time, but he wouldn't change. She had even threatened to leave him; still he wouldn't stop.

"*Why is he like that?*" Nan asked, remembering his brother fondly.

"*Depressed.*"

"What? Depressed?"

"*Yes. He just can't take heart from anything,*" chimed in his father.

Nan felt it strange that Ning, formerly a cheerful young man, had degenerated like that. Before he had left China, Nan had never heard the word *depressed*, which his mother now used like an everyday term.

Nan gave his parents each five hundred dollars, saying he'd had to leave Atlanta in a hurry, so was unable to bring them any gifts. At the sight of the green banknotes, his parents beamed. His father picked up a crisp twenty from the wad of cash and narrowed his weary eyes to observe it against the sunlight streaming in through the window, as if to ascertain its genuineness. *"This is twenty dollars,"* he said. *"I never saw American money before."*

"It's real." Nan nodded.

"I've never thought the almighty dollar looks so ugly."

His mother interjected, *"What a silly thing to say. No money looks ugly."*

The old man chuckled and sucked in his breath. *"That's true. Just one of these banknotes can buy me a hundred noodle meals."* He turned to Nan. *"Now tell me, how much can your restaurant make on a good day?"*

"Around a hundred?"

"Five of this!" He fluttered the twenty in his hand. *"No wonder people say America is the richest land."* The wrinkles around his snub nose turned into grooves as he grinned and clucked his tongue.

Nan didn't say more. Instead, he went to wash and brush his teeth. Then he undressed, got into bed, and slept eight hours on end.

10

TOWARD DUSK Nan went out to the riverbank with his brother, Ning. He pushed his father's Phoenix bicycle through the back alley lined with piles of garbage, but when he came out of it and got on the bike, he couldn't ride it steadily anymore, and pedaling zigzag, almost ran into a young couple. His brother, tall and rawboned, shook his head, crying, "*Use the bell!*" Squeals of laughter rang out around them.

Nan dismounted instead, and together they walked to the Song-hua River. They turned onto Central Boulevard, which stretched north about a mile, all the way to the riverside. Nan had once been fond of this cobbled street built by the Russians in the nineteenth century, but somehow it was nothing extraordinary now. He felt the street rather confining, probably owing to the numerous business signs overhanging the buildings.

The Wu brothers entered the plaza that formed the center of Stalin Park, in the middle of which stood a slender monument erected in memory of the victory over a huge flood in 1957. A struc-ture supported by stone columns, resembling a giant horseshoe, curved behind the monument. Somehow this piece of architecture that had impressed Nan greatly for many years now looked flimsy, no longer giving any feeling of magnitude. The two brothers went deeper into the park and reached the waterside. The riverbank was different from what Nan had remembered. This place had once been like a park, filled with flowers and trees, but now most of the plants were gone and there were booths and kiosks everywhere, selling foods, fruits, drinks, souvenirs. People were bustling around with their purchases in string bags carried in their hands or slung over their shoulders. There were also flocks of tourists strolling about, and some were cracking spiced watermelon seeds and spitting the shells on the ground. Not far away to the east rose a cluster of tall residential buildings that blocked the view of the grassland. In fact, the riverbank was now like a marketplace. The ground paved with concrete slabs was strewn with melon rinds, ice cream cups, crushed eggshells, Popsicle sticks and wrappers, cigarette butts. Nan and Ning leaned against the guardrail atop the embankment, watching a houseboat wobbling near the other shore, with a grapnel dangling over its stern and with foamy wavelets tumbling in its wake. The surface of the water had shrunk considerably, only about two hundred yards wide now, revealing a broad band of sandy beach. "*Where are all the ships?*" Nan asked his brother.

"*There has been a drought. The water is too shallow for the ships to come up here.*" Ning licked his thick lips. His baby face, narrow at the top and wide at the bottom, puffed up a little, his gaze focused on a moored rowboat.

"*The river has changed so much. I never thought it was so meager,*" Nan said. He had dreamed of the Songhua many times and always seen it as an immense body of water like a lake. Now he guessed that the Hudson or Lake Lanier must have mingled with this river in his dreams.

"*You should come and see what it's like here in the morning,*" said Ning. "*It's thronged with people, like a sports ground. People exercise and dance everywhere.*"

"*Didn't they build an amusement park over there some years ago?*" Nan pointed at the wooded land in the middle of the river called Sun Island, over which a biplane was flying slowly, bobbing like a giant dragonfly caught in the wind.

"*Yes, but if I were you I wouldn't go there. It looks better from here. It's too crowded there, just a tourist trap.*"

Indeed, viewed from this shore, the island was lovely, with picturesque buildings and bright-colored houses. It had been covered by bushes twelve years before. In his late teens Nan had often swum across the channel in the afternoons and napped on the warm beach that was now occupied by pavilions, boathouses, and a long platform on stilts which must have been a pier. He told Ning, "*I thought I'd go and see the island, but there's no need now. The water is so narrow I feel I can wade across."*

"Like this river, China has run out of strength. It's already rotten to the core. Brother, you made the right choice to stay in America." Ning took a swat at a horsefly hovering around his head but missed it.

"Life is hard there too," said Nan.

"Still, you have hope there, don't you?"

"I don't know." Nan wanted to say *"What hope?"* but he held back, not wanting to upset his brother.

"Nan." Ning looked rather shy. *"I'm thinking of going to Australia."*

"For what?"

"To emigrate."

"That'll be very hard, Ning. It will take ages to get all the papers through. If you were a young woman, your life in Australia may be less difficult. Chinese men are often at a disadvantage compared with Chinese women in foreign countries."

"Why so?"

"Chinese women are more likely to be accepted because white males like them. Also, generally speaking, Chinese women can take more hardship than Chinese men. If you go to Australia with your wife, it'll be less difficult for her to adapt. To be honest, Minyan may not stay with you forever once you reach Australia. I've seen many broken marriages among the immigrants in America because the wives changed their hearts. I'm lucky. Pingping has been loyal to me. She can endure more suffering than I can. Without her I couldn't have survived there." He had to stop because a surge of emotion seized his heart and drove him to the brink of tears. Then it dawned on him that Minyan, his sister-in-law, might have wanted to take Ning to another country so that he'd have to give up his gambling friends here. Nan had met Minyan a few hours ago and liked her, but he didn't feel she was very reliable. She was a looker, also quick-witted. He was sure that if she and Ning went to Australia, she could make it there, whereas Ning, sensitive by nature, might get lost and lapse into his old ways, frequenting casinos and betting on horses.

His brother, the youngest in the family, had always been the baby and didn't have the strength to grapple with fortune in a foreign land.

Ning sighed. *"I don't see any meaning in my life here. My job makes me go to parties almost every night. I hate alcohol but have to guzzle it, to get drunk a few times a week, or others would think I'm dishonest. I'm sick of this kind of life, sick of having to smile at the people I don't like to meet, sick of attending banquets at which I have to blab like a windbag. I want to go abroad for some peace and quiet."*

"At least you have many friends here," Nan said. *"Our life in America is very solitary. It would be hard for you to endure a lonely existence in Australia."*

"I'm not afraid of loneliness, which is better than hopelessness. This place is totally ruined. You should see what it's like here in the winter—the smog is so thick that sometimes even the sun has changed its color, and whenever you go out, you have to wear a surgeon's mask, or your nose will be blocked by soot. I don't know if you've noticed that millions and millions of Chinese have lung problems, because China has no lungs anymore—all the forests are gone. Worst of all, there are lots of criminals roaming around. Too many people have lost jobs and are desperate to get along by any means. A colleague of mine was stabbed last spring under the bridge right outside our office building, because he didn't have enough cash on him for the mugger. In this place it's impossible to live honestly—you have to lie constantly because everyone else lies. If you don't, others will take advantage of you. In the marketplace more than half the scales are crooked. Our neighbor, Aunt Niu, bought a sack of sweet rice dumplings from a peddler one evening last January, but when she got home she found they were actually frozen donkey droppings. A friend of mine, a policeman, lost his marriage because he returned to the owner a full envelope of cash he'd picked up on a bus. His wife called him 'mental,' and even his parents-in-law said he was a dope."

"Look at it this way, Ning. You're almost thirty-five and don't speak any English. Even if you're lucky and get to Australia eventually after spending a fortune, it will take several years for you to

settle down. In a foreign country it's almost impossible to restart your life once you're past forty, unless you have a lot of money or extraordinary talent. The struggle is too overpowering and can drive you out of your mind. Ning, you must think carefully before you decide to go to Australia. To my mind, you belong to this place. At least you have a comfortable job here and people respect you as a reporter."

"Actually, Minyan wants to go abroad more than myself. She's been attending a night school to learn English."

"I see. Think twice before you make up your mind, will you?"

"I will."

A man began bellowing a folk song from a rowboat up the bank. A freight train blew its whistle, trundling across the dark, old bridge downstream built by the Japanese more than half a century ago. Numerous lights were already on, flickering lazily on the river. A moment later the two brothers turned back, each wheeling his bicycle with one hand on the handlebar. On their way home Nan gave Ning three hundred dollars and made him promise to let his wife keep the money.

11

NAN gave the same amount of cash to his sister, Ying, who didn't really need the money since her husband owned a profitable landscaping company. But the dollars were a hard currency, which pleased her.

Nan told his parents not to buy braised chicken or fresh fish for him because he ate those things every day in America. He just wanted homely food, like millet porridge, cornmeal gruel, plain noodles with soy paste, fried toon leaves. These things were easy to make. His mother didn't even have to go to the marketplace to buy anything. His aunt, living in the countryside and having four toon trees in her backyard, would mail his parents a large sack of the leaves every spring. Although Nan had missed these foods, he didn't enjoy them as much as he had expected. Somehow everything tasted different from what he'd remembered. Maybe he'd lost some taste buds. Or maybe all the memories of those toothsome foods were just the remaining sensations of his childhood.

The next afternoon he and his mother were at home alone. His father had gone to a memorial service held for a former colleague of his who had just passed away. Putting a clay pot of chrysanthemum tea on the side table for Nan, his mother sat down and sighed.

"*What's wrong?*" he asked.

"*I miss Taotao.*"

This was strange, because Nan remembered that she had never liked her eldest grandson and had once even refused to watch over the boy when he and his wife had to attend a meeting together. For that Pingping still held a grudge against her. Nan told his mother,

"*Don't worry about him. He's fine. He's a stellar student and will have a good future.*"

"*I want to see him.*"

"*All right, I'll talk to Pingping and see if we can bring him back next summer. That way he can learn some Chinese from you and my dad.*"

"*No, I want to go to America to see him and Pingping.*"

"*Why do you have to go yourself? At your age it's not safe to travel that far.*"

"*Why? I'm not that old.*" True, she had just turned sixty-five.

"*I'll try to send Taotao back to stay with you next summer, all right?*"

"*I want to see America myself.*"

"*Mom, you have a very comfortable life here. If you fall ill there, you could die abroad. Don't you have arteriosclerosis and dizzy spells?*"

"*I'm well now, and I'd like to see America before I die.*"

"*Truth be told, for old people life there is harder than here.*"

"*I don't mind. I can work.*"

"*Work, at your age?*"

"*Yes, there's no shame in working. Everybody knows how easy it is to make money in America. After you gave us the cash the day before yesterday, your dad said to me, 'Damn, we've never had so much money in our whole life. See how easy it was for Nan to toss out a thousand dollars. In just twelve years he has become such a rich man.' My son, you know, that amount you gave us is enough for us to live on for a whole year.*"

"*We make more there but have to spend more too.*"

"*Don't you own a restaurant?*"

"*Yes, I do.*"

"*I can work for you. I can make dumpling wrappers, wonton wrappers, noodles, all kinds of buns and pies. For five dollars an hour I can earn forty a day. In a year that'll be more than ten thousand, enough for your dad and me to spend in our remaining years. Nan, I'll stay with you just a year and then I'll come back. Please take me to America.*"

"*How about my dad in the meantime?*"

"He'll stay home."

"But he can't cook."

"He can always hire a maid."

Nan realized that his father wouldn't go because he had many friends here, because he could play mah-jongg every night, and also because he'd have to be around to collect their pensions and take care of this home. Nan said, *"I'll have to talk with Pingping about this. I can't decide by myself."*

His mother's face dropped and a few folds appeared on her throat. She said, *"Who's the boss in your home? If you insist on your right as her husband, of course Pingping will obey you."*

"Mom, I can't do that. She owns half the business too. We two are partners, like a team."

She seemed to intuit that Pingping wouldn't let her come to America because the two of them had never gotten along. She sighed and went on in a flat voice, *"You're not your old self anymore. Having your wife, you no longer need your old mother, the same as your brother and sister. Heartless. Every one of you is heartless."* She pursed her lips, her nose crinkled.

Nan wanted to say, "Where were you when Pingping suffered and struggled with me all these years? Did you ever weep with me when we lost our baby? Were you ever worried when we couldn't pay our bills? You only know how to take advantage of us and ask for money. Greedy. Both of you are greedy." But he held his tongue, lowered his eyes, and muttered, *"Mother, you don't know how hard life has been for Pingping and me. If she were another woman, she'd have walked out on me long ago. She's the mainstay of our family."*

"I see, your old mother is useless to you now." She rose and shuffled away. Her shoulders sagged.

Nan rested his head on the back of the sofa and closed his eyes. The conversation saddened him. He remembered how the day before, when he mentioned Pingping's miscarriage, his mother had merely said, "If you're more filial to your parents, no misfortune like that will strike again." Those words still rankled him. Now how could he make her understand that she was no longer a member of his immediate family? How could he convince her that Pingping was the only person he could rely on? Greedy and vain, his mother just dreamed of making a fortune and showing off to her neighbors and friends. Ning had told him that their parents often bragged to others about going to America for a vacation and to see their grandson. His mother had even promised some friends of hers that she'd persuade Nan to help their children study in the United States when the kids grew up. As a result, many people had begun to ingratiate themselves with his parents. Nan realized that the old man and woman couldn't possibly commiserate with him and Pingping over the fear and misery they had gone through in America. How lonely he felt in his parents' home, as though he hadn't grown up in this very apartment. Perhaps he shouldn't have come back in the first place.

12

"I CANNOT *imagine marrying a man younger than myself.*" That sentence, spoken by Beina sixteen years before, had been reverberating in Nan's mind ever since he'd been home. In fact, she was just four months older than he. His memory of the proposal still stung him. Fat snowflakes had fluttered around as he proposed to her, saying he'd do everything to make her happy, including most of the household chores. He also promised her that they'd eventually live in a city south of the Yangtze River because she disliked the cold climate here. And with trepidation he waited for her answer. A few sleepy birds croaked in the treetops, whose branches had all caked into masses of snow. Her voice was flippant, which unsettled him, though he had steeled himself for the worst. When the final answer came, he felt crushed and wounded, leaning against the bole of a young birch crusted with ice. "*I've got to go now. Good night,*" she said, and walked away, fading into the darkness. Tears, hot and unstoppable, coursed down his face.

If only he had cut his ties with her right then and there. But instead, he had returned to her later on and gotten enmeshed deeper and deeper in her maze.

For several days now he had been thinking about her. Has she been happy? What does she look like now? Like a middle-aged woman? That's unlikely. She always knew how to take care of herself. Does she still remember me? Does her husband, that fellow with a rabbit face, really love her? Would she like to see me? Will my reappearance disturb her? What does she do? Still working as a translator in the information office of the sewing machine factory?

He hadn't asked his siblings about Beina, and nobody had mentioned her either. But he was determined to see her before returning to America. He wouldn't expect to rekindle her feelings for him. All he wanted was to see her once more so that he could preserve her in his memory as a lovely woman beyond his reach, as someone who still possessed his soul, so that the flames of inspiration would blaze in him again.

On Sunday morning he set out for Daoli District, for Beina's home. He walked the entire two miles, first along Thriving Peace Street and then along Worker and Peasant Boulevard. The poplars on the sidewalks were twice as large as when he had last seen them, but most buildings alongside the streets were grimier as if coated with coal dust. Since coming back, he had taken some herbal boluses that helped relieve his allergy, so he could breathe normally now. He turned onto a small lane after he passed the sewing machine factory, which, according to one of the signs on the gate pillars, now manufactured motorcycles as well. He found Beina's bungalow easily, which was tucked away behind two rows of tenements and which he had thought might have been torn down. This Japanese-style house had appeared in his mind from time and time, usually surrounded by cherry blossoms and tulips, but now, standing before it, he saw only a few aspens that seemed to have withered. The grape arbor and espalier that used to shade the east side of the house were gone, replaced by a small garden grown with eggplants, bell peppers, tomatoes, fava beans. The large willow under which he had often watched Beina's window on the second floor looked ragged, as if it had been struck by lightning, its stringy branches floating in the breeze. He stood under the tree for a while to collect himself. Then with a throbbing heart he climbed up the brick steps and knocked on the door. He backed up a little, his stomach aflutter.

A noise came from inside, and a svelte young woman in a pastel sundress came out. She looked familiar, but Nan wasn't sure if he had ever met her. *"Who are you looking for?"* she asked in a voice full of sleep, her eyes fixed on him.

"Beina Su. This is still her home, isn't it?"

"Sure. Do I know you?"

"I'm Nan Wu."

The woman's eyes widened with a dreamy light. *"Oh, I heard of you. Come in. I'm Beiya, Beina's half sister."*

She showed him into the spic-and-span living room. Once he had sat down on a chintz sofa, she asked what he'd like to drink, tea or beer. The latter was a household beverage in Harbin, enjoyed by both men and women, even by children. *"Just boiled water will be fine,"* Nan told her.

Having placed a cup of tepid water before him, she sat down and said, *"So you went with Beina for some time, didn't you? In fact, she often mentioned you. Didn't you go to America in the eighties?"*

"Yes, twelve years ago."

Nan scrutinized her face. Her little nose and thick-lashed eyes didn't resemble Beina's at all. A baby boy in blue open-seat pants was playing with a rubber ball in the room. He wagged his fleshy buttocks as he crawled and toddled around, chasing the ball. Beiya lifted him up and sat him on her lap.

"Your sister men-mentioned me?" Nan's voice caught. He lifted the cup and took a gulp, the water reeking of chlorine.

"Yes. She said you must be a rich man by now."

"I'm just getting by."

"So you haven't met Beina in America?"

"What? You mean she's in the States too?"

"Yes, in Illinois."

"She's there alone?"

"No, with her family."

"When did she leave?"

"About five years ago."

"Oh, if only I had known." Stupefied, he suddenly felt drained. A strange emotion overcame him, as if he had been taken in. He asked for Beina's address and phone number, which her half sister jotted down for him with a red fountain pen. By her manner and knowing smile he guessed she knew Beina had once turned down his proposal. In her voice there seemed a touch of sadness and sympathy.

"How is she doing in Illinois?" he managed to ask.

"She complains a lot. She's working hard to support her family."

"In the beginning it's always hard. You have to struggle to put down roots in America. Usually it takes ten years to settle down."

"*So you already have a green card?*"

"*I'm naturalized.*"

"*That's awesome. My sister hasn't got her green card yet.*"

"*That shouldn't be difficult for her.*" He grimaced.

He wanted to ask more about Beina, but restrained himself. The baby was hungry and wanted to suckle, so Nan seized the moment Beiya turned to give her breast to her son and got up to take his leave.

On his way back he felt dazed, dragging himself eastward absentmindedly. His hand patted the trunks of the poplars lined along the sidewalk as he passed them. Some pedestrians turned to look at him as if he were a lunatic. Approaching home, he forgot to enter the compound through the back alley. Instead, he walked into the front gate and even nodded at the people sitting in the guard office. One man recognized him and pointed him out for the others in the room. A few men gathered at the opened window to observe Nan, who was an overseas Chinese now. They whispered, "*Look at his face, so pink. He must've drunk cow's milk every day.*"

Nan pretended he hadn't heard them. However, the moment he rounded the corner of the first building, Uncle Zhao appeared, holding a galvanized kettle. The mousy old man, pock-faced and beetle-browed, froze midstride, then approached Nan, saying, "*Big nephew, you don't remember me? No? You have such a short memory.*"

Nan recognized him, but also remembered his father's admonition to avoid this old codger. He forced a smile, his face blushing blotchily. "*Of course I know you, Uncle Zhao. How are you?*"

"*I'm good. When did you come back? Why didn't your father breathe a word?*" He looked upset, a frown gathering on his bulging forehead.

"*I didn't tell him about my return either. I'm on a business trip and dropped in to see my parents.*"

"*Have you been home for days?*"

"*No, I arrived yesterday.*" Nan had to lie to exonerate his father. "*Uncle Zhao, I've got to go. My mother's waiting for me.*"

"*I understand.*" Despite saying that, the old man looked sour, his face a little crumpled as if Nan had slighted him.

•

Uncle Zhao phoned early that afternoon to invite Nan and his father over for dinner the next evening. Nan's father kept thanking him while apologizing for Nan's inability to come. He said, "*He's leaving tomorrow morning. He didn't plan to come home. He just took a break from his business engagement in Beijing. . . . No, this evening is out of the question. We're going to Peacock Pavilion for a family gathering. Nan hasn't seen his nephew and niece yet. . . . You see, he's really in a hurry. . . . Ahem, why did you say that? Of course he's grateful. Only because he doesn't have time to see anybody here. Listen, Old Zhao, he brought back something for you. I won't tell you what it is now. . . . Don't work up your temper like this, all right? . . . I'll see you soon.*" He hung up.

Nan was uneasy about his father's promise to Uncle Zhao and said, "*What are you going to give him?*"

"*That will be up to you. How much do you want to spend?*" His father grinned, a tea leaf on his eyetooth.

"*I don't have time to get anything for him.*"

"*No problem. You can leave some money with me, and I'll buy a gift for him and say you brought it back.*"

"*But he'll be able to tell it's a hoax.*"

"*Don't worry about that. Give me two hundred dollars.*"

"*For what?*"

"*I can buy a small air conditioner for him. It isn't much, really. You owe him—he gave you four of his best paintings. Any one of them could be worth that amount. This is cheaper than to arrange his visit to America, isn't it? He always dreams of holding a one-man show there.*"

"*All right, all right.*"

Nan took out his billfold and gave his father four fifties. He felt this was a good arrangement, since he'd have to repay the debt to Uncle Zhao one way or another. If he had gone to the old man's home for dinner, he was sure that the geezer would have tried every way to make him promise to help arrange a show of his paintings and calligraphy in New York, or D.C., or Atlanta. He was afraid of meeting that monomaniac again.

13

AFTER a series of loud hisses, the train bound for Beijing thumped, threw Nan forward a bit, then began pulling out of the Harbin station. He waved good-bye to his parents and siblings on the platform. His mother and sister broke into tears while his eyes filled too. He felt he might never be back again.

He was seated in a sleeper compartment and rested his cheek against the frame of the window. Outside, the grassland slid by. The convex plain stretched into a mist wavering in the distance. Along the railroad track a low fog was gathering, so thick that the nearby fields seemed covered by a layer of fresh snow. A moment later a swarm of town houses emerged, surrounded by vegetable fields in which women and old men were squatting on their haunches, tending seedlings or spreading manure with bare hands. Nan could tell that the ceramic-tiled houses, before which were parked some cars of Japanese and German makes, were inhabited mostly by rich people. Satellite dishes stuck out of the roofs like huge mushrooms. If he had moved back to this city, he could have afforded to live in such a place, but he'd have felt uncomfortable about the sight of the poor peasants who toiled in the fields in the same way as their ancestors had done centuries before. It seemed that the harder they worked, the poorer these people would get.

Villages and hamlets came up and flitted away. They hadn't changed, and some showed little life in them except for a few columns of cooking smoke rising from the thatched roofs. In front of a schoolhouse a bunch of children chased a soccer ball, all wearing nothing above the waist. Nan guessed that perhaps most of the able hands in the villages had left to seek work in towns and cities.

Indeed, many of the fields looked disused, as if the people had abandoned the land, whose dark soil is so rich that the plain is known as China's "granary."

In the same compartment sat two other passengers, a bulky old woman and a trim salesman. They were chatting about bureaucratic corruption while smoking a pack of Red Pagoda Hill cigarettes. The heavy-faced woman, who must once have been a ranking official, kept saying she missed the leadership of Chairman Mao, who had been not only concerned about common people's livelihood but also cleaner than any of the current national leaders. Her words put Nan in mind of the memoir by Mao's personal doctor published in the United States recently, which debunked the myth of the great man's integrity and honesty. Evidently these people here didn't have access to a book like that. They had no idea of the huge royalties Mao had reaped from his own books, particularly the little red one, during the time when in the whole country no one else received royalties and all writers had been paid merely small contribution fees. Neither did they know that the great leader had bedded women like changing clothes.

The squint-eyed salesman sighed and said one of his cousins' families was so impoverished that they hadn't been able to send their son, whose stomach was perforated by an ulcer, to the hospital and instead had hired a sorcerer to chant and dance around to exorcise the evil spirit said to have possessed the boy. As a consequence, they'd lost their only son. But in their local county many officials had used public funds to build houses for themselves, some even for their mistresses, and one bureaucrat had constructed a mansion for his grandchild, who wasn't even conceived yet.

The woman sighed and told the man, *"I've seen so many poor people these days that I often wonder why we Communists started the revolution in the first place. My maid's brother in the countryside named his little daughter 'Color TV,' because he and his wife always dream of having a television set."*

Reluctant to join them in their conversation, Nan climbed to the top berth and lay down to doze off despite the *clip-clop-clip-clop* drumming of the wheels. To some extent, he regretted having come back to see his parents and siblings, who seemed more distant from him than ever before. He wondered why so many overseas Chinese would retire to this mad country where you had to bribe and feast others to get anything done. Clearly a person like him wouldn't be able to survive here. Now he wanted all the more to live and die in America. How he missed his home in Georgia.

14

DANNING told Nan that Shaoya, Mrs. Liu, whose husband had passed away five weeks before, wanted to see him. Nan had liked Mr. Liu, though he didn't share his nationalistic zeal. He had always felt that the old man was partly blinded by his patriotism. Danning called a cab and together the two of them set out for the Lius'. Although the distance was less than three miles, it took them almost forty minutes to get there. The streets were jammed with traffic—automobiles, bicycles, tricycles, and even a few horse carts. Nan wondered why so many people wanted to buy cars in Beijing. He had seen a row of Cadillacs and BMWs parked before a multistory apartment building. Beyond doubt, some of the families had put more money into their vehicles than into their housing.

Shaoya received Nan and Danning warmly and brewed a pot of Puer tea for them. Wearing a puce tunic, she looked slightly older than she had eight years ago, but her face was sunny, as if she enjoyed living alone. She had a favor to ask Nan. Her husband's dying wish was to have his ashes taken to Canada, where their daughter was studying chemistry at the University of Alberta. Shaoya wanted Nan to help realize Mr. Liu's wish—once he took the ashes to the United States, he could mail them to their daughter from there.

The request surprised Nan and evoked mixed feelings in him. Mr. Liu had been a fervent patriot, but why would he want to have his cremains shipped out of their native land? Had he changed his mind about China? Didn't he love this country anymore? He must have been bitterly disillusioned. Nan's mind was spinning with questions, yet he said to Shaoya, *"I can take his ashes with me, but I can't guarantee you that they'll reach your daughter."*

"*China's customs may confiscate them,*" added Danning.

She said, "*I've thought about the risk too, but I can't mail them from here. Our mail is monitored.*"

"*How about letting me take half his ashes?*" Nan suggested. "*Just in case the customs seize them.*"

"*That's what my husband desired—he wanted a part of him to remain in China. I packed only half the cremains.*"

She got up and went into an inner room. Nan sighed and sipped the hot tea, which tasted a little grassy. Danning whispered to him, "*Mr. Liu used to say he wanted to be buried in a clean place.*"

"*Do you think he missed North America?*"

"*Probably. He once said he wanted to 'uncage' his soul.*"

Shaoya returned with a package the size of a brick, tightly wrapped with blue plastic cloth, a small envelope taped to its top containing a letter for her daughter, and she placed the parcel on the tea table. Nan lifted it with both hands. It was light, less than a pound. Carefully he put it into his shoulder bag.

They went on talking about some common acquaintances living in New York City. Shaoya said she wished she could have lived in America three more years so that she could have earned enough points to qualify for U.S. Social Security, but she'd had to return with her dying husband the year before. Now she depended on the remittances her daughter sent from Canada, because her salary was just enough for food and rent. She planned to leave China, but it looked as though she might not be able to do that in the near future. The police had kept her passport and wouldn't return it to her.

Coming out of the Lius', Danning took Nan to a nearby street, saying they should see another person before heading home. Nan followed his friend into a brick building that housed the headquarters of an American fast food company named Cheers. They went up in an elevator to the third floor and found the accounting department. In a stentorian voice Danning greeted the secretary, a young woman wearing eyeliner so thick that it appeared as if her lids had grown into multiple folds. He told her, "*I want to see your boss.*"

"*She's on the phone.*"

"*Tell her an old friend is here to see her.*"

"*All right.*" She turned away as if eager to interrupt her boss.

Suddenly the silver cell phone on her belt chimed and she switched it off.

"Heavens, that sounded like a fire alarm and scared a sweat out of me," said Danning.

Tittering, she nodded at him, then went into the office.

To Nan's astonishment, Yafang Gao came out, smiling and waving at Danning. "Welcome," she said pleasantly in English. She wore wire-rimmed glasses, a beige Peter Pan–collared pantsuit, and open-toe stilettos. Though trimmer than before, she looked aged and had laugh lines. At first she didn't recognize Nan, but then her face lit up and she held out her hand. *"Nan Wu! When did you come back?"*

"A few days ago."

"Are you going to work in Beijing?"

"No, I'm leaving for the States tomorrow morning." As he spoke, he saw a shadow cross her face. She kept fluttering her eyelashes.

She took them into her office. Walking behind her, Nan noticed that one of her high heels was shorter than the other one. The moment they sat down on the sectional leatherette sofas, the secretary came in with a tray holding three cups of coffee. Yafang was the director of the accounting department here, and her company had a number of fast food chains in China. As she lifted her cup with her left hand, Nan saw a diamond ring on her finger and remembered she was a lefty. Obviously she was engaged or married, but he wasn't sure if he should ask her about that. They talked about life in Beijing and about those who had returned from abroad. Many of them had made a fortune, owning houses, cars, and even companies, but the pressure was tremendous as a result of cutthroat competition in the business world. Nan didn't say much about his life in Georgia and just told her that he still ran his tiny restaurant and still tried to write poetry, but in English now. He expected she'd comment on his persistency in writing, but she didn't respond to that. He felt a little mortified and believed that to her he must be a poor man and probably a failure.

Although she invited them to lunch at a nearby Korean restaurant, Nan declined, saying he had to go shopping for his family in the afternoon. She didn't insist and rose to see them leave. In the hallway, Danning went into the men's room, leaving Nan alone with

Yafang. She stepped closer and whispered to him, "*I was a silly girl when I went to America seven years ago. I'll appreciate it if you don't talk to others about what happened to me.*"

"*I'm not a chatterbox. My lips are sealed.*" Indeed, Nan had never mentioned Heng Chen's assaulting her to anyone except for Pingping.

"*I've tried so hard to forget that nightmare, but I can't. It still hurts.*"

"*Think of it this way: Heng Chen has got what he deserves and is totally ruined. You're doing so well now—that's the best revenge.*"

She smiled, this time gratefully. "*I know you're a gentleman, Nan. Sometimes I miss New York, but this is home.*"

"*I wish I could say that.*" His throat contracted, his voice a bit shaky.

She looked him in the face, her eyes radiating a tender light. She said, "*You must have a happy family. Few men who come back from America are as calm as you.*"

"*I'm lucky that my wife prefers a solitary life.*"

Danning appeared down the hall, coming up to them. Yafang hugged Nan and said, "*Take care. Good luck with your writing.*"

"*My, that's really close,*" Danning said to her. "*You always just shake my hand.*"

Before she could respond, the elevator jingled and opened, and they both stepped into it. On their way out, Danning told Nan that Yafang's husband was a senior official in the Trade Ministry, a man about town who had earned a Ph.D. from the London School of Economics. The husband and wife were popular and influential figures in the business circle in Beijing, also notable for their private foundation that funded several elementary schools in the countryside. Danning had known them for just about a year. In fact Yafang had said a lot of good things about Nan.

15

NAN returned to Atlanta bone tired and with a stomachache. Ping-ping massaged his back to help him get the gas out, but she couldn't stop his fits of hiccups. As she was working on him, she asked, *"What did you eat that gave you so much gas?"*

"Nothing indigestible. I was just disappointed."

He told her how his mother wanted to come to work for them and how Uncle Zhao still set his sights on holding a one-man show in America. The whole trip had been mostly torture, and he should have listened to Pingping, who had warned him not to go. He had just wasted time and money. *"I felt out of place wherever I went in China,"* he told her. *"Trash, trash everywhere, so many places were like a garbage dump. I had an awful time, awful."*

Pingping was relieved that he hadn't promised his mother anything. She not only disliked the old woman but also was frightened of her. Every once in a while she'd have nightmares in which her mother-in-law jabbed her fingers at her face, sneering or calling her names. From the first days of their marriage she had wanted to live as far away as possible from Old Yulan, Nan's mother, yet Pingping could never break off with her completely, no matter where she was. Whenever she opened a letter from her, she couldn't help but shudder a little, and she often heard her abrasive voice at night. If only she could banish that old woman from her mind altogether. On the other hand, she liked her father-in-law and felt grateful to him because the old man had often carried Taotao astride his neck and allowed the boy to play in his large office. Once Taotao squeezed his grandfather's toothpaste all over his desk and sofas, but the old man didn't throw a fit and just made him promise not to do it again. So the five hundred dollars Nan had given his father didn't bother her, and even the money for an air conditioner for Uncle Zhao was well spent, having cleared the debt they had owed him.

With more devotion Nan resumed working at the Gold Wok, and the long hours didn't bother him as much as before. He was grateful to Pingping, who had over the years spent more time at the restaurant than himself. For better or worse, this place was their own, and with it they could make an honest, decent living. But a few weeks later Nan grew restless again, scribbling poems whenever he had free time. A new concern began to trouble him as well. By now they had saved almost $30,000, and the money, sitting in the bank, would hardly accrue. Should they buy another restaurant? He and Pingping talked about this but couldn't decide what to do, because a new business would mean they'd have to hire some people, whose wages would consume most, if not all, of the profit.

Then Janet suggested that Pingping consider buying some stocks. She loaned her a few issues of *Money* magazine. Through reading them Pingping began to understand what mutual funds were. Janet also told the Wus that Dave's retirement money had been invested entirely in mutual funds, so Nan and Pingping were convinced that it wouldn't be too risky to buy the stocks. They bought $20,000 worth of 500 Index. From then on Pingping would pay close attention to the Dow Jones, but Nan didn't bother to think about money. He was occupied with work and some poetry books.

Recently he had fallen in love with a volume of poems, *The Lost Geography,* by Linda Dewit, who lived in Vermont according to the biographical note on the back of the book. He liked her dark lyricism, which reminded him of Kent Philips's paintings. How strange this coincidence was. That man painted landscapes in Montana, whereas the old poet wrote about people and things in New England, but their works seemed to have some kindred spirit. Perhaps the dark luminosity had stemmed not from without but from within, from the depths of their souls. Nan also believed that the beauty of Dewit's poetry might be due to the always present awareness of mortality in the speaker's mind, even when she celebrated nature and life. Her lines were elegant, supple, honest, and always intelligent, for example, "Imagine, in a northern dusk / even a breeze brings you extra light," and "I hate the erosion of your affection / and will stop wearing smiles." Nan was fascinated and pored over Linda Dewit's poems whenever he was free. He even hand-copied the pieces he liked most.

One day he was surprised to receive a letter from Bao Yuan. His friend had written on the inside of a card bearing a pair of swans in rippling water:

August 26, 1997

Dear Nan,

By the time you read this letter I'm already on my way back to China. Life in America is too difficult for me, and I am reluctant to have my wife live here. She is the youngest child of her family and might not be able to endure the loneliness or survive the struggle we would have to wage if I stayed. Besides, her parents wouldn't let her live far away from home. Also, they are obssessed with their granddaughter, my baby girl. Now that I am a U.S. citizen, I can travel back and forth, so I made up my mind to settle down in our homeland. I'm sure I will miss the Blue Ridge Mountains, but I plan to stay and work on the mountain for three or four months a year. That's to say, from now on I will live as a world citizen. When I come back, I'll let you know beforehand. Meanwhile, may your business and writing both flourish.

As ever,
Bao

To Nan, Bao had been a remarkable success, so the letter threw him deep into thought. What had made Bao retreat to China? Hadn't he already bought a building lot for his future home in Cobb County? Why had he changed his plan all of a sudden? He seemed to have given up too easily. Clever, that man was too clever.

Nan couldn't picture Bao's actual situation, but he was sure that the reasons his friend mentioned in the letter might not be the real ones. He suspected that Bao must have suffered a setback in his art. Perhaps his agent, Ian Bernstein, had lost interest and confidence in him after the debacle of Bao's Shanghai series. In retrospect, Nan could see that this had been bound to happen, since Bao rushed too much and fell prey to moneygrubbing instead of aspiring to a higher order of artistic achievement. Even in this capitalist land a true artist ought to spurn the temptation of money. Indeed, China was probably more suitable for a man like Bao. Nan thought of writing back, but his friend had given no return address. Bao must have left in a hurry.

Later Nan heard that Frank, the lawyer, had sold the piece of land on which Bao's studio sat to a developer, which all of a sudden rendered his teacher homeless in this country.

16

ONCE in a while Nan would call Dick using phone cards he had bought at the World Bookstore; calls within the United States were only three cents a minute, and they didn't show up on the phone bill, so Pingping couldn't complain or suspect that Dick might mislead Nan into something shady or even take him away from her. In the fall Dick invited Nan to visit him, saying that if Nan liked the Iowa Writers' Workshop, he would try to get a scholarship for him, provided Nan worked hard on his poetry and came up with some strong writing samples with which Dick could convince his colleagues of his talent. Despite his distrust of such workshops, Nan was intrigued and eager to see his friend. Pingping wasn't happy about the idea and said to him, "*You just came back from China two months ago. You can't leave this place to me again.*"

"*Only this once, please. I won't do it again, I promise.*"

"*No.*"

"*Please let me go and see what the writers' workshop is like.*"

"*I've said no.*"

That topic came up every day, and a week later Pingping caved. They asked Shubo to stand in for Nan and he agreed readily. Shubo was unemployed again because the marble quarry had shut down. Mr. Mu, the backup chef, had left for Alabama to work for his nephew who had just opened a restaurant in Mobile. Though Shubo couldn't cook as well as Nan, Pingping could give him a hand in the kitchen if need be. Nan promised his wife he would be away for just five days at most.

There was another motivation he hadn't revealed to Pingping, namely that he planned to visit Beina on this trip. He knew this was crazy and that the woman might not be pleased to see him, but he couldn't help himself, as if a supernatural force possessed him, driving him toward her. To his mind, even if she wasn't happy about his reappearance, the sight of his first love in this land might rekindle the intense passion he needed for writing poetry, for which he wouldn't mind exposing himself to new wounds.

He knew he was acting like a reckless, love-crazed youth, but despite his uneasiness, he couldn't wait to see her—as if his sanity depended on such a meeting. He was going to drive the hatchback he had bought secondhand the previous winter after his old Ford's clutch had gone. This reliable Dodge should make the trip enjoyable and less tiring.

He set out before daybreak on Monday, September 22, and drove northwest along I-75 and then switched to I-24. He enjoyed driving through the mountains and forests in Tennessee, but Kentucky was a bit too flat to him, although the cruise was smooth and pleasant, there being little traffic. Now and then a shower blurred the view of farmsteads—the corn, soybean, and tobacco fields, some of which had just been cut, were a dappled brown. At some places kudzu had engulfed abandoned farmhouses, shacks, and barns. Nan disliked this kind of lush vegetation because it suggested there were snakes and animals lurking in it. He often missed the forests in the North, which had a sparse undergrowth. Toward evening, a fog began gathering and even obscured the road signs along the way, so he got off I-57 and checked into the Thrifty Inn at Mt. Vernon, Illinois. The motel was in a three-story brick building, its rooms having wide windows. A plump woman at the front desk gave Nan a clean, comfortable room on the top floor, which was five dollars cheaper than those below. Nan cooked himself noodle soup for dinner and ate it directly from the pot, with a jar of kimchee, while watching a CNN interview with a blue-helmeted general of the U.S. peacekeeping force in Bosnia. After a hot shower, he went to bed and slept nine hours on end.

He didn't make breakfast the next morning and just ate two chocolate cookies and drank a large mug of coffee provided by the motel in its lobby around the clock. He set off rather late, after eight, because there were only about four hundred miles left.

It was a fine day and the farmland was dark, loamy, and boundless. The land was so flat that even the sky seemed lower than the day before. At one place a swarm of windmills was scattered among prairie grass like a flock of giant birds in flight. Nan especially enjoyed seeing the corn and soybean fields, in some of which combines were rolling, often accompanied by trucks. He was amazed to see cascades of the kernels pour into the backs of the trucks directly so that the farmers wouldn't have to do threshing and winnowing afterward. He had seen harvesters of a less advanced type back in the northeast of China, but they had all been owned by the state farms, each of which consisted of at least five hundred people. In contrast, here every individual family used such a machine.

Pulling up on the roadside, Nan stepped out of his car and sat down on the grass to watch a combine reaping corn. The sight touched him as he remembered that in middle school the students of his grade had once gone to the countryside to help the peasants gather in crops. After all the ears of corn in a field had been plucked off by hand the previous day, each of his grade-mates took charge of a row and sickled down the plants, which the villagers would peel and use the skins to weave mats. How tedious and backbreaking that work was! Within two hours most of them began to complain of backaches and had blisters on their hands, yet they had to continue for a whole day to finish cutting that field of corn plants. By comparison, here the combines shredded the stalks and left them in the fields to fertilize the soil. Furthermore, a regular-size field here, much larger than those in China, could be harvested by two people in just a few hours. As Nan was observing the rolling machines and remembering how human labor had been wasted back in China, tears welled in his eyes and blurred his vision. He wished he could tarry longer to watch the harvesting some more.

The vast land was so sparsely populated that occasionally it looked desolate. Some farmsteads were decayed—the red barns with gambrel roofs, the silos topped with silver domes, and even the white farmhouses seemed to have fallen into disrepair, though beyond them meadows were dotted with fresh hay bundles and with milk cows grazing indolently. Nan couldn't help but wonder how lonesome those farmers living far away from the highways must have felt, especially in the wintertime when they were snowed in.

He didn't reach Iowa City till six p.m. as a result of an accident near Davenport—an eighteen-wheeler sideswiped a pickup and caused a standstill on the highway. Without difficulty he found Dick's apartment in a brick building with a mansard roof. Dick was relieved to see that Nan had arrived safely. He had to moderate a students' reading that evening, and Nan was too exhausted to go with him. Instead, Nan took a shower, then cooked himself a simple meal. After dinner, he looked through Dick's collection of poetry books, most of them hardbacks, which filled four tall bookcases. Dick also had hundreds of CDs and DVDs, some of which were Hong Kong kung fu movies. Nan was fascinated but too tired to go through all the disks stacked against the wall. He made his bed on the long sofa in the study and lay down to sleep, having left the floor lamp on.

A frost fell that night, and the city was blazingly bright the next morning, the warm sun shining on the streets, roofs, electrical wires, and trees, though the sidewalks were plastered with wet leaves. Nan loved the cool weather and took a walk in the bracing air. Dick didn't accompany him because he had to prepare for the afternoon poetry workshop and would have meetings the whole morning. Nan enjoyed seeing a few white houses with red roofs, red jalousies, and red porches, as if they were gigantic toys. Passing a small pond, he came upon some yellow lotus flowers, which he had never seen before and which, though wilting, delighted him. A few lotus pads were as big as coffee tables. And with a flashing plop, a tiny fish skipped out, disappeared, and left behind expanding ripples. Strolling on such a fall morning in this midwestern town, he felt rejuvenated and full of expectations, as if he were a graduate student again. The dark soil of the roadside fields smelled familiar and brought Manchuria back to his mind. Now and then one or two cyclists passing by would greet him heartily or give him a cheerful nod.

Early in the afternoon he went to Dick's workshop. He found the Creative Writing Program easily, in a white wooden colonial on North Clinton Street, its shutters, windows, doors, and eaves all blackish green. Before its front entrance stood a young oak and around the house were maples, their leaves showing their pale undersides whenever a wind ruffled them. The interior of the house was much nicer than its exterior, with fine woodwork and a few stained-glass windows. The seminar room was in the back of the first floor, and Nan went in without saying a word to anyone. Sitting against a wall, he quietly observed the students seated around two large tables pushed together. At the other side of the room stood a tall metal cabinet. Dick didn't introduce Nan to the class and just mentioned they had a visitor today, then he went ahead to conduct the workshop. Behind him two chalkboards hung on the wall; one of them still bore three lines left by a past class illustrating the metrical pattern, marked with alliterative ticks. Nan liked the ambience of the seminar, which was cozy and informal. Most of the aspiring poets were smart and articulate, full of nervous energy, but he wasn't impressed by the poems being discussed, which were too light and too arty to him. One piece addressed the speaker's own breasts as a pair of little friends, and another was about the palatal sensations produced by mint chocolate.

These beginning writers seemed quite fragile and seemed to be writing poetry mainly for themselves or for an elite readership. True, they argued heatedly with reddened cheeks, flashing eyes, and sly smirks, but the passion seemed to have originated more from personal feelings and the obsession with linguistic devices than from the love for ideas and deep emotions. To a degree, poetry had become an esoteric art here, somewhat deprived of its vitality and earnestness. It was hard for Nan to imagine fitting in such a group. He was afraid they might laugh at his ineptitude for English and attack him where he was weak.

A passionate exchange broke out between a Latino man and a myopic blonde over whether it was music or meaning that gave poetry the power to captivate the audience. The man, wearing a crew cut and an earring, emphasized that genuine poetry must sing, like the blues, and that meaning must come secondarily, whereas the woman argued that melodic sounds without meaning would be empty and valueless, so semantics ought to take priority in poetic composition. While she was speaking, she kept glancing at Nan over the top of her rimless glasses as if she expected him to disagree with her. Dick intervened and talked about "the auditory understanding," saying that sometimes even though we didn't get the meaning of a poem, we could still be moved just by listening to it, so there must be some inherent connection between the sound and the meaning. Ideally speaking, the sound should echo the sense, as Alexander Pope said three centuries ago. Despite the teacher's explication, the two students didn't seem reconciled, staring at each other from time to time. Nan wondered whether there had been some personal friction between them. Dick announced a ten-minute break, and Nan left without returning to the second half of the workshop.

Late in the afternoon, over a glass of Merlot, Dick asked Nan, "What do you think of my students?"

"Very impressive, especially zer nearsighted blonde."

"You mean Samantha, the tall one?"

"Yes. She's smart."

"Samantha knows more than the rest of the class. Actually, she's published a chapbook. Don't you want to come and join us here?"

"I cannot decide now. I have to be very careful about zis. You know I have a family and a business to take care of."

"As I told you before, you should try to become a professional poet eventually." Dick's voice then turned solemn. " 'The intellect of man is forced to choose / Perfection of the life, or of the work.' "

Nan knew he quoted some poet, but whom he couldn't say. He asked, "Why does it have to be one way or zee other? Why can't one have a middle way?"

"Like how?"

"Do you have to live a literary life to produce literary work?"

"Well, poetry has its own logic. If you want to be a poet, you may not have perfection of both the work and the life. It all depends on how much you're willing to sacrifice."

"Is zat why you don't have a family?"

"To some extent, yes."

"Zis is too much for me. Let me think about it, okay? I will let you know my decision soon, very soon."

"All right. Keep in mind that you have talent, but you need to give up a lot in order to develop your talent."

"I can see your lawgic, but I cannot rush to a decision."

"I understand. Some of our students had good jobs before they enrolled in our program. Remember the black guy with a mustache?"

"Yes. He's smart too."

"He used to be a physician in Milwaukee, with an M.D. from Duke. He came to the workshop because he wants to be the next Langston Hughes."

"Well, he would be better awff if he worked as a sailor or waiter."

Dick didn't seem to catch the irony. Yet at his own word "sailor" Nan's lungs constricted. Before he met Pingping and after Beina had jilted him, he had dreamed of joining the merchant marine and sailing around the world, just as Langston Hughes had once worked on freighters. As a sailor he could have had a lot of time to read and write, which would have been a good way of becoming a writer. He sent query letters, together with his one-page vita, to several marine shipping companies, but none of them bothered to write back. People must have thought he was a freak, since they never expected applications for jobs, which were all assigned by the state regardless of personal preferences.

Dick offered to take Nan to a French place that evening, but Nan preferred not to dine out. He was tired of restaurant food and wanted to have something simple and wholesome. There was some long-grain rice in Dick's cupboard, so Nan boiled porridge and scrambled four eggs with diced tomatoes and panfried a pack of Polish sausages. Dick enjoyed Nan's cooking, which he said was the only thing he missed about Atlanta. They drank two bottles of wine between them and talked deep into the night.

17

DRIVING back by I-74, Nan got off at Red Cedars, Illinois, where Beina was living. On entering the town, he stopped at a food mart and bought a bag of beef jerky for Taotao. He asked a saleswoman for directions, and she said Huron Road was in the north, about half a mile away and close to a cemetery. Without further delay he drove into Red Cedars. It was almost midmorning, yet the town, more like a big village, seemed still asleep, white clapboard houses wet with rainwater and some partly obscured by gray bushes. After Nan passed a traffic light, a café appeared, but it looked empty inside despite four cars parked before the yellowish cottage. In some front yards of the homes along the streetside, apples and pears were strewn under trees, half eaten by birds and animals, and yellow jackets buzzed into or exited from the holes in the fruit the birds had made. With little difficulty Nan found Beina's place, a pinkish house with peeling paint and an overhanging second story. It sat on a slope at the end of the narrow street. His heart was thumping. Would she be in there? It was Thursday and she was probably out at work. He went up to the front door and rang the doorbell, but it was either broken or disconnected, no sound coming from inside. So he clanked the brass knocker shaped like a horseshoe, hoping her husband wouldn't be the one to come out.

An old Chinese woman in a powder blue housedress appeared, holding the door ajar. "*Who are you looking for?*" She sized Nan up, her eyes glassy and shrewd.

"*Does Beina Su live here?*" asked Nan.

"*Yes. You are . . . ?*"

"I'm a former classmate of hers, back in China, I mean. Is she home?"

"No." Her face didn't change. "She's at her office, at Fifty-seven Chauncy Street, near McDonald's. Go down the road and take a left at the second light. That's Chauncy. You won't miss it." She pointed at a large orange sign in the south that claimed AMAZING BARGAINS!

Nan was surprised that she treated him as if he lived nearby. He asked, "Aunt, are you her mother-in-law?"

"Yes. I'm taking care of their kids. My son is in—he's correcting his students' homework. Won't you come in and talk to him?"

"No, no need to trouble him. I have to go along without further delay."

He thanked her and drove away slowly, feeling lucky that he hadn't run into Beina's husband, that rabbit-faced man, who might have been able to guess who he was.

Having taken two turns and passed a few stores and a McDonald's with a fenced-in playground for children, Nan found 57 Chauncy Street, which was a two-story brick building housing several business offices. He regretted not having asked the old woman what kind of work Beina was doing, but looking through the directory in the vestibule, he saw "Oriental Healing Arts Studio" and "Yoga Workshop." He decided to go to room 206 first, where the studio was. As he climbed up the stairs, the wooden steps edged with cleated iron sheets, sharp creaks shot up from under his feet. He tried to walk lightly; still the noise wouldn't go away. He looked up and could tell that the building must once have been a factory, the ceiling at least fifteen feet high and massive wooden pillars visible in places.

For some reason his heart was calm, as if this were a regular visit to an insurance agent or a physician. Beside the frosted-glass door of room 206 stood a small artificial pear tree in blossom, planted in a plastic pot. Nan knocked on the door, but no one answered. He turned the handle and went in.

At the sound of the door chime, a woman cried from an inner room, "I'll be with you in a minute." Nan recognized Beina's voice, which sounded lively but a little forced, neutral in the tone adopted for business use. She then asked someone in a subdued tone, "How do you feel when I twist this needle?"

"The tingling is gone," said a man.

"And this?"

"Don't feel a thing."

"Good. I can take out the needles now."

Wordlessly Nan sat down on a high-backed bench like the kind in a train station and closed his eyes, his legs crossed at the ankles. On the right-hand wall hung an old oil painting of a windjammer surrounded by rowboats, and on the desk near the window stood a lamp capped with a white metal shade. Again Nan tried to imagine what Beina looked like, but somehow he couldn't conjure up a clear image. He put his thumb on his wrist to feel his pulse, which was unrushed, about seventy a minute. He wondered what was wrong with him.

A tall whiskered man in a flannel shirt, jeans, and work boots ambled out of the inner room while saying over his shoulder to Beina behind him, "This really helps me relax. I can sleep much better now."

"I told you so" came her sugary voice.

At the sight of Nan the man called out, "Howdy."

Nan returned the greeting and stood up as the patient made for the door. Beina saw him and came over, stretching out her hand, smiling as if she were expecting him. She wore a pink dress that gave her a flattish figure, and on either of her wrists was a jade bangle. It dawned on Nan that her half sister must have informed her of his appearance at their home in Harbin, and that her mother-in-law must have called her just now; otherwise Beina couldn't possibly have been so at ease. Still, he was puzzled. Hadn't she played fast and loose with his heart? Didn't she feel bad for the wound she had inflicted on him? Didn't she assume he might hate her? Why was she so placid?

"*Come sit here,*" she said with a smile that revealed her tiny canines, and patted the back of a chair next to her desk. After making two cups of tea, she proceeded to sit down in her swivel chair. "*What brings you to Red Cedars?*" she asked.

"*I went to visit a friend at the University of Iowa,*" Nan said, seated beside the desk. On its mahogany top spread a trapezoid of sunlight. He observed her closely. She was almost a middle-aged woman now, her face slightly sallow, and her bangs had begun to gray. A few thin wrinkles appeared on her neck as she lowered her head. Despite her smiling eyes, despite her full lips, somehow she seemed subdued—the fire, the coquetry, and the insouciance that had once set his entire being aflame were no longer there. Even her voice had lost its crisp, bright timbre. She was just an ordinary woman with listless eyes and an incipient double chin.

Nan tried to appear natural but felt his jaw go stiff whenever he attempted to smile. He kept lifting the tall teacup to his mouth so that he didn't have to face her all the while. He didn't talk about himself and just listened to her. She said she envied him because he had gotten a green card without spending a fortune on an immigration lawyer. If only she and her husband had come to the States before the Tiananmen massacre. That way they too could have been granted permanent residency automatically. Nowadays it was so hard to get the papers that she wasn't even sure if their lawyer could really help them.

Then she offered to take Nan to McDonald's, where they could talk over lunch, but he declined, saying he ate restaurant food every day and the cup of oolong tea she'd made for him was good enough. Also, he'd have to hit the road soon. *"Do you like it here?"* he asked, hoping she'd say something negative.

"I don't know—I guess I do. Hongbin, my husband, is studying toward his degree, so I have to work to support my family."

"What's he studying?"

"Public health."

"Related to Japan?"

"No, he has almost forgotten his Japanese, which he doesn't use here."

"I see. Does he help you in this studio?"

"No. I do acupuncture by myself, just to make a couple of dollars. I spent a whole year learning how to do it before we came to America, so I passed the exam and got the license here. How about you? I heard you owned several restaurants."

"*We have only one, very small, and I don't like running it. I've been writing.*"

"*Nan, I can see you haven't changed much, still a dreamer. Your heart is still young.*" She smiled and shook her head as if in disapproval.

"*I guess so. Besides dreams, what else can I have?*" He said that as if to himself, realizing he could no longer share his thoughts with this woman for whom he had almost lost his mind sixteen years ago.

She lifted her teacup and took a sip, then went on telling him more about her life in this town. "*Hongbin and I won't mind settling down here. The town has good public schools, well above the average in the state. On top of that, real estate is cheap here. For a hundred and fifty thousand dollars you can buy a big house, even with a pool in the backyard. You saw my mother-in-law just now. She's all right and takes good care of my kids, especially the younger one, just two years old. Did you see my son Michael, the younger boy?*"

"*No.*"

"*He's absolutely adorable. The problem with my mother-in-law is that she's too stingy and always translates dollars into yuan when she spends money. She can never get accustomed to American life. But she loves my kids and I appreciate that. My kids are the center of my life. Now I know what parental love is like and why Confucius taught people to be filial to their parents. I would do anything for my kids, even die for them. See, I'm a dutiful wife.*"

"*Also a good mother.*"

"*You're right.*"

"*Still, you must rule the roost at home.*" He managed a smile as a twinge tugged his insides. He raked his fingers through his thick hair.

"*Tell me, why did you come to see me?*" She curled her lips, her round cheeks coloring a little.

"*To see if you're like the Beina I often dreamed of.*"

"*Well, you came too late, to be honest. Eleven years ago I asked you to help me come to the United States, but stupid you, you didn't seize the opportunity. I had no children then and I was thinking of leaving Hongbin.*"

"*You mean, you might have come to join me here?*"

"Well, that was a possibility. I always had a soft spot in my heart for you because you hurt me."

"I hurt you?"

"Yes. You gave up on me too easily, as if I was not a woman worth your effort to compete with Hongbin. Worst of all, you burned all the poems you'd written for me. That's like you gave me a gift and then took it back. You humiliated me, you know."

"Wait a minute. I was a poor man you despised, and I couldn't buy you anything like the red scooter Hongbin got for you from Japan."

"But later you came to America. Couldn't you promise me a red car? Even just lie to me?" She forced a titter in an attempt at levity, her thumb rubbing her ring finger.

"I see. I became a man of means to you, but what made you think I'd be willing to buy you a car?"

"Because you loved me."

"So you believed I would abandon my wife and child for you?"

"Wouldn't you? Didn't you come all the way just to see me? I bet your wife has no idea where you are." Her eyes flashed, and for the first time since he came a familiar vixenish look crept on her face. Then she lifted her chin with annoyance, apparently aware of Nan's eyes riveted on the pocket of flesh hanging under it.

He said in a half-flippant voice, "Don't assume I'll come and slobber over you whenever you whistle from far away. I'm too old to be a slave of love anymore. Besides, how can you be sure I'm still smitten with you after so many years?"

"I'm your first."

"What's that supposed to mean?"

"For a man like you, the first love is always the flame consuming your heart. You cannot stop your torch song."

"You've underestimated me. I know what true love is like now. You've never loved any man devotedly, whereas my wife loves me and is always ready to suffer with me."

"Still, you don't love her, do you? I'm pretty sure you'll come to see me again. But don't take this as an invitation."

"Well, you think you still have your hooks in me?"

"Try to get them out."

"We'll see." He chortled but couldn't laugh it off. His chest tightened.

Deep down, he knew this trip was a mistake—all the years' longing and anguish had been caused by a mere illusion, and all his pain and sighs had been groundless, wasted for the wrong person. What an idiot he had been!

But this disillusionment was perhaps necessary for him to sober up and begin to heal. Indeed, he didn't feel the old numbing pain anymore despite sitting so close to Beina. Something tickled his throat and made him want to laugh, but he checked himself lest he go into hysterics. He felt as if there were a wall between her and him. Probably she had already set up such a barrier in her mind before he came, or such a wall might be just another ploy of hers. Even without her doing that, he could no longer imagine getting closer to her.

A few minutes later he took his leave. A wind swept through the empty street and tossed up a tuft of his hair from behind. He stepped into his car and pulled away. Beina hadn't asked for his phone number or address but had given him her business card, on which a pair of cranes was flying to the realm of longevity. In his heart he knew he wouldn't contact her again. Coasting along the on-ramp to I-74, he rolled down the car window and flung out her card, where it blew into the wild grass.

18

NAN had been ill for several days, though he went to work as usual. The trip to Iowa had plunged him into a depression, also a bone-deep exhaustion. In a way he hated Beina, who had changed so much, or was so different from whom he'd imagined, that she had shattered his vision of her. He felt sick at heart, but he began to be extraordinarily considerate to his wife. Pingping was alarmed by his sudden change and urged him to get some medical attention—at least go see an herbalist, who wouldn't charge a lot. She feared he might be having an early midlife crisis, a sort of male menopause. But he replied, *"I have a heart problem no cardiologist can diagnose and no drug can cure."*

Despite his despondency, he resumed working on his poetry, with greater effort. He mailed out another batch of poems to a small journal called *Yellow Leaves,* which he had noticed published some Asian American authors. He had no hope of acceptance and just submitted his work routinely. He called Dick and told him that he wouldn't be coming to study with him because he preferred to stay with his family. Dick said this would be a huge loss to Nan, who was already forty-one, and that it would be too late to develop his talent if he didn't concentrate or make the necessary sacrifice soon. Nan thanked him, but was adamant about his decision. He knew that from this point on he'd have to be on his own, and that probably Dick and he would drift apart in the future, since as a famous poet Dick always had a crowd around him. In other words, Nan would have to accept isolation as his condition and write for no audience, speaking to emptiness.

One afternoon the phone rang at the Gold Wok; Nan picked it up and heard Danning Meng's hearty voice. *"Hey, Nan Wu, I want to see you,"* his friend said.

"Where are you?" Nan was thrilled.

"I'm in Washington, D.C."

"Doing what?"

"Attending a writers' conference and doing a tour. A playwright was supposed to come originally, but she had a stroke, so I filled in for her."

"Can you come to Atlanta?"

"Of course. That's why I'm calling."

Danning would stay with the Wus for two days, then go on to catch up with the rest of the Chinese writers' delegation in Oxford, Mississippi, to see the town, the prototype for the capital of Faulkner's Yoknapatawpha County, and to visit the great novelist's home, which was said to have been the biggest house in his hometown when he was alive. Both Nan and Pingping were excited about their friend's visit. That night they tidied up their home a little, though, exhausted by a whole day's work, they couldn't do as much cleaning as they wished. Danning would stay in Nan's room. Nan was happy to give up his bed to sleep two nights with Pingping, but she frowned when he grinned at her meaningfully. Despite loving him, she didn't like sharing her bed with him, since he'd turn in late, often in the wee hours, and snore loudly. She had to rest well to work the next day and didn't want to have sex too often.

Danning arrived two days later and thanked Nan on behalf of Mrs. Liu for having mailed her husband's ashes to their daughter in Canada. He presented Pingping with four of his books, which didn't impress her much, but she gave him a hug for the gesture. She still couldn't enjoy his fiction. Over the years she had read a number of his novellas and short stories published in magazines and disliked most of them, so she knew what kind of books these were. Despite her low opinion of his writings, she was glad and hospitable since he had come all the way to see them. Also, she was happy in Nan's happiness.

Danning was very impressed by the Wus' restaurant and brick ranch, and by the lake in their backyard. He walked around the house and said to Nan, "*Your home has great feng shui. Look at those trees, absolutely gorgeous. And you own them all. I won't have a blade of grass in Beijing that I can call mine after we move into an apartment building next spring.*" At the sight of the waterfowl he exclaimed, "*My goodness, what a peaceful haven you have here. How nice this all is! I could never dream of living in such a tranquil spot. Nan, you're a lucky man and have everything you want. I'm burning with envy.*" He sounded sincere, genuinely moved.

At lunch he told Nan, "*Your life here is so clean and decent. You made the right choice to remain in America. I wish I hadn't gone back and had stayed to make an honest living like yours.*"

"*But you've become a famous author.*"

"*Others can say that, but I know what I've accomplished— nothing. Serious writings are a kind of extension of one's life. But I've just been wasting my life and making noises that will disappear in the blink of an eye. What price fame? Just more troubles. The only meaningful thing, the only salvation, is your work, but significant work is impossible in China at present. Besides the censorship, the country's too hectic, and everyone is in a rush to grab off something. People are all obsessed with getting rich, and money has become God.*" He sighed, looking tearful.

Nan said, "*You don't know how hard Pingping and I have worked.*"

"*Of course I can imagine that. But you got your reward. You have your own business and your home, and even two cars. You're a solid businessman. Here you do hard work but live comfortably. What's more, Taotao is a fine boy, and you won't have to worry about his education. My daughter is going to take the entrance exams for high school next spring, and she has already started cramming day and night. She loves painting, but we have to dissuade her from planning to major in the fine arts at college. At most she can specialize in ad designing. By contrast, your son can follow his own interests, his own heart. This is a fundamental difference in our children's lives.*"

"*My son is doing well because his mother has helped him every day.*"

"*You're such a lucky man. Your wife is not only pretty and hard-working but also loyal.*" Somehow Danning's voice choked. He swallowed and wiped his teary eyes.

"*What's wrong?*" Nan asked with a start.

Danning heaved a long sigh. "*Sirong just had an affair with a colleague of hers. Nowadays it's so common, even fashionable, to have a lover outside your marriage.*"

Nan ventured, "*Does she mean to leave you?*"

"*No, that's the hardest part. My daughter is very attached to her, more than to my parents, so we have to stay in this marriage.*"

Later Nan thought about their conversation. He knew Danning had told only his side of the story. He was sure that his friend had seen other women, at least some of the girls in the bars, hair salons, and nightclubs. Indeed, his own philandering might have driven his wife to have the affair, and nobody but himself should be to blame.

•

The next day Danning wanted Nan to take him to Chinatown. Pingping again asked Shubo to stand in for Nan, so after dinner the two friends drove west along Buford Highway toward Chamblee. Entering Norcross, they saw a road gang in orange vests and caps gathering garbage on the roadside, where stood a blue van hauling a trailer loaded with shovels, rakes, and barrels. Danning wondered who these young men were, still working at this hour. "*Prisoners,*" Nan told him.

"*This is a good way to reform them. I didn't know American prisoners also work.*"

"*Some of them do. I once saw a prison detail planting trees and flowers.*"

The sight of the convicts reminded Nan of their mutual friend Hansong, who had gone crazy and shot an old man eight years earlier in Massachusetts after he heard that his girlfriend had disappeared in Tiananmen Square. Nan knew Hansong hadn't completed his prison term when he was deported three years ago. He asked Danning, "*Do you happen to know how Hansong is doing?*"

"*You haven't heard he's married?*"

"*You mean, he was released from jail?*"

"Yes, but he can't find a regular job in China. Nobody wants to take English lessons from him, so he's been a freelance translator."

"He was a smart man. What a waste."

Nan felt sad as a lull set in. The traffic light turned red and he hit the brakes. Somehow he caught every red light today, which gave him a premonition that there might be trouble this evening.

As they passed a shopping center near the Korean supermarket, Danning cried, *"Stop! Double back. I saw a strip bar over there. Let's go have some fun."*

Nan hesitated but jammed on the brakes. He did a U-turn and pulled into the plaza. The parking lot was full, so they left their car behind the building of the strip club, in front of an adult movie theater. Nan wondered if he should go in first to scout this place out, but his friend was already heading toward the bar's front entrance, so he followed him. The second they stepped in, a brawny, hard-faced man boomed at them, "Five dollars a head."

Nan gave him a ten. It was foggy and clamorous inside. They took a table near the passageway to a small room blazoned with VIP on its door, since all the tables in front of the dance platforms were occupied. From where they sat they could watch the performances from the side. Along the walls stood some Mexican workers wearing cowboy hats and nursing beers. They seemed reluctant to take a seat at the tables, which would amount to inviting a girl to do a lap dance or table dance. A short-haired barmaid in a lavender skong came and asked Nan and Danning, "What would you like to drink?"

Though he'd already downed a few glasses of wine at dinner, Danning ordered a shot of bourbon and a mug of lager. Nan asked for a Molson. He was afraid his friend might have had a drop too much, but he said nothing. Among the tables several topless girls were doing lap dances. In a corner, a girl in a blue bikini raised her bony rear end, swaying it at a stocky Mexican man, who, holding a tall can of beer, seemed intimidated but couldn't retreat further, his back already against the wall. On the string of her briefs several dollar bills were flapping as she thrust her backside at him. She was so thin that her ribs showed. Unlike the standing Mexicans, the white men sitting at the tables seemed at ease, though naked girls were wriggling in front of them or gyrating on their laps. None of them looked excited, and at most some were amused.

With a twang the metallic music resumed, and two young women wearing high heels went onto the central platform and began dancing. One of them jumped up and gripped a chrome pole and with one leg spread out revolved around it. The din was so deafening that Nan's eardrums itched.

He was giddy, never having been to such a place before. He had passed this club every Monday morning on his way to the World Bookstore to buy the Sunday newspaper and had thought that it must be stylish in here and that at most the girls would be topless when they stripped. Now he was astonished to see that some of them didn't have a stitch on, and that a few women, already over thirty, wagged their wide, ungainly bottoms tagged with a bunny's tail as they walked around bartending. He looked at Danning, who was ecstatic, grinning, his eyes aglitter. Danning tapped the table gently with both palms as if playing a drum to accompany the music. The room looked so hazy and so crowded that Nan felt as if he were in a ship's cabin.

A tall brunette came and asked them while batting her dark eyes, "Would yuh care for a lap dance?" Her accent betrayed that she must be a recent Eastern European immigrant.

Nan lowered his head and saw a tattooed butterfly on her inner thigh. "How much?" he mumbled, and felt his cheeks flushing.

"Ten bucks."

Before Nan could say another word, Danning banged the greasy tabletop with the heel of his palm and crowed, "Yes, dance for us."

The girl turned around, swaying her hips, and began slipping out of her bra little by little. Nan lifted his eyes and saw her youthful breasts, the nipples erect and the areolas pink, flecked with a few pimples; he forced his eyes farther up, to her face. She was affectedly ogling him, the tip of her tongue wiping her teeth and lips, while she raised her rump at Danning, wagging it from side to side. She craned her neck, gently kissed Nan below his ear. He wondered if she'd left a smudge there. She groaned in a whisper, "Don't you want me?" Smiling, she opened her mouth, a tiny pearl sitting at the center of her tongue. Nan was breathing hard, his mouth dry, and he had no idea how to answer. He wondered whether the pearl had been fixed to her tongue permanently. How could she eat with that thing in her mouth? It wouldn't be easy for her to brush her teeth either. What did it stand for? Why did it have to be kept in there? As he was speculating, she lifted her upper body a little and began grinding her behind against Danning's lap. The music went faster and noisier while her gyration turned wilder. Danning's laughter grew louder and louder as her bottom kept revolving.

"Ouch!" she cried, and straightened up. "No tarching!"

Danning laughed, baring his buckteeth. "Keep going!" he grunted.

She resumed lap dancing, but a moment later stopped again. She looked annoyed and sputtered out at Danning, "If you tarch me again I'm gonna tell security."

Danning grinned and kissed the tips of his plump fingers. "You're delicious," he said.

Nan glanced at the front entrance, where a big hulk of a man, wearing a flattop, was looking in their direction, flexing his corded arms and bulging pectorals; the top of his right ear was missing. But Danning was already too befuddled to care. He said in Chinese to the girl, who refused to dance anymore, "*You, little whore, you want to throw me out? Do you know who I am? Look at this face.*" He pointed at his nose. "*Don't you know me? I'm a major novelist, an award winner, famous in the whole country. Give us a good dance. We want the same service for our money. You danced for that man longer and better just now. Why don't you smile at us like you smiled at him?*" He pointed at a hairless white man, whose eyes were half closed while a girl leaned supine over him with her arms raised backward, hooked around his neck.

"Stick to English," the lap dancer fired back. "I don't know Korean."

Nan was frightened. He stood up and handed a twenty-dollar bill to her. "Take zis, miss. Keep zer change. I'm sawrry, he's drunk. I'm taking him away."

The girl stretched out her right leg and pulled open the elastic string around her thigh, with which some singles and fives were already attached. Nan inserted the twenty, but a bill fell on the floor.

He picked it up and put that in as well. She smiled and gave him a peck on the cheek, whispering, "Thank you, sweetie." Then she went away to the bar counter to join the girls perching on the mushroom seats.

Danning took out a business card that bore his official titles as a committee member of the Beijing Writers' Association and an adjunct professor at Peking University. "*Let me give her this, all right?*" he said to Nan, grinning, then turned to the girl.

"*Please, let's go!*" Nan grabbed his upper arm.

The hulky bouncer came and helped Nan support Danning toward the door. The business card dropped on the floor, faceup.

19

IT WAS Sunday the next day, and Danning wanted to go to the morning service. The request puzzled Nan, but he drove his friend to the Chinese church in Duluth where Mr. Shiming Bian had been a pastor. There was little traffic on the street, and most of the shops weren't open yet except Dunkin' Donuts. A shower had poured down the night before, so the trees and roofs looked cleaner, their colors fresh and sharp. Nan pulled into the church's hedge-bordered parking lot, which was partly filled, and backed into a space. Walking toward the front entrance, he chaffed Danning, saying, "Are you going to the confessional box?"

"No, just to attend the service. I feel awful. I was out of my head yesterday evening."

Nan made no comment, still troubled by the scene at the strip club. Together they entered the foyer of the church, but to Nan's surprise, the schedule had changed—the service in Mandarin wouldn't start until eleven and they were one hour early. However, the English service was about to begin in a chapel next to the nave, so they decided to go to that. In the chapel there were rows of chairs in lieu of pews, and in a corner was a black organ at which sat a small woman. On the chancel, which was just a regular platform below a large cross on the wall, stood a soft-faced young woman wearing a bob, as well as two young men, one holding an electric guitar and the other, the bespectacled one, a sheaf of paper. As soon as Nan and Danning sat down in the last row, the nearsighted man invited the congregation to rise and the three young people at the chancel started a hymn, the words projected on the front wall for the worshippers to follow. The three singers sang into the microphones with their eyes half closed. From the front ceiling hung a pair of Yamaha amplifiers. The music was expansive and uplifting, played by both the organist and the guitarist, while the entire room sang: "Come, now is the time to worship, / Come, now is the time to meet God . . ."

The song moved Nan. Danning, caught by the music, was singing loudly with the others. His baritone voice was as distinct as if he were leading a choir. Nan was amazed that his friend could sing the hymn with such abandon. Danning shook his head from side to side as he was chanting. After the song, they belted out another one. Then Mr. Bian went to the front and read out his prayer in English. He spoke haltingly as if his tongue were stiff and his nose blocked, but his voice was charged with feeling. He begged God to bless the parish, to forgive the sinners among them, to console a family who had just lost a child in a traffic accident, to provide strength for everyone in this community so that they could fight evil and do more good. Mr. Bian was thinner than he had been two years earlier, but his face was radiant and his manner more dignified, as if he were no longer a dissident but a pure clergyman. He looked energetic and even his hair seemed thicker than before. Unlike the others, who all bowed their heads, Nan lifted his eyes from time to time to observe the pastor. Mr. Bian had published several articles in the past two years to revise his political views and urge people always to differentiate China from the Chinese government. He argued that with such a distinction in mind one could resist the Communist propaganda and avoid letting patriotism dominate one's life, because there were values higher than a country or nation.

After Mr. Bian said the prayer, Reverend Robert MacNeil, tall and skeletal, took the lectern and delivered a sermon entitled "Take Advantage of Our Opportunities." He read out Ephesians 5:8–20, then elaborated on the phrase "making the most of every opportunity, because the days are evil." He said God's mercy was like a big party to which everyone was invited. Whenever a sinner repented, God would delight in his return to him. But the sad truth was that the majority of people wouldn't attend God's party because they were like sleepers who wouldn't wake up, too lazy and too foolish. That was why the Lord announced, "For wide is the gate and broad is the road that leads to destruction, and many enter through it. But small is the gate and narrow the road that leads to life, and only a few find it." The reverend declared that the genuine way to rejoice in God's love and generosity was to avoid evil and spread the words of the Lord. Every real Christian must work constantly to lead others to Jesus Christ. Nan was impressed by the preacher's eloquence. The old man quoted from the Bible without touching the book and even pointed out the exact numbers of chapters and verses. He urged the congregation to seize every day to follow the Lord's way. He also mentioned that Sir Walter Scott had gotten these words carved on his sundial: "I must home to work while it is called day; for the night cometh when no man can work." Because Scott was always aware of the approach of death, he had never wasted his time and managed to finish his books.

Nan listened, fascinated. Yet unfamiliar with the New Testament, he couldn't understand everything Father MacNeil said. Meanwhile, Danning was totally engrossed, his eyes glued to the reverend's shriveled face. As Nan glanced sideways at his friend, a red offertory bag was handed to him. He hadn't expected this and hurriedly pulled a dollar out of his pants pocket and put it into the bag. To his amazement, the instant he passed the bag on to Danning, his friend thrust his fist into it. Obviously Danning had prepared his offering like a regular churchgoer.

When the reverend was done with the sermon, people rose to their feet and sang another hymn, following the lines projected on the wall. As they were singing the last refrain of the song, Nan saw Danning's face bathed in tears. His friend was genuinely touched and chanting with the others:

> *And we cry holy, holy, holy*
> *And we cry holy, holy, holy*
> *And we cry holy, holy, holy*
> *Is the Lamb!*

Father MacNeil raised his leathery hand and gave a benediction in a sonorous voice: "May God grant us the wisdom as bright as daylight. May God give us the courage to expose ourselves fully to the Holy Spirit so that we can make ourselves new every day. May God bless us with joy and love so that we can spread his love to everyone in the world!"

"Amen!" the whole room cried.

The dark-complected woman struck up the relaxing postlude on the organ, and the reverend announced, "Now you are dismissed."

Once in the foyer, Nan asked Danning, "*Do you want to attend the Mandarin service as well?*"

"*No, I've had enough for today.*"

Through the opened door to the nave Nan saw hundreds of people sitting in the pews in there and waiting for the service. Mr. Bian was seated on the chancel, about to deliver his sermon in Mandarin. In the lobby a few men stood around engaging in small talk, and two women at a long table were handing out flyers to new arrivals. Nan and Danning went out of the church. The pavement was glinting a little in the sunshine, and the air seemed brighter than it had an hour before. Pulling out of the parking lot, Nan asked his friend, "*Could you understand everything the old preacher said?*"

"*No, but he made me feel better, much better. I'm cleaner now.*" Danning sounded serious and meditative, as if exhausted.

"*Do you believe in Christianity?*"

"*Not really, but I like to attend the service once in a while. In Beijing I can't go to any church or temple because I'm a petty cadre at the writers' association. I'd get into trouble if I went.*" He sighed. "*Ah, like a small fish I too yearn for clean water.*"

Slowly Nan followed the traffic on Beaver Run Road, still puzzled by Danning's claim to be cleaner than before. On the other hand, he was convinced that if his friend had often gone to a church or temple or mosque, Danning might indeed have become a better man.

•

Nan was broody after seeing Danning off on a quarter-filled Greyhound bound for Oxford, Mississippi. He felt he might not see his friend again. Danning seemed tormented by a kind of desperation, which might not subside as long as he lived in Beijing and held his official position. Nan had never thought that his friend would go downhill as a result of his fame, which seemed to have let loose the demon in him.

Danning's visit had upset Nan. For the following week he went on telling his wife that success was the mother of failure, transposing Chairman Mao's famous quotation "Failure is the mother of success."

20

EVER SINCE his return from China, Nan had been restless for another reason as well. He couldn't make any progress in his writing. As he had failed in his search for an ideal woman, his project on a bunch of love poems had come to a halt. He wondered if he was suffering a writer's block. One afternoon, when the busy lunchtime was over, he was sitting at the counter and had his nose in a book entitled *Good Advice on Writing*. Both Pingping and Niyan were taking a break, seated at a booth, drinking tea and cracking spiced sunflower seeds. Janet was with them and from time to time lifted her cup and blew away the tea leaves. She was talking excitedly about how happy she and her daughter were in the weekend school at Emory, which, managed by a Chinese graduate student, had more than 160 pupils now. Time and again she uttered a word or phrase in Mandarin.

Nan stopped at a quotation from Faulkner. It stated: "The writer must teach himself that the basest of all things is to be afraid; and, teaching himself that, forget it forever, leaving no room in his workshop for anything but the old verities and truths of the heart, the old universal truths lacking which any story is ephemeral and doomed— love and honor and pity and pride and compassion and sacrifice."

The first part of the sentence jolted Nan, who suddenly understood the real cause of his predicament. For all these years he had bumbled around and shilly-shallied about writing because of fear: the fear of becoming a joke in others' eyes, of messing up his life without getting anywhere, of abandoning the useless, burdensome part of his past in order to create a new frame of reference for himself, of moving toward the future without looking back. It was this fear that had driven him to look for inspiration elsewhere other than in his own heart. It was this fear that had misled him into the belief that the difficulties in writing poetry in English were insurmountable and that he couldn't possibly write lines that were natural and energetic. Now this realization overcame and disgusted him. He read Faulkner's words once more. His mind hardly registered the meaning of the second part, but the first half again astounded him. Tears were rolling down his cheeks. How he hated himself! He had wasted so many years and avoided what he really desired to do, inventing all kinds of excuses—his sacrifice for his son, his effort to pay off the mortgage, his pursuit of the American dream, his insufficient command of English, his family's need for financial security, the expected arrival of a daughter, and the absence of an ideal woman in his life. The more he thought about his true situation, the more he loathed himself, especially for his devotion to making money, which had consumed so many of his prime years and dissolved his will to follow his own heart. A paroxysm of aversion seized him, and he turned to the cash register, took all the banknotes out of the tray, and went to the alcove occupied by the God of Wealth, for whom they had always made weekly offerings. With a swipe he sent flying the wine cups, the joss sticks, and the bowls of fruit and almond cookies. Around him were scattered pistachios and salted cashews. The three women in the booth stopped chatting to watch him. He thrust a five-dollar bill on the flame of a candle and instantly the cash curled, ablaze.

"My God, he's burning money!" gasped Janet.

They all got up and rushed over. Niyan clapped her palm over her mouth as Nan was setting aflame a whole sheaf of banknotes. "*What are you doing?*" his wife cried, and yanked his shoulder from behind.

His fell on his bottom, the cash still blazing in his hand. He looked entranced and dewy-eyed. Pingping yelled again, "*Don't burn our sweat money!*"

Niyan wrenched a few unburned banknotes out of his other hand, and he tossed the rest at the smiling God of Wealth. Pingping shoved him aside and tried to save the flaming bills while Nan flung up his hands and cried, "I want to burn it all, all zis 'dirty acre.'"

"He must be having a breakdown," Janet said.

"I hate this mahney, this 'dirty acre'!" he yelled in a voice verging on a sob. His eyes gave a flare.

"What he talking about?" Pingping asked Janet, who shook her head, having no clue either.

Nan had meant to say "filthy lucre," but in the throes of frenzy he got the idiom wrong. He picked himself up from the floor and stamped on the half-burned cash, saying through his teeth, "Dirty acre! Dirty acre!" His face was misshapen, his eyes smoldering with pain.

The women were too confused to respond. He turned and stormed away to the kitchen. Pingping was wiping her eyes while Niyan clucked her tongue and said as if to herself, "Why he hate money so much?"

Janet wagged her chin. "Maybe his mind just snapped. It often happens to people who have too much stress."

"He's really crazy," Niyan said, as if out of schadenfreude.

"He's just sick man," Pingping wailed, and doubled over, her face twisted. "Now you see this is real Nan. He always want to torture me."

Nan thundered from the kitchen, "Yeah, I'm sick, sick of everysing here, sick of myself, sick of every one of you, sick of zis goddamned restaurant!"

They were stunned. None had expected he had such a harsh, menacing voice. "Maybe he should go see a shrink," suggested Janet, patting Pingping on the back as she continued to convulse with sobs.

Nan went out the back door to traipse around the shopping center awhile, his mind still whirling. The sun was scorching overhead, and in no time perspiration soaked the back of his T-shirt. The walk calmed him down some, though he still couldn't focus on any thought. Near the entrance to the photo studio toward the east end of the plaza, a mottled gray pigeon that had to be a crossbreed of a pigeon and a dove limped over, walking on the back of its crippled left foot. Its head kept bobbing at a cockeyed angle as it tottered toward Nan, who had often fed it. Nan fished in his pockets but found only a handful of coins, so he stepped aside to avoid obstructing its path. Before the pigeon passed by, it paused to flutter its wings, which suddenly gleamed in the sunlight. If only Nan had had some crumbs or leftovers on him. He liked this lone bird, which was tough, unafraid of people.

When Nan went back to the Gold Wok twenty minutes later, he became himself again, and without a word set about cutting a basket of eggplants, which were all tender and seedless, handpicked by Pingping at the Cherokee farmers' market. For the rest of the day he was very quiet and did everything he was supposed to do.

21

PINGPING was still angry with Nan for burning the money. For three days she'd avoid rubbing elbows with him at work, and neither would she speak to him. However hard he tried to induce her to talk, she'd compress her lips. At most, she'd give a faint smile if he said something funny or silly.

On Monday morning the truck that delivered groceries came as usual and left two crates of celeries and napa cabbages and a bucket of tofu at the back door to the restaurant. Without telling Nan, who was supposed to move them, Pingping began carrying them in by herself. As she was lifting a crate, suddenly a tearing pain shot through her back and her knees buckled. She fell on the cement doorstep, unable to pick herself up. "Nan, come and help me!" she called out. Two flies, startled, took off from the tofu, whirling around at a high pitch.

Nan rushed out with a towel over his shoulder and saw his wife lying on her side. Her face was contorted while her hand covered the small of her back. "*What happened?*" he panted, bending over her. "*Why didn't you use the hand truck?*"

"*Oh, I broke my back!*"

"*Can you move?*"

"*I can't. My back snapped.*" On her eyelashes tears glistened.

As Nan tried to help her get up, she gave a loud moan, which frightened him. He left her there and hurried to the parking lot to fetch their van. He wasn't sure if she had really broken her back, but she looked partly paralyzed. He must take her to the hospital immediately. He told Niyan to ask Shubo to come in and help. If her husband was unavailable, she could just close the restaurant for the morning.

Pingping was rushed into a small room in the ER at Gwinnett Hospital. A lanky male nurse said she couldn't have broken her back. "Maybe she slipped a disk, you know," the fellow told Nan.

Then a tall, rugged-faced man stepped in and introduced himself as Dr. Gritz. He looked at the bruise on Pingping's elbow, already bandaged by the nurse, and then began pressing her back here and there. "Does it hurt here?" he kept asking in a soft voice.

The injury was on her spine, just above the small of her back, but to the naked eye there seemed nothing abnormal. The doctor said to Nan, "I'm going to give her an X-ray to see if there's any bone injury."

"Sure. Do whatever is necessary, please."

The X-ray showed everything was normal, so Dr. Gritz decided to use MRI, which could reveal muscle and ligament damage. Following the male nurse pulling the gurney with his mealy hand, Nan pushed Pingping through a long corridor to the scanning lab. In the semidark room, a woman technician and Nan helped Pingping lie on a narrow table. Before sliding her into the tube of a stout MRI scanner, the woman told Pingping, "If it bothers you too much, just raise your leg to let me know." Pingping nodded, then her head disappeared into the tube. The technician began to produce the images of her lower back.

The machine made rumbling noises like a rickety washer while Pingping lay still as if asleep. Nan wondered whether she was hurting. That was unlikely, as she seemed at ease.

The film of the MRI indicated that a disk was protruded, pressuring some ligaments between two vertebrae. Dr. Gritz said this didn't look like a ruptured disk, so it wasn't an emergency case, and all Pingping should do was rest in bed for a few weeks. He prescribed ibuprofen and a steroid and told her not to move around too much until the pain subsided. She could walk a little when she felt up to it, but she mustn't do any hard exercise. Gritz also referred her to Dr. Levin at a clinic in Norcross. "I'm an orthopedic surgeon," he said to Pingping. "A back pain specialist can do more for you."

Though their substandard medical insurance covered a larger part of the cost, the first hospital bill surprised the Wus, altogether more than three hundred dollars. Both Nan and Pingping were unsettled, knowing this was just the beginning. If only they had bought a better policy. Nan took his wife to Dr. Levin two days later and paid another eighty dollars for the visit. From now on she'd have to see Dr. Levin twice a week. If her pain persisted in two months, the specialist said, they should seriously consider a surgery that helped most back pain patients recover fully. Despite the professional assurance, Nan and Pingping didn't believe it necessary for her to undergo an operation, fearing that any mishap might mess up her spine and paralyze her.

Besides that fear, they had no idea how much they'd have to spend for her medical bills, which became a concern because the restaurant hardly made any money these days—most of the profit went to Niyan and Shubo. What's more, Pingping might have to see a physical therapist or chiropractor, according to Dr. Levin. Goodness knew how long those therapeutic sessions would take. Every day Nan wrapped a hot water bottle with a towel and tucked it against Pingping's back. He also gave her massages, manipulating her spine gently in hopes of restoring the slipped disk fully to its original position. She groaned whenever he touched the injured area, yet after each massage she felt slightly better, so she let him work on her twice a day. She was easily depressed, irritated at herself, and often said she was a total nuisance.

"*That's all nonsense,*" Nan would tell her.

He was afraid Pingping might never be normal again; worse still, that she might suffer sciatica even if the injury healed. Dr. Levin had said that Pingping's long working hours had taken a toll on her lumbar muscles, which must have precipitated the disk prolapse. This also meant it might be difficult for the Wus to continue running the restaurant as before. These days Nan had been thinking of looking for a full-time job that provided full health care benefits. If he found such work, he'd sell the restaurant. He talked to his wife about his thought, and she agreed to let go of the Gold Wok, though she wept afterward, hating to part with their business. Yet both of them knew this might be the only sensible thing to do.

22

NAN told Shubo and Niyan of his decision to sell the restaurant, and to his relief, they wanted to buy it provided the price was reasonable. Nan said he would let them have it for $25,000, the same as the original list price, if he found a full-time job elsewhere. He knew he could have sold it for a few thousand more, but the two were friends and the Wus wanted to leave the Gold Wok in their hands.

That settled, Nan began reading ads in newspapers and hunting for a job. There were many openings advertised, but few offered medical insurance. In two days he went to nine places—three restaurants, four stores, and two offices, and filled out forms and questionnaires and was told to wait for them to call him. The working hours at all the places were in the daytime, and only one of the jobs offered decent health care benefits, but he wouldn't be entitled to them until he had worked three months at the store. He was frustrated, convinced that none of those places would hire him. What he needed was a job that provided full medical insurance right away.

At last he went to Sunflower Inn on Buford Highway, a motel owned by James Lee, a Korean man. It had advertised in *World Journal* for a front desk clerk. Nan was offered the job on the spot, probably because Mr. Lee was impressed by his English. The boss, licking his arched lip, said, "We only have night hours at the moment."

"Zat's all right," Nan replied. "As long as you offer good health insurance I'll take zer job. I have a child and can't run zer risk of not having my family cahvered."

"We do provide that, but you'll have to pay about three hundred dollars a month. Actually, some of our employees don't join the policy even though we offer them that. It's too expensive for them."

"I understand, but I would love to buy zee insurance from you."

So Nan started to work at the front desk the following night. His shift was from eleven p.m. to seven a.m. He'd be alone in the motel until six o'clock when the cook, Genia, a middle-aged Korean woman, came in to prepare the continental breakfast. Nan liked the job very much. After midnight it was quiet in the lobby and he could read and think, though his mind often turned to Pingping, who was still housebound. These days she, despite her pain and weakness, would cook for the family when Nan wasn't home. She herself could hardly eat anything other than a few spoonfuls of the grain porridge she made for herself. Her calves were so cold that she had to wear leg warmers all the time. Nan urged her to rest well and eat more, saying she might die if she didn't have normal meals. He couldn't imagine himself functioning without her. She had become an integral part of his life, having suffered silently and sacrificed unconditionally for the family all these years. The more he thought about her life, the more remorseful he felt. He hoped it wouldn't be too late for him to make atonement, to cherish and love her devotedly. He even prayed to God for her recovery.

23

HAVING followed the physical therapist's instructions, Pingping exercised lightly every day and began to feel better. The small of her back was less numb and painful than before, all the symptoms somewhat alleviated. She had also regained her appetite and color. At length Nan and Taotao were relieved to see that she was on the mend.

"*I want to work at the restaurant when I'm well again,*" Pingping said to Nan one afternoon. She regretted having sold the business in a rush, but she too had thought she might not recover at all. Two days earlier, despite Nan's objection, she had phoned Niyan, who had assured her that, after her recovery, Pingping was welcome to work at the Gold Wok.

"*That's fine,*" Nan told her. "*I'll talk with Shubo. They may need your help, but you should rest at least a few weeks more. I'm done with the restaurant myself. I like my job at the motel. Besides, I must have the health insurance for us.*"

A week later Nan went to talk with Shubo about Pingping's wish. To his astonishment, Shubo said Nan should have sold him the restaurant for less money if he had intended to leave Pingping at the Gold Wok, so now Nan mustn't interfere with his work. Infuriated, Nan blasted, "*This is really low. I let you have this place at a big discount because I thought you were my friend. But when I need your help, you just give me a bunch of hogwash. What kind of friend are you?*"

"*Business is business,*" Shubo snorted, but he avoided looking Nan in the eye.

"*I never thought you were such a businessman.*" Nan slapped the top of the karaoke machine Shubo had just installed.

"*We're living in America now and should be coolheaded about this sort of thing.*" Shubo's voice was harried, while his fingers were thrumming a table. Behind him a carpenter was busy building a bar.

Niyan said to Nan, "*We don't have an opening right now. When we need Pingping's help, we'll let her know.*" Unconsciously she combed her upper lip with her teeth. Beyond her, on the beverage machine was taped a bottomless-cup sign.

"*Yes, you can let Pingping fill in for you when you have to go to a party,*" Nan sneered.

"*Wait a second,*" Shubo butted in. "*Was I not a handy stopgap for you for several years?*"

"*So? That was how you learned this trade. That was a procedure for your apprenticeship!*"

"*Nan, you have a penchant for going ballistic. Truculence is your Achilles' heel, you know.*" Shubo sucked his cheeks, his wispy mustache bristling.

"*Only because I'm too gullible about people. With a good buddy like you, who needs an enemy?*"

"*We really don't have an opening now. You're being unreasonable.*"

"*At least I'm not out of character—haven't forgotten how I started. All right, thanks a million!*" Too sick to argue with Shubo anymore, Nan wheeled around and stalked out of the Gold Wok.

"*Such a hothead,*" Shubo said to his wife, and cracked the joints of his fingers.

"*I did promise Pingping to let her work here.*"

"*So what? We've changed our minds. We own this place now and must run it in our own way. Once Pingping is here, Nan will poke his nose into our business for sure.*" He passed into English: "Too many dragons cause a drought."

"*The right American idiom is* 'Too many cooks spoil the soup.'"

"*You know what I mean.*"

"*But aren't Pingping and Nan our friends?*"

"No friendship is unconditional."

Niyan breathed a sigh and said no more, believing he was right. In this place one had to take care of oneself. Friendship was largely based on mutual usefulness—only personal interests could bind people together.

24

EVER SINCE Nan began working at the motel, he had kept a poetry journal, which was a traditional practice of ancient Chinese poets. On the first page of his blue spiral notebook he had copied these lines from Frost's "Oven Bird":

> *The bird would cease and be as other birds*
> *But that he knows in singing not to sing.*
> *The question that he frames in all but words*
> *Is what to make of a diminished thing.*

At night he often read those lines before writing down his ideas and reflections on poetry and writing. He regretted not having started the journal earlier, which helped him organize his thoughts and also provided material for his poems. When he sat at the front desk alone, he felt at peace with himself. At long last he could sit like this, thinking and writing devotedly. How mysterious and miraculous life was! Even Pingping's back injury had done him a service, forcing him to change his life. He couldn't help but wonder whether it was the working of some supernatural power that had lifted him out of his old rut. How fortunate he was to have Pingping as his wife and fellow sufferer.

Every day he told her she must concentrate on her recuperation and mustn't work too hard on her paper cuttings, which she had begun making for Janet's store and which she enjoyed doing very much. She and her friend would split the money from the sales of her artwork, and Pingping wanted to study many patterns, improve her scissor work, and develop her craft. She imagined that someday she'd show her mother the cuttings, which would force the old lady to admit that her oldest daughter was superior to her in the art. Nan fully supported Pingping's plan and bought her rolls of paper of different colors and a set of scissors, large and small. But he advised her to take the paper cuttings mainly as a hobby, not as a profession. In other words, she mustn't give herself any pressure and must rest well, not sit too long and hurt her back again. He also told her to avoid going to the Gold Wok, which she might hate to see now. Shubo and Niyan had reorganized the business, and nowadays many Chinese customers, including a foursome glee club, would go there and sing karaoke songs until midnight.

The Wus talked about what Pingping might do after she recuperated. Ideally, she thought she'd like to get a degree in library science and work as a librarian eventually, but that was not feasible. Besides being unable to write in English and having to pay high tuition, she couldn't leave her family for college. Taotao would need her help in the next few years, and she'd feel restless when away from home. As a compromise, she thought she'd like to open a clothing store at Beaver Hill Plaza. They could import fashionable clothes from China and other Asian countries and sell them here for a good profit. They had known people in this business doing quite well in Massachusetts. So Nan went to see the owner of the plaza, who agreed to rent the Wus the suite next to Janet's store, which had been vacant for more than half a year. The Wus planned to open their shop in two or three months.

At last free of the restaurant, Nan somehow felt wary of food and had deliberately curbed his hearty appetite. These days he ate just one meal a day, usually in the evening. If he was hungry at work, he'd drink a cup of coffee with a lot of milk and sugar in it, and if hungry during the day, he'd eat a banana or an orange, as though reducing his food intake could strengthen his body and mind. He didn't know how long he could continue to do this, but he wanted to exercise his willpower fully so as to live a life different from before.

One morning, as Nan was about to leave the motel, Mr. Lee called him into his office. His boss narrowed his small, kind eyes and said, "Nan, would you like to be the manager of this place? I will give you a big raise for that."

Without thinking twice Nan replied, "No, I want to work zer night shift so zat I can take my son back from school in zee afternoon. He has some extracurricular activities." True, for the first time Taotao could join the chess club, though he wasn't good at any real sports thanks to lack of participation over the years. Before Nan had changed to his current job, the boy had had to return home immediately after school, by the bus. Now Nan would pick him up late in the afternoons, and on Thursday evenings he'd drive him to the Red Cross office in Lawrenceville for public service. Sometimes father and son talked about where Taotao would go to college. The boy, already a freshman in high school and half a head taller than his mother, always said he'd go to the Northeast for college, partly because he was still a Red Sox fan. These days he had been talking about sociology as his college major. Nan, knowing Taotao might again switch to another subject in the humanities or social sciences, didn't discourage him and just asked him to come back to see his mother at least twice a year. He suspected that his son might want to meet Livia again, and worried that she might still do drugs, but he didn't ask him. He was sure they still had e-mail contact. In time he'd try to dissuade Taotao from going to college in the Northeast, since Pingping would prefer to have him closer to home.

Mr. Lee, having expected that Nan would jump at the offer since almost a third of his wages went to health insurance, was moved by Nan's explanation and said, "You're a good daddy. I understand."

The offer saddened Nan in a way. It reminded him of his interview seven years ago with Howard, the owner of Ding's Dumplings in Manhattan. Howard too had meant to make him a manager eventually. Nan's life now seemed to have come back in a circle to the starting point. Yet he could see that he was no longer the same man. He had been toughened by the struggle, by the mistakes he had made, by the necessary process of acclimatization that a regular immigrant like himself would have to go through. What's more, his family had a relatively stable life. He could even say he was a better man now, wiser and more capable, and determined to follow his own heart.

When sitting at the front desk in the small hours, he'd think about his life, especially about his twelve and a half years in America. Many things previously unclear to him had become transparent. The notion of the American dream had bewildered him for a good decade; now he knew that to him, such a dream was not something to be realized but something to be pursued only. This must be the true meaning of Emerson's dictum "Hitch your wagon to a star." To be a free individual, he had to go his own way, had to endure loneliness and isolation, and had to give up the illusion of success in order to accept his diminished state as a new immigrant and as a learner of this alphabet. More than that, he had to take the risk of wasting his life without getting anywhere and of becoming a joke in others' eyes. Finally, he had to be brave enough to devote himself not to making money but to writing poetry, willing to face failure.

On Christmas Eve, which was a Friday, he wrote a poem for Pingping for the first time in his life. The lines came naturally and effortlessly as he jotted them down in his notebook. Seeing the words on the paper, he was moved, also awed, his vision blurred a little. The poem went:

Belated Love

So many years I wandered around
like a kite scrambling away from your hand
that held a flexible string.
How often my wings collapsed,
soaked by rain or shattered by wind.

Still, I went on scouring the clouds
for a face that might blow the shimmer
of my brain into blazing lines.
With a seething heart I wobbled through
the air, chasing a sublime haze.

Now I'm at your feet,
no zest left in my chest,

my wings fractured,
my mouth foaming regret,
my words too jumbled to make sense.

What I mean is to say,
"My love, I've come home."

Having read the poem once more, he wept, tears wetting his fingers. Never had he been able to write with such fluency and feeling. He revised the poem numerous times, rearranging some lines and replacing a word here and there. He worked hard at it.

After four o'clock sleep finally claimed him. He rested his head on a rubber pad on the counter and dozed off. His *Collins Cobuild Dictionary* sat beside his elbow, on top of which was a volume of Linda Dewit's poems. By now he used only monolingual dictionaries so that he could understand the definitions of words more accurately and learn the language faster.

"Merry Christmas!"

"Merry Christmas to you too!"

Nan was wakened by the joyous greetings in the corridor leading to the kitchen. The low-pitched lobby smelled of fresh coffee and muffins. He rubbed his eyes and smiled as Mr. Lee, in a gray anorak, stepped in to replace him. Even though he had to work on the holiday, Nan felt genuinely happy. "Merry Christmas!" he said to his boss.

Mr. Lee looked at him in perplexity, though he greeted him back. "I thought you'd be upset about working tonight," he said inquiringly.

"No, I'll be happy to work here every night." Nan beamed despite his tired face.

As Nan headed for his car, a homeless man, Jimmy, who was a veteran of the Vietnam War and often mooched cigarettes from passersby, was sitting on his heels with his back against the wall of the motel. He stood up, grinning at Nan, and said, "Merry Christmas, sir. Can you spare some change?" He put out his dark-skinned hand, his ring and little fingers missing.

"Merry Christmas!" Nan cried back. He thrust his hand into his hip pocket, pulled out four singles and some coins—all the money in there—and gave them to Jimmy.

Jimmy said, "You gave me a real holiday, sir. Thank you!"

"Buy yourself a cahp of coffee and a doughnut."

"I will."

Nan could feel Jimmy's eyes following him all the way to his van. The sky was overcast and the wind chilly. It threatened snow. He lifted his head to watch the low nimbus clouds. Snow would make today more like Christmas, and Pingping and Taotao might roll a snowball again in their backyard. Nan felt sleepy, his forehead numb, yet he was strong in spirit. He pulled out of the parking lot and turned on the radio, which was playing a swelling carol. He reminded himself that he mustn't nod off on his way home.

EPILOGUE

EXTRACTS FROM
NAN WU'S
POETRY JOURNAL

January 3, 1998
THE OTHER DAY, at the used book store Book Nook, I picked up a volume of poetry, *A Peculiar Time,* by Dabney Stockwell. Having read it through, I feel it's a remarkable book: fresh, elegant, intimate, and full of mysterious lines. But there's no way to find more information on this poet, who should be in his seventies if he's still alive. Neither Barnes & Noble nor Borders carries his books. This saddens me, because it shows how fragile and ephemeral a poet's reputation can be. In the acknowledgments, Stockwell listed the magazines in which most of the poems had originally appeared. Obviously he was known, if not famous, when the book was published in 1969. No matter how good one's poetry is, its survival seems to depend on chance. Therefore, one shouldn't expect any success. In the end there may be only failure.

January 30, 1998
I have found that the addressee, the "you," in lyrical poems is vital in shaping the poetic voice. It functions like a sounding board that helps determine the level of diction and the volume and tone of the speech. Generally speaking, it's more effective to identify the addressee in a poem so that the readers can be clear who is speaking to whom.

March 9, 1998

Good news. *Yellow Leaves* accepted two poems, "Pomegranates" and "The Drake." Though it returned my other three pieces, this is my first acceptance, which I hope portends an auspicious beginning. The editor suggested only one minor revision—deleting a comma. I revised four other poems slightly and sent them out to *Still Water Review.*

April 7, 1998

For a long time I couldn't decide in what kind of English I should write. I used to avoid using American English because some of my poems were set in China. These days I feel I must depend on the American idiom and stop confining myself to the neutral English like that used in the Holy Bible, NIV. My subject matter would eventually be American, so I should get myself ready for the task of speaking in the American idiom. I mustn't live in the past and must focus on the present and the future.

May 4, 1998

Heard from *Arrows* today. Its editor, Gail Upchurch, urges me to quit writing poetry. She wrote, "I admire your courage, but I should let you know you are wasting your time. English is too hard for you. You may be able to write prose in English eventually, but poetry is impossible. So don't waste your time anymore. Do something you can do. For instance, write a memoir about the Cultural Revolution, which I'm sure will be marketable. Or write some personal essays. In brief, the way you use the language is too clumsy. For a native speaker like myself, it almost amounts to an insult."

Screw the memoir! It's a kiddie form. I don't mind insulting someone by my writing. A poet is supposed to outrage people. Gail Upchurch spoke as if I hadn't known I was waging a losing battle, and she didn't know I already accepted myself as a loser who has nothing to lose anymore. To write poetry is to exist.

June 13, 1998

Chinese poetry does not have the concept of the Muse. As a result, the poetic speech can originate only from the human domain.

This is an interesting phenomenon, which marks the fundamental difference between Chinese poetry and English poetry. Perhaps this can explain why Chinese poetry is more earthy and bound to the affairs of this world. Should I believe in the Muse? I don't know, but I can see that such a belief may empower a poet. Still, how can we be sure what work has divine sponsorship and what does not? Even if we are sure, can't our convictions be but illusions? In other words, how can we trust our own visions? Probably to stay within the human domain is a better way to go.

July 6, 1998

Tu Fu wrote, "Writing is a matter of a thousand years; / My heart knows the gain and the loss." It seems he was quite certain that some of his poems would last a millennium. Although he is a great poet, if not the greatest in Chinese, his confidence verges on megalomania. The mortality of one's poetry is contingent on many factors mostly beyond the poet's control. By contrast, Horace said he hoped his work would survive himself by a century. This is more human, aware of his finitude.

July 20, 1998

Talked with Dick last night. He is bored in Iowa and said he'd try to see if he could work out a deal with his university so that he could teach only one semester a year. He misses New York, especially the nightlife. He is opposed to the idea of self-publishing, because a vanity press book is looked down upon by professional poets. Screw the professionals! William Blake published *Songs of Innocence and of Experience* at his own expense; so did A. E. Housman with *A Shropshire Lad*. I should not exclude self-publishing once I have enough poems for a book.

August 22, 1998

Fives poems were rejected by *Poetry,* but the editor wrote an encouraging note, saying he saw "a glimmer of talent in every poem." He seemed to address me as a young woman. I've been revising the poems and will send them elsewhere soon.

September 6, 1998

Too many people call themselves poets in the U.S., just as too many people call themselves artists—here even a con man is called con artist. I don't believe in the "art" of poetry. For me it's just a craft, not very much different from carpentry or masonry. It's a kind of work that can keep me emotionally balanced and functioning better as a human being. So I write only because I have to.

September 27, 1998

Gail Upchurch wrote again and said she still couldn't see any progress in my poetry. She quoted Yeats, who in a letter declares that no poet who doesn't write in his mother tongue can write with music and strength. I was disheartened by the quotation, as I do love some of Yeats's poems. I felt as if a brick had hit me in the face. On second thought, I believe Yeats's statement might be true only of his time. Nowadays TV and radio are everywhere, and you can hear native English speakers talk every day, so it may be less difficult for a writer to choose to write in his adopted tongue.

On the other hand, Gail Upchurch did raise a serious question. She wrote: "The reason I have advised you to write prose is that the main function of prose is to tell a story. But poets should have a different kind of ambition, i.e., to enter into the language they use. Can you imagine your work becoming part of our language?"

I have no answer to that xenophobic question, which ignores the fact that the vitality of English has partly resulted from its ability to assimilate all kinds of alien energies. From now on, I won't send my work to *Arrows* again and will avoid Gail Upchurch, that killjoy. She even said, "So don't continue until you learn how to rhyme 'orange.' "

October 2, 1998

Today I heard on NPR that Linda Dewit had passed away two weeks ago. At the news I wasn't sad somehow, probably because I felt her poetry became more precious to me. I went to Borders and bought two of her books, though I already had her *Collected Poems*. I'm glad that her death in a way consecrated her, and now to me she exists solely as a genuine spirit embodied in her work. Had I met her in person, I might have been disappointed, just as I was by Edward Neary. It's better this way, letting Linda Dewit's poetry shape her image and keep it intact in my mind. A poet's work should always be better than the poet. That's why one writes—to make something better than oneself.

October 30, 1998

Sent out five poems to the *Kenyon Review* this morning.

These days I have tried to memorize a few lines by Auden every day. Sadly, my memory is no longer as strong as ten years ago. Today I can hardly recall what I learned yesterday. Probably my creative powers have passed the peak and I started too late. Yet for me there is only trying, and I will be happy if I can work this motel job for many years.

POEMS BY NAN WU

Revelation

Suddenly he saw his mother's ugly face
after seeing her smile for thirty years.

Suddenly he heard his mother's monstrous voice,
having remembered all her lullabies.

Suddenly he found his mother's secret cookhouse
stocked with human flesh and blood.

For the first time he tasted tears of rage
and hated the nickname she called him.

He soon left for a distant place,
where he has lived secluded.

A Contract

Long ago I was promised a contract.
This made me feel rich and brave.
In return I pledged all my faith,
eager to serve and praise.
I was a normal child, sure about
what to love and what to hate.

When I grew up I was given the contract itself.
In it was the map of a whole country,
there was no mention of money or property,
but it guaranteed me a happy future.
I knew nobody merited my envy
and nothing else could make me succeed.

I took my contract to another land,
where I showed it at an international bank.
People cringed and whispered.
A large man burped and said to me,
"Sir, this doesn't mean anything."
Choking back tears, I muttered, "Thank you."

Homeland

You packed a pouch of earth into your baggage
as a bit of your homeland. You told your friend:
"In a few years I'll be back like a lion.
There's no other place I can call home
and wherever I go I'll carry our country with me.
I'll make sure my children speak our language,
remember our history, and follow our customs.
Rest assured, you will see this same man,
made of loyalty, bringing back gifts
and knowledge from other lands."

You won't be able to go back.
Look, the door has closed behind you.
Like others, you too are expendable to
a country never short of citizens.
You will toss in sleepless nights,
confused, homesick, and weeping in silence.
Indeed, loyalty is a ruse
if only one side intends to be loyal.
You will have no choice but to join the refugees
and change your passport.

Eventually you will learn:
your country is where you raise your children,
your homeland is where you build your home.

My Pity

I pity those who worship power and success.
When they are weak they close their borders,
which when they are strong they expand.
They let a one-eyed ruler lead them
into a tumbling river, where they are told
that under the water stepping-stones
form a straight path to the other shore.

I pity those whose wisdom is all worldly.
They take the death of the young calmly,
but when the old die, they will collapse,
pounding their chests and wailing to heaven
as if they were willing to go with the dead.
Their sense of life is circular,
so their solution to crises is to wait,
wait for the wheel of fate to turn.
"History," they're fond of saying,
"will sort out things by itself."

I pity those who love security and unity.
They're content to live in cellars where
food and drinks are provided for them.
Their lungs are unused to fresh air
and their eyes bleary in sunlight.
They believe the worst life
is better than a timely death.
Their heaven is a banquet table.
Their salvation depends on a powerful man.

Spring

In the late afternoon a chorus of birds drifts
and sways a boat brimming with hopes,
forgotten but still floating in the bay.
If your heart is full of longing for
a distant trip, it's time to go.
You must set out alone—
expect no company but stars.

In the early twilight golden clouds billow,
suggesting a harvest, remote yet plausible.
Perhaps your soul is suddenly seized
by a melody that brings back
a promise never fulfilled,
or a love that blossoms only in thought,
or a house, partly built,
abandoned . . .

If you want to sing,
sing clearly.
Let grief embolden your song.

A Change

You didn't come. I was there alone
watching drenched dragonflies cling
to the grapes under your trellis,
listening to a flute that trilled
away in the shuttered nursery.

Alone I stood in the rain, crooning
to the wind, and let my songs
be carried off by the wings
that still cleaved the hazy evening.
I saw my words fall on a mountainside
where trees and grass were dying.

Now and again
your little gate would wave
as if to say "Go away."

Afterward, weaned from love
and sick of everything,
I thought I would stop singing.
Yet words lined up, kept coming,
though in my voice I heard
a different ring.

A Love Bird

How I would like to be a bird
    kept in your cage of love.
You called me Sparrow but preferred
    an eagle or a dove.

You shooed me off your cozy eaves
    and made me use my wings.
How I cried for fear, for relief.
    You merely said "Poor thing."

Across oceans and continents
    I've traveled, wrestling winds.
My heart, homesick, often regrets
    my strong and spacious wings.

I've lost my sparrow's melody
    and cannot find your house.
Many times you must have seen me
    as one born in the clouds.

Pomegranates

Another rain will burst them—
full of teeth, they will grin
through the tiny leaves

that used to conceal their cheeks.
I'll take a photo of my pomegranates
for you, the only person

I care to show. Like others
you craved the fruit
so much, you overlooked

the crimson blossoms wounded
by worms and winds.
You could not imagine

some of them would swell
into such heavy pride.
I can tell you, they are sour.

A Good-bye in January 1987

"All aboard!" cried the train attendant.
My father was holding my three-year-old son
to watch me leaving for another continent.

"Good-bye, Taotao." I waved,
but my child was silent
staring at me with a sullen face,

his tears trickling down.
If only I could have brought him along!
The wheels hissed, about

to grind. "No good-bye,"
he cried finally, "no good-bye, Mama."
I forced a smile, then climbed

the ladder, stabbed by pain.
The village platform began to fall away,
blurred, and disappeared in the plain.

Since then his tears, mingled with mine,
have often soaked my bad dreams,
although he did join me in '89.

I swear I'll never say good-bye
to my son again, not until
he graduates from Parkview High.

The Donkey

Mama, do you remember the donkey
who collapsed on the street that afternoon?
And the overturned cart, its wheel still moving,

mussels and clams scattered in heaps all around?
He lay in a ditch, his belly sweating,
heaving, while blood flowed from his mouth.

The old one-eyed driver was kicking him
and yelling, "Get up, you beast!"
Only a long ear twitched, as if to say "I'm trying."

I swear, he was too tired to get on his feet.
Unlike a horse playing sick,
he was too weak to pretend.

Mama, I can still see that mountain of seafood,
the driver standing on it and cracking his whip.

My Doves

All night long I hear my doves cooing
to tell me there's a snowstorm gathering.
Their feathers, once intensely white,
are gray and tattered, though the whistles
I tied to them eleven years ago
still scatter notes of brass when they fly.

They tremble a little from cold.
Their short bills having lost the jadelike translucency
are more fragile than before.

Who feeds them now?
Under whose eaves is their cote?
Do they still go to the aspen grove to look for worms?
Do the cats still attack them and steal their young?

Time and again they seem to cry,
"Nan, Nan, come and take us away."
They make my morning blue,
bluer than a freezing dusk.

All day long I see the shadows
of their wings flitting about—
through my lawn, along the asphalt,
across the walls of the dining hall,
on the kitchen floor, around my wok . . .

Groundhog Hour

As the groundhog enters our yard
all the noise ceases in our house.
I dare not raise my voice
to tell my family in the kitchen
that we have a little visitor,
a portly guy in a brown coat.
If he hears any sound in here
he'll run away, rocking his ample rump.

He stands up on his hind feet,
clasps his hands below his ursine face,
and looks right then left as if to make sure
his shadow hasn't followed him.
Soon he roams the grass casually,
sampling our clover and alfalfa,
catching an insect or snail.
He never jumps like his cousin the squirrel.

How can I tell him he's always welcome?
A humble guest, he has no idea
we celebrate a day in his name.
I keep my face back from the window
so he can enjoy a quiet meal,
or even a sunbath as
he often does back home.

Whenever he's here
my winter shrinks, green-faced.

The Drake

Oh, what human bastard threw the lines
and hooks into the lake?
Instead of a fish they caught me,
slashed my tongue, mangled my wings.
All my ducks thought I was finished
and left me to die on this shore.
I know they're fighting over my post,
their voices shrilling in the woods—
ka, keck, quack.

Oh, even a god dies alone.
I won't complain or sob,
although my heart is sore,
gripped by numbing sleep.
I must remain mute like an earthworm
and dense like a tree.
If only I could rise and swim again,
again commanding my clan—
ka, keck, quack.

Oh, how can I thank the Wus enough?
They cut the lines and dislodged the hooks.
They cleaned the maggots off my wounds
and even gave me a pill before
they put me back into the lake.
Now I'm going to rejoin my tribe
and tackle their new chief.
First they should know I'm still alive—
ka, keck, quack.

Nan, a Fantasizing Husband

I dream of becoming an idle Nan,
in whose calendar all days are blank.
Don't blame me if I am such a man

who goes to ball games as a major fan
and whose job is to draw cash from the bank.
I dream of becoming an idle Nan.

Scientists, artists, statesmen do what they can,
but I would have my good fortune to thank.
Don't scold me if I am such a man.

Trouble will always come if you have a plan
to attack front and flank.
I dream of becoming an idle Nan—

in the morning I'll eat omelet with ham;
if it's fine, I will roam the riverbank.
Don't pinch me if I am such a man!

Time will crush everything into one span.
Why strive for money, power, fame, and rank?
I dream of becoming an idle Nan.
Don't kill me if I am such a man!

A Father's Blues

Again I'm back at square one,
where every street says "Dead End."
I thought my daughter, unborn yet,
would show me an outlet.

Again I'm back at square one
to face an empty yard where a house once stood.
My child was a vision I lost myself in.
If only I had unlearned selfish parenthood.

Again I'm back at square one,
holding a little casket I cannot inter.
My child died before she grew a lung.
If only I knew where they dumped her.

Again I'm back at square one,
where a man has to restart alone.
Let me unsee my daughter's twinkling pulse
so I can search my soul for a milestone.

A Mother's Blues

I had my baby with me again last night.
She curled up at my side,
saying, "Mommy, your bed is so nice.
It's cold out there,
I'm so scared."

"Don't be, my child."
I patted her silky hair.

She told me,
"I won't wet your bed, Mommy."
I said, "Don't be silly—
you're not big enough to pee."

I woke to find her tiny coffin against my cheek,
still stuffed with her little quilt and mattress.
Oh if only I could hold her again inside me.

Again I saw my baby this morning.
She was on the deck, toddling.
Now and then she peeked in through
the glass door, prattling.

Homework

Under his pencil a land is emerging.
He says, "I'm making a country."

In no time it blooms into colors.
A blue bay opens like a horseshoe on
the shoulder of a glacier.
Below, a chain of mountains zigzags,
greened with rain forests.
Farther down he places mines:
aluminum, silver, copper, titanium,
iron, gold, uranium, tungsten, zinc.
Two oil fields beside branching rivers
are kept apart by a sierra called Mount Funfun.
In the south a plain stretches
into vast fertile land, where
he crayons farms that yield oranges,
potatoes, apples, strawberries,
wheat, broccoli, cherries, zucchini,
poultry, beef, mutton, cheese.
(There's no fishery
because he hates seafood.)

On the same map he draws a chart—
railroads crisscross the landscape;
highways, pipelines, canals
entwine; sea lanes curve
into the ocean, airports
raise a web of skyways.
He imposes five time zones.

For a child a country is a place
unmarked by missiles

and fleets. He doesn't know
how to run it with the power
to issue visas and secret orders
and to rattle nuclear bombs like slingshots.

Her Dream

was to be free of responsibility,
to be born the youngest in her family,
pampered by her parents and humored
by big brothers and sisters,
and later to marry a man of mild temper
who would worry alone about money,
business, household duties, the authorities.

But born the oldest child,
she had to tend her siblings,
cut grass for ducks and geese,
gather firewood in the valley,
and walk miles to shop in the villages.
She'd cook supper
if patients delayed her mother.

Like many women of her generation
she cannot recall a happy episode
in her childhood. Yet she's resolved
to give her children a loving home
so that they won't be bowled over
if someone whispers to them "I love you."

Status

They are referring to the photo
I mailed them last May.
In it I wear a cell phone on my belt
and lean against my rusty Chevrolet
parked before the medical building.
Their letter says my brothers both
have well-paid jobs in Shanghai now—
one is a consultant at a foreign bank
and the other manages a soccer team.
"They each carry a phone like you
but they haven't bought a car yet."

My parents have forgotten that I wear a phone
as a custodian at the hospital . . .
to get the call when a toilet needs cleaning.

An Admonition

All your sufferings are imaginary,
all your losses not worth mentioning
if you keep in mind what you used to see—
peasants eating husks and tree leaves in the spring,
workers feasting their bosses to get a raise,
police rounding up the villagers who refuse to relocate,
women getting sterilized after their firstborn,
newlyweds setting up house in cattle sheds,
worshippers arrested and forced to live
on rotted food if they do not repent—
by comparison, all your misfortunes are imaginary.

Here in America you can speak and shout,
though you have to find your voice and the right ears.
You can sell your time for honest bread,
you can eat leftovers while dreaming
of getting rich and strong,
you can lament your losses with abandon,
if not to an audience, to your children,
you can learn to borrow and get used
to living in the shadow of debt . . .
Still, whatever grieves you has happened
to others, to those from Ireland,
Africa, Italy, Scandinavia, the Caribbean.
Your hardship is just commonplace,
a fortune many are dying to seize.

Immigrant Dreams

She too sells her hours in America.
Her dream has evolved into a house
on two acres of land with a pool.
She once dreamed of becoming a diva
or movie star or a painter
who specialized in fish and bamboo.
But she gave up art school
and came here to expand her selfhood.
At least that's what she planned to do.

He didn't know that at heart
she was a mother and wife,
a woman who would love burgers and fries.
Indeed, dollars can equalize most lives.
If only he were twenty again
or could stop patching his dream
with diffident feet and rhymes.

Heaven

for Dick

Every religion promises a unique heaven
where there's no sickness, old age, pain, or death.
In Pure Land Buddhism, heaven is said
to lie somewhere in the west,
and you can get there if you do good,
recite Amida's name every day, and never kill.
You'll be reborn into that vaulted domain,
not from the spasms of a womb
but from a lotus flower—such a birth saves you from
falling back into a lesser incarnation on earth.
Once you settle in the Pure Land
you'll suffer no extremes of cold and heat;
you'll be provided with beautiful clothing
and gourmet food, always ready and warm.
There will be no anger, greed,
jealousy, ignorance, laziness, or strife.
The place is resplendent with precious stones,
towers built of agate, palaces of diamonds.
Huge trees of various gems bear
blossoms and fruits, always fresh.
Giant lotus flowers diffuse fragrance everywhere.
Pools inlaid with seven jewels
hold the purest water, which adjusts itself
to the depth and temperature each bather needs.
Under your feet spreads the ground paved with jade.
Day and night flowers fall from the sky shaded
by nets of gold, silver, and pearls.
In the air waft celestial music and aromas.
Not to mention living with Buddha and bodhisattvas.

Born of flesh and consumed by care,
how can I not marvel at those wonderful things?

How can I not think of mending my ways
to earn entrance to that splendid place?

Yet tired of travel and tangled in the web of dust,
I will pray to the almighty power:
let me be a tree on earth after I die,
a tree that blossoms into fruit every summer.

A Eulogy

Yes, praise—let me think of someone,
who, in suffering, still holds
happiness as his birthright;
who, searching in vain for his misplaced gloves,
remembers those who have no hands;
who, while keeping an eye on his god,
does not frown on the gods of others;
who, having lost a contest, is ready to salute
the one who has just outperformed him;
who, in a bustling street, still hears
birds in distant hills;
who, though able to mix with crowds,
is not rattled by their clamor;
who, loving a country, never lets this love
outweigh his love for a woman and children;
who accepts disaster and triumph equally,
making friends with neither;
who treats a limousine just as a vehicle,
a palace as no more than a dwelling;
who, while having coffee with a dignitary,
doesn't hesitate to step out the door
for a breath of fresh air.

An Exchange

You have been misled by your folly,
determined to follow the footsteps of Conrad
and Nabokov. You have forgotten
they were white Europeans.
Remember your yellow face
and your puny talent—unlikely
to make you a late bloomer.
Why believe you can write verse in English,
whose music is not natural to you?

You have betrayed our people,
scribbling with the alphabet out of
contempt for our ancient words,
which stand like rocks in time's river,
against the tides of gibberish.
Carried away by hatred,
you have mistaken diversion for devotion.

Even if you're lucky and earn a seat someday
in the temple housing those high-nosed ghosts,
do you really think they will accept you
just on the merits of your poems?
Be warned—some of them, who were once SOBs,
will call you a clever Chinaman.

•

For God's sake, relax a little.
Stop raving about race and loyalty.
Loyalty is a two-way street.
Why not talk about how a nation betrays a person?
Why not condemn those who have hammered
our mother tongue into a chain

to bind all the different dialects
to the governing machine?
Our words, yes, once like a river,
have shrunk into a man-made pond
in which you are kept, half alive,
as a pet to obey and entertain.
So, I prefer to crawl around at my own pace
in the salt water of English.
As for the great ghosts in the temple,
why should I bother about their acceptance?
The light of dawn does not discriminate.
A tree, or butterfly, or stream
(unlike the dog corrupted by humans)
does not notice the color of your skin.

To write in this language is to be alone,
to live on the margin where
loneliness ripens into solitude.

Another Country

You must go to a country without borders,
where you can build your home
out of garlands of words,
where broad leaves shade familiar faces
that no longer change in wind and rain.
There's no morning or evening,
no cries of joy or pain;
every canyon is drenched in the light of serenity.

You must go there, quietly.
Leave behind what you still cherish.
Once you enter that domain,
a path of flowers will open before your feet.

ACKNOWLEDGMENTS

My heartfelt thanks to the John Simon Guggenheim Foundation for a generous fellowship that enabled me to complete the first draft of this novel in 2000, and to the Virginia Center for the Creative Arts for a residency during which I worked on "Poems by Nan Wu."

I am grateful to LuAnn Walther for her comments and suggestions; to Lane Zachary for her critique; to Wilborn Hampton for reading the beginning pages of this novel; and to Dick Lourie and Donna Brook for their comments on the appended poems.

ABOUT THE AUTHOR

HA JIN *left his native China in 1985 to attend Brandeis University. He is the author of the internationally best-selling novel* Waiting, *which won the PEN/Faulkner Award and the National Book Award; the novel* War Trash, *which won the PEN/Faulkner Award; the novel* The Crazed; *the story collections* The Bridegroom, *which won the Asian American Literary Award,* Under the Red Flag, *which won the Flannery O'Connor Award for Short Fiction, and* Ocean of Words, *which won the PEN/Hemingway Award; the novel* In the Pond; *and three books of poetry. He lives in the Boston area and is a professor of English at Boston University.*